AT FIRST IT WAS THE M
BECAME REV

Summer, 1928, Rusty loses his job as a Lake Erie tugboat deckhand and can no longer afford his charter boat business. Out of work, out of hope and with a family to feed, he desperately turns to hauling grape juice for the mysterious Trapani clan despite his suspicions. After several successful trips, Al Trapani offers him an opportunity to run illegal alcohol from Canada. Rusty reluctantly agrees to try it just once.

As Rusty slips into the underground world of rum running, he comes to realize he is losing far more than his principles—he is jeopardizing his marriage and his life. But getting out is not easy. Hunted by a sadistic renegade Coast Guard captain, Rusty soon finds himself in the captain's crosshair, forcing him to challenge not only his principles, but his perception of good and evil.

The 1920s roar to life as Rusty's rum running legend grows.

COMMENTS FROM READERS

"With intense description and characters you'll love (or hate), R. C. Durkee holds readers on course and breezing through this engaging tale of love, wickedness, revenge and morality."—*Rick Porrello, author of To Kill the Irishman, "Best true-life crime caper since Goodfellas-San Francisco Examiner."*

"...a believable plot based on historical fact...brings history and events to life through Rusty's eyes and experiences. It's all these elements, wound into a satisfying and realistic story line backed by historical fact, that make *Rum Run* a winning account."—*D. Donovan, Senior eBook Reviewer, Midwest Book Review.*

...a hit with boaters, Lyman owners and anyone who loves a good read."—*Heidi Langer, Program Manager, LBOA*

RUM RUN

R. C. Durkee

Moonshine Cove Publishing, LLC

Abbeville, South Carolina U.S.A.
FIRST MOONSHINE COVE EDITION November 2014

This book is a work of fiction. Names, characters, places and incidents are products of the author's imagination or are used fictitiously. Any resemblance to actual events, locals or persons, living or dead, is entirely coincidental.

ISBN: 978-1-937327-55-2
Library of Congress Control Number: 2014918270

Book interior design by Moonshine Cove staff; original cover art by the author, used with permission.

Acknowledgements

Thanks, Dad for believing I could write a book and get it published. This is for you.

Thank you also to my family: Roger Atkinson, Shirley Durkee, Derek Durkee, Kurt Durkee, Judy Poll, Ralph Genco and Susan Genco. I really appreciate your feedback. Thanks for believing in me.

Thank you Fred Backstrom, of Grafton-Midview Public Library reference staff, for your help in locating information when I hit a brick wall and for helping this technically challenged author with formatting and computer troubles.

Also, thanks again Roger, a former Lyman and Skiff Craft boat owner, for sharing your experience boating on Lake Erie.

I would like to acknowledge the United States Coast Guard who keep our waters and lives safe. I have great respect and admiration for them.

Cousin Ron & Deb –

Enjoy!

R.C. Durkee

Dedication

This book is dedicated to my Grandpa.

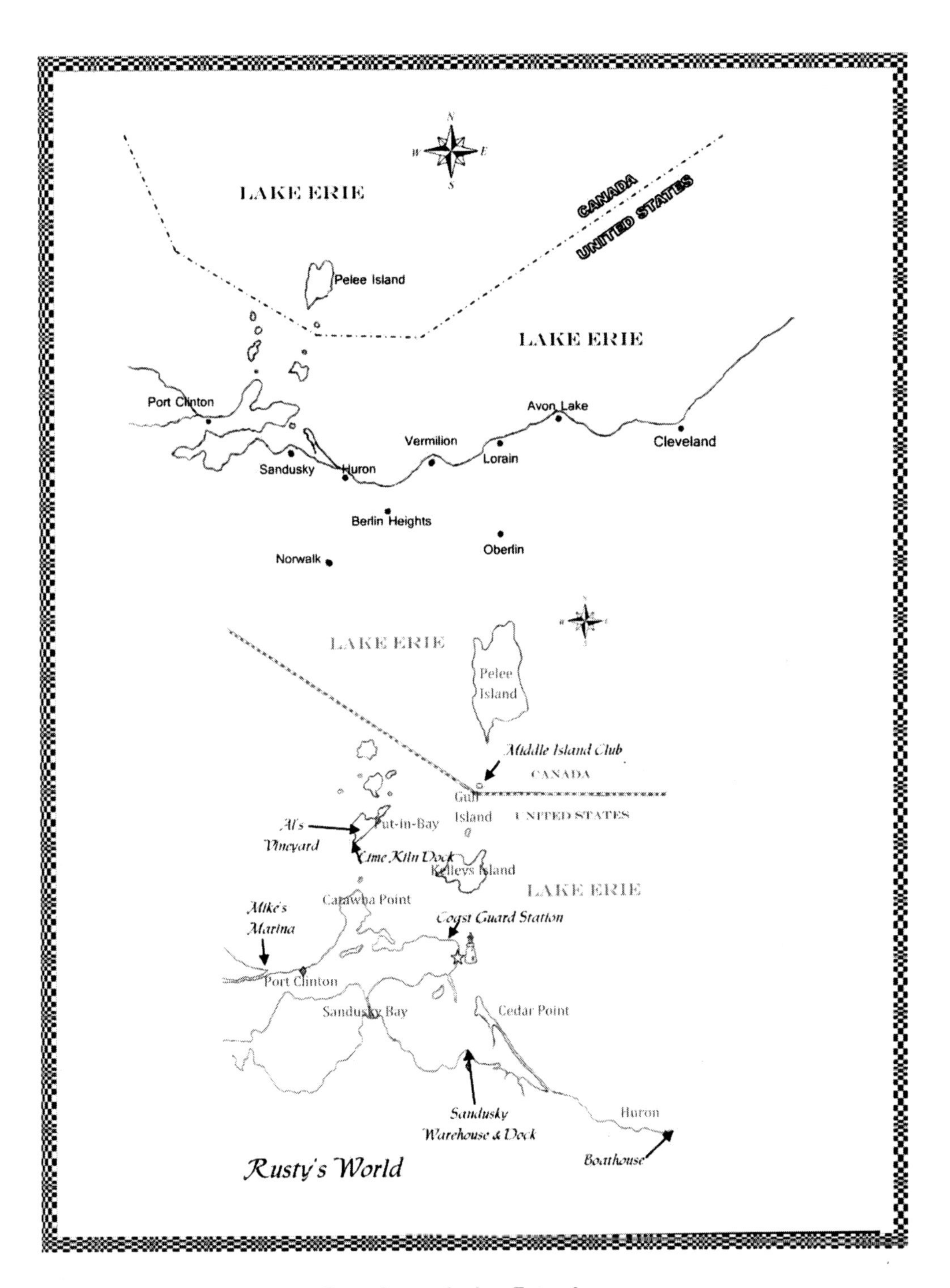

Southern Lake Erie Area

Historical Note:

Demon Rum. That was the moniker given to alcohol by temperance groups and clergy long before the nation's Prohibition Law went into effect. Drinking wasn't the problem but drunkenness was and it was looked at with disapproval as far back as the founding of our country. In America's early years, alcohol was an acceptable drink as water was often contaminated, juice was seasonal and milk would not keep. [1] Alcohol was also used for medicinal purposes, business transactions and for celebrations but many could not or would not practice restraint. Temperance groups calling for moderation and self- control (the true meaning of temperance) began taking root in the 1700s, and with the backing of the church, they blamed unrestrained consumption of alcohol for social evils such as immorality, abuse and idleness. The term *teetotaler* came into being at this time as those who supported temperance placed a letter "t" by their name on temperance rosters to indicate their "total belief" in temperance. The term teetotaler would later become synonymous with anyone who abstained from drinking. By 1830, Americans, on average, were *consuming 1.7 bottles of hard liquor per week.*[2] The cry for prohibition increased. Radicals such as the hatchet-wielding Carrie Nation took to saloon busting. Women's suffrage groups gathered in front of saloons singing hymns, holding prayer vigils and petitioning saloon keepers to shut down their "Dens of Inequity." A number of states passed prohibition laws but these were not enforced and with neighboring states calling prohibition unconstitutional, the movement could not get off the ground. With the outbreak of the Civil War, the nation became preoccupied with war and the movement towards prohibition was abandoned.

After the war, American consumption of alcohol grew to quantities that have not been equaled since.[3] Organizations such as the national Prohibition Party and the Women's Christian Temperance Society were born. The WCTS took on more than demon rum, they also championed social reforms such as women's rights, labor reforms, and the Americanization of immigrants who were flooding into the country. Their focus of concern was mainly urban and industrialized settings. In small towns and rural America, Americans were becoming concerned about the influx of immigrants and growing urban power. The Prohibition Party found supporters in these areas and the pulpit was used to reinforce the evils of demon rum. It would not be until the powerful Anti Saloon League, formed in 1895 and born out of the Prohibition Party, would the pressure for a national prohibition of alcohol gain momentum. Henry Ford and other industrial giants jumped on board and advocated the ban of alcohol citing squandered paychecks, domestic abuse and workplace idleness pointed to alcohol abuse. Ford was so adamant that he sent social workers to his employees' homes to evaluate their home life, and if drunkenness, abuse or alcohol use was witnessed or even suspected, an employee would be fired.

So powerful became the pressure for a nationwide ban of alcohol, the 18th Amendment was ratified on January 16, 1919. It prohibited the manufacturing, transportation and selling of alcohol. Only sacramental wine and alcohol (mainly whiskey and brandy) for medicinal use was exempt and one would need a prescription for that. In order to enforce the law, the Volstead Act was passed on October 28, 1919. An outcry followed. Many considered the law unconstitutional. *How do you legislate morality?* they cried. They felt the law was an affront to returning WW1 veterans who had fought for democracy. Others felt it was class discrimination because the wealthy would have the means and money to acquire the banned alcohol, the working class would not. And immigrants took it as a personal attack on them as alcohol was part of their culture (Italians-wine, Irish-whiskey and Germans-beer). Never the less, the law went into effect the following year on January 16, 1920 and within an hour of its effect, two train boxcars loaded with alcohol were robbed at gunpoint at a Chicago rail yard.[4]

Americans, rebellious by nature, found ways to skirt the law. Some made homebrew for personal use. After all, the law did not say it was illegal to drink alcohol. Others feigned illness to get medicinal whiskey or brandy from the local druggist who had a stack of doctor signed blank prescriptions for alcohol "medicine." Prescriptions flew off the pad as willing druggists made at least $3.00 on an alcohol prescriptions and at least another $3.00 on the "medicine."[5] Moonshiners flourished, selling home brewed corn-based alcohol and giving rise to the bootlegger and speeding automobile on dusty roads. But there was a market for top grade alcohol and smugglers responded to the need, crossing borders- especially Canada's, to bring first-rate brand alcohol to the thirsty. A man with a small motorboat loaded with alcohol obtained from a mother ship across the border could resale an $8.00 case of purchased scotch for $65.00.[6] It just wasn't bandits or gangsters breaking the law, now it was every day people becoming criminals to make extra money to supplement their modest or low income.

Gangs and gang warfare erupted. Hijacking alcohol cargo became common place. Innocent people became victims of mistakes or crossfire. Enforcement of the law was like "an old cat catching a young mouse."[7] Crime was rampant. The latter half of the 1920s saw money pour into law enforcement. Federal agents were added and their firepower updated. The number of Coast Guard vessels were increased and upgraded for speed. Atlanta's Rum Row was finally busted, but Great Lakes smuggling remained out of control.

The latter half of the twenties, Al Capone was a celebrity. The cocktail, born to camouflage bad alcohol, was popular. Football's Red Grange was a sports star and controversy still raged over the "long count" in the Dempsey-Tunney fight. Babe Ruth hit his 60th homerun and the nation was engrossed in the Sacco and Vanzetti murder trial. Buster Keaton was still getting laughs and Greta Garbo was smoking the big screen. The Twenties were losing a little of their roar as daring hemlines became a little longer and flappers began to fade. But speakeasies boomed and gangland crime intensified. This is where the story *Rum Run* begins. And for some, *Blue Skies* and *S'Wonderful* were not always the case.

---

[1] Wayne Lewis Kadar, "The Prohibition Era: 1920-1933," *Great Lakes Heroes & Villains* (Gwinn, Michigan: Avery Color Studios, Inc., 2009) 133.
[2] David Von Drehle, "The Demon Drink. How Prohibition Turned Tipplers into Criminals, Teetotalers into Lobbyists- and Remade U.S. Politics," *Time*, 24 May 2010, retrieved 27 May 2014 <http://www.content.time.com/time/magazine/article/o,9171,1989146,00.html >.
[3] William A. Meredith, "End of Prohibition: What Happened and What Did We Learn?" *The Great Experiment: Thirteen Tears of Prohibition 1920-1933*, graph: "Per Capita Consumption of Alcoholic Beverages (Gallons of Pure Alcohol) 1910-1929," 29 April 2005, retrieved 15 April 2014 <http://www.albany.edu/~wm731882/future1_final.html>.
[4] Frederick Stonehouse, "Rum Running," *Great Lakes Crime: Murder, Mayhem, Booze & Broads*, (Gwinn, Michigan: Avery Color Studios, Inc., 2004) 41.
[5] Stonehouse, 42.
[6] Stonehouse, 43.
[7] Wayne Lewis Kadar, "The Prohibition Era: 1920-1933," *Great Lakes Heroes & Villains*, (Gwinn, Michigan: Avery Color Studios, Inc., 2009) 151.

Preface

Lake Erie shoreline, Vermilion, Ohio. June 1928.

The evening was exceptionally quiet. The lapping of waves and lowing of a cow from a barn situated near the shore was all Hank Krause heard as he hurried across his yard to the barn. He had gotten home late from a game of cards, and the cow was letting him know just how late he was. The light from the glowing lantern he carried washed the ground around his steps, making the surrounding night seem extra dark. He glanced toward the dark void which was the lake. It merged with the moonless, starry night sky in an eerie edge-of–the-world look. Out there, beyond the void, lay the Canadian shoreline, too far to see even in daylight. *A Great Lake indeed*, he thought. A flash of light caught his eye in the abyss of water and sky. It was low on the lake he judged. He halted to a stop as he searched the blackness beyond the shore. Nothing. He waited a moment or two and took a few steps toward the lake, raising his lantern to avoid tripping over Edna's rock garden. The light from the lake flashed again. This time, it was closer to shore. Krause quickly realized what was behind the mysterious light and set his jaw. He extinguished the light from his lantern and hurried back to the house, picking his way in the dark.

"Edna," he said, his voice measured, "Call the sheriff." He grabbed a 20 gauge shotgun from its station at the kitchen door.

Edna wrung her hands, her eyes growing wide. "What's going on, Hank? Why do you need the gun?" Her voice was anxious.

"Tell the sheriff there's a signal light from a boat off shore. They think I'm signaling to them with my lantern." He cracked the barrel open to assure himself the shotgun shells were in the chamber despite the fact it was always at ready. He snapped the barrel back in place and burst out the door with Edna on his heels.

"Don't go out there, Hank, please. Let the sheriff handle this."

Hank ignored her pleas. "Get back inside and call the sheriff. Now!"

Krause rushed to the shoreline behind his barn just in time to make out the shadowy form of a boat beaching on his sandy shore. He raised his shotgun to his shoulder. "Get the hell out of here," he shouted, and shot a round over the boat. The flash from the gun blast blinded his night vision. Unable to see, he cocked his head but heard no sound from the boat so he shot again to show them he meant business.

Flashes of staccato lights and rapid report erupted from the boat as it returned machine gun fire. The boat engine barked to life, and moments later its dark shape roared away from the shore until both its sound and shape was swallowed by the blackness of the lake.

Krause lay upon the sandy beach, his shotgun next to his side and the sand growing dark about him with his blood. The only sound was the lapping of waves and the lowing of a cow.

Chapter 1

"Excuse me, is this your boat?"

Rusty looked up from mooring the boat to the pump dock and shielded his eyes from the mid-morning sun. It was already hot and humid. "Yea," he said to the obscure figure eclipsing the sun.

"Would you give me a lift to the mainland?" the figure asked.

Rusty climbed out of the boat and the figure, no longer an umbra, came into view revealing a wiry, young man with snapping dark eyes, a cocked smile.

"Ferry will be along about 11:30," Rusty said and began pumping gas into his boat.

The lanky, young man fished in his pocket and then pulled out a handful of bills. "I'll give you 25 bucks if you take me to Sandusky now," he said, swaggering towards Rusty flapping the bills from his outstretched arm.

Rusty was not sure he had heard him right. That was $10.00 more than he made on weekend charters. He sized up the anxious, young man and judged him to be about 8-10 years younger than himself, making him roughly around 25 years old. His hair, black as his eyes, was slicked back from his occasional habit of running his fingers through it like a comb. The exception was a devilish lock that flopped defiantly about his forehead. His clothes were crumpled and mud-caked despite the fact that he had tried (unsuccessfully) to brush both mud and wrinkles out. Rusty guessed he had spent the night in some wallow behind an island speakeasy. How he got to Middle Bass Island a mile and a half away was anyone's guess, and the fact he had $25.00 on him was intriguing. But what made him do a double take was the way the young man was dressed. From the waist down he wore regulation World War I Army uniform pants wrapped with puttees and a regulation belt and buckle. He topped it off with a soiled white sleeveless Tee shirt. It looked as though his clothes were a part of him like his skin or hair. This made the young man all the more peculiar considering the war had ended a decade ago. There has got to be a story to this character, he thought, returning the gas nozzle to the pump. "You must need to get there pretty bad," he said, glancing at the money the young man dangled before him.

"Just like to get there as soon as I can." The young man said, flashing a grin as the money danced in his hand.

Rusty put his hands on his hips and looked towards Sandusky. The sun was already hot and the shoreline was hazy from the heat. The island of Middle Bass was approximately 17 miles from Sandusky located on the southern Lake Erie shoreline in Ohio. If he opened her up he could make it back in time for the Put-in-Bay charter plus make an easy $25.00 to boot. He motioned the young man towards the boat and began untying the mooring lines.

The young man sprang into action and began untying the stern line.

"Hold it," Rusty said as the man was about to jump aboard, "Money first."

The young man winked and plopped the money into Rusty's extended palm.

Minutes later, the boat, with both men aboard, was churning its way to Sandusky Bay.

***

Sandusky in June of 1928 was a typical boating town. Each business, each lifestyle was touched in some way by the lake. Townsfolk lived, worked or played on Lake Erie and its shore. Not as industrial as the lake city of Lorain to the east, Sandusky was occupied by fisheries, small boat building and the excavation of limestone. Named from the Seneca Indian word *San Too Chee* meaning *Cold Water* (though some say for a 1700 fur trader named Sodowsky), its bay was protected by two peninsulas: Cedar Point to the east and Marblehead to the northwest. With a population just over 23,000, it was a jumping off point for the Lake Erie islands of North Bass, Middle Bass, South Bass, Kelleys, Rattlesnake, and Mouse plus the Canadian island of Pelee lying north of the international border that cut Lake Erie horizontally in half. Boaters, ferries and charters scurried back and forth between Sandusky and these islands. For the most part, island populations were light as access was dependent upon ferries and weather. Winter isolated them from the mainland and islanders had to wait until the ice grew thick enough to support vehicles fitted with skis or horse drawn sleighs to cross the frozen lake to the mainland. But summer saw a swell in numbers as mainlanders flooded the islands for summer getaways (with the exception of tiny Rattlesnake and even tinier Mouse islands remaining deserted due to their size and rocky terrain). South Bass with its boardwalk town of Put in Bay was already popular among the bourgeois as a summer retreat where restaurants, cottages, bike and boat rentals, water tobogganing, dance halls and underground caves to explore catered to the seasonal crowd. But no one had to tell men like Rusty what the lake offered. Whitefish, Herring and Blue Pike provided commercial and recreational fishing which was the basis of Sandusky's livelihood. Then there were the limestone quarries in Sandusky and on islands like Kelleys to the north which provided foundation rock, stone and gravel for construction in the growing region. With the city of Lorain's steel mill and ship building to the east and Toledo's industries to the west, the lake was bustling with industrial freighters, cargo ships, tugboats, charter boats and pleasure crafts from mid-March to November's stormy end when, bone-chilling arctic wind from Canada would sweep across the lake, thickening the ice and closing shipping lanes, locking the lake in a frigid, barren, silent world of frozen waves.

The Roaring Twenties and Prohibition affected the town much as it had other cities its size. Though not as popular as a smugglers' port as the nearby sleepy town of Vermilion, its location still made it a port of call for smugglers sneaking

bootlegged alcohol from wet Canada to the dry Ohio shores under the eyes of vigilant Coast Guard and federal agents. Lake Erie provided the perfect corridor to transport quality liquor legally made in Canada to the shores of Lake Erie via swift boats dubbed rumrunners where contacts along less populated rural areas would retrieve the contraband and disperse it throughout the country. However, remote places were not always a guarantee of safe passage. Although some big cities like Toledo turned a blind eye to bootlegging, smaller towns were split on upholding the 18th Amendment, and some citizens, whether out of boredom or morality were vigilant to any peculiar activities. During the open water seasons of Prohibition, the Coast Guard stationed out of Marblehead Point was kept busy patrolling the shoreline, apprehending rumrunners and dumping confiscated alcoholic contraband overboard into Sandusky Bay off Cedar Point. For the most part, these rumrunners were locals with small boats looking to put food on the table while other runners did it to get rich quick and have a thrill doing so. Ferrying the illegal booze from Canadian shores or anchored "mother" ships just over the border that divided the lake in half, a small-time boat pilot could make an easy $50 on a nights run. That was twice the money than a man could make working an entire week at an honest job.

***

"Live on the islands?" the young man asked as the bow of the boat smacked the choppy waves.

"No, Vermilion. I run charters out of Sandusky on weekends."

"Is this your boat or do you work for a company?"

"My boat," Rusty dug two cigarettes out of his shirt pocket and offered one to the young man. Idle chatter was not Rusty's favorite way to pass the time, but it was necessary to beat one's gums with the clientele on the charters. Treating them more like a friend instead of a meal ticket was one way to insure repeat business. The young man, however, had an air of adventure about him that made him more interesting than the usual white collar executives or celebratory birthday fishing trips that frequented his charters.

"So what's your day job?

"Deck hand on tugboats. I work out of Lorain," Rusty said, raising his voice over the drone of the motor, "Shipyards— push-pull ore freighters at the steel mill."

The young man raised his brows, seemingly impressed.

"When the shipping season ends for the winter, I work for Lyman's building boats. Just temporary until the lake opens again in spring," Rusty said. The young man made conversation easy.

"A man of the lake," the young man said.

"Not always. I worked two years at the steel mill in Lorain. Two years too long."

The young man smiled and nodded. “I’ve heard men tell that furnace is like looking into the jaws of hell. How they find anyone to do that job beats the hell out of me.”

“When you need dough, you would be surprised what you’ll do,” Rusty said as he flicked his spent cigarette into the lake. “Say, I didn’t catch your name?”

“Pete!” the young man said as he bounded towards Rusty with an extended hand.

“Rusty. You from Sandusky?” It was Rusty’s turn to quiz.

“Toledo.”

“So what’s your day job?”

“Don’t have a regular day job, so to speak, but I do okay.”

“I bet you do,” Rusty said, thinking of the 25 bucks so freely offered. Spray shot up from the bow of the boat as it smacked a wave.

Pete chuckled. “There is money to be made if you look in the right places.” He took a deep drag on his cigarette. “And it ain’t at a damn blast furnace.”

“So where do you look?” Rusty said. There was a hint of suspicion in his voice.

Pete’s eyes snapped and his smile tightened. “Is this a cross examination or you just curious, Red?”

“It’s Rusty, not Red.” Rusty’s voice was thick.

Pete drew a deep breath and leaned back onto the rail, and watched the green, frothy wake created by the boat. “There’s easy money to be made out there.”

“No such thing as easy money.”

Pete snorted and stared trancelike at the water.

Rusty decided to change the subject. “You see some action?” he said with a nod to the uniform covering Pete’s lower half.

Pete flicked his cigarette butt overboard. “Naw, I was too young for the war,” he said, looking down at his pants. “The old lady running the boarding house where I lived was throwing these things out and I said, ‘whoa, now that’s too keen to throw out.’ Great as a dame magnet—they think I saw action.”

Rusty’s rolled eyes went unnoticed by Pete. The word keen or magnet did not come to mind when he was fighting for his life and that of his mates onboard ship in the Merchant Marines. He may have felt keen standing in line for enlistment at the drug store in Toledo, and being a dame magnet did cross his mind when he saw himself in uniform for the first time. Keen, or rather excitement came to his mind when he arrived for training in Massachusetts—his first time out of Ohio, then pride when he was assigned to a steamer in the north Atlantic. But once the torpedoes began launching from Heinie U-boats with his ship’s name on them, he no longer felt keen or magnetic but scared shitless.

A large white boat emblazed with emblems approached them off starboard, bringing both men back to reality. Rusty recognized it as a newly built picket boat. The numbers CG157 were displayed on the bow’s hull.

“Coast Guard,” Rusty said over his shoulder to Pete.

“With a bastard on board for a captain,” Pete muttered as he moved to the starboard rail to watch the cutter sweep by. It left an undulating wake in its aftermath that rocked Rusty’s boat back and forth.

“Is that Captain Connors’s boat?”

“It’s Captain Kid all right,” Pete said.

“Many think Connors a hero of sorts,” Rusty said, casting a wary eye at Pete. “But then I guess it has to do with what side of the fence you’re on.”

“It also depends what your view of a hero is.” Pete folded his arms and leaned against the rail, facing Rusty. “I personally don’t consider a guy who gets his kicks ripping a man apart with a machine gun a hero.”

“It does have a way of discouraging bootleggers/”

Pete didn’t laugh. “Does it also discourage fishing? Last month the hero riddled a fisherman full of holes by accident and nothing ever came of it.”

“The buzz at the docks said the fisherman’s boat was used as a rumrunner.”

Pete ignored the remark. “Shoot first, ask questions later—Connors’s motto.” He held his hands up to simulate holding a machine gun. “Rat-tat-tat-tat-tat,” he mocked as he “shot” at a phantom boat, then turned his imaginary gun towards the back of the disappearing Coast Guard cutter and continued to “shoot”.

Rusty shook his head. One thing for sure, Pete made the trip interesting as well as lucrative. With the throttle opened up, the boat no longer fought the waves but skimmed across the water, making the ride smooth and fast.

“A farmer was killed in Vermilion last night,” Rusty said. “Apparently bootleggers mistook him for a contact.”

“Sounds like more to that story.”

“Guess the old man opened fire on them when they came ashore on his beach and they shot back.”

“Then Wyatt Earp was asking for it.”

“What he was asking for was to be left alone and milk his cow.”

With the skyline of Sandusky emerging from the haze and growing sharper by the minute, Pete calmed and took a seat near Rusty. “*Rising Sun*, good name for a fishing boat though she doesn’t look like your typical charter cruiser.”

“She’s a Lyman—a runabout,” Rusty said. “I wasn’t looking for big charter jobs, just something that could pay for itself while having some fun with it.”

“She’s smooth.”

“Lyman is known for building a good boat that can handle this lake’s chop. That’s why the ride is so smooth.”

“She fast?”

“That’s why I wanted one. Fast but smooth.”

“Dream boat, uh?”

“I guess you could say.”

“*Rising Sun*,” Pete said, stretching the name out. “The early bird catches the worm or in this case, the fish.”

A faint smile crossed Rusty’s face.

"I don't see too many rising suns in my business," Pete said.

Rusty wasn't sure if Pete wanted him to comment on that remark, so he decided not to pursue it. He turned the topic back to the boat. "Actually, I named it for a place here in Ohio about 50 miles inland, south of Toledo. Farming country, and like you said, it also makes a good name for a fishing boat."

Pete waited for him to continue, but Rusty seemed lost in his thoughts. "You raised there?" Pete asked, bringing him back.

"No, I was raised in Toledo. When my mother died I was ten so I went to live with a widowed aunt who had a farm in Risingsun."

"Sounds boring."

Rusty smiled. "I grew up working her farm and living on potato soup." *Chrissake, he was spilling his guts to this guy.* "There were back payments that she did not…could not pay and the bank doesn't cut any slack for a widow woman and fourteen-year-old boy. She lost the farm. I returned to Toledo and got a job on the docks. By seventeen, I was working as a trainee on the tugs doing everything from scraping hulls to swabbing the deck. Then the war came and I joined the Merchant Marines."

"Liked the water better than the dirt, uh?"

"Little more excitement on the water…but it would be nice to have the farm back if just for the sake of it. Listen to crickets instead of gulls for a change."

Pete noticed Rusty's smile was fading. "What makes you think the farm is still there?"

Rusty eyed the tall profile of the Marblehead Lighthouse marking the entrance into Sandusky Bay and nosed the *Rising Sun* eastward toward Cedar Point.

"It's probably long gone."

He cut *Rising Sun* between the peninsula of Marblehead on their starboard and sprawling Kelleys Island off their port side before making a right turn into the mouth of the bay whose entrance was flanked by the lighthouse on one side and Cedar Point on the other.

They both fell silent for a few minutes until Pete broke the silence. "You married?"

Rusty raised his brow. Pete was just one question after another. "That's where the steel mill comes in." Lake gulls began circling the boat as Sandusky grew larger and landmark buildings were now easily distinguishable.

"When I got back from the war, I met my wife-to-be in Lorain. Her Dad and brothers worked at the steel mill. They got me a job there. Steady income, job security, the whole bit. It got me this boat, nice cottage and a happy wife and I hated every minute I worked there. When I started the charters, I quit and went back to the tugs. Her family thought I was nuts giving up a job like that." He began backing down the boat's engine. "You married?"

Pete stood for a better view of Sandusky. "Yeah, right," he said. "Last thing I'm looking for is a manacle on my finger."

As they entered the bay, Rusty cut the engines, and minutes later they were docking. When the boat was secured, Pete turned to him and extended his hand. "Perhaps we'll meet again," he said with a grin.

"Stranger things have happened," Rusty said, shaking Pete's hand.

Pete laughed as he jumped onto the pier.

Rusty gathered some stowed fishing tackle in the bow storage for the scheduled charter and when he looked up again, Pete had vanished into the dockyards. Smuggler, he thought. Pete definitely had to be a smuggler. It wasn't uncommon for the Coast Guard to kick a smuggler off onto one of the islands after seizing his rum running boat and booty. That would explain Pete's disheveled appearance and need for a ride back to the mainland. He wondered if it was Connors who left Pete stranded on Middle Bass Island. No, he decided, if Connors had caught him, Pete wouldn't be hitching a ride home. There was some truth to what Pete had said about the Coast Guard captain's shoot first, ask questions later policy. It was common practice for Connors to riddle a boat and its occupants with bullets before demanding surrender from whoever was left to respond. His punishment was as ruthless as it was self-righteous. As commander of the rum chaser CG157, he was as much a swashbuckling hero as he was a relentless scourge. His trademark was a Savage Lewis .30 caliber machine gun which he toted like some men carried pistols. Capable of firing 500-600 rounds per minute, Connors and his infamous gun set a record in the summer of 1927 by catching a rum smuggler every other day for a seven week period. But his ethics were questioned by fellow guardsmen and civilians alike, and the line between hero and sadist was often blurred.

The fisherman Pete had referred to was using his boat to smuggle liquor from Leamington, Ontario across the lake to Lorain. His destination was a restaurant that resembled a medieval castle built on the shoreline. The castle's basement had a tunnel that opened to the lake, and rumrunners arriving from Canadian shores laden with bootleg would pull into the tunnel to an underground dock and be met by the restaurant's personnel who unloaded the smuggled liquor. It was rumored that Al Capone ate at *Castle Erie* when meeting with his Cleveland cohorts. Whether or not the rumor was true, it made great publicity for the restaurant, so the owner perpetuated the rumor with reports of phantom sightings of Capone.

On board the fisherman's boat that particular night of the run was a small-time hood from an Italian mob out of Toledo. Connors had caught wind of the run and at nightfall, he positioned his cutter just off the Lorain shore near the restaurant, switched off the running lights and cut the motor. Just before midnight, the rum running fishing boat arrived and as it was entering the tunnel the pilot caught sight of the shadowy cutter positioning itself to block the opening into the tunnel. The small rumrunner gunned the engines and nimbly maneuvered out of the tunnel's entrance and attempted to outrun the cutter, but the CG157 was fast and closing with Connors blazing away on his .30 caliber machine gun. The smugglers' boat ran a zigzag course to no avail and after an hour long chase, the .30 caliber's bullets succeeded in ripping the mobster nearly in half. Meanwhile, Connors's first mate sent a bullet through the head of the pilot of the runner. The pilot slumped forward, landing on the throttle, pushing it up to full throttle. Crowds, attracted by the gunfire, had gathered along the shore to watch the spectacle as the runner zigzagged, circled and sped out of control until it crashed into a jut of rocks off Avon Point and exploded into a ball of fire that sent a firework spray of orange sparks raining onto the dark water. It was never proved who shot first or if indeed the rumrunner was returning fire. Connors, whose crew of two was button-lipped and as maverick as he, was never questioned. The incident was met with uncertainty and unspoken suspicion by Connors's peers. Most Coast Guardsmen were content with stranding the runner and crew on one of the islands and seizing the boat to auction off later. It was not so much as a virtuous gesture as it was one of practicality because despite a solid case against the smuggler, attorneys usually managed to exonerate them over some obscured detail, making a mockery out of the Coast Guard in the process.

Stranding a smuggler and seizing his boat, then dumping the booty overboard gave the Guard some sense of satisfaction despite the fact a smuggler could always find a willing skipper to take him back to the mainland for a few bucks. A few days later, the smuggler would then buy his boat back without contest at auction. Running rum, after all, was a very lucrative business.

The guardsmen at Erie's southern shore stations felt Connors's hollow victories came with a price that they had to pay, for now the smugglers and runners no longer took chances and began to fight back. Some armed themselves, others armored their runners. Either way, none wanted to end up in the sink courtesy of Connors. The captain had a dark side and how he managed to put together a crew in league with him eluded the other Guardsmen, but he got the job done and superiors were happy, so they looked the other way. They nicknamed him Captain Kid. It was meant as a joke, but Connors's relished the moniker and it fed his zeal all the more.

Rusty backed the boat from the dock, nosing her bow towards the islands. Like most people, he hungrily followed the newspaper accounts of bootleggers, rumrunners and gangsters. Still, they were stories on paper whereas Pete was flesh and blood. Di would be intrigued but upset to know he had had a brush with a real hoodlum. It was one thing to be shocked and fascinated by the exploits of Capone, Dutch Schultz and the Purple Gang in the newspaper where they were safe on print. She would not understand how incidental the whole thing was with Pete. Besides, he didn't figure it out himself until he was already in route to Sandusky that Pete was a runner. But it didn't matter, twenty-five bucks was twenty-five bucks, and if he hadn't taken Pete, someone else would have. No skin off his nose. As he headed for Put-in-Bay, Rusty checked his watch—forty-five minutes until the next scheduled charter. If he really *opened her up* he could make it to the island by a gnat's ass. He pushed the throttle forward and *Rising Sun* sent up cascading spray as she slapped the waves then rose out of the water and planed on top, skimming the water on her dash to Put-in-Bay.

Thirty-five minutes later as he pulled into the dock, he checked his watch and chuckled.

Chapter 2

Di did not find Rusty's adventure as exciting as he had hoped. Her mind was elsewhere and that disappointed him.She was never bored to hear his stories—like how one of the great stone freighters had its load shift, causing it to list dangerously, and how the tugboats, with him on deck, had pushed it upright and held it till the load was evened, or how Shorty Samuels got his foot crushed between a tugboat and dock on a windy day. She had held her breath as he told about being caught in a waterspout on a charter run with a group of Lorain steel executives out for a fishing trip, and how he was hired to take the wealthy Miss Pendleton and a group of her society friends from her father's Kelleys Island mansion to a picnic at Put-in-Bay. It was by the widening or narrowing of her eyes that he could tell what impact his stories were having.

Tonight, though, her eyes were far away and he knew his story about Pete would be lost in an ocean of thought. He studied her face for a clue as to what she had on her mind, and as they took their seats at the kitchen table, with his eyes fixed on hers, he asked, "How was your day?"

For the first time since he had come home, her eyes focused on his. She hesitated, rummaging through her mind, and then her eyes sparkled. "A bootlegger came to the door this morning…he needed a place to hide because agents were hot on his tail, so I hid him in the root cellar in exchange for a case of beer. He's still there. Wanna beer?"

He stared at her as he registered what she had said then he burst into laughter.

She laughed too. "Okay, so it was the milkman with a bottle of milk, but that's as good as it gets."

The old twinkle was back in Di's eyes. Relieved, he attacked his plate of potatoes, peas and pork chops while Di pecked at hers.

***

He had met Di the day after a monster tornado hit downtown Lorain. She was a volunteer with the Salvation Army and he was a volunteer for clean-up in the aftermath of destruction. Her job was filling plates of three squares a day for storm refugees and volunteers; his was digging through rubble for the injured and dead, then cleaning the debris of what was once a bustling city center. The June 28, 1924 tornado brought Rusty and Di's lives together in what Di would later proclaim as fate.

Di's family lived southwest of the city where the land turned rural. Uncle Fritz, her mother's brother who lived with them, had noted their barometer steadily falling and mentioned to Di and her mother a storm was coming.

They were picking strawberries in the garden when the mother stood to straighten her back and noticed the black sky and white rolling squall line of clouds plowing ahead by the advancing storm like a snowplow pushing snow. "Grab your basket, Di, and head for the house. We are in for a blow."

Born in the farmland southwest of the city of Sandusky shortly before 4:30 p.m., the tornado touched ground and began its 52 mile journey to the east, bulldozing everything in its path, heading directly for the unsuspecting city of Lorain.

Rusty, who was working seven day shifts at the Lorain dockyard, had just docked and secured the tugboat as the first big raindrops fell. He just made it to the cover of the wheelhouse as the rain came down in torrents. He and the rest of the tug crew watched as pea-sized hail bounced on the deck alongside pounding raindrops.

As they hunted the skies, the tugboat's engineer was the first to spot the tornado.

"Look, it's a twister!" he shouted, and Rusty and the first mate flew to the front windshield of the pilothouse and watched as the tornado bore down upon the city.

Passing too close for comfort, they watched as the destruction of Lorain unfolded before them. As quickly as it had come, it had left, leaving the crew stunned as they stared through the blurred windows trying to distinguish shapes and landmarks through the ensuing sheets of rain.

"Looks like we are in for a long night, boys," the boat's master said with grim expression, breaking the silence.

Rusty pulled on a raincoat, grabbed a flashlight and the ax that hung on the wheelhouse and led the solemn procession down the wharf towards the city.

The State Theater had collapsed, killing 15 people and burying others alive. Seventy-three people in total were killed and 200 needed emergency surgery. With electrical, telegraph and street car lines down and streets piled high with rubble and trees, Lorain was cut off from the rest of the world, and night was closing in. For the first time, the bustling industrial city of Lorain was silent. Soon flashlights and lanterns appeared. Voices called out. Word got out, and by 10 o'clock that night, doctors and nurses from Cleveland began arriving by tugboats by means of Lake Erie. Before the night was over, the city's hospital was full.

The light of the following morning revealed a scene that was apocalyptic. Broadway Avenue was reduced to piles of rubble. Neighborhoods were indistinguishable. Roads, if recognized, were impassable. Residents were dazed. One thousand homes were damaged; five hundred homes and two hundred businesses were destroyed.

The Red Cross was the first to arrive and immediately established an emergency relief hospital in the city's high school. The Salvation Army followed and set up canteens to feed the storm refugees and the rescue workers. As word got out, people began arriving from surrounding communities to offer help. Rusty was among those who volunteered.

It was in the supper line at the Salvation Army's canteen that Rusty first laid eyes on Di as she plopped meatloaf on the extended plates of tired volunteers and storm refugees. When it was his turn, she had looked him directly in the eye and with an infectious smile said, "Is that enough gravy?"

Only he heard, *I'll have your baby.*

He saw her three times a day for the next two days, making sure he always got in her line and if she happened not to be on duty, he waited until she was. She asked him where he worked when he wasn't cleaning up after twisters and he said *with towing at the shipyards and steel docks.* He asked her if she had ever been to the dance hall at Ruggles Beach up the road. She said *yes.* When she asked if he liked to dance, he said *no but would go if she would be there.* So she said, *Ab-so-lute-ly!* He then said *how about the Saturday after this coming one... we could use a break from this,* to which she said, *Ducky!*

Six months later, they married and bought a cottage on the lake in the town of Vermilion. The cottage was a bargain as it had sustained damage from the large, crashing waves that accompanied the tornado as it skirted Vermilion on its way to Lorain. Rusty was handy with a hammer as years on the farm molded him into a self-taught carpenter and within six months, the cottage was restored, only better than before. And Di, an accomplished seamstress—one of the skills forced upon her by her mother while growing up, transferred the cottage into a home that made any man glad to come home to. Together they made a team.

Chapter 3

It was after they were married that her brothers got him a job in the steel mill. More money and job stability were the incentives and with every drive to work, he hated the job more. When he left the mill two years later, her family nearly disowned him except for her Uncle Fritz who had listened impassively to his announcement and explanation to the family of why he was quitting the mill and returning to tugboats. To put it simply, he preferred the open water to entombment in a volcano and no amount of money could even the scales. As they sat around the supper table, he assured her family that he had it all figured out. He had taken the Coast Guard test and was certified now as Able Bodied Seaman which was a higher ranking than deckhand, meaning more responsibility and pay. He would work his way up to mate which was right under master—another name for captain. On weekends, he would charter *Rising Sun* for fishing excursions and ferrying people and freight. When asked what he would do when shipping lanes closed for the season and Erie freezes over, he replied that Lyman Boat Works, a company he worked at before the tugboats, was moving from Cleveland to Sandusky and with his prior experience of boat building with them, he should have no trouble getting employment over the winter. If he hustled at chartering and got the promotion to mate, he could draw the same pay. When he had finished his plan of execution, he was met with a wall of silence until Di's father broke it by saying, "Well it sounds like you have thought this through." Her brothers, on the other hand, scowled at him through the rest of the meal.

While Di's brothers had declared his quitting of the mill *a stupid thing to do* and her father said *looking a gift horse in the mouth*, Uncle Fritz sat quietly by taking in all the commotion caused by that announcement. He was a robust man with ruddy cheeks who was short on words and long on laughter which consisted of a rolling, ongoing chuckle. He wasn't laughing though on the day he followed Rusty alone out into the yard after Rusty had dropped the *quitting the mill* bomb during the family's Sunday meal.

"The mill will put money in a man's pocket but it will take his soul in return," Uncle Fritz had said, "And a man shouldn't be without his soul." No ongoing chuckle followed. After a silent pause, Uncle Fritz had then poked Rusty in the ribs and added with a twinkle in his eye, "Separating you from the lake would be like separating a German from his beer." He then broke into his signature chuckle, only cranked a notch louder and smacked Rusty on the back. No one laughed harder at their own jokes than Uncle Fritz. And no one made better homemade beer.

***.

After the tears quit flowing and his new course of action proved it could still pay the bills, Di decided to get a job as a lace maker in the nearby town of Elyria for "fun money" as she called it and for something to do as most her friends now had jobs. Each weekday morning at 6:00 a.m., she caught the LakeShore Electric's interurban streetcar downtown, rode it to Lorain where she caught the Yellow Line interurban for a fifteen minute ride to Elyria where it deposited her downtown. From there, she caught a bus to Elyria's industrial center and walked the remaining distance to the lace factory where she worked. As the streetcars whizzed down the tracks shooting a shower of white and blue sparks from its connector to the electric lines, she would immerse herself in Virginia Woolf's *To the Lighthouse* or Ann Loos's *But Gentlemen Marry Brunettes* (of course being a brunette herself she already knew) or whatever novel of rage was being currently devoured by a public hungry for excitement. At the factory, her job was rolling finished lace unto spindles—a boring job nonetheless helped along by her humming of tunes such as *Wish I could Shimmy like my Sister Kate* or *I'm Just Wild About Harry*, substituting Rusty for Harry in her head. But break time was seasoned with gossip and laughter as women shared cigarettes over news such as Joan Crawford's hottest look or laments over Valentino's death. New boyfriends, bad boyfriends, husbands and the hot-looking delivery truck driver were also topics of conversation.

Her job was a mere ripple in home life being no children involved and supper still appeared on the table at its usual time or close to it. With the extra income, she could remain in fashion and fad—something that made her happy, and therefore Rusty. Often while waiting for the bus home she would slip into the Five and Dime for the latest *Vogue* or *True Stories* or a pack of Luckies so she didn't have to bum cigs off Rusty. She used her money to buy silk material with pink peonies and black trim to sew a kimono to wear to her Saturday afternoon Mah-jongg games to the delight of her friends who showed up the following week also clad in kimonos and waving Oriental hand fans. That was the same week she added a parasol made of bamboo and rice paper to her ensemble. The extra income from the lace factory also allowed Rusty and her to attend the talking pictures and theater on a regular basis at the newly built Palace Theater in Lorain (formerly the State which was destroyed by the tornado), although Rusty could do without the plays preferring Tom Mix westerns and Buster Keaton's *The General* over *Funny Face* and *An American in Paris.* And with the mill no longer having a strangle hold of shift turns and overtime on him, Sunday afternoons (when there were no charters) could be spent picnicking on Put-in Bay or riding the coaster and merry-go-round down the road at Crystal Beach Park in Vermilion. Although Di would have dearly loved to shimmy at the area's many dance halls and cheer on a dance derby now and then, she knew it would be asking a lot of Rusty. It wasn't much of a sacrifice for her as she considered that phase of her life as the *pre-alter years* and was quite happy with her present situation.

Chapter 4

The tugboat yard where Rusty worked after leaving the mill was located in the Lorain Harbor where the mouth of the muddy Black River met Lake Erie. An immense breakwater was constructed off shore to protect the harbor from the lake's choppy waves gnawing away the shoreline. An assortment of tugboats, including those of Erie Towing where he was employed as an AB Seaman, assisted the big freighters (called lakers), barges and ships of National Tube of U.S. Steel (a.k.a. the steel mill) and American Shipbuilding, both located a short way up river.

When Rusty arrived at the towing yard early Monday morning, the day after meeting Pete the smuggler, he heard a commotion coming from the docks outside the dispatcher's station. From what he could see, it looked like the dispatcher and the boss's son, Eliot were squabbling in a pretty heated argument. The dispatcher and Eliot, both tomato-faced were squared off and yelling in each other's face. Eliot was making wild gestures toward a new trainee who stood quietly to the side.

Despite their obvious yelling, he could not hear a word they said over the clatter and screech of arriving coal cars and incessant banging of the mill beating ingots of ore into steel. Added to the mix was the riveting and hammering from the shipyards and the clamorous cat-like squawks overhead from aggravated lake gulls squabbling over garbage and fish guts.

Frank Kopinski, the mate from the tugboat, *Cherokee*, had now joined the fray and Eliot, like a dog trying to decide who to bite first, split his time between screaming at the dispatcher and the mate. Rusty shook his head.

Eliot was an asshole from the get-go according to the employees at Erie Towing, and they felt this badge most likely extended beyond the world of the dockyard. Having his father as owner of the company gave him a ticket to say or do whatever he wanted to whomever he wanted, completely ignoring the hierarchy of the job. It also gave him a ticket on the express lane to becoming a tug master. No one wanted to work with him and when trouble arose, which it eventually did, the dispatcher would shuttle him off to another crew, passing him off like a bad check. After Eliot joined Erie T, Rusty noticed mysterious little things happening. Sometimes he'd find his tools broke or missing and things would be out of place and it grated him as he was adamant that things be placed properly for safety's sake. There was not enough evidence to point the finger, but in his heart he knew it had to be Eliot behind all this as these things did not happen before he joined the company. Too make matters worse, he had to go behind Eliot and fix his mistakes. Like babysitting, he told the tugboat's engineer.

At this point, Eliot was the same rank as him—an AB Seaman although their rationality and abilities were poles apart. Rumors floated that a position would be opening for mate on the tug, *Iroquois* after the winter hiatus making Rusty and Eliot both eligible for the coveted slot despite Rusty's seniority. The *Iroquois*'s master, Captain McIntyre pushed for Rusty, and Rusty also had the popular vote among the crews for the position but being the boss's son held water. Still, Eliot harbored jealously and resentment over Rusty's wisdom and high regard among the crews.

Rusty decided to avoid the quarrelling knot of men, and head the long way around to where his tug was docked awaiting the day's orders. The shipyards around the towing company docks glowed in luminous orange as the morning sun breeched the sooty hills of coal and iron ingots, carving rays of gold through the tall metal and brick canyons. The steel mill on the west bank of the harbor resembled a sprawling medieval fortress made of metal, rust and soot with tall smoke stacks for turrets. It glowed orange with the first rays of light—the best its grimy façade would look all day until sunset gilded it in pinks and oranges. At the river's bend, across from the mill, American Ship Building spread along the banks of the Black River. The fingers of golden sunlight found their way through the enormous dry dock cradling the skeleton of an immense laker under construction and bounced sunlight off the sheets of steel and hammer heads as men crawled like ants around and through the developing hull.

The sky above was already swarming with gulls and the air, like always, stank like rotting eggs from the steel mill's pickling vats. Thick, yellow sulfurous smoke circled the city surrounding the mill, burning noses and coating throats. Monstrous machinery moved and bellowed like prehistoric creatures. Tall smoke stacks venting Vulcan furnaces shot flames of orange and blue into the sky, licking the heavens with fiery tongues. Metal groaned, and grit and red-orange ash fell like dirty confetti.

As Rusty approached the *Iroquois*, Davey Reynolds, the tugboat's engineer, poked his head out from the engine room where he was running checks. He was lanky and tall and bent slightly forward like he was always ducking a low doorway. His face was agreeable and radiated a contentment that bore no lines despite its middle age. His hat, grease smudged and a bit flat in the crown, sat back on his head and his sparkling blue eyes and lively voice told his love of his work.

"Watch it, Rusty," he said with a chuckle, "Eliot has worked himself into a lather earlier than usual this morning. You may be next on his hit list."

Rusty snorted. "Maybe his old man cut him out of the will?"

Davey laughed. "The new kid is probably getting a taste of Eliot's guiding principle of placing the blame on others."

"Idiot needs to go soak his head."

He dubbed Eliot Idiot after his third major slip up nearly cost a crew member his life. Anyone else would have been fired at that point. In the last incident, Eliot tried to pin it on Rusty but Cap McIntyre, high in his wheelhouse, saw the whole thing and gave Eliot three days without pay. And that was the beginning of the bad blood between Eliot and Rusty. From that day on, Rusty never missed an opportunity to substitute Idiot for Eliot. It was "Idiot, make a square knot to secure this" or "Idiot, Cap wants to see you." Eliot ignored the dig, but his face would turn beet red, and he was often seen making obscene gestures behind Rusty's back.

Davey joined Rusty on the deck of the tug where Rusty had busied himself checking towlines.

"Did ya hear what happened west of Vermilion at the road blockade on 6?" He said, vigorously rubbing grease off his hands with a rag. Rusty shook his head, so Davey continued. "This bootlegger was driving a hearse with a coffin loaded with hooch. He figured he couldn't make it through the road block being it was close to dusk so he hired a tow truck to pull him like he had broken down, and he gets waved straight through the blockade."

Rusty grinned.

"So then," Davey continued, "He gets to Sandusky where he is suppose to meet up with some guys with a boat but they never show. It's pushing midnight and he's getting antsy, so he heads for Bucyrus without the tow truck and runs into another road block. Well, this time, deputies smell a fish and search the hearse. When they open the coffin lid they hit jackpot—it's loaded with Seagrams and Corby's Select."

"Sounds like he should have stuck with the side roads," Rusty said.

"He did, he did," Davey said laughing. "The area is crawling with cops and federal boys—probably Capone's train car was spotted on the sidetrack at Bucyrus or something. It's crazy out there, Rusty. Seems like every hoi polloi and their grandmother is making, storing or running booze."

"Either way, he's dumb. He should have waited till broad daylight and thrown a widow woman on board complete with hanky, tears and a bogus priest," Rusty said to which Davey laughed all the more.

As Rusty began readying the deck gear for the day's work, he wondered if the boat that didn't show, the one the hearse was waiting for, involved Pete. Made sense, he thought. Pete's boat got busted, and Pete and company got dumped off on the island. The lack of shouting from the dispatcher's terminal caught his attention.

"Looks like the row has been settled," Davey said, ducking back into the engine room.

"That or Kopinski tossed Idiot to the fish." Rusty said.

A few moments later, the new trainee appeared at Rusty's tugboat. His hands were buried in his pockets and he looked like a dog that had just been kicked.

"I have been reassigned to your boat," he said sheepishly.

"Sounds to me like you got a promotion," Rusty said. "Come aboard, kid."

Chapter 5

Erie Towing was one of a few towing companies that served the lake's southern shore. It was a small company providing harbor tugs for push—pull services for shipping companies using Lorain's harbor. Like other companies its size on the Great Lakes, it was at risk of losing clientele to bigger companies who could provide more services and lower costs due to volume. One particular conglomerate who operated out of most of the ports of the five Great lakes shared Lorain harbor with Erie Towing. They provided not only the same services as Erie Towing, but push boats for barges, firefighting tugs and big ocean going tugs to assist ships in trouble further out in the lake—a job too difficult for Erie T's smaller tugs. Competition was stiff as towing companies were pressured by the shipping industry to provide quality service at the lowest cost and only the big companies with their large fleets and specialized services could survive the competition. Erie Towing was beginning to feel the pressure.

The fleet of Erie Towing consisted of five harbor tugs whose ownership had passed father to son for three generations. They were called screw tugs because their propellers, located under their hulls, turned like a giant screw. Unfortunately, this made them more vulnerable to the wash or wake of a large moving ship than the newer stern-driven tugboats so the dangers of capsizing or being sucked under the ship were increased. Erie T, as they called themselves, recently upgraded three of their five tugs from steam to diesel power at considerable cost. Diesel meant more power and power was what tugboats needed in order to manipulate a 20,000 ton, 600-foot super freighters that were now being built.

The *Iroquois*, *Cherokee*, *Wyandot*, *Shawnee* and *Delaware* of Erie T were emblematic of the classic tugboat. They had hulls of thick plated steel painted black and rolled fenders for protection against ships' impacts. Tractor and truck tires were chained to their sides as additional bumpers. Hunks of old towline were layered over their bows giving the boats a shaggy sheep dog nose look. This also offered additional protection to the bow from the jarring impacts the tugs (and crew) would endure on a continual daily basis as the tugboats pushed, pulled and towed large cumbersome ships in or out of harbor.

As a deck hand aboard the *Iroquois*, Rusty's main job was manning the towlines. Made of hemp rope, these towlines could measure from 6-12 inches in diameter. His duties included throwing the line to a ship and then securing it to the giant steel H-bitt where, like a hitch on a vehicle, the stress of towing was centered. It was his responsibility to make sure the line was properly guided through the molgoggers and Norman pins along the bulwark to keep it straight and taunt during a tow. If his line was positioned at a wrong angle, the tugboat could capsized or be pulled into the ship in an event called girding. If he allowed the line to go slack, the tugboat would lose control of the big ship or foul the tug's propeller by entangling the line in it. Along with such vital duties, he also had the mundane tasks of maintaining the equipment and keeping the tugboat clean and painted.

The other crew members of the *Iroquois* consisted of Nick Petrakis, the mate who supervised the deck and was second in command under Cap McIntyre, Davey—the engineer whose knowledge of the new diesel engine was invaluable and Jimmy, the greenhorn rejected from Eliot's tugboat.

***

Friday brought a choppy lake and no sun. Beyond the breakwater, the lake was an endless expanse of whitecaps and the west wind, though warm, whipped through the harbor and tore unsecured caps and hats from heads. The towing companies were hustling and bustling trying to keep up the demand the weather had put on them in assisting wind-tossed ships and barges through the channels and harbor.

The *Iroquois* had just pulled into dock upon returning from replacing a channel marker when the dispatcher met them. He had to raise his voice to be heard above the wind. He had papers with orders for Cap McIntyre. Rusty and the trainee moored the boat while McIntyre and Mate Nick disembarked and approached the dispatcher. Davey stuck his head out from the engine room, trying to catch bits of the conversation sailing past him on the wind.

"There's a ship just beyond the breakwater that is having a helluva time trying to get into port," the dispatcher said, the wind snatching the words from his mouth. "She's a five hundred foot ore carrier and could use three tugs but the *Cherokee* is down for repairs."

Captain McIntyre winced. "Well, the steamers are out—they just don't have the power. We have to stick with the tow diesels and make do."

"I'll give you Kopinski and Eliot from the *Cherokee*. That will give you a total of two mates and two hands plus the trainee," the dispatcher said with finality. With a nod from Captain McIntyre, he hurried back to his office.

Rusty didn't hear him say Frankie's name, but he did pick out the name Eliot and that made him groan. No one wanted to work with Eliot, but he the least.

Captain McIntyre called the crew together once back on deck. "I don't know if you heard, but we got a freighter beyond the breakwater and just two tugs to do the job in this blow. She's gonna be like a sail in this wind. Frankie is going to assist Nick as Second Mate and Eliot will help Rusty on deck." He looked Rusty straight in the eye. "I'm counting on you Rusty."

Rusty nodded.

As soon as Frankie and Eliot were aboard and the mooring lines freed, the *Iroquois* cleared the dock, and Captain McIntyre throttled up the engine. The tugboat with the big letter E on the side of its wheelhouse headed out the channel with the tug, *Wyandot* close behind.

The freighter, as the dispatcher had said, was a 500-foot ore carrier out of Superior, Wisconsin. She was heavy in the water with her load of ore which gave her some stability but the expanse of steel that made up her hull was catching the west wind and pushing her sideways as she struggled to pass the breakwater and enter the harbor.

The *Iroquois*, with her veteran crew, would position itself at the bow as the head tug while the *Wyandot* would take the stern. Both positions posed its own unique dangers of collision, capsizing or being run down by the moving ship, potential events accelerated by the wind and waves.

As the *Iroquois* approached the ship's starboard bow, Rusty tied a monkey fist knot the size of a muskmelon at the end of the tow lead in order to add weight and momentum to the line for the throw from the tug to the ship. Above him, two crew members of the ore carrier looked down upon him and watched anxiously as they waited for Rusty to throw the line up to them. The wind was whipping their shirts and pant legs wildly. The throw would be tough.

Captain McIntyre brought the *Iroquois* alongside the swaying ship and fought the swells and wind as he labored with the wheel and throttle to position the bouncing tug accurately. His eyes were everywhere, scrutinizing the ship, Rusty, the bow and bulwarks, Eliot at the bollard and the tug's portside. Instinctively, he used wheel and throttle to make corrections. He was well aware his crew's lives were dependent on his snap judgments, but his face did not betray his concern. Only a furrow between his eyebrows revealed his concentration.

Rusty, with rope in hand, positioned himself at the bullnose and steadied himself by standing wide legged. He began swinging the section of rope with the knot in it to build its momentum as he eyed the men above him who were at one moment close and a second later, too far away as they rocked up and down with the rolling ship. He knew second or third chances would be few and far between. He synchronized the rock of the tug, the up and down action of the ship and the swing of the rope, calculating the movements. Suddenly, all aligned and he reacted in split second. Every muscle tensed and released as he threw his body weight into the throw. The rope snaked up, uncoiling as it rose up and outwards towards the men straining over the rails to catch the end with the monkey fist knot. They caught it. Skill, more than luck, guided the line and it would not have been unusual for a seasoned deckhand to miss the line's mark in these conditions.

The towline, now affixed to the ship by the men, ran from the ore carrier to the tugboat, back through the tug's bullnose ring, passed through cleats and back to the towing bollard where Eliot was rapidly wrapping and securing the tow line around the H—bitt.

Cap McIntyre reversed the engines and struggled with the wheel and throttle to keep steady strain on the taut towline to avoid fouling or loss of control. It was not an easy feat as each roll of the ship or dip of the tug threatened to sag the line.

With the line secured to the bollard, Eliot ran back to the safety of the wheel house as the line began to tighten between the two vessels.

"Rusty, get your ass back here," McIntyre yelled at Rusty's hesitation. He followed Rusty's stare to water level where the big ship's hull was displacing the flow of water. He knew instantly as did Rusty an interaction was occurring-interaction being the displacement of water under the ship's hull. It meant the flow of water around the massive hull of the ore carrier, coupled with the wind and swells, created an area of low pressure adjacent to the ship's starboard bow right where the *Iroquois* was positioned. This situation had a suction-like effect and if the *Iroquois* could not be freed of the ship's drag, it would be sucked under the freighter's hull.

The towline strained against the molgoggers. Rusty kept a wary eye on them. If these guides failed, the towline would sweep across the deck and the *Iroquois* would most likely be capsized and or overrun by the huge ship.

McIntyre fought to keep control of the tugboat which bashed against the ship. The tug crew grabbed whatever was solid close to them to brace themselves from the jarring impacts. Then the *Iroquois*, like a slow motion wreck, began to be pulled toward the ship's massive bow, resisting the reverse of the powerful diesel tug engine. She had to be freed and fast or she would go under. Rusty instinctively sprang for the bollard to slip the line and slammed to a stop, staring in disbelief at the rope hitch Eliot had tied. Eliot had failed to turn up the towline. "Turning the rope up" was a means of tying a towline that allowed for quick release in an emergency and this was an emergency plus. Rusty cursed. No time. A fire ax hung at the front of the wheelhouse just behind the bollard. He lunged forward and snatched it from its rack as the tugboat list to port side and began to nose down, throwing Rusty up against the bollard. Davey, his blue eyes no longer dancing, came on deck to see why the tug was listing, grabbing the rail of the wheelhouse steps to brace himself from falling on the rebounding deck. At stern, the trainee slipped and fell, then clung to the bulwark once he got his feet. He eyed the life preserver on the back of the wheel house.

McIntyre, never taking his eyes off the bow roared at Eliot. "Get your ass out there and help him."

Rusty straightened and steadied himself before the bollard, then swung the sharp ax at the rope wrapped around the bollard. He swung again. The rope split and the line flew through the bullnose, whipping towards the ship. Instantly, the *Iroquois* righted, and was pushed aside by the wake of the ship as it passed by. The tug's crew, who had taken cover just before Rusty split the line, rose up from their ducked positions out of harm's way from the whip of the unleashed line. Rusty stood by the bulwark and looked up in awe as the massive wall-like hull of ship passed close in front of him. He felt his strength draining away, but it didn't last long because he spotted Eliot coming up behind him.

"You son-of-a-bitch." Rusty sprang at Eliot and threw him against the wheelhouse. Eliot slammed into it hard and winced. "You didn't turn up the rope on the hitch. It's one of the first things a deckhand learns!" Rusty slammed him again, wanting to do much more.

Eliot drew back from the heat off Rusty's red face and the burn of his blazing eyes, and he winced, anticipating a blow but Rusty backed away, throwing his hands in disgust at him. Davey, Frankie and Nick cautiously approached.

"That son-of-a-bitch could have killed us all!" Rusty growled, stabbing his finger toward Eliot who was still up against the wheelhouse, too frightened to move.

"It will be taken care of," Nick said, raising his hands to calm Rusty. He glared at Eliot. "Wheelhouse, Eliot," was the best he could choke out in his anger.

Eliot peeled himself from the side of the wheelhouse. The back of his head throbbed where it had taken the impact of Rusty's rush. He raised his hand to rub it, but instead straightened his disheveled shirt and slinked to the wheelhouse.

As Eliot climbed the steps to the helm, Rusty hollered up to him, "You're an idiot, and you know it and your ol 'man knows it. Your constant screw-ups are going to get a man killed."

The crew fell quiet as they watched Eliot skulk up the steps.

Inside the wheelhouse, up in the pilot house, Captain McIntyre felt a headache coming on, and it wasn't just Eliot's appearance before him. He couldn't say anything to Eliot at that moment. He had to say something other than a string of cursing and name calling, but for now, cursing and throttling Eliot was all that came to mind, so he sat there gathering his composure for a moment and then told Eliot to report to the dispatcher's office upon docking. A meeting concerning his slack habits would be reviewed and discussed. He excused Eliot and turned his attention back to the tugboat and began to prepare once again to tackle the troubled ore carrier. With the crescendo of the engine noise, the crew returned to their posts with Eliot distancing himself from Rusty. Frankie took Eliot's position assisting Rusty and working the bollard. Davey returned to the engine compartment and Nick orchestrated all. The new trainee remained standing in the aft deck clutching a life preserver, his eyes wide.

***

Eliot was given three days off work without pay. What he did with his time off no one knew, but Cap McIntyre requested he be re-trained with emphasis on knot tying. He was. But sometimes it's hard to breach a thick skull and armor made of Daddy.

Chapter 6

If ever there was a time Rusty could use a beer it was now. It wasn't so much that a bottle was hard to get, heck, he could get one from Di's Uncle Fritz and not any of that needle beer either but some good stuff from German recipes. He just needed to go home and get Di first. Maybe take her to dinner. Anything besides sitting at home. He felt too agitated and restless for that.

Prohibition put only a slight dent in the consumption of spirits. In fact, alcohol consumption actually grew. Like anything forbidden, it became all the more coveted and sweeter when one thought they were pulling the wool over the eyes of law enforcement. Prohibition was considered not only unenforceable but an infringement of their rights to get blotto.

Alcohol could be purchased at many establishments in Vermilion or from any of its dark corners or alleyways. With the right signal, a nip of whiskey could appear in your soda at the ice cream parlor, a beer could be passed to you in the bathroom closet of the pool hall, and hair of the dog could find its way into your cup of joe. At the dance hall on the beach, there was always a stash of liquor in the floorboards behind the band stand or the hollowed out bed of a pickup truck parked in the darkest corner of the parking lot. You could pretty much tell which pickup held the giggle juice by the steady traffic of young men with center-parted hair, oxford bags and bow ties that beeline to the truck like drones to a hive. Though most of the speakeasies were located out of town, there were still places within Vermilion that secret knocks or passwords could get you a ticket into a backroom juice joint. And since pharmacies were allowed to dispense medicinal alcohol, many people became afflicted with the "bug" and prescriptions for small bottles of "medicine" flew off the prescription pads.

When Rusty walked through the kitchen door, Di was sculpting ground beef into meatloaf.

"Put on your lipstick and glad rags," he said. "We're going to Rauscher's for supper."

She gave him a puzzled look, raising her gooey, greasy hands from her culinary project. After all, it wasn't Friday or Saturday. "What about this?" She pointed with her chin to the ground meat in the bowl.

"Icebox it, Di, and we'll have it tomorrow night."

She paused for a moment, then grabbed a towel, wiped her hands vigorously, tossed it in the sink and pulled off her apron. He stepped aside as she dashed to the bedroom to change.

He loaded the mound of meatloaf into the icebox, and when she emerged, she had on the pearl beads he had got her for their second year anniversary and a new cloche hat pulled down on her head. Her eyes sparkled under the rim, and he was glad he came home for her instead of going to Sam's Billiards for the beer.

***

Rauscher's Restaurant was a popular new restaurant located on the bank of the Vermilion River right where the river bends as it winds its way towards Lake Erie. With its close proximity and easy access to the lake, the restaurant took full advantage of its location and lined its waterfront with boat docks and picnic tables to snag the pleasure boaters and fishermen from the lake for a bite to eat. This section of the Vermilion River was like an aqueous road with boat traffic almost constant particularly on summer weekends. It was on these weekends that the river was choked with every small craft imaginable—fishing boats, powerboats, sailboats, rowboats, canoes, rafts, inner tubes—anything that could float inhabited the river during the long, warm days of summer weekends. Across the river from Rauscher's was the business side of boating: boat ramps, storage, docks, repairs, canvas shops, marine gas pumps, fish cleaners and bait and tackle shops. They lined the bank and on a typical summer weekend, it was often hard to find a place to dock. Fred Rauscher, recognizing the benefits of the view and the entertainment provided by the activity at the wharves, installed a wall of glass that ran the length of the dining room facing the river, making the tables along the glass wall a much coveted spot to dine.

With it being a weekday evening, Rusty and Di had no problem getting a table by the window. As she slid into her seat and settled in, she hunted for a hint from his face.

"So what's the occasion?"

Not dying? Happy to be here instead of the hospital? Just glad to be alive? He did not know exactly what to say and he knew she would be upset when she heard what happened. She never did trust the lake. It was more fickle than a flapper she would say, quoting her Uncle Fritz. Violent storms popped up and disappeared just as fast, and good swimmers drowned in it. *Should have stayed at the mill out of harm's way, where your soul would be safe and sound in the rolling mill department far from the treacherous waves of Erie.* She didn't actually say that but he knew she thought that. So he decided not to tell her and ruin the evening for both of them.

"Do I have to have a reason to take you out for supper?"

"No, just thought there might be one."

"If you need a reason, how about a warm summer evening with the best looking girl in town and her new hat."

She smiled shyly and fluttered her eyelashes, feigning demureness. It made him chuckle. The waiter came and they both ordered fried Whitefish with home fries and a side of coleslaw. She ordered a coke and he lemonade. It was cold and tart and made him forget about the beer.

While they waited for their meal, they watched the boats chug slowly up and down the river. It was a peaceful scene that was further enhanced by the setting sun sparkling off the broken water left by the wakes of boats. A parade of mallard ducks headed down river, bobbing as they rode each wave, and gulls circled lazily overhead with only a caw here and there. Weekends had an entirely different atmosphere with the fishing and pleasure boats and the popular canoe rentals jamming the river on Saturday and Sunday afternoons. Sounds of motors, people's chatter, laughter, squealing kids and squawking gulls would fill the air. The doors of commerce along the banks would be thrown open and the docks and riverbank would swarm with activity. The smell of diesel and oil from the busy marinas would mix with the dank, fishy smell of the water and the fried pike wafting from Rauscher's outdoor grill. And all day long the river would be choked with watercraft as the mallards would scoot from bank to bank in fear of being run over. This evening's tranquility, without the weekend hubbub, was exactly what Rusty had sought and found.

The meal came and he asked for another lemonade. As he dunked a sliced potato into ketchup and took a bite, he noticed a Coast Guard harbor patrol boat plying its way up river towards Rauscher's on the heels of a small Chris Craft speedboat. The Chris Craft was slowing and the patrol boat was coming along side it to ease it towards the docks of the restaurant right below their table.

He poked Di's arm as she was nibbling on a fish filet and nodded toward the window for her to look.

A guardsman at the bow called through a megaphone to the pilot of the small boat to *heave to and come about.* They wanted to board.

She wiggled in her seat. "This is exciting and we got front row seats."

"Probably a routine check."

"Probably a bootlegger," she said, ignoring her food.

"You mean rumrunner. Bootleggers are dry land, rumrunners are water," he said matter of fact. He took another potato slice and dunked it in ketchup.

"You told me the Coast Guard has no jurisdiction inland."

"Only if there is no local law but since there is a force here, they probably got permission from Chief Bales to continue their pursuit of this boat up river."

The Chris Craft docked, and the patrol boat slipped in behind it. From their vantage point, Rusty and Di could look down upon the decks of the two boats and see that there were two men in the Chris Craft and what appeared to be two Coastguardsmen in the patrol boat with one indicating to the men on the Chris Craft to disembark. The two men disembarked, one muttering to the other. They stood stiff-legged with arms folded facing their boat. As Rusty and Di watched the scene unfold below them, one guardsman boarded the Chris Craft while the other remained with the patrol boat standing guard at the helm. All four men appeared to be quite tense. The guardsman who boarded the Chris Craft walked about the boat, first in cockpit, then the forepeak, then aft deck, stopping at times to poke about. In the stern was a bench seat with stow away doors on the front below the seat. The guardsman crossed over to it, knelt down, opened the doors and looked inside using his flashlight's beam of light to poke around the interior of the stowaway compartment. The two men on the docks were no longer talking as their attention was riveted on the guardsman looking into the storage space. The guardsman pulled out a couple of life jackets, a blanket, a rope and a tool kit onto the deck. The compartment was now completely empty. The guardsman sat back on his heels. The men appeared to relax.

"He smells a fish," Rusty said. "Those boys aren't out of the woods yet."

The guardsman was not getting up, but remained staring at the now empty stowaway compartment. Rusty could almost hear the gears turning in his head. The two men on the dock must have also sensed his wariness for they began fidgeting and exchanging glances.

Di and Rusty ignored their food and watched the guardsman as intently as the two men on the dock watched him.

After a few tense seconds passed, the guardsman pulled the tool box towards him and opened it. He pawed through it and removed a hammer and screwdriver, and then, with the hammer and screwdriver in each fist, he dove head first into the compartment until his upper body was lost under the bench seat and the remaining half stretched out on deck. The sound of wood splitting could be heard from the stowaway compartment. Rusty and Di could hear the squeak of nails being torn from their clench on the boards of the floor. After a minute passed, the guardsman wiggled back out and triumphantly held a bottle of Cotton Club Gin up for the guardsman on the patrol boat to see. The patrons in the restaurant burst into applause and cheers startling Di and Rusty who didn't realize the other diners were also riveted to the action. She joined in the applause while he smiled and wolfed his coleslaw.

The two men were arrested and handed over to Chief Bales, and Di and Rusty spent the remainder of their meal watching bottles of bootlegged beer and gin being excavated from below the Chris Craft's bench seat storage area. When all was done, six cases of beer and four of gin were stacked onto the dock of the restaurant before being loaded onto the patrol boat. The guardsmen untied the empty, rum running Chris Craft and towed it behind the patrol boat down the river towards the lake, its destination, most likely, Cedar Point. And the sun had yet to set.

***

The evening felt warmer as the gusty wind of the day had finally subsided. After they left Rauscher's, Di suggested a walk to the nearby small sandy beach where the Vermilion River met Lake Erie. The evening was too nice to be tucked inside, and Rusty was more than willing not to rush home. The beach was on the opposite bank of the restaurant, so they crossed the village's road bridge over the Vermilion River and strolled through downtown, following the river's curves until they reached the small patch of beach. The sun was just touching the water to the west where the cities of Huron and Sandusky were only blurs on the horizon. The lake was calm and bluer than the pea green of the day and the skies clear except for a few remaining thin clouds to the north and east left over from the day. It was a complete contrast from earlier and Rusty never ceased to marvel at how quickly the lake's conditions could turn about. The golden sunlight shimmered off the expanse of water as they took a seat on a bench where the street dead-ended into the little beach. They watched the sun turn a soft creamy orange as it touched the water and began melting into the lake. He put his arm around her shoulder and she laid her head on his shoulder but their serenity was short lived as a splash of water and muttering of indistinguishable cursing came from behind a rocky out crop to left of the beach. They looked at each other with raised eyebrows, then turned to the rocks and waited to see what was sloshing its way through the water towards them. Emerging from behind the boulders and rocks, a boy, tall for his age and gangly, appeared with his pants legs rolled up to his knees, clutching a fish net scoop in knee-deep water. He was preoccupied with probing the waterline with his scoop, oblivious to the sunset spectacle behind him. Above him on the rocks was a large black and tan German Shepherd dog who was dividing his attention between watching the boy and watching the shoreline. The dog was an instant tip off that the boy was Eddie.

Eddie was an eleven-year-old going on forty. He had eyes in the back of his head and wide open at that, and nothing happened in town without his knowledge. Forget the barber's, forget Sam's, you wanted the skinny, you went to Eddie. He knew where Sam hid the booze and who delivered it, who was sneaking to the dark backdoor of Mrs. Pergotti when Mr. Pergotti was out of town, who was beating his wife and who was poisoning the towns dogs, although he didn't actually see the face of the shadowy figure who snuck about at night. If it was secrets you wanted to keep, you had better be a bigger tipper than the next guy. His world was the shoreline and streets of Vermilion, and he was never seen separate from his duckbill cap or his sizeable, athletic shepherd dog by the name of Prince. Prince had an intimidating way of standing with his hind legs apart, tail down and head lowered with piercing eyes-on-target anytime anyone approached Eddie, and no one wanted to put the dog to the test by coming between the two of them. The dog had an unnerving way of staring at you and cocking his head as though he was listening and understanding every word you said. In fact, Rusty swore that dog did understand every word and often said if that dog had vocal cords, it could probably carry on an intelligent conversation more than most people he knew.

It was Rusty who gave Eddie a slingshot when Eddie told him about the poisoned dogs. Eddie told him that Prince was too smart to fall for the bait (and Prince was), but Rusty had showed up the next day at Eddie's hangout at the docks and gave him a sling shot "in case things got ugly." So Eddie practiced with a can placed on the piles of the pier while Prince stood watch.

As the last peek of sun disappeared with a flash and the sky above spread with rose and pink hues, Eddie emerged from the rocks with his fish scoop heavy with bottles. He held them up for Rusty and Di's approval.

"I knew those waves would kick more up," he said with a triumphant grin. "Got me a good one, too." He fished out a bottle of Old Crow whiskey. "An easy twenty simoleans."

"If you were my child, I would smack your bottom for monkeying around with that stuff," Di said, causing Eddie to grin. She liked Eddie as did most people, and Eddie liked her. In fact, there were times when his old man was fried and would beat the tar out of him that he secretly wished and tried to imagine what it would be like if Rusty and Di were his parents. He also imagined what Prince would do to his father during the beatings if Prince would be allowed in the house. He pictured Prince tearing his old man's throat out while his father's final gasps would be "sorry Edski." There was no mother to act as a buffer between him and his old man so he, along with Prince, lived mostly in the backyard shed and streets of Vermilion, putting as much distance between him and his lollygagging father and where he was always welcomed by the locals. They bought him free sodas and ice cream cones, and Sam made him hamburgers. He was offered meals here and there by women of the church or widow women looking for someone to spoil. He and the dog had their rounds about town which always began at the crack of dawn at public beach at the dead-end of the street.

Being a street waif gave him the one luxury on being the first boy on the beach to hunt and gather bottles of alcohol that had washed ashore from rumrunners either dumping their contraband when they were about to be busted or wrecking their boats and spilling their cargo during a pursuit. Boys spent their summers combing the beaches not for shells or trinkets, but for booze which could bring anywhere from one to twenty-five dollars, depending on the brand, at the dance hall down the road. These budding entrepreneurs often made more money per bottle than their adult bootlegging counterparts. And if the lake was a bit stingy in belching up the booze, the boys would help themselves to the stashes hidden by smugglers about town in truck beds, coal bins and ice houses much to the fury of those who would find bottles, sometimes cases missing. For kids a bit shy about operating their own "business," the town's ice cream shop, used as a front for illicit spirits, was a place a kid could earn some pocket change. At the shop's back door, kids would be given bottles of liquor to sell and then paid when the bottles were brought back empty. If the bottles were returned washed, the kid would get a few extra cents.

As evening settled in and the gulls took to roost, Rusty took Di's hand and they walked back towards home, but he wasn't sure if he was ready to go back yet. The night was young and he still felt edgy.

"Do you feel like shaking a hoof, Di?"

She looked at him with surprise. "You wanna dance?"

"Yea. I do."

She raised her eyebrows. "Now I know something's afoot."

He sighed. "Okay, okay, we'll bowl instead."

"Nope, we are going to dance." She wrapped her arm snuggly through his and he felt like it was more of a trap than a gesture of affection.

The dance hall was located down from the beach on the other side of a long, wooden pier. An out of service, dilapidated lighthouse was situated at the end of the pier and was in danger of collapsing into the lake and bets were placed which season's squall would claim it. There was a mystery about the lighthouse because—besides being a ghostly-looking ruin, a secret entrance through a hole in its foundation led to a manhole cover on the first floor of the lighthouse. Initially, the secret passage was said to be a former rendezvous spot on the Underground Railroad, but with Prohibition, rumors and speculations circulated that the place was everything from a cargo lair for rumrunners to Al Capone's hiding place. But mostly it was a hot spot for young adults looking for whoopee, a scare or a smoke. And kids around Eddie's age used it for a place to hold a rite of initiation into one of many secret clubs floating about town. Eddie easily won membership in a coveted club for staying the entire night alone during a full moon and thus retaining his neighborhood title as most fearless kid.

Just past the lighthouse, the dancehall was brightly lit like its own beacon of refuge for souls looking to have fun or forget the day's troubles. Music of Basie, Ellington and Jolson spilled through open doors and windows and carried out over the lake on soft breezes. Light pouring from the windows made patterns of bright squares on the dark sand, and the strings of porch bulbs surrounding the eaves of the one story, clapboard building, sent streams of light into the dark night, sparkling off the gentle waves that lapped the shore just off the back porch. Inside, heads were bobbing, bodies shaking and laughter mingled with the blaring refrain of *every morning, every evening, ain't we got fun?* And booze flowed.

As Rusty headed for the porch steps he caught a glimpse of Eddie stationed around the corner of the building in the shadows. Eddie grinned at him and Rusty feigned a scowl. As Di pulled him up the steps, he looked back over his shoulder to Eddie and whispered, "Hey, kid, save me a beer."

Chapter 7

As Rusty walked past the open door of Erie T's dispatcher's office the following morning, the dispatcher checked his watch.

"You're here early," he said, rolling his cigar from one side of his mouth to the other.

"Got a line to splice," Rusty said over his shoulder as he headed for the *Iroquois* moored on the bank.

Despite the early hour, the harbor was just as he had left it the evening before—bustling with activity and noise. Just beyond the line-up of tethered tugboats, incoming railroad hoppers loaded with coal were being raised from the railroad tracks by specially built elevator-like dumpers that lifted whole sections of railroad hopper cars at a time and dumped them sideways in unison. It was like pouring out the contents of a string of buckets. The coal spilled out of the cars and onto black, sooty hills of coal to be transported later to the steel mill to fuel the giant blast furnaces. The banging, clanking, screeching, hammering and riveting never ended. It was the same scene, the same noise day after day.

He hopped onto the deck and made his way to the bow where the towline he had chopped with an ax the day before was coiled and waiting repair. Lake gulls, who had been observing his approach from their perch atop the wheelhouse, flew off as he neared, scolding him for the disturbance.

Davey arrived. "Hey, Rust, you're here with the cock's crow," he said as he jumped aboard and disappeared below deck into the engine room.

Hmm, Rusty thought, *so he does go home at the end of the day. That blows that theory.* He had this image in his mind of Davey being a permanent resident of the engine room. His relationship with the engines was like that of a doting father and when they "purred" (as he put it) he was filled with pride. Davey seemed like a perpetual fountain of laughter and sanguinity and that was reason enough to make him likeable, and he wondered if the man had ever been angry or said a harsh word in his life. Had Davey been married with children, he would have been a loving husband and doting father and could easily be taken advantage of if the wrong woman got her hooks in him. He respected the fact that Davey was methodical and knowledgeable in his trade and cool under pressure, but he wondered if the owner of Erie T knew just what a gem they had in him.

Erie T was being pinched and the owner was scrimping as much as he could without hurting his wallet and that included grossly underpaying Davey. With his expertise and experience, any operator would jump at the chance to snag him for their engineer but loyalty was another trait of Davey's. He started with Erie T and most likely would end with them. Loyalty aside, he knew Davey couldn't bear the thought of another engineer screwing with his beloved engines.

Rusty took hold of the ends of the coils where the cut was made. The line was heavy in his hands. Made of thick hemp rope, it was as thick in circumference as his wrist. He began unraveling the severed ends and while doing so, caught a glimpse of the trainee arriving. He heard Davey from below deck call out "here's another early riser," and it made him smile.

"Well, I see we didn't scare you off with yesterday's excitement," Rusty said, eyeing the young man as he leaped onto the deck. "Ready for another exciting day at Erie T?"

"Yes, sir," the trainee replied.

The trainee had a mop of curly blond hair that he tried to control to some success under his cap and was of average build with nothing really outstanding about him except his doe-eyed gaze and quiet manner which could easily be mistaken for shyness. His eyes were blue-green like the color of the lake. At eighteen years of age he was considered a late starter by some accounts as many greenhorns cut their teeth at 15 scraping hulls, painting rails and assisting the deckhands. He was mannered and quick to learn and Rusty never had to tell him twice, or as he put it to Cap McIntyre, he was everything Eliot wasn't. He liked the trainee but couldn't get past his quiet façade to know what he was really like. He was just as much a closed book as Davey was an open one. His name was Jim Watson or Jimmy as they called him. If a name could end with an "e" sound, it was tacked on the end like Davey, Rusty or Frankie. It made things friendlier that way Nick had said. Nick made it clear, however, that only his mother could call him Nickie, and so he remained "Nick."

"You're just in time for a lesson in rope splicing. So come on over here and grab that end." He pointed to a spot on the rope a length down from the cut. "Unravel it back to here. Then I'll show you how to marry the two."

The two sat opposite of one another immersed in the unraveling and weaving of the hemp coils when their concentration was broken by Davey who joined them on deck.

"Get a load of this," Davey said tipping his head toward the *Cherokee* docked behind them.

They followed Davey's gaze and saw Eliot emerge from the wheelhouse looking rumpled and sleep-drunk. It was obvious to them Eliot had spent the night onboard the tugboat.

"What in the hell is he doing here? I thought he was laid off for three days," Rusty said.

They watched as Eliot stretched, then ran his hand over his hair to smooth it in place. He then glanced about the dock, doing a double take when he spotted them watching him. He glowered at them and jumped onto the dock. When he walked past the *Iroquois* and saw Rusty holding the partially spliced towline he snorted and headed up the riverbank towards the direction of the all night diner on Broadway.

Davey looked to see if Rusty had caught Eliot's glare and figured he had as his jaw was tight.

At length, Rusty stood up and held the repaired towline with the freshly woven spliced area suspended in his hands like a boa constrictor.

"Let's see how good this splice is. Grab her and pull hard," he said to Jimmy.

Jimmy grabbed the opposite side of the repair and he the other. Both pulled in a tug-of-war manner that Rusty could have easily won, but instead Rusty pulled with equal force to Jimmy's.

"Good to go from this point. The real test will be when she gets some real pressure on her," Rusty said, relaxing his pull. "We'll do that later today. Meanwhile grease the capstan."

***

The day for the most part went uneventful. Eliot did not return for work due to disciplinary punishment and that made the crews in good spirits. Rusty and Jimmy made some minor repairs to the deck and checked the tugboat fore and aft for any damages that might have occurred during the incident the day before. When Captain McIntyre arrived, the *Iroquois* was squared away and ready for action. The day's business included replacing a harbor marker that had been run over by a freighter and towing a barge of scrap iron up river to the steel mill. On the way back down the river, the *Iroquois* offered assistance to a harbor patrol boat whose engines stalled leaving it to drift at the mercy of the current but the offer was refused. Since it posed no problem or congestion in the river they left the Guardsmen to their repairs and drift of the current.

After lunch, with little else to do until the arrival of a small freighter due in from Michigan, Rusty decided it was a good time to clean the tugboat top to bottom. Jimmy swabbed the decks while he crawled up the exterior of the wheelhouse to clean the windows. Brass was polished and equipment wiped down and neatly stowed. He sharpened the ax blade to assure its edge was razor-sharp for the next time it was called into action while Jimmy scrubbed the spackle of gull droppings dribbled over the painted big letter E on the side of the wheelhouse.

The Michigan ship, Cap McIntyre informed them, radioed that it would be arriving later than expected, stretching the day out longer than the crew of the *Iroquois* had wished. With unusual lull in action and the maintenance caught up, Nick, the mate declared a break which was both rare and much coveted by the hardworking crew.

Rusty took a seat up on the bulwarks and moments later, Davey emerged from below deck into the sunshine and world beyond the stuffy engine room. He took a seat next to Rusty, squinting as he adjusted his eyes to the brightness of the sun mirroring off the water.

"I'd say it was good to be up in fresh air but there's no such air in all Lorain," Davey said. "It could gag a maggot today."

Rusty offered him a cigarette and the two sat relishing the rush of nicotine as they watched a giant jaw-like Hullet shovel bite into a 500-foot freighter's cargo of ore and dump the load onto one of the many mountains of ore stockpiled along the riverfront.

"That's a lot of ore day in and day out, when you think about it," Davey said.

They sat in silence for a moment or two then Davey sighed. "I think I was born in the wrong era," he said, staring at the activity at the ore terminal. He took a pull on the cigarette and exhaled a deliberate long stream of smoke. "I would have liked to have been a cowboy."

Rusty digested Davey's revelation for a moment. He took a pull on his cigarette. "Still can," he said finally.

"Nah, I mean one when there was still Indians and no train tracks crisscrossing willy-nilly over the Plains. Nothing for miles but buffalo grass and a good horse for company along with cattle and antelope."

"Where the deer and the antelope play?"

Davey ignored him. "I'd have me a Paint horse. Black and white with four white socks. Chief-that's what I'd name him."

"Four white socks is bad luck," Rusty said matter-of-fact as he watched the huge bucket lower into the ship and bring up a load of ore, and then swing over to the mound and release the load in a loud, crescendo "whish" of sliding ore followed by the bone-jarring bang of the giant bucket.

"It's my horse! Okay... two socks."

Rusty raised his brows.

Davey continued. "Under that big empty sky surrounded by miles of open prairie..."

"You got that out on the lake, only water instead of grass."

"It's different, Rusty," he said, his gaze following the river. "I wouldn't have to worry about ships running over me or being capsized by a rogue wave or sent to the sink in one of those crazy storms."

"What about the Indians and rustlers? And rattlesnakes?"

"Ah shucks, Rusty, I hate snakes."

Davey's daydream came to an abrupt end as Captain McIntyre's voice bellowed from the pilothouse, "The Michigan is in sight."

The crew jumped into action. Davey vanished into the engine compartment, and Rusty and Jimmy slipped the mooring lines. A short time later, the *Iroquois* was churning its way down river heading for its mouth and the break wall beyond to rendezvous with the Michigan ship. The splice on the rope performed to perfection during the towing.

***

That night at 3 a.m., a shadowy figure poked around the moored tugboats of Erie T. The docks were deserted except for a lone police officer walking his beat along the docks who was distracted by the siren of a Coast Guard Harbor Patrol boat as it raced past him heading down river. The dark figure went unnoticed as it slipped onto the deck of the *Iroquois* and headed for the bow. Forty minutes later, with stars as the only witnesses, the figure slipped off the boat, slithered up the bank, and headed for Broadway in the direction of the all night diner.

Chapter 8

The morning sun, looking like a giant egg yolk, finally emerged above the tree line where it had been playing peek-a-boo through the trees. The glare blinded Rusty as he rattled east in his Model T truck heading for the dockyards. The light was already strong and promised to be hot. The route to work ran along the shoreline making the drive a mixture of pleasure and agony—pleasurable because of the panoramic view of the lake augmented by the rising and the setting of the sun on his way to and from the harbor, agonizing because he'd rather be out on the lake than in the harbor of Lorain. His mind at the moment was not on work or even the blinding sun that caused him to squint, but on a particular automobile he had dreamed of owning since he first saw it parked out front of the dealership on his route to work. He stopped once to inquire about it, and then again to see if it really matched up to his first impression. The fantasy was no longer a wisp of imagery in his mind but taking solid form as money was steady and his secret nest egg had grown enough to make the vehicle a reality. The stash was a well-kept secret from Di as he planned to surprise her on their anniversary knowing she would love it as much as he would love the look on her face when she saw it. Then again, he figured, she would love anything besides the pick-up.

The truck, like the cottage, was a victim of the Lorain tornado. Rusty had found it under a heap of wood and plaster lying upon its side and wedged against the remnants of a hardware store at 4th and Broadway. Its windshield was cracked and the left headlamp dangled but remained attached by a spaghetti of wires. The body was a bit battered but not beyond repair and in the hands of the right handyman it could be restored. The pickup truck, a 1923 Ford, was hauled to a nearby salvage yard where it and scores of other vehicles and wreckage from the tornado awaited claim to ownership. Rusty kept his eye on it and after some time had passed and no one laid claim to it, he purchased it for a song. He knew the engine, axels and frame were good and that he could patch it back almost as good as new. The truck served its purpose as a work truck for him and a means for Di and him to break beyond the limitations of streetcars, trains and buses.

But his dream automobile would be just the thing for them to paint the town and it teased him each time he passed by it from the lineup of parked automobiles and trucks at Harbortown Ford. It was a 1928 Model A Roadster two door breezer with a Rumble seat and a spare tire on the running board in front of the driver's door. Di, he envisioned, would call the roadster thc bee's knees. He already had planned the first trip to the Pavilion at Beach Park in Avon Lake for a picnic and dance followed by an evening show at the State in downtown Lorain where he hoped a talkie or vaudeville show would be on the marquee and not a Bugsy Berkely-type song and dance on that particular night. Originally, he planned their first trip to the Crystal Ballroom on the eastern outskirts of Vermilion in hopes of catching a big act like Glenn Watkins or Ray Miller but that was going to take more jack than he would have after buying the roadster. He would need to save again for that sashay. The Crystal Ballroom would have to wait for her birthday and when more dollars than sense was had.

The thought of Di and him breezing along in the open air through town and country brought a smile to his face as he maneuvered his truck through the streets of Lorain heading for the harbor. But for now, the truck would suffice, and they were lucky for that as not everyone had an automobile or even a need for one for that matter. Townsfolk used streetcars and country folk walked or used horse drawn buggies and wagons to get where they needed to go. Buses and trains provided for those times when one needed to go a bit farther. The automobile, though, was growing in popularity and many buggy lanes were quickly converting to dusty or, if it rained, muddy automobile roads. The image of his new roadster hitting a hogged-out mud hole made him grimace.

He parked the truck in Erie T's parking lot along the river and hesitated before exiting it, staring at the lake beyond and at the hazy blue hue that blurred the line between sky and water. The blue seemed endless and made the lake seem like a vast void. Today, the waves were still and the near flat waters gave the illusion one could walk on water and he knew eight miles out the lake surface would be like glass. Erie was soft and beckoning and he wished he was taking the *Rising Sun* out for a run and getting lost in the calm blue abyss of the lake instead of the garish colors, hard edges, noises and stench of the harbor that awaited him once he left the compartment of the truck. He sighed and opened the door, gathered his lunchbox and gloves and slid out of the cab.

As he slammed the door shut, he notice an excited knot of men gathered about the moored *Cherokee.* The knot consisted of the *Cherokee*'s mate Frankie Kopinski, its engineer Bobbie Peets, Lloyd Robson the greenhorn deck hand, and Davey, Jimmy and Nick from the *Iroquois.*

As he approached, Frankie spotted him.

"Here's Rusty. Hey Rusty come over here and tell us what you think this is," Frankie said, nodding to the *Cherokee*'s portside hull.

Rusty walked up to where the gathering of men had parted to allow him up to the spot on the tugboat's portside that was the focus of their attention. He leaned forward for a closer look at the hull and poked his little finger into a perfectly round hole. When he straightened up, eager eyes were focused on him, waiting for his verdict.

"A bullet hole," he said, matter-of-factly.

"Told ya," Frankie said to Nick who rolled his eyes.

"We all figured that, Frankie," Nick said.

Frankie ignored Nick and continued. "Damn thing got shot last night while moored here."

"Bet it was Coast Guard going after a runner on the river," Lloyd said with a nod from Bobbie Peets.

"What are ya talking about, this baby has been shot from the bank," Nick said.

"You were in the war, Rust,' Davey said. "What type of bullet made this hole?"

"I think .30 caliber, but it wasn't shot in the river or the bank. Not enough damage for that close of range." He studied the hole. "This was shot from some distance and I bet there is more than one hole." He scanned the side of the tugboat. "There. And there," he said, pointing each hole out.

The men gawked at the boat. A wide spray pattern of holes and chunks of splinter and chipped wood quickly revealed themselves to them.

Eyes quickly jumped from one to another.

"You mean out on the lake?" Frankie said, his eyebrow flying up. "This tug doesn't go out on open water and we sure in the hell would know if we got hit by this," he said, thumbing toward a bullet hole.

Rusty shrugged. "That's what it looks like to me. The pattern of spray is wide because it was shot from a distance. Those holes would have been closer together had it been a close rake."

Frankie ran his hand over his face. He was growing red. "So what in the hell do we do about this?"

"Why don't you ask Eliot," Davey suggested with a glance towards Rusty. "He spent the night on the boat. Maybe he knows what happened?"

Frankie and Nick exchanged glances.

'Where is Eliot?" Frankie growled, scanning the docks. "He should have been here by now."

"Laid off," Bobbie said.

"Oh, that's right," Frankie said, catching himself. He narrowed his eyes as he mulled the information over in his head. Finally, he heaved a sigh, "I'll go see the dispatcher and he can tell the old man the *Cherokee* was shot up last night. They can take it up with Eliot." He started down the dock towards the office and said back over his shoulder, "Better tell Cap Brumfield someone doesn't like his boat."

Rusty and Davey headed down the dock towards the *Iroquois* with Jimmy in tow.

"What do you think, Rust?" Davey asked.

"I think the *Cherokee* got shot."

"Yea, yea, but why…and where?"

"Someone probably felt sorry for the old girl knowing Idiot was a deckhand on her and decided to put her out of misery."

Davey guffawed and a moment later, sighed. "So now we got to worry about getting shot."

"Sounds like the old west, uh?" Rusty said and chuckled.

***

Captain McIntyre's arrival at the *Iroquois* was delayed by Captain Brumfield of the *Cherokee* who had just been informed of the bullet hole.

Rusty, Davey and Jimmy watched from the deck of the *Iroquois* as Nick pointed out the holes and damage to McIntyre while Frankie, back from reporting to the dispatcher, paced back and forth with his hands on his hips. Captain Brumfield stood quietly with his arms folded and stared at the holes while listening to Nick's theories.

Rusty lit a cigarette and offered one to Davey who passed on the offer and Jimmy wasn't offered at all. They waited and watched and finally, Captain McIntyre broke away from the group and headed for the *Iroquois*.

"Are we all clear?" he asked as he boarded.

"Aye, aye, sir," Rusty said.

"By that I mean of bullet holes as well?"

"We gave her a once over and she's clear."

"For God's sakes, keep your eyes and ears open," McIntyre said swinging into the pilot house. "Someone has either a personal vendetta with tugboats or a terrible aim."

Rusty and Jimmy untied the mooring lines and the *Iroquois* was the first tugboat of the day underway with the *Delaware* and *Wyandot* not far behind. The *Cherokee*, with the novice deckhand, Lloyd Robinson, was resigned to odd jobs around the harbor.

The first mission of the day was like most days, assisting an ore freighter into the harbor to the terminal. The ship, out of Duluth, Minnesota, was a self unloader and would not require the service of the Hullet bucket. Instead, a conveyer belt running the length of the ship would unload the ore out of the hold and onto the dock at the terminal. The expansive ship, Rusty guessing close to 600 feet in length, had a black hull that rode low in the water and on either side of its bow, painted in 7 foot bold white letters was its registered name, *HIAWATHA*.

Rusty and Jimmy marveled at the size of her as they approached.

"*By the shores of Gitchie Gumee, by the shining big-sea-water…*," Rusty said as he looked at the name.

"Uh?" Jimmy said looking puzzled at him.

Rusty gathered the line. He had already tied the monkey knot on the line's end on their approach to the ship.

The black hulled freighter dwarfed the *Iroquois* which had taken its position at the bow just under the monolithic white letters of *Hiawatha*. The *Wyandot* slid into position at the stern and both tugs synchronized their speeds with the freighter which had slowed on its approach to the harbor. The *Delaware*, positioned near the river's mouth, waited for securing of the tow line which would signal it into action to use its bow's steel and hemp rope bumper to push and jockey the cumbersome freighter's hull mid-ship so as to hip it up to the dock for unloading.

Rusty took his station at the bow of the tugboat. The lake was calm and the wind nonexistent so he knew the throw would be easy for the most part despite the turbulence caused by the ship coursing through the water which rocked the tugboat. It was nothing unusual and the throw would be a snap compared to days when the lake was agitated.

As predicted, the throw was easy for him, and the man at the *Hiawatha*'s bow caught the line effortlessly. With one end of the line secured to the ship and the other to the H-bitt at the tug's bow, Rusty gave a thumb up to McIntyre who responded by reversing the throttles.

"Steady strain, Jimmy," Rusty shouted to the novice deckhand over the sound of the engines. "Slack in the line is dangerous. If the line sags, it can foul the propeller, stop the power and cause us to collide with the ship. Always keep steady strain on the towline."

The *Iroquois* began backing up, stretching the towline taut between the *Iroquois* and *Hiawatha*. The screw propeller of the tugboat dug at the water like an auger and the muscular tugboat, dwarfed by the huge ship, shuddered then began pulling the bow of the freighter slowly around into the mouth of the river and clear of the breakwater. The line was rigid under the strain of the weight of the ship.

From his position behind the H-bitt, a safe spot where he could duck behind in case a line broke, Rusty watched the towline's placement between the molgoggers and its alignment with the bullnose cleat at the bow. He scanned the section with the splice which was now positioned halfway between the two vessels. There was a lot of pressure on the line, but he knew the splice was good. He must have done hundreds of them and they never failed and he prided himself at that. He checked the line placement again. Everything looked good. His eyes traveled the length of line again to the splice. His eyes narrowed. The splice wasn't right. It didn't look right. All of a sudden, the hemp started fraying as it began to unravel. In that split second, he knew the way the splice was separating and unraveling, it was not the method of plaiting he used.

Rusty hollered to Captain McIntyre and signaled to him to cut the power. The words were indistinguishable, lost in the noise of motors, but Cap McIntyre knew what he meant. McIntyre throttled back, making the line slack without sagging. The commotion made Davey poke his head out from the engine room. Unable to get the gist of what was happening, he come up on deck for a look, remaining close to the doorway of the engine room

The momentum of the ship, still in motion from the initial pulling of the tugboat, caused it to continue turning, and McIntyre reversed the tugboat to keep the line loose but suspended between the two vessels. But the motion of the big vessel was too much in play like a giant's fulcrum being pivoted by the unaware *Wyandot* which was 600 feet away and pulling the freighter's stern around.

Nick radioed the *Wyandot* to cease action.

Then the big ship rolled and the line stretched taunt between vessels like an over drawn rubber band. With pressure resumed on the line, the hemp rope commenced unraveling only this time at lightning speed. Davey, recognizing the situation, spun around and darted for the engine room doorway.

Rusty ducked behind the H-bitt just in time as the air cracked like a bullwhip above him as the line snapped and sent the half of line attached to the *Iroquois* whipping wildly across the deck with lethal intent. Rusty heard a yelp, then a moan. He waited for the line, like a snake cut in half, to stop its spasm, then he jumped up from behind the security of the bitt and raced around the wheelhouse, jumping over the now limp and harmless line. He found Davey lying face down half way down the steps of the engine room. Davey's moans were twisted in agony and sent chills down Rusty spine. He swiftly but gingerly stepped over Davey and picked him up by the shoulders. In a flash, Nick had a hold of Davey's legs and was helping him carry Davey inside the wheelhouse where they laid him on a bench.

"I think his back may be broke," Nick said.

"Yea," was all Rusty could choke out.

It was that day that he came to believe fate had a hand in the scheme of life as Di had always said. It was not like Davey not to be manning the engines at such as critical time. It was not like Davey to come on deck when a line was under pressure. Fate, it had to be, he assured himself. There was one thing he knew for damn sure and that was the splice was not his. But how could it not be? He struck the side of the wheelhouse with his fist.

Captain McIntyre radioed for help—first to the dispatcher to get an ambulance dockside, then to Erie's T's rival, the big Great Lakes Towing Service for one of their tugboats to take over for the *Iroquois* as Erie T had no extra tug to replace her.

As soon as the big company's tugboat arrived and lines were cast and released, The *Iroquois* made haste for the docks.

An ambulance was waiting and Davey was loaded in.

"I'm going with him," Rusty said to McIntyre.

"I need you here. Nick will go with him. Soon as we button down, we'll all go since Great Lakes has us covered."

Rusty grimaced. The next hour seemed like an eternity.

Chapter 9

It was just after three in the afternoon when Rusty walked out of the cavernous hospital's big white double doors and into the harsh sunlight. He felt as though all the blood in his body had pooled to his feet and each step down the stone stairs felt anchored with its weight. Davey was not dead but his back was broken like they had suspected. The doctor had explained to them that more than likely Davey would be paralyzed from neck down or at best, from the waist down. Might as well be dead, Rusty thought when the doctor's words turned to garble after the initial disclosure.

Nick had called Erie T's dispatcher from the hospital with the prognosis and was informed that Davey's mother with whom he lived had been contacted. She had seemed a bit confused and upset, the dispatcher told him, and had no means of getting to the hospital. Davey's mother was frail and *ancient as dirt* as Di referred to her, and Rusty wished like hell the dispatcher would have held off until she could have been told in person considering her delicate condition. He would see to it, he assured Nick, she got a ride to the hospital.

He left the hospital and drove straight to Davey's home. It was an older two-story fading clapboard sandwiched between two houses of similar design and condition on a side street just south of the city center of Lorain. It was a neighborhood of aging owners and tenants whose houses had aged along with them. The tornado of '24 had missed this old neighborhood which, despite the era of *permanent prosperity*, would have suffered irreplaceable loss to its older residents. As he pulled into the driveway, he saw the next door neighbor lady leaving Davey's house. When she saw Rusty pull in she waited, pulling her sweater around her despite the warm day. She was elderly herself, but hale and hearty compared to the older Mrs. Reynolds. She met Rusty at the truck door before he had a chance to get out. She was a robust woman and *officious as all get out* according to Davey who was at times grateful to have such a meddlesome neighbor next door to keep her eye on his mother while he worked.

"I work with Davey," he said through the open side window of his truck. "There was an accident at work."

"I know," the neighbor said. "Mrs. Reynolds called to me from her window and told me what happened, poor dear. I am taking her to the hospital." There was a sense of excitement and eagerness about her. A woman on a mission, he thought.

He hid his relief. He really hadn't looked forward to going back to the hospital so soon and Mrs. Reynolds's grief would make it twice as difficult. "He's at St. Joseph, second floor. His room is about halfway down on the west side..."

"I'll find him," she cut him off. "Thank you."

"Thank you," he said feeling released. He backed down the driveway and headed for home.

***

The ride home seemed too fast. Di wouldn't be home for another two hours and he wasn't too eager to be alone with his thoughts. He splashed water on his face and grabbed a soda out of the icebox then walked out to the back yard with a bang of the wooden screen door. He walked to the back edge of the yard where the land met the lake and sipped the soda and watched the waves collide against the rocks below. Theirs was not a sandy beach. The edge of their property ended abruptly as a rocky cliff dropped approximately two stories to the lake below. The rocks created a natural breakwater in slowing the waves' erosive action upon their shoreline.

He was glad it wasn't a beach. Watching the greenish waves break against the rocks and dissolve into white froth as they pulled away from shore to gather for another hammering against the rocks was mesmerizing. If the lake was in one of her nastier moods, her energy sent geysers of spray that nearly reached the top of the cliff when the waves broke and he could feel the spray upon his face. It was times like this that made his blood course quicker and his blue eyes darken in excitement. There was something near hypnotic in the push and pull of Erie's waves as they rolled onto sandy shore and smashed into rocky coastline. She was the other irresistible lady in his life. You had to keep an eye on her though as she was fickle as a flapper like Uncle Fritz and Di had said. Ever the seductress, she would beckon a sailor onto her calm waters, luring him from the safety of shore, then abruptly change to five-foot white caps or grueling chop with a mere shift of wind direction. Salts knew to keep an eye on the sky and a nose on the horizon as storms were legendarily instantaneous and Erie liked to catch one off guard. Few sailors lost sight of shore or a place to put in, yielding the middle of the lake to larger vessels and freighters. To him, the lake was as unpredictable as a temptress— one minute she loved you, the next, bring you to your knees. Today, though, the lake was gently lapping the rocks below. He breathed deep, allowing his nostrils to fill with the fresh, damp breeze that swept off the lake.

He checked his watch. Four o'clock. Di wouldn't be home till 5:30. He headed back to the house, looked in the icebox. There was left over fried chicken but he didn't feel hungry despite missing lunch.

He jumped in his truck and crossed the bridge over the river into downtown Vermilion. He cruised around the small town for a bit before turning a corner and spotting the sign for *Sam's Billiards.* He had only been in there a couple times when passing through before he was married. Sam's wasn't the kind of place you took a lady when you went out on the town.

He pulled off the road and parked in front of Sam's, instantly smelling an intermingling of hamburgers, onions and sausage drifting out of the door. Any other day, the smell alone would have enticed him in, but today he was in no mood to eat. As he stepped up to Sam's door, he caught the hindquarters and tail of what looked like Prince, Eddie's German Shepherd, disappearing around the corner of the building into the alleyway. Rusty headed inside the billiard hall. It was dark and cool inside, and the concentrated smell of grilled food filled the air. After his eyes adjusted to the low light, he could see the place was empty except for two men playing billiards in a separate room to the right. Smoke hung like a fog above them. They turned to look at him when he came through the door and Sam raised his head from the counter. He took a seat at the counter.

Sam's Billiards was about as commonplace as Sam himself. The only thing that gave it any character at all was the characters themselves who frequented the joint. They were men of the lake for the most part—pilots, sailors, fishermen, longshoremen as well as marinas and bait shop proprietors. Men like Duffy Waltrip who owned a small fleet of fishing boats chasing pike and herring and Big Red Stoefen who, as a stevedore, spent day in and day out, loading and unloading freighters at Lorain's dockyards. It was a gathering place for ferry boat captains and deckhands, boat builders and fish cleaners and it was the lake that gave these men common ground. It was the kind of place men got together and hashed over fishing and freight, wages and strikes and who had the best bootleg beer. It was a quieter place than the basement bowling alley full of steel men at Joe's in Lorain, but its patrons were no nonsense men just the same.

Sam's was the place a man could get a coffee with an extra jolt or a beer disguised as a soda. The phrase *how's your mother in Scranton, Sam* would get you a bottle of imported beer hidden under a load of cord wood in the back of Sam's pickup truck parked in the alleyway. Never mind Sam's mother was long dead.

And Sam's was the place a bootlegger looking for a runner could find a sure pilot and trusty crewmen to ferry his contraband liquor across from Canada. It was not unusual to see money flash at a dimly lit corner table and handshakes exchanged. Stories were swapped, close encounters disclosed and the mere mention of the name Captain Connors of the Coast Guard vessel CG157 brought a collective snort from the patrons.

"Yours is a familiar face," Sam said to him as he watched Rusty settle in to the counter stool.

"It's been a while since I've been here," he said.

Sam studied him. "Looks like you had a tough day."

Rusty sighed. "Friend of mine got hurt at work."

"Bad?"

"Damn near killed him. When he comes to he'll probably wish he was dead."

Sam raised one brow.

"Doctors say he's paralyzed. Permanently."

Sam shook his head and reached under the counter for a glass. "How did it happen?"

He stayed quiet for a moment or two s replaying the accident in his head.

Sam waited for him to continue.

"We work on tugboats with Erie T. A line broke. It whipped back and cracked my buddy across his back. Fool wasn't even supposed to be on deck."

Sam winced. He disappeared behind the counter, rummaged around and came back up with a bottle of whiskey. He poured a shot in the glass. "Here. John Barleycorn can't help your friend but it might make your day go down a little easier."

Rusty tossed it down and when Sam went to refill it, he covered the glass and Sam nodded.

"I know I know you," Sam continued. "I've seen you about town. Help me out here."

"I live on the edge of town and have my boat docked here. I own a small charter business."

"That's it—the charter business. My brother-in-law chartered a fishing trip with you. Your name is Red…"

"Rusty."

"That's it. The hair's an easy tip off. My brother-in-law had good things to say about the trip. Would book you again. Said you knew some hot spots to fish."

"That's what I'm paid to know."

Sam smiled. "There are a lot of ol' boys that get paid and don't know a damn thing. When a man's got a good reputation at the helm, word tends to spread."

"Tends to spread when he's got a bad one as well."

Chapter 10

Rusty braced himself for Di. He was two hours late. Time had escaped him and although he avoided his watch, he couldn't avoid her.

She had seen his lunchbox on the table and knew he had come home early. The lunchbox was there, and he was gone and no note. At first she worried he was hurt, but then it dawned on her he could not have been too badly injured or sick as he was able to drive the truck. Hours passed, and anxiety and anger rose simultaneously. When his truck came rattling into the driveway, she wasn't sure if she should hug or slug him.

As he approached the kitchen screen door, he saw the room had grown dark with the setting sun and he could make out her silhouette leaning against the sink. The drawn out red glow from the end of her cigarette tipped him off she was dragging heavily on it which she did when she was upset. He opened the screen door and entered the kitchen with a wary eye cast on her and the smoldering tip on the cigarette.

Moments of silence hung suspended then she said, "Its nine o'clock, Rusty. Can you tell me where you've been?" Her voice was measured and cold.

"Sam's."

"Sam's?" She said it with ice.

He crossed over to the table and plopped down and sighed.

"You better have a darn good reason to be gone so long without so much as a note. And Sam's?" She emphasized each word with her cigarette hand, wielding it like a scolding rod. "Christ, Rusty, you had me scared to death and to think you were having a high-ho time at Sam's." She turned her back to him and faced the sink.

Rusty sat forward in the chair and rubbed his hands over his face.

"Di, Davey got hurt real bad today," he said to her back. "I took him to the hospital this morning. Spent most of the day there." He sighed heavier this time. "He's bad." He looked toward the open screen door and watched the orange and red light of sundown spread across the sky. "I should have gone back to work but I didn't. You weren't here and I was... I forgot the time."

She stood for a moment absorbing the information, then dabbed her cigarette out in the sink. "Is he going to die?" She said quietly, the chill melting from her voice.

"Doctor says he is going to be paralyzed."

More silence followed. She turned around to face him.

"His whole body? Or just his legs?"

Just his legs? Rusty thought. "I don't know."

Di crossed to the table and slipped into a chair next to his. "Well, what did the doctor say?"

"I just told you. He'll be paralyzed."

"Is that it? Not how much? For how long? For the rest of his life?" Extracting information from him was like pulling teeth.

"I don't know…they don't know."

"How did it happen? Was it on the tug? Did he fall? What happened?" Her voice grew increasingly agitated.

He sat in silence.

"Is he going to walk again?"

"I don't know."

"Will he be bed ridden or in a wheel chair. Can he be in a wheel chair?"

"I don't know."

"I mean, is he conscious? Does he know?"

"I don't know! I DON'T KNOW!" he shouted, slamming the table with his fists.

Di fell quiet.

He covered his mouth and reached his other hand over and placed it on top of her hand on the kitchen table. "I'm sorry, Di." He slumped in his chair. "I just *don't* know," he said weakly. He felt miserable for biting her head off and he had enough to be miserable about as it was. "A line broke during a strain. It snapped back and cracked him on the back like a whip. I'm talking about a rope the size of my wrist hitting him," he encircled his wrist with the fingers of his other hand for emphasis. "Davey shouldn't have been on deck…"

Di searched his face. The fading light emphasized a furrowed line between his eyes. His face looked drawn and pale and his eyes empty and sad.

She laid her hand on Rusty's forearm. "Accidents happen, Rusty," She said gently.

"The break happened at a splice—a splice that was fine the day before. A splice that took the strain all day yesterday and each time I checked it, it was fine. I know that splice was good."

"Accidents happen."

"That should not have happened." He sounded as though he was scolding himself.

"But it did. Things like that happen. That's why they call them accidents."

"You don't get it, Di. I was the one who repaired the splice. I was the one who should have checked it again this morning," he said, ignoring her pity. "I crippled Davey."

Chapter 11

Everyone was quiet around the docks of Erie T the following morning. Even the sky was heavy with clouds, and the lake, looking gray and sullen, promised an afternoon chop.

Erie T had one tugboat down for repairs, one tugboat short a deckhand, and now one short an engineer.

"They'll probably lay-off and consolidate crews," Nick said to the group.

"They'll probably go under," Bobbie Peets muttered.

"Just my luck now that I landed the job of deckhand," greenhorn Lloyd Robson said.

Frankie glared at him. "Go tell Davey your hard luck story."

That was about the extent of the day's conversations while the crews patched the bullet holes in the *Cherokee* and the *Iroquois*'s splice was mended again then checked and rechecked by the mates.

***

That evening, Rusty and Di picked up Mrs. Reynolds for a visit to Davey at the hospital. Rusty had exchanged his truck for his father-in-law's 4 door Model A after work so there would be room to take Davey's mother.

"Hold it," Di said, grabbing his arm in front of a flower vendor stationed near the hospital entrance. "Buy Mrs. Reynolds some flowers to take to Davey," she whispered.

"Davey might not even be awake."

Di lightly slapped his arm. "That's not the point."

Rusty bought a small bouquet of nosegays as selected by Di.

"Here, Mrs. Reynolds, for Davey," she said.

Mrs. Reynolds's dull, red-rimmed eyes brightened a little. "Thank you, dear."

***

Rusty was shocked to see Davey awake.

Davey followed the three of them with his eyes as they entered the room and approached his bed. They looked as though they were walking on eggs. His eyes rested upon his mother and tears began to fill them as she went to his bedside. Mrs. Reynolds leaned forward, her frail frame trembling, and kissed Davey on the forehead.

Di steadied her while Rusty busied himself looking for a vase or glass to place the flowers. A lump had lodged in his throat and he couldn't swallow it down.

"Are you....okay, Mom?" Davey said with difficulty.

Mrs. Reynolds stroked his hair. "Fine, son, I got good people looking over me. How is my boy doing?"

Davey's eyes rolled over his body. "They got me doped up on something so I don't feel a thing. I don't know if I'm coming or going."

She forced a weak smile. "You need the rest." She patted his shoulder.

Rusty's hands shook as he tried to fill the vase with water from a drinking pitcher.

"Rusty?" Davey said.

Rusty nearly dropped the vase. He turned to him and feigned a cheery smile.

"Are they managing okay without me?"

Rusty placed the flowers on the table by the pitcher and cautiously approached the bed. "It's only been the one day."

Di glared at him.

"But we can handle it till you get back," he quickly added.

"Hold the fort for me, buddy. And don't let Peets touch my engines." He smiled feebly and shut his eyes.

"I won't." Rusty choked.

They stood silent for a minute and watched as Davey slid into sleep.

Mrs. Reynolds lost her stoicism and began to sob. Di placed her arm around her and gently ushered her from the room. Rusty hesitated then started to follow them out.

"Hey, Rust," Davey said barely audible. He was drifting in and out of sleep.

"I'm here, Davey," he said, his voice almost a whisper as he sidled up to the bed.

"What happened?"

Rusty felt every muscle in his face tightened. He felt his throat tighten. He fixed his eyes on the vase of nosegays. "We had strain on a line with this monster of a tanker out of Minnesota…*Hiawatha…*," he spoke slow and deliberate. "Her name was *Hiawatha*," he repeated almost dreamlike. His mind drifted back to the scene, and he could see the big white letters spelled out on the hull. "Everything was going well…the throw, the tie off…the line used was one that had been spliced the day before. It worked like new under pressure the day of the repair. The *Hiawatha* was the first tow of the next day…the line could take the strain…should have taken the strain… because I spliced it myself…"

Davey's snores interrupted him. He peeked over at Davey and saw he was fast asleep.

He swallowed a sigh of relief and felt his muscles sag. He paused for a moment before heading to the door, and then with one more glance back to Davey, he slipped out.

Not today. Davey will find out soon enough that I spliced the line that crippled him. I just can't do this today.

He caught up with Di and weeping Mrs. Reynolds just as they reached the main doors. He felt like bolting through the opening and running for the automobile, but instead he held the doors open for the women to pass through and escorted them to the vehicle.

Chapter 12

Eliot was back. Rusty spotted him in the dispatcher's office when he arrived at work the next day. He wasn't sure but it felt like his top lip had visibly curled back into a snarl upon seeing Eliot. Only thing missing was a low growl. *Where was Prince when you needed him?*

He hurried past the office and jumped onto the *Iroquois*. Eliot was the last *thing* he needed to see, and if Idiot had any sense at all (brains were out of the question), he would give him a wide berth.

The rest of the morning, Rusty buried himself in his work. He only spoke with Jimmy and Nick, and when Bobby Peets asked him how Davey was doing, he told him he had standing orders from Davey to keep him away from the *Iroquois*'s engine room.

This made Peets laugh. "That old rascal, I am going to pay him a visit and tell him I made some adjustments and McIntyre says it runs better than ever."

Peet's laughter over his plan to rib Davey echoed down the dock and could still be heard after he had boarded the *Cherokee*.

The day was slow and no orders came down as Erie T was short in both tug and manpower. The crew watched as Great Lakes Towing was dispatched on call after call. They watched from the bulwarks of their tugs as the modern, more powerful tugboats passed by them in the channel on their way to jobs that Erie T could have handled.

"This doesn't look good," Nick, arms folded, said to Rusty and Jimmy. "Maybe I better mosey over to Great Lakes and see if they need a mate."

"Is it really that bad for us?" Jimmy asked as they eyed a big ocean-going tugboat head out on a mission.

"Elementary, my dear Watson," Rusty replied.

Jimmy looked at Rusty. "My *dear*?"

Nick scoffed at Jimmy's remark. "Sherlock Holmes, Jimmy. Rusty's not going Jane on us."

The day ended with the same blanket of gloom that had started the day. Rusty grabbed his lunchbox and jumped onto the dock. He was anxious to get out of there.

"Hey, you gonna see Davey," Peets called to him.

"Gonna stop on the way home."

"Tell'em I was poking around his engine room. I'm going to swing by the hospital later and I want to see his reaction."

Rusty smiled. If anything could make Davey get out of bed that would be it. As he headed down the dock towards the parking lot he saw Eliot approaching.

Shit, he thought.

As they passed, Eliot clipped him with his shoulder and snorted a laugh. "Who's the *idiot* now, smart guy?"

Rusty dropped his lunchbox, spun around and cold cocked Eliot flat on the nose. Eliot hit the deck hard, landing on his ass. He sat up, and both hands flew to his nose. Blood was making an appearance between his fingers.

"You broke my nose you son-of-a-bitch," Eliot cried, holding his nose.

"I'll break more than that if you get up." Rusty said, clenching his fists and holding them like a boxer with a right lead. His eyes were wild, wide and black and the look terrified Eliot who wisely chose not to get up.

Peets and Nick ran up. Each one grabbed an arm of Rusty and pulled him back from Eliot who remained seated on the dock.

"Damn it, Rusty," Nick yelled, "Fighting will get you fired."

"He's been asking for it."

"And you gave it to him and more. You made your point."

Rusty's eyes burned into Eliot, making him squirm.

Peets and Nick could feel Rusty's muscles coiled tight as springs.

"We are not letting go until you calm down, so relax, damn it," Nick said.

"Breath it out, buddy," Peets said in a calming voice. "Come on, it's over. You gave him a good what-for."

They felt his muscles loosen. Both men hesitantly relaxed their grip, but remained hanging on in case he changed his mind.

Rusty took a deep breath. "I'm okay."

Peets and Nick let go of his arms.

"I'd get the hell out of here, Rusty, before the dispatcher gets wind," Nick said under his breath. Then he added, "Eliot's been looking for a reason, and I am afraid you gave him one."

Rusty scooped up his lunchbox and headed for the parking lot.

Peets helped Eliot to his feet.

Eliot's face was red and blood caked his nostrils. "Consider yourself fired," he yelled to Rusty's back. "My old man will have your ass for this." He dabbed the back of his hand under his nose and examined it for fresh blood.

Rusty continued walking.

"He's going to pay for this," Eliot mumbled to Peets and Nick, "And I don't mean money-wise, though it is coming out of his pay."

"Shut up, Eliot," Nick said. "Next time I'll let him clean the deck with you."

"Next time?" Eliot glared at Nick. "There's not going to be a next time."

Chapter 13

"Rusty!" The dispatcher shouted as he passed the office's open door the next morning.

Rusty pulled to a halt. He drew a deep breath and hesitated before turning around and heading back to the doorway. He knew it was about the punch to Eliot and each step back to the dispatcher's office felt as though he was walking through molasses. He had slept well last night despite the threat of repercussions from the fight, and not even the stickiness of the muggy night, which would usually make sleep difficult, fazed him. Eliot had festered in him, and punching him was like draining a wound of pus. He set his jaw and walked through the open doorway.

The dispatcher was seated in the middle of a raised wooden u-shaped desk cluttered with mounds of paperwork, radio microphones, a panel of knobs and dials and a telephone placed on the hard right. Empty coffee cups and a stapler anchored stacks of paper in the event a cross breeze kicked up between the open door and windows. An ashtray overflowing with spent cigar stubs took prominence near the microphone. The desk configuration and four walls of glass allowed the dispatcher to have a panoramic view of traffic up and down the river, the dockyards, the ore terminal with its railroad cars, the mounds of iron piggots, and of course, Erie T's moored tugboats along the riverbank. The dispatcher was sweating profusely, not because of his meeting with Rusty, but because the hot and humid morning was playing havoc with his rotund body and no breeze brought relief into the box-like office. When Rusty walked inside, the dispatcher paused over paperwork before looking up to address him.

"Damn Coast Guard wants a copy of the dispatches from three nights ago. As if I don't have enough to do," he grumbled through his stub of a cigar. "You know why I called you in here, Rusty?"

Rusty folded his arms. "I have a feeling it's not about the promotion to mate."

The dispatcher snorted. "I saw what happened on the dock yesterday with you and Eliot, but I didn't rat you out. The kid bitched to his old man and he gave me a call. He wanted me to fire you, but I told him you would be a major loss. He doesn't have a clue about this operation, and since money is his only concern, I convinced him that where you go, so goes the business. Still, you can't punch out the boss's kid without expecting consequences. You might as well hit the old man himsclf."

"Eliot had it coming."

"Shit, everyone knows it, but you're the guy who decked him and has to pay the price. He's gotten under your skin like a chigger and you're letting him dig deeper. Don't think for a moment I don't know what's going on. I see what he's doing but I didn't figure you for being so thick-headed that you can't see he is goading you into losing the promotion or worse—getting fired. You are playing right into his hands."

"I am trying to do my job and it doesn't include babysitting an idiot who doesn't know the difference between knotting shoestrings and tow lines."

"That's the difference between being Joe Blow and the boss's son. He can be the biggest asshole in the world and still have job security."

The dispatcher saw him growing red. "Rusty, I know it, the crews know it, the ships know it—hell, the entire harbor knows you are the best but it doesn't matter. Do you hear me? It doesn't matter because what matters to your boss is his son, and he wants Eliot master of a tugboat sooner than later. Do you understand what I am saying? Even Brumfield and McIntyre are at risk if the old man decides Eliot should be master tomorrow." The dispatcher snapped his fingers to emphasize the snap decision.

Rusty unfolded his arms. His face felt hot. "Just keep that s.o.b. out of my way."

"I am," the dispatcher said with finality. "That's why you are laid off for the rest of the week. Boss's orders." It was like a judge bringing down the gavel on a verdict.

Rusty looked stunned. "What about pay?"

"No work, no pay. You know the score."

Rusty felt gut punched. The dispatcher turned back to his paperwork. End of conversation. To argue more would be pointless.

He spun on his heel and stomped out the door.

Nick was stationed outside the door, and Rusty ran into him. He brushed past Nick without saying a word.

Nick had overheard the end of the conversation. He stormed into the office.

"Rusty is not just a deckhand, he's my right hand man. Things are bad enough as it is and now you are taking away our best man."

"Just following orders," the dispatcher mumbled. A radio call came in.

Nick scowled. "The old man and his kid are deep-sixing this company!"

The dispatcher raised his hand to shush Nick so he could hear the call.

Nick waved his hand in disgust back at him and stomped out. He hurried to catch up with Rusty.

"Rust, it's just a cool down period. That's all. Don't make it more than it is."

Rusty slammed to a stop. "Don't make it more than it is? Nick, Davey is laying in St. Joseph perhaps never to walk again, my promotion to mate is looking slimmer every day, and that rat bastard who has been harassing me since the day he arrived is now hitting below the belt and I am without pay for a week. What part of *not more than it is* do you mean?"

Nick was quiet.

Rusty turned and began walking towards the *Iroquois* to retrieve his belongings.

"Rusty," Nick called after him. He caught up with him again. "Rusty, maybe this is for the best. I mean, we've all been talking about the company struggling lately. These tugs are being patched together. Hell, the *Shawnee* has been inactive for a month and a half for lack of repairs. While they're falling apart, the rest of the world is going diesel and getting bigger and better rigs. The old man doesn't put any money into them anymore, he's just wringing them dry. We can't compete and one of these days the calls for Erie Towing will stop." Nick shot a glance around. "We're going down the tube. I am even thinking of jumping ship and going to Great Lakes to see if there is an opening. Come with me. Guys like us are in good standings along the lakeshore. Hell, companies will be fighting over us."

Rusty snorted. "And back to square one climbing the ladder and waiting for an opening for mate for God knows how long. I was this close to being a mate," he said, pinching his fingers an inch apart to show how close.

"We were all that close to something more but it's going belly up and even if it doesn't, Eliot sure as hell will be made mate over you. Christ, his dad's the boss."

"Then I better give some good thought about jumping ship with you."

Nick patted Rusty's shoulder.

"See you next week," Rusty mumbled as he jumped onto the deck of the *Iroquois* and grabbed his gear and then headed for his truck.

***

From the deck of the *Cherokee*, Eliot feigned stowing gear and checking lines as he watched the scenario at the office and dock out of the corner of his eye. He couldn't hear what was being said, but he had an idea watching Rusty's and Nick's body languages. A grin spread across his face and he chuckled.

***

Rusty passed the driveway to his cottage and headed through downtown Vermilion and straight to Sam's. He smoldered the whole drive there. When he got to Sam's, he bee-lined it to the counter and plopped onto a center stool.

Sam turned around and a smile washed his face. "Hey, Rusty, right?"

He nodded.

"You're here early."

Rusty was silent.

"Interest you in some scrambled eggs and a cup of joe?"

"Sounds good."

"No work today?"

"No."

Sam sized him as he poured the coffee. "One of those days, uh?"

He grunted in response.

"Well, there's always something for what ails you," Sam said with a wink. He nodded towards the coffee cup steaming in Rusty's hand. "Add a little hair of the dog?"

Rusty shook his head. "Too early in the morning for that."

Sam chuckled. "It's never too early for that."

Chapter 14

The clock above Sam's counter chimed 9:00 a.m. A whole day had managed to cram itself into a few morning hours. Rusty raised himself from the stool and dropped a couple of coins on the counter.

"Leaving?" Sam asked, the clinking of coins causing him to turn around.

"Yeah."

"Taking the boat out today?"

"Depends on the weather. Got that look and feel to it."

"This mugginess could bring on a doozey, all right," Sam said, as he removed Rusty's dish and cup then swept the counter with a dishtowel. "You ought to stop by on the way back. Gets interesting in the late afternoon and evenings when the fishing crews and dockwallopers come to roost. There's always something brewing in the pot."

Rusty smiled. He wasn't sure if Sam meant that figuratively or literally-probably both.

The moment he stepped out of Sam's door, he hit a hot and sticky wall of heat and humidity. Good Lord, if it's this hot already what's noon going to be like, he wondered.

The drive to Sandusky was breathtaking for the Cleveland-Sandusky Road hugged the lakeshore offering sweeping vistas of the lake, interrupted only by trees, quaint little fishing villages and public beaches peppering the route. He could feel the tension of the morning trickling out of him as each mile passed by. The morning heat had already hazed the lake, and when he passed the sandy peninsula of Cedar Point, he could barely make out the land mass which was practically obscured by the blue haze that hung over the water.

It was the kind of day a seasoned sailor kept an eye on the cumulus clouds that popped up like popcorn in a bowl of blue sky. He would watch these harmless cotton balls of clouds feed off the heat and moisture that rose from the lake, growing, expanding and gathering until their mushrooming mass grew so big that he hoped like the devil he could beat them to shore before their transformation into thunderheads. It was the kind of day a seasoned sailor kept the shoreline within sight.

Lake Erie's claim to fame is instantaneous storms. It can go from calm to storm back to calm in almost the blink of an eye, leaving bewildered Lake Erie greenhorns to wonder what just hit them. In thirty minutes, wave action can go from mere inches to 4 feet at the approach of a storm and if a sailor is not already heading for shore, it may be too late to make safe harbor. Erie's storms are fast forming, short and violent. Its shallow waters react violently to wind, and the lake's southwest to northeast position makes a perfect wind tunnel for the Prevailing Westerlies to funnel across its full 241 mile length, gaining speed and strength to create instant 25 plus foot waves and 60 to 70 m.p.h. gale winds. Her shallowness also causes wave crests to overrun themselves and collapse, making them choppy and confused. A vessel that can survive an ocean storm can sink in a gale on Erie. Even the day after a storm, Erie can remain agitated and restless, lashing out with six foot waves to keep small craft at bay.

It was the kind of day fish bit and the sky was watched, but he was not interested in the fish today. He was looking forward to using his impromptu free day to cruise the *Rising Sun* up to Port Clinton to pick up a new battery operated bilge pump for the boat and hoped the weather wouldn't echo the morning's bad start. He had heard talk around the docks how handy these battery operated ones were as opposed to the old style that used exhausting hand pumping to clear the bilge of water. He was directed to a small shop in Port Clinton where a mechanic, highly regarded among fishermen, was building them cheaper than Rusty could buy elsewhere. Besides, the trip to Port Clinton was a good excuse to use the boat. Not that he needed one.

He removed the tarp covering the *Rising Sun* and it was like taking the wrappings off a coveted gift. He drew a deep breath as his eyes swept her stem to stern. She was 22 feet in length with a 7 foot beam and made of white oak and mahogany with a lapstrake hull painted white and varnished mahogany trim with brass fittings. A runabout with an open cockpit, she exposed Rusty to the elements which was fine by him. That's what it's all about, he would say, when ask if the sun got too hot, the breeze too brisk or the rain too hard. *If I wanted to be closed up, I'd stay indoors*, he would say. Wooden hatches in the deck covered compartments within the hull that were used as bait wells and fish boxes. In the bow, more storage space allowed for stowing tackle and gear, tarps and equipment. Her motor, unlike the typical Lyman outboard, was an inboard motor located under her belly with a screwdrive shaft that ran down the center underneath the hull to the propeller under her stern. The hull was semi-planing with tapered soft entry and round chine with very little deadrise at the stern. It was because of the boat's hull shape and construction that made Lyman boats legendary for handling Lake Erie's rugged chop with grace and speed. Only *Rising Sun* was anything but standard.

He first spotted *Rising Sun* when she arrived at Lyman's Boatworks in Cleveland where he worked before the steel mill. She was battered and ragged—just barely a shell, or as he had described her, "rode hard and put away wet." It was debated whether to rebuild or scrap her out for parts. No one knew her story, but Mr. Lyman remembered building her. She had been custom ordered with specifics that included a length of 22 feet which was seven feet longer than Lyman's longest standard built boat. The client was a steel executive from Cleveland and what the boat was used for and what happened to her to reduce her to shambles remained a mystery. Her hull was badly damaged, the dashboard smashed and missing a dial and throttle lever and her windshield broken with only shards of glass protruding from its frame. From the shell that remained, Rusty could envision the boat she once was and could be again plus more. He asked the boss if he could personally rebuild her and have her in lieu of pay, and was granted his request providing it was done on his off time. Throughout the long nights of that summer, he worked alone in the shop sawing, sanding and fitting as he restored her back to her former self and much more. Slowly (to some, painstakingly but not to him), a sleek and durable boat began to emerge under his skillful and patient hands, and his dream of owning a chartering service was finally within reach. The Lyman family and their skillful boat builders watched with curiosity often adding suggestions. With the modifications, she emerged into a small fishing charter boat built to his specifications with added bench seating, fittings for fishing poles and a hold for the catch of the day. She was, for the most part, a Lyman boat and yet she wasn't anything like a standard Lyman. She was unique and one of a kind and would turn heads and make boatmen scratch their heads in wonder about this mysterious runabout that had the signature Lyman look.

When she debuted on a warm, late fall day, the employees and owners of Lyman applauded as she was rolled out. The decrepit, discarded old boat had rose like a phoenix out of her ashes. *Rising Sun*- how appropriate Mr. Lyman had said when he read the name Rusty had painted on her transom. Also painted to the right of the name was a small painting of a yellow sun rising up from a horizon of blue water. She would be the fulfillment of his dream to be a full time charter captain while working the off season building boats at Lyman's. But when he met Di and asked her to marry him, his dream was reduced to weekends and as extra income as it would take more than charters and seasonal boat building to support the two of them and a home. And that also was fine by him because he still had the two loves of his life.

He folded the tarp and stowed it, and then gave the boat a once over. After checking the oil and fuel levels, he started the motor and she purred to life. He smiled, thinking how Davey could appreciate that sound. With everything checked out, he untied the mooring lines, and *Rising Sun* was set free. He eased her away from the dock and puttered through Sandusky Bay until he cleared the peninsulas of Bay and Cedar Points that guarded the bay's entrance. Then he throttled her up. Now he was set free.

***

The trip to Port Clinton was the perfect remedy. The lingering tension of the morning fell as the sound of the motor rose and the velocity increased. The breeze created by the speed of the boat stripped away the sweat from him and the calmness of the hazy waters allowed him a smooth, relaxing ride without fighting a chop. *Rising Sun* skimmed the water. Days like this, he reminded himself, was the real reason he built her.

As he rounded Marblehead Point with its limestone lighthouse reflecting the morning sun on its brilliant white tower, he blasted his horn in greeting to Cap Huddleson, the lighthouse keeper who shot back a hearty wave from the grounds of the lighthouse. *Rising Sun* slipped through the channel between Marblehead Peninsula to the south and Kelleys Island to the north and headed into open waters of Erie toward the tip of Catawba Island where she would then make her turn west for Port Clinton. He rounded the tip far enough from shoreline to avoid the shoals that rimmed Catawba's point and once cleared, dashed for Port Clinton and the little marina with the bilge pumps.

When Port Clinton emerged from the hazy shoreline 45 minutes later, he felt a sense of regret how quickly the time went by. He could have gone slower to drag the cruise out, but then, what was the point of the trip if he couldn't cut her loose.

***

The little marina of Rusty's destination sat at the point where the Portage River spilled into the lake. Its operator, clad in saggy coveralls, worked as a marine mechanic and tinkered as a machinist which justified his grease stained hands. It was this one man operation who pieced together the battery driven bilge pump that could compete on a local level with those sold at the big marinas for double the cost and cause men like Rusty to seek him out. The operator was not motivated by the fact he could make good money selling these pumps, but driven by the desire to rid him and fellow boaters of the pain in the ass hand pumping in order to empty the bilge of water that had washed overboard. The rest, the orders and sales by word of mouth, just naturally followed, and necessity turned to pride that he could offer the average man a well-made product at a lower cost.

When he looked up from an engine repair and saw Rusty, he proclaimed, "*Rising Sun Charters*! Here for the bilge pump." It was the unique custom Lyman that made *Rising Sun Charters* memorable, not to mention the fact that the operator never forgot a face. But first, he was determined to give Rusty a tour of his shop and operation, and Rusty knew that you weren't just buying a pump or whatever from this fellow, you were buying a piece of him.

He reminded him a lot of Davey—a simple man who loved his work and took pride in a job well done. He gushed about his pumps and how he built them as if they were children he begat, raised and sent out to the world the best they could be. Must be a mechanic thing, he thought, with Davey and his love affair with his tugboat engines coming to mind.

After retrieving the pump he built for Rusty, he gave him quick instruction on how to operate it while Rusty silently marveled at how something so simple could make life so much easier.

"Yeah, these babies are the cat's whiskers. Those hand pumps are long a thing of the past," the operator said, passing the crate housing the pump to Rusty after he boarded *Rising Sun*. "I'm getting orders up and down the lake. I even had to hire a kid to help me out. At this rate, I might wind up with a full blown assembly line like Henry Ford," he said with a wink. "Hey, you want me to hook this baby up."

"No, I can manage. Besides, I got to be heading back." He figured there would be an installation charge and the pump set up was too simple for that.

"Well, I hope you are not going too far," the operator said with a nod of his head toward the lake behind Rusty.

Rusty looked over his shoulder and saw the sky had grown dark along the horizon to the west and northwest. Its indigo color contrasted sharply with the sun that still shone over Port Clinton and points east. Rusty checked the waves and saw they were no more than ripples of a few inches. "I'm heading to Sandusky," he said.

"If you kick her in the ass you might make it," the operator said, backing from the boat. "Then again, you might want to button down here."

"The lake will be a mess after it passes," Rusty said, knowing how agitated the lake could be following a storm. He scanned the skies. "No, the sun is still shining where I am heading and the waves haven't kicked up yet. I think I'll be okay. This girl is pretty quick and can handle a chop. Besides, I have to get back before five."

"Well, if it sneaks up on you, I would put in at a lee harbor on Catawba or Lakeside if I were you."

"Once I round Catawba, I'll be home free."

The operator shook his head. "You're either fearless or foolhardy. That's a small boat for rough weather. Me? I wouldn't take the chance but then again, I'm longer in the tooth and have had enough of my share of excitement out there."

Rusty smiled and fired up the motor. *Damn weather.* All he wanted to do was make a quick run. Blow off the stink of the morning. *Damn the weather.*

The gale warning flags were up and flapping gently in the light breeze as he motored past them heading out of port.

The run back was not a straight shot west to east. He had to reverse the way he came by going around the big L-shaped peninsula of Marblehead whose bottom of the L ran west to east and its vertical "thumb" jutting to the north with its tip called Catawba Point. He would have to head north for approximately 8 miles before rounding this point and then head southwest for another 7 miles to the eastern most tip of the L where Marblehead Lighthouse stood. The run would be in open water up to this point with no land mass to blunt the force of a storm from the northwest. Not only would the wind from this direction be unchecked, it would produce large waves and heavy following seas. Once he rounded Marblehead Lighthouse point, he would then have to drop south and make a dash for another 7 miles south to Sandusky. This part of the run would have some protection from the peninsula's landmass he just went around, but it wouldn't be until he cut through the small peninsula points of Bay and Cedar flanking the entrance to Sandusky Bay that he really could- *could* be home free. Until a boat made harbor, it was a crap shoot on Lake Erie in a storm.

He throttled up once he cleared the harbor and breakwater and headed north to Catawba Point with a wary eye to his left. The color indigo had begun bleeding into the entire western half of the sky and it had grown considerately darker than when he had first observed the storm's approach on the western horizon from the dock. Overhead, a thin veil of clouds covered the sun and made it milky, but to the east, the sky was clear and bright and beckoning. He wrestled with the idea of turning back and taking the grease smudged mechanic up on his advice. He looked to the clear east and decided to press on. He reached the halfway point to the tip of Catawba without incident, but the waves had kicked up to about a foot. Still, it was nothing *Rising Sun* could not handle. She glided over the waves as if they were as flat as glass. *Damn she handled good*, he thought. The sun was fading overhead behind a blanket of clouds but it was still bright to the east. He decided to go to the point.

Rising Sun flew over the water as he fixated on the tip of land he had to round as though by intently staring at it he could make the distance close faster. A long roll of white clouds assembled low on the western horizon, extending the entire length from south to north. Their snow-white appearance contrasted sharply against their background of blackened sky. He shot a glance at the cloud bank as it formed ranks and felt the hair on his neck stand on end. The sight was intimidating and he suddenly felt very small. He concentrated his sight back to where the land mass ended at the point of Catawba and focused on it. He pressed the throttle to make sure the engine was wide open.

The water for some distance beyond the point was no more than hip deep and with swells it was even less. The urge to cut close to the tip was enticing with the storm bearing down, but he knew he would have to swing extra wide to avoid going aground.

The squall line, marked by the long, low shelf of white clouds being pushed ahead of the storm by the wind, began its roll across the lake. He watched the eerie white rolling line of clouds against the indigo black sky with dread as it grew in size and plowed towards him as if it were snow pushed by a gargantuan snow plow made of wind.

His only chance now was to round the point ahead of the squall's impact, but at this point, he was on a collision course with the storm. He cursed himself. He called himself a dummy. *What in the hell were you thinking?* He wasn't thinking- he was too intoxicated by the run to think. You stupid, stupid asshole played over and over in his head. It was too late to go back, and no place to put in. He would have to press on, round the point and try to put the peninsula's land mass between him and the storm, then head south until he came to the first available harbor. But the approaching storm had him cornered. His only escape from a broadside hit with the squall line was rounding the tip of Catawba. The waves were now whitecaps and *Rising Sun* was beginning to buck. The race to Sandusky could never be won, and the thought of safe harbor on Catawba's lee side was diminishing fast. It now became a race to put the storm behind him and round

Catawba Point instead of getting hit broadside and yet he didn't relish the thought of being pushed around the point by a heavy following sea which was dangerous in itself.

The tip of visible land at Catawba's northern point was close now, but he had to swing *Rising Sun* wide to avoid the shoals and it made him cringe to have to go farther from shore and further out into the lake. He arced her starboard and barely cleared the shoals. The waves lifted the bow and sent her nose diving into the next swell, and he could see the rocks lurking below the surface on each downward plunge. As maddening as it seemed, he had no choice but to steer her even further north out into the lake and closer to the storm. He didn't need to see how close the squall line was; he could feel it breathing down his neck and see the shadow of the descending black cloak of sky as he cleared the shoals and turned the boat again to the east to attempt to round the point.

A gust kicked off his hat, and then it grew still. It was an unsettling stillness-the calm before a storm kind, and he knew not to be fooled by the sudden lull. The storm was only taking a deep breath and at any second would exhale. He pressed the throttle again to make sure it was buried to reassure himself she was wide open. The squall clouds were bearing down on him like a pack of wolves chasing a deer and he could hear the wind howl within them. Darkness like a shroud began to cover him. He raised his eyes and saw the tumultuous roll of white clouds above him, like some giant marble rolling pin about to flatten him. Their turbulence promised violence. His choice to try and beat the storm now put him at great risk. He had gambled and lost. He gripped the wheel with both hands.

He made a hard turn right to starboard, cutting across the crest of a 5' wave on a 45° angle in hopes of avoiding being hit broadside or aft by the powerful wind racing across the open waters towards him. He braced himself.

Sixty-six miles an hour winds slammed into the *Rising Sun*'s stern just as he swung her about. So great was the collision, the stern began to lift and the bow to dive despite his efforts to keep the waves from slamming into his transom. The boat yawed to starboard. Over the howling wind, he heard the motor begin to crescendo and race as the propeller began lifting from the water. He cut back on the throttle and steered slightly to port. The boat righted itself. The wind roared through, around and past *Rising Sun*, buffeting her as she bounced and bucked on the waves. It tore at his clothes and raked his hair forward. It ripped water from the crests of the waves and blew the resulting spray on a horizontal drive across the lake that engulfed him in mist and water pellets, and for what little he could see all around him, it was a watery world of whitecaps, spray, and foam.

The squall line's frontal blast of gale force winds swept over and past him, and the wind that followed settled into a moan that rose and fell with the waves. Waves, six to seven feet high and determined, rolled eastward following the frontal line. They rammed and crashed into the backside of *Rising Sun*, washing over her stern and threatening to swallow her with each swell. He was running before the sea and knew he was in danger of broaching should he over react on the steering wheel or throttle. He rode the undulating waves like a broncobuster calculating and second guessing the moves of a wild horse. He played the throttle up and down, fast then slow to allow the waves to go under him and not against him, aware that timing the approaching waves and their speed was everything if he were to get out of this intact. Too fast, and he would bounce recklessly along the tops of the waves like a skipping stone and risk losing his propeller and control of the boat. The boat could yawl dangerously to one side and possibly broach—a situation where the stern comes out of the water during a yawl, causing the boat to roll sideways into a trough between waves. Then the following wave rolls the boat over. If too slow, the waves would rush under the boat, pushing the stern up and nosing the bow into the wave ahead causing it to dive into the water and awash the boat. Sinking was a high probability in both cases.

Beads of rain mixed with sweat on his brow as curtains of rain began sweeping the lake, pulled along by the racing squall line like boxcars attached to a raging engine. Lightning laced through the sky and thick bolts connected water and sky. Thunder responded in crashes and booms, and the ripping sounds of lightning bolts split the air as they hurtled to earth before ending in an explosive crack. Feverishly, he worked the throttle up and down while maintaining a course of control. It was the first time he felt fear since the war and the adrenaline racing through his veins made everything sharper and clearer. All five senses and his awareness became focused. His reactions and skills became razor sharp. Instinct kicked in and it made him feel alive—truly alive.

The rain enclosed him and *Rising Sun* in a "snow globe—like" world of water where nothing seemed to exist beyond the confines of the boat. The compass was his only sense of direction now, and between mopping rain and lake water from the dial and his eyes plus fighting the wheel and throttle, he wished he had a third hand and before long, a fourth.

Playing the waves seemed eternal but the adrenalin jolt kept exhaustion at bay. With his watch and compass as his only guides, he estimated where Catawba's harbors should be, but with zero visibility and the tempestuous wave action, it would be a risk guessing the shoreline and maneuvering into harbor.

Rising Sun had rounded the point and now crossed over to the lee side of Catawba. She was handling the waves as her bow cut across row upon row of closely packed waves as opposed to diving into them. To break concentration and timing in order to look for harbor did not seem like a good idea at this point, so he decided to maintain his course and head for Marblehead Point and the Fresno beam from Cap Huddleson's lighthouse that would show him the way home. As his eyes grasped for a pulse of light, he prayed for his endurance to hold out and a bolt of lightning not to find him in the deluge.

A shaft of light cut through the curtains of rain. "God bless you, Cap and your beautiful light," he whispered. But he knew he was still not out of danger for the storm was following the same track as him and he could not go faster or slower to get out from under it. It dogged him like a hound on his scent. He had to keep pushing until he rounded the lighthouse point and dropped down Marblehead Peninsula's eastern coast. It would be then that he would finally find some respite from the wind and waves in this more protected coastline.

Rising Sun coursed on through the heavy seas guided by the pulse of light. More minutes passed, and then, squinting from the onslaught of water dousing his face, he thought he saw a shape. He mopped his eyes and saw the misty form of the lighthouse tower emerging before him. He breathed deeply for the first time since the ordeal began and felt heady with relief. As the rain blurred lighthouse grew larger, so did his confidence. He tooted his boat horn like a trumpet heralding the return of a victorious warrior. *Beat me will you?* As he rounded the lighthouse point, the rain—merciless and driving for most of the trip, scaled back to a downpour. He checked over his shoulder and saw a band of light stretching along the western horizon which had been black minutes before and he knew he was in the tail of the storm and although the storm was not yet over, he had survived the worse. Still, there was enough lightning dancing overhead to make him wince, but each boom or rumble reassured him that particular bolt did not have his name on it.

As *Rising Sun* zoomed passed the lighthouse, Cap Huddleson watched the misty, rain obscured boat through a water-blurred window from the comfort of the keeper's house and wondered who it was that managed through such a blow in such a small craft.

The course, due south towards Sandusky, was not smooth sailing. The waves along the eastern Marblehead Peninsula had decreased to 3 to 4 footers thanks to the protection offered by the land, but still posed a formidable challenge to small craft due to its chop. *Rising Sun* rocked side to side, and rose and smacked down with each wave. She was beginning to feel logy and not responding as well to Rusty's handling of her. He recognized the problem. While he was all consumed in wrestling with the wheel and throttle she had taken on too much water and was in need of bailing. The storm's roar had now become a retreating growl making it possible for him to free up a hand to pump the bilge. It was an arduous job made more difficult by the fact that his energy was expended combating the storm and exhaustion was rushing in to take its place. He pumped and pumped back and forth on the handle that led to the pump below until his shoulder ached. Slowly the bilge emptied. The lake no longer tossed water inboard and the hard rain became a summer shower and for that he was grateful as he felt he could no longer muster the strength to go another round.

"Where's *baby* when you need her," he said, casting a glance with disgust at the crate housing the battery-operated bilge pump as he pumped and pumped and pumped by hand.

Ahead, like two goal posts, was Bay Point and Cedar Point, marking the opening into Sandusky Bay. He cut back on the throttle and entered the bay. The waves here were reduced to 2-3 feet due to protection on three sides.

As he motored up to the dock and eased into his slip, the rain became a drizzle. He killed the engine and tied off *Rising Sun.* She sat silent, rocking gently against her mooring lines like a race horse brought off the track, cooled down and stalled. He was soaked, and his clothes plastered to him were burdensome, and he was trembling all over.

It was also the first time since the war, after a submarine attack when the adrenaline rush was draining away, that he had trembled so and felt his arms and legs turn to gelatin. *No*, he thought as he re-boarded *Rising Sun*, *more like wet noodles when they've been boiled too long.* He sat down on the bench at the stern and watched his hands tremble. He felt drained and his shoulder ached. He fished in his pocket for a cigarette and pulled out a rain-soaked one. He grimaced and stuffed it back in his pocket and sighed.

After a few minutes passed, he raised himself from the bench. His body still vibrated from the remnant of adrenalin, but there was still much to do. He finished pumping the bilge out, wincing from the ache in his shoulder and then threw a mooring tarp over the boat and fastened it down. Tomorrow he would dry her down and rig up the new bilge pump.

As he walked to his truck parked in front of the boat slip, he looked at the sky. The clouds were breaking up and clearing to the west, but now the horizon to the east and southeast, the direction the storm was heading, was black and ominous. A feeling of victory washed over him. He beat it. The storm had reminded him what it was like to be truly alive, and it wasn't until then that he realized how dead he had been.

He removed his wet shirt, shoes and socks. Although the storm was the result of a cold front sweeping down from Canada by way of Michigan, it was cold in name only causing some fluctuation in temperature, dropping it from a stifling 92° to a clammy 75.

He drove back home to Vermilion in his bare feet. It wasn't until he passed Huron that he remembered his hat blowing off into the wind and cursed having to find a replacement, knowing all too well good hats are hard to find.

***

Rusty checked the kitchen clock. Di wouldn't be getting off work until 5, and that was a few hours away. He had changed his clothes and felt restless, so he decided to drive to Elyria in hopes of shaking off the excitement of his "adventure" and pick Di up from work and have supper there. She like surprises, but the fun derived from picking her up and taking her to supper would soon shrivel like a balloon with a hole once he told her of the lay off and why. Dare he tell her of the close call on the boat, too?

It was still drizzling when he got to Elyria, though the worst of the blow was over. The thought that he would spare her waiting for the bus and streetcar in the leftover rain pleased him. With time to kill, he splashed his way through puddles and went into Woolworth's Five and Dime, bought a newspaper and took a seat at the lunch counter. He ordered a soda from the cook-waitress who was built like a fullback, lit a cigarette and unfolded the papers. It seemed surreal to him that just hours ago he was fighting for his life out in the lake. He tried to wrap his mind around the thought that prior to the storm, he was at the Lorain docks and got time off. *All in one day, hmm, hmm, hmm.* Perhaps it had all been a dream. No, if it had been, he wouldn't be sitting at a counter in Elyria having a cig and soda and waiting for Di to get off work.

He sighed and unfolded the newspaper. The headline on the front page read, *Great Tide of Bootlegging on South Shore of Lake Erie.* He read the article as he drank the soda and smoked his cigarette. He was about to turn the page when a grainy photograph on the bottom of the page caught his eye. It was of a Coast Guard picket boat with a crew of three posed on deck with stacked cases of alcohol. Two were chief motor machinist's mates. The tall one had his foot up on a case like a big game hunter with his trophy, the second one stood wide—legged with his hands on his hips and his chest thrust forward. His issued hat sat cockeyed on his head. He wore a smug face. The third one, the captain, stood front and center and was of average height and sturdy built. He brandished a Savage Lewis .30 caliber machine gun. As grainy as the photograph was, the captain's eyes, hooded by the visor of his cap, seemed to burn through the paper. The caption read *Connors Cleared of Charges of Attempting to Kill Port Clinton Fisherman.* His mind flashed to Pete and what he had said about Connors. He read on. The article said that Connors opened fire on a fisherman returning to port at dusk. The fisherman was wounded and his boat sustained damages. A thorough search of the boat, under the watchful eyes of a gathering at the dock to where the boat was towed, produced only a chest of Blue Pike and Herring. Hardly, as one bystander was overheard saying, something to get shot over.

How, he wondered, did Connors get out of that one? He finished reading the papers, folded it and tucked it under his arm. He wanted Di to see the infamous Captain Connors. After dropping some coins on the counter, he headed for the truck, all the while wondering whatever became of the mysterious Pete.

The rain had stopped by the time Di stepped out of the factory. The sun had returned and as it burned the wet surfaces, it evaporated the remnants of rain into a ground hugging mist, turning it twice as muggy as before. The temperature rebounded to 86° and it felt sticky and close.

He was leaning against his pickup when he spotted her, called to her and waved. She spotted him, grinned hard and waved back. She looked happy to see him.

"God, it smells of earthworms out here," was the first words out of her mouth as she slid onto the truck seat, leaned over and planted a kiss on his cheek.

"Hi to you, too," Rusty said, grinning. "Where do you want to eat?"

Di didn't hesitate. "Let's get a sandwich at the counter at Woolworth's! They make great sodas."

Rusty's brows flew up. "Okay," he said, not taking his eyes off the road.

When they arrived at the lunch counter and took their seats on the stools, the same big, buxom waitress with the look of a prison matron turned to them.

"Back so soon? Musta been good," she said with a wink.

Di looked at Rusty. "What's that all about?"

Rusty blushed. "I was here earlier- got a paper and something to drink while I was waiting for you to finish work."

"Don't blame you, it's hot as hell," Di said, fanning herself with her hand.

Rusty waited till the big woman, took their order and moved to the grill area. He turned to Di and lowered his voice. "Di, I left work early this morning…"

Her eyes widened. "Are you sick?"

"I wish." He fell quiet for a moment, feeling her eyes upon him, examining his face. "I was laid off for a week."

She frowned and looked toward the back of the woman building their sandwiches. "The company is going under," she said with finality.

"No. Not yet. Can't be too far behind, though, from the chatter around the dock." He paused. "I belted Eliot and broke his nose."

"You what?" Di said, sitting bolt up on the stool.

"I punched Eliot and got a week off without pay for discipline." There-it was all out.

"Are you off your nuts?" She said in a loud whisper. She took a swig of soda and slammed the glass down.

He could see she was chewing her lip like she was holding back words she might regret letting out? She would demand a reason why, so he beat her to it.

"It was over Davey," he said, hoping she would then feel that the defense of Davey, whom she adored, was justifiable. Besides, how many times had she said, "someone oughtta punch Eliot's lights out"?

They sat in silence until their sandwiches arrived. Then she spoke.

"So, now what?"

"I'll see if I can pick up some charters this week to make up for it." Then he added, "I have a charter on Saturday out of Vermilion. I'll dock there overnight Friday, charter Saturday, and keep the boat overnight there again so Sunday we can take the boat to Avon Point and have a picnic."

"Jeepers, Rusty, I don't know if I'll feel like it."

"Why? Because of the week off? I told you I will make up for it."

"It's not just that, it's the whole thing- you fighting with Eliot, the company, I don't know."

Rusty felt a sinking feeling in his gut. "It will work out. It will. I got the boat, you got a job…Erie Towing isn't the only work on the lake." He rubbed her arm. "Don't worry, if all else fails, we can always bootleg Uncle Fritz's beer." Di snorted a laugh, and quickly covered her mouth.

Rusty felt relieved. "A day of boating and picnicking will fix what ails you, my girl. I guarantee you'll feel better."

"Not if the weather is crap."
Rusty grimaced. Maybe he better keep the storm story to himself, he decided.

Chapter 15

There were no charter runs that week. *Rising Sun Charters* was advertised as a weekend business and that could explain why no one sought him out but he had hoped hanging about the docks would scare up some sort of business. Most people worked during the week, he realized, saving excursions for the weekend, *but didn't anyone need a part run or small freight hauled to the islands?* He kept *Rising Sun* docked for that week opting to remain around the docks to make himself available. The week was spent cleaning and making minor repairs on the boat as well as routine maintenance. He touched up spots needing paint and varnished the woodwork. He even repainted the name, *Rising Sun* on the stern even though it didn't really need it. The battery-driven bilge pump had been installed the day after the storm.

In between chores, he found time to chew the fat around the docks and marinas, catching up on news and acquaintances he usually did not have time for on weekends because of the charter bookings. He also made a daily stop at Sam's either coming or going for breakfast or lunch. He finally told Sam about why he was off work that week and the story had made Sam laugh. Sam said sometimes fists got to settle what words can't. On Friday night, Rusty drove the truck to Sandusky and parked it by his slip for the weekend so he could cruise *Rising Sun* back to Vermilion to be ready for Saturday's early morning charter. Di initially was going to ride along, but changed her mind at the last minute-weather too risky she said, despite Rusty protesting there wasn't a cloud in the sky.

Chapter 16

"Hey, Rust, two guys are looking for ya." Eddie used his chin to point to *Rising Sun* docked along the channel of the Vermilion River. He was perched on a salt barrel behind the fishery with Prince sitting at attention by his side.

The afternoon sun was hot and the air was thick and smelled of fish and dank lake water. Rusty's shirt stuck to him and he smelled of sweat. He had just wolfed down a sandwich at Sam's after the all morning charter in an area of water near Hole-in–the Wall, a rocky cove known among local fishermen as a hot spot. The sunlight reflecting off the lake was intense and the reflection made him squint as he inspected the men in the distance who lingered in front of his boat. They didn't look like fishermen. He put his hands on his hips. "Did they say what they want?"

Eddie shrugged. "Don't know. I asked them and they said it was none of my beeswax, the assholes."

"Watch your mouth," Rusty said. He dug in his pocket and produced a dime. "Get yourself an orange pop, kid," he said, tossing the coin to Eddie who snagged it mid-air.

Eddie jumped off the barrel then headed off with Prince in tow. Rusty started down the row of docked boats with a wary eye on the two men who had now straightened as they realized the man who was approaching them was the skipper they were looking for.

"Rusty?" the smaller of the two asked. His face was soft and burnt and his smile relaxed. He wasn't dressed for fishing. He wore a white shirt with the sleeves rolled to the elbows, black pants and a narrow black tie. A fedora shaded his dark, bright eyes. The larger man's dress was copy, only a number of sizes bigger. They looked of Italian descent.

"Yeah," Rusty said, stopping before them. "What can I do for you?"

"You were recommended to us by a mutual friend. I own a vineyard on Put-in-Bay and need to hire a charter to haul grape juice from the island to Sandusky on Friday afternoons from August through November if the weather holds out," the smaller, fleshy man said.

Rusty sized the larger man to the right. "I have a job through the week and charter on weekends. I can do it on Saturdays in the afternoon, after the morning fishing charters."

"Nah, no good. What time do you get off on Fridays? Maybe you can do this after work? It would be about two hours of your time and enough money to make it worth your while."

The man's pushiness, despite his cheeriness, irritated Rusty. "It would take more than two hours. I work in Lorain and dock in Sandusky. Hell, the drive there and back is more than two hours."

The small, fleshy man looked at the larger man. The larger man shrugged. Rusty could almost hear the gears spinning in the smaller man's mind. A few moments passed as the smaller man hashed out his thoughts while the larger man, it appeared to Rusty, appeared to draw a blank.

"How early on Saturday?"

"My first charters are at six, sometimes earlier. Fish bite early."

The small man frowned, and the larger man studied him for any indication of what he was thinking.

Finally, the smaller man said. "Friday night- it's gotta be. Pick up is at the Lime Kiln Dock at the island's southern tip. If you decide to do it, be there at 8. That should give you enough time to get there and it will still be light enough on your trip back. I guarantee you'll be paid more than your Saturday morning charters total. I'll even pay you in advance."

Rusty mulled it over in his head. "Where would I be taking the juice?"

"Back to Sandusky! See, no big deal-it's right back to where you started from."

"I don't know," Rusty said. "I'd have to talk it over with the wife. Friday nights we go out for supper."

"Well chew on it for a few days. With the extra money, you'll be able to take your old lady to a real fancy place on Saturday nights. Make her happy." The man slapped him on the back and Rusty stiffened.

He wasn't sure what grated him more- the reference to Di as an old lady or the slap on the back. He'd chew on it all right.

As the men walked away, Rusty called after them, "Hey, how do I get a hold of you if I decide to do it?"

"No problem," the small man called back, "Just leave word with Sam."

***

The Lake Erie Islands had ideal soil and weather conditions for the growing of grapes, and vintners who had migrated from Germany recognized this asset and established numerous highly productive vineyards on the islands. Their wines rivaled those of France and were shipped all over the United States as well as abroad.

The first blow to the island vineyards came in the late 1800s when a fungal disease attacked the grapevines and wiped out most of the vineyards. Those that survived had a second blow in the form of the government's ratification of the 18th Amendment to the Constitution in January 1919 which banned the manufacturing, sales and transportation of alcoholic beverages. When Prohibition went into effect, it devastated the island's economy and many vineyards went bankrupt and fell into ruin. A few resourceful vintners managed to survive by making and selling grape juice, something that quickly became popular. Cases of juice contained a warning stating that under no circumstances should you add yeast, sugar and store for a period of time because the grape juice will turn to wine which is illegal. That, of course, was the point behind its sudden popularity and the salvation of many vineyards.

Chapter 17

Despite the gentle ripple of lake waves, Di got seasick. It wasn't actually the trip itself that made her stomach flip and flop, but the rocking and swaying the boat did at dock and before it got up to speed in the open water. It usually took a chop to get her sick but Rusty had been noting the past few weeks that she seemed quieter than usual. He tried to distract her by pointing out the area of his charter the day before at Hole-in-the-Wall as it was located on the way to Avon Point. She feigned interest but Rusty could tell her attention was concentrated on trying to keep the queasy feeling churning in her stomach at bay.

"Don't stare at the water, Di," he said, "Look at the horizon. See up ahead, that jut of land is Avon Point."

She raised her head to look. She was white as a sheet and her lips were drawn. He knew her lips would be as pale as her face under her red lipstick. He felt a twinge of guilt. She loved picnics and the vacation like atmosphere that came with lake living, but she was wary of small boats and harbored a total distrust of the lake. To her, the lake was not pleasing in itself, but something you had to deal with in order to have your pleasure. It was like paying her dues to get to do what she wanted. Not all boats bothered her. The criterion was they just had to be big and crowded with people. Less isolation and bigger boats equaled security in her mind. She loved to take the big ferries from the mainland to the islands and daydreamed about cruising across the lake on the big cruise ship, *Goodtime*, but what gave her the "willies" were small boats on vast Lake Erie. "So help me, if I can't see the shore I will never set foot in the boat again. I mean it, Rusty," she said each time they took the boat out in the lake.

He knew she meant it. That was one thing about her- she was good to her word.

***

The Pavilion at Beach Point, where Avon Point reached out into Lake Erie, was a popular spot for swimming, picnicking and socializing. It was known for its sandy beach, towering oaks, aromatic flower gardens, nice bathhouse, and 15 varieties of ice cream. The Pavilion, standing two stories high, served as a community hall for socials by day and a dance hall by night, with people living as far as Cleveland arriving by the interurban or by passenger ferry to the popular spot. On summer weekends, crowds swarmed to the park to swim, picnic and listen to barbershop quartets, jazz bands and orators and attend the ever popular ice cream socials.

Once they were docked, he helped her out of the boat. Her legs wobbled a bit and he held onto her arm until she steadied herself. It wasn't until both feet planted on solid ground that she let out a sigh of relief. After a quick inventory of her belongings, she straightened her gown, thrust her head erect and marched towards the beach. She toted a wooden handled, black peacock printed cloth satchel stuffed with beach blanket, towels, a bathing cap, nose plugs and a change of clothes including swim wear for Rusty lest he changed his mind about swimming. She had worn her swimsuit under a pink and black kimono-sleeve robe trimmed in tiny beads and deceptive enough to pass for a stylish dress. This way, she could avoid changing in the bath house, reason being more of a time-saving factor than anything else.

He carried the picnic basket she had packed with fried chicken, her mother's German potato salad, pickled beets and lemonade. She purposely excluded dessert as ice cream from the stand at the bath house would provide them with that indulgence.

They arrived on the beach with belongings in tow, and Di immediately set about assessing the sand full of people, scanning for an open spot and selecting it as carefully as though it was permanent real estate. *Don't want to be close to kids with beach balls, crying babies or disgusting people* she had warned Rusty as they trudged through the squishy sand, lugging the satchel and picnic basket. She located a spot, and they staked their claim by spreading the blanket. Di began to unload the picnic basket. After the contents where arranged on the blanket, she took one look at the potato salad and then the fried chicken and felt her stomach churn again. She pressed her lips together and stared at the food as if it were poisonous.

"You okay? You're a bit green around the gills."

She gulped. "I'm going to take a quick dip first." She dug through the satchel for her bathing cap and nose plugs. "Help shake off the woozies."

"Okay," he said, watching her as she struggled on her cap and slipped out of her robe. "Besides, you'll get a stitch if you eat first," he said to her backside as she trotted towards the water, positioning the nose plug as she went. He tried to imagine how going back into the waves would make one shake off the woozies. He lay back on his elbows, watching her as she dove into a breaker. She popped up from the surf moments later to his relief. She seemed fine so he settled back to soak up the sun and sights, and eventually his thoughts drifted to the grape juice men and their proposal. He knew Di would be upset about skipping Friday night suppers as she looked forward to it as much as he did. Work separated them enough as it was she would often complain. Friday nights were near ritual and the routine pretty much repeated itself each weekend with few interruptions. Friday was supper, Saturdays were charters for him and her day for errands, shopping and lunch or Mahjong with friends. Sundays were morning worship, then parks or picnics or visits to Di's family farm. Friday evenings and Sundays were their together days.

No. No. He didn't need the money. They were doing well as it was. Okay, so he could get Di that roadster a whole lot sooner with the money from the Friday evening charters, but it was not like they had to have the extra money. He kicked it around in his mind, and before she joined him on the beach blanket after her swim, he decided to not even mention it. Made no sense to concern her with something that was not about to transpire.

She trotted up to their blanket while pulling off her bathing cap and to his relief, her color had returned as well as her enthusiasm. "Let's eat. I'm starved."

He grabbed a plate and heaped it with food and handed it to her, but she did not reach for it. He watched in puzzlement as the color drain from her face again. He lowered the plate to the blanket in front of her. "One minute you're sick, the next you're not. What's going on?"

She stared at the plate of food and he could tell there was an internal struggle within her whether to take a bite or vomit.

"You're not pregnant are you?" he said, picking up a chicken leg and began gnawing on it. When he glanced back to her, her eyes were locked on his. He lowered his stripped chicken bone. "It was just a joke."

She burst out crying.

A woman sunning on a blanket next to them raised her head and looked at them when she heard Di's sobs. She narrowed her eyes at Rusty.

A man reading a book seated in front of them also turned to look.

Di tried to rein in her tears to a whimper.

"You want to go home?" Rusty began repacking the meal into the basket.

She shook her head no and dabbed at her wet eyes with a napkin.

"Let's go see the flowers then." He stood up and offered his hand to her, pulled her to her feet and wrapped the robe about her.

He took her hand and walked silently through the scented paths winding through the grassy picnic area. Though she no longer cried, her blotchy face and red eyes and nose betrayed her. Each time someone passed near them, she feigned interest in a rose or a daisy so they could not see her face.

"Better?"

She nodded again.

"Are you coming down with something? Do you feel sick?"

"It comes and goes." She sniffed.

"You sound pregnant."

"What if I was?"

"Are you?"

"I don't know?"

"What do you mean *you don't know*? Of course you'd know."

Di stopped abruptly and turned to him. "It's not all that black and white, you know."

He was quiet for a moment, allowing the sting to subside. "Well, that would be great, wouldn't it…if that was the case?"

She was silent. The bounce in her step was missing. He felt confused.

They continued walking in silence and finally ended up back at the beach. After they gathered their belongings in silence, Di smiled at the woman who had raised her head again to look at them. Rusty helped her into the boat, and soon they were heading back to Vermilion. Taking her on the longer trip back to his dock in Sandusky seemed out of the question. Telling her about the Friday night grape juice men seemed just plain crazy.

Chapter 18

Monday arrived too soon. He knew his time off would be the buzz around the docks. Actions and words would be twisted. He would be pitied by most, doubted by no one. God, he hated having to look at that bastard again. It would only be a matter of time before he would be choking once more on one of Idiot's shit sandwiches. That was inevitable as the sunrise.

Nick had given him a pat on the back upon seeing him as he boarded the *Iroquois.* Jimmy had smiled at him and told him he was glad he was back and Cap' McIntyre, from the rail of the wheelhouse above him, nodded to him.

The morning flew by as they were busier than usual.

When they shared a seat on the bulwarks for lunch, Nick told Rusty that during his absence, the *Shawnee* was sold for parts. Rusty showed no reaction as he quietly ate his lunch of fried chicken and pickled beets leftover from the picnic meal the day before.

"The old man's also working out a deal to sell the *Delaware* to some private firm in Buffalo," Nick continued.

Jimmy glanced at Rusty to see his reaction.

A few moments passed silently as Rusty seemed to concentrate on spearing a beet with his fork. Finally, never looking up from his plate, he said, "Well, the *Shawnee* has been junk and without a crew for some time, and the *Delaware*, being steam powered, really hasn't been much use except for odd jobs or in a crunch."

"It's the beginning of the end," Nick said. "The company is cutting back instead of growing."

"What about *Delaware*'s crew?" Rusty asked.

"Peets is going to train Evans on diesel so he can replace Davey. Evans is only experienced in steam engines," Nick said to clue Jimmy. "The experienced guys are going to replace the greenhorns on the other tugs."

"That means me," Jimmy said.

"You'll do okay, Jimmy," Rusty said. "You got what it takes to make a good pelican and getting a job won't be hard for you."

Jimmy smiled halfheartedly.

"Yep, the old man is pissing the business down the hole," Nick said.

"We still got three tugs. That's what we've been using anyways," Rusty said.

"And how long do you think Erie T will stay afloat?" Nick said as he snapped his lunch box shut and stood up. "You heard the rumor the old man's got a gambling debt. Do you think he's going to put the money from those two tug sales back into the company because if you do, you are a sap." Nick started for the wheelhouse. "Keep your eyes open, Rust. We're being wasted here."

Jimmy watched Nick walk away. "I would have left anyways if you and Nick left."

"I'll put in a good word for you, Jimmy. I know Nick will do the same."

"Thanks, Rusty."

***

A week later, the *Delaware* chugged her way down the Black River and past the Lorain Breakwater Lighthouse at the mouth one last time. She was bound for Buffalo and her crew dispersed among the *Iroquois*, *Cherokee* and *Wyandot*.

On Jimmy's last day, Rusty and Nick got on either side of him and on the count of three, tossed him overboard into the river. After dragging himself out laughing and onto the dock, he gave each of them a soggy but hearty handshake.

"I'm gonna miss you guys," he said, growing serious. "Rust, I can't tell you how much I appreciate you showing me the ropes."

"That's literally!" Nick laughed.

They all laughed.

"I mean it," Jimmy said.

"Don't go soft on us, kid," Rusty said with a playful punch to Jimmy's shoulder.

"Yeah, you're killing us with kindness and we ain't use to that around here," Nick said.

Jimmy grabbed his stow and headed down the dock, turning one last time to give a half wave-half salute to the guys gathered for his farewell. He sloshed and slogged and left a wet trail in his wake.

"Don't take any wooden nickels, kid," Rusty yelled after him.

***

A week after Jimmy's departure, Nick burst through the door of the *Iroquois*'s wheel house, startling Rusty and Evans. Nick's face was ashen. "The old man has pissed away the *Iroquois* and *Wyandot*!"

Rusty and Evans jaws dropped.

"I told you he was in hock and now they are coming to collect! Erie T is no more." Nick jumped back onto the dock and headed for the *Wyandot* moored behind the *Iroquois*.

Rusty and Evans looked blankly at each other.

"He didn't mention the *Cherokee*," Evans said, finally breaking their silence.

Rusty was too stunned for words. With a baby on the way, he felt gut punched.

Chapter 19

"They're right, you're going to have to find something pretty quick. Di can only work so long, and then kaput, the money's gone." Uncle Fritz took a swig from a bottle of his homebrewed beer. He was seated next to Rusty on a bench overlooking his garden he shared with his sister, Di's mother. It was a large garden bordered by grapevines on one side and wild blackberry bushes on the other. In between, Di's mother grew cabbage, potatoes, beans and beets to name a few and some of the tastiest corn Rusty had ever ate. Uncle Fritz gave special attention to his grapevines, hops patch and the field of barley he shared with Di's father. Lessons handed down and taught to him by his German-born father had not gone to waste and even Prohibition failed to make a ripple in his brewing of beer and fermenting of juice from grapes, blackberries and dandelions. Weather and insects were the only obstacles in Uncle Fritz's pathway to a perfect bottle of amber beer or sweet glass of wine to share with family and friends.

He had said the samc thing to Rusty that Di's father and brothers had said, only he had a way of putting it that did not rub Rusty's hairs the wrong way. It was for reasons like that, Rusty sought out the company of Uncle Fritz during his visits to Di's family.

"I hope you buried a money jar in the back yard for times like this," Uncle Fritz said.

"Di puts half her money in a savings account, and I have a nest egg put aside from the charters. I was planning to surprise her with a roadster. Something nice besides the old truck." Rusty sighed.

"No. No car. Baby is coming and you have no job. Right now, the truck will have to do. A roof is more important than a fancy car."

Rusty frowned and took a sip of beer. Uncle Fritz was right. That's what stung.

***

The moment Di broke the news to the family about the dissolve of Erie T, the brothers had jumped on it by declaring *I knew it* and *I told you so.* Jobs on the water, they affirmed, were never stable. The mill is always hiring, her Dad had interjected. Good job security and better pay, he added, to the nodding heads of the brothers. With that, her brothers immediately began mapping out plans for Rusty's return to the mill. That's when he got up and went out to the backyard to seek out Uncle Fritz, locating him by following the sound of humming coming from the garden.

"They're already lining up work for me at the mill," he told Uncle Fritz.

"You have other plans?"

"I plan to poke around the docks between Lorain and Sandusky first thing Monday morning to see what I can scare up for work, tugboats, ferries, barges—whatever floats. I'll go to Cleveland or Toledo if I have to. I am an AB Seaman and I'm not going to piss away all that learning and all those years climbing the ladder toward captain for a factory job. There's a demand for experienced seamen like me."

Uncle Fritz raised his brow. "Well, then, since you're so popular, you have nothing to worry about."

Rusty's face reddened with embarrassment. He wasn't one to blow his own horn and here he was crowing to Uncle Fritz.

"What I meant..."

Uncle Fritz waved the comment off. "I know what you meant. You are a good sailor and it's what you know. You are a man of the water, not steel. There is a difference and if you cross them up, all you get is a very unhappy man who does not do his job well. You've been down that road to know." Uncle Fritz paused. "It's a big lake out there, and I am sure there is plenty of work for good deckhands or pilots. Besides, if you can't find a job or make enough money for three," he poked Rusty in the ribs with his beer bottle, "*The mill is always hiring.*"

Rusty snorted.

"Just don't get desperate. I'd hate to see you at Cedar Point Park operating the pedal boat rides wearing a silly captain's hat."

Rusty grinned. His eye caught Di flagging him from the back of the house. He rose from the bench. "Thanks for the beer. You know, you could make a killing selling this."

Uncle Fritz chuckled. "The hops make it special and it's extra good because of the love I add to it for my family and friends—not to mention forbidden fruit always taste best." As Rusty walked away, Uncle Fritz called out, "Remember, any port in a storm, Rusty." Only Uncle Fritz meant the steel mill, whereas he thought of anything but.

***

The next morning, he was at Lorain Harbor- partly out of habit, mostly sniffing for work. Despite Nick's optimistic assumption that he and Rusty would be in demand, he found no openings around the harbor for his current level.

He had high hopes that Great Lakes Towing would take him. They were a nice company- growing, paid well and treated their employees and tugs with respect. The only thing they lacked because they were so big was the family-like atmosphere the Erie T crews shared among themselves, the bond that made these guys not just fellow workers, but friends. But he wasn't there to make friends, he was there to get a job. He was disappointed to learn Great Lakes at their Lorain base was not currently hiring. *Don't think our Toledo or Cleveland stations are hiring at this time, but I know our bases in Detroit and Buffalo are always looking for deckhands with experience*, he was told at the Lorain office of Great Lakes Towing.

Could you keep me in mind if an opening appears locally-Toledo and Cleveland included? Rusty had asked, writing his name and address on a paper and handing it to the personnel man.

***

He returned to the hunt for work, becoming increasingly exasperated as his quest hit dead-end after dead-end. Despite the explosion of industry and construction after the war which created thousands of jobs, there were also thousands of men who were able and eager to fill those jobs. It was boom time, and unemployment, if not by choice, was generally short-lived. The glut of able body workers meant few openings and because of that reason, men hung on to their jobs with tenacity.

He had fooled himself in thinking that finding good work locally would not be a problem for him even if it meant a step back and fewer wages, so the day had been a cold slap in the face. There were still many ports to check out, he told himself.

He decided to set his sights next on Sandusky's busy harbor, but thought he'd first stop by Huron's port with its complex of tall grain mills that exported flour and grains across the lake. There were tugboats and barges there, he told himself reassuringly, and Huron was closer to home.

As he was about to leave, he heard his name shouted.

"Rusty! Rusty!" The voice came from the river.

He looked up and down it and heard his name shouted again.

"Rusty! Up here!" The voice came from a lake freighter plowing its way up the Black River. He spotted someone leaning out of the wheelhouse. The figure was flailing his arm out the window to draw attention.

"Rusty, hey Rust, up here."

Nick was attached to the waving arm and booming voice. He was all grins.

Rusty waved back. He was grinning, too. "What in the hell are you doing there?" he shouted back.

"Harbor pilot! Great job!" Nick yelled to him. "Have you had any luck?"

"Not yet."

"I'll keep an eye out for you, Rust," Nick said with a final wave as the freighter glided by.

Rusty shook his head with a smile. *Good for Nick.* It would have been a waste had he been anything less. He watched the freighter as it passed by, then started for his truck parked in its old spot when he still had a job. A man who had overheard him earlier looking for work approached him. He said he heard Rusty was looking for work and had a tip. *Someone told him that someone else said that Able Barge was looking for a deck hand.* Rusty thanked him and decided to check it out. To his disappointment, the skill level was low and the pay reflected it. The moment he had appeared at the small dockside office of Able, he knew he didn't want the job. Able was looking for someone that could serve the dual job of deckhand and longshoreman for off and on loading of freight. The turnover rate of employees (as admitted by Able personnel who said they were always in need of help) sent up a red flag to Rusty. The hard work didn't scare Rusty, but the fact that he had to start on the ground floor again for money that paid squat repelled him. He rejected the offer by telling the company he would get back to them, figuring since he had just started his search, he wasn't eager to bite at the first lousy job dangled before him. But with Di's income soon to cease and the drain on the saving account soon to begin plus a third mouth to feed, he decided he wouldn't write the job off until he exhausted the options.

Rusty crawled in his truck. Huron, then on to Sandusky harbor and the islands was the plan. Those places were like a second home to him and there are plenty of tugboats, ferries and stone freighters at those places. Somewhere, someone had need of a deck hand or dock worker. Plus they were close to where *Rising Sun* was docked.

It was a long day with his name taken instead of his skills. Most companies, since it was well into summer, had their help for the season. *We will be hiring for sure the start of next season—your experience will be most welcomed. Come back in early spring.* He felt a touch of panic setting in. He needed work now, not spring. Sandusky and the islands buzzed with commercial activity and he figured there had to be an opening somewhere. His last stop was a ferry company operating between islands. *Any openings? It doesn't have to be for just deckhand. I am open for almost anything.* He was sounding desperate. *Begging was for the hopeless,* his aunt had always said when he was growing up on the farm. He wouldn't make that mistake again. He had set a trawl line of hooks baited with his experience and reputation with high hopes that something would bite, but it was too late into the season and positions were filled. Check back in a week or two became the mantra of many companies. At the end of the day, at his last stop, something, rather someone, did take the bait. It was a freighter company that hauled lime, limestone and flux out of Kelleys Island to the industrial ports of Gary, Buffalo and Duluth. They could use an experienced deck hand. It involved lake travel, long hours, and overnight layovers and he would make more money than a forty hour work week at Erie T. But it came with a price as the shifts were long and grueling and his status lower. But he would be on the water.

Rusty wrestled with the opportunity. It was not what he had exactly hoped for. It would mean separation from Di when she needed him most. It would also mean she would need the truck. That would not be a problem, he figured, as he could catch the Lakeshore Railroad in Vermilion and take it to Sandusky, hop the ferry to Kelleys and walk to the quarries. But again, there was the issue of being separated for days on end. That alone would have been bad enough without the pregnancy and baby heaped onto the pile. And what if she needed him? What if there was an emergency and he was halfway across the lake? It would take time, maybe days to get to her. He didn't marry her to be away from her especially now that she needed him the most. She would be alone for the most part unless she moved back to the farm until—until what? Until a phantom job opening like the one he had? He flashed to the mill. The mill would be six or seven days a week, twelve hour shifts depending on the department, but they could stay in Vermilion and he would be home each day—even though he would be half dead from exhaustion and either sleeping or working. Either way, he would have to stop the charters, and the thought sickened him for he had hoped and dreamed, as his reputation and business grew, to make it a full time business during the lake's open season. And would he ever be able to remove the tarp from *Rising Sun* again? The thoughts bounced about his mind like ricochets. He didn't know how to answer the offer and it troubled him because he felt he should know the answer. Could he sleep on it? God, how dithering that sounded.

Sure. There is always a need for good hands with our company.

He started back home. He would try Cleveland's harbor tomorrow and if that didn't pan out, he would search in Toledo, he strategized as he passed Huron. *Those harbors are so big, they have to have job openings.* His thoughts of all that happened to him in the last two weeks were like a jumbled mix of marbles that were poured into his head and wildly rolled about, scrambling his sense of reasoning. His perfect world had fallen apart in a snap of a finger. Di and he had played it carefully. They had chartered their course and saved and dreamed. Life was…life was…ducky. It was one of Di's expressions, not his, but at the moment he was at a loss for any other word. *At what point did it start to go wrong? Was there a warning flag?* He decided—no he knew—there was a red flag. Nick had said all along about the problems dogging Erie T but he, like the other crew members stuck his head in the sand, ignoring Nick's hunch. He should have split when Nick first suggested it when Great Lakes was hiring. He had backed the wrong horse and lost. Now, instead of being happy about the baby, he was sick with worry. And what if the baby was born sick? What if Di had a bad labor? What if Di got sick? What if he got hurt? What if…what if…what if? "What if frogs had wings?" he would say to Di when she was on a *what if* roll. *Then they could fly*, she would always answer.

He chewed over and over the mushrooming of recent events, sorting and trying to make sense until his head felt like it would explode. He drove east on Cleveland-Sandusky road heading back towards Vermilion, never once looking at the lake.

Chapter 20

"No. Stone freighter is out of the question. And you can forget Toledo, too. Don't even bother to look there." There was finality to Di's statement. The door to her mind had slammed shut when Rusty mentioned them and he knew he would need more than a crow bar to pry it back open.

"Di, if Cleveland doesn't pan out, I am running out of choices."

"Choices of harbor work, you mean. I can understand you not wanting to work at the mill, but there are all sorts of factories in Elyria. One of them has to be hiring. The lace company is surrounded by them."

He sighed. "I'm a seaman, Di, not a factory worker. If I have to take a job far from home, it will only be temporary while I keep looking closer to home. I'll just keep dogging places until I find an opening. At least we can keep the cottage with the money I would make and you can stay with your mother if you like while I'm gone. Then, by the time the baby is here, I should have a job close by because I plan to keep looking and spring will bring all sorts of possibilities."

If she was listening, she didn't show it. He waited for a response and when there wasn't any, he went to the screen door, hesitated, and walked out and into the back yard. His head throbbed. He headed back to the edge of the property and smoked a cigarette while he watched the waves pound the rocks below. Bullheadedness wasn't uncommon for Di, but the undercurrent of anger that now coursed its way through her was. He missed the old Di, the happy Di, the adventuresome Di, the *we can do it*, Di. Things were hard enough as it was and now there was no pleasing her. He finished his cigarette and flicked the butt into the breakers.

He went to bed that night with hope and a headache. Cleveland, being such a major harbor, had to have a job somewhere for him. He played that thought over and over again in his mind until he fell asleep sometime after midnight. Meanwhile, Di slept with her back to him.

When he awoke the next morning before the sun, the darkness hid the fact she was not in bed. He heard faint rustling outside the bedroom. He sat up and saw a soft wash of light coming from the kitchen. The smell of coffee and cooked ham drifted into the bedroom. He felt her side of the bed and it was empty. He pulled on his pants and followed the smell of frying ham and coffee and found her standing in front of the stove frying eggs.

Without looking up from the stove, she said, "You're going to need a good breakfast for the day ahead," as he came into the kitchen. He poured himself a cup of coffee and took a seat as she brought him his plate. It was his favorite—eggs in a nest, sunny side up in the center of hollowed out slices of toast with a slice of ham on the side.

He looked up at her, and she looked sheepishly back. He rubbed her arm. "Thanks," he said. His smile was warm.

She reflected the smile and a wash of relief spread over her. She sat down next to him. "I am sorry about…"

Rusty cut her off. "It's okay. We'll get through this patch. Together."

Her eyes brimmed with tears. "I know this is a pickle for you and I am not making it easy…"

"It's a pickle for you, too. But we'll get through this."

She sighed. "It's a test."

"No, Di. It's life."

She looked so small and childlike at that moment. He leaned over and pulled her toward him, kissing her on the forehead and then sat back. A twinkle appeared in his eyes. "If you want to think of it as a test, think of it as separating the men from the boys. Come on, Di, are we men or boys?"

She snorted a laugh. Her eyes were suddenly shining. "We're *men*!" She giggled. She shot forward and planted a kiss on his cheek. Then she picked up her coffee cup. "Here's to good hunting," she said, raising her cup.

They touched cups.

He felt a rush of warmth inside before he even drank. Di was back.

***

From the window of the Lakeshore Electric's interurban, Rusty watched the Terminal Tower emerge from the thick fog of smoke and soot that enveloped downtown Cleveland. Like a stake marking the city's center, the tower was the only visible sign that the city of Cleveland lay beneath the opaque blanket of haze. The Cuyahoga River came into view. Looking brown and sluggish like an Anaconda snake, it coursed and wrapped its way through the city as it headed for Lake Erie.

Everything about Cleveland's industrial harbor on the Cuyahoga River was louder, bigger and busier, but it couldn't beat Lorain in smell although it came pretty close. Rusty figured it was because the Cleveland factories were more spread out whereas Lorain's industrial section was concentrated.

His search area would be more expansive in Cleveland and included a long stretch of the winding Cuyahoga which was lined as far as the eye could see up and down the river with sooty industrial plants, railroad cars, barges and freighters of every size in an area known as *the flats*. At the Cuyahoga's mouth, the wide harbor hummed with tugboats and barges hard at work. Lying off shore within a stone's throw from the harbor, a small island, called Whiskey (which really wasn't an island, but a peninsula carved out by the river), groaned and banged as it processed ore with the help of giant steel grasshopper-like legs and Hullet shovels that had the size and bite of a giant dinosaur. Like Lorain, railroad hoppers along the river slammed and banged, only here, noise and activity was multiplied times over. Cleveland's harbor was big, gritty and impersonal and one could easily lose himself among the workforce.

He walked along the bank as he headed towards an assembly of tugboats, pausing to watch a huge freighter slip up river. It was a sight he never got use to, but this time, he quickly lost interest in the ship itself as he noticed the wake and eddies created by its passing. They were yellowish-green in color and moved with the consistency of milk with a smell that was a potent cocktail of metals, sulfur and rotted garbage. The floating dead fish added to the mix.

He grimaced, and then continued toward the tugboats.

Numerous tugboat companies dotted the river and shoreline. Some were monopolistic like Great Lakes while others were privately owned like Erie T. Since he knew Great Lakes wasn't hiring, he skipped over it and headed for the first company he came to. To his surprise, they were hiring—temporarily. A deckhand had been badly hurt two weeks ago and needed another two weeks off according to his physician. Rusty was welcome to replace him but was warned that the former deckhand gets his job back upon his return. He agreed. The fellow's break became his break. The only downside was he would have to work Saturdays and most of his charters were Saturday bookings. He wavered at the thought, but didn't show it and shook hands with the tug owner while hoping he could convince those already booked to move to a Sunday charter. It would mean missing church and Di would be upset about that as well as him working on the Sabbath, although he knew working on Sunday would really be more about missing out on their afternoon picnics and roller coaster rides than keeping the Sabbath holy.

The tug job would take him into August. Plenty of charters in late summer and fall when fishing is best anyways, he told himself. But he would still need a job to pick up when this one ended. This one will at least buy him time to sniff around the harbor in Cleveland, and meanwhile, maybe he could sell himself to the tug company.

He felt pleased with himself. He had a job with tugboats, though temporary, and Di would not be alone and would have use of the truck as he could take the rail into Cleveland and walk the distance between the terminal and the industrial flats. For tonight, he could give his mind a rest and start thinking all over again tomorrow.

But as of now, the tugboat company needed a hand immediately, and Rusty was put to work right after the handshake.

***

The week was grueling and he fell asleep before his head hit the pillow. The freighter and barge traffic at Cleveland's harbor was non-stop and so was the tugboat service. At Lorain's smaller harbor, the pace was not as hammering and there were moments of down time that could be spent on tug maintenance peppered with laid back conversation. He hadn't felt so ragged out since he was a wet behind the ears deckhand in Toledo. Only now, he was longer in the tooth and the ache in his muscles didn't disappear overnight. Di even noted he seem to crawl out of bed on all fours in the morning like a dog. *Like a dog all right...dogged and dog-tired.* The longer commute to the city with all the walking and rail riding, not to mention waking up in the wee hours in order to make it to work on time, only heaped another layer of tiredness and soreness on his spent body. There were evenings that his head hung so low, Di thought she may have to pick it up before he fell asleep face first in his supper plate. On Sunday's visit to the family farm (the charter booked for Saturday, not wanting to switch to Sunday, canceled altogether), Uncle Fritz referred to the new job as dog-tiring after sizing up Rusty. Her brothers called it more money than Erie T but not as much as the mill. Rusty hadn't heard their remark as he was still taking note of the dog reference used again.

As the second week was drawing to a close, he wasn't so gung-ho about selling himself to the tugboat line or any line for that matter. It was bad enough that his prospects of being made a mate within the year would not come to fruition. He could begrudgingly accept that but to start all over again as low man on the totem pole was almost unbearable. Working harder for less, he groused, but only to himself. He could handle the harder if the pay was on par. If he just knew this was all leading somewhere, to something other than the void it seemed to be headed. The climb back up to mate would be a long one, and there were no old deck hands.

Thursday arrived like a bolt out of the blue. He realized not only did he have just two days of work left with the tug company, he had no other job lined up. He had been so consumed in work, he had not had the time to look or even think about job hunting. It was getting down to the wire and the tug line had yet to extend a job offering as he had hoped. He consoled himself with the thought that they would most likely make the job offer on his last day. Meanwhile, the charter scheduled for the coming Saturday also canceled when he asked if they would be willing to switch to Sunday.

It was also on Thursday that he realized he hadn't seen Davey for a while and felt a pang of guilt for the lapse in time. Before he left for work, he told Di he would be late as he would be getting off at the Lorain stop to see Davey in the hospital. *You can't go there looking worse for wear*, she had answered. He told her he was going to the hospital, not the theater. He had no time to come home and change before visiting hours ended.

When the interurban stopped at Lorain's depot that evening after work, he got off and boarded a waiting street car that deposited him near the hospital. His clothes were a collage of oil, dirt and wrinkles and stunk with sweat and when he stopped at the front desk, he suddenly felt very aware of his appearance.

"Who are you here to, see, sir?" The receptionist inquired. She seemed not to notice nor be concerned with his grubby look.

"Dave Reynolds."

She leafed through papers until she found who she was looking for.

"Mr. Reynolds has been discharged."

"Good. That's good news. Back home then?"

She studied the paper. "No, sir, he has been taken to a nursing home in east Lorain. I can give you the name and address."

He was stunned.

"Sir? Would you like to know the name of the facility? Sir?" She paused and instead of waiting for an answer, began writing the name and address on a piece of paper. She handed it to him and he half-heartedly accepted it.

"Do you know what kind of shape he is in?"

"Sir, I am just the receptionist. You will have to talk with his nurse or doctor."

He looked at the words on the paper but did not read them. He stuffed it slowly in his pocket. "Thank you."

"You're welcome." She gave Rusty a quick scan, shook her head and returned to her work.

He walked out of the hospital in a daze. It was not what he expected to hear. He was expecting Davey to be sitting up in bed or in a wheelchair or walking with the aid of canes or a nurse, joking and anxious about getting back to his engines. He was expecting to hear Davey would be back to work in the fall. What he wasn't expecting was to hear Davey was in a nursing home. Davey was supposed to be better. He had to be better.

He headed back to the trolley stop in a daze. Well, no charters on Sunday, he thought when his mind returned to thinking after Davey's news had caused it to jump the tracks of rationality. *I'll see Davey then—without Di. God knows what's in store. Then I'll break it to him about Erie T. That ought to break his heart enough to go along with his back.*

Chapter 21

Sunday arrived brandishing a double-edged sword. He was again out of a job and it was the day he would see Davey. He wasn't sure which made him glummer and decided it was an even draw.

Di insisted on going with him, but Rusty was firm. This was something between Davey and him, he said. Man talk.

The drive from Vermilion to Lorain's east side went quicker than he had would have liked. As he crossed the bridge spanning the Black River in downtown Lorain, he could see the docks once occupied by Erie T. The only tugboat moored there was the *Cherokee.* A small barge consumed the space where the *Iroquois* and *Wyandot* once moored. He felt a twinge in his gut. A part of him said to look away, but he defied the sense behind it and craned his head to look over every niche of the dock and harbor as if he was seeing it for the last time.

The nursing home was built out of sandstone quarried from the nearby town of Amherst. Unlike the hospital, it was unassuming. Thc whole feeling surrounding it was more pastoral than urgent. "Out to pasture…out to die," he muttered as he pulled into the parking lot. A grassy area to the right of the entrance had large elm trees with umbrella-like canopies that offered shade to picnic tables beneath them. To the left of the entrance, a sandstone sidewalk lined the front of the building and served as a walkway from the parking area as well as a sunny spot for residents of the home to sit and soak in the warm rays.

Since it was a sunny Sunday afternoon, the walkway was lined with wheelchairs of nodding residents, and the picnic tables and lawn were filled with ambulatory residents with their visitors.

Rusty skirted past the wheelchairs, noting that Davey was not among those seated. He walked inside and was instantly met by a stern looking woman with graying hair and a set jaw behind a large oak desk. He wasn't sure if she was more guard than receptionist. She sized him up as he stood before her scrutinizing eyes. He was glad he was in his Sunday clothes.

"Good afternoon. I was told a friend of mine is a resident here. Dave Reynolds."

She flipped through her file box. "Dave Reynolds-Room 31."

Short, but not sweet. He hoped for Davey's sake the nursing aides were warmer than the bucket of ice stationed at the door.

He headed down the corridor, dodging tottering old men with canes until he came to Room 31. The number seemed to shout out at him. He hesitated at the door. It reminded him of a magic act he and Di saw at Crystal Beach two years ago. *What's behind the door?* The barker had teased. *A lady or a tiger?* The door to Room 31 was a no-brainer. He had a good idea what was behind it. He knocked softly. A voice from within said, "Come in."

He pushed the door slowly open.

"Rusty!" Davey's face brightened. "You've found me out!" A soft chuckle followed.

"You betcha. You can't get away from me that easy."

Davey chuckled again, only this time more heartedly. He was prone in bed and looked pale and gaunt, and his sunken cheeks exaggerated his high cheek bones. Davey was lean to begin with, so there was little meat to spare and weeks of bed rest had whittled away at his muscles. But the ashen skin bothered Rusty the most. Davey's tan was lighter than the crew's to begin with because he spent most of his days in the engine room, but it wasn't until he saw him lying in bed, that he realized just how tanned Davey had been when he was with the tugs and how pallid he looked now.

"Pull up a chair," Davey said, pointing out a wooden straight back chair.

Rusty's brows shot up. "Davey, you're able to move your arms!"

"I surprised myself, and then the doc said since it was my back and not my neck, I probably would be good from the waist up."

"Then you can get around in a wheelchair."

"That's the plan, I hope. Right now, that seems to be a ways away as I am weak as a kitten."

Rusty pulled the chair up to the bed and sat down. "How are you feeling otherwise?"

"Could be better, could be worse."

Worse, you would have to be dead to be worse. "Has there been any improvement? I mean, are you sitting up, getting out of bed?"

"Oh, Christ no," Davey said. "They sent me here because they couldn't do anything more with me. And Ma, bless her heart, can't take care of me at home until I can get strong enough to use a wheelchair."

Rusty sat quietly, digesting the information. "What happens next?"

"Nothing."

"Nothing?"

Davey looked towards an open window in his room. Birdsong could be heard. "This is it."

Rusty felt a surge of panic but didn't show it. "You're young. You're strong. You'll get in that wheelchair and get the hell out of here. We'll get you back to new."

"There's no fixin nerve like a bone or muscle, Rusty."

"So what you are saying is at the best, you'll be wheelchair bound?"

"Unless the good Lord lays his hands upon me and heals me, or you strap me standing upright in a handcart and wheel me about, this is it."

Rusty looked down at his own hands folded upon his lap. They were leathery and lined, and if he had notion to turn them over, he would see rough calluses marring the palms. They looked blocky and strong.

Davey could see he was at a loss for words. "So, what's the skinny at work? Peets got his hands all over my engines?" Normally, Rusty would have laughed at his comment about Peets, and Davey sensed something was troubling him more than his condition. "Rusty, you look hang-dog. What's gnawing at you?"

The dog reference again. He looked Davey squarely in the eyes. *The roller coaster is at the top of the hill and the first car is dangling over the top. No stopping it now. Here it goes, wheee…* "Erie T was sold to settle the old man's gambling debt." It was blunt and to the point but Rusty knew Davey would want it laid out on the line. *He may be paralyzed, but he is a man and can take it on the chin.*

Davey was quiet in a reflective sort of way.

Rusty waited for a response.

Finally, Davey raised his brows. "I'll be damn. To tell you the truth, I am surprised it lasted as long as it did. The old man was always an asshole and pot chaser. After all, Eliot had to inherit his shit-for-brains from someone."

Rusty's laughter burst out like a valve letting go on a steam boiler. He surprised himself how loud it came out.

Davey joined him and both men laughed uncommonly long.

After they had composed themselves, Davey asked, "So what happened to the *Iroquois*?

"It went to Toledo. *Delaware* ended up in Buffalo, *Wyandot* to Detroit. *Shawnee* was parted out and sold for scrap.

"And the *Cherokee*?"

"It's still docked in Lorain. It was never sold."

"Hmm," Davey said.

Rusty could tell he was kicking something around in his head.

When Davey failed to reveal his thoughts, Rusty said, "Davey, about that day, the day of the accident. You asked me what happened and I never got to finish telling you."

"Water under the bridge, Rusty. I came on deck under a strain, the line snapped, and I got hit. Lines break, and I was a horse's ass for going topside. I knew better."

Rusty searched Davey's eyes. Once they twinkled constantly, now they sputtered and sparked here and there like misfiring cylinders, struggling to fire back up to life.

Davey's acceptance of the blame for his actions didn't lessen the burden of guilt Rusty felt for tying the splice. "How's your mother?"

"She's due in here in about an hour," Davey said, glancing at the clock. "Folks from church take turns bringing her up to see me on Sundays and the neighbor lady brings her on Wednesdays. I know folks are looking out for her but she's not use to being alone so much and she's a bit rickety. I'm sick with worry about her."

Davey had a point. Mrs. Reynolds was well up in years and it didn't look like Davey would be home anytime soon. He felt that twinge in his gut again.

"Di and I will stop in every now and then and check on her. You know Di, she likes to fuss."

Davey smiled. "She must—she puts up with an old bullhead like you."

"I'll let you get some rest before your mother gets here," Rusty said, standing up.

"Yeah, God knows I'm exhausted from lying in bed all day watching the flies on the ceiling."

"I'll grab some Zane Greys for you on my next visit."

"Get along, little doogie," Davey said as he watched Rusty head for the door.

Rusty smiled despite his sinking heart.

Chapter 22

Tuesday found him at the docks of Lorain again, then Huron and Sandusky. Even though he was bumped by the Cleveland deckhand's return, he still felt he had a chance of being hired back there at some point. After all, the company's boss and tug master had nothing but praise for him. If anything, they may float his name around the docks of the Cuyahoga as being a first-rate deckhand and someone shorthanded, like the company where he had temporarily worked, just might contact him. Just to make sure, he spent Monday wandering the industrial flats, passing his name and place of contact to any and all companies using the Cuyahoga River and Cleveland harbor for commerce. At any rate, he knew his chances would be better in the spring. Good names and good reputations spread like a grassfire during hiring time.

By the end of the day on Tuesday, his cup was empty again. Lorain, Huron and Sandusky had no openings. Not that he had expected any as it had only been just over two weeks since his last check. He would have to speak again to Di about Toledo.

He missed taking *Rising Sun* out. The thought of her being docked for three weeks grated at him. He missed being on the lake, too. It was on its waters he felt truly alive and his troubles erased by the waves. He once read in a magazine about a man from India—a yoga or yogi or something that said you had to find your quiet place in order to center yourself. He wasn't exactly sure what the mystic man meant by centering, but he was sure that being not centered was likened to a broken blade on a propeller that caused a boat to shudder, falter and break down. He had the place to "center." It was out there on the blue-green waters of the lake; he just couldn't get to it. A couple missed weeks is a lot of time lost in Lake Erie's short summers and the realization of it set off an alarm bell in his head, warning him of the dwindling days of boating season.

So while in Sandusky, he made a point to stop by his dock and check on the boat, hoping just seeing the *Rising Sun* would be enough to squelch the mushrooming feelings of frustration, angst and bitterness that had taken root in his gut. It was getting too late to take her out for a cruise (Di would have supper waiting), but as he stood on the dock watching the sun glint off the crests of waves, he vowed he would not let the week go by without taking it out for a cruise. Sunday for sure. He'd be damned if he spent Sunday afternoon at Di's farm listening to the virtues of working at the steel mill.

Life was short. Davey proved that point. Who knows what shoals lie under the still waters of life waiting to ground you, rip your hull or sink you? *Make the most of it, but keep your nose clean while doing so.* That's what his aunt on the farm had told him. Then the bank took her farm away—her clean nose and all.

The ride back to Vermilion was reduced to all the bad things in his life—his mother's death, his father shipping him out to live with his elderly aunt, the seizure of her farm from the bank, the school of hard knocks as a sixteen year old deck hand alone in Toledo, the war, the years of crap and scraping and trying to get ahead only to lose everything you gained...Davey...

The poisoned thoughts compressed themselves so tightly in his head, they left no room for all the good that had happened to him. He had made lemonade out of lemons. But the positives evaded him like whiffs of smoke on the wind as he coursed his way home. He felt like a Spanish bull that had been stabbed by the barbed lances of picadors and was now having the matador's red cape flaunted before him.

On the way home, he stopped at Sam's. It was pushing eight o'clock when he got there. The joint was packed and loud. Sam was right. The place really popped after hours when the businesses closed and fishermen came in from the lake. The counter seats were filled, so Rusty weaseled his way between two stools and waited for Sam to notice him.

"Hey, hey, Rusty, how you doing?" Sam called out upon spotting him.

"You got a Coke with lots of ice?"

"Your name is on one!"

"I'll be seated over by the wall next to the checker table. I want to ask you something if you get a chance," Rusty said.

"Couldn't catch that," Sam said, raising his voice over the noise.

"Got a question-I'll be seated by the checkers," Rusty called out, as the crowd swallowed him.

"I'll bring your drink over to you," Sam called back.

Moments later, Sam appeared with a glass of Coke bobbing with ice chunks. A dishrag was draped over his shoulder. "You wanna ask me something?" He appeared patient and easy despite the hubbub around him.

"Is it really grape juice that I would be hauling for those men from Put-in-Bay if I decide to ferry for them?"

"Sure," Sam said nonchalantly.

Rusty looked him dead in the eye and Sam could see Rusty was serious as the grave.

"I mean it. Just grape juice?"

Now Sam grew sober. His voice softened to reassure Rusty who looked tense. "Yeah. Just grape juice."

Rusty leaned back against the wall. "How do I contact them?"

"I'll let them know. You just show up at the Lime Kiln Dock at 8 on Friday."

Rusty nodded.

Sam gave Rusty a reassuring wink before he headed back to the counter.

Rusty sighed. He took a sip of the Coke and almost choked. He wasn't expecting that. Sam had put a shot of rum in it.

Chapter 23

He checked his watch. It read 7:40. Rusty took a seat on the bench at the boat's stern, lit a cigarette and watched the sun slowly slide towards the western horizon. It was high enough in the sky to still be warm and bright, but not low enough for the colors of sunset. The lake was calm and had grown a darker shade of blue with the sun's angle. *Rising Sun* rocked softly against her tethers with only the sounds from ripples of waves lapping against her hull while Lake Gulls, circling the dock in spirals, cawed to one another as they searched the area for food scraps leftover from the day. He was oblivious to their noisy company for their presence was as constant as the waves.

Lime Kiln Dock was located on the southernmost tip of the island of South Bass. It was here limestone, quarried from the island, was crushed and placed into large kilns where it was superheated down into a powder called lime. Once cooled, it was then loaded onto freighters to be shipped to various ports in the Great Lakes to be used as whitewash paint and alkaline for farm fields. Because of the dock's location off the beaten path of tourists, it was also used for receiving and exporting shipments of goods and freight between the island and mainland, thereby by-passing the crowds who choked the passenger ferry and public docks in downtown Put-in-Bay on the opposite side of the island where the action was happening. One passenger ferry, however, ran hourly service back and forth from Lime Kiln Dock, serving the island's locals wishing to avoid the same swarm around the docks the small harbor town attracted during summer.

He had passed that last departing ferry of the day from Lime Kiln on his way to South Bass and noticed it was mostly empty. The locals had apparently got their business abroad taken care of and were settled in for the night and those aboard heading back to Sandusky were most likely seasoned day-trippers avoiding the wait for crowded ferries.

It was pushing 8 o'clock when he heard rattling followed by the putter of an approaching vehicle. He rose from the bench seat and stepped up and onto the dock next to *Rising Sun.* Minutes later, a flatbed truck fitted with swaying racks motored around the wooded bend in the dirt road and pulled up to the dock in a cloud of dust. The truck bed was stacked with wooden crates that he presumed housed the grape juice. A man, somewhere in his twenties, sat on the open back of the truck bed with his legs dangling over the edge. Two dark silhouettes of men sat in the truck's cab. After the truck came to a stop and the engine turned off, a small man got out of the passenger side and Rusty instantly recognized him as the grape juice man he had met on the docks in Vermilion.

"My charter man, hello, the wife must have wanted that fur coat after all," the man said grinning as he walked over to him with an extended hand.

The comment grated Rusty but he took the remark in stride. There was always one in every group, at every job—a wise guy who gushed with fountains of bogus enthusiasm and bullshit. All you had to do is watch where you stepped when they were dropping a load.

The man grabbed his hand and shook hard with a trap-like handshake that made Rusty feel ensnared. He had an impulse to pull away in fear he would be ensnared.

"My name is Al. That's my younger brother, Lou in the truck and my baby brother, Joe in the back."

Rusty sized each man as they were introduced, exchanging stiff nods with them. Despite the family reunion type introduction conducted by Al, he felt uneasy.

"So… we good with the grape juice run, then? All set to go?" Al said.

"All set," Rusty said.

Al clapped his hands like he was rallying troops. "Let's get unloaded so Mr. Rusty can get home by dark."

Lou swung out of the truck and headed to the back of it while Joe jumped into the bed and grabbed a crate and handed it off to Lou. Lou started towards the boat.

"Hold it!" Rusty said, placing himself between Lou and *Rising Sun*. "First, I want to take a look at what I am hauling."

Lou froze and looked at Al.

"Why grape juice, of course, but by all means feel free to examine. After all, you're the captain," Al said. He signaled Lou to open the crate. Joe tossed Lou a pry bar from the truck cab, and Lou pried the lid off. He pulled out a bottle filled with deep purple liquid and passed it to Al. Al handed it to Rusty, but Rusty didn't take it.

"Open it," Rusty said.

Al looked surprise. Lou and Joe stiffened and exchanged glances.

"I want to know if that's really grape juice in them bottles or hooch."

Al breathed a sigh of relief and uncorked the bottle with his pocket knife. He passed the bottle to Rusty.

Rusty took the bottle as he focused on Al's eyes. He took a whiff, then a sip. It was grape juice. He handed it back to Al.

The three brothers stood as though frozen in place, their eyes locked on Rusty as they awaited the verdict.

"That's damn good stuff," Rusty said.

Al laughed with a slight shake to his voice, and Lou's and Joe's stances thawed. They rolled their eyes at one another.

Lou tapped the lid back on and picked up the crate. He was about to board *Rising Sun* when Rusty ordered, "Wait."

Al drew a deep breath and his face began to flush. "What now, Mr. Rusty?"

Rusty extended his palm. "You said you would pay me ahead."

Al forced a smile. "Indeed I did," he said through his teeth. He reached into his pants pocket and pulled out a roll of bills secured with a rubber band. He removed it and peeled off two bills—a five and a twenty. He handed them to Rusty. It was more than Rusty made all week busting his ass at Erie T. "That should cover your expenses and time," Al said. "Square?"

Rusty shook his head. "Square!"

As Lou was about to step over the rail, Rusty said, "Just… be careful there. Keep the crates on the deck floorboards, all right?"

Joe and Lou silently loaded the crates onto the *Rising Sun.* All in all, about twenty crates were arranged on the deck. If she had to, she could easily hold another ten between her bench storage and aft space. But there was only twenty.

It was pushing 8:30 when everything was secured and readied.

"Where am I going with this?" Rusty asked.

"Sandusky, like I said before. Joe will show you when you get there."

Rusty looked surprised. "He's going along?"

"Of course," Al said. "How else do you expect to make the connection or unload the boat?"

Rusty frowned at Joe who was already making himself comfortable on the bench seat at the back of the boat. "Yeah, right," he muttered and boarded *Rising Sun.* He turned over her engine. "Get the mooring lines, will ya?" he said to Joe.

"See you next Friday, Mr. Rusty," Al said as he and Lou stood side by side on the dock watching the boat ease away from it.

Rusty didn't wave or comment. He'd reserve the cordialities until after he had seen how it played out tonight.

The ride on the lake and across the Sandusky Bay did not take long with silence hanging between the two men for the entire trip, which was fine by Rusty.

As they drew close to Sandusky's public docks, Joe directed Rusty to the right towards the warehouse district that lined the waterfront. Numerous docks privately owned by the companies for shipping and receiving jutted into the water edging the warehouses. Joe pointed out a long and narrow concrete dock, and Rusty steered over to it. He hugged the dock as Joe grabbed a mooring line and jumped out and tethered the boat. Rusty killed the engine and tossed the aft line to Joe to secure, keeping an eye on him to make sure he tied off correctly.

The sun was now on the horizon and, as though having spent its energy, dimmed to the color of a pale lemon. The waters had darkened to shades of navy blue and indigo with pastel blues cresting the tops of soft waves as the low, weak rays of sunlight passed through them.

The warehouses, shut down for the day, loomed dark and cavernous in the growing twilight except where windows caught the fading sunlight and reflected it back, giving the appearance the vacant warehouses were aglow from within.

"Give me a minute," Joe said, the first words he had uttered since Rusty met him. He jumped out of the boat and walked up to a solid wood door at the back of a four story grimy red brick warehouse and knocked.

Rusty remained in the boat and watched and waited for the door to open and reveal whom or what was behind it. He felt uneasy. It seemed so clandestine for grape juice.

Moments later, a wide wooden door on a track next to the door Joe had knocked on, rolled open, and two men pushing hand trucks walked out. Rusty could hear them exchange greetings. They followed Joe to the boat and he jumped down onto the deck and began passing crates to the men who stacked them on the hand trucks in silence. When the crates were stacked high on the hand trucks, the men then wheeled them back to the doorway and disappeared into the warehouse only to return minutes later and retrieve another stack of crates. Rusty sat and watched. Neither man from the warehouse acknowledged him the entire time.

When the last of the crates were loaded, one man turned to Joe. "Is this it?"

"Twenty for now," Joe answered back. "My brother wants to see how it goes tonight before increasing the number."

The man shrugged and pushed the last load towards the open sliding door with Joe in tow.

Rusty watched with a mixture of curiosity and caution with caution being the larger of the mix.

"Oh, you can go now," Joe said over his shoulder, leaving Rusty to untie his own mooring lines.

Rusty headed back to the public docks a short way down from the warehouses and then docked the *Rising Sun* at his private slip. As he pulled the tarp over the *Rising Sun* and tied it secure, he couldn't help but wonder why the vineyard did not use the local ferry to haul the juice. Since it's legal, what's the big deal, and it would be a heck of a lot cheaper in freight charges than what they paid him. And if business is so good as to pay him a week's worth of wages for one haul, why don't they buy their own boat? It all seemed shady for grape juice. He didn't know what to make of the night other than it created more questions than answers.

He was in his truck and heading for Vermilion by the time the sun had slipped below the horizon and dusk had firmly settled in. It would be dark by the time he got home. Di was going to be pissed. Pissed at how late. Pissed at not going out for supper. She hadn't been in too good a mood lately as it was and he hoped the twenty-five bucks in his pocket would change that along with supper and a talkie on Saturday. *God, twenty-five smackeroos for taking the boat out for a cruise.* He couldn't beat that with a stick. Sorry about the mill, boys, he said under his breath. But as he pulled into the driveway of his cottage, he couldn't help but feel dirty.

Chapter 24

"How can one charter run pay a week's wage at the tug yard?" Di asked as she crunched on toast smeared with her Mom's sweet strawberry jam from June's crop. The seams on her Sunday dress were taut around her mid-section and it wasn't until this morning when she put the dress on, that she finally surrendered to the fact that she would need a larger size. Morning sickness, which for her was actually *anytime sickness*, had finally subsided.

Rusty was at the helm of the stove, scrambling eggs. It was a question he himself had pored over. "Apparently, they have more dollars than sense."

"I *bet* its grape juice."

"It's grape juice, I checked."

She narrowed her eyes. "If it looks like a fish, swims like a fish and smells like a fish, it's a fish!"

Rusty scrapped the eggs onto plates. "The fish tasted like grape juice, Di." But like her, he too had a hard time swallowing the legitimacy of the circumstances. She would crap if she knew he was delivering to a deserted warehouse, he thought. When she had asked, he told her the drop off was at a dock in Sandusky not far from *Rising Sun*'s slip. He hadn't lied. He just didn't tell her everything, such as the vintners were three elusive Italian brothers, the delivery was to a vacant warehouse and the men who off loaded his boat were shady-looking. It wasn't like him to keep secrets from her, and he hated himself for not having her privy to all the details. She might even enjoy the air of mystery surrounding it as long as there was no danger to him or no laws broken and together they could sort out the possibility of an underlying covertness to the business. But for now, with her condition, he just couldn't risk getting her upset over nothing. It was grape juice, and the men apparently wanted to avoid the congestion of public docks on a Friday night. There, the mountains went back to mole hills.

***

The number of cases of grape juice increased on *Rising Sun* as did the baby in Di's belly. Rusty was now stowing crates of juice in places that held fishing tackle and bait as well as the hold for the day's fish catch and he took extra care in calculating the weight and distribution of the load and setting limits. The five extra smackers paid for every ten crates over the twenty meant squat if the boat was overloaded.

September's sunsets came earlier and cooler and by the time the crates were unloaded and the fishing gear reloaded and the boat prepped for the Saturdays fishing charters, it was always dark when he left Sandusky.

It was also in September that Rusty bought a wheelchair for Davey, so he could leave the nursing home and return home. Giving him that chair made Rusty feel like he opened a door on a bird cage and set the bird free. Never mind that bird had a bad wing, he was free.

Davey's homecoming was nothing short of a hero's homecoming. Rusty wasn't sure of the connection between a broken back and cake and ice cream, but the crowd that greeted Davey when Rusty and Di drove him into his yard, seem to think there was. As the wheelchair was unloaded and Davey lowered into it with the help of Nick and Bobby Peets, the crowd broke into applause.

Rusty muttered to Di under his breath, "What would they have done if he had walked out of the car?" To which Di jabbed him smartly in the ribs with her elbow.

Peets wheeled Davey toward the back yard of the house, parting the clapping and cheering crowd with the wheelchair. Rusty recognized half the faces, some crew members from the former Erie T, a number of the Reynolds's neighbors, and a few he guessed were distant kin. It was hard to miss the meddling next door neighbor as she was in charge of the homecoming and directed the course of its action like a traffic cop. Di had complained earlier to him that the neighbor had taken over the planning of it from her and Mrs. Reynolds when it was supposed to be a joint effort. Mrs. Reynolds was like driftwood in the neighbor's self-appointed managerial flow, and Di, who wasn't a stranger to swimming against the current, chose to let *bossy knock herself out*! Rusty knew then and there the pregnancy had taken a lot of wind out of her sails.

"Get over here, Rusty!" a voice from the back of the yard shouted.

He looked over the bobbing heads packing the lawn and saw the group from Erie T. He grinned and dodged his way back to them. Besides Peets and Nick, Frankie Kopinski, Lloyd Robson, Cap McIntyre and Cap Brumfield were there. He didn't realize how much he had missed them until he saw them gathered there and after the hearty handshakes and back slaps stopped, he said, "Eliot couldn't make it?" and the group roared with laughter.

"Fill me in what you all are doing now," Rusty said. *God, it felt good to be with them again.* "You still harbor pilot in Lorain, Nick?"

"Yep, and Peets and Brumfield are also in Lorain, working with Great Lakes."

"I tried there and their other stations but they didn't need a deckhand."

"Yeah, there is no shortage in that," Nick said. "Lloyd's having the same problem, but he did land a job with a barge company."

"The job stinks and pays crap but at least it's in Lorain and it's a job," Lloyd said with a shrug.

"Frankie, here, had to go to Cleveland," Nick said.

"I wasn't happy about the move, but the pay is great," Frankie said. "I'm with a shipping company hauling lumber across the lake from Canada. That pilot job just got a whole lot farther away. I am bumped down to second mate."

Rusty looked at McIntyre. "How's it with you, Cap?"

"I decided to hang up my captain's cap, Rusty. I feel too old to go rummaging around for a new job, and I want to stay put." Cap McIntyre paused. "I suppose if Great Lakes has an opening for a pilot, I might jump at it. Brumfield's got a word in for me."

"Anyone heard from Jimmy?" Rusty asked.

"Nope. I haven't seen Jimmy since that last day we were altogether," Nick said.

The rest of the crew nodded in agreement.

"What about you, Rust?" Nick asked.

Rusty looked down into his glass of lemonade and swirled the ice around in it. "I decided to go fulltime into charters."

The men waited for him to elaborate but he didn't.

"Business must be good then. That's great, Rusty!" Nick said, breaking the silence. "It's what you wanted all along."

Just then, Davey wheeled up to the group, causing a break in the conversation. He had overheard the chatter on Rusty's chartering business on his approach. "You're gonna lose all that muscle and get baby hands," he said with a tease.

Rusty snorted, and the men snickered.

"You boys better get some ice cream before it melts," Davey added.

***

Monday morning, Di crawled out of bed and came into the kitchen where Rusty was sipping coffee and smoking a cigarette. She was bent and holding her side and she was as white as a ghost.

He hid his alarm. "Morning sickness back?"

"Different. It's shooting pains. I'm also spotting blood."

His heart landed in his throat. He jumped to his feet and pulled a chair over to her and lowered her on to it. "I'll get the truck. We're going to the doctor."

"I'm not going in my nightgown."

"The hell you are."

She glared at him. "I'm not going anywhere in my night clothes. That's final."

Rusty rolled his eyes. "Fine." He went into the bedroom and came out with a dress.

"Not that one."

"Yes, this one." He helped her off with the gown which she did begrudgingly and pulled the dress over her head. She did not make the task easy and it felt as though he was dressing an obstinate two year old. After the dress was wrestled on, he tried to help her to her feet but she didn't budge.

"My hairbrush."

He muttered under his breath and went back into the bedroom for it.

He bit his lip as she sat there painstakingly brushing and arranging her hair. The moment she sat the brush down, he took her hand, pulled her to her feet and ushered her to the door. As she reached the threshold, she stopped abruptly, causing him to collide into her backside.

“Do you need to be carried to the truck?” he said, his voice anxious.

“My hat and purse. Can’t go without a hat and purse.”

He set his jaw and rolled his eyes again. “What are you trying to do, give me a heart attack? Come on, Di, this is no social outing.”

But she had dug her heels in like a mule and he knew she wouldn’t budge unless he carried her or retrieved the items. He decided the latter would be easier and avoid the consequences of rankling her further. He searched the kitchen to locate the hat and purse.

“Bedroom,” she called from the doorway.

Rusty grumbled all the way to the bedroom and back. He plopped the hat on her head and slipped the purse strap over his arm. “This is it, Di, no more, you are getting in the truck if I have to carry you.” He took her arm and steered her towards the vehicle then loaded her in like she was a stack of egg-filled crates. The thought flashed in his mind that he should nail the door shut so she couldn’t get back out.

The ride to the doctor’s office in Lorain didn’t take as long as it did when he drove to work at Erie T.

***

“No work. No heavy housework. No dancing. No long walks. Just take it easy. Sit and read and relax.”

The *sit and read* part was fine with Di, but the *no work, no dancing, no walks*—why hadn’t he just come out and say *no life*. She’d planned to work a few more weeks, and definitely didn’t plan to live cloistered like a nun. Her pregnancy would have gone unnoticed at this point had a couple of her co-workers not noticed the slight weight gain and dark circles under her eyes. Surely, she could have eked out a few more weeks.

The part that really grated her most was when the doctor had told her she was no spring chicken for this being her first. If this wasn’t your first,” he said, “it wouldn’t be such a problem pregnancy.” She would have thought he was full of hooey except for that episode she had in the morning.

All the way home, Rusty said, “I told you to quit work. I told you so. I told you shouldn’t be on your feet so much. Didn’t I? Look how swollen your ankles are. Didn’t I tell you to stay off your feet?” He was like a stuck needle on a phonograph.

Di stared out the window in silence until she couldn’t take his chiding any longer.“Stow it, Rusty. You’re squawking like a parrot.”

Rusty scowled the rest of the way home, with one eye on the road, the other keeping a close watch on her.

Chapter 25

"You interested in making some extra clams?" Al asked as he and Rusty watched Lou and Joe load the *Rising Sun* at Lime Kiln Dock. It was 7 p.m. and the sun was already setting, forcing the meeting time an hour earlier to keep pace with the light of the shortening days.

Rusty didn't answer right away. This was his fourth chartered run with them. He was making a week's wage which would have been sufficient, but the pending baby, Di's doctor bills and Davey's medical bills weighed heavily on his mind. He tossed his spent cigarette butt to the ground. "What are we talking?" he finally asked.

"Our shipment goes east and west out of Sandusky. Our trucks haul to Port Clinton and Lorain and from those points, Toledo and Cleveland. Now, Port Clinton is not a problem, but Lorain is a drive. We figured if we shipped by boat from Sandusky to Lorain, we would be saving ourselves some dough and a whole lot of headache. You see, the boat would have a straight shot and get the job done faster and that would make everyone happy including you with some extra dough."

"Why not bypass Sandusky altogether and go straight to Lorain from Put-in Bay?"

"Do I look like a dummy? It doesn't work that way. It goes to Sandusky first, then to Lorain. Sheesh!"

Wisenheimer. "What's the arrangement?"

"Wednesday morning. Same dock in Sandusky that you unload. Pick up a load of juice there, and then drop it off at a dock off Beaver Creek where Oak Point Road dead-ends into the lake east of Lorain. Twenty simoleans plus gas, deal?"

"Depends, are we still talking grape juice?"

Al feigned hurt. "Mr. Rusty, did I insult you with just twenty clams? I'll make it twenty-five."

Rusty had a ready answer for that, but kept his mouth shut. "Twenty-five plus gas," then he added, "And don't think you can pull the wool over my eyes and slip in something extra. I'm not risking my boat for twenty-five."

A smile crept across Al's face. "I wouldn't expect you to."

***

It wasn't a difficult decision. Di's difficulties cost extra and then there was Davey. On the visit a week after the party, when Rusty was alone with Davey, he had worked his way around questioning Davey about his lack of income and bills. It was a delicate subject and the chance being misconstrued as prying into another man's business, but Rusty was careful how he navigated through it. Davey was a proud man, but Rusty never gave him reason to believe that he snooped for the sake of nosiness. Davey, who understood Rusty as well as Di and Uncle Fritz did, knew that his inquiries were based solely on concerned for a friend.

"Are you and your mother managing?"

"We're holding our own. Neighbors bring food over off and on, like they're taking turns or something. The lady next door checks in each day and the grocer sends a boy over with groceries once a week. Priest stops by Sunday afternoons. God knows, she won't leave me not even for church." He shook his head.

It wasn't exactly what Rusty had meant. He wanted to know if and how the bills were being paid. He knew the house was paid for because he remembered Davey describing how he burnt the mortgage paper in his driveway then treated his mother and himself to a root beer soda at the fountain on Broadway. When he finally worked Davey around to the subject of money, Davey's face grew solemn.

"House is paid off, so we don't have to worry about a roof over our heads. Don't have a car- never had need for one here in town, not that I could use one now," he said, looking down at his legs. "I have enough saved away for Ma and I to live off of, but not enough for the hospital or nursing home bills. If I pay them, it takes the savings away and soon there's no money for electricity, gas or taxes. And since I can't work, there's no income." He stared hard at his legs. "Either way, I'm scared to death I'll have to sell the house. Then where will Ma go? Old agers home? I'd probably end up in a government home for cripples. Can't stand the thought of Ma leaving her home and being all alone."

Rusty thought he heard Davey sniffle, but didn't want to look. He remained quiet, and silence fell over both men.

At last, Rusty spoke. "Davey, don't worry about your mother, or losing your home. We are going to work this out. I got some money set aside I'll pay towards the medical bills."

Davey looked at Rusty with raised brows. "Rusty, you ain't got a job, and you got a baby on the way! Unless you know how to crap money or find it growing on trees, you aren't in position to be offering what you don't have. Jeeze, Rust, that baby's going to take money, as well it should, and you are not denying Di or that little one because of my troubles. I won't hear of it." Davey began wheeling toward the porch door.

Rusty was afraid he had offended him. "I do have a job. Makes good money. And don't tell me what I can and can't afford. Di and I have a nest egg, too, for your information."

Davey stopped wheeling and spun around. "You better guard that like a dog guards a soup bone, 'cause you never know what lies ahead." Davey sounded cryptic.

***

So when Al had asked him if he wanted the extra run, Rusty didn't need to think long or hard.

Chapter 26

Now that he was unemployed, it gave him a different perspective on the activities during the weekdays outside of the harbor of Lorain. Life for him these days moved at a slower pace in which he watched the cyclic bustle of the business day as though he was observing it through the eyepiece of a nickelodeon. Even the harbor at Sandusky had a different air than the one he experienced on weekends. Pleasure craft and weekend sailors were replaced by vessels of commerce, commercial fishermen and longshoremen during the week. The atmosphere, like that of a typical workday in Lorain, radiated business instead of pleasure, and he found himself enjoying the break from routine while observing the action from the point of an onlooker.

He found time and was able to catch up on projects that had been stowed or placed on the back burner, waiting for that rare empty day. He also rediscovered his love of woodworking by making a crib for the baby. But priority was given to the patching and tinkering of the pickup truck, realizing it and not the new roadster would remain their mode of transportation. *Permanent prosperity* was leaking through his fingers like sand no matter how hard he grasped.

On Wednesday morning, he rose before daybreak and fixed himself toast and coffee. Halfway through eating it, Di stumbled out sleepy-eyed and yawning.

"You should have wakened me," she said, burrowing her knuckles into her eyes.

"Go back to bed. You need the rest. It's still dark out."

Her response was a big yawn.

"On my way back from Lorain, I'll stop in Vermilion with the boat and we can have dinner together before I take it back to Sandusky."

Di nodded, her eyes blinking in slow motion as she fought back sleep. Having him around more gave her piece of mind even though she was doing better. "Do I make it, or are we going out?"

"We'll go out. See what's cooking around town midday." A break in the monotony of being home all day now would do her good, he thought, although he felt boredom would have a hard time setting up shop with her as she was absorbed in converting the small storage room off the bedroom into a nursery decorated the color of Easter eggs. A point he felt he should be prepared to counter with sailor knots and toy trucks in case the baby was a boy.

***

The sun had crested the southern end of the lake's eastern horizon and immediately began burning off the low ground fog that had wrapped itself around the bay area as he idled up to the same Sandusky warehouse dock he used on

Friday night runs. He cherished early fall on Lake Erie as the season brought with it the warm, sometimes hot, temperatures of summer without the blistering overhead sun and stifling humidity. On the other hand, fall also brought waterspouts and whitecaps. Those were the days that the air temperature failed to reach sixty degrees and the wind cut from the north. Small craft were wise to avoid the lake for the same reason that caused the foggy mornings. Crisp, cool air colliding with the warm air rising off the lake resulted in 5 to 7-foot waves topped with whitecaps and agitated skies with a low, tumultuous cloud deck capable of spawning tall, ominous waterspouts powerful enough to capsize a small boat or tear up a dock. The wind and temperature of water and air could go two ways on the lake. They could move together like a ballet creating a perfect boating day or they could struggle like two wrestlers grappling for dominance, their collision generating violent weather. A seasoned lake sailor paid close attention to his barometer, wind gauge and gut feeling.

Today, though, was to be warm and promised a calm lake typical for September. As Rusty waited at the dock, he watched the first ferry of the day cast off and head across the bay on its way to an island destination.

The placidness of the scene was interrupted by a clanking noise over his shoulder. He turned to look at the warehouse from where the noise emanated and saw the doors of the warehouse rattling open on the tracks. A moment passed as he watched to see who or what would emerge from the dim opening. The squeaky sound of wheels preceded hand trucks pushed by the same men who had unloaded Friday shipments only this time the procedure was in reverse. The hand trucks were stacked with crates and the men began loading the same crates Rusty had delivered on Friday night back onto the boat. Rusty watched, his brow drawn together in puzzlement. One man's crate bumped into the hatch opening that led into the bow. "Hey, be a little more careful," Rusty said with a sharp edge to his voice. The sullen man cast him a brooding look and disappeared into the bow with the crate.

Ten minutes passed and the boat was loaded. One of the men, not the sullen one he had barked at, dug into his shirt pocket and pulled out a folded paper. He unfolded it and handed it to Rusty. It was a hand drawn map of the area where Beaver Creek spilled into Lake Erie. It was crudely sketched, but self-explanatory. An outline of a dock marked the location where the lake, Beaver Creek and a road paralleling the creek converged. The words "oak point rd" were scrawled with an arrow pointing to the drawing of lines representing a road and an "X" was drawn on the outline of the dock.

The man tapped his index finger at the location of the dock. "Here there will be a milk delivery truck waiting. We ain't got around to painting it yet, so it will say *Paradise Farms Dairy* on the sides."

Rusty's brows drew together and he cast the man a wary look.

The man glared at him. "What? You got a problem with dairies?"

Rusty snatched the map and crumpled it into his pocket. "I better not."

The man snorted, grabbed his hand truck and pulled it away, trailing the other man into the warehouse. The big doors slid shut, leaving Rusty alone.

They ought to paint The Smart Ass Grape Company over the dairy name, he thought.

He untied the mooring lines and started the engine. As he eased from the dock, he felt his boat rock sharply to port at the same moment he heard a thud. He spun around and saw a wiry man had jumped on board. His heart skipped a beat, and then his jaw dropped. Standing on the deck was Pete, the cocky fellow he had given a lift from Middle Bass Island to Sandusky back in June—the one he suspected was a smuggler.

"What in the hell are you doing in my boat?"

"I'm going along to help unload," Pete said. "And hello to you, too."

Rusty was stunned. He had yet to throttle up *Rising Sun* so the boat was drifting on its own away from the dock. "What do you mean *unload*? You with them?"

"If by *them* you mean Al, Lou and Joey from Put-in-Bay, yeah. They're cousins of mine."

Rusty immediately reversed the engines and backed the boat to the dock. "Get out. And tell your pals to get these crates out," he snapped.

"Whoa. Hold on partner. Why the bug under your skin. What happened?"

"You're what happened," Rusty said. "Now get out or I'll throw you out."

Pete looked surprised. "Can you at least give me a reason? Something I can tell cousin Al."

"Yeah, tell *cousin* Al I think you are, no, I know you are, a smuggler and his grape juice that smells like a fish has been confirmed to be a fish by your presence."

Pete's eyebrows flew up. He held his hands up in surrender fashion. "Whoa, chief, let me explain. You're right. I was a smuggler. You picked me up after the Coast Guard seized the boat some fellas and I were using- okay, *smuggling* with, and dumped us off on Middle Bass. Talk about scared. I thought for sure they'd arrest us or shoot us. But instead, they stranded us. My pals ditched me and that's when you came along." Pete nodded towards the open lake. "Things are getting tense out there. The C.G. is getting serious-real serious. They're getting faster boats and arming them with .30 calibers and they mean business. Some runners are packing guns now, so the C.G. doesn't want to take any chances. I figured I wouldn't be so lucky the next time, and with crazy Connors out there shooting at anything and everything that moves on the lake, I decided my ass meant more to me than the easy rubes. So I quit. I stopped the day you gave me a lift back to Sandusky. Next day, I went to see cousin Al to see if he needed help with the business."

He took a seat on a stack of crates and continued. "The family had a vineyard on the island and thanks to prohibition, they had to tear the vines out and replace them with juice grapes. At first it was rough for the family, which is why I decided to run booze to help the family out and get back at the feds for causing my family's hardships. Then the juice grapes took off and so did the business. So I ran booze as a lark. It was exciting and easy. You can make big dough doing nothing but running and I'm talking big mazuma. But that close call put me on the level." Seemingly proud of his conversion to legitimacy, Pete smiled and regarded Rusty with the righteous eyes of a born again.

Rusty scowled. For some reason, he had a hard time buying what Pete was selling. He certainly didn't sound reformed on the boat trip back from Middle Bass which he claimed was a turning point. He folded his arms. "The boat is not leaving the dock until I taste what's in those bottles and it better be grape juice for your sake and Al's."

"Don't go having a kitten," Pete said. "You got a screwdriver or pry bar?"

Rusty tossed him a pry bar he kept in the cockpit for more reasons than prying.

Pete caught it and forced open a crate from the stack on deck. He removed a bottle and tossed it to Rusty.

Rusty took out his pocket knife and dug out the cork. He smelled it and took a swig. It was the same great tasting grape juice as before. He sat the bottle down on a flat spot at the helm. "I'll give you the benefit of doubt for now. But all I need is the slightest of reason and..."

"I get it...save your breath," Pete said, tapping the wooden lid back on to the crate. He looked at the bottle in Rusty's procession and grimaced. "You owe them for that, you know."

Rusty picked up the bottle and, with an eye on Pete, took a long pull, drinking it half down before removing it from his lips. "Consider it a perk of the job."

***

Just like in the drawing, a lone wooden dock jutted into Lake Erie at the point where Beaver Creek and Oak Point Road converged. It was surrounded by reedy marshes where cattails grew tall and herons and frogs flourished. It was a deserted spot off the beaten path, which is why it was favored by duck hunters and an occasional fisherman, both who saw to the dock's maintenance for their use.

As *Rising Sun* approached the dock, Rusty saw the milk truck parked nearby with the words *Paradise Farms* painted boldly on its sides. It looked oddly out of place in such a desolate, marshy location. He throttled down and guided the boat up to the dock. The milk truck's driver stepped onto the dock and caught the line Pete threw and tied the boat off. The man was a lot like Pete—young, jaunty and far more cheerful than the men at the Sandusky dock. He and Pete embraced one another the moment Pete stepped off the boat.

Rusty observed cautiously from the helm of the boat.

"Vince, this here is Rusty. He is our pilot," Pete said, after breaking from the hug.

Vince reached down into the boat and offered his hand to Rusty.

Rusty shook it.

"Pete said you were a bell bottom in the war."

"Merchant Marine."

"Ooh," Vince said. "Sink any Heinie subs?" Without waiting for a reply, he added, "That would have been darb. Hey, Pete, get back in the boat and let's get this unloaded."

It took longer to unload than load, and with no hand trucks available, they had to carry the crates from the boat to the milk truck. When the two men had finally finished and the doors of the truck shut, Vince again shook Rusty's hand. "Till next time, Bell Bottom."

Rusty opened his mouth to say, *it's Rusty*, but Vince was already bounding to the truck with Pete close behind. The last thing he saw before the truck started up was Vince pulling on a white jacket and a white deliveryman's cap.

***

"You look like you've seen a ghost," Di said as she and Rusty took their seats at Rauscher's.

"I kinda did." He had docked in Vermilion to meet her for dinner as he'd said. The whole Beaver Creek incident seemed surreal to him.

Di waited patiently while the server took their order and when they were alone again, she said, "For crying out loud…are you going to keep me in the dark?" She could tell he was wrestling with the idea of whether or not to tell her. "What? You think because I'm pregnant you got to handle me with kid gloves? I got a news flash for you; women have babies all the time. They were pregnant and having them in covered wagons fighting Indians." She folded her arms. "Jeepers, I need some kind of adventure in my life. I'm so damn bored that I'm going out of my head."

Was she pouting? He rested his head in his hand and studied her. Her eyes were snapping. She was as beautiful as ever and still the firecracker. He wondered if motherhood would toss a wet blanket on her zest. He hoped like hell it wouldn't. "I saw Pete. Remember Pete, that fellow I gave a ride back from Middle Bass in early summer?"

"The smuggler?"

"Yeah, or was. Claims he's on the level now."

"So how did you run into him?"

"That chartering job with the grape juice."

"The fishy smelling one?"

He nodded. "It seems to stink more with each run. Seems Pete is related to those guys and works for them."

She raised her brows.

"This morning, he gets on the boat to help make the delivery to Lorain. And here's the best part—the truck they loaded the juice into had Paradise Farms Dairy written on the sides. It was a milk delivery truck."

Di had just taken a sip from her root beer and the news caused her to choke on it, followed by the burning fizz of carbonation coming up through her nose.

"Jeez, are you okay?" he said, grabbing a napkin for her. "I shouldn't have said anything."

She dabbed the napkin at her nose and blinked her watery eyes. A minute passed while she composed herself. "Jeepers Creepers, if it hurt that much going down as it does coming up, I'd never drink the stuff!"

He smiled.

She then narrowed her eyes and grew serious. Pointing her finger at him and using it to emphasize each word, she said, "Don't let them make you a sap, Rusty. I think Pete is as legit as a cat in a canary cage. Grape juice, bushwa!"

"I checked again, and it was grape juice. That's what's so strange. It really is grape juice."

Di drummed her fingers on the table and pursed her lips. Her narrow eyes told him she was deep in deliberation.

"You know what I think," she said, breaking from her thoughts. "I think grape juice doesn't cost enough to make the money you are being paid for two runs a week. I also think the milk truck is a ruse. It may be grape juice now, but keep your eyes wide open because I really think they are testing the waters to see if it's safe to go in." She nodded her head with a wink and took another sip of her root beer.

The server brought their food and set the plates before them. They dug in, and Rusty felt relieved her appetite was back.

He was glad he told her. Not only did she confirm his suspicions, it made the juice runs feel less like a dirty secret. Together, they could sort this out. At this point, there was nothing wrong or illegal, but just enough of an air of uneasiness and dubious circumstances to make it suspect. *Eyes wide open, that's for sure.*

***

On their Sunday afternoon visit to Di's family's farm, Uncle Fritz motioned to Rusty to follow him to the shed where he made his beer. The shed was more like a summer kitchen. Copper kettles, funnels, glass bottles and hoses were hung and shelved neatly. Grain boxes lined one wall. Once inside, he fished in the dark for the cord to the light bulb, found it, and pulled it, causing light to flood the shadowy interior. In the middle of the shed sat a new wooden rocking chair still smelling of polish. Uncle Fritz took a deep breath, his chest swelling. "It's for Di and the baby."

Rusty nodded in approval. He hadn't realized Uncle Fritz's talents extended beyond gardening and beer making. He ran his hand across the headrest and followed the grain down to the armrest. It was made of hard ash and sanded as smooth as the surface of glass. He pictured Uncle Fritz spending hours alone on just the sanding. The tight grain and the soft light caramel color of the wood were then brought to life by the sure brush strokes of varnish over its surface The ladder back rocker was as finely made as any he had ever seen in swanky furniture stores in Lorain and Elyria. He was impressed with Uncle Fritz's craftsmanship.

"Is there anything that you're not good at," he asked, after admiring the rocker.

"According to my sister, I'm not good at listening." Uncle Fritz then went on to explain how he had wrestled with the idea of whether or not to paint it, preferring the natural beauty of the wood grain. The natural wood would stick out like a sore thumb in a child's room painted floor to ceiling in pastels, so he considered white paint—*neutral*, he explained to Rusty. But in the end, he couldn't bring himself to paint it.

"This way it's still neutral so it doesn't matter if it's a boy or girl."

"This way, it's an heirloom, and she'll love it. You are quite the carpenter. And all this time I thought beer brewing was your forte."

"Oh, it is," Uncle Fritz said with earnest. "My beer is way better than my carpentry." As if reminded, he went over to a shelf in the back corner and grabbed two bottles. "This is summer's batch. We'll see how it's coming." He opened the bottles and passed one to Rusty. The rocker was temporarily forgotten.

"I got a question for you," Rusty said, as they stood over the rocker, sipping their beers. "You know those grape juice charters I was telling you about?"

Uncle Fritz chuckled. "*Ja*, grape juice."

"Well, it gets better." Rusty proceeded to tell him about Pete, the milk delivery truck and the desolate dock.

Uncle Fritz nodded as he listened.

'So what do you think," he asked when he finished relaying the latest grape juice episode.

Uncle Fritz lowered his beer. "Pete is a rotten apple and since he's in the barrel with the others, all the apples are kaput. Sooner or later, all the apples around Pete will be bad and that includes you." Uncle Fritz took the last swig and burped. "Hey, that's good stuff!"

"That's what Di said. She thinks they are testing the waters."

Uncle Fritz chuckled again. "That Di, she's a smart one."

"So what do you think?"

"I just told you what I think."

"What I mean is, should I stop the grape juice charters?"

"Have they given you a reason to stop? Pete says he is on the up and up. Maybe he is. Maybe he did have a scare. But I wouldn't trust him or his cousins further than I could throw them."

Rusty reflected for a moment, absorbing what Uncle Fritz had said. "The thing is the money is paying our bills. Fishing charters have tanked since the fish have been scarce. And I'm having a hard time finding a job this time of year."

Uncle Fritz regarded Rusty. "The family will help you pay your bills, you know that. Fall is good fishing, they'll be back."

"That's not the point. I have a job that is paying our way."

"Well then, see no evil, hear no evil, speak no evil."

"What do you mean by that?"

"Just what it means. If you are going to make your money running grape charters for the Italians, be an ostrich and collect your money."

"And if I find out I'm running wine? I'll be breaking the law."

Uncle Fritz chuckled. "What do you think you are doing now?" he said, motioning to the bottle in Rusty's hand.

Chapter 27

It came as a surprise. But it shouldn't have. Rusty, loaded with juice and "baby brother" Joe, departed from Lime Kiln Dock on what appeared to be another uneventful Friday run among the last of the day's boaters and fishermen who were taking advantage of the warm, September evening. The lake was as flat as glass and a shade darker than the soft blue sky as Rusty settled back in his chair and headed for Sandusky Bay.

Just as he was about to throttle up to speed, a Coast Guard picket boat rounded the tip of the island coming from Put-in-Bay's windward side. Rusty instantly recognized it as one of the new 38-footers that replaced the slower 75-foot Six-bitters the Guard had been using through the mid 20s.

Once the Guard broke up Rum Row off the Atlantic seaboard in '25, they moved their picket boats as well as extra rum chasing vessels to the Great Lakes (Rum Row was the nickname of the spot where ships anchored side by side just over the U.S. maritime border to supply small rum running boats with high quality Canadian, European and Caribbean alcohol). Rum running speedboats, up to now, had pretty much ran unopposed by the understaffed Coast Guard and their slow Six-Bitters and harbor patrol boats on Lake Erie, but these new pickets were made with rumrunners in mind. They were capable of 24 knots with crews of three manning .30 caliber machine guns and Browning Automatic Rifles called B.A.R.s, both fully automatic and capable of over a mile range with accuracy up to a half mile. Though serious rumrunners still had faster boats, the runs from the Canadian shoreline across the Great Lakes to the United States coast had become a bit more challenging. The Coast Guard was determined to do on the Great Lakes what it did to Rum Row in the Atlantic and to do so, more Guardsmen, faster boats and bigger guns were brought to the lakes.

Rusty hoped it was a coincidence, but soon realized the picket boat's course was aimed directly at him, and its intention was to intercept the *Rising Sun.* His gut told him this was no random boat safety inspection. Despite being clean, he felt uneasy. Hell, if he thought this grape juice business seemed shady, why wouldn't the Coast Guard? As the picket boat bore down on *Rising Sun,* he took a few deep breaths and leaned back in the pilot chair, attempting to look as nonchalant as he could with a thumping heart—until he read the call numbers on the picket boat's bow, CG157— the number of notorious Captain Connors's vessel. He felt his heart drop to his stomach. Connors and crew had a reputation of being overly zealous and excessively destructive in their searches, descending upon a boat, suspicious or not, like a pack of hyenas ripping and tearing after meat. Rumors also floated that mysterious bottles of whiskey or scotch would be “found” by the crew despite ardent denials by the pilot of the boat being probed. *Who ya gonna believe?*

A megaphone barked orders from the Coast Guard vessel. “Return to dock, *Rising Sun.*”

Rusty gritted his teeth and eased the boat around and headed back to the dock. He searched the shoreline for Al or Lou, but there was no sign of them.

Once *Rising Sun* neared the dock, the picket boat came up from behind boxing her in. “Prepare for boarding,” the megaphone crackled. Joe jumped onto the dock and tied off *Rising Sun*, while another line was thrown from the picket boat and two guardsmen jumped aboard, one affixing the line to her.

Rusty killed the engine. He wasn’t sure if he felt more worried or angry. Had it been any other Coast Guard crew, he wouldn’t have been so uneasy. With any other guardsmen it would be a search—*can’t blame you boys for your suspicions, you’re just doing your job*, and, with no contraband found, off they would go—*sorry for the inconvenience, sir*—no one knocked around, no bullet holes in the hull, no damage to the boat except for a pried board or two at the most.

But with Connors and crew, upholding the law had little to do with it. It was like Davey had said during a lunch break on the *Iroquois* after Connor’s latest act of shooting up a ferry he swore had rum aboard. The position gave Connors and his pack of dogs an excuse to be gunslingers, bullies and ruffians, all within the confines of the law. Rusty had always straddled the fence between his opinions of the CG157’s captain but the half sinking of the shot up ferry changed his mind. Pete was right. Davey was right. Connors was a rogue and the Guard needed to rein him in.

One guardsman, the larger of the two on board, ordered Rusty to disembark and stand next to Joe. Rusty recognized the man from the newspaper photographs, the smaller one, too. Having seen their images staring out from the newspapers, brandishing pistols and rifles and looking more like pirates than guardsmen, he never imagined he would be meeting them face to face. Davey should see this, he thought, they do look like wild-eyed gunslingers right out of the pages of his western novels.

The smaller of the two had beady, ready eyes and the taller one had an edgy swagger. Both sported .45 automatic pistols. The taller one with a swagger kept his hand floating above his piece in quick draw mode. Rusty knew right off these men were gasoline and just looking for a lit match. *Howdy ma’am* would be as foreign on their lips as *sorry for your inconvenience, sir.*

As Rusty and Joe watched from the dock, the guardsmen began their ransacking of the *Rising Sun.* Bottles crashed, boards squealed in protest as they were pried, crates crashed as they were thrown from the hold and storage under the bow.

Rusty’s face was hot and his breaths came rapid and shallow. They were roughing up *Rising Sun* for shits and giggles and there was nothing he could do or say about it. He glared at the picket boat’s wheelhouse and could see the shadowy, motionless silhouette of what he presumed was Connors. The only indicator the shadow was alive was the on and off red glow from a puffed cigarette, like the intermittent glow from a warning light on a buoy to warn sailors of danger.

With each loud crash of glass and crunch of crates or screech of forced nails, Rusty's muscles drew tauter like the string on a bow before the arrow launch. His fists were clenched so tight, his knuckles were white. He would have throttled anyone else for doing less to his boat. Their asses would have been long overboard. He cast an eye towards Joe who had pulled out a cigarette and was smoking it as laid back as if he was watching swimmers at a beach. He figured Joe wouldn't be so cool if booze was hidden among the bottles of grape juice—a thought that Uncle Fritz put in his head when he asked him if the grape men always selected the bottle for him when he demanded a sample.

The ransacking lasted for fifteen minutes before it ended in the bilge.

"It's clean," Rusty overheard the larger man mutter to the smaller. The smaller man gave a half-hearted thumb down sign to the shadowy figure in the wheelhouse. The two guardsmen appeared disappointed.

No feast for the hyenas today.

After kicking a few more bottles around on the deck (for spite, he figured) the larger man untied the line, freeing *Rising Sun* from the CG157. He then jumped back onto the picket boat. Just before the small man joined him, he turned to Rusty. His beady eyes were snapping. "We're watching you, *Rising Sun*," he said, then boarded the boat.

Rusty and Joe waited silently on the dock till the picket boat was under way. Then they scanned the *Rising Sun*'s deck, their eyes soaking in the broken glass, the escaping purple juice seeping out onto the deck boards and trickling into the hull and the jumble of deck boards, some pried up, others removed completely.

Finally, Rusty broke the silence. "Sons of bitches."

Joe grunted in approval.

Rusty climbed into the boat, gingerly stepping over the wreckage.

"You know, you're not gonna get paid for tonight. The terms are for safe delivery," Joe said.

Rusty gave Joe a hard look. He crossed the deck towards the dock, his fist clenched again. Joe took a step back even though Rusty remained in the boat. "*You know*, you're not gonna get a ride back to Sandusky if you don't get your ass on this boat and help me clean up and salvage the unbroken bottles," Rusty said, his eyes smoldering.

Joe shrugged, and climbed on board. He began packing the good bottles into unbroken crates, while Rusty tossed the busted bottles and smashed crates overboard. The cleaning and the repairs would have to wait until he got back to his slip in Sandusky.

Between the two of them, they managed to salvage half the load.

Twilight had settled in by the time *Rising Sun* arrived at the Sandusky warehouse dock. This time, no knock at the door was needed for the hand-truck men had stationed themselves on the wharf. As the boat pulled up, Rusty could see they were pissed and anxious.

As Joe jumped out of the boat to fix the mooring lines, one man crossed over and cuffed his head.

"What took you so long, moron," he yelled.

"Hey, watch it," Joe shouted back. "We got stopped by the C.G. and they busted us up."

"Tell it to Sweeney," the man said, sneering.

Rusty stepped onto the dock. It was the first time he had gotten out of the boat on these runs. He went up to the man, who took a step back. "He's telling it straight. We got searched by Connors's crew—you do know Connors?"

The man nodded. His eyes were uneasy with a bit of fear thrown in.

"Then you know we didn't come out of this too good." Rusty's voice was low and thick as he looked the man in the eye. "We were able to salvage half the load, so I expect half the money. Since your business gave cause for me to be searched and since my boat got busted up in the process, I expect to be paid the other half for repairs, *capisce?*"

The man was taken back at first, and then he narrowed his eyes. He jabbed his thumb on his chest. "I'm not the boss, tough guy, so save the lather. All I do is ship juice and collect my money. You got a problem, see Al. *Capisce?*"

***

The next morning, Rusty stepped off the passenger ferry along with the weekend tourists onto the dock in downtown Put-in-Bay, having left *Rising Sun* in her slip in Sandusky in need of repairs. Last night, on the ride home, he had decided against telling Di about the roughed-up boat, telling her instead he was late because the Coast Guard had stopped him and searched the boat and found nothing. He then told her he had business on the island Saturday with the grape juice men and had no idea how long he would be gone, therefore, he would take the Lake Shore interurban to Sandusky so she could have the truck.

Halfway across the bay, he realized he didn't know the last name of the men he was working for. Hell, he thought, it's a small island populated by German descendants so how hard would it be to find a couple of Italians with a vineyard anyways.

With the summer over and fall settling in, most tourist shops lining the island's downtown lakefront were either closed for the season or opened weekends to snag the last strangling revelers hoofing it at the dance hall on the main drag.

Rusty stepped into a diner that was opened year round, ordered coffee and when it was served, asked the waitress if she knew an Al who grew grapes on the island.

"You mean the Sicilian?"

"That would be him."

"They're on the west side of the island over by the cemetery. The old Schmitt place. Bought it off the poor bastard when he went under. First the worms, then Prohibition. Hermann Schmitt made wonderful wine. What a waste."

He didn't want to appear too anxious about Al or the family's business, so he waited until her next round with the coffee pot. "Does Al come to town a lot?" That wasn't really what he wanted to know. He wanted to know if the locals viewed them as an upstanding family or a den of thieves.

"Nah, they keep to themselves pretty much. Seem okay when they are out and about. They are a generous lot, though. Great tippers. Even donated an engine for our only fire truck when the old engine blew. Said it was no big deal as they benefit from having the fire truck as well. That was a buzz on the island for a while."

"I bet. I have to see him on business and not sure how to find the place."

"Take that road to Catawba Avenue then turn right at the cemetery. Just look for their sign that hangs on a stone wall next to the driveway. It says, *Vietato l'Ingresso.*"

"Name of the vineyard?"

The waitress grinned. "The English translation is underneath. It means *Keep Out.*"

Chapter 28

Finding the place was not hard, but how to get past the two Doberman Pinschers who were eyeing him like a steak as he stood in front of the closed gate would be. They must have felt he lingered too long because they rose from their sunny spots on the lawn to await his next move. His plan was to catch Al off guard, but fat chance now. Not only would the dogs sound the alarm and ruin the surprise, they became a wall of teeth between him and Al. He was pissed, but not enough to be mangled by the family pets.

He stared through the bars for signs of life other than the two eager canine sentries. The place, what he could see of it, looked beautiful from behind the bars of the gate. The driveway cut through an oak and cedar dotted lawn and beyond that he could make out a large two story limestone house with a large wrap-around covered porch trimmed in white. Beyond the house was obscured by more cedars and bushes. Unlike the touristy end of the island, this side was so quiet, he could hear the wind rustle the oak leaves and birds call to one another from the treetops. If it hadn't been for the two sentries and the welcome sign at the gate, he would have thought it a real haven. He grasped the gate bars without thinking and one dog woofed a warning. There was no reaction from the house, so he shook the bars and hollered "hello" sending the dogs into a barking frenzy as they rushed the gate. The scenery now consisted of teeth, gums and flying slobber, and he hoped like hell the gate was strong and the stone walls high enough.

After a minute filled with the sound of raging dogs, a man built like an ice box walked down the driveway. As he drew closer, he hollered to the dogs in Italian and motioned them away from the gate. They slinked away, obviously disappointed, sat nearby and growled like two motors on standby.

"What do you want?" the man said as he approached the gate.

"I want to see Al."

"Nobody said nothing about an appointment with Al."

"Al is not expecting me. I work for him and need to see him about work."

The man looked him over. "What kind of work?"

"I am the pilot of the boat that makes the juice runs."

"Which run?"

"Put-in-Bay to Sandusky."

"You just don't waltz in here without an appointment," the man said with a snort.

He glared at the man. "Look. I came quite a ways to see Al. Would you tell him Rusty wants to see him."

"What about?"

"Tell him there has been a problem."

"A problem? What kind? Rusty who?"

"He'll know who it is," Rusty said with an edge to his voice.

The man grimaced and headed back up the driveway. The dogs remained, eyes locked on Rusty in a staring match to see who would make the first move.

Five minutes passed, and a smaller man emerged around the corner of the house. His walk was brisk as he headed down the drive. Rusty recognized him. It was Al.

"Rusty!" he called out. "How is my man?" He was all smiles as he approached the gate. "I'm sorry Giuseppe did not let you in. But...he is careful, you know." The growling dogs assembled behind him as he unlocked the gate. Al stomped his foot at them. "Get the hell out of here." They scattered a short distance.

Rusty hoped the ice box man would not confuse Al's command as an order directed at him, but the ice box did not appear.

Al swung open the gate and shook Rusty's hand as he invited him through, then locked the gate behind him. He was as effervescent as a glass of cola. "I am glad you stopped by to visit."

"This isn't really a social call. I had a problem last night. You may have heard about it?"

Al grew thoughtful. "Ahh, yes. I heard the Coast Guard searched you."

"Not just searched me, they busted up my boat pretty good."

Al nodded, his brows knitted together. "Ay, don't worry about the shipment. I'll still pay you full price."

"I also expect compensation for my boat repairs."

Al's smile faded. "That is something you should take up with the Coast Guard. They were the ones who damaged your boat."

"But the juice from your vineyard gave them the reason."

Al frowned. "The Guard does this regardless of who, what or where. Tell you what. Since we are friends, I'll pay for repairs this time." Al reached into his pocket, pulled out a wad of bills and peeled off two twenties. "Let me know if you need more."

Rusty collected the money and instantly felt its calming effect.

Noting his reaction, Al said, "Since you are here, let me take you on a tour of the vineyards and our operation."

Rusty hesitated. Stepping into Al's world felt like a stepping into the underworld, but he needed some answers.

"Come on," Al motioned as he started up the driveway. "You should at least know something about the product you are hauling. And, it gives me the chance to show off my little darlings."

***

The *little darlings* turned out to be the purple and red bunches of grapes swollen with sweet juice that dangled from row upon rows of vines that grew in the loamy-sandy fields behind the house. It was orderly and well-tended, and smacked of pride, reminiscent of Uncle Fritz's endeavors. About a dozen pickers armed with snips and bushel baskets dotted the field. Two barns, one limestone, the other wood flanked the left side of the fields. The size of the vineyard was impressive considering it was on an island.

"Concords here, Niagaras there," Al pointed out. He removed a scissor-looking snip from his trousers' pocket and severed a bundle of deep blue Concords from the vine and presented it to Rusty. "Don't tell me this isn't the sweetest grape you ever ate."

Rusty pulled a grape from the bunch and popped it into his mouth. The slightest pressure of his jaw caused it to explode into a juicy pulp both sweet and tart. No question Al could grow a great grape as well as make great grape juice. But could he get rich off of it?

Al caught him glancing toward the barns. He placed his hand on Rusty's back, "Let me show you how we turn these darlings into the best juice this side of the pond," he said beaming.

As they crossed through the vineyard, Al unraveled the story of how he came to be the vineyardist of this place.

"These islands have perfect growing conditions for grapes. The surrounding waters act like a mirror, soils are light and there is an extended growing season in fall. Grapes need that extra time. The lake acts like a giant greenhouse to keep the island warm when the rest of Ohio is freezing its ass off with frosts and early freezes. The extra-long season is the key ingredient for maximum ripeness which equals maximum sweetness.

When the Germans arrived here years ago, they recognized these islands would be perfect for vineyards and wine making. They purchased properties on the islands, imported vines from their homeland and with sweat, muscle and God's Grace built themselves vineyards that produced prize-winning wine that turned the Frenchies green with envy. Them Heinies know what they're doing when it comes to booze.

This place belonged to a kraut named Schmitt. He specialized in Riesling and Sauvignons. His Rieslings took top prize at some big shindig with the Europeans. The crop and winemaking were going great guns for old man Schmitt until this little worm comes along- rootworm it's called—and it burrows into the vines, killing the whole plant. Schmitt and his fellow islanders lost over half their vineyards to these little devils. Had to tear out vines and burn them. A real disaster. Some vintners lost everything, but old Schmitt managed to hang on, saving healthy cuttings, re-grafting and replanting and building his vineyard back up. Just when things started looking up for him, *bam*, Prohibition broadsides him, and he is stuck with a vineyard of wine grapes that he cannot make into wine and sell. Poor bastard went under just like the rest."

He shook his head. "This place was dead. Schmitt's wife died meantime, too. Few vintners switched to juice grapes, but Schmitt, now old and alone, just grew turnips and potatoes. What a waste." He opened the door to the wood-clad barn and invited Rusty inside. "This is where the pickers bring the grapes after picking them. They dump them here, and then these two fine ladies sort them," he said, nodding to two women with scarves knotted upon their heads.

Inside, benches heaped with grapes were surrounded by stacks of bushel baskets. The women sorting through the mounds of grapes looked up and smiled. The air was heavy with the foxy, sweet smell of ripened Concord grapes.

"Looks like a bumper crop," Rusty said.

"I am very happy," Al said. They walked out, and Al led him to the stone barn. "This is where the juice is extracted and bottled." He opened the door to the stone barn.

This barn was brighter with whitewashed walls, and round bins, barrels, wooden paddles, funnels, bottles and crates filled the space. A large grape press dominated the side wall to the right. Next to it, on an adjacent wall, a sliding door opened to the wooden barn located fifteen paces away.

"This is where the sorted grapes are brought in by a wheeled cart to the press," Al pointed out.

At a bench on the opposite side of the building, Rusty saw a man was corking bottles and passing them down to a woman who stuck labels to them. She then placed them in a crate and when it was full with bottles of juice, the corker would carry the crate to join other full crates stacked next to another sliding door.

Rusty knew he would be seeing those same crates at Lime Kiln Dock on Friday.

"Do you still stomp the grapes in those bins with your feet?" he asked.

Al smiled. "I don't stomp grapes." He guided Rusty back out into sunlight. "Where was I… ah, yes. Old man Schmitt was broke. When Prohibition started, I was helping with my family's vineyard in Upstate New York. We grew Pinot Noir, Cabernet Sauvignon- red wines, you know. Suddenly, we are in the same boat with guys like Schmitt. Can you imagine telling an Italian he can't have wine with his manicotti? There's years of cultivating, toiling and perfecting in each bottle of wine. A vintner is a farmer, a chemist and an artist all rolled up into one. It's not one season that goes into a bottle, its years and damn if my old man and nonno were going to tear up everything they worked hard for. But that's another story…

So I heard about these islands on my business travels to Ohio, and with grape juice getting real popular, I looked into it. I heard about an old vineyard on Kelleys for sale but didn't get too excited about it. That's when I heard about old man Schmitt on South Bass and his troubles. So I went to see the old man. At first, he didn't want anything to do with me. I have to admit I didn't like him either, but I sure liked his farm. Told him about my family vineyard in Upstate, the absurdity of the law and next thing you know we are talking grapes and wine-making. I may have been an Italian, but I was a brother vintner, and that helped sweeten him up. Or was it the money?" Al looked thoughtful. "I made him a real nice offer."

A bell clanged at the house, and the grape pickers dotting the vineyard raised their heads like hungry baby birds.

"Hey, dinner is ready. I insist you join me."

"No…my wife is expecting me back." Di really wasn't as he had told her he could be a while.

"She needs to let up on the nose ring every now and then." Al laughed.

Rusty didn't find the jab at Di funny or the insinuation he was brow beat. "So what happened to Schmitt?" he said to change the subject.

"He went to the mainland. Island life can be tough when you are old and alone. Now let's finish our conversation over dinner."

Rusty shook his head. "Thanks, but no thanks. I have a bit of a trip ahead of me and…"

"I am insulted you are not joining me. My feelings are hurt," Al said, placing his hands over his heart and faking a wince. "But the wife waits, and I too am a married man and know their tempers. Another time, my friend. I will hold you to it!" He shook Rusty's hand. "Giuseppe, see Mr. Rusty to the gate so the dogs don't have sport with him."

Rusty started down the driveway with the ice box man, then paused and turned back to Al. "Just what is your last name anyways?"

"Trapani!"

Chapter 29

Rising Sun was back in Vermilion the following day. Since he wasn't quite sure the extent of work she would need, he felt having her close to home would make the repair job easier as supplies were close at hand and he could work off and on. He would also be near Di in case she needed him plus she would have access to the truck. Since it was Sunday, she was off to her parents' farm after church, and the chance of her dropping by and seeing the damage to the boat was minimal. Boat maintenance was not unusual, so he wasn't questioned when he took a rain check on Sunday's dinner with the family by saying *Rising Sun* needed some repair—he just didn't say what or how much. He felt like a heel for not telling her what really happened to the boat, but making her upset in her condition outweighed the whole truth. Still, he felt lousy. He had always been on the level and couldn't help but think his lack of total honesty pointed to his association with the Trapanis.

Today, the weather was kind to him, giving him a clear, warm day to work on the boat, although he wished he was out on the lake instead of sidelined. He sighed as he gazed at the glass-like water as it stretched to the horizon until it met with the empty sky the color of a robin's egg. A sharp horizon line separated the two hues of blue. Perch were biting, and the harbor of Vermilion and its river were crawling with small fishing crafts taking advantage of the gift of a pleasant fall day. As much as he wished he could be among them, he was thankful it wasn't cold or rainy to make the job worse than it already was. The day before, he had stopped in Elyria and picked up lumber and hardware with Al's money. He had three fishing charters booked for next week and the pressure was on to get the boat repaired by the first charter on Tuesday. Between fuming over the damage and being lost in the ripping out of the damaged decking, he didn't notice he had company until a familiar voice startled him.

"Holy Christ!" Eddie said as he approached *Rising Sun* with Prince in tow. "What happened?"

"I got to do some patching."

"And how! Looks like pirates attacked the *Sun*."

"Does look like it at that." Little Eddie had hit the nail on the head. As much as he would have liked to confirm it was indeed pirates, he instead said, "I hit the pier in Sandusky when I was coming in the other night."

"Hooey! The only way you'd crash into anything is if you were fried."

"Hey, watch your mouth, wise guy. And I don't get *fried*."

"So what really happened?"

Rusty feigned a scowl. "You sure you're not related to Di?"

"I wish." Eddie sat down on the dock next to the boat and Prince settled next to him. He fell quiet as he watched minnows dart about the piles supporting the dock.

Rusty glanced at him. Eddie's face had turned suddenly solemn and he knew his remark hit a sore spot. "Any new news, exciting or otherwise, with you?" he said to change the subject.

"Another dog was found dead this side of Beaver Creek. Poisoned. Duck hunters came across it."

Beaver Creek! A look of alarm flashed across Rusty's face. He stared at the back of Eddie's head. "When did this happen?"

"Guys found the dog Saturday morning. Said it looks like it had been dead for a few days." Eddie rose from the dock. "I'm scared about Prince, Rusty."

Rusty sat back on his heels. A deep furrow plowed its way between his brows. Dogs were being poisoned from Huron to Lorain by smugglers not wanting the four-legged alarms to alert the community to their covert operations. Now this dog shows up dead at the Trapanis' dock. *Looks like a duck, walks like a duck, quacks like a duck...*Di would say. She had a saying for everything. He returned from his thoughts and regarded Prince at Eddie's side. The *ever-loyal Prince- the only constant in young Eddie's life*. He dug into his pocket. "Here." He handed Eddie a five dollar bill. "Keep Prince well fed... and keep an eye on him. You watch him... you hear me?" He searched his pocket again and found one dollar and two bits. "For you at the diner." It was all he had on him. "You still got that slingshot?"

Eddie stuffed the bills in his pocket and mumbled thanks then said, "Practice all the time."

"Good. How did you hear about the dog?"

"At Sam's. The hunters were there."

Rusty frowned. "Why are you hanging around there?"

Eddie ignored the remark knowing Rusty already knew the answer to that one.

"That's no place for a kid. Your old man around?"

"Too much as far as I am concerned. Every time he gets zozzled, he manages to find his way back home. That's when me and Prince skedaddle."

"How old are you now?"

"Eleven."

"Too young to be on the streets."

"Yeah... well you're not the one getting knocked around for nothing. I'll take the streets over a thrashing any day."

Eddie had a point.

"You going to school every day?"

"Have no choice. They'll put me in an orphan's home if I don't go or miss too much. Got held back this year as it is."

"That doesn't surprise me with all the days you miss."

Eddie shrugged.

Rusty grimaced. He wanted to blurt out *your Dad should have his ass kicked from here to Toledo,* instead, he said, "You shouldn't be on your own so much."

"Me and Prince manage fine. Besides, I got you and Hoot and Widow Donovan looking out extra for me."

Rusty put his hands on his hips and snorted. "I'm talking about a guardian or step parents, not a motley crew."

"Jeezus...don't *you* start. You know how I feel about do-gooders."

Rusty shook his head. Like a feral dog who growled when it saw a leash, Eddie was warning him he had gone a bit far. Eddie may have been slick to a point about concealing the depth of his situation, but he was hanging on by his nails. With each passing year, his father became more invisible and the talk of a boy's home became more solid and it made Rusty feel guilty to know the situation on both sides but do little about it except brush it under the rug. Hoot and Mrs. Donovan perhaps shared his guilt.

Hoot was the town's night watchman, and since Eddie was an occasional creature of the night when his old man was home, his and Hoot's friendship was inevitable. Hoot liked the company and Eddie liked an adult ear to bend. And Hoot didn't treat him like he was a scallywag. The old man was given the nickname years ago when a railway accident involving two boxcars ended his days as a switcher. He lost his leg below the knee as well as his job. Few job opportunities presented themselves for a one-legged man with a ninth grade education. Hoot began his downward slide into the role of town bum. Eventually, he got a wooden leg and began doing odd jobs around town but he drank anything with enough alcohol in it to *take the edge off* without being noticeably drunk—a habit, along with his leg, that limited his job prospects. It was the town's police chief, and only officer, who approached him years ago to offer him the job as night watchman. It was an uneventful job that paid middling, requiring that he simply watch over the town during the night and if something seemed amiss or a problem arose, he would call the sleeping chief. For twenty-three years and through two police chief reigns, Hoot kept a nightly watch on the sleeping town. It was Bert, late owner of hardware store that nicknamed him Hoot right after he became watchman, alluding to the night owl. The name stuck, and a whole generation later knew his name only as Hoot.

Mrs. Donovan, also known as Widow Donovan, lived in a modest clapboard house on a tree-lined side street in the center of town. The view from her kitchen window included Sam's back door one street over where she often saw, to her disapproval, Eddie loitering. She had lost her husband and young son in the flu of 1918. Her older son went to war and never came home and was buried in France. She kept to herself mostly and had a fondness for cross-stitching, lemon cookies and Eddie. On Sundays, she cooked shepherd pie, and on Wednesdays she made corn beef, cabbage and boiled potatoes and Eddie, knowing the routine, made himself available outside her home around supper time those nights. It was because of Eddie, that her love of baking was rekindled, so cookies, cake or pie was also in the offering. She didn't ask questions or lecture him or tell him he should be in state care...she just fed him and gave him her son's clothes from her attic as needed. She treated him with the same kindness she would with an amiable stray dog, knowing full well if she tried to collar him, he would turn and run and be gone for good. She would make a good grandma Eddie once told Rusty.

Rusty's thoughts returned to his task, and he went back to work hammering planks in place.

Eddie crawled onto the boat to watch. "So when is Di going to have that baby?"

"Most likely during a big snowstorm in March."

"You oughtta name him after me."

The remark took Rusty back. "What if it's a girl?"

"Edith...no, Edie."

A smile flashed across Rusty's face, erasing the furrow between his eyes. "I'll pass it on to Di."

Eddie's face brightened. For the next hour, he helped Rusty remove damaged wood, hammer new deck boards and passed tools until he spotted two fishermen in a rowboat heading towards the marshes east of the pier. "I gotta go."

Rusty looked up and saw the boat. He shook his head as Eddie and Prince scurried towards the marshes.

Recently, the Coast Guard had hired local fishermen to dump some of the confiscated booze in the marshes of Vermilion. Not all the bottles broke on impact giving determined fellows like Eddie an opportunity to make a few bucks fishing them out of the tangled reeds and foul-smelling muck, and not all the bottles made it into the marsh either—just enough to make it look good.

Chapter 30

Five miles south of Pelee Island, *Rising Sun* dropped anchor. Pike were biting here and the clients were excited except one fellow who was a bit green in the face and kept asking Rusty if the lake was always this choppy. Rusty was happy. It was getting harder to find fish as there was no such thing as quotas to limit the amount of fish caught and the search forced him farther out into the lake. A tip-off led him to anchor just off Canada's island, Pelee where schools of pike were rumored to be found. As one Huron fisherman told Rusty over coffee at Sam's two days earlier, "the lake is just plum fished out." It was that man who told him about Pelee.

As the morning wore on and less fish bit, Rusty checked his watch.

"It's time to pull the lines, gentlemen. Looks like fish for supper."

The clients reeled in their lines and he assisted those more awkward with the gear. They were in high spirits, and the green-faced man looked relieved fishing was over.

After the catch was stored and gear stowed, Rusty weighed anchor.

A boat appeared on the east horizon first as a small dot then growing in size. He watched its approach as he turned over the engine and started for the Sandusky harbor. The approaching boat veered from its course and headed directly at them. He kept a wary eye on it as it drew closer. When he realized it was a Coast Guard vessel, he felt his heart sink into his stomach. When the vessel drew close enough, he could see it was a cutter and not Captain Connors's boat. He sighed with relief. The cutter reduced speed and a megaphone said, "Ahoy, *Rising Sun.* Come along side."

"Did we do something wrong?" he heard one of the men in his charter say.

The cutter sidled up to them."Captain, this is a routine inspection. Grab the line and tie it off on your bow."

A line was thrown and Rusty grabbed it and tied it off at his bow cleat. Though it felt like *déjà-vu,* he knew it was really happening again. The charter men were whispering nervously among themselves.

"It's okay," he reassured them. "It's a routine inspection." He had trouble convincing himself, though. He counted six guardsmen.

Two men boarded. They were business-like, but friendly. He was guarded and awkwardly friendly back.

"Captain, we are checking for proper licenses, safety equipment, capacities, and catch—the routine. Gentlemen, excuse us, it's for your safety as well."

Rusty showed one man his charter license and boat registration, while the other man looked over the boat.

"You boys don't have contraband on board, do you?"

"No sir," they replied in unison.

"Just fish, sir," Rusty added.

"Looks like a nice batch of pike, the searcher said, looking into the hold. "Can't stand the smell or taste of fish myself." He put the hatch cover back on and continued checking for life preserve rings, lines, first aid kit, and fire extinguisher, and then he checked the boats running lights, navigational equipment and charts. He looked over the fishing gear as well. Rusty glanced over the shoulder of the guardsman checking his papers and noticed the searcher seemed satisfied with what he saw.

"Everything appears to be in order," the guardsmen said, handing back the registration.

The searcher nodded in approval.

"Sorry for any inconvenience. Just doing our job to keep the lake, its coast and you safe," they said, re-boarding their vessel. "You men enjoy your fish supper. Captain, thank you for your co-operation."

Rusty nodded and untied the line and tossed it back to the cutter. It wasn't until the cutter started to pull away that he realized he was holding his breath. He exhaled and instantly felt tension melt from his muscles.

"Wow. That was something," one of the men exclaimed.

"Yeah," said another. "They were nice and all, but it was kinda scary. I felt like I did something wrong."

"Bushwa, it was routine. They're just looking out for our safety," the green-around-the-gills man said.

"I bet they were searching for stowaways or booze," the second man countered.

Rusty snorted. "That's exactly what they were doing."

***

With the three charters in the bag that week, he felt good about himself again. He even told Di about the inspection off Pelee Island and how he felt it was an excuse to check for contraband. After all, illegal aliens and liquor from Canada were popular cargo for cashed starved fishermen or opportunists like Pete, *before he saw the light.* The only fly in his idyllic ointment of charters was the Friday night grape juice run that broke the chain between the fishing trips. You couldn't count on charter bookings as steady income, but you could on the Trapani runs, so he kept Friday and Wednesday afternoons clear. He felt he was two different people now, the *Rising Sun* Charter Captain with a great wife and home, and the Grape Juice Runner with shadowy missions and secrets—the long lost doppelganger who had finally developed and freed itself from the confines of Happy Captain Rusty to become its own entity.

***

On Wednesday's juice run from Sandusky to Lorain, he had three questions for Pete. Two he had planned to ask Al that day at the vineyard, but forgot during the course of the impromptu tour, the third question was for Pete himself.

After he and Pete left the warehouse dock in Sandusky and were on their way to the desolate dock at Beaver Creek, he asked Pete the first question that had been simmering on the back burner of his mind. "Wouldn't it be more cost effective if the Trapanis owned their own boat?"

"Well, yes and no. First of all, they charter a couple of boats—you just have the run for this area."

"You mean there is more than one area they are delivering to?"

"Heck, yeah. And picking up. Do you really think that vineyard on Put-in-Bay can put out that much grape juice?"

Rusty was taken back. "Where are the other places and runs?"

"Different places all around the lake."

"Upstate New York?"

"Yeah, Al's old man and grandfather have a vineyard there, too. You won't be doing that one, though, that pilot is in solid."

Rusty was stunned. Pete's answer pretty much took care of the second question, but he asked it anyways. "Why don't they use the freight ferry from the island to Sandusky? It would be cheaper."

Pete's face screwed up. "That doesn't make sense. We would have to go to the ferry dock to unload and truck back to the warehouse. It's more convenient to have a boat pull right up to the dock. And second, the ferry runs on a schedule. They cut back on trips in fall when we need the service the most—when the grape harvest and bottling take place."

Rusty fell quiet. Both answers made sense. For a while, the only sound was the engine hum of *Rising Sun* as she sliced through the water. But Pete's answers inspired another question. "Can grape juice be *that* profitable?"

Pete shrugged. "I don't see the books, I don't know the business. I just do what I am told and collect my pay. Like you. But apparently, since wine and booze has been outlawed, grape juice is real popular and big demand means big profit. Imagine that? If you ask me, juice is a pretty poor substitute."

Rusty nodded in agreement then added, "But grape juice can be made into wine."

"Can. But it's a far cry from the Real McCoy."

"It's still wine."

They both fell silent.

The third (actually it became the fourth) question gnawed at him until it made its way out of his mouth. He wasn't sure how Pete would take it, but he had to know, and since he didn't want an answer that beat around the bush, he decided his question shouldn't either so he asked bluntly, "Did you or Vince poison a dog near Beaver Creek?"

"What?" Pete's face was perplexed.

Rusty repeated it staccato. "Did you or Vince poison a dog near the Lorain dock last week?"

Pete's face turned to a scowl. "What in hell kind of question is that? Vince and I like dogs. We don't poison them. What in the hell made you ask that?"

"A dog was found dead by duck hunters there and rumors have it the dog was poisoned."

Pete glared at him. "And you think we did it?"

"I think bootleggers did it."

"Well maybe a bootlegger did or didn't, but it sure in hell wasn't Vince or me." He angrily wrestled a cigarette out of his shirt pocket, lit it and took a drag. The smoke he exhaled looked like dragon breath. "What kind of guy do you think I am anyways?" He took another forceful drag. "I may be a lot of things, but I'm not a killer!"

"It was a coincident. Same place, same time…"

"And you naturally assumed it was us." Pete puffed his cigarette and exhaled dragon smoke again.

"It seemed…"

"It seemed all right!" Pete flicked the cigarette overboard. His face was dark.

"I apologize."

"Yeah, you apologized all right."

"Hey, I said I'm sorry. You don't have to get all pissy over it."

"And you don't have to assume so much."

Now Rusty was growing agitated. "That's why I asked. End of story."

Before Pete could retort, a fast approaching boat caught his attention, distracting him from continuing the argument. Despite the lake being void of watercraft in their vicinity, the speeding boat was on the same course as *Rising Sun.*

"Hey, check it out," he said to Rusty as he nodded towards the stern and the closing boat.

Rusty looked over his shoulder and saw the vessel flying across the water and closing fast. He reached under the dash, pulled out binoculars and tossed it to Pete. "See who in hell it is."

Pete went back to the stern and spun the focus rings back and forth until the vessel's image in the glass sharpened. "Shit. It's Connors."

"Shit!"

Pete voice was anxious. "What do we do?"

"We maintain, until told otherwise."

Pete no longer needed the binoculars. "I don't know, man, but he's flying. He's going too fast to stop us."

Rusty looked over his shoulder again. He was shocked to see how close the CG157 was. "If that bastard doesn't give way, he's going right up our ass."

Pete hurried back to the cockpit. "What do we do?"

Rusty ignored him.

The CG157 let out two short blasts on its horn startling Pete.

"He's going to overtake us on port side," Rusty yelled over the CG157's engines' roar. Refusing to be bullied by Connors by slowing or changing course, he set his jaw and maintained speed and stayed the course. "Hang on. We're going to get hit with a bow wave."

Pete grabbed the windshield frame with one hand and the port rail with the other and braced himself.

The CG157 roared by so close, the *Rising Sun* yawed to port.

"You son-of-a bitch!" Rusty yelled as the speeding picket boat almost side-swiped the Sun. He glared purposely into the cockpit and got a good look at the boat's pilot, "Captain Kid" Connors. What he saw in those passing seconds was a cold face chiseled with high cheek bones and a dark band where Connors's eyes should be, the band being caused by the shade of his hat's bill. Connors stared straight ahead as if *Rising Sun* was not there, though Rusty knew he was watching out of the corner of his absent eyes like a shark. His suspicion was confirmed when he saw Connors do a double take as he passed. He followed the direction of Connors's attention and saw it was Pete that had caught Connors's eye. It could have been his imagination, but he swore Connors bared his teeth.

The picket boat swept by them with great force and as it pulled away, its wake made *Rising Sun* then yaw dangerously to starboard, throwing Pete to the opposite rail. He scrambled to catch himself from going overboard, grabbing and clinging onto the starboard rail along the bulwarks.

Rusty worked the wheel and throttle to right the rocking boat. When *Rising Sun* finally settled, he asked Pete if he was okay.

A trickle of blood oozed out of a cut above Pete's brow.

"You must have hit your head."

Pete touched his brow and looked at his red fingers tips. "He did that on purpose."

He looked shaken.

"He's a bully."

"He's mad in the head," Pete said.

"One thing's for sure, he seemed to recognize you," Rusty said, glancing askance at Pete.

Pete stumbled back to the cockpit bench seat next to Rusty. "Fucking asshole. Someone ought to put a bullet in his head."

"Is he the one who dumped you off on Middle Bass?"

"I wouldn't be sitting here if it was Connors. But we did have our run-ins and he could never nail me on anything." Pete lit another cigarette. His hands were trembling. "I always managed to jettison the cargo just before he got close and if you knew him, you would know how much he hates being outfoxed."

"I sure in hell hope he knows you're on the level now."

Pete grunted. "Connors believes what he wants to believe."

They watched the stern of the CG157 grow smaller and smaller until it disappear on the eastern horizon.

"Must have had bigger fish to fry than us."

"If he hurries, he may be able to catch the departing ferry from Avon Point and get in a few pistol whips on the crew and passengers."

Under different circumstances, the comment would have made Rusty grin, but somehow it didn't seem all that absurd, and besides, a new worry had taken root. "Seeing you on board here might be bad for me. I think I'm already on his shit list even though I was clean when he searched me."

"Who can say? If he's already got a taste of your blood, he'll pursue you until he devours you."

"You got a point. He had no idea you were on board when he pulled that stunt. Just thought he would have a little fun without anyone around to witness. We could have capsized. As it was, you damn near went overboard."

"Yeah," Pete muttered, "and I don't even know how to swim!"

Chapter 31

Four fishing charters later, it was Friday evening at Lime Kiln dock with Rusty waiting as Louis and Joe had stacked the last crates on *Rising Sun.*

"See you got the boat patched up real nice," Al said, glancing at the boat while he counted out the money for the run. "You oughta build a boat sometime."

"I did build boats years ago."

A hint of surprise flashed across Al's face. He handed Rusty the money. "Any more problems with the coasties?"

"They're stepping it up," Rusty said, stuffing the money in his pocket.

"That's 'cause they are moving all their boats to the Lakes 'cause Rum Row has been busted up. But those boats of theirs are slow as ox and just as clumsy."

"Not all of them. They built some new pickets and harbor patrollers that have some get up and go to them."

Al shrugged it off. "Runners can go through them like water through a sieve. No contest."

Rusty chuckled. "I heard they are now using confiscated rumrunners and commissioning them into the fleet as Coast Guard vessels. Using the runners own boats against them."

"I know for a fact, boat builders are building C.G. boats and runners alongside one another. The boats look the same, are built the same but its apples and oranges 'cause the runner can afford all the bangs and whistles that give him the faster boat while the feds half-ass it 'cause of costs."

Rusty smiled and untied the bow line. He was about to cast off when Al called to him.

"I almost forgot." He reached into his shirt pocket and pulled out a small envelope. "You and your misses are invited to my vineyard estate for the Harvest Party. You won't want to miss it. Every year, as the season is wrapping up, before the lake gets too cold, we throw a big party to celebrate the grape harvest. Everyone is there and those not invited wish they were. It's black tie and champagne, so dress to the nines."

Rusty removed his cap to scratch his head. "I don't know…?"

"What's there not to know? Last Saturday in September at 6 p.m. We privately charter a ferry out of Sandusky to bring guests over and take them back."

"I'll see what my wife says."

"Oh, she'll say yes if she loves to party, hoof it, eat Caviar and drink champagne. We even have a live band and it's always a big name but we keep it a surprise for the guests and they are never disappointed. Tell you what. I'm expecting you already. Remember that day at the vineyard when I invited you to dinner and you couldn't stay and I said next time? Its next time, and I'm holding you to it. It's settled."

Rusty raised his brows. "I'll run it by her."

"And make sure you are at the dock at 4:30 'cause the ferry leaves Sandusky at 5 p.m. sharp."

Rusty waved in acknowledgement.

Moments later, he and Joe were cruising their way to Sandusky. The last thing—the only thing—Joe said to him when the final crate was unloaded onto the dock was, "Don't bring any hog legs. You'll be checked at the door. We like our parties clean."

***

"Gosh, I don't know. I mean, it will be dark when we leave. I've never been on the lake in the dark on a small boat. It's scary enough in the day. And what if the lake is rough?" Di furrowed her brows.

"If it's rough, we don't go. And as for the dark, the ferry will be lit up like a carnival and we'll be with lots of people."

She grew quiet in the dark cab of the truck as it puttered and rattled through the shadowy countryside. The afternoon at the farm helping her Mom shred cabbage and pack it into sauerkraut jars had exhausted her and at the moment, the last thing she looked like and felt like was a party.

"We don't have to go. It's just that I know how you always loved to dance and party, and I haven't taken you out lately. Besides, this party sounds swanky and I thought you might like to see the estate. Al says they put on the Ritz. We'd be like those movie stars you read about." He glanced over at her but was unable to see her expression in the dark interior. "It's really up to you. As for me, I can take it or leave it."

"How would that look if you didn't show up at your boss's party especially after he practically threatened you for standing him up for dinner?"

Rusty laughed. "He didn't threaten me, Di. That's the way he talks. He was teasing."

"He's a gangster. How do you live like that on grape juice?"

"I told you, it's probably old money. His family has vineyards in Upstate and in the old country. They probably set him up here. Besides, grape juice consumption is at an all-time high." He heard her snort. "Like I said, it's up to you and I won't go if you don't."

"You got that part right. I don't know. I can't dance now anyways."

"I know, but you can listen to the music, rub shoulders with high society and eat caviar. Caviar, Di! Can you image us at a party that serves caviar? Think of what your Mah-jongg group would have to say about that?"

She giggled, and quickly added, "I would need an entire outfit."

"Of course. We'll go to Cleveland for that."

"Oh…oh…and you would need a tuxedo, Rusty." Her enthusiasm suddenly awakened and began mounting with each new thought. "And I would have to get my hair and nails done. Oh my God, when was the last time you were at the barbers?"

Rusty smiled. It wasn't so much the fact that she had decided to go that made him happy, it was the fact that the old Di– the one with a spirit as light as butterfly wings had resurfaced.

***

One tuxedo, one haircut, one set of polished Oxfords; one Esther Ralston-style finger wave taken from the cover of April's *Motion Picture* magazine, one *Youth Glow* facial clay treatment, one makeup makeover, one beaded emerald green silk and chiffon Basque gown with handkerchief hem (that Coco Chanel herself would approve of), one bronze beaded black net evening cap with metallic braid, one bronze beaded black purse, one pair of embroidered green silk stockings and one pair of T-Bar strap heels with rhinestone buckles later and they were ready to paint the town, or rather island, red.

In the time it took him to exchange the truck with Uncle Fritz's Model A and then change into his tux, Di was still not ready.

"Come on, you have been preening all day. By the time we get there, the ferry will be gone if you don't shake a leg."

Fifteen minutes of pacing passed before she emerged from the bedroom. She looked as glamorous and beautiful as any movie star on the cover of *PhotoPlay* and for a moment he couldn't believe what she saw in him. Still slender, no one would ever guess she was five months with child beneath her gown. "We should have left twenty minutes ago," he muttered, checking his watch.

"My coat…not that one, the one with the fur collar."

Rusty stifled a grimace. "You'll be the belle of the ball if you get your butt in the automobile so we can go, Miss Swanson. The ferry leaves at 5 and we have a ride ahead of us!"

She sniffed as he held the door open while she climbed inside.

He milked the Model A all he could for speed as they raced to Sandusky. Fritz would have a fit if he saw this, he thought with his foot heavy on the accelerator, dodging pot holes dotting the road. She was quiet for the most part, grunting and grabbing her stomach each time he missed and the vehicle hit a hole. The Model A clipped along, but despite its best efforts, they arrived at the dock just as the ferry was pulling away.

He banged the steering wheel. "God damn it!"

She stared at the ferry's stern with her mouth agape, and then burst into tears.

Silently, they watched the ferry head out into Sandusky Bay towards the islands.

He broke the silence. "Come on, get out of the car."

"What?"

"Just come on. We'll take *Rising Sun.* She just docked over there."

"Rusty?"

"Dry your eyes. You can touch up your makeup on the boat." He climbed out of the car and hurried toward the boat's slip. "Come on," he shouted, waving her on over his shoulder as she remained seated in the car.

She opened the door and stepped out hesitantly. "Rusty, I don't know if this is a good idea." But he was too absorbed in untying the boat's tarp to hear her.

She stepped lightly towards the dock, picking her way over the gravel in her heels. "Rusty, I don't know about taking the boat. It will be dark when we leave."

"We'll be fine." He glanced at the shrinking ferry as it passed through Bay's and Cedar Point's peninsulas. "We may even beat the ferry getting there."

"I am talking about afterwards- when we leave the island."

"Di, you have been on the *Goodtime* at night."

"It's a big boat. It had over a hundred people on it!"

"So, we'll stick with the ferry on the way back. We'll be in its lights and earshot of the crowd on board. And you won't have to worry about some rummy stepping on your toe or putting the moves on you on the cross back." He pulled the tarp cover off, folded it hastily, then stowed it in the bow. "Come on, Di, we can catch up with the ferry."

She stood stiffly on the dock, pulling her coat tightly around her.

He looked up at her, saw she was balking and sighed. "The water's calm. There's going to be a half moon tonight. The sky is clear." He waited a moment, then crawled out of the boat and went to her on the dock. "Opportunities like this don't come one's way too often. More than likely, this will be the only chance we get to do something like this."

She bit her lip and nodded.

He took her arm and helped her into the boat, and waited until she took a seat on the bench seat in the cockpit, then he cast off the lines and jumped in. He wasn't sure if it was the face powder or fear that made her face look pale. He stroked her shoulder as he sat next to her on the bench seat behind the wheel. "I am fully capable of this ...it's what I do, and *Rising Sun* is a sturdy and stable boat."

She shook her head in agreement.

He started the motor and eased from the dock. "Keep behind the windshield and your hair and cap will be fine." Within minutes, they were gaining on the ferry.

***

They docked soon after the ferry. He had decided to take it slow and tail it so as not to mess up her hair and to also know where to dock.

The ferry was half unloaded when he tied off next to it at Lime Kiln Dock.

"This is the dock where I pick up the grape juice on Fridays," he told her as he helped her out of the boat. "Of course it usually doesn't look like this."

The dock had taken on a different look and atmosphere. Colorful Chinese paper lanterns were strung about the dock in a festive mood and attendants in bow ties waited to assist departing passengers. Nearby an open sided bus that he recognized as the island's tour bus sat idle as it waited for guests to board and transport them to the vineyard estate.

"How exciting," she whispered as they slid into two empty spots on the bus.

The bus was loud with laughter and joviality as it made its way on the gravel tree-lined road toward the vineyard. She watched the headlights make shadows dance in the darkening woods beyond the highlighted trees bordering the road, adding to the mystery as to what lie ahead. But the mystery seemed limited to her alone.

Everyone seemed to know one another, but no one seem to notice them. The party that apparently began on the ferry had carried over to the bus. Rusty winced over the raucous. She poked him in the ribs and giggled.

After a short trip, a glow of lights could be seen through the dusky trees. The bus headed for it as though it was a beacon. They rounded a corner and a large double story stone house came into view.

She leaned her head out the bus and could see the high stone entrance as the bus passed through the open iron gates leading into the estate and headed up the torch lined driveway. It came to a stop at the brightly lit front porch of the manor house.

Rusty noted the absence of the Dobermans, but he guessed Giuseppe would be close.

He helped Di off as the guests spilled out from both sides of the bus. A familiar voice boomed from the porch which was lit up like a theater marquee.

"*Benvenuto*, welcome, come right in, my friends." It was Al, dressed to the nines in tails, cigar smoke encircling his head. "Come in, come in," he repeated as the guests made their way to the porch.

Rusty could see Di's eyes were wide and taking in every detail. Her eyes swept over the limestone walls, Greek Revival architectural detailing, white porch pillars and two four feet high stone Venus de Milo statues flanking the doorway. Jazz music spilled from the open doorway. They stepped up onto the porch.

Al greeted each guest with a hug or handshake. "He seems personable enough," Di whispered.

"He's got the market cornered on that," he whispered back.

Al gushed when he spotted them. "Mr. Rusty, you came. I knew you would and I finally get to meet your beautiful wife." He shook Rusty's hand vigorously, and kissed her hand lightly.

Rusty noticed her blush.

"Now I know why Rusty always rushes to get home."

"Thank you for the invitation, Mr. Trapani," she said, blushing again.

"Enjoy…enjoy," Al said with a slight bow and swept his hand to the open door.

Did Di bat her lashes? Rusty wasn't sure. He took her arm and led her into the foyer before she became too tangled in Al's web of charm and almost ran into a wall named Giuseppe. *Ah, there he is.*

Giuseppe circled him and moved close. *Here comes the frisk Joe had mentioned*, he thought, but out of the corner of his eye, he caught Al giving Giuseppe a discreet shake no of his head. Giuseppe backed away.

Rusty sighed with relief. Giuseppe had a way of making you feel guilty even if you weren't. "Hello, Giuseppe," Rusty said cautiously testing the waters.

Giuseppe grunted in response. Rusty put his arm around Di. She was always a good ice breaker.

"I would like you to meet my wife…Di. Di, this is Giuseppe. I apologize for not knowing your last name," he added.

Giuseppe's eyes, like two steel marbles, rolled over to Di. His dour face softened. He held out a hand that resembled a bear's paw. She placed hers in it. His hand could have swallowed hers, but it didn't. He held it lightly as if it was fragile. "Nice to meet you, Mrs.," he said with a thick Sicilian accent.

"The pleasure is mine," Di said coyly and slipped her hand from his. As she turned away she made bug-eyes at Rusty. She grabbed his arm and they walked through an arch and a two story reception hall packed wall to wall with laughing, dancing and drinking guests spread out before them. For Di, it was like walking onto a movie set; for Rusty, it was like walking into money.

The hall was decorated in Art Deco design from its geometric wall sconces to the bold, contemporary furnishing, but the paintings were Italian classical scenes reminiscent of Caravaggio and Titian. Tall Parlor and Sago Palms dotted the room and Boston Ferns cascaded from columns. In the center of the floor, an eight foot high water fountain lit with orange and green lights spouted while goldfish swam beneath in a small pool. The black and white checkered board floor was made of imported Italian marble and an open staircase gracefully curved to the second floor balcony where a twelve piece band was playing. Rusty looked up and saw a crystal chandelier the size of a Model T overhead. He poked Di and pointed up. *Hubba-hubba* escaped her lips.

The band finished *I'll See You in My Dreams* and went right in to *If You Knew Susie*.

"Tell me that's not who I think it is," Di said, looking up at the band on the balcony.

"It very well could be. They were just over at the Crystal Garden and Al says he gets big names."

Di dropped her jaw and looked at Rusty. "Guy Lombardo?"

"And his Royal Canadians."

She muffled her squeal. "Good lord, Rusty. Who is this Al anyways?"

"I am not sure, but if I see Capone, Dalitz or the Licavoli brothers in the crowd, we are definitely going to cut bait and run, caviar or not!"

"Pos-i-lute-ly!"

"Capone? Did I hear the name Capone?"

Rusty turned around and Pete was standing there. He was holding two drinks and a burning cigarette. At first, Rusty didn't recognize him as Pete was all polish from his Valentino—parted hair to his spats. Oddly, he looked good spiffed up in a tux.

"I was just teasing my wife that Capone was…um…that he is rumored to come to this area."

"I wish," Pete said.

"Are you serious?" Di asked. She was all eyes.

"This is my wife, Di," Rusty interrupted. "Di, this is Pete. You remember me talking about Pete."

"So you're Pete. I am glad to meet you. My husband tells me you help him on the charters." She understood now how Rusty could take an instant liking to him. He was easy and amiable with movie star looks.

"I'd offer you my hand, but…" Pete held up the two glasses.

"Now that's what I'd call a two-fisted drinker," Rusty said.

Pete laughed. "One's for my date. She's the one standing by the tall plant putting on more munitions. A real Dumb Dora but she's a hoofer on the dance floor and a bearcat in…uh," Pete flushed and avoided Di's gaze. "I mean, we're not serious or anything." He cleared his throat. "To answer your question if I am serious about Capone…"

"Capone, again…aarrrggghh. You're not boring them too about your life's ambition to see Capone, are you?" The tall, thin "Dumb Dora," in her early twenties, lifted one of the glasses from Pete's hand. She wore a short sequined copper colored dress trimmed with a fringe hem that shimmered when she walked. A rhinestone headband with an orange feather sat upon her bobbed dark, almost black, brunette head. A long gold and black silk scarf wrapped around her neck with one long end draped over her shoulder in front and the other end over her back. Her eyes were heavily made with deep purple shadow and thick black liner and her brilliant red lipstick screamed *fire*.

Di felt suddenly conservative.

The flapper leaned into Di as though sharing a secret. Her breath smelled rank with liquor. "He heard rumors that Capone has been seen at the Castle in Lorain and that he gets his hair cut at an underground city in Bucyrus." She snorted, and Di winced. "So now he's always on the lookout for him like he's Lindbergh or Valentino or something."

Pete glared at her. "He's famous just like your movie stars, doll. Besides, Valentino is dead." She sneered at him.

"More like infamous," Rusty said. "Either way, he's one guy I would rather see from afar than up close and personal."

The band struck up *Yes, Sir, That's My Baby* and the flapper began dancing in place. Di stepped back to avoid getting splashed by her drink.

"Come on…let's hoof it," the flapper said and grabbed Pete by the arm.

Pete looked at Rusty and rolled his eyes as she dragged him off in the direction of the dance floor.

A waiter in tails appeared before Rusty and Di and presented them a tray of glass flutes filled with champagne. They each took a glass.

Di took a sip, blinked her eyes and rubbed under her nose. "That's got a tickle to it!"

A small round woman in a long black and silver sequin and Deco beaded evening gown and a rhinestone tiara with a long peacock feather picked her way through the crowd towards them. Her black hair was pulled back tight into a bun at her nape, and a cigarette burned at the end of a long cigarette holder she held poised.

"Welcome to our party. I am Constance Trapani." She extended a gloved hand to Rusty. "My husband, Al, pointed you out...Rusty and his wife, Di. We are delighted to have you as a guest at our home and so happy you could attend the party. We throw this every year to celebrate the end of harvest and rejoice its success with family and friends. It's also a way to thank our employees for their dedicated service."

Rusty had to stop himself from transfixing on the long peacock feather which swayed, bobbed and whipped above her with each head movement.

"I see you have champagne already, but there is also a bar in back and banquet tables brimming with culinary delights along the side wall over there at your service," she said pointing her cigarette holder to each area.

"Thank you, Mrs. Trapani," Di said, but Mrs. Trapani was already turning away.

They watched until she was absorbed by the laughing, dancing, drinking crowd, her tall peacock feather and circle of smoke the only visible signs of her whereabouts.

Di turned to Rusty. "I don't think Prohibition is working."

He smiled. "You know the old saying about forbidden fruit?"

"Let's go check out the food, and I want to see Guy Lombardo up close. Jeeze, I wish my friends could see this! I feel like a movie star."

"I feel like a fish out of water."

That night they slow danced, ate caviar, drank champagne and the Trapani family's red Madeira. They made small talk with business owners, police and fire chiefs, councilmen, judges as well as many of the island's locals. They were also introduced to Trapani employees and extended Trapani family members. They even met Al's nonno from Upstate New York, although the conversation was strained as the old man spoke no English. But it wasn't until actor, Dean Swenson with Broadway star, Leena Lee on his arm showed up halfway through the night with an A list entourage that Di went weak in the knees.

"I'll be damned," was all Rusty could say under his breath, trying not to look star struck.

The party roared into the night.

***

"How are you doing?" He asked Di, noting she was looking peaked.

"The spirit is willing, but the flesh is weak. I feel tired and a bit lightheaded."

He checked his watch and his brows flew up. "No wonder, it's past one!" He looked about the room.

The party was in full swing with no indication of breaking up. Booze was flowing and couples were crashing into one another as they danced the Lucky Lindy on the crowded floor.The bar was lined shoulder to shoulder and Dean Swenson was boasting loud and slurry about the misery of having to work with directors like DeMille and stars like Crawford while Leena Lee draped herself in a Peacock chair with a cocktail in one hand and a cigarillo in the other and rambled on endlessly one Broadway tune after another. The oversize room suddenly became too hot and too loud and too small.

"I don't think the ferry will be leaving anytime soon," Rusty said, raising his voice over the raucous.

"Doesn't appear so," she said.

"We don't need the ferry for security. It's just over sixteen miles from here to Sandusky and we can see shoreline lights along the way."

She grimaced.

"The lake is calm. We'll be perfectly safe and from the looks of it, home in bed before the ferry even leaves the island's dock."

"This isn't working like we planned."

"Never does."

She heaved a sigh. Her eyes were so tired, they were having trouble focusing. In fact, the last conversation she had with Judge Lintly's wife, she had to fight to keep her eyes focused and her lids from drooping, hoping the chatty woman wouldn't notice.

"I'll tell Al we are leaving and get our coats."

She made a face and shook her head *no.* "Let's wait another thirty minutes or so. They've got to be getting tired, too."

He looked about the room. "You think so, uh? The second band is still going strong." Lombardo and his Royal Canadians had wrapped up at 11 p.m. and was replaced by a popular local band that performed at area ballrooms and dance halls along the north shore. When the band struck up *Tiger Rag*, some began dancing in place while many were half under the table.

"I'll get our coats," he repeated.

***

"I was hoping we could find time to talk in the billiard room," Al said when he learned of their leaving.

"Di is tired. She's with child, so she wears out pretty fast."

"Oh," Al said, and then added, "But the ferry isn't ready to leave yet."

"We used my boat to come over."

"Oh," was Al's response again. "Well, we can talk another time. But to give you something to think over, I was going to propose an additional route to you since we are expanding."

"I'll give it thought. Till then, thank you for the invitation. My wife really enjoyed herself."

Al broke into a grin. "I told you so."

"Could you also thank your wife for us? I know Di wanted to personally thank her but can't seem to find her in the crowd."

"Yes, yes of course. Take your wife with your little bambino home to rest." Al snapped his fingers to a man in tails waiting nearby. "The gentleman would like his and his missus's coat, and tell Mario to get the Packard and drive them to the dock."

As Rusty and Di stepped out into the fresh night air, Rusty caught a glimpse of a hulking dark figure standing in the shadows at the end of the porch. It looked like the shape of an icebox with a head on top.

"Goodnight, Giuseppe," he said and heard a grunt in response.

A 4-door '27 Packard pulled up to the steps. A baby faced, round-headed young man resembling Al minus twenty or so years sat behind the wheel. Rusty helped Di into the automobile, and they rode to the dock in silence.

After a thank you and goodnight to Mario, they found themselves alone on the deserted dock under the colorful glow of the Chinese Lanterns. Beyond, laid the black void of the lake. The sound of water lapped against the ferry whose lights were dim and appeared vacant. Perhaps the captain and crew are catching a few *zzzs*, he thought, or are at the party. He started to untie the mooring lines securing *Rising Sun*.

"One moment," she said, placing a hand on Rusty's arm just as he was about to board. "I just want to savor this a little longer." She gazed at the lanterns and looked wistfully towards the direction of the house. "This really happened, didn't it?"

"My imagination couldn't come up with this, so it must have."

"Could we just rest on the boat until the others arrive? That way the night wouldn't end so soon, and we wouldn't be so alone out there."

"So soon? We've been here for over seven hours!" He then sighed. "I'm pretty worn out myself, and those people might whoopee all night. Be there when the sun comes up, most likely, passed out with hangovers and swollen ankles and what not..." his voice trailed. He stepped into the boat and reached for her hand.

She didn't notice it, for she was transfixed on the black waters of the lake.

"If you look straight ahead, you can see the lights along the shoreline of Catawba Point from here. Once we get under way, we'll see lights from Kelleys Island and Lakeside. We'll always be in sight of lights. See, there's Marblehead Light shining across the water. Remember how beautiful you said its light looked on that moonlight cruise from the deck of the *Goodtime*? You said it was so romantic. Well, this will be too. The waves are just a ripple, the moon is shining, we are in constant sight of shore lights, and we have the lighthouse showing us the way from here to the bay. Cap Huddleson will probably be watching us from his window, sipping his tea as we go by."

"Cap Huddleson will be sawing logs." She felt a shiver despite the warm night air rising from the tepid lake, still radiating summer's heat it had been collecting and storing all season.

Another shaft of light reached out from Marblehead Light and swept across the water. It did not reach them, but it showed the way. She watched the light pass over the water, and then stepped into the boat. "I'll keep my eyes closed and pretend its daylight."

"At this rate, it soon will be." He untied the mooring lines and started the engine. As the boat drifted from the dock, she stiffened. He saw her eyes riveted on the dock and its bright colorful lights as he turned the boat to head out into the inky open water under a black canopy filled with stars and waxing moon.

As they headed southeast in the waters between Catawba Point and Kelleys Island, he made small talk about the beauty of the night and their progress lest her eyes were truly closed. He pointed out landmarks in case she was watching, and then turned the subject to the party hoping that would take her mind off the ride.

Twenty minutes had passed since they left the dock. "We're over halfway to Sandusky," he said with cheer in his voice. "If you open your eyes you will see how close we are to the lighthouse. It's practically blinding."

Di flashed open her eyes. The sight of the sweeping beams from the rotating Fresno lens and the lights highlighting the white pillar-shaped lighthouse gave her reassurance.

Rising Sun glided past Marblehead Point and the lighthouse and began her arc towards Sandusky.

"Since its going good, we can cut off a lot of driving time if you want to take the boat straight on to Vermilion instead."

"No!" was the curt reply.

No sooner had she said that, then the air seemed to split over Rusty's head. He jumped, and then heard a far off splash followed by a loud report. For a split second he was stunned. He recognized the sound but thought it not possible. Another crack of air was heard as it split over the bow causing an instantaneous change in air pressure, another far off splash followed by a report. It was a sound he prayed he would never hear again—a sound he last heard in the North Atlantic during the war, a sound that had chilled his blood with fear before rallying him to fight.

"Down!" he yelled to Di as he pushed her to the floor. He jammed the throttle wide open and *Rising Sun* rose in the water. Her bow parted the waves until she reached a planing speed then she skimmed over the dark water.

His eyes, wild with alarm, searched the dark void where he had heard the sound of the report. Using the intermittent beams of light radiating from the lighthouse, he tried desperately to try to catch a glimpse of what lie beyond out in the dark lake from where the gunshots emanated.

"What is it? What's happening?" Her voice was frenzied.

"Just stay down," he ordered. *Rising Sun* flew towards the two peninsulas that guarded Sandusky Bay's entrance.

He heard a hollow thud to his port bow and highlighted by a shaft of light from the lighthouse, saw wood splinters fly into the air followed by another report. This time, he caught a muzzle flash piercing the darkness off his portside towards the northeast. Between the strike and the flash, he figured the shooter was a mile way.

"Chrissake," he cried, and clenched his teeth. He could feel the hair on his neck standing on end. He made a sharp turn to starboard to cut closer to shore. The boat listed to right and Di rolled into the steering column.

She began screaming hysterically, covering her head with her hands as she crouched in the bow.

"Are you all right? Are you okay? Di?" he shouted.

"Rusty, what's happening," she screamed.

He hated to tell her. "We are being shot at."

She began to cry.

He quickly assessed his advantages. He knew where the shots were coming from and the distance they were traveling from. He also knew the bullets were .30 caliber. Whoever was shooting at them was using the big stuff, and they had apparently been lying in wait like a barracuda in a reef. *Had they mistaken them for someone else?*

Another shot hit the water near the stern and Di's sobs turned into wails. *How in the hell can they be so accurate in the dark and at that range?* He began ticking off in his head each possible culprit. A rumrunner would be more interested in running and if armed, they usually used handguns, shotguns or rifles; a hijacker would have chased him down or intercepted him and they wouldn't be using big artillery as they would not want to risk damaging the goods; fishermen-no way; that left Coast Guard. Less than half their boats were equipped with .30 caliber guns—the biggest issued, but they were known to fire a warning shot across the bow if they suspected a rumrunner as their objective was to capture not sink. Whoever was out there on the lake lurking in the darkness wasn't interested in scaring or discouraging or arresting. They were interested in destroying. Only one man, one crew fit that ticket. The same ones that had been dogging him since the grape juice charters.

Shoot first; ask questions later. Pete's words echoed in his head.

"Di! Di! Listen to me. Listen! Put the life ring on. Di, are you listening?"

"I'm too scared to move."

"I know, but you got to."

"I don't want to die."

"That's why I want you to put the ring on- just in case..."

"What? In case what?" She was choking on her tears.

"In case..." *damn he didn't want to scare her more*, "In case something happens to the boat."

He heard her rustling around in the bow. She was blubbering and beginning to hyperventilate. He had never heard her make those sounds before and it curdled his blood.

"Is it on? Di? *Is it on*?"

Silence.

"Di!"

"Yes, damn it!"

He checked over his left shoulder to see if he could see anything. Whoever it was, they were just beyond the shafts of light from the lighthouse, lurking in the darkness, and *Rising Sun* was silhouetted each time a beam swung around, something no doubt planned.

The same instant he heard an incoming whistle, he felt the boat shudder. One pounder. They were using cannon. Shards of wood flew all directions and he ducked, covering his head to avoid being hit by splinters. The muzzle flash caught his eye again, only this time it was brighter and the report was quicker and more earsplitting. The assailant had closed distance and was using cannon with one pound balls. He heard the sound of water rushing into the bilge. *Rising Sun* had taken a hit amidships just below the waterline, simultaneously halting her engine. His heart landed in his throat.

He scrambled for the bilge pump. Water was pouring in, but he refused to accept the fact that the pump could not keep up. Di's screams punctuated the silent darkness.

He grabbed her arm and shook it. "Di, quiet, I don't want them to hear us."

He grabbed his flashlight and pull started the pump anyways and watched in horror as the water slowly swallowed the pump. He felt the little world of *Rising Sun* begin to move in slow motion. Di's screams seemed so far away. Like *Rising Sun*, he felt heavier and heavier. Like a dream that seems to go on and on but in actuality lasts only a split second, so did his daze. The alarm went off in his head and Di's screams became sharp again and the world sped back to normal. He sprang into action. Grabbing a coil of rope, he pulled Di out from the bow and lashed one end around her and the life ring. As he did, she shook uncontrollably but fell eerily silent, and he knew she was most likely going into shock. As he lashed the other end around himself and grabbed another life ring and the flashlight, he could feel lake water about his ankles. *Rising Sun* was slowly sinking, and they were a half a mile from the nearest shoreline which was Marblehead's east coast. His brain scrambled for advantages. The water was warm, still holding the heat of summer. They were within the light of the lighthouse and Di was a good swimmer. But she stood stiff as a corpse and white as a ghost. Her lack of tears and screams chilled him more so than the hysterical screaming. The water was half way to his knees now, and he knew it was a matter of time before they would have to abandon the shelter of *Rising Sun* and be at the mercy of the lake and their attackers. He reached under his steering wheel and grabbed the crow bar just in case their attackers came after them, but it was heavy and awkward and would only be a hindrance when he swam, so he let it slip into the water on the deck.

It was an odd feeling he felt-waiting to sink... waiting for the water to swallow the last vestiges of his boat and in turn, casting them into dark, bottomless waters. *Just waiting and riding it out to the bitter last.* He had no radio, and yelling for help would be a useless waste of energy that would only give their position away to whoever was out beyond the light, letting them know there were survivors. He would swim for shore, dragging Di and pray she wouldn't fight him or surrender to the water. He felt empty, but wired. His senses were full throttle to hyper sensitive making him feel like a caged animal looking to fight or flee. He searched the black void, his ears aching for a sound. The *Rising Sun* was now disappearing below him. He shook Di hard. She had to be responsive and ready to act. He grabbed her hand and pushed away from the submerged boat, pulling her away with him...

***

The second shot woke Cap Huddleson out of his sleep in his chair by the window, an open book resting in his lap. His tea had long gone cold. He stood and stretched. He had a habit of falling asleep while reading when the night was quiet and no storms or distress calls required his vigilance. *Was it cracks of thunder that awoke him? Fireworks from Cedar Point Amusement Park?* He grabbed a light jacket and walked out into the night air. It was silent except for the soft lapping of the water against the rocks, and above him spread the stars and a half moon. He walked to the rocky shoreline next to the lighthouse and gazed across the water at the distant lights of Cedar Point still blazing away. No fireworks, just business as usual on a Saturday night. The amusement park and its dance hall were a good marker to the bay's entrance as was the lighthouse, he thought. He checked his watch. The ferry from Put-in-Bay should be coming by any time now, he figured. That's when he heard another report. *Was that a gunshot?* He strained to listen for any sound in the direction it came from. *Was that a woman's scream?*

Cap Huddleson ran for the lighthouse and bounded up the steep, winding steps. He was breathless by the time he reached the three story window facing east. Huffing and puffing, he threw the window open and leaned out with the binoculars and caught sight of an object half a mile off shore out in the lake. Each time the shafts of light swept past that area, it spotlighted the object for a second. He could see it was a boat.

"My God. It's the ferry!" He muttered. Just then, a flash of light on the horizon caught his eye, followed by boom. His mouth fell open. *Are they being fired upon?* He rushed down to the radio and contacted the Coast Guard Station located on Marblehead.

"We have a MAYDAY. There's a boat in trouble about a half mile east-southeast of the lighthouse. I think it may be the ferry from Put-in-Bay!" He gave the coordinate. The Coast Guard said they were on their way. He then telephoned the police chief whose jurisdiction covered Marblehead, Lakeside and Catawba.

"There may be people in the water," he explained. "Help and an ambulance on standby are needed. Oh, and chief, I think the ferry may have been hit by gunfire." With that, Cap Huddleson grabbed a spotlight and a lantern and hurried to a small boat equipped with an outboard motor moored near the lighthouse. He was underway, headed for the boat in distress when he heard the fifth and final shot.

***

Rusty pulled his way with one arm through the water, the other arm looped around Di's life ring. His life ring was cumbersome and made swimming difficult and slow, but he didn't want to take a chance with exhaustion or hysteria from Di without it. He had seen too many guys gamble without preservers in the war and lose. Thankfully, calm water and a calm Di made the arduous task less difficult. He prayed it was his shaking her to her senses and not shock that made her so quiet and compliant. He alternated swallowing and spitting water while keeping one eye on the dark shoreline and one on her. Minutes earlier, after *Rising Sun* had been swallowed by the black waters, he had heard the motor on their attacker's vessel turn over, then the rumble of engines that soon trailed into the distance heading northeast until he could no longer hear it. He thanked God that the hunters had abandoned their prey.

A spotlight in the direction he was swimming suddenly blinded him. A beam of light swept the waters around them until it finally rested on them. Rusty winced in the brightness of the light. He then heard the hum of an outboard motor. A voice behind the spotlight called out.

"Ahoy. Rescue is on the way."

It was then that he heard Di begin to weep and knew she was okay.

***

When Cap Huddleson arrived, he saw only two people in the water and no boat. He reached for Di and with Rusty pushing below from the water, pulled her into his boat. She was soaked to the bone and coughing water. Her dark hair was plastered to her head. She had no coat and was missing one shoe. His heart sank when he saw her pretty gown, drooped and waterlogged, and her lovely face ashen and her eye make-up smeared, giving her a ghoulish, hollow eye-look. He then reached for Rusty and dragged him aboard. Once aboard, Huddleson saw him go limp. His face was drained, and his coat, from what Huddleson surmised was part of a tuxedo, was missing. The fine shirt clung to Rusty's body and his soggy pants dripped with lake water. The bow tie was missing as was his shoes.

"Where is the ferry?" Cap Huddleson asked. There was alarm in his voice.

"It's still at the dock at Put-in-Bay," Rusty said between coughs of water.

Cap Huddleson looked puzzled. "That wasn't the ferry?"

Rusty shook his head no.

"Are there more or are you the only two?"

"Only two of us." Rusty put his arm around Di who had begun to shake uncontrollably. "We left the party ahead of the ferry. We were in my Lyman heading for Sandusky when a vessel, stationed about a mile northeast, opened fire on us and sank us."

"*Rising Sun*." Cap Huddleson recollected. "I recognize you now."

"If I find that son-of-a-bitch who did this I am going to kill him."

Cap Huddleson's face fell grim. He grabbed a blanket he had brought along and he wrapped it around them. He didn't respond to the comment, but he looked troubled by it.

He started for shore.

They could see flashlights appearing along the bank. Then a bright spotlight switched on them. Vehicles were being positioned to shine their headlights out into the water. Cap Huddleson looked at Di. "Don't you worry, missus, the cavalry has arrived."

A loud motor from the water caught Huddleson and Rusty's attention. Rusty stiffened at first until he realized it came from the opposite direction of the attacking vessel. It was a Coast Guard harbor patrol boat rounding the tip of Marblehead. Their spotlights swept the water. A guardsman's voice yelled, "Ahoy!"

***

A small army of hands were reaching to assist Di and Rusty from the boat once it landed. Cap Huddleson steadied Di as she staggered out and into the arms of the rescuers. He then took Rusty's arm and passed him off to Police Chief Stoddard and a volunteer fireman. It was then he noticed blood on the floor of the boat. He scrambled after Rusty.

"Did you get shot or hurt?"

Rusty shook his head.

"What about the missus?" Cap Huddleson's voice was anxious.

"No. I don't think so." He noted Huddleson's tone and it made him uneasy. "Why?"

Cap Huddleson pulled him back towards the boat and pointed his flashlight beam at the small pool of blood.

A wave of panic crossed Rusty's face. "Oh my God…the baby."

Chapter 32

Uncle Fritz and Di's mother rushed to the reception desk of Sandusky's hospital. Her mother's face was wrought with angst and she was breathing short and shallow. Rusty had called them after he and Di had arrived at the hospital, forgetting he had taken the Model A and leaving them only with the two-seater truck. Di's mother burst into tears when she spotted Rusty pacing in the adjoining waiting room. They hurried to join him.

"How is she?" Uncle Fritz asked.

"She is hemorrhaging. They rushed her back, and I wasn't allowed to go with her. I haven't heard anything since."

Uncle Fritz rubbed his chin. He watched his sister muffle her sobs with a handkerchief over her mouth."You said someone shot the boat up and it sank."

"Yes."

Uncle Fritz was grim-faced. "Do you have an idea who did it?"

"Yes."

"Did you tell the police and Coast Guard about your hunch?"

"No."

Uncle Fritz looked puzzled. "Why?"

Rusty ignored the question. "Where's Di's father?"

"You took the four-seater and left us the truck. Di's father is contacting the brothers at the mill. They're working graveyard shift now. He'll ride up with them in their auto."

A nurse walked into the room. Her face was somber. Rusty froze. She looked at Fritz and the mother.

"They're with me. They're family," he said.

She crossed over to him and in a low and sympathetic coached voice said, "I am sorry to have to tell you that your wife lost the baby."

Rusty went weak in the knees. "And my wife?" His bottom lip was shaking.

"She's resting. She's lost a lot of blood and is traumatized by the events. We gave her something to relax and sleep, but she needs to stay here for a while under observation and until she can get her strength back."

"Can I see her?" He could hardly breathe.

The nurse looked at him. His eyes were rheumy with tears and his face worn and beat. His damp tuxedo was half missing, and his hair disheveled. Her face softened. "Okay…but just a peek." Then she added to the others, "Just her husband."

***

Although she was asleep, she didn't look peaceful. Her face looked scrunched and strained. Now and then, she would toss or moan. As soon as he stepped away from her door and into the hall, he pounded the concrete wall and wept. He waited until he could compose himself, and then headed back to the waiting room.

Uncle Fritz watched him anxiously as he approached, noticing his red eyes.

"She's asleep. They assured me she should be all right," he said in a tight voice.

"Thank God," her mother cried.

Uncle Fritz was silent as he processed the information, then said, "That's good, ja? Some bed rest, some home rest..."

Silence followed until Rusty broke it. "What time is it?"

Uncle Fritz took out his pocket watch. "Two minutes to five."

"I'll be timing it just about right. Can you hold the fort for me here? There's someone I need to see."

"It better be the law," Uncle Fritz said.

"It will be," he said with an edge.

Uncle Fritz didn't like the way he said that. "Don't go off half-cocked. We have enough on our plate."

Rusty set his jaw and started for the door. "Our plate's only half full!"

The comment grated Uncle Fritz. He grabbed Rusty by the arm. "Listen. Di is like a daughter to me. I don't have children of my own. She is as my child, and I have a right to know who's behind this as well as what you're up to. What you do affects Di and that affects me!"

Rusty was hesitant. Uncle Fritz's eyes were burning holes through him and his grip was tight. He never saw him so intense before and realized he had underestimated Di's uncle as a gentle man. He relented. "I had my hunch. Then I overheard something the lighthouse keeper said to the police chief when we were getting into the ambulance."

Uncle Fritz grip tightened and he shook his arm as though shaking out the information. "What did you hear?"

Rusty lowered his voice. "The keeper said he caught a glimpse of the vessel just after the last shot. Apparently, the vessel got a little too close and the light beam from the lighthouse caught it for a split second as it was turning away."

Uncle Fritz was riveted.

"Said it was a picket boat... a Coast Guard picket boat."

Uncle Fritz felt the blood drain from his lips. He relaxed his grip. Rusty might as well as cold cocked him with the revelation. "Will the police chief investigate?"

"I don't know." He pressed his hands on his forehead as if to hold his thoughts together, then he looked up. "It's hard to tell the good guys from the bad guys anymore. The chief may even cover for them. For all we know, they could be in cahoots together."

"Cahoots for what? Shooting at innocent boats?"

“They may have thought I was someone else… or running liquor. That’s what I got to find out.”

“Wait. I’ll go with you. Di’s father and brothers should be here any moment now, then you and I will go together. This is going to need a cool head.”

Rusty shook his head. “You’re needed here.”

“So are you!”

He ignored the remark. “I’m taking the truck. The guys can drive over to the dock in their auto to pick up the Model A and bring it back here.” He started for the door again.

“Wait. They’ll be here soon. I want to go too.”

But Rusty wasn’t waiting. He pushed through the doors.

“Don’t do anything stupid. Di needs you more now than ever,” Uncle Fritz called to him.He cursed under his breath as he watched Rusty go. He felt like running after him, more to stop him than to go with him. He saw the look in Rusty’s eyes. They were dark and snapping like electrical wires short circuiting. He looked at Di’s mother slumped in a chair and sobbing. He felt ripped in two. He cursed again, wishing his brother-in-law and nephews would hurry.

Chapter 33

Rusty stopped the truck just beyond the Coast Guard Station but within view of the dock. Just as he had figured, CG157 had just docked after an all nighter out on the lake. He had watched as a harbor patrol boat cast off moments before CG157 arrived to begin its shift, and a moored Coast Guard tug was active with preparations to begin its day. He yanked the parking brake, cut the engine and stormed towards the station doors. He wasn't halfcocked like Uncle Fritz had said, he was full cocked. He jerked the door open, and in doing so, the heads of two guardsmen and a dispatcher simultaneously snapped up from their tasks, their eyes riveting on him. They knew instantly that he was upset.

"I want to see the captain of CG157!" His voice was thick and his eyes smoldered like hot coals.

The guardsmen straightened up, eyeballing him.

"Okay," the dispatcher said. "But tell me what the problem is."

"It's between me and the captain."

The dispatcher frowned. "You just don't come busting in here and making demands. There's protocol to follow."

"Then I'll wait here until he shows up."

The dispatcher slammed the pencil he had been holding to the desk. He sat back in his chair and sized Rusty. "The captain may have left for the day. He just finished his shift."

"Then check!"

"You're not the one giving orders here, fella. You mind yourself. You're dealing

with federal law here."

"Law my ass. You want to talk about law, then you tell Connors and his crew to get their crooked asses in here and we'll talk law all right."

The guardsmen exchanged cautious glances.

The dispatcher stiffened. "Now you listen, buddy, if this is about a grievance, you fill out this paperwork here and it goes through the necessary channels." He passed a paper to him, but Rusty refused to take it. "If you know what's good for you, you best not make trouble or I'll throw your ass in the brig."

'What do you want to see him about," one of the guardsman said.

"That's between me and him."

The guardsman swaggered towards Rusty. He was tall and lanky. The dispatcher held out his arm to stop him, but the guardsman brushed it aside. "For your information, wise guy, me and him," he said thumbing to the shorter guardsman, "happen to be the crewmen of CG157, so maybe you can tell us your problem."

Rusty muscles tensed. He recognized their smug faces from the newspapers. "You and Captain Kid shot up my boat with *my wife* and me in it. We were coming back from a party on Put-in-Bay. The shooting took place off Marblehead Point." His face felt as hard as granite and his words hissed like steam through his clenched teeth. "You bastards sunk my boat. My wife almost drowned...you killed my baby. So you tell your captain to get his ass in here because I got a score to settle with all of you!"

"You said a baby was killed?" The dispatcher shot a look to the tall guardsman who ignored his questioned.

"What's this about a score to settle...did I hear you right? Because if you got something to settle, we *will* settle it here and now."

Rusty and the guardsman crossed towards one another, and the dispatcher jumped between them. A verbal fracas erupted between the two men with the dispatcher sandwiched between them. The second guardsman moved closer. He had his fists doubled.

From the back of the room, hidden by a half wall, a third man rose from where he had been sitting and listening unbeknownst to Rusty. "Pipe down!" the voice boomed.

Rusty's eyes shot towards him. He knew instantly it was Captain Connors. Coldness oozed through his dark and stabbing eyes. For the first time, he was able to see the face clearly. Connors's cheekbones sat high and sharp, chiseled out of a marble hard face. The cool façade, though, was betrayed by the piercing, burning eyes. When he spoke his voice was deliberate and booming in a theatrical way as if he were addressing more than one man. It instantly silenced the room. "What makes you so sure it was Coast Guard that sank your boat?" He had an audience to please.

"Because the shots came from a Coast Guard picket boat."

"You seem pretty sure about it."

"I am."

"And when was this?"

"Last night. After midnight."

"And you could tell—the dark of midnight, that not only was it a Coast Guard vessel, it was specifically a picket boat?"

Rusty glared at him.

"How far was this vessel from you when you were struck?"

"Struck my boat three times, first almost a mile, then a half a mile away. At that distance, it had no reason to fire upon me."

"A half mile away, and you assume not only was it a picket boat, it was specifically the CG157?" Connors swaggered up to Rusty. He looked at the two guardsmen and shook his head as if in disbelief. "This man must have supernatural eyesight since he claims he can see call numbers half a mile away in the dark."

The two men snickered.

Connors circled Rusty like a shark looking for a place to bite. Despite his cool and collected demeanor, his neck was beet red, made more obvious by the white collar of his uniform, and his eyes burned like windows to a furnace. "There are two things you need to learn, boy. One, never assume, and two, I or my crew never do anything without reason." He leaned close to Rusty. "I don't know what you and your wife were up to that would provoke someone into sinking you, but to assume it was us… well, that's…"

"I know it was you!"

"You know shit," Connors yelled. "You were probably drunk and hit a rock."

"I have never been drunk in my life."

Connors sneered. "Well, that settles it. Then you're a liar."

Rusty rushed him, but before he could reach him, the two crewmen snagged his arms on either side, stopping him in his tracks. They held him tight.

"Attacking a guardsman? A captain, no less. You just threatened the law, boy." Connors swaggered up to Rusty then punched him hard in the stomach. Rusty doubled over, suspended by the two guardsmen.

The force knocked the wind out of him, and when he caught his breath, he coughed. Then he exploded to life, wriggling free from his human bonds and rushed Connors, tackling him to the floor. He drew back to punch, but before he could get the punch off, one of the guardsmen kicked him in the back of his head and sent him sprawling. Then they pulled him to his feet, passing him back and forth as they took turns beating him bloody until he could no longer pick himself up from the floor and remained a limp heap.

Connors straightened his uniform and snatched his cap from the floor. "Throw that garbage out the door."

Each man grabbed an arm, and began dragging him towards the door.

Just as they reached the door, he mustered his strength, spit out blood, picked up his battered head and said, "There was another witness. He saw you."

The dispatcher looked confused. He turned to Connors.

Connors shrugged. "He's bluffing." He nodded to the men and they threw him out the door.

***

Rusty staggered towards his truck, crawled inside and rested his head on his hands holding the steering wheel. He could taste blood and his head pulsated like a giant heart. A sharp pain in his side each time he took a breath, told him he had a broken rib or two. He felt so rubbery and drained, driving the truck seemed more like calisthenics, so he just sat dazed and nodding until the light from the rising sun shone through the window of the cab, bathing his face in light and warmth and rousing him from his lethargy. He checked his watch. It was 8:35 a.m. *How time flies when you're having fun.* He started the truck, shifted it into gear and headed back to the hospital.

The look on the face of the receptionist told him he looked as bad as he felt. When she asked if he needed medical attention, he asked only for directions to a restroom. Di doesn't need this, he thought as he stared at the puffy, blood smeared face looking back at him in the mirror. One eye was swollen half shut, the other filled with blood. His hair was caked with dried blood, and his once white tuxedo shirt was ripped and stained with a palette consisting of dirt and blood. He splashed water on his face and winced. His head throbbed. *How does one pull off presentable when they look like this?*

Uncle Fritz rose when he saw him, and Rusty could see his face fall the closer he got to him. Uncle Fritz said nothing, but the grave look on his face spoke volumes.

"Is she awake?" Rusty said.

"Her mother is with her," Uncle Fritz stammered as he looked him over. "I can see what happened to you…but how did it get to this?"

"You could say I went looking for a fight and found one."

"I could say that and more. By the looks of you, I would say you were the small dog in the fight." Uncle Fritz shook his head and sank down on the waiting room's chair. "Well, you tipped your hand when you should've been poker-faced. How do we get to the bottom of this now that you got the pot stirred?"

Rusty said nothing.

Uncle Fritz frowned. "The rest of the family is here. They are in with her. Something I advise you not to do in that condition. She'll cast a kitten if she sees you like that. Thought I'd wait for you out here, and by the looks of you, I'm glad I did."

Rusty sat down gingerly, holding his side and winced.

"You need a doctor. Looks like some cracked ribs."

"Guess I'm at the right place for that."

Uncle Fritz rose and went to the receptionist. "This gentleman will need to see a doctor." When he returned to his seat, he said, "Well, we know how the Coast Guard feels about your suspicions. Now we'll see what the police will do about it."

"I think the picket boat was an isolated incident involving the CG157. The Guard itself isn't behind it. At least, I think. The dispatcher looked upset when he heard what happened. As far as the police…we could be opening another can of worms. For all I know, they could be in cahoots with Connors."

"In what way?"

"Catching smugglers…or smuggling themselves."

Uncle Fritz grimaced. "Either way, we need to scout this out and see just how big this cahoots is before we make another move. But first, let's get you checked out. Then we'll go see that lighthouse keeper and find out exactly what he saw. Something tells me we are going to need him as a witness."

Chapter 34

It was going on noon when Uncle Fritz, behind the wheel, and Rusty drove up to the lighthouse at the far tip of Marblehead Peninsula. The two-story keeper's house sat about a hundred feet from the tall, columnar light pillar and was painted in white with red trim that echoed that of the lighthouse and made for a striking contrast to the cobalt blue backdrop of water and sky. The place was tidy and the grounds manicured more than Uncle Fritz had expected. The mums and marigolds that lined the picket fence and the red and pink rose bushes flanking the walkway told him the keeper had a love of earth as well as water.

There was no activity. Rusty went to the house and knocked at the door while Uncle Fritz drank in the sight of the graceful lighthouse perched on the rocky shore overlooking the Sandusky Bay and the distant peninsula across the way where Cedar Point Amusement Park sat. The crisp fall air made visibility clearer and farther than it normally would be in summer's haze.

"Hey, I can see the roller coaster from here," he called to Rusty.

Rusty knocked again. After waiting another minute, he walked around the side and checked the garage. Huddleson's Model T was parked inside.

"Probably asleep," Uncle Fritz said, joining him. "Most likely he was up all night like you."

"Let's check the lighthouse," Rusty said.

"What is his name again?"

"Huddleson. Folks call him Cap Huddleson."

"Seems like everyone along the lake is named Cap this, Cap that..."

Normally, a comment like that would have made Rusty smile, but he and Uncle Fritz were beyond jokes and smiles. He opened the door to the lighthouse and was about to step onto the landing at the bottom of the steps when Uncle Fritz grabbed his arm and yanked him back.

"Jesus Christ All Mighty!" he said, pointing to the floor of the landing.

Rusty jerked back at seeing a body he almost stepped on lying crumpled at the bottom of the winding staircase. "Oh jeezus...it's Huddleson. Huddleson! Huddleson!" he shouted, kneeling next to the keeper. He shook him.

"Is he dead? He looks dead."

Rusty rolled Huddleson over and listened to his heart. "I can't hear anything." He placed two fingers on Huddleson's neck where the carotid artery was located. He concentrated while he waited for the slightest pulse of blood.

Uncle Fritz froze and held his breath so not to make the slightest sound.

After a long minute, Rusty drew a sigh of relief. "There's a weak pulse. Really weak, but there." He sat back on his heels. "Thank God he's still alive."

A rush of air escaped Uncle Fritz. "He needs a hospital. I'll pull the car up to the door."

Huddleson moaned when they lifted him.

"It's okay, Cap. We're taking you to a hospital," Rusty said in a soothing voice, trying to cover the shake in it.

They lugged him to the car.

"Something told me to take the A with the backseat, "Uncle Fritz said, grunting as they hoisted him in. He buried the accelerator as they flew west along the roads of Marblehead headed for the Bay Bridge leading to Sandusky and the same hospital where Di was hospitalized. He glanced at Rusty. "Did you see that empty bottle of Scotch next to him? Think he was drunk and fell?"

Rusty was quiet for a moment as he stared at the road ahead. As long as he could hear Huddleson moaning in the backseat, he knew he was alive. "If he fell drunk down the stairs, why didn't the bottle break? And wouldn't there be booze on the floor and steps where it spilled out?"

"Ja…and his breath doesn't smell of alcohol. Did you notice the bottle—how it was in the crook of his arm? A little too odd for a tumble."

"Hmm-mm. The man just rolled down God knows how many steps and an unbroken bottle remains tucked upright in his arm."

They exchanged glances.

"You want to know what's really at odds? Huddleson's is a teetotaler—been that way even before Prohibition."

Uncle Fritz glared at the road ahead. "He was pushed!"

"Someone hoping to eliminate the witness perhaps?"

Uncle Fritz set his jaw. He gripped the wheel tighter. "Looks like that can of worms has been opened and the worms already out."

***

After Huddleson was wheeled off to surgery, Uncle Fritz offered to drive Rusty home and get a clean change of clothes, but Rusty refused. They needed to be there to talk to the surgeon afterwards, and then and only then, would he go home and change, he said, adding that they would have to hurry back so he could see Di before visiting hours were over. Uncle Fritz agreed, but mumbled under his breath that the surgery could be long and visiting hours ended at eight.

As they waited, they poured over the events, sifting through facts and considering possible scenarios.

"Huddleson is not out of danger. Whoever did this left him for dead and may come back to finish what they started," Rusty said. "The hospital will want to report this to the police if we tell he was pushed, but what if the police are in on it? Reporters would soon flood the hospital and the word will be out about Huddleson's attack and an investigation will get under way and then what? A "visitor" comes calling to his hospital room and…"

"Snuffs him," Uncle Fritz finished.

“We need a plan. Huddleson’s accident and the fact he’s alive will get around quick. Whoever is involved will be paying close attention. First, we need to talk to the nurses to keep track of those who visit him. I know a nurse I can trust.” He blushed. “I dated her a couple of times before I met Di. Then we need to get word out that Huddleson doesn’t remember anything, not even the rescue off Marblehead. Say he’s got amnesia. Then, God willing, if he does have his senses and remembers, we need him to pretend he doesn’t remember anything.”

“What about the police? They have to be told this looks suspicious.”

Rusty paced the floor. “If…*if* he comes to and is okay, we’ll keep his faked amnesia between the three of us. Huddleson will just have to pretend he has a mental block of that night and morning. It happens all the time in accidents or bad events. Hell, I saw it happen to guys during the war. If he wants to save his ass, that’s what he’s got to do.”

“Let’s hope he’ll be in a position to pretend. He didn’t look good,” Uncle Fritz said with a sigh.

“I know. But either way, we got to get to the bottom of this before someone really gets killed.”

“Someone was already killed. An empty rocking chair and crib is proof of that.”

Chapter 35

They took Di back to the farm. The loss of blood had made her frail in body and the loss of the baby made her fragile in mind. She needed care, and her mother would have no one other than herself to see to her daughter's tending. Spinach and liver were a few of the remedies her mother pushed, while Uncle Fritz insisted on calf's heart for the blood and the broken heart. An organ for an organ, he would say.

Rusty was there often despite the cool reception from the brothers. *He knew Di was fearful of the lake. He worked for bad elements which gave the Coast Guard reason to suspect. He should have stayed at the mill.* The mill speech was like a stuck phonograph needle. When the heap would get too big from the shovel loads of guilt they piled on him, he would head to Sam's. Only Uncle Fritz remained in his corner, offering guidance much the way a shepherd kept reign on a wayward sheep in his flock.

He wasn't sure of anything now, when Di would come back home…if he would ever get a boat again…if he would ever be a charter captain again…if he and Di could ever be the same? But mostly, he agonized over Di and the baby and when and if she came back home, if things would be the same before their world was turned on its head, though deep in his heart he feared and knew it would never be the same. What he was sure of was he had no baby, no job, no boat, no home life and no Di so to speak.

Di was treating him cool. He wasn't sure if it was out of melancholy or blame or seeds planted by the brothers. Whatever it was, or perhaps all three, talking to her was like talking to a wall of glass—transparent and hard, but fragile. If pressed, she would answer, but not initiate, and her responses were short and often curt. He could see the changes in her eyes as the days passed from dull to indifferent to dark then brooding. Whatever was going on inside her head, she would not let him in, and that chilled him to the bone. It hurt him that she did not acknowledge the fact he was suffering too.

He and Uncle Fritz frequently visited Huddleson at Sandusky Hospital. Each time they asked to see the visitor registration, noting Chief Stoddard and the Coast Guard dispatcher, both who had known Huddleson personally for years, were on the list a number of times. Reporters, despite denials to interview him, gobbled up any scraps of information they could find and relayed it in their newspaper columns. One local headline read, *Lighthouse Keeper: Hero, Then Falls.* The byline reported that Huddleson fell down the steps of his lighthouse after a night of dramatic and exhaustive rescue and is suffering amnesia. Rusty read the article out loud to Huddleson. The article described Huddleson's rescue of a husband and wife he heard crying for help when their boat was mistaken for rumrunners and sunk by a mystery boat. Then it went on to describe his fall down the lighthouse steps in the early hours of morning most likely from fatigue from the overnight rescue, and being found by two sightseers visiting the lighthouse. It described him as physically improving, having a sense of awareness but totally blank about the rescue and fall. Not unusual for such head trauma, the doctor was quoted. There was no mention of the bottle of scotch.

But Huddleson remembered everything and agreed to keep his awareness between Rusty and Uncle Fritz. He told them after the ambulance had taken Rusty and Di away, most of the crowd remained behind at the lighthouse until dawn mulling over the events of the shooting and rescue. The talk said Rusty and Di were mistaken for rumrunners and a misplaced bullet, meant to stop the craft, unintentionally sunk the boat. More than likely they were victims of a turf war. Neither he nor police Chief Stoddard, who took a statement from him at the lighthouse right afterwards, mentioned that a Coast Guard picket boat was suspected. He remained at the lighthouse until the final person left, and then he wrapped up, fixing to call it a day. As he was shutting the door to lighthouse, two men drove up in an older Chevrolet and asked for a tour of the lighthouse. They wore black overcoats and had fedoras pulled down on their heads, shielding their eyes. One was tall, the other short. He told them it wasn't a good time...asked them if they could come back later. But the tall one said they were passing through on their way to Detroit and couldn't wait. Despite feeling uneasy about the way they looked and their mannerism, he unlocked the door and led them inside. He gave a quick history and described the Fresno lens, then told them he had a long night, was beat and didn't relish going up the steps again, but they insisted he lead them up the stairs.

Huddleson had a funny feeling they were there for more than a tour and history lesson. He got thinking maybe they were there to scope out the area or sabotage the light. They must have sensed he was uneasy and suspected them of foul play because they got impatient. *Let's go, pop*, the shorter man had said, nodding to the stairs. He recognized his voice. It was the same voice he often heard on the ship to shore radio—a real distinct voice. He asked, *is that you, Bill?* And the question seemed to agitate the two men. The fellow that sounded like Bill said, *it looks like you need some help, Cap.* With that, they each grabbed an arm and began pulling him up the winding stairs. When they got about two thirds up, the tall one said he was whipped and had enough, said *this should do.* That's when they pushed him down the stairs. He got lodged about halfway down and they kicked him loose until he began rolling the rest of the way down. He really didn't remember the rest of the fall, or their leaving, but apparently they were satisfied he was dead. At first he thought they were goons from a bootlegging ring out of Detroit. That is until he heard Bill's voice.

No, Rusty had said. *Professional goons would have seen to it you were dead, and they would have staged the scotch more convincingly. These sound like idiots trying to cover their tracks. Who's Bill?*

"Chief motor machinist's mate—on CG157" was Huddleson's reply.

***

Unbeknownst to them, on the night of the shooting, Chief Stoddard had gone directly to the Coast Guard Station after seeing Rusty and Di off in the ambulance and talking with Huddleson. He asked the Guard dispatcher for the log that night and asked questions about what boats patrolled where and when. He asked specifically about picket boats that night. He was told CG157 was on patrol that night but nothing in the log about being in the NE quadrant.

Is there a chance they could have been just passing through there and not recorded their course in the log?

The dispatcher told him records are pretty tight and gasoline consumption monitored. *Why does he want to know?*

Just hoping they might have seen or passed a vessel out there that night that could help me with the investigation of that sinking off Marblehead. I'll stop back later after they come in and see if they saw or heard anything unusual last night. Thanks.

Chapter 36

Rusty drove back and forth to the farm to see Di each day for a week before he visited Davey, his first visit since summer. When he realized how much time had passed and the condition he found Davey, guilt struck him like a board on the head. Davey had whittled away since their last visit, having peaked in weight and strength when he first came home. His body before the accident had little to spare to begin with and now it looked like bones without meat under the sleeves and trouser legs. His cheekbones were grotesquely exaggerated making the area below them dark and sunken like the sockets of his eyes. He looked like one of the prisoners of war at Andersonville Rusty saw in books about the Civil War. Then there was the feeble Mrs. Reynolds who could not recall who Rusty was until Davey insisted she knew him. Clutter littered the house and a thick layer of dust told him house cleaning had been neglected. At least the dishes had been washed and drying in a drain rack.

When Davey saw him, he straightened up in his wheelchair and grinned from ear to ear. Something, Rusty felt, Davey hadn't done of late. How pathetic, he thought, that his visits, like a scattering of bread crumbs, were the spice in Davey's life.

"I'm plum out of soda pop to offer you," Davey said to him as he peered into the empty void of the icebox. Rusty looked discreetly over his shoulder and noticed a quarter loaf of bread, an inch of milk at the bottom of a bottle and a casserole dish. "How about some coffee? I think there's still some left in the pot."

Before Rusty could stop him, Davey had wheeled to the sink and excavated two cups from a pile in the drain rack and headed for the coffee pot, determined to be a good host. "I know you drink it black, but I take mine with milk. Could you grab the bottle for me?"

"I know you do," Rusty said, reaching for the bottle. He saw the food in the casserole dish was nearly gone. What remained looked cracked and shriveled and dried out. Had it been there since the party? He checked Davey and saw he was preoccupied with pouring coffee so he took a whiff of the milk and recoiled. "Whoa partner, I think your milk went to sour cream on you."

"It's not going to kill me. Go ahead and put a shot of it in the cup."

"Might give you an upset stomach."

"Might give me the squirts!" Davey said with a chuckle.

Rusty raised his brows. Somehow he didn't find the sour milk funny and the empty refrigerator disturbed him. "Neighbor lady still looking in on you?" He asked, trying to sound casual.

"Up until she left for Indiana a few weeks ago, visiting her daughter for a month or so. She had a baby. Asked me to watch her house and make sure it doesn't get robbed or burn down while she's gone. I told her that's about all I can do is watch." He chuckled again.

Rusty failed to find humor in Davey's quips. "So who's been looking in on you?"

"Oh, the church does off and on." Davey sipped his coffee, seemingly oblivious to Rusty's summation of his circumstances. "So what's new with you?"

Such a little question with such a big answer. Where would he begin, he wondered, and did he want to dump on him when Davey has his own ongoing hard luck story? They could have a *can you top this* contest if they weren't careful. Or would it be a diversion for him—something to stir Davey from his doldrums and make his blood run again? He sipped his coffee, relieved it wasn't too old, while he contemplated. After a few moments of deliberation and coffee sipping, he opted to tell Davey. After all, Davey liked a good western and weren't the themes of those potboilers comparable to his story—good guys versus bad guys? The premise was always good triumphing over evil but first *good* had to go through hell before popping out on top of the shit pile- at least in Zane Grey's world. He decided to start small and work his way up. "I don't have a boat anymore."

Davey looked up from his cup. "You sold *Rising Sun*?"

"She sunk."

Davey fell quiet for a moment. "Go on."

So he did from the juice runs and searches to the beating at the station. When he got to the part about the shots and sinking, tears welled in Davey's eyes. And when he told him about Di and the baby, the tears spilled over and rolled down Davey's ashen cheeks and he cussed. It was the first time he had ever heard him swear.

The story took an hour and when it was finished, Rusty fell quiet. By the stunned look on Davey's face, he began wondering if it was a good idea to have told him.

It was Davey who finally broke the silence. "So what's next?"

He shook his head.

"You need to go above heads. Not just at the Marblehead Station, either—go to the top."

"It will be considered an accident. A boat coming from the islands area after midnight is most likely a rumrunner."

"And it's okay to open fire and sink a runner, possibly killing those aboard?"

"The coasties fire warning shots and give chase. Their objective is to confiscate the boat and the liquor, destroy the booze then auction the boat. Most runners aren't even charged let alone shot. Connors is a different breed. He's a renegade and mad in the head. Besides, there's no proof saying it was even him. There's no denying we were shot and sunk, but hijackers will be blamed."

Davey scowled. "Hijackers are after the booze and they want it intact. Besides, have you ever heard of any hijackers using .30 caliber machine guns? They'd blow that booze to smithereens or sink the boat—like what happened to yours. Then they'd have nothing."

"They'll say it was a score to settle or turf war and my boat was mistaken for another.

Davey shook his head. "Well you thought it all through haven't you, and yet here you are without help from authorities, without a boat, without a job, without a baby and a wife who has left you."

"She didn't leave me. She needs care. Her mother insisted on taking her back until she's stronger."

"You're forgetting one thing," Davey said, holding up his finger, "Your ace in the hole…you have a credible witness who saw, not assumed, saw a Coast Guard picket boat! Like you, he also heard a large caliber gun from that direction. And Huddleson is not a man to be bought."

"No, but he could be silenced."

"But it sounds like you have taken care of that with the amnesia story."

"As long as it keeps working. What if this gets pushed under the rug like other incidents involving Connors?"

Davey leaned forward. He narrowed his eyes. "We'll know the truth."

Their eyes locked and Rusty could see in Davey's eyes a fire had been ignited deep within his shell.

***

A number of hours had passed when Rusty finally checked his watch. He didn't like it as much as his old wristwatch that got damaged when he was in the lake. "I got to get going," he said standing. He paused for a moment, "Hey, I got to run up to the store for some things. How 'bout I grab a few things for you and drop them off before I head home."

"Well, if it's not out of the way, I guess we could use a few things. Mom got confused the other day when she went to the store. Ended up down by the post office. A flatfoot brought her home and she thought he was the grocery clerk." Davey's laughed but it hinted of sadness. "There should be some money here somewhere," he mumbled as he began rifling through a kitchen drawer.

"Don't bother. I got it. You can pay another time or settle with a soda pop next time." Rusty said, waving him off.

He left depressed. It was obvious that Davey and his mother needed more help than groceries or casseroles. They needed a housekeeper or a caretaker—someone to cook, clean and shop. Maybe a nurse once a week, too. That would take some money. Money they sure in hell didn't have. And here he was with no income now. He had some money saved from the juice charters, but with his own medical bills and living expenses, he would burn through that like a grassfire in August. He drove to the grocers. He didn't really need to go there but Davey didn't need to know that. While he was there, he grabbed a pack of cigarettes and a Zane Grey paperback for himself.

Chapter 37

A month and two weeks had passed since the sinking of *Rising Sun*, and with it came a sharp, icy wind out of Canada. He braced himself from the whipping wind as he stood on the shore of his backyard, listening and watching as angry, monstrous green waves roared towards shore, lashing and biting hunks of sand and rock from the coastline. Visibility was less than a quarter mile, creating a gray, wet shroud in and along the lakeshore from Detroit to Buffalo. He squinted and blinked, fighting to keep his eyes open from the sting of foam and spray being ripped from the waves and hurled inland. Anyone who saw him would have thought him mad for standing in such an onslaught of wind and wave.

Generations of lake sailors, forecasters and locals throughout the Great Lakes called this fierce tempest, *The Witch*, or more specifically, the *November Witch*, and the mere mention of its name would send chills up a sailor's spine and evoked images of shipwrecks. Like an extortionist, it came calling each November for its pound of flesh in exchange for the fair weather, smooth sailing and biting fish in the summer season.

The rain and spray stung too much. He shuddered, half from the bone chilling soaking, half from trepidation. Though he had stood there for less than ten minutes, it felt longer. He hurried back to the house, peeled off his cold wet clothes and hung them over the furnace grate to dry and then changed into dry clothes. The house was dim from the lack of sunlight and felt dead as if Di's absence was more than a temporary move to the farm. He looked for traces of her around the house, coat, hats and purse—gone; clothes—missing, shoes too and an empty vanity. Not even a comb. *Hell, a dead person left more behind.*

He checked the clock on the mantel. It was only 8 a.m. He had slept little that night, and what sleep he had was as tempestuous as the gale battering the lake and shoreline. He sunk into his chair in the living room and lit a cigarette. The howling wind and sleety rain made the room seem even bleaker, but he refused to switch on the lamp. The only thing he felt like, the only movement he wanted to make was to punch his fist right through the wall. He pictured the plaster shattering under the impact of his knuckles, and the spiky pain that would race from his fingers to his shoulder. He imagined it, but he didn't do it because all it would accomplish was a sore, stiff hand and plaster repair. He wished fate was three dimensional with the ability to feel. Something you could get physical with, threaten it if it tried to play games with you. You could walk outside and there it would be, like a life-size jack-in-the-box, bouncing in glee and snickering no doubt after the last hand it had dealt you, and you could walk right up to it and *pow*, bust it on its snout.

But there was no such thing, so he smoked his cigarette down to the butt while he stared at the wall, waiting for a respectable time to head for the farm.

***

Sam's was packed when he stopped there around 11 p.m. after a day at the farm with Di. Since no one could be on the lake that day or wanted to be home that night, the crowd was restless and eager to whoop it up. They jammed the joint shoulder to shoulder, and Rusty had to squeeze his way into the door, his pardons lost in the din of music, laughter and cracking cue balls. He hadn't been to Sam's since the accident.

When he finally worked his way up to the counter, Sam, spotting him, rolled his eyes to the right and mouthed the word *fed.*

He then proclaimed in a loud cheery voice, "Good weather for a cup of coffee and a bowl of soup." He poured Rusty a cup of coffee. "Eddie caught a whopper of a snapper in the marshes, so turtle soup is the soup of the day."

"Shouldn't they be digging down in the mud this time of year?"

Sam winced over a belly laugh that exploded next to him. "What? You mean Eddie or the snapper? I didn't catch what you said."

As people shuffled about the counter as though playing musical chairs, Rusty soon found himself next to the man Sam had warned was a federal agent. The man had just finished scraping the bottom of his bowl of soup and was now nursing a cup of coffee.

"Soup any good?" Rusty asked.

"To be honest, it's probably the best tasting soup I had in a long time," the man answered.

"The hamburgers here are good too."

"Must be why this place is so popular," the man said.

With that, Rusty decided to drop the conversation. He drained his coffee, and headed towards the pool tables. By the sounds of the cheering and clapping, someone was clearing the table of balls much to the dismay of his challenger. Rusty wormed through an opening in the crowd to watch and did a double take. The man sinking the balls left and right was none other than Pete. He took a step back, allowing the crowd to swallow him, and hoped Pete was too preoccupied to have spotted him. *What's he doing here?* He turned abruptly to head back to the counter area and ran smack into Sam's big barreled chest. Sam's voice was low, but earnest.

"Rust, we heard what happened. Damn it all to hell, it just tore us up."

Rusty was taken back. He gave Sam a quick nod and tried to go around him, but Sam blocked him.

"Do you know who did it? Rumors are flying it was Coast Guard. Everyone around here is pissed. And Al, he's just going crazy over this. Says he's been trying to get a hold of you but it's like you're avoiding him. You know he likes you, we all like you. You're more than just an employee to the family so when that happened to you and your missus...and then... Al says there was a baby. Son-of-a-bitch."

Rusty felt his throat getting tight. As far as he was concerned, he was finished with the Trapani clan. He had no boat for their runs, therefore no need for any more contact, shoulder rubbing or dealing. It was a job and it was over. All he wanted to do was distance himself from them and get his head together.

"If you know...if you got even an inkling who did this to you...you let me know."

Rusty nodded half-heartedly.

Sam grabbed his arm tight, forcing him to look him in the eye. "I mean it...you got a hunch...we want to know." He then released his grip and patted Rusty's shoulder sympathetically to dismiss him.

Rusty squirmed past. He wasn't really sure who *we* were or what *they* would do about it if he told him the finger pointed to Connors. And was it because of the Trapanis that he had been singled out by Connors, he wondered? As far as he knew, the Trapanis, though mysterious as all hell, were on the up and up. And why was Pete here? Was it coincidence or connections to Sam or was Pete looking for him?

A loud cheer went up. Apparently, Pete had won. Rusty pushed his way to the door. He didn't want to see Pete or talk to him. He just wanted to distance himself from that world and stow the incident for now until he could patch things back the best he could. He couldn't forget what happened, and he damn well didn't want to let it go. There would be a reckoning, but he needed time to think and investigate without Pete, Sam or anyone else gumming the works. And he needed to rebuild his life and Di's faith in him. He had already taken his first step. He was to start Monday afternoon—at the mill.

Chapter 38

Working turns- that's what it was called. One week, he would work seven to three, the next week, three to eleven and the week after that, eleven to seven. Then the rotation would start over. The country was hungry for steel and the mill was running 24/7 to fulfill it. Most men eagerly embraced the extra hours. Wages were great as it was but overtime hit the ball out of the park and put two cars in garages, prime rib on the table (never mind the chicken in the pot) and new shoes on the family's feet. To Rusty, it was the closest thing to a prison sentence, time he had to serve to pay his debt literally and figuratively.

Monday afternoon found him in the steel mill's underground tunnels, shoveling up scrap pieces and chunks of ore that fell from the grates above where the ore was pared and shaped into ingots before heading to the giant furnaces. He shoveled the scrap into a wheelbarrow and wheeled it to a huge bin the size of a trolley. When full, the bin would be hauled away by large overhead cranes to a place beyond his realm. It was an eerie world of orange light and black corners where he labored under sweat, soot and grime; a place where shadows and darkness were punctuated by dusty orange shafts of light spilling from the furnaces above; a place of slag hills and thick stratums of graphite dust and metal chips that smothered the floor; a place where a macabre pseudo fog of orange steel dust hung suspended in the air making laborers look more like mythical trolls than men. To cope with the dust, he spent the workday with a handkerchief wrapped around his head to cover his nose and mouth which, when removed, made him look like a raccoon. It was a job, he told Uncle Fritz, any moron could do. It was a place men bid out of and where openings were always available, and before the week was out, he had his bid in for the rolling mill department where he had last worked before quitting there so many years ago.

***

Thanksgiving was around the corner, and as he sampled Uncle Fritz's wine in the brewing shed at the farm, he was quiet.

Uncle Fritz noted his brooding. "What do you think of this one as the table wine for Thanksgiving dinner?"

Rusty took a sip and swirled it around in his mouth before swallowing. "I'm not a big fan of wine, but it has good berry taste and sweet."

"Blackberry. *Ja*, I think this will do just fine." He glanced at Rusty whose brows were furrowed and face scrunched tight like a fist. He had worn this scowl since the accident. "You have a lot to be thankful for," he said point blank.

Rusty snorted. "How about pointing it out for me as I'm having a hard time finding it."

Uncle Fritz corked the wine bottle and replaced it on the shelf. He kept his back to Rusty, becoming absorbed in organizing and straightening bottles filled with wine and beer. It was Uncle Fritz's version of the silent treatment.

Rusty felt a twinge of shame. "Fact is I feel more sorry than thankful."

With his back to him still, Uncle Fritz said, "Thankful, you were not killed, thankful Di did not drown or die at the hospital, thankful the lighthouse keeper saw you, thankful you have a home, thankful you have family who looks after you, and thankful you have a job for starters. I can go on…"

"No. It's not necessary. I get your point. I just see it from a different angle. I lost a lot and thankful is not a word that comes to mind right now."

Uncle Fritz turned around. "It will. Most things happen for a reason."

He always hated that expression, but when Uncle Fritz said it, it seemed almost plausible. He gulped the last swallow of wine and set the glass down. "I gotta head out. See you tomorrow."

Uncle Fritz, still busy at the shelves, looked over his shoulder. "Sure. Sure. Tomorrow."

***

Di was sitting at the kitchen table drinking coffee with her mother when he returned to the farmhouse. She had lost weight as well as her sparkle, and her eyes stared vacant from the dark circles that encircled them. Still, it was good seeing her out of bed and dressed. She wore a perpetually sober face, and he wondered if she was like that right along or just when he was there.

Her mother looked up when he came in and gave him a weak but kind smile. Di remained fixed on her coffee.

"I got to be going. Catch me a nap before starting graveyard shift tonight." He waited for a response from Di, got none, and then gave her a peck on the forehead.

"I'll see you tomorrow," he said half to her and half to her mother.

"Remember Thursday is Thanksgiving. They do let you off for that?" the mother asked.

He smacked his forehead. "They run around the clock, but I don't start until 11, so I will be able to be here most the day."

"I hope so. I have a twenty pound turkey reserved and three pies to bake. Di is going to help me with apple and two pumpkins, isn't that right, Di? Catch some sleep before coming over. Dinner won't be until 5. Oh wait," she crossed to the icebox and pulled out a small sack wrapped with string and handed it to him. "Couple of meatloaf sandwiches for work."

He nodded *thanks* and smiled gratefully, and then glanced back at Di just before heading out the door, but she was preoccupied with stirring her coffee. *Coffee over him.* Maybe I should ask Uncle Fritz if that's on the thankful list, he groused to himself as he headed for the truck. He drove out the driveway, unaware she had gone to the door and was watching him until he disappeared out of sight.

Chapter 39

The steel mill was made bearable by the fact cold weather was arriving on a strong Canadian wind, bringing with it an advance guard of sleet. Some days, when the weather broke and offered a freak warm day and a calmer lake, he went out by the docks at break time to smoke or eat his lunch. It was on these days he would watch the last vestiges of the season's boaters heading out for one last fling on the lake before surrendering to the weather. They gambled they would have time before fall slipped into winter to store their vessels for the season—a task most boaters had already completed by Thanksgiving. Those stubborn few were guys like him, mostly fishermen, who wanted to wring out one last sail or cruise before packing it in. It was watching those boats head out that bore a hole in his already aching heart.

It was the last day of November and Di remained at the farm. It had been a little over two months since the incident and when he asked her about coming home, she said she could not bear the sight of the nursery and crib. So he spent two days before his afternoon shift dragging the crib and all the nursery accessories to the back of the lot, tossing them in a heap and then setting them on fire, watching as the wind whipped the ashes away. He then wallpapered over the pastel paint with a rural motif of farms and sunflowers. Among the pattern was a scene of little cows next to a red barn surrounded by green, rolling pastures. It reminded him of the Paradise Farms milk truck and Vince. The last time he saw him, Vince was three sheets to the wind and dancing with the grace of a duck with Pete's flapper girlfriend at the harvest party. He and Di had practically fell down laughing at his clumsy attempt and determination to Charleston while the party goers shouted "get hot, get hot, get hot."

When he punched out the following week after his day shift, he wasn't sure if it was fate or his thoughts of Vince and the party that made Pete suddenly materialize at the mill's exit where the workers departed after their shift. Pete was leaning against a light pole, lighting a cigarette and watching the sea of tired, gritty men pour out of the mill when Rusty spotted him first.

As soon as Pete made eye contact, he straightened up and waited Rusty's approach.

"What the hell are you doing here?" Rusty said as he brushed past Pete.

"Looking for you," Pete said, hustling to catch up. "We heard you're working at the mill now…man, from the looks of you, it's worse here than I thought. You look like hell."

"I feel like hell."

A few snowflakes began to fall. Pete pulled his collar up around his neck. "We're real sorry about what happened that night of the party. In fact, we're mad as hell. Al took it personally."

Rusty cast him a sideways look. "*He* took it personally? I'm the one that got shot!"

"Al thinks it's personal because they have been watching his place. He feels you got caught in the middle. You know our warehouse in Sandusky got raided a few days later?"

"My plate has been pretty full so forgive me if I haven't been keeping up on your affairs."

Pete continued. "Yeah, well they busted the place up pretty good and beat Joe for no reason. Broke his arm and nose. Said it was to get our attention."

"Who's *they*?" Rusty quipped.

"Feds! The Coast Guard has been patrolling the island all summer and dogging our boats. Then we hear two Feds are on the island renting one of the cottages at Peach Point. Heard they've staked an outpost on Kelleys Island, too."

"You should have warned me Al was being watched. I figured it was just me the Guard was hounding."

"We didn't think there was any reason to. Besides, the warehouse came after your sinking. So did hearing about the Feds on the islands."

They reached Rusty's truck in the parking lot, and Rusty tossed his lunch box on the seat of the passenger side. "They find anything?"

"Course not. We're not stupid. But hundreds of gallons of grape juice were destroyed not to mention Cousin Joe. Al's really pissed."

Rusty walked around to the driver's side and jerked open the door.

Shivering from the cold, Pete said, "Do you know who shot you?"

"It was dark."

"But do you have an idea. We really want to know."

"So the hell do I." Rusty crawled inside the truck.

Pete reflected for a moment, and then hurried over to the driver door. "Al wants you to come see him."

"Don't have time." He started the truck.

"He's got a proposition. He wants to help you. And after seeing this place, you really may want to consider what he has to say."

He put the truck in gear. "So long, Pete. Don't take any wooden nickels." He then drove off.

***

The next day, a black Packard zipped through the parked cars at the mill in the lot where Rusty parked, and cut him off as he was headed to his truck. The passenger door flung open and Giuseppe exited like a big bear emerging from his den. He then swung the backseat door open and, with his permanent deadpan expression and frosty voice, said, "Ciao, Mr. Rusty, the boss wants to talk to you."

Rusty hesitated. He knew Giuseppe would not take *it's been a long day and I just want to go home, clean up and eat* for an answer. He leaned forward and saw Al sitting in the backseat.

"A moment of your time," Al said.

Giuseppe held the door, his hooded, dark, eyes fixed on him like a panther waiting to see his move.

There was really no choice, so he crawled inside and the door slammed shut behind him. His palms began to sweat.

"Rusty, Rusty, Rusty," Al said. "My heart is broken for you." He placed his hands over his heart to emphasize. "When we got the news, the first thing Giuseppe said was 'tell me who, boss'. That's how much you mean to us."

He wasn't sure if he should thank Giuseppe for the concern.

"Drive around for about ten minutes," Al said to the driver. He then turned again to Rusty. "Pete said your time is little, so I'll make this short and you don't have to give me an answer right away. In fact, I insist you don't. I want you to sleep on it. First, how is the missus?"

"Better."

"Good. Good. And the lighthouse keeper who rescued you—how's he doing?"

"Better. He's out of the hospital. Coast Guard is operating the light until he can manage again. He can't remember a thing about that night."

"Hmm. That's too bad. I was hoping he'd seen something."

"So does everyone else."

"How's the mill job."

"Pays the bills."

A few seconds of silence passed. "Does it pay enough for a new boat?" Al asked.

"I'm not worried about that now."

"Of course not." Al fell quiet again, and then said, "Rusty, I feel bad. I can't change what happened, but I can help."

Rusty shook his head no.

"Ah-ah-ah… let me finish. Your world has taken a big turn, my friend. You lost a lot by no fault of your own. I lost, too but it was money. A lot of kale was left on the floor of the warehouse, but what really steams me is the beating of my baby brother, Joe. For what? Grape juice!" Al's face grew dark and brooding. "Think about it. You're gonna bust your ass at this hell hole and you'll still be out a boat, a baby and a wife."

"What do you know about my wife?"

"I know she's not home with you. And what did you do wrong? Nothin'!"

He started to speak but Al cut him off.

"Here's how I want to help. The Coast Guard is auctioning off confiscated rumrunners at its Cleveland station next Saturday. There is suppose to be everything from runabouts to cabin cruisers, many modified for running, others good for fishing or cruising- all sizes, all shapes, all makes. I want you to go with Pete and pick out a boat for yourself. Whatever tickles your fancy. It's on me."

"Why?"

"Because one, I feel responsible. You were there because of my party. Two, I know you will never get another boat with your money situation and three," he drew a breath, "I want you to pick out a runner for me. Something fast that can carry a load-say, 75-100 cases."

"You don't need me for that. Pete can pick one out."

"But you know your onions when it comes to boats and boating."

"So I pick you out a runner and that's that."

"No. You pick yourself out a fishing boat and then I want you to chew on this. The runner will need an ace of a pilot- someone who knows the lake, the shoreline and boats. Someone tough and not easily bullied—that's where you come in. You got first crack at it."

Rusty slowly shook his head no. "I don't think I want to do that again."

"You won't be doing grape runs again."

His eyes shot to Al to search for a meaning.

"We're both in a situation where we can't win, but we have nothing to lose. We both need money, lots of it, and we both have scores to settle that are along the same lines." The usual cheerful spark in Al's eyes was gone, replaced by two dark bottomless whirlpools.

Rusty felt uneasy, like he was teetering on the edge of an abyss that was trying to suck him in.

"You're a straight shooter, so let me put it to you point blank. I want to run booze out of Canada. None of that rot gut either, the pure stuff. I will need a fast rumrunner and a savvy pilot. A guy like you belongs on the lake not in the nether lands of some filthy mill. Look at you. You're a waste here. A pilot can make a 50 to 100 simoleans easily for each run. Couple days a week—well, you figure it out. How much you make at the mill busting your ass seven days a week?" Without waiting for an answer, he continued, "I already have the first leg worked out; the second leg will be the toughest. That's where you come in."

Rusty was stunned. "Why rumrunning? All that investment and you're dumping the juice business?"

"We're still working grape juice *and* turning water into wine. But rumrunning is where the big money, the fast money is made and if we're going to be treated like criminals anyways, might as well jump aboard. Besides, it puts me, us, where we need to be to clean things up."

"So you're asking me to break the law?"

Al snorted. "The law? Where's the law in this mess. Can you tell me honestly who are the bad guys and who are the good? Law abiding fishermen are running just to make ends meet. Guys like you and Joe are getting fucked up by the so called law for nothing' and meanwhile law enforcement is doing shakedowns and hijacking booze to line their pockets. The government, the one you laid your life on the line for, is poisoning alcohol with methyl alcohol killing hundreds of citizens and sickening or blinding thousands more. How's that for morality! Prohibition has made criminals out of the average Joe and corruption in the legal system. Legitimate vintners like Schmitt and my family in Upstate had the carpet yanked out from under them then went under and for what? So a bunch of teetotalling old grannies don't get offended when they see a glass of whiskey. We never made trouble or asked for it, but it found us. Is Prohibition really working or is it just another way to make money 'cause I see more booze flowing now and more corruption than I did before the 18th passed. So tell me, Rusty, who are the bad guys?"

Rusty face tightened. "How about you tell *me* something? I think my sinking and the grape juice runs are connected. You're feeling guilty about more than just us leaving your party. The last time my boat got roughed up you said it wasn't your responsibility. Why now?"

Al scratched his chin. Rusty could see his eyes clicking in his head, searching for the appropriate answer.

"I'll make it easy for you, Al. I was hauling doctored grape juice from the warehouse to Beaver Creek dock where it was hauled away by a bogus milk truck to your contacts. When I questioned what was in the bottles, I was always *handed* a bottle. I should have picked one out at random. Maybe I should be mad at you instead."

Giuseppe turned and looked over the back seat first at him then Al. Rusty clammed up.

Al nodded to Giuseppe who then turned back around. "You're a smart guy, Rusty. If you had suspicions, why did you go along with it? Lot of money for running grape juice, uh? And just for the record, you were hauling plain grape juice from the island to the warehouse."

"But you weren't level with me. You lied to me about the run from the warehouse to the dock. It was wine I was hauling then wasn't it?"

"Lie is a strong word. I never said that second run was plain grape juice and you never asked me. It was still grape juice, only it had a little kick. I asked if you wanted to make more money hauling cases from the warehouse to the dock. You said you wouldn't risk your boat for twenty, so I upped it to twenty-five with gas. And you took the money. A lonely dock, a milk truck, come on, Rusty. You're no dummy. You knew it, or chose not to believe it. And it wasn't like it was hard liquor."

"Next you're gonna tell me it was sacramental or medicinal wine."

"No I'm not. I don't give a rat's ass what or where it goes. There is a big demand, and guys like you and me supply that demand and we get paid big money to do so."

"Then the Coast Guard had a right to suspect me."

"Each time the coasties stopped you, you were clean. Am I right? So they hassled you—they hassle every Joe Blow on the lake. But shooting at a boat to hit it—to sink it—a boat that was always clean…? That's a whole new ballgame. You, my friend, are either a mistake, a mark or a personal vendetta."

The car drove back to the same parking lot and pulled up to the spot where it had picked up Rusty. Giuseppe got out and waited for a signal from Al before opening the back door on Rusty's side.

Al placed his hand on Rusty's arm. His eyes were more pleading now than intense. "I owe you because I wasn't completely straight with you. That's why I want you to pick out a boat. I can't call it square because I can't give you back your baby or your life. So you're still calling the shots. If you want to run for me, I'll make it worth your while—no strings attached. You can quit when you want. If you don't, I beg you to still pick out a runner for me. You don't have to, but I wish you would because I trust you."

Rusty was quiet. Trust. Al was a fine one to speak of trust. He felt deceived by him and the Trapanis. What a fool he was. And yet, there was always that cloud of doubt that had hung over the activities—a wave of suspicion that he would suppress when it tried to surface. Maybe Al was right—maybe he chose not to believe it.

Al nodded to Giuseppe and he opened the door. Rusty crawled out. "Pete will be at Sam's at 7, Saturday morning. He'll leave for the auction in Cleveland from there. If you want to go, be there by 7:30. Auction starts at noon. And Rusty, if you don't go…I 'll understand."

Chapter 40

A guy nicknamed Blinky got the job opening in the rolling mill. Another guy called Moocher was burned by dripping molten ore. They were instantly replaced by two new guys. *More rats swarming into the nocturnal underground world than crawling out,* Rusty mumbled to himself. He coughed a lot in these last few weeks and missed seeing the sun—what little sun that could be found in northern Ohio in November and December.

When he left work Friday afternoon, he told his foreman he needed to take a day off on Saturday for personal reasons.

A glow along the eastern horizon promised daybreak soon when he arrived at Sam's early Saturday morning. He was in no rush to leave his truck. Crossing the threshold into Sam's on this brisk morning would be a step into another world—one he was not really sure if he wanted to enter. As he sat there deliberating whether to leave the truck or head back home, an abrupt double bang on the roof of the truck made him jump. He turned and saw Pete grinning at him from the passenger side's window. Pete's ears and nose were red from the cold. Rusty opened the door, hoping Pete hadn't seen him jump.

"Hey, you beat me here," Pete was saying as Rusty climbed out of the truck. "I wasn't sure if you would even come. Man, I could use some coffee. Have you had breakfast yet? We have time."

Before Rusty could answer, Pete was bounding into Sam's.

The aroma of thick, dark coffee rolled out the door and beckoned to Rusty. He crossed the threshold. There were two other diners besides himself and Pete. Most of the patrons were likely in bed or nursing hangovers from celebrating Friday's payday. Sam wasn't there but that was no surprise since he was a constant presence from noon until the wee hours, six days a week. A short, gray haired woman with thick arms stood before the stove grilling sausages that sizzled and spit. She nodded at Pete as he took a seat at the counter and automatically reached for three eggs.

"What's your friend having?" she said, without looking up from the grill.

Pete looked at Rusty.

"Whatever you're having," he said.

"Ditto that, Ruth and shake your tail feathers on that coffee, sweetheart."

"Sweetheart my ass," she said, scrambling the eggs. She was smiling when she brought the pot and two cups.

Pete had decided early on he would drive to the auction so if they bought a boat Rusty could pilot it home. Rusty had said he wasn't keen on taking a boat out that he hadn't inspected and tested, but Pete still insisted on driving the '28

Chrysler supplied by Al. Since he had no car of his own, this gave him an opportunity to drive, he said. Rusty was fine with it as it meant not having to burn his own gas for the likes of Al, although fifteen minutes into the ride he wondered if it was such a good idea. Pete sped along the lakeshore road like a man pursued. Halfway to Cleveland and he had already chalked up a stop sign running and a near t-bone. He wondered if Al would be so generous with his new automobile had he known how his little cousin drove. Then, again, maybe that was why Al looked outside his circle for a pilot. After all, runners and bootleggers were risk takers, not reckless. Like bold sailors, careless runners didn't last long.

As they raced towards Cleveland hitting every bump and dodging near misses, Pete chattered away non-stop, covering topics from hot Cleveland speakeasies to the "bearcat" he was dating. Eventually, Capone's name came up, just like his "bearcat" had accused him of "yammering on" about at the harvest party.

"Just once I'd like to see him, not meet him ...you know, just see him. Like at a counter in a fancy juice joint tossing back a shot or passing him on the street. Then, I could say, 'yeah, I've seen Big Al. He comes to the same juice joint I hang at when he's in town on business.'" He was grinning ear to ear just imagining it.

Rusty rolled his eyes. "Cleveland is not his turf, so I doubt you'll see him around here, and I wouldn't go confusing him with the likes of Jesse James or Robin Hood."

"No, but he's just as famous and he makes headlines."

"So did the Purple Gang."

***

The lake was slowly releasing its grip on summer's heat so the air felt a slight bit warmer at the Cleveland harbor than it did inland. It had the reverse affect in spring when the frozen expanse radiated cold like a block of melting ice, chilling the lake shore residents to the bone while miles inland, beyond the lake's reach, people basked in warmth and sunshine. Still, it was nippy enough that Pete pulled his collar up on his coat.

"We're freezing our nuts off here, while Capone is getting sunburns on Palm Island. Must be nice." Pete said through clicking teeth.

"It has its price."

"Yeah, but it's worth it."

"Could you do what he does to get what he has?"

Pete didn't hesitate. "If it gets me a ticket out of this iceberg to a warm, sunny beach surrounded by dolls in bathing suits, maybe..."

Rusty snorted.

It was an hour before the auction was set to begin, so they wandered through the maze of boats along the station's harbor, stopping for a double take or once over whenever one would catch their eye. The bigger vessels were docked in the water while the smaller ones were lined side by side ashore. Some were dry docked, others on the ground. The arrangement followed rank, with the simple rowboats first to be auctioned. The "big boys," the ones that would hold the crowd, would be last to sell. He was amazed at the variety of boats and found everything from row boats to sail boats to modified motor boats used as rumrunners. He saw a Lyman smaller and older than his plus a small, narrow wooden Punt boat built by a local fellow he had met a few times who built this type of boat for use in the marshes off Sandusky and Catawba. Apparently, the Coast Guard felt this particular little boat did more than duck hunt or slog through marsh reeds.

"Check this out, Rust," he heard Pete's excited voice from behind a large 35-foot Hacker cruiser.

He rounded the cruiser's stern and saw Pete ogling a 26-foot Chris Craft runabout that looked like new. It was sleek and had a 100 horsepower Curtis aero engine in it.

"I bet it was a runner. This is it. This is what we bid on." Pete ran his hand over the boat's gunwales like he was checking the lines on a horse even though Rusty felt confident he had never been close to a horse in his life.

"It's the bee's knees. Al would like this baby."

"That's the problem," Rusty said. "It looks like a fancy boat."

Pete looked puzzled.

"It's too obvious. A boat like this is going to get nailed for sure."

"But you can tell its fast just looking at her. It can outrun anything the coasties got."

"Forty tops. Come here a minute, Pete." Rusty walked over to the wharf where the Guard had its personal arsenal of boats moored. When Pete caught up with him, he pointed to a 33-foot Garwood former racing boat modified for cargo. "That's a runner. Now check out the engines on it. 500 horsepower Liberty airplane engines... 50 miles per hour easy."

Pete stared.

"It's not in the auction because the Guard is using it to chase down runners. They are seizing powerful, fast boats like this from rumrunners, commissioning them into their fleet and using the rumrunner's own custom built boat to capture other runners. In other words, fighting fire with fire."

Pete looked disappointed.

"Now, do you think that Chris Craft, as is, can outrun this coasties' runner?"

"We'd modify it."

Rusty headed back into the maze of boats for sale.

"I'm gonna buy it, Rust," Pete called out.

"Do what you want, it's not my money."

Rusty spent the remaining time looking over the boats, more interested by them in general than actually searching for a runner or fishing boat.

After a time, he noticed the auctioneer climbing onto a makeshift podium made from an overturned crate. He had a megaphone in hand. An assistant with paperwork sidled up next to him.

Pete appeared with a bidding ticket. "What did you find?"

"Nothing."

"Nothing? What do you mean nothing? You telling me out of all these boats you can't find jack?"

"Yeah."

Pete shook his head in disgust. "Well, I am bidding on the Chris Craft."

"You do that."

"Al wants a boat."

"Al wants a runner."

Pete threw his hands up and stormed off towards the small crowd gathering for the auction.

"Let's get this show on the road," the auctioneer said through a megaphone.

Rusty found Pete standing in the middle of bidders and joined him. A number of guardsman perched around the wharf to watch the action.

The auctioneer singled out the Punt boat to begin, said a brief description, briefer history and why it was so necessary to own…then he launched into number rattling, his prattle competing with the mew of gulls circling overhead.

Halfway through the sale, the Chris Craft came on the block. Rusty felt relieved. He was cold and had lost interest and knew they could leave after this regardless if Pete bought it or not.

The auctioneer opened with a bid of seventeen hundred dollars. Said it was a fine boat and an insult to start lower.

Someone in the crowd yelled, "One thousand."

"Shame on you, sir," the auctioneer cried, but began the prattle at one thousand.

"Don't appear too eager," Rusty said in a lowered voice. "Let it ride up."

Pete listened much to his amazement. When the price stalled at eighteen hundred, Pete raised his ticket. The bid then bounced around until it reached twenty-one.

"Al gave me four grand, but that was to cover your fishing boat, too," Pete whispered.

"I wouldn't go over twenty-two," Rusty said under his breath.

When the price jumped to $2,175.00, Pete froze.

Rusty looked at him, and saw he was transfixed on the man bidding against him.

Pete looked uncomfortable. He shook his head to the auctioneer to indicate he was through.

The auctioneer rattled on a few more seconds, paused then shouted, "Stolen for $2,175.00 to bidder number 12!"

Pete pushed his way through the crowd, heading towards the car.

"What the hell just happened back there," Rusty said, catching up.

Pete halted. "See bidder 12 and those two guys with him?"

"Yeah?"

"They're connected to Cleveland's Mayfield Gang. They can have the damn boat."

***

Pete dropped Rusty off at Sam's. "What do I tell Al?"

"Just what happened, Rusty said. "We didn't see anything that measured up."

Pete looked disappointed. "I'll tell him we are keeping our eyes open."

"Stay out of trouble, Pete… and don't go looking for it either."

Pete gave him a faint smile before driving off.

Rusty climbed into his truck and started for home. As he crossed through the intersection in the middle of town, he looked out of habit at the fishery on the river just before crossing the bridge. Its small fleet of fishing vessels was beginning to trickle back up the river after a day on the lake chasing late season fish before the ice settled in and grounded them until spring thaw. One vessel, one that had not been there previously, sat in dry dock. It was a small but typical Lake Erie trap net boat, built for commercial fishing and rough weather. It looked more hardy than fast and had capacity for cargo. A "for sale" sign leaned against the wooden structure the boat sat upon.

Rusty craned his neck over his shoulder for a final look at it before crossing the bridge. A thought hatched in his mind. He checked his watch; it was just after five. Dinner at the farm was at five. He winced. He drove past his cottage and headed straight for the farm. He would be late. He would have to explain his tardiness more out of politeness than fear of chastising. He would apologize to his mother-in-law who would be keeping his food warm in a low oven then to Di. As he drove into the growing darkness of early December's short days, it allowed him the time to think and the thought that had planted itself in his head when he had seen the fishing tug had taken root and was emerging into an idea. By the time he reached the farm, he knew what he needed to do. Whether he did it or not would depend upon Di. He hadn't felt this heady since Lyman sold him the ramshackle boat that would become *Rising Sun.* He hadn't felt this hopeful since its sinking.

He apologized unabashedly to his mother-in-law when he arrived, smacked a kiss on Di's forehead and attacked his supper with gusto. Di and her mother exchanged glances. He seemed as one who had caught a slight breeze in a doldrums sea. His mother-in-law shrugged to Di and disappeared from the kitchen, leaving them alone.

Di sat opposite of him at the table regarding him with an air of suspicion. Although she sat over an arm's length away, he was always grateful she remained instead of disappearing along with her mother. It was enough to keep him encouraged at least. So not to chase her away, he usually kept the conversation light, chatting about the mill and the characters there or current events or the latest books or movies, non-threatening topics that she normally would have been interested in. Over the past weeks, he had conditioned himself not to be hurt by her distancing or vague replies.

But about every two weeks, after the small talk had wrapped up, he would ask her bluntly when she planned to come home. Her answer was always very clear and adamant—"I never want to see the lake again." The reply stabbed his heart each time, but still he asked, hoping upon hope that time really did heal wounds and she would eventually relinquish her stance and return to her once beloved cottage. So when he asked her again this time and she just shook her head in disbelief that he would ask again so soon, he knew he had his answer as to what he would do next. Meanwhile, he would wait for her as long as it would take.

Chapter 41

Sunday morning Rusty skipped church. He had told Di the night before to go without him. Sunday, he had explained, was the only day he could do this particular task because of his work schedule. He would join them for Sunday dinner, though. Consensus of opinion was that he was probably shopping around for a house inland.

His "task" took him to the downtown fishery's wharf where the fishing boat he spotted the day before sat in dry dock. The fishing fleet was in and moored for Sunday rest. Upon his arrival, big snowflakes began floating down. The place was deserted, or so he thought as he made a beeline for the trap net fishing boat with the for sale sign. He was under the hull when he heard a familiar voice.

"Gonna buy it?" It was Eddie. Prince sat next to him with cocked head.

"Thinking about it." He came out from underneath the hull. "Why aren't you in church?"

"Why aren't you?"

Rusty feigned a scowl. "Wisenheimer."

Eddie grinned.

"You're a man-about, is anyone from the fishery here today?"

Eddie pointed towards the company's ice house. "I saw a fella go in there a few minutes ago."

Rusty walked to the ice house with Eddie and Prince in tow. "Hello," he called in the doorway.

A small man with a double layer of gloves came out. His teeth had a slight chatter. "Just inside warming up," he said, winking at Eddie who rolled his eyes. "What can I do for you, Rusty?"

"That boat for sale…what's the story on it?" he said.

"It's from Port Clinton Fish Company. It needed work and since it was basically surplus, Walt decided to sell it."

They ambled towards the boat.

"Does it float?"

"Hell yes."

"What's he asking?"

"Not asking, he's telling. He wants two thousand, five hundred."

"Mind if I climb aboard and look around?"

"Be my guest."

Rusty climbed up and into the boat while the man and Eddie waited below and Prince snapped at snowflakes.

The boat was heavily constructed and larger and far bulkier than *Rising Sun*. It was 33 feet in length with a beam of 10 feet 2 inches and powered by a 40 horsepower diesel engine mounted below the pilothouse. The shaft drive of the propeller was enclosed and the propeller positioned underneath. It had a shallow hull and was carvel planked with Longleaf yellow pine then tinned over with steel sheeting. The pilothouse, located forward amidships, was tucked under a sturdy canopy with four square windows for a windshield. Unlike the fishery's other boats, this one had an open deck with no obstruction between the pilot seat and stern. It also relied on a bilge pump instead of scruppers to remove excess water that washed overboard. The trap net boat as a whole was void of any detailing beyond practical needs. What *Rising Sun* had in its graceful lines and rich mahogany decking and trim, this boat lacked. It was a commercial fishing boat built for the sole purpose to catch and hold fish and handle battering waves in its capacity as a daily working vessel.

Rusty examined the engine compartment, bilge and hold and then poked around the pilothouse. By the time he crawled down, a light coating of snow had accumulated on the man's and Eddie's hats and shoulders and Prince's back.

"Twenty-five hundred, uh?"

"Uh-huh."

"Thanks for letting me check it over."

"Sure thing," the man said. "Walt will be in bright and early tomorrow if you need to talk to him." He hurried back, passing the ice house, to the building housing the office leaving Rusty and Eddie alone.

"Hey, kid, how about some breakfast on me? I could go for pancakes on a day like today."

Eddie brightened and tapped the bed of the truck for Prince to jump in and then scrambled into the passenger seat next to Rusty. They each ate a double stack while Prince wolfed down two hamburgers.

Monday started the second shift swing giving him plenty of time to head back to the fishery to see Walt. Following his own advice to Pete, he put his game face on and walked into the office as nonchalant as he could.

"Hey, Rusty," Walt said with a big smile when he walked through the doors. "How've you been?"

"I've been better."

Walt's smile slowly faded. "Yeah…what happened was a downright disgrace. How's Di?"

"She's okay."

"How's it going at the mill?"

"It's a paycheck."

Walt nodded. "So what brings you here on such a lovely day?" Outside it was snowing.

"I was wondering what price you needed for that trap net boat in dry dock?"

Walt raised his brows. "You interested in that thing?"

"Depends on the price."

"Are you fixing to use it to replace *Rising Sun*? I mean, it's like comparing a delivery truck to a Model A."

"I know."

Walt rubbed his chin. "It would make a nice good size charter boat, but I got to level with you, Rust, it needs work."

"I see that. That's why I'm hoping we can deal."

Walt crossed over to the window and looked at the boat. It was almost obscured by the falling snow. "I wish I had an opening for you on the fleet." He sighed. "The fish are getting harder to find and if anything, I'll be laying off instead of hiring come next spring if it doesn't turn around." He turned from the window. "Two twenty because I'd like to see you back on the water."

"$1,900.00 if you really want to see me."

Walt chuckled. "You're twisting my arm. I already gave you a deal…but I'll let you have it for $1,975.00 since it needs some work."

"Would you hold it for fifty bucks until I can get the money?"

"Sure. Who else would want this but you," Walt laughed. "You see diamonds where other men see stones."

They shook hands.

Rusty fished out a twenty and three tens from his wallet and handed it to Walt. "You know anyone who would want to buy a cottage?"

Walt took the money without counting it. "You're not talking about your place, are you?" He looked surprised.

"I am."

"Eh, Rust, this boat's not worth selling your cottage for if that's your plan."

"It's more than that. Di doesn't want to live on the lake anymore. I'm thinking of getting a place inland."

Walt's brows furrowed. "I can see her point of view." He grew thoughtful. "You got yourself a nice place there. Right on the lake… " He paused. "If you are serious and have thought this out…well, I might have someone in mind."

"I'd appreciate it if you pass the word along."

Walt's expression had gone from cheerful when Rusty had first walked into the door to somber now. "I just hope you haven't bit off more than you can chew."

"That makes two of us."

He had enough change left after his down payment on the boat for lunch, so he walked to Sam's to grab a sandwich before heading to work, unaware Eddie had been tailing him.

"So, you're gonna leave town without telling me," Eddie snapped. "That's just jake." He was fuming.

"I wouldn't leave without telling you." Rusty shot him an askance look. "And how did you know that? Eavesdropping on my conversation with Walt?"

Eddie ignored the questioned. "What the hell am I suppose to do? You said you would always look out for Prince and me. That makes you a liar."

Rusty stopped abruptly. "You watch your tone with me." Then he saw the hurt and desperate look on Eddie's face. "Listen kid, I do and will watch out for you. It just that things change and I can't live here anymore. It's not like I want to leave, I have to leave." He gripped Eddie's shoulder. "When I find a place...before I move...I promise you will be the first to know and I will give you an address and a telephone number where you can reach me. You can call from the drugstore. I'm also going to talk to Mrs. Donovan. She'll keep an eye on you."

Eddie pulled away and kicked at the air. "Blast it, she's nosy enough already!"

"That's because she cares about you. Like me."

"I see how you care."

"Stop it, Eddie. This has been hard enough on me. I'm not ditching you, understand?"

Eddie scowled. "Yeah, I understand all right. Just like my old man asks me if I understand that it's the booze and not him that beats me when he's drunk."

Rusty sighed. "I'm going in for a sandwich. Want one?"

"Nope. Might as well get use to you being gone starting now. Come on, Prince."

Rusty frowned as he watched Eddie and Prince heading down the sidewalk. In a way, he was dumping Eddie and it made him feel like crap. The load was getting heavy. Davey made him feel like crap. And Di most assuredly made him fell like crap. He walked into Sam's, took a seat at the counter and ordered a hamburger when what he really felt like was a beer.

Before he left, he handed a folded note to Sam to pass on to Pete. Without opening it, Sam tucked it between a jar of pickles and a can of baking powder. Had he opened it, he would have read *Pete, tell Al I got his runner, Rusty.*

***

Pete was stupefied as he stood before the homely boat astride the wooden structure at the fishery. "Tell me you were drunk when you bought this and wrote me the note."

The remark rolled off Rusty. "There's a runner inside there, you just don't see it."

"You sure in hell got that right. I thought we were talking about speedboats."

"You were talking speedboats. I was talking sneaky boats. Things aren't always what they seem."

Pete shot him a sideways glance. "Well, you certainly fooled me so how about spelling it out so I can convince Al why he should pay for this?"

"Al won't need convincing once it's explained. In fact, he'll like the idea."

"Then convince me because apparently this bird has flown over my head."

Rusty circled the rugged vessel as he explained. "It's a trap net commercial fisher and will remain so. It will head out into the lake just like any other commercial fishing vessel and lay a string of nets."

Pete looked blank.

Rusty grinned at Pete's clueless expression and continued. "Only the fishing grounds it will be heading for will be the pickup spot for the booze, and when we string the nets out in the lake, bottles of bootleg will be bundled in those nets, marked and waiting under water to be picked up later that night. Bottles instead of fish. Its fish hold will be filled with more than whitefish and herring and operating right under the Coast Guard's nose. If they snoop around, they'll find fish in the hold and some fishermen just casting their gill nets."

"A wolf in sheep's clothing."

"Now you're on the trolley."

"Damn, somehow it doesn't have the same kick. You are relegating me to the role of a fisherman on a…a worn out fishing boat? What a come down after my previous rum running career."

Rusty smiled. "The money will make you feel better."

Pete snorted.

"Before you get your shorts in a knot and decide to jump ship, come over to the truck. I want to show you something." Pete followed him to the truck, and Rusty opened the passenger side door and pulled out a long, bulky bundle wrapped in cloth secured with string.

He untied the string and removed the cloth wrap, revealing a detailed wooden model of a boat.

Pete looked over his shoulder. "What's this?"

"This, Pete, is your runner. Actually it's my runner. We will use it along with the trap net boat. Fishing boat by day, runner by night."

Pete's eyes shot to his. "Kind of small ain't it?"

Rusty scowled at him. "Funny, wise guy. It's a model."

"I can see that."

"I made it to scale. One inch equals one foot. This is 32 inches long, so the boat itself will be…"

"Thirty-two feet," Pete finished. "You building a runner?"

"Uh-huh."

"Then there is a speedboat involved."

"Trap net boat drops off and speedboat picks up and delivers."

Pete looked like someone who had just figured out a magic trick. "I know where you're headed with this. The fishing boat picks up the booze across the border and smuggles it back over. Once it reaches its "fishing grounds," she drops her nets loaded with sauce. The runner then retrieves it later under the cover of darkness."

"And you said you didn't get it."

Pete studied the model. It was beautifully crafted right down to the detail of the dashboard and bench seats under the removable (on the model version only) pilot house. The replica represented a long, sleek runabout of 32 feet in length with a beam of 9 feet. It showed the pilot house located forward, streamlined low and enclosed with small square windows on each side and a narrow but wide rectangular windshield, angled back aerodynamically. Only one small window overlooked the after deck and was located in the center between the two seats. The deck was also completely enclosed with a slight barrel shape to the decking with one large hatch access to the engine amidships and two hatches fore and aft of the engine compartment. There was no doubt to her looks that she would be all business and she left no question as to her role on the lake. She was the sturdy, big sister to the Chris Craft Pete had wanted, but he didn't seem to mind. She looked fast, muscular and mysterious.

"How much cargo can she hold?" he asked.

"I figured about 80 cases. 100 if we bundle them in burlap. The weight of engine and crew as well as the weight of the steel plating will determine how much cargo weight we can carry."

Pete's eyes glazed. "Twelve bottles to a case—that's 1200 bottles. Case costs around $8.00, sells across the border at $50-60.00—that's an easy $50,000.00! And that's not even cut! We're going to be rich!"

"The trap net boat will hold three hundred cases worth if you go by the pounds of the fish it can hold," Rusty continued, but he wasn't sure if Pete was even listening as he seemed to be stuck back on the profit to be made and kept running numbers over and over again.

***

Walt's hunch was right, someone, his sister actually, wanted the cottage. Within a week, she paid Rusty for it and gave him thirty days at his request to pack and move. No hurry, she had said, as long as she could be in by spring. He paid off the remaining mortgage and Walt for the balance on the trap net boat and spent the week looking for a place to rent. He already had an idea as he had, like Walt had questioned, thought it out painstakingly after his last visit with Di. In fact, it was on the ride home from the farm on that occasion that the decision to sell the cottage was cemented. *Too many memories. Too empty.* It became just an address without her.

Chapter 42

"Petey comes running back to me and tells me I gotta lay out some serious dough here for two boats. I asked him, *why do I need two boats when I already got one lined up and just need one other?* And he says we're gonna sneak booze in right under the coasties' noses and we need a big fishing boat for that." Al leaned back in his chair and took a puff on his cigar. He, along with his brothers Lou and Joe and cousin, Pete had met Rusty at a corner table in Sam's. A freezing rain was falling and Al was antsy that the trip back could be dicey. Giuseppe did not come along, and Rusty figured with the brooding Trapani siblings, there was no need for Giuseppe's strong arm. "I can see how the fish boat can hold more booze and how it can pretend to be fishing. That's sneaky. What I fail to see is how it can make connections on shore…I mean a damn commercial fishing boat heading for a remote inlet or unusual dock is going to look suspicious."

Rusty almost expected a snicker from the two brothers but instead they sat stone face, staring at him.

"It won't be making deliveries," he said, "That would be fishy. Instead, she will drop her gill nets as though we are stringing her line, only her nets will be a string of bundles attached at intervals to the line. Inside the bundles will be bottles of Canadian booze. The bogus fishermen, namely us, will cast the booze-filled nets into the water. To the observer, it looks like a fishing boat is stringing its line. The net, with bottles attached, sink and stay put with the help of net weights. Should the Coast Guard inspect or search the vessel, no booze is found. After dark, the speedboat retrieves the bundles and delivers to the contact. Coast Guards will be watching the islands and boats coming across, but we will be leaving from our base on shore and not heading far out in the lake. As for the speedboat, since I am building it, I plan to keep it for myself and pay for the materials. You would be, basically speaking, chartering it like the *Rising Sun* plus a cut of the merchandise it will be hauling. The trap net fish boat is yours. It will be an easy sell when you no longer have use for it. I'll just take my cut that we agree upon for the cargo and piloting of it."

Al was quiet and puffed his cigar as he sized up Rusty. Finally, he said, "Why do I need your runner?"

Rusty proceeded with caution. "Because the speedboat retrieves the string of net bundles overnight and make the deliveries quickly. It can also act as a decoy if needed. It can get in and get out fast."

"How do you know where the nets are in the dark?" Lou said.

"Map coordinates, lights on shore and net markers floating on the water to mark the spots the nets are located. There is nothing suspicious about that. Fishermen use net markers to mark their string."

Al said, "Why bundle the bottles in the first place and how do you keep them from breaking when you toss them overboard?"

Rusty felt uneasy as if he was seated before an inquisition as all black Trapani eyes were latched on to him and every word he said.

"You can haul more bottles by bundling them together because you are eliminating the bulkiness and weight of cases, and because of their flexibility, you can also stack in more bundles than you can cases. Instead of 300 cases, you could fit…say 100 cases more if the bottles are removed and bundled into netting. That's just an estimate."

Rusty could see Pete was struggling to stay quiet. He was excited and bursting to put in his two cents to convince the Trapani siblings that this was a good plan. "Pete, why don't you tell them how they bundle the bottles based on what you've seen when you were running."

Pete was eager to tell. "Between 25-50 bottles could be bundled together by placing them in burlap stuffed with straw to keep the bottles from clinking together then wrapping net around each bundle. The net is drawn tight so there is no bottle movement. Then each bundle is tied at 50 foot intervals and tossed overboard and strung in a long run like you were stringing gill nets. Probably a run of…" he looked at Rusty for the answer.

"500 feet—just like the gill nets."

"The nets," Pete continued, "are marked with net markers to help locate them later just like the gill nets are marked," he said with a nod to Rusty. "Like Rusty said, to anyone watching, it will look like we're fishermen stringing our gill nets."

Al narrowed his eyes. "Who's gonna unpack those cases and bundle them bottles?"

"Well," Rusty said thinking, "there are guys on the Canadian side that will do it for a price…"

"Or we can do it ourselves. There are enough of us leftover from the warehouse," Pete added.

"Can't go to Canada to do that," Lou said.

"No," Al said, leaning back in his chair. "But we can set up shop on the Canadian side on Middle Island. That's the first leg of our operation anyways, and the same fella who is letting us use his shanty to store booze for the second leg pickup will more than likely jump at the chance to take a cut to let us bundle bottles in it. Hell, Joe, you're over there as it is, boozing with the Canucks and rumrunners at that club house there." The more Al talked, the more he was getting into the idea of the fishing boat and the bundles. "Coasties head out for the islands about 4 or 5 in the afternoon to get in position to snag runners coming off them—the islands being big staging areas for rumrunners. It was going to be a trick sneaking off Middle Island and crossing over with a speedboat, but with the fish boat we'll be loaded and underway before the coasties even leave port. We'll probably even wave to them as they pass while we string our so-called nets." The thought made Al chuckle.

"To be accurate, the trap net fish boat will need to retrieve the cargo before dawn and be ready to string the line at daybreak," Rusty said. "That's when fishermen do it. Then sometime after midnight, Pete and I will collect the bundles and deliver them to the drop. If I do this right, we should be hard to detect, but if not, I plan to be faster than the fastest boat the Coast Guard has—even with a load."

Al's eyes were shining. "When will we be good to go?"

"First of April."

Al chuckled again and took a puff on his cigar. "Heh-heh-heh…April Fools."

Chapter 43

"Here's the deposit and two months' rent," Rusty said.

The man fingered through the wad of bills, double checking Rusty's count.

The action irritated Rusty and after completing the count, the man nodded in satisfaction and stuffed the bills in his pocket.

A river rat was the image that came to mind as he assessed his new landlord whose narrow face merged into a point at his large sharp nose, hooding his tobacco stained buck teeth. He even squirreled the money away like a rat would candy wrappers.

"Like I said, I make my rent collections the first day of the month so either be here or bring the money to me on or before the first. And none of this *I'll have the money tomorrow bullshit either."*

"Got you the first time," Rusty muttered.

The place was a boat shanty directly on the bank of the wide Huron River in the small coastal town of Huron. The shanty sat a stone's throw from where the river joined Lake Erie offering him a view of the lake between another boat shanty and a sail loft that sat between him and the open water. The river was only a few yards from his backdoor and the view, besides that of the sluggish river, included the stone yards and mounding hills of limestone gravel on the opposite bank. In front of the shanty, a one lane dirt road dead ended at the lake. Across from him, a short row of weather beaten Cape Cod-style cottages lined the opposite side of the road. A long rocky pier took up where the dirt road left off, jutting 600 feet into the lake. What Huron lacked in the rugged beauty of his cottage's coastline and Vermilion's New England-style charm, it made up for in its practicality of a small, hard-working fishing village. Di, he felt, would not have liked it.

His boat shanty was two stories high if viewed from the road and three stories if viewed from the river. It looked like a barn with peeling, gray painted clapboard siding and sliding barn doors on either end of the ground level floor. The ground level, with its barn-like interior was used as a garage and workshop with an open area large enough to store or build a boat within. The second story was accessed by an outside open staircase that ran up along the side of the building. It was made into a small efficient apartment with a kitchen area big enough for a stove, icebox, sink and small table, and two bedrooms big enough to squeeze in a twin bed and dresser in each. There was electricity available and a water closet on the first floor in the boat garage which, despite being within the building, still had to be accessed from the loft by going outside and down the staircase- not much different than using a backyard outhouse with the exception of better facilities.

The lowest level was a boat garage off the river. One could drive a boat from the river into the watery garage under the shanty. A rugged staircase, built upon a platform running along the interior, served as an access to the ground level floor. There was also a trap door where one could access the boat from the middle of the ground level garage directly onto the boat. He couldn't ask for more.

He had chosen Huron not just because he was familiar with it, but because it was located midway between Vermilion and Sandusky and it was not that far within reach of Di's farm which was now southeast of his new location whereas in Vermilion, it was more south. But it was a considerable drive to the steel mill in Lorain which would be a problem when ice and snow settled in.

When he first told Uncle Fritz he planned to sell the cottage and move to Huron, Uncle Fritz was taken back. *Why sell? Why Huron? Why not stay at the farm with Di?* He protested until Rusty reminded him that Di's return to the cottage was about as possible as pigs flying to which Uncle Fritz agreed. The cottage meant nothing to him now, he explained, and he would be closer to Lyman Boatwork's new facility in Sandusky where his skills as a former boat carpenter could resume at spring's hiring.

But Di...you should be with her, Uncle Fritz had pleaded.

She has been distant. Has she said she wanted me to stay here? Rusty had asked. *The farm is her refuge from me. Am I right?* Uncle Fritz didn't have an answer to that to which Rusty told him reaffirmed Huron for the time being until she mended.

With that being said, Uncle Fritz offered to explain the sell and move to the family but Rusty, he said, would have to be the one to break it to Di.

***

Her reaction was like a pendulum ranging from indifference to rage. One minute she didn't care because she never wanted to see the place or the water again; the next, she ranted and cried because he had no right selling it without asking her to which he agreed wholeheartedly and apologized over and over.

Why Huron? She had demanded.

Because it offered an opportunity for him to make more money to get them a place inland, he had answered. *It also was halfway between her and Lyman's boat company.*

So you're going to dump the mill as well? What's next- me? This was followed by the door to her room being slammed in his face.

Damned if I do; damned if I don't, he thought feeling more confused than ever.

A week later, Uncle Fritz and Di's brothers helped him move the majority of the cottage possessions back to the farm and into a storage barn, and then they helped him move the necessities he needed to Huron. They didn't say much when they saw the boat shanty but the look on their faces were bewildered. One brother suggested he best take the interurban to Lorain than to drive to work—*save on gasoline and catch some zzzs coming and going.* A thought Rusty already had prior to handing over the rental down payment.

Once he settled in, he had two things to do right away—take Eddie by interurban to Huron to show him the boat shanty and the ins and outs of the electric railway that ran from Vermilion to Huron. He showed him the route from the depot to his place on the river, hoping it would give Eddie some piece of mind that he was not a world away. If he needed help or just wanted to visit, he need only catch the interurban in Vermilion and he would be in Huron in a short time, he reassured Eddie. He had already talked to Mrs. Donovan. He left money with her for trolley fare to Huron and he would pay Eddie's fare back to Vermilion, a resolution that made Eddie a bit more at ease; the second thing he needed to do was to have Pete help him get the trap net fishing boat to Huron. As the fishery lowered the boat into the Vermilion River by crane, he hoped like the dickens Walt was right when he said it would float and power on its own as the cold lake was no place to tests the waters both figuratively and literally.

Pete was no sailor but he was eager and listened and that held water for Rusty. The twenty minute cruise went without a hitch. She was no *Rising Sun*, but she handled better than he expected and that pleased him. Besides a bit of structural work, the engine was telling him it needed tuning. He breathed a sigh of relief when they finally docked up river at a marina that had agreed to dry dock the fishing boat for winter. He noticed Pete was grinning while they secured the boat. He may not have like the idea of playing the part of a fisherman, but Pete seemed to relish the thrill of their clandestine enterprise.

Chapter 44

He began to wonder if perhaps he was a bit too optimistic when he had told Al the boats would be ready the first of April. Christmas was fast approaching and each passing day meant less daylight as time raced towards the shortest day of the year. Sunlight was at a premium and by the time he stepped off the trolley in Huron from his day shift at the mill, sunlight was no more than a milky glow just above the western horizon.

The next two evenings he spent arranging his shop below the apartment. He had one light bulb in the center of the first floor's barn-like garage and one over a workbench along a side wall. Normally, the lighting would be adequate, but for the intricate building of the boat, he would need more illumination. He located two dusty kerosene lanterns on a shelf and an empty metal can. He added kerosene to his mental note of supplies for the hardware store.

He checked the wood stove in the corner for creosote buildup, webs and mouse nests. There was no wood, so the trip to town would have to include firewood and coal lumps with enough for the stove upstairs in the apartment loft as well. As he hung his tools on the wall over the workbench and set up the jigs, he mulled over how he could fit work, boat building, Di and sleep into 24 hours. He could not afford to compromise any, but Di, he finally decided, would have to be Sundays and a day or two during the week—a thought he could not bear, but a thought made justifiable that absence would make her heart grow fonder. It could also backfire and reveal she could do without him. He pushed the thought out of his head as fast as it had popped in. Now sleep he could handle. He would grab forty winks on the trolley to and from the mill. After all, if he could catch winks onboard during the war, he could sleep on the noisy trolley. Then there was Christmas around the corner, getting in the way. He already had holiday plans with her and did not want to compromise there. No, he couldn't and wouldn't miss any opportunity she allowed him to be with her, even if it meant checking your pride at the gate to take her ice skating at the park's rink. Yes, he would grab sleep here and there like in the war and hope like hell both the relationship and the boats would be good to go come spring.

Using Al's reimbursement money for the trap net fishing boat, he bought supplies he needed to build the runner. By Christmas Eve, he had a load of lumber stacked in his shanty consisting of white oak, hard maple and Louisiana red cypress, cartons of nails of various grades and sizes, cartons of brass screws and three wrapped gift boxes containing a diamond clip (the latest in hat accessories he was assured), blue silk stockings with a crossword puzzle-like pattern at the calves (also assured as vogue) and the novel, *The Bridge of San Luis Rey* (a

Pulitzer Prize winner he was informed). Once Christmas and New Year's Eve was out of the way he could get down to business, he assured himself as he drove to the farm in a fresh powder of snow to pick up Di for Christmas Eve church services.

Her mother was pulling an apple strudel out of the oven as he opened the kitchen door and let the aroma of cinnamon and nutmeg escape out into the night. Sticky pecan rolls and creamy cheesecake topped with a layer of sour cream already graced the table. Damn, Christmas smells good, he thought as the spicy scents swirled around him. At some point he thought he whiffed rice pudding. His stomach growled, and he hoped the minister kept it short tonight. After all, they all knew the story, and the rice pudding would be getting cold.

The rest of the family followed their noses into the kitchen. Di's mother smacked the youngest brother's hand as he reached for a caramelized pecan on an end roll.

"Christmas morning," she said.

As the family began pulling on their coats and hats for church, Di motioned Rusty to the parlor. She pulled a package from under the Christmas tree and handed it to him. "I thought you might want this before church."

He looked at her quizzically, and removed the wrapping. Inside was a pair of black oxfords dress shoes like the ones he had kicked off his feet in the water just after *Rising Sun* had sunk. His former shoes, like *Rising Sun* and his dreams now rested in the bottom of Lake Erie. He felt a lump in his throat.

He was lost for words as he stared fixedly on the shoes. She felt a twinge of panic. She hadn't expected that reaction.

"You needed shoes for church. I knew how much you liked your old ones," she stammered. Her face felt suddenly hot. *What was she thinking?*

He swallowed his lump and reached for her hand. Their eyes brimmed with tears. "This is exactly what I needed. I needed dress shoes and these are perfect. You are right…I do like these shoes."

"It's hard to find something you like."

"I like everything you give me. You know what I like."

She brushed away a stray tear.

He removed his boots and put the shoes on and stood up. "Joe Brooks or what?" he said with a grin, trying to make her laugh.

She nodded and smiled, though faintly. But it was a smile.

"Di! Rusty! *Schnell!*" Uncle Fritz called from the door.

They loaded up in the automobiles with Di climbing into the truck seat next to Rusty. It felt like old times. Or at least damn close.

Chapter 45

Rusty lit the wood stove and the kerosene lamps. It was two days past Christmas, and he was already behind. He gathered an assortment of 2x4s and 2x8s, nails and a hammer and began sawing and hammering until he had a wooden jig big enough to hold and support the framing of the boat. The howling arctic wind shook the shanty's walls and seeped around the barn-like doors like icy fingers, but he felt quite comfortable inside, and when his fingers got too cold, he warmed them up at the wood stove. It took hours to build the wooden support structure, and when he finally nailed the last piece and stepped back to critique it, he checked his watch and was shocked to see the time. Hunger had eluded him and offered no clue as to the time. He killed the stove and lamps and buttoned up the shanty, clocking in with only a minute to spare for the start of the afternoon shift.

The first thing he did the following morning was dig out a clock with chimes—one of three they had received as wedding gifts years ago. He mounted it in the workshop over the workbench. After lighting the stove, he removed two of the thickest planks of white oak, one being the longest; the other, the widest. He began with the wide plank- the one he had carefully selected at the lumberyard for the curvature of its grain. He traced a curved pattern that he had drawn on paper onto the wood to correspond with the curvature of the oak's grain. Satisfied, he began to saw on the drawn lines. By the time work rolled around, the crude semblance of a stem—the part that rises from the keel at its forward end creating the bow—had emerged from the plank of wood.

The remainder of the week was dedicated to shaping and smoothing the stem and then laying out the keel from the longest plank of oak. Once the keel was cut to width and length and placed atop the jig, he used a planer to mold and shape its form, shaving and chiseling here and there until a sturdy backbone emerged.

Often he clocked into work with less than a minute to spare. More than once he fell asleep on the trolley and had to be jostled awake at his stop. The farm visits were no longer daily, but he made sure to join the family at supper during evening shifts and to be there on Sundays. He was burning the candle at both ends, and his foreman was growing more perturbed with each passing day as his productivity fell. His lack of sleep and a schedule that crammed 36 hours into 24 made him slack at work. He felt like an overloaded circuit about to blow a fuse.

The boat project came to a halt for another holiday hurdle—New Year's Eve. He had traded shifts with another fellow at the steel mill so he could surprise Di with a masquerade ball at the Crystal Ballroom courtesy of Al and Constance Trapani. Normally, she would have given her eye teeth for such an invitation but she declined, pointedly stating if he couldn't get why she was in no mood, well, he just didn't get it. Oh, he got it. As difficult as the boat would be to build, it was going to be far easier than building back their relationship, he ruminated. So on New Year's Eve, while Al popped the champagne cork in the Vermilion ballroom and Pete threw up on his bearcat in an East 9th Street speakeasy, Rusty played pinochle, drank pilsners, and ate pork roast smothered in sauerkraut with Uncle Fritz and family. When midnight rolled around, he toasted it with a glass of elderberry wine and dropped a bombshell of a kiss on Di to her surprise.

***

The following week was dedicated to splicing one inch oak boards and shaping them into the transom. It was at this point he began to drift away from the typical Lyman construction he used when he was employed by the company. The Lyman family, however, was also involved in the popular sport of boat racing and racking up trophies and championships with their legendary boats, so building the racers gave him first-hand knowledge of how to make a boat fast. His plan for the runner was to marry the Lyman technology of endurance and racing speed with the best of designs culminated from legendary speedboats and runners that would promote speed, flexibility, and endurance enough to carry a payload at a high rate of speed with maneuverability. This boat would also need to offer protection for cargo, engine and crew and an engine big enough to complete the demanding task. And with that in mind, he set about building a boat that might have peers, but no superiors.

The transom would contribute to that goal by being narrower than the beam at mid-section to reduce drag so the water would have no resistance as it passed around the sides of the boat. The bow would be straight up and down in keeping with the Lyman traditional design, but it would be narrow and razor-sharp like a wedge point to split the water before getting up to planing speed.

When the transom was completed, he secured it to the aft end of the keel. With the stem and transom attached to the keel, he had a strong, solid spine on which he could now add the bones, muscles and guts.

To start the skeletal framework, he attached wooden molds he had constructed weeks earlier from patterns based on his blueprints and model. These molds, strategically placed at intervals along the topside of the keel would provide a frame on which the strakes and ribs could be shaped into position and secured. Once the framework was in place, the molds would then be removed and the boat's shape first revealed.

But building the skeleton would not only take time, but need an extra hand. He thought of Uncle Fritz. His woodworking skills would be advantageous (not to mention he owned every tool under the sun), but then he would have explaining to do as Uncle Fritz would know the boat atypical and be curious. And what would Fritz say when he learned he was building a rumrunner boat? It would make him an abettor to rumrunning. Damn. Uncle Fritz should not be involved, not this way at least, he decided. Then there was Pete and company—worthless as tits on a bull when it came to manual labor. Probably thought a hammer was a weapon instead of a tool. As for Davey, he already had plans for him to help install the engine. Whether Davey would help or not remained to be seen. But maybe, he thought, Davey would like to be involved from the ground up to give him something—anything to do. That is, if Davey didn't object to being a partner in crime. And if he did agree, there would be no one more capable or button-lipped to help him, save Uncle Fritz. There was one thing to do—go see Davey.

***

That all too familiar guilt pang in his stomach that he had come to know the last six months stabbed him in the gut again as he pulled up to the curb in front of Davey's home. The driveway was filled in with snow and the house had the look of a place long deserted.

The front steps to the porch were drifted, so he stepped through the snow to the side door. The stoop was hidden beneath eight inches of snow. He knocked on the door and waited a minute or two and then, banged on it. A frosty window on the neighbor's house next door opened. The neighbor lady stuck her head out.

"Open the door and holler in. He's probably asleep."

He acknowledged with a wave and cracked the door open. He called out hello, and then waited. There was no response so he took a step inside. "Hello! Davey? You home?" Five steps led from the door directly up to the kitchen. There was no response. He started slowly up the steps. The house had the musky smell of vacancy. He called out again. "Davey? It's Rusty. Hello? Hello?" Reaching the top of the steps, he scanned the kitchen. A casserole dish and plates in various stages of use littered the table and counter tops. He grimaced. "Davey? Mrs. Reynolds? It's Rusty." A feeling of anxiety began to creep over him. The nosy neighbor woman would have known if they were not home, so they had to be here, he thought. As much as he felt like an intruder, he felt compelled to search for them. No longer sensitive to his trespassing, he searched the rooms one by one until he entered the back bedroom and found Davey slumped in his wheelchair at the window. Rusty's heart landed in his throat. Davey looked dead. He rushed to him and shook his shoulder vigorously. Davey jumped awake.

"Jumping Jesus!" Davey shouted. His eyes were the size of ping pong balls.

"Chrissake, Davey, you scared the crap out of me."

"You? I'm the one who got snuck up on and had the crap scared out 'em."

Rusty wasn't sure who was shaking more- him or Davey. "I'm sorry as all hell, but when you didn't answer…I thought the worse."

"There you go thinking again." Davey straightened himself in the chair. "Not sure if I'm happy to see you or not. You scared the be-geezers out of me."

"You should lock the door if you are such a sound sleeper.

"Why? You probably would have kicked it in and then I would have a door to fix along with my heart."

"You're welcome." Rusty sunk wearily on the bed. "Where's your mother?"

Davey's face suddenly fell, sending a wave of dread through Rusty. "Why, Rusty, she went into an old timers home just before Christmas," he said in a soft voice. "She thought she saw her cat out in the snow and went after it. She hadn't had a cat for thirty years!" He shook his head. "Police found her wandering in the middle of the road three blocks over. Said she was so covered with snow she looked like a snowman. No shoes. No coat. And here I sit like a bag of guts unable to do a blasted thing about her wandering off but to call out to the neighbors for help." He looked down at his legs. "Worthless. Worthless."

Rusty hung his head. "I wish your neighbor would have let me know. It twists me to think your Christmas was alone. You could have spent Christmas with us. Di's family is very welcoming." *Would have, could have, should have.* He should have thought to have stopped in before the holidays. He should have bought them a duck or ham…groceries, for crying out loud. But no, he was too wrapped up in himself. "I'm sorry about your mother."

Davey shrugged. "She's better off. She's getting the care she needed. Half the time, she didn't even know who I was—thought I was a burglar once. Hollered and carried on so, it's a wonder the neighbors didn't call the police."

Rusty sighed. This probably was not a good time to bring up the boat. Then Davey opened the door in the conversation.

"So what have you been up to?" he asked, snapping Rusty out of his thoughts.

"Still at the mill. Di still at the farm. Sold the cottage. Been building a boat."

"Whoa, there—sold the cottage?"

"Di never wants to see the water again."

Davey frowned. "Are you living at the farm?"

"I got a boathouse in Huron."

Davey raised his brows. "That must be the building the boat part of the story."

Rusty nodded.

"I'm glad to hear you're building a boat. Can't say that about the rest of the news. She gonna be another *Rising Sun*?"

"No…not really. I guess, though, you could say it is a charter." He was scrambling for words.

"I could say if you fill me in on the details."

"Well, it's bigger…"

"Uh-huh."

"Faster. Going to have a bigger engine…"

"Uh-huh, uh-huh."

"Stronger, more solid all the way around…better protection."

"Can't blame you there."

"Basically, a cargo hauler instead of a fishing boat."

Davey raised his brows again. "No longer a fishing charter?"

"No. Not at this point anyways."

"Hmm. That was always your dream."

"Well, we all had dreams at one time. Most the time they just stay dreams. I at least had a shot at mine. Short but sweet."

Davey nodded his head in agreement.

“It’s going to have two engines. Big ones.” It was like a confession.

“How big we talking?”

“What would you say if I said Liberty engines, that is, if I can find someone who deals with them?”

“Whoo-wee,” Davey said, leaning back in his wheelchair. He looked perplexed. “Oh, you can find them all right, but what in blue blazes would a charter boat need one aircraft engine for let alone two? What kind of cargo are you hauling anyways?” His eyes narrowed as he searched Rusty.

Rusty guessed he had a pretty good inkling.

“You’re not building what I think you are building?”

“What do you think I’m building?”

“I think you graduated from grape juice.”

Rusty looked out the window at Davey’s street view. Row after row of double story houses lined the street like peas in a pod. What a sight for a man who dreamed of being a cowboy, he thought. “I need your help with the engines and mechanical work, but could really use your help building the boat overall.”

Davey followed Rusty’s gaze out the window. “Is this something you really think you should do? You’ll be dealing with bad elements all the way around. That Coast Guard captain fellow, well, you’ll also be giving him the reason he needs to take you under.”

“He’s already taken me under. Besides, what makes you think he’ll get me again?”

Davey shook his head. “Money and revenge—the driving force behind man.” He shook his head. “Does your wife know about this?”

“No. And I plan to keep it that way.”

“Can’t you put that energy to better use? Build another fish charter boat, buy a home…if not for your own hide, than do it for Di’s sake.”

“It is for her sake and more.”

Davey wheeled himself to the center of the room. There was wistfulness in his voice. “How did we end up this way, Rust? What happened? We had a good job, good crew…life was good…” his voice trailed off.

“Sometimes you eat bear, sometimes the bear eats you.”

“I guess. Everything…everyone has changed.”

“Life is change and I’m going to change it again. That’s why I’m going to do this. I can’t change what happened but I’m going to try to make things better than they are now.”

“By involving yourself in a deadly game of chance?”

“Life is a chance, Davey. We took a chance each day we went to work on the tugs—a deadly chance at that, too.”

“Maybe so, but it wasn’t a game and it was honest money.”

“Maybe. But this is no game, either.”

Davey was thoughtful. They sat quietly for a minute, and then he asked, “How’s Di doing?”

"She's okay. Still bitter. Just got to give her time. Doctor said trauma like she had takes time to get over. He said don't be surprised if it's pushing spring."

Davey nodded. "Keep at her, don't lose her."

"I won't. But I'm going to build this boat and I could sure use your help."

Davey narrowed his eyes. He looked deep into Rusty's eyes. "There's a bad man out there calling himself the law."

Rusty remained quiet. He wasn't sure where Davey was going with this, but whatever was going through Davey's mind, it made his eyes grow dark.

"If you're hell bent on doing this, I know where we can get our hands on some airplane engines."

Rusty looked at him with surprise. "You'll help me then?"

"I'll help you stay out of trouble. God knows what you're getting yourself into."

***

He and Davey spent the next two days boarding up the Reynolds's house as it was obvious Mrs. Reynolds would not be returning. Having Davey move in with him at the boat shanty had a threefold purpose—help him build the boat, to give Davey a purpose and to look after him so Davey wouldn't be alone to wither away. He had decided after visiting Davey the last few times that the neighbor lady seemed more preoccupied with snooping than helping. He also resolved no matter how busy he was, he would take Davey to visit his mother once a week at the least.

With the water closet on the first floor, it was decided that Davey should sleep in the garage and a bed and nightstand was set up by the wood burner creating a simple, but warm nook. It would be a temporary arrangement until Rusty could come up with a better arrangement, which he set upon soon after Davey's arrival. He built a harness and block and tackle pulley system so Davey could lift himself out of his wheelchair, slide into a swing-like harness and pull himself up to the second floor or down to the first like a bucket in a well. He also purchased a second wheelchair for Davey's use on the second floor. That would give him a wheelchair on each floor.

It would be the harness assembly that would give Davey greater mobility and options. It would be the boat building that would give him back his spirit.

***

The first part of January was spent cutting, bending and attaching the stringers and ribs to form the framework. To get the wood flexible to bend into shape, Rusty built a steam box out tin roof sheeting, stove pipes and a five gallon metal container that held water to make the steam. He fashioned a long, tin "box" and connected it to the water container with the stove pipes. The wood stove provided the heat source for the water. When the water reached a boil and steam found its way through the piping into the tin box, he placed the wood pieces in the long tin box and after thirty to forty minutes, the wood- so hot they needed gloves—was ready to bend into shape. He and Davey worked quickly, bending and screwing the wood in place before it cooled and became rigid again. Instead of oak, Rusty chose maple for the ribs. Maple, he explained, was strong, but lighter in weight than oak. He also shaved them down a tad more than usual like they did on the Lyman racers to further reduce the weight.

Mid-January brought a squall that crippled the lakeshore from Huron to Avon Point. Electricity went out, roads were blocked and a trolley car derailed by a snow drift made the local newspapers' front page. From the warmth of the loft above the workshop, Rusty and Davey had watched the river and lakeshore form an ice crust and then, with each passing day, watched as the crust grew thicker.

Mid-January also brought a visit from Uncle Fritz as soon as the roads were cleared.

Chapter 46

"Here you are," Uncle Fritz said, stepping into the barn, the sound of hammering having led him there. The cavernous room glowed with light from the electric bulbs, kerosene lamps and glowing stove, a sharp contrast to the cold, blue dusk outdoors. His eyes immediately fell on the skeleton of the boat. "So this is why you weren't coming around as much." He walked towards the boat setting upside down upon the jig. Spotting Davey, he nodded, "Mr. Reynolds."

"How are you, sir," Davey replied.

Uncle Fritz's eyes scanned the boat. "What kind of boat is this? It certainly isn't another *Rising Sun.* Is it a new charter?" His eyes returned to Rusty. They were full of questions and wonder.

"It's neither," he said, pausing from hammering. He lowered his hammer and felt suddenly awkward.

"I'm afraid I know little about boats, so you'll have to enlighten me," Uncle Fritz said.

"I'm sorry, Uncle Fritz..."

"Sorry? Sorry about building a boat or sorry that I don't know? It's good to see you are back at it."

"I'm sorry I haven't been around as much. Between work and this..."

"We were just worried about you. Di has this gloom and doom thing going that you aren't well. When she decided you fell off the pier and was washed out into the lake, I said *enough already,* I'll go check on him."

"It's nice to know she cares."

"Hmm, yes," mumbled Uncle Fritz. He circled the boat, studying the construction, and running his hand along the chine. "You should have told me about this. I would have brought my tools and helped." He poked his head through the framing. "There's something exciting about building a boat. Chairs and tables are fine, but a boat...a boat is not fixed to one spot—it goes somewhere. It's adventure...it's freedom." He removed his head from between two ribs. "Ah, but perhaps I read too many books and daydream like the landlubber I am."

"Nothing wrong with that," Davey said, wheeling towards the workbench.

Rusty set the hammer down on the jig. "I could really use your help, Uncle Fritz, but I'm not sure you'll want to be a part of this." *This is going to get real thorny.*

Uncle Fritz looked puzzled. "Why?" He noticed Rusty shifting uneasily. "What's wrong with me helping on this?"

"You are not what's wrong. The boat is what's wrong."

Uncle Fritz raised his brows. "What's wrong with the boat?"

Rusty frowned. His vagueness was only compounding the mystery. "Its purpose is questionable."

"What are you saying, Rusty?"

Rusty hesitated, glancing almost sheepishly at the boat. "It's a charter boat for cargo hauling—for rum running," he finally said. There. It was out.

Uncle Fritz was quiet for a moment, absorbing the words. He then cleared his throat. "And who is this rumrunner you are building the boat for?"

Rusty was silent.

Uncle Fritz could tell he was wrestling with an answer. He looked intently at him, waiting for one.

"Me."

"You?"

"Yes."

Uncle Fritz sank onto a nearby stool, removed his hat and rubbed his hand over his hair. His lack of response was worse than a reaction.

Rusty glanced at Davey who had buried himself into a chiseling project at the workbench but was all ears.

"And when did you decide this undertaking?"

"When Di was in the hospital. That's when I decided to build the boat. The running for money was an afterthought."

"If you needed money…"

"I don't need money!"

"How much do you need?"

"I don't want your money!"

Uncle Fritz's eyes shot to Rusty's. They hardened. "My money is no good?"

"That's not what I meant."

"Then what is it you mean?" Uncle Fritz said, rising to his feet. "What in the hell do you think you're doing?"

Rusty didn't have an immediate answer and he could feel Uncle Fritz's eyes chiseling into him like the blade of Davey's knife carving into the wood.

"I made a deal."

"A deal? With who? The devil?"

"With the man I was chartering grape juice for."

"The Sicilian? Then you may as well be doing business with the devil. I thought you were smarter than this. What do you owe them? Tell me. I will give you money to help get out from under them. What do you owe them?"

"Nothing. Just my word. I made a deal to run beer and liquor for them. They needed a pilot. I needed a boat and out of that hell hole mill."

"That is not an answer. You need money and that *hell hole* pays your bills. That *hell hole* is respectable work that any man would give his eye teeth for."

"A respectable man wouldn't be down in the pit breathing in sooty shit and dodging molten rain."

"How dare you say that! It's an honest job- one that takes a *real* man to go to each day...not like some hood smuggling horse liniment for the likes of the mob."

"They are not the mob, and I'd say that's pretty ennobling coming from a man who has a shed lined with rows of homemade beer and wine...you're a regular little factory."

"How dare you. *How dare you.*" Uncle Fritz took a step forward and shook his finger. "The law, and I emphasize *the law*, allows me so much for personal use. And even if I share a bottle or two with friends and neighbors, I don't take a damn nickel for it. And you, my son, have crossed a line."

"The law allows you homemade wine not beer! Beer is *verboten*!" He regretted his comment the moment it launched from his lips. He had turned on Uncle Fritz like a cornered feral dog. *Lower than a dog.* "Uncle Fritz...I'm sorry. Sorry as hell. I'm way out of line." He looked off into space. "You're the...the only one that's been there for me. I'd understand if you can't forgive me, hell, I can't even forgive myself."

Uncle Fritz waved his hand and lowered himself back onto the stool. "Let's stop with all this hullabaloo and boo-hooing and get down to brass tacks. You are playing with fire and are going to get burnt. And to think I always thought you were level headed. Well, this is certainly a turn around. It's obvious a cool head is needed here." He glanced at Davey. "Are you in on this, too?"

"Me?" Davey said looking up. "I'm just building the boat. What he does with it is his business. I worked with him long enough to know how pigheaded he can be when his mind is made up. I figured I would do my best to keep him safe at least by helping him build a good one. He's going to run no matter what we say."

Uncle Fritz nodded, perhaps half in agreement and half in defeat. He turned his attention back to Rusty and lowered his voice. "You're going off on a tangent, son. You need to focus on getting your life back and rum running is not the answer. To make these people happy, build the boat and give it to them. Whatever remains owed, we'll scrape money up to buy them off the rest of the way."

Rusty shook his head. "There's more to it than money."

"More to what? More than breaking the law and getting yourself killed by mobsters, hijackers or the Coast Guard? Convince me that what you are about to do is not stupid or self-indulgent."

"Don't you remember that Di and I were almost killed—that the intention was to kill us?"

"Like yesterday. And that's what we should be focusing on, bringing those responsible to justice."

"That's exactly what I'm doing."

Uncle Fritz did a double take at him. "It's about revenge is it?"

Rusty was silent.

"You don't even know who's responsible?"

"I know. You know. Cap Huddleson knows."

"We assume"

" Huddleson said it was a Coast Guard picket boat."

"But what if he made a mistake? It was the dead of night. And who is to say what guardsmen were involved if it indeed was Coast Guard?"

"It's Huddleson's job to know! And what about the men who tried to kill him? He recognized one of them as Connors's mate."

Uncle Fritz's face fell ashen.

"Don't you see…two plus two equals four!" he said as he approached Uncle Fritz.

"So now you're Wyatt Earp."

"Jesus Christ, Uncle Fritz, this will happen again if I don't stop it. I'm marked. It doesn't matter if I cruise, fish or piss in the lake. Connors has it out for me. He *knows* I suspect him. He *knows* Huddleson saw him. You saw what he's capable of."

Uncle Fritz rose again from the stool. Rusty could see he was brooding. Uncle Fritz hesitated for a moment then crossed over to the corner of the barn to where a shovel hung on the wall. He grabbed it. "Here." He tossed it to Rusty who caught it in mid-air. "I once read a Chinese proverb in a fortune cookie that says when you go out for revenge, to dig two graves: one for your enemy, one for yourself.

Rusty swallowed hard.

"You're above the law now, so I guess you won't need me," Uncle Fritz muttered. He turned to the door. "I'll tell Di you got a part time job with Lyman's. Their shop is up and running in Sandusky now. She'll believe it. Despite all, she at least still believes in you." He went out the door into the cold dusk. They could hear his engine start and the sound of his wheels crunching in the snow.

Rusty threw the shovel to the back of the barn where it crashed with a clatter. It was enough to make Davey jump, put aside the chiseling and turn towards him.

"He's right you know."

Rusty set his jaw. "And so am I."

Chapter 47

When Sunday rolled around, he headed for the farm as usual. Uncle Fritz's words had played over and over in his head like a stuck needle on a phonograph and driving him just as crazy. It was with a mixture of eagerness and dread that accompanied him on his drive there—eagerness to see Di and dread having to face both her and Uncle Fritz, knowing full well their dissatisfaction with him though each for different reasons.

While he waited in the parlor for Di, Uncle Fritz passed through, spotted him and grunted. Rusty stopped him before he could leave the room.

"Please, Uncle Fritz, I'm sorry about the other day. I beg your pardon and hope you'll forgive me."

"Pardon? Forgive? Do I look like a priest?" Uncle Fritz's stern brow softened when his eyes met Rusty's—they looked desperate and searching. "Would it change your course if I did forgive you?"

He shook his head no.

Uncle Fritz grimaced.

Rusty glanced at the doorway. Footsteps could be heard approaching the room. "I want you to understand why I'm doing this."

Uncle Fritz checked the doorway also. "Son, this is not like the war. Do you think there is anything to be really gained by doing this? I don't know what's in your head, but I know what's in your heart and as I see it, you have more to lose than gain."

Di appeared in the doorway. "What did you lose?"

"Nothing, *liebchen,* "Uncle Fritz said. "Just talk between men about work." He exited the parlor, leaving her and Rusty alone.

She raised one eyebrow inquisitively at him.

He shifted. "I lose more, uh, money by being a boat builder then, uh, being a factory worker."

"That's not news.

"Di, why do you do this to me?"

"Do what?"

"Treat me like this."

She looked surprised. "I don't know what you're talking about?"

"You have treated me like shit since the accident and I want to know why."

"You're full of hooey!" She spun around and headed for the doorway.

He grabbed her arm and spun her around. "This is what I'm talking about. You always digging at me, and I don't know what I did to deserve this treatment. I want to know what's in your head? You make me feel like what happened that night was my fault."

"It was your fault." She jerked her arm from his grasp.

"My fault?"

"If it hadn't been for your boat and...and your charters and those damn vineyard people it would have never happened. We wouldn't have been on the lake and we wouldn't have been attacked and I wouldn't have lost our child!"

He was flabbergasted. "How can you say such a thing?"

"You asked what's in my head, so now you know." She marched out of the room.

He stood stunned. The beating at the Coast Guard Station didn't hurt this bad. He stood in silence for a moment, absorbing the blow. Then he grabbed his coat and hat.

The next thing Uncle Fritz heard was the truck engine turn over. He melted a spot on the frosty window with his hand and looked through the clear spot in time to see Rusty drive away. "Oh no," he whispered. "Oh no."

Rusty threw himself into the building of the boat. The customary trips to the farm ceased. He was a moth to her light, and she had turned off the light.

Davey noted the change in him, edgy and driven, as well as the absent trips to the farm he so ritually had kept but he didn't bring it up. He would give his friend the space he needed and watch with sadness as Rusty's world fell more apart.

The block and tackle system worked flawlessly, and Davey's overall strength and zest grew along with the muscles in his arms and upper body. He could now expertly maneuver himself in and out of the wheelchair and raise and lower himself at a quick pace between floors.

By the end of January, the chine and bottom planking on the boat were completed and the side planking ready to begin. He explained to Davey they were going to use the lapstrake hull planking and "clinker-built" method Lyman boats were famous for with some modifications that the Lymans used on their personal racing boats. The lapstrake planking and clinker built construction gives the hull extra strength with more flexibility as well as cushions the ride," he said. "As each individual lap hits the water, it will do its own small part to absorb the blow and smooth out the ride. Makes one hell of a difference at higher speeds in the lake's chop."

"Bearing in mind I'm a mechanic, what exactly is meant by clinker built?" Davey asked.

"How the planks are fastened to the framework. It's also called clinch-built. A steel block is placed in the inside of the hull at the exact spot a nail is driven in on the outside of the hull. When the nail is pounded through the plank and frame and hits the steel block on the opposite side of the hull, it causes the nail to bend or "clinch. Adds to the hull strength."

"I know about clinch nailing, just didn't know that's what clinker built meant."

"Now you know." Rusty pulled a board from the stack of lumber. He'd spent a good hour at the lumber yard in December inspecting and selecting each board destined to be a hull plank.

"Not mahogany?" Davey asked.

"No. Louisiana Red Cypress. It's lighter, but just as strong. We used it on the racers."

Davey nodded in approval.

"Here's the thing. We are going to do the usual lapstrake planking from the gunwale to the waterline. From that point on, we'll reverse the lapstrake pattern. Above the waterline, the planks will overlap as usual like clapboard siding, but below the waterline, the pattern will be like clapboard siding turned upside down. In other words, we'll work our way down to the waterline, then work our way up from the bottom up until the two patterns meet at the waterline."

Davey raised his brows. "And why is that?"

"The reverse lapstrake planking creates less drag in the water thereby increasing the speed. Lyman had us plank the racers like this."

"Little did you know you would be using those same racing tricks yourself?"

He sighed. "Yeah. Life's funny that way."

Davey wheeled over to the stove and tossed in a chunk of coal. "Looks like a long day ahead."

"I'll fill the coffee pot," Rusty said. He grabbed the pot and headed outside for the stairway and almost ran right into Uncle Fritz standing outside the door.

Fritz was bundled in a wool coat with the collar up, a wool cap with ear flaps and a wool scarf wrapped around his neck. In the falling snow, he looked like a snowman with a bulbous red nose, and Rusty wondered how long he had stood outside the door wrestling with himself whether to go in or turn back.

"Uncle Fritz?" A myriad of thoughts raced through his head.

"You haven't been around. We want to make sure you're okay." Uncle Fritz said. There was caution in his voice.

"Go in and get to the stove and warm yourself. I'm making a fresh batch of coffee."

"Thank you. Coffee sounds good."

With the ice coating formed by the last two confrontations cracked, a warm wash of relief swept over Rusty. Fritz hadn't written him off. Not yet anyways.

Uncle Fritz stepped inside, scanning the room and the boat still upside down on its supports. With the framing complete and the transom finished, he was able to clearly see the boat's distinct size and shape. He crossed to the wood stove and raised his hands before it to warm them.

"Just stoked her," Davey said, backing away to make room. "She's putting out some heat now."

Uncle Fritz unwrapped his scarf, then removed his hat and placed them on the workbench.

Rusty returned with the coffee pot and placed it on the stove. "I don't suppose you brought your carpenter's apron along?"

"You supposed right," Uncle Fritz declared. "Stove warms this place up pretty good," he said looking over the workshop as he rubbed his hands. He spotted the pulley system and examined it. The board seat, like one would set upon on a child's swing, was a tip off. He turned to Davey. "This for you?"

"Yep. I can pull or lower myself between floors like a bucket in a well."

"Ingenious, ingenious," Uncle Fritz said.

Rusty could tell he had something more than curiosity on his mind. "Is everything all right at the farm?"

Uncle Fritz glanced towards Davey. It felt awkward talking personal business with Davey in the room but Davey was a fixture of the boathouse now and that left him with little choice but to say what he had come to say. "Everyone is well and good. We miss your visits, of course. And Di…" he sighed, "Di cries a lot. Your absence has caused concern. One day she is sure you have fallen through the ice, the next, you are stricken in bed with tuberculosis. Then she's convinced you hate her and have left her for good. She hasn't thought of the interurban running over you. That will most likely be next week, so I thought I'd beat her to the punch and find out if you're all right."

"Tell her I'm fine."

"So I see." He turned back to the stove to warm his hands again. "Come to Sunday supper," he said point blank.

Rusty grimaced. "I'm not sure if that's a good idea."

Uncle Fritz turned around to face him. His brows were drawn. "It's a good idea."

Rusty lined up three coffee cups on the workbench. "Di doesn't want to see me."

"Bullshit! She's a train wreck since you've been away."

"She blames me for the accident. For the baby."

"So you crawl under a rock instead of fighting back."

"I don't want to fight."

"Not with her…for her!"

"What do you think I've been doing for four damn months?"

The room fell silent, making Davey feel awkward to be in the thick of another discussion between the two men.

Uncle Fritz finally broke the silence. "Come to Sunday supper. No one judges you. Di needs you. She wouldn't be pining about and imagining every possible worst case scenario if she didn't care. Really wearing on the rest of us, I might add." He paused. "I understand why you're doing this," he said with a nod towards the boat. Don't think for one minute that a part of me doesn't want to grab a hammer to help build that boat and hunt down the monster who shot at my loved ones and destroyed their lives."

Rusty allowed the words time to absorb.

“So…come to supper. My sister’s making stuffed pork chops. Your favorite.”

The old dangling the stuffed pork chop on a string to entice me. He grabbed the coffee pot and filled the cups and then passed them out. “And if Di is upset that I’m there?”

“You’ll still get a good meal out of it. She’ll be fine. She thinks you abandoned her so she will be relieved to see you. May even mind her tongue better.” He took a sip of coffee.

The wall clocked chimed and he glanced at it. “I have been instructed to stop at the grocers on the way home.” He finished his coffee. “Sunday supper, ja?”

Rusty nodded.

Uncle Fritz hesitated before going out the door. “I said I understand you. Don’t confuse that with sanctioning your actions.”

Rusty nodded again.

Chapter 48

By Sunday, the planking between the keel and chine was complete. Rusty felt more than a twang of guilt about leaving Davey behind to eat leftover cold fried chicken while he himself would be sitting down to a full blown, all-stops-out hot supper at a table lively with folks. It wasn't in their nature to exclude someone like Davey from their table, so he knew the lack of invite was purposeful to iron out this latest ripple in family business. The *meal to heal,* he thought of it.

The table conversation was light and cautious, but reassuring. No wisecracks, no talk of factory or money. He wasn't asked why he stayed away, but was reaffirmed he was family and Di's mother said family needed to stay together. Collective nods at the table backed her. "Try to keep Sunday's supper if you can," she added.

He wasn't expecting Di to throw her arms around him when he arrived, nor did it happen, but when she saw him her eyes sparkled with excitement and she hung on every word he said. She watched him closely and he thought he detected a look of sympathy in her eyes now and then. Uncle Fritz was right. Not one cross word or digging comment found its way out her mouth. When he left that night, with a plate of food and piece of pie for Davey, she walked him to the door. She asked when she would see him next. He felt as high as a kite.

***

Two weeks and one smashed thumb later the planking between the chine and gunwale was complete. It was time to turn the boat right side up and for that he would need more help than Davey could offer even if he wasn't bound to a wheelchair.

Rusty recruited the man who owned the bait shop two doors down to help. The bait shop owner in turn recruited his fishing buddy to assist, interest in boat building and, more so, curiosity being the key draw for both men. With additional block and tackle in place and a whole lot of grunting and straining muscles, the men rolled the boat to an upright position. When it was finally settled into place, the men stepped back in silent reverence.

"Wow. Some boat," the bait man said, breaking the silence.

"A picture of grace," his friend added.

"That's no fishing tug for sure," Davey said.

"No sir. Say, what's it for?" the friend asked.

"It's a racer. Can't you tell," the bait man said, chiding his friend.

"Oh yeah."

"I helped build racers for Lymans," Rusty said.

"Gonna give racing a shot, uh? Lyman's not going to be happy about this," the bait man said. "His former builder using the tricks of the trade against him," the bait man added turning to his friend and both chuckled. "Let me know when and where you'll race. I'd like to put some money on her!"

Righting the boat was a small victory that was celebrated with boat talk, lake stories and fishing bull that lasted longer than Rusty would have liked. But he kept the coffee flowing and the wood burner stoked as the wind howled and shook the shanty.

When the group finally broke up at dusk and Davey gone to bed, he finally got his first chance to be alone with the boat, upright for the first time on the supports. It had a commanding look from atop its perch. He walked around it. It was only half way finished but his mind's eye saw it complete. Tough built and sleek with quick lines, it looked fast at a standstill, and he had this funny notion that if he opened the sliding rear door, the boat would lunge from its perch, dive into the river and bolt for the lake. The more he looked it over, the more it pained him to think that this striking boat, emerging out of stacks of lumber and sweat, was being created for one sole purpose.

***

"You're kidding? That's the same guy I bought my bilge pump from," Rusty said as he and Davey drove to Port Clinton on Davey's suggestion that a fellow mechanic running a marina was the man to see if you wanted airplane engines. The next step on the boat was building the engine stringers and for that it was necessary to know the size, weight and space volume of the engines. "So you're saying this quiet old fella is supplying aero engines to runners?"

"That quiet old fella was a runner! Ran everything from illegal aliens to coke to scotch in a ferry boat," Davey said. "One night a storm snuck up on him and he hit the shoals off Catawba. Luck would have it on that particular night he was only running 'brown plaid'. The ferry broke apart and sunk and he damn near lost his life, owing his hide to a life ring and the shallows. After the storm, folks for weeks collected bottles of scotch washed ashore."

"When was this?"

"'Bout 23 or 24. Before the tornado, I think."

"Is he still running?"

"Heck, no. Took the accident as a warning from the All Mighty. Oddly, it hasn't spooked him from coaching from the sidelines. Local runners seek him out when they need a part or advice or an engine," he said with a sideways glance at Rusty.

"How did you know about this?"

"He's a boat mechanic- like me. Talk always travels up and down the lakeshore among colleagues."

"Huh." Rusty's thoughts drifted back to his own storm run after buying the pump and the marine operator's words of caution concerning the approaching squall.

They pulled into the marina, and he helped Davey into the wheelchair and wheeled him through icy slush to the shop, unaware they were being observed by the marina operator from within.

The door jerked opened. "Davey? Davey Reynolds is that you?"

"Mike, you rascal, how are you?" The two men locked hands and embraced.

"I'm doing fine, but what in the hell happened to you?"

Davey scoffed. "I'd like to say I fell off a horse, but the fact is it was an accident on a tug. Line broke and I was the recipient of the ensuing back lash."

"Damn. I always thought that was dangerous work. Hey, you bought a pump off me last summer didn't you?" he said, turning to Rusty.

"I could've used it before I got back to port." Before he could explain farther, the operator turned his attention back to Davey.

"Gee, it's good to see you. Davey here was my ace student," he said to Rusty.

Rusty raised his brows. *Student of what, mechanics or running?*

"He was a natural with engines," the operator continued, answering the question for him.

"Still is," he added.

"So what brings you fellows here? I'm guessing it's not ice fishing."

"Liberty engines. Can you get them and how much?" Davey said to the point before Rusty could even formulate his words.

Mike, the operator, chuckled as he lowered himself on to a stool. "What do you need airplane engines for," he asked cautiously with a half grin.

"A racing boat," Rusty said.

"A runner," Davey said.

Mike's eyes jumped back and forth between Rusty and Davey.

"You fixing to run, Davey?"

"I'm fixing to fix Liberty engines on a runner."

The man exhaled loudly and pushed his cap back on his head. "You sure you want to get messed up in that, Davey? I mean, it's a step out of character for you."

Davey' s face grew solemn. "A lot has happened between my days as an apprentice and this set of wheels."

Mike's brows furrowed and he nodded. "You still in Lorain?"

"Huron."

Mike nodded again. After a pause, he said, "Can I get the engines? Yes. What do they cost? Figure between $125-150.00 apiece. How many engines you thinking?"

"Two. If one dies, I still have the other," Rusty said.

"In line or side by side?"

"I was thinking…"

"Side by side," Davey blurted. "Twin screws."

"Good boy," Mike said. "You boys want some coffee?" Without waiting for an answer, he got up and retrieved the coffee pot and three cups. He sat them on the workbench. “Now, let’s talk business. If you’re going to run, you gotta do it right.”

Sleet drummed on the tin roof of the marina shop as Mike poured out coffee and advice. Hours later, with handshakes, ideas and two engines on order, Rusty and Davey headed back to Huron.

Chapter 49

The engines' stringers needed to be amply fortified as each engine weighed 844 pounds. Rusty was concerned. He was expecting around 1500 lbs. total and the combined dry weight was 1688. Add to that the fuel, fluids and cargo of alcohol plus the weight of two men, himself and Pete, and he began to wonder if the boat would set right in the water let alone maneuver. He pictured a barge tug dodging picket boats and speedboats in his mind's eye. *Like pitting a water buffalo against a tiger.* He just had to trust his calculations were correct and the proof that they were—or not—would be in the shakedown run.

He and Davey used dense oak for its strength in the engines' bed and a generous share of heavy brass screws to attach the stringers. The bed took up a sizeable portion of the bilge as each engine measured 41.5 inches high by 67.375 inches wide by 27 inches deep.

At one point, he overheard Davey mumble something about a sledge hammer when a regular hammer might have worked and since Davey wasn't using a hammer, he guessed the reference was to the engines.

When the engine bed was complete, he placed a phone call to the Port Clinton marina operator. "We're ready, Mike."

The following morning, Mike arrived with a flatbed loaded with two aero engines. "Packards," he said as they loosened the tie-downs. "V-12, water cooled, boys."

By supper time, the Liberty engines were mounted in place in the engine bed, and the men celebrated with a steak dinner on Rusty at the restaurant downtown.

***

While seeing a boat shell emerge from the stacks of lumber was rewarding and the placement of the engines thrilling, the next project would be complicated and tedious because it could not be rushed. Rusty felt as though the assembly and connections of the boat's mechanics were cranked down to a state of slow motion—gas tanks, carburetors, pumps, twin screw propellers, fuel and electrical lines—the list went on. Each day the routine was repeated. They got up, put the coffee pot on, stoked the wood burner and set to work on the boat's guts. The Liberty engines, rising tall and imposing from the bowels of the boat was their inspiration. Twelve—cylinder, liquid cooled pistons in a V-shape configuration with six cylinders on each side boasted a 5" bore and a 7" stroke with a displacement of 1,649.3 cubic inches. Each cylinder had one intake valve and one exhaust valve operated by its own single overhead camshaft which individually worked each cylinder's two valves. *Beasts*, Davey called the engines and he named them Odin and Thor from the mythical gods in Norse legends. Like idols worshipped, they slaved on toward the goal of feeding these hungry beasts to awake them from their dormancy.

***

It was mid-February. The lake was frozen. Beyond the shoreline, beyond sight, the wind and frigid temperature had carved ice sculptures from the final waves before the lake was locked in a cover of ice. Each splash of open water or wind-whipped mist added a coat of ice onto the frozen wave, building the ice structures higher and higher as the water froze on impact. Looking across the frozen tundra of lake, the icy sculptures looked like ghosts that had been frozen in place as they trudged across the lake. Ice fishermen, ice breaking ships' crews, and bold bootleggers running with Model A's fitted with skis replacing the front tires were the privileged few who saw this frozen phenomenon. Eerie yet beautiful especially when the winter sunlight—bright in a crisp, clear sky—poked its tempered rays around and through these icy monuments.

Sundays at the farm were going well. There was more laughter at the table, and Uncle Fritz, never one to hold a grudge, was always anxious to share his beer. So Rusty, not wanting to jeopardize the present harmony, decided to leave out the minor detail of quitting the mill a month ago. Davey came along now and then on insistence from the family. He kept it occasional so as not to interfere with the mending of his friend's relationship with Di.

"You know Tuesday is Valentine's Day," he told Rusty as they ran piping from the auxiliary gas tank to the engines.

"Shit. I forgot. Thanks."

"That's what friends are for."

***

White Oaks was packed. It was an upscale restaurant on a creek that not only provided a scenic overlook but offered an access from the lake to the restaurant's cellar where a speakeasy buzzed with liquor, laughter and dance.

The hostess led Rusty and Di down a hallway to the back dining room, and Di caught a glimpse of what she guessed was the infamous "secret door" with a reputed peep hole for screening clientele. Rusty pulled her past it lest her curiosity raised concern. The hostess seated them, not by a window as he had hoped, but at the only open table in the far corner. The creek was out of view, but they could still enjoy the sight of the wooded ravine enchantingly aglow with floodlights. So far, so good, he thought.

She looked radiant in the glow of candlelight and he noticed she was wearing the silk stockings he got her for Christmas and the pearl necklace from their first anniversary. It looked promising.

The dinner conversation was light. She asked how work was going. He said, "Well." She asked how he liked his place in Huron. He said "Okay." She said Davey looked great and he thought how she should have seen him the day he found him alone in his house in Lorain because she would have said *really great* compared to that day.

Dinner was going well, and then he said, "I miss you."

It made her fall silent. He watched her eyes become moist and saw the light from the candle glistening off them. *I blew it.* He put his hand to his mouth and stared at his empty plate. The bus boy appeared out of nowhere and whisked his plate away. They sat in silence. He shifted in his seat. Just when he thought he couldn't stand the silence any longer she said in a soft voice, "I miss you, too." Her words were like a hammer on a glass wall.

He closed his eyes and felt tears welling.

She reached for his hand. It was warm. He opened his eyes to make sure he wasn't dreaming. He allowed time to savor the moment, and then he reached into his pocket and pulled out a tiny wrapped box. It seemed like the perfect moment for his Valentine Day gift to her. He pushed it across the table towards her. She looked at it with the curiosity of a cat seeing a mouse. She removed the wrapping and opened the box. It was a diamond ring. Her eyes shot to his.

"Will you marry me?" he said. His eyes were anxious.

She looked at him with puzzlement. "Rusty, we *are* married."

"It's a rhetorical question. If you had to do it over again…would you say yes?"

Her eyes searched his. She saw his were intent, perhaps a bit fearful. It was as though he was searching for a life linc to be thrown. "Yes. In a heartbeat."

He hung his head and teardrops dotted the tablecloth.

***

Later that evening after he parked the truck at the farm, he leaned over to kiss her before they got out. She kissed him back. He then engulfed her in his arms and began kissing her harder. She pushed away and got out. He wasn't expecting the icy mitt after the evening and it bit like frostbite. He sighed and then also got out of the truck and stood next to it. She was about to open the door to the house.

"You coming in?"

He could see her breath in the frosty air. "No. I should be heading back. Roads are a bit icy and it will take me longer than usual."

She nodded.

He was just about to get into the truck when he heard her call out.

"I love the ring, Rusty. It was a wonderful night. Thank you. See ya Sunday." The last part was almost a question. "See you Sunday," he said.

Chapter 50

"Now pay attention. You use this button at high speeds. If you use too little, you'll blow the engines. Too much and you shit yourself… literally," Davey said, pointing out a button on the dashboard of the boat. "This button releases drops of castor oil to the carburetor. When she starts running rough, you give it some drops to smooth it out. It will also keep the cylinders cool. Bear in mind, a shot of the oil is like a kick in the ribs, so you better hang on to your hat when you press that button.

Rusty leaned over the rail for a closer look. "Fighter pilots used castor oil to increase horsepower."

"And crapped themselves from inhaling the oil fumes," Davey said. "Kinda takes the romance out of a dogfight when you picture the aces with a nasty load in their pants."

Rusty chuckled.

Davey continued his schooling. "If you use the castor oil at low speeds you'll clog the carburetor and stall the engines. So remember—it's to be used at higher speeds only and for that extra boost of power." He moved back amidships where the engines were located. "The engines are going to consume one to two quarts of regular oil an hour. That's why I put in the auxiliary oil tank with a cooler." He pointed it out to Rusty. "It's installed under the waterline in a water tight casing, see?"

Rusty leaned in for a better look.

"Remember to keep these engines cool and lubricated or you'll find out the hard way if you don't." Davey settled back into his wheelchair. "You already installed an auxiliary gas tank as back up but don't become dependent on it—remember, its purpose is to provide extra fuel to see you back should you get in a pickle and burn through the main tank."

"Aye, aye, sir," Rusty said straightening up.

"So, are we ready?" Davey's eyes were shining.

"Ready for what?"

"To light these babies up!"

"Now?"

"Why not. We have to see if they turn over and run before we get ahead of ourselves."

Rusty looked surprised. "I just thought we had to wait…"

"For what? Until the boat is varnished and in the water?"

"I guess we are all hooked up..."

"So open the doors and hit the starter and we'll see how healthy Thor and Odin are."

Rusty slid open the barn doors. It was the perfect day for the test as it was clear and the sun felt good streaming in. He poured gasoline in the fuel tank and checked the water and oil levels. He gave Davey thumbs up, pulled out the choke and pushed the starter button to engine one. The engine made cranking sounds, then a weak whine—almost in protest. He feathered the choke. The engine fell silent. He pulled the choke and pushed the starter button again. Another whine, then a chug. Then another chug. The engine sucked in the fluids and the fluids gave it strength. It cranked faster and turned over then rumbled to life. The throaty rumble vibrated the barn walls and Rusty could feel the vibration penetrate his chest cavity and shake his heart. A grin spread over his face.

Davey listened to the engine settle into loud big cat purrs and began laughing. "Sounds healthy."

Rusty then repeated the process with the second engine and once it too ran smooth, he reached for the throttles and Davey stopped him. "Not yet. Give them time to break in and remember how to work. We gotta go easy and work them up to a gallop."

***

He and Davey had just finished the final work on the propellers days later when the sound of a vehicle rattled to a stop outside the shanty. They could hear a car door shut then the sound of footsteps treading up the stairway to the above apartment.

Rusty cracked open the barn door. The vehicle wasn't familiar. He looked at Davey and shrugged. The visitor banged on the apartment door above their heads. He was not within sight of Rusty.

"Salesman?" Davey whispered.

Rusty shrugged again. They remained quiet as the stranger knocked again. Then they listened as the footsteps descended down the stairway. Rusty put his eye to the crack and waited with anticipation to see who would appear. It was Pete. He threw open the door.

"Pete, you rascal, you gave us a start."

"What are you doing? Hiding down here?"

"I wasn't expecting anyone. I want to keep this under wraps and I sure don't need anyone nosing around."

"Well you can relax now." Pete spotted Davey.

"Pete, this is Davey. He's helping me build the boat. He was the engine man on my tug. A-1 mechanic and good buddy."

Pete glanced at the wheelchair.

"Davey, I want you to meet Pete. Pete's family owns the vineyard that charters me. He's gonna be the co-pilot on this venture."

Pete crossed over to Davey and they shook hands.

"So you're the fellow that gets to ride shotgun," Davey said. "Heard you've had some experience in these matters."

"A bit. You could say I'm coming out of retirement."

"You're in luck," Rusty said, "we were just about to crank these engines up and give them some throttle for the first time."

Pete walked over to the boat. "Wow, this is really something." His eyes glowed like a kid in a toy store as he examined the boat inside and out. "Holy shit, those engines are the berries. Where did you get them?"

"Friend of Davey's. Makes that Chris Craft at the auction look like a lead sled, huh?"

"And how. What's the top speed?"

"Should do fifty easy, but we're hoping at least sixty—or more on flat water," Davey said.

Pete laughed and clapped Rusty's back. "Can I hear them?"

"Sure. Planning to fire them anyways."

Rusty slid open the barn doors, then went up to the boat's dashboard. Pete was over his shoulder as he pulled the choke and pushed the starter button. The engines turned over and barked to life at the first try and settled into a pulsating rumble.

Pete let out a whoop.

Davey nodded to Rusty to go ahead. "But no more than two thirds on the throttle. They're fresh engines and we don't want to blow them."

Rusty pushed the throttle slowly up, stopping half way. The engines roared louder with each advancement of the throttle lever.

They exchanged glances, their eyes wild with excitement.

Davey held his fingers about an inch apart signifying little and then pointed up with his thumb.

Rusty eased the throttle forward a bit more. The engines howled with power and shook the walls of the shanty. They laughed wildly but could not hear one another over the thunder of engines.

Rusty cut back on the throttle and the men continued to laugh and whoop.

"That's not even wide open," he said. Something caught his eye at the barn door. It was the bait shop man. He was bug-eyed and jaw dropped. Rusty flipped the engines off.

"Holy smokes. I heard this noise and felt the shop shake and thought the grain elevators blew up," the bait man said coming in to the shanty. "What kind of engine you got in that thing?"

"Liberty aero engines," Rusty said. "Two." They were still coming down from their laughing high.

The bait man circled the boat. "Who-wee, I got to bring my buddy over to see this. What are we looking at here?"

Davey wheeled over to him. "Surplus aircraft engines made for fighter planes by Packard. V-12 and water cooled. Five hundred horsepower at 2,000 rpms.

Power to weight ratio is 0.53 horsepower per pound." It was more information than the bait man needed or understood.

The bait man grinned. "I definitely want to put money on this when it races."

Pete glanced at Rusty who gave a discreet wink.

"Mind if I bring that fellow over that helped flip the boat?"

"Only if you two can keep this between yourselves. Don't want the competition to get wind of it. Then they'll all be doing it."

"Don't worry, mister. Dark horses make money. We'll be as silent as the grave."

Pete looked at Rusty for his reaction. "I'm counting on that."

The bait man was in no hurry to leave and it aggravated Rusty that he couldn't talk freely with Pete. He looked at his watch. "Guys, I'm going to button up for the day and get something to eat uptown."

"Afraid I can't join you," the bait man said, "I 'm in the middle of a project myself." He shuffled around a bit, realized the conversation was dead and headed halfheartedly towards the door. You boys take care," he said. With that, he was gone.

Rusty sighed with relief.

"Does that bird think this is a racing boat?" Pete said.

"I hope he does."

"Rusty told him we are building a racer and so far we think he and his buddy are buying it—we think," Davey said. "For how long, remains the question. When this boat starts heading out after dark a couple nights a week, it may raise some brows."

"He lives close by?"

"He lives above the bait shop a few doors down."

Pete made a face. "He might be a problem."

Rusty bolted the barn doors. "Folks here tend to mind their potatoes. That's why I came here. That and because we are not the only rumrunners using this river."

His answer seemed to satisfy Pete.

"Still, if there's a problem, we know where to look first," Pete said.

Rusty wasn't sure what Pete would do if there was a problem and just what it would bring about for the friendly bait shop man. He hoped he didn't have to find out.

Pete went back to the boat. "So, besides the hull design and engines, what other advantages are we looking at?"

"Well, for one thing," Davey said, "we got self-bailing scruppers to eliminate the need for fussing with a bilge pump."

"Self-bailing, I like the sound of that."

"Well you won't if you take on water less than 20 miles per hour. Then you better activate the bilge pump or grab a bucket."

"So what's a scrupper?"

"Drain holes in the hull that draw off the water that washes over the deck before it can get into the bilge and cargo hold," Rusty said. "High speeds create a vacuum in the scruppers as they pass over the water and that vacuum causes suction which pulls water from the bilge. Like a siphon. They also serve as deck drains to try to eliminate water that washes overboard from going below deck. Flaps keep the water out when the boat is stopped or running slow and need to be manually opened and closed."

"And this is very important," Davey said, "when the ride is over- close the scruppers because water will run back into the open drains, fill the bilge and sink the boat."

"Gotcha," Pete said nonchalant.

Davey looked at Rusty and shook his head. Pete was already heading under the boat and examining the propellers. Pete seemed as reliable as a cheap watch and he hoped he was wrong about him, but to be sure, the closing of the scruppers would have to fall upon Rusty's shoulders.

"What's the deal here," Pete called out from beneath the boat.

"Inboard twin screw propellers—so we can beach it. Also allows more maneuverability at high speeds."

"You sure know your onions when it comes to boats," Pete said, sliding out from underneath.

"Let's hope I know what I'm doing when it comes to running."

"That's where my expertise comes in. Hey, did you hear about Bugs Moran's gang getting rubbed out at a garage in Chicago? Mowed down by wise guys with Chicago typewriters and sawed-offs posing as cops."

"Couldn't miss it. All over the front pages and on the radio. Capone's got a long reach from Florida."

"Pos-i-lute-ly. Big Al's expanding his business."

"More like Scarface is expanding his territory by mopping out the competition. Which reminds me, this has a bullet proof windshield and windows,"

"I wouldn't expect less," Pete said rapping the glass. "That had to set you back a few clams."

"I expect to recoup it real soon."

"Trust me. You will."

"So where have you and Al been? I expected you guys to be dropping in now and then."

"Al's in Florida. He won't be back until Mid-March. Me? I've been busy."

"Busy what? Button shining on 9th with the flappers?"

Davey snorted a laugh.

"Ha-ha, funny man. A real hot sketch. For your information I've been busy lining up our contacts. And also for your information, Father Time, flappers are on the way out."

"Such a loss," Rusty said to Davey who sat grinning in his wheelchair.

Pete ignored the remark. “Al’s expecting you to be ready first of April. Are you gonna make it?”

“The over decking needs to be done. Cockpit work, too. Steering wheel, dials, seat, stuff like that. Also some minor work on the fish tug. It would help if you were to lend a hand.”

“I’d like to, but I can’t. In fact,” he checked the clock over the workbench, “I need to get going. I’m meeting Vince at the Castle in Lorain.”

“Some other time then.”

“Yeah. Sure.”

After Pete left, Davey looked at Rusty. “That’s one groundhog who saw his shadow. You won’t see him again until the end of March.”

Mid-week, a telegram arrived and notified Davey his mother had passed. He took the news in quiet stride. She had been slipping. The funeral was small with a few attending including the nosey neighbor, Di with her parents, Uncle Fritz and the *Iroquois*’s former master, Cap McIntyre to Davey’s surprise and gratitude.

Chapter 51

It was decided that Joe and Lou would be crew members. The days were getting longer and warmer. The wind still had a bite as it swept across the yet frozen lake onto the shore, but if one could find a windbreak like the south side of a building, the sun felt warm and promising.

Rusty noticed the longer days when he stepped out of the shanty for a break and a cigarette. Over in Vermilion, Eddie did, too. For him, it meant less time indoors and more time away from his old man who hibernated at home during winter, basting in his easy chair with a bottle of busthead at his side.

It was March and an ambitious spring was trying to oust the stubborn winter. One could tell just by listening to the lake and rivers groan and pop as the ice began to shift. Rusty turned a wary eye towards the Huron River in anticipation of the ice jams that were soon to come. His shanty would be at risk as melting snow would make the river rise and its flow, barricaded by the ice covered lake, would have nowhere to go but over the banks and flood the area.

Hoot and Eddie also listened and watched from the banks of the Vermilion River wondering if the old lighthouse and rickety pier could handle another spring bombardment of refrigerator-size ice chunks propelled by the rushing river water.

To the west, from his lighthouse perch on Marblehead Point, Huddleson watched too, only he kept an eye out farther beyond the rivers and into the lake. He watched through binoculars the Coast Guard's ice breaker carved its way through the lake's thawing icy mantel to open lanes of clear water so ships could resume commerce and rivers could flow. While inland at the farm, Uncle Fritz saw and heard spring too in the yellow blooms of witch hazel and the whisper of wings overhead as flocks of ducks and geese returned north.

The signs were as an alarm bell for Rusty. April 1st would not be held back like the river. He and Davey labored into the wee hours, adding brackets, racks and strapping to secure the forthcoming liquid cargo. Then they varnished the interior. Rusty mixed a concoction of flat paints until he got a dark charcoal color and together they painted the hull. Then they began armor plating, swathing each completed section of plating with the same dull dusky paint.

Eighth of an inch steel plating, Mike had instructed. *Place strategically to protect the engines, the hull and your ass. Use judiciously as it will add weight and weight means less speed and more fuel.*

As he riveted the steel plating in place around the boat's hull and the cockpit, all Rusty could think about was the sound the bullets made as they ripped overhead and struck *Rising Sun* with dull thuds and splitting wood and it made him smolder. He pictured Di crunched under the forward deck in terror and the look on her face when she realized they were sinking. Her cries pierced his heart over and over again, often waking him nights in a cold sweat. There was even a moment when he was beating the plating into shape around the cockpit's frame that he visualized it as Connor's head with his cruel eyes and smirk. He was not going to be Connor's sitting duck again.

Davey knew what was playing at times in his friend's mind by the look that would come over him. It was as though a dark curtain would draw over his face, and he wondered if his usual passive temperament was only a façade and it worried him. Rusty was going to do whatever was in his head and heart, and he knew he couldn't stop or change his friend's course, so he suggested a layer of sand between the cockpit's wooden walls and steel plating as extra buffer of protection. Rusty liked the idea and sand was purchased before the week was over.

***

The calendar said spring had officially arrived, but it didn't feel like it. The wind was raw and there was dampness in the air from thawing earth that chilled Rusty to the bone. He paused to button his coat as he pushed Davey towards the wharf where the fishing tug was moored. The rum running boat was finally complete and all that was left was working out any kinks the trial run might reveal but for that, the weather needed to break so he and Davey set their focus on the fishing tug.

Rusty noticed Davey whistled and hummed while working on the engine mechanics in the old fishing vessel, something he did not do while working on those of the rum running boat, and he figured Davey felt more at home with the tug than he did with the other. He often heard Davey singing some cowboy ballad from within the engine compartment like he did in the days of Erie T and he hoped he didn't put Davey in a compromising position by asking him to help. If Davey had his way, he figured, the fishing tug would be exclusively used as a fishing tug—and that would be the end of this ordeal.

***

"Thought you fell off the face of the earth," Sam said as he poured Rusty a coffee.

"I'll probably wish I had come summer." His trip to Vermilion was just as much about old habits as it was checking on Eddie.

"You still working on that ole fish tug you bought from Walt?"

"She's overhauled and running good. Damn near makes me feel guilty for what I paid for it."

Sam laughed. "Al's back from Florida. Have you seen him yet?"

"No. He kinda fell off the earth, too."

"Well, he's back and he should be getting in touch with you any day now I imagine. He's as tan as this countertop."

Rusty sipped his coffee. "Seen Eddie about?"

"Once in a while I see him leaving old lady Donovan's place. He came in here about a month ago with a black eye and I asked him if he got in a fight at school and he said his old man popped him."

"Son of a bitch."

"And then some."

Rusty tossed some coins on the counter and stood up.

"Al know how to find you now that you've moved?"

"Yeah. Pete's been to my place already, so Al should find it."

Sam gave a wave.

Rusty headed straight to Mrs. Donovan's house nearby. She looked glad to see him when she opened the door.

"I got that boy going to school more than not," she said with pride as she served Rusty tea. "Helping with his homework, too, but he's a job, I'll tell you, and he tolerates me just so much. When he gets his nose in the wind, I lose him. He'd rather keep company with that darn dog and Hoot than with the likes of me."

"You wouldn't see him at all if he didn't like your company."

"You mean my biscuits and pies."

He gazed out her window, noticing Sam's alley in part of the view. "I'm sorry about asking you to watch over him. I didn't mean to burden you."

She sighed. "It's not that I don't mind giving him a meal or helping with the books...it's just not right...a boy that age running about like a feral dog. Lord knows what going to become of him especially with that lowlife of a father."

He reached into his wallet and pulled out a couple of bills. It was the last of his money from the sale of the cottage. "Here, take this to help pay for his food."

She snorted and waved her hand in protest. "For goodness sake, I don't need that. I enjoy having someone to cook for. Besides, I consider him my good deed...my charitable contribution to society and Christian duty."

"Just take it. If you don't need it, give it to Eddie for anything he needs."

She hesitated at first and then took it. "I'll save it for the boy."

"When you see him, could you tell him I was looking in on him and hope to see him next time?"

"I will."

He headed back to Huron.

***

The next two events were more than he had expected, and both occurred on the last weekend of March.

The first was the arrival of Al during the shakedown run of the rum running boat. The lake was open thanks to a stretch of warm temperatures and sunny days, and Rusty was anxious to put the months of toil to the test.

He and Davey spent Saturday morning going over the rumrunner before agreeing it was ready to go. At noon, Rusty slid both the front and rear barn doors open and winches were attached after he had rigged planks and rollers in which to slide the boat down to the water's level. It would be a short slide down to the water but it needed more help than Davey could provide. The bait shop man and his buddy would be eager beavers to assist, he thought, and he tossed the idea of using them in his head, but he loathed having to involve them anymore than they already were. That's when the black Packard showed up and Al, Pete, Joe and Vince exited from it.

"Hey, hey, my man, Rusty, how are you?" Al gushed as usual. "I come to see the ballyhoo that has Petey jazzed up. He's been chin wagging about this ever since he seen it." Sam was right. The Florida sun had browned Al like a basted turkey.

"Come see for yourself," Rusty said leading the way for Al and Joe. Pete and Vince had already disappeared into the shanty during the hellos.

Davey backed his wheelchair into the corner to make room for the group.

"Al, this is my friend Davey. We worked together at the tug yards and he helped me build this boat. He'll be our mechanic. Davey, meet Al, his brother Joe and cousin, Vince. These are the fellows that chartered me for their grape juice deliveries." He knew Davey recognized them right off but he introduced them anyways.

Al crossed over to Davey and shook his hand while Joe nodded and Vince said "glad to meet ya."

"First, a little red ink compliments of the vineyard for you and your friend," Al said producing a wine bottle from inside his coat and handing it to Rusty.

"Thanks," Rusty said. He sat the bottle on the work bench.

Al clapped his hands together and into a rub. "Let's see what we got here."

Rusty opened the engine compartment. "It's got two V-12 Liberty aircraft engines that will each push 500…"

"Yeah, yeah. Pete's been yammering on something about that. Spare me the details, Mr. Rusty. I'm a simple man. I know food, grapes and money. All I want to know is how many cases this tin can haul and can she stay ahead of the game?"

Rusty raised his brows. He saw Davey do the same with a twinkle in his eye. "Eighty, maybe one hundred cases if they are bundled instead of cased."

"Maybe? We need to know a number. Maybe is not a number."

"There is already a lot of extra weight to begin with. I'll know better after a few hauls."

Al circled the boat, brushing Pete aside who was preoccupied pointing out points of interest to Vince. Al ran his hand over the armor plating and then rapped his knuckle on the windshield. "Bullet proof glass?"

"Uh-huh."

Al circled back to the beginning. "I'm very impressed. Very." Then he turned serious. "Do you believe in fate?"

Rusty shifted. "I used to believe everything happened for a reason."

"Well, I *do* believe in fate, and I believe it was fate the day you gave Petey a lift because that ride brought us together. We're going to make quite a team." He clapped him on the back. "April first is around the corner. Is she ready for business?"

"Just got to get her into the water and give her a trial run. That's what we were about to do when you arrived."

"Then what are we waiting for? Boys, help the man get his boat in the water and let's see if this bird flies. Petey, pay attention to what Rusty tells you to do, you hear?"

Rusty doled out instructions and positioned Pete, Vince and Joe along the sides of the boat to steady and guide it down the ramp. Davey situated himself so he could see underneath the hull, stating he was closer to the ground and therefore had a better advantage of how the rails and boat were aligning. Rusty, then, stationed himself on the winch at the bow. Al stepped back and watched from the opening of the front doors.

It took an hour to jockey and slide the boat and when it finally slid into the water, it plunged into the river with a splash like a barracuda released back to the water, causing the water to undulate in swells around it. They waited for the boat to finish rocking and settle. Rusty sighed with relief, not realizing that he had held his breath as she slid in. When she had settled, he jumped aboard and began inspecting the seams and bilge as Pete and Vince tied the boat to a set of on shore bollards.

"She gonna be safe parked here?" Al asked no one in particular.

"There's a slip under the shanty that connects to the river."

"Ah, a boat garage out of sight."

After a couple minutes passed, Rusty appeared on deck and flashed Davey a thumbs up.

The boat looked at home in the water. Its smoky dark, plain built form looked powerful and athletic, giving it a sense of authority.

"Hey? Where's its name. It's gotta have a name," Al said, searching the transom, "or it will get busted for sure."

"It's there," Rusty said with a wink to Davey.

"Where? I don't see it?"

"On the transom. Right where you're looking."

Al squinted and scanned the back of the boat all the harder. "What are you, futzing with me?"

He could see Al's face reddening. "Her name is *New Moon*. And like the new moon, it's there but you just can't see it."

"*New Moon*? Oh, I get it, wise guy. The runner will be invisible in the dark like a new moon. *Rising Sun*...*New Moon* you're playing with words here. But ya still gotta have a name that is visible."

Rusty went into the cockpit and came out with a sign with wires attached. The words *New Moon* were painted on it in bold white block letters, a contrast to the graceful, cursive font of *Rising Sun*. He affixed the sign to the transom. "There—

it's legal. But once she's on a run, we will remove it so she can't be identified should we get chased."

Al chuckled. "Clever man. What's the deal with the waterline? Am I right- that is the waterline above the water? Did you screw up or is that on purpose?"

"It's what you could call an optical illusion," Rusty said. "I made it high so when the boat is loaded and low in the water, it will look like normal level and not look like its setting low with a load."

"Gee, you're full of tricks. Petey, did you give Rusty these ideas, being an ex-runner and all?"

"No," Rusty interjected before Pete could answer.

Pete appeared next to him. "Can I go on the test run since I'm going to be riding shotgun?" he asked.

"Davey gets that honor, Rusty said, "Besides, I need his ears and know-how to make sure all is operating like it should and in case the engines die." He grabbed a pair of binoculars from atop a toolbox on the pier next to the boat and handed them to Pete. "If we break down, you guys will need to come tow us with the fishing tug." He looked at the group gathered on the deck and suddenly realized that would be like asking pigs to fly. "Do any of you know how to operate a boat?"

The group shuffled a bit and exchanged glances.

Al looked at Pete and Joe. "You two have been around boats." He stared at Pete. "You use to run rum. Didn't you ever have to operate a boat?"

"A fish tug is not a speedboat," Pete muttered.

Al shook his head in disgust.

"There is a difference," Rusty said. "Listen, if we are setting still for more than a half an hour and you see me waving my arms, go to the marina where the tug is moored and tell the owner we are testing a boat and it broke down and needs a tow. And for heaven's sake don't let him call the Coast Guard. No, on second thought, go two doors down. There's a bait shop. The owner lives upstairs. Tell him Rusty is testing his boat and it broke down and needs a tow. He'll be more than happy to help." He hoped like hell he would not need to involve the bait shop man. "All right, let's do this. You boys help me get Davey on board." He wheeled Davey up to the boat's side, and Pete and Joe helped ease him into the boat and onto a seat in the cockpit. "Tool box," he motioned to Pete once Davey was seated.

Pete grabbed the toolbox and passed it to him. Rusty then took his seat at the pilot's chair. "Wish us luck, boys," he said, turning over the engines.

"Wait...wait," Al shouted. "We got to do this right." He disappeared into the shanty and moments later emerged with the bottle of wine he had brought. "It's not champagne but it will do." He went to the bow and raised his voice over the low rumble of idling engines, "I christen thee *New Moon*,.." he said and smashed the bottle against the bow, spraying shards of glass and red wine in to the air and river.

Pete and Joe untied the lines and tossed them into the boat. Pete flashed the thumbs up to Rusty.

Rusty eased the boat from the dock. It felt good to feel that sensation of buoyancy again. It felt more familiar to him than solid ground. The boat swayed as he backed it away from the dock, its engines purring like content tigers. He gently spun the steering wheel and the boat responded correspondingly as the bow turned towards the lake. He tapped the throttle lightly and the engines deepened to low growls as they motored down the river to the open water. *New Moon* was like a collected race horse heading to the track. He looked at Davey and saw him grinning.

"Kind of like the calm before a storm," Davey said, his smile broad.

"I feel like I'm holding onto the reins of a thoroughbred before the starter's pistol."

"Just don't give her head—she needs time to break in."

Al, Pete, Joe and Vince watched with intensity as the runner cleared the rocky breakwater and headed into the open water.

They took turns watching through the binoculars as Rusty cruised the runner at slow speed, and then add throttle and maneuvering the boat one way, then another. They would repeat this routine over and over.

Thirty minutes passed and Al checked his watch, Pete sighed and Joe lit a cigarette.

"When are they going to open it up?" Vince wondered aloud as he watched the runner through binoculars head east until it was almost out of eyesight but still within binocular range.

A few minutes later, the runner sprinted back into view heading west in a cloud of spray. It was moving at a good clip and they could hear the rumble of the engines following close behind. The runner arced and headed back east then made another pass.

The action arrested their attention and they watched with renewed interest. On the last pass it slowed and headed back towards the breakwater and river.

"Is that all?" Vince asked with disappointment in his voice.

"New engines got to be broke in slow," Pete answered, repeating what Davey had said the day he stopped by.

Rusty came alongside the dock and Pete and Joe caught the lines and tied them off.

"What's the verdict?" Al said, leaning down to look at him in the cockpit.

"There's some bugs to work out," Rusty said, crawling out. He headed back to the engine compartment and opened the hatch and poked around the engines.

"Carbs needs adjusting, number eight valve is tapping and there is a slight vibration in the drive shaft," Davey reported as Pete, Joe and Vince lifted him out and into the wheelchair.

"I couldn't feel the vibration, but if he says there is, then there is," Rusty said stepping out of the boat on to the dock.

“What’s that mean in layman’s terms?” Al said. “It sounds bad.”

“Fixable,” Rusty said.

Davey explained further. “The drive shaft that runs the propeller is off center a bit and the carburetors need adjusting for better gas flow. The tapping sound in the valve means adjustments- all new engines need tweaking and hot ones like these need constant fiddling. All and all I say they did splendid, uh Rust?”

“How fast were you going?” Vince asked.

“We were at half throttle when we were making the passes towards the end,” Rusty answered.

“Whoo-wee,” Pete said. “Half throttle,” he repeated. “You won’t be able to keep your eyes on it when it’s at full throttle, Vinnie.”

Al started drifting back to the shanty. “I am glad to hear that. For a minute I thought it was all show with no go. I mean, a tugboat could keep up if that was top speed.”

Davey followed him, and Rusty caught up and pushed the chair over the uneven ground. “Think of her as a race horse,” Davey told Al. “You just don’t take a thoroughbred out from pasture and expect it to win a race. You got to break it in, warm it up. Work it up to racing condition. When she’s ready, she’ll run. And boy, will she run.”

Al smiled. “I’m pleased to hear that, Mr.…?”

“Reynolds.”

“Mr. Reynolds. Hey, remember what I said about fate and serendipity,” Al said stopping abruptly and turning to Rusty. He pointed at Davey. “Fate. Your man was destined to be here.”

Davey looked up at Rusty and raised his brows.

When they returned to the shanty, Al pulled out a map and a paper and spread them on the work bench.

The map was of the western basin of Lake Erie which included the U.S. and Canadian islands. Al placed a hammer, planer, screwdriver and a jar of nails on each corner of the map to keep it flat as the men gathered around him.

“Middle Island is here,” Al said, stabbing his finger at a small dot on the map. “A horse fly can shit bigger than that. It is the southernmost point of Canada, south of Pelee and just over the border. The fishing tug will make its pickup at a fish shanty at a cove on the northeast side.” He placed a paper with a hand drawn map of Middle Island on top of the map and smoothed it out. Landmarks, piers and buildings were penciled in. “Here’s the cove where the shanty is located. Joe will direct you to it. He knows the island like the back of his hand, it’s his second home as he practically lives at the clubhouse there, hey, Joey?” He continued. “The shanty is where the cases of booze will be delivered, unpacked and repackaged in bundles and loaded onto the fishing tug. My Airedales—the ones that worked at the warehouse in Sandusky—will be doing the packing along with some Canucks that are friends of Joe. Where you dump the load and how you pick it up with the runner is your problem. The only thing that concerns me after the load leaves the dock is the bottles get delivered where and when you are instructed. Like I said, you are responsible to get the cargo to its destination and on time. That's why your cut is so generous."

Rusty made no comment. He looked over the drawn map of Middle Island and then he said, "Who's responsible for getting the cargo from the island to the lake drop-off?"

"Joe."

"Does that mean Joe will be onboard the fishing tug?"

"Yes."

"We need a crew to help run the boat and cast the net line. Will Joe be helping to do that?"

"Yes, and Lou. You remember Lou who loaded you along with Joe at Put-in-Bay? Do you think you'll need more? Pete should be available. Vince can't as he will be your land contact."

"Hey, if I'm out all night on the runner when do I sleep and have a life?" Pete said.

"Two will be fine if Lou's been around boats and can cast nets," Rusty said.

"He's a fast learner," Al replied. "You gonna pilot the tug?"

"It depends. Like Pete said, it may be rough being both places."

Al nodded.

"You haven't seen the tug yet. How about checking it out while I go over it with Joe."

Al shook his head and blew out a plume of smoke. "Gotta run. Another time. Joe, you bring Lou and Pete back for a fish boat lesson. And make it pronto as we start next week."

***

"So that's the Trapani clan?" Davey murmured as he took a card from the deck. A cold spring rain was falling as they sat at the kitchen table.

Rusty studied his cards. "Most of them. Too bad you didn't get to meet Giuseppe. I don't think he's related, though. Probably got him from the appliance section of the hardware store."

Davey grinned and took a sip of his root beer. "I wonder if that wine tasted any good?"

Rusty raised his brows as he pulled a card from his hand and tossed it onto the table. "What difference does it make, you don't drink anyways."

"That's why I was wondering," Davey mumbled as he studied his hand.

Rusty shook his head in amusement and then turned serious. "That tug is going to need a pilot with know-how. I'm not sure I can work both ends, and Joe and Lou will need overseeing."

"You mean you don't have faith in Tweedle Dee and Tweedle Dum?"

"About as much faith as Prohibition lasting another decade."

"Cap McIntyre's retired. Mentioned at my homecoming he'd be willing to come out of it if he found a local job that made it worth his while."

Rusty studied his hand. “What about you?” He glanced up from his cards to see Davey’s reaction.

“Me?”

“You know how to pilot a boat.”

“You want me to skipper the fish tug?”

“You know how to pilot and you know the lake.”

Davey remained quiet as he shuffled his cards about.

“Forget it, I shouldn’t have asked you. You’re involved too much as it is.”

Davey spread his cards out on the table. “Read ‘em and weep.”

Rusty tossed his bad hand down without revealing it to Davey and pushed back from the table. “You’ve beat me every hand.”

“Hope your luck’s better at running,” Davey said scooping up a pile of pennies and nickels. “To answer your question, I’ll need to sleep on it. I mean, that would be reining me in a whole different direction. But truth be told, I can’t say I haven’t enjoy working with you on the boat even if it’s for the wrong purposes.” He backed his wheelchair from the table and stared at his legs. “I’ll give it strong consideration. But it’s gambling with more than small change.”

He was surprised Davey was giving it consideration and instantly regretted asking him. “Gambling with our lives to be exact. Dave, it’ll be dangerous. We’ll be breaking the law and there will be hijackers out there.”

Davey took another sip of root beer and studied the bottle. “One more thing, Rust. It’s my second chance, too.”

***

Before he reached the back door into the kitchen, Uncle Fritz called to him from the doorway of the chicken coop located behind the house. The spring air around the farm was filled with different sights, sounds and smells than those that lingered over the lake and shoreline in springtime (and not all bad ones like the coop or hog pen). It was like two different worlds. He could smell fresh dirt from the thawed earth and the sweet cherry blossoms from the nearby orchard. Spring Peepers- tiny little frogs, who live in the woodlot and around the small pond, peeped earnestly while crows cawed and birds chattered noisily from treetops over territorial rights. Overhead, he heard a familiar cat-like sound, looked up and saw about three dozen lake gulls who had come inland to hunt, circling over the broken fields searching for worms and insects kicked up by the plow.

“What’s going on with the boat?” Uncle Fritz said in a hushed voice as Rusty approached him.

“It’s finished and in the water.”

“Still going through with it, uh?”

Rusty didn’t answer.

Uncle Fritz heaved a sigh. “I was hoping after six months…with spring…” He faded off.

“Has Di had a change of heart in six months?”

Uncle Fritz stepped from the coop, shut the door and latched it. "Time heals wounds."

"Not if they're festered."

Uncle Fritz motioned for him to follow him to the pond. "What do I tell Di if you're arrested or hurt or, God forbid, killed? What do I tell her family? And say you come out of this all right, can you live with yourself if you have harmed or killed someone?"

"I'm rum running like three quarters of the pilots out there, and I'm not looking for a fight—but if it comes my way, I'll be ready."

"That's looking for trouble."

"No. It's making big money fast to make Di and Davey's life better and yes, it's thumbing my nose at the law but it's a stupid law that is about to be repealed because the law makers have woke up and realized how asinine it is."

"But as of this moment it's the law! Besides, the reason behind the repeal is because of men like you and your hoodlum friends. People are dying over this."

"Just a minute. There is a difference between bad men and good men. Ask Huddleson, ask Di."

"Ah… so you are judge, jury and executioner?"

"We've been all through this before and I'm not going to defend my position over and over."

Uncle Fritz saw Rusty's face growing redder so he fell silent.

They paused at the pond's bank and watched a muskrat swim about. "You're like a son to me…that's why I care so much about you and want to save you from yourself. I can see a train wreck about to happen, but I'm helpless to stop it."

"Perhaps you should have more faith in the engineer?"

Uncle Fritz sighed. "Perhaps, but not under the circumstances. Let's head back. Di will be wondering why you didn't see her first and dinner should be soon."

That evening, after Rusty said his goodbyes and Di kissed him goodnight and he was left alone in his pickup truck about to start it, Uncle Fritz approached him, coming up to the window of the truck. "Open up your hand, I have something for you."

Rusty stuck his hand out and Uncle Fritz placed a round, flat object in it. He looked at it and saw it was a compass. It was Swiss made and looked expensive.

Rusty looked at him for a reason.

"To help you find your way back."

Chapter 52

Rusty had planned to name the fish tug *Chief* since that was the name Davey had said he would call his horse had he been a cowboy but Davey stopped him before he painted it on the transom and suggested *Calamity Jane* instead, stating Jane was a calamity and alcoholic thereby an appropriate name for a rum running fish tug. Rusty agreed but wondered if it would be a tip off of the boat's real mission since the real Calamity Jane died of alcohol poisoning.

Its hull was already clad in steel which was typical of many trap net fish tugs due to the battering they took, so modification entailed extending the sides of the pilot house back three feet on each side and replacing the glass to bullet proof glass. The bill was forwarded to Al who didn't bat an eye. But the pilot house was open in back and offered no protection to pilot or crew from behind and to modify it could raise suspicions. It was a dilemma Rusty and Davey hashed over and a situation that made Joe and Lou uneasy. They would literally have to *hit the deck* if they came under fire and Davey, well it would be to his benefit not to expose the boat's stern if pursued.

When Pete, Joe and Lou showed up for their first lesson with the boat, Rusty informed them that Davey was going to be the pilot. They accepted it without question as their only concern was to get their lessons underway so they could leave while the day was still young.

Davey coached lesson one—starting and maintenance of the boat's diesel engine. Lesson two was Rusty's domain—maneuvering the boat. The bilge pump, a joint tutorial, rounded out lesson three. That was followed by Coast Guard regulations briefing and a crash course in seamanship and emergency procedures or as Davey called them, "calamity" dealings.

"Tomorrow we'll teach you about the fish nets and running a line and take the boat out to see what sunk in," Rusty said, rapping his knuckle against Pete's head. He overheard Lou mumbled something about *another day shot.*

***

"Get to know one another's faces, boys," Al said as he introduced Rusty and Davey to the packing crew at the fish shanty on Middle Island.

The old fish shanty was snug back into a rocky cove concealed by Cedar and Hemlock trees. A long worn wooden pier ran from the simple barn-like structure out into a calm inlet. It was an older building that was abandoned for fish when prohibition started and turned into a secret storehouse for rumrunners. The Trapani's latest pursuit involved renting the property and modifying the shanty into a packing and storage warehouse, though one could never tell from the outside as it still looked like an abandoned fish shanty. There were no windows in the building and the floor was open except for a couple of round, rough cedar posts supporting the roof. Wide doors were situated at either end to allow fresh breezes and daylight to come inside. Empty wooden benches were arranged about the dirt floor in packing house order and lanterns dangled from long wire hooks over each bench. Nets and ropes draped across benches and hung from hooks on the wall, and all looked ready to receive its first cases of alcohol. Seven men—five looking like they could call themselves part of the Trapani clan, had gathered there to get final instructions from Al and to meet Rusty and Davey.

Al singled out two men. "These fellas will be delivering the booze to the shanty from the mainland." They did not look Sicilian and they spoke their salutations with a Canadian accent.

"This guy," he pointed to Davey, "will be the skipper that will haul our product from the shanty on the fish tug. And this guy, Rusty, will be the runner who picks up the product in the lake and makes the deliveries. These fellas are in charge on water and you answer to them," Al said, sweeping the men gathered with a stern look, "and I expect no grievances from any of you be it on terra firma or H_2O. Now, does everybody got everything they need and set to go before I get the ball rolling 'cause I don't want any surprises or flies in the ointment, *capisce?*"

***

Al followed Rusty and Davey out to the trap net fishing boat moored to the pier and watched as Rusty helped Davey board and get seated, then waited as Rusty jumped back out and onto the dock to untie the lines as Davey fired up the diesel engine. "Hey," he said under his breath to Rusty, "Is that buddy of yours going to be okay? I mean he can't get around without help."

"Joe and Lou will be with him."

"Yeah, but they might be kinda busy, you know. Besides, if things get ugly out there, they'll have their own skins to worry about."

Rusty walked up to Al. He looked like he had a bad taste in his mouth. "I don't doubt that for one minute. Davey and I are both aware of the circumstances and neither of us expects Joe and Lou to be his babysitter. We expect them to cover his backside, though, just as Davey would cover theirs, but if you don't think your boys are capable of that then perhaps you should consider a pilot and co-pilot of your choosing."

Al was quiet as he puffed on his cigar and scrutinized Rusty. "The boat only needs one pilot. It's not my fault your friend is a cripple. If he needs a co-pilot it comes out of his cut. As it is, I thought you were going to pilot both crafts but I went along with this arrangement owing mostly to your case that his knowledge of mechanics would be invaluable to us. You could say his share of the pie is more for his expertise as a mechanic than it is for driving the boat."

"His share includes overseeing Lou and Joe who you know don't know from nothing when it comes to boats. I'd say with Davey you got three for the price of one—a pilot, an ace mechanic and a babysitter."

Al ground his cigar stub out on the wood of the pier. A strained smile crept across his face. "You're a clever man, Mr. Rusty, clever man. That's why I wanted you with me in the first place." He drew a deep breath and looked across the quiet inlet. "If he feels he needs a co-pilot, let him have one. I'll bump his share up a bit not for a co-pilot but because your friend wears so many hats. If Joe and Louie don't work out, we can have a crew change—from my stable. Deal?"

"Deal." Rusty cast the stern and spring line on to the boat and jumped aboard. The diesel engine rumbled as Davey gave it throttle.

Al raised his voice to Rusty, "Remember, I'm here to make money, not to shell it out so everyone can have a turn at playing cops and robbers."

***

First light appeared low on the eastern horizon and somewhere in Huron a rooster was crowing. Davey was already aboard when Joe and Lou arrived in Lou's gray '26 Buick. Joe yawned repeatedly to which Davey overheard Lou muttering to him something about staying out too late when there is a job the next day.

Davey's spirit had grown in step with his independence. Rusty had built a ramp from the ground to rail level on the fish tug that would allow him to wheel up to the rail, swing his legs over and lower himself onto a series of "benches" with hand rails that led to his seat behind the steering wheel. The configuration allowed Davey to go to and from the boat and to his pilot station without assistance. He could now get out of his bed on the second floor, go down to the first floor, cross the backyard to the dock and board the fish tug on his own. A third wheelchair had been purchased and stowed within arm's reach of Davey's captain's bench in case he needed to move aft or leave the boat other than at its home dock which, if that were the case, he would then need the aid of Joe or Lou. It was a situation he hoped would not come to pass.

He was checking the dashboard gauges and the cousins were stowing their gear when Rusty came out of the fish shanty with a twelve gauge double barrel shotgun cracked open in the crook of his arm. He slid a shell in each chamber as he walked up to the tug and then snapped it shut and headed straightway to the pilot house without acknowledging Lou or Joe. Davey swung his legs aside as Rusty placed the shotgun within arm's reach of him on a rack installed above the windshield. "Just in case," he said.

Davey smiled. "Justin Case, glad to meet you, and I hope I don't have to introduce you to anyone."

Rusty felt that all so familiar twang of guilt in his gut. Davey was too gentle and decent to be thrown in a mix of riffraff and wrongdoing. He hesitated and looked at Davey. "You still want to do this? Because I can pilot this if you have a change of heart. In fact, I wish you'd change your mind. Helping me with the boat was more than enough."

"Already got my feet soiled doing that," Davey replied, staring hard out into the lake to avoid Rusty's eyes. "Besides, it feels good to be back on the water."

"You don't have to be on the water this way. We can cruise or fish whenever you want."

"What I *want* is to be useful." He spoke with an edge to his voice as he turned back to the dials and gauges on the dash.

Rusty hesitated, and then stepped out from the pilot house. "You boys ready to make it happen?"

"Ready as ever," Joe answered.

He caught a glimpse of a revolver in Joe's waste band. It looked like a .38. "I'll be co-piloting and helping you boys string lines for the first couple trips just to make sure things run smooth and everyone knows what to do and how to do it."

Lou pulled a .45 semi-automatic handgun from the bundle he brought aboard. He pulled the chamber open, looked in the barrel, shucked it shut and then stuffed it in his waistband as well.

"This is it then," Rusty said, looking over the crew. He jumped out of the tug and untied the bow and spring line. "Joe, get the stern."

Back on board, he gave the thumbs up to Davey who eased the fish tug from the dock and turned her nose down river. With the bow pointed towards the lake, he gave the engine some throttle and a black puff of dark smoke belched from the exhaust stack. The *Calamity Jane* began chugging towards the mouth of the Huron River.

Rusty stood along the gunwale, facing out towards the lake. A soft blue glow washed the horizon signaling the forthcoming sunrise. The lake water spread before him like a collage of indigo and cobalt blue broken only by small ripples of waves reflecting the luminous cerulean blue of the eastern sky. A fresh breeze off the cool waters washed over him. Overhead, lake gulls mewed and cawed as they gathered to circle the fish tug. He knew he should be feeling guilty and anxious, but he felt neither. He felt just too damn good.

Chapter 53

The *Calamity Jane* arrived at the inlet just as the sun broke over the horizon. The cove was muted by a gray mist that had yet to burn off and the old fish shanty, tucked among the trees and rocks, looked as though viewed through gauze. What little noise from sloshing waves and first birdsong was muffled by the veil of mist. It wouldn't be long before the gulls found the boat.

Rusty, Joe and Lou stood on the deck, straining their eyes and ears for signs of activity as Davey idled up to the pier. Joe was first to spot a cousin descending the rocks near the shanty where he had been stationed as lookout. The cousin, cradling a .222 rifle, waved them in.

"Late start," he said, leading them inside the shanty. "Aren't fishermen on the job at the crack of dawn?"

Lantern light glowed inside and Rusty could see burlap bundles wrapped in fish netting assembled by the door. Wooden crates, some broken, were tossed into corners and men mixed about the floor. Cigarette smoke hung in the air like a smog bank. As soon as the men realized the fish tug had arrived, they snapped to work and began gathering the bundles and hauling them toward the boat. The bundles, packed with bottles of high grade whiskey, had been placed in burlap sacks stuffed with straw, then placed into a square of netting and drawn tight with rope as directed by Al on Rusty's instructions.

"Hey, Joe," Rusty heard one man say, "Check out the pike!" The man was holding a bundle like it was a fish he had caught.

No one spoke to Rusty or Davey. Rusty directed spots to place the bundles which were rapidly piling up while Davey, sitting sideways on his bench seat, watched in curiosity.

Rusty counted each bundle as it came aboard. There were one hundred bundles and each was heavy. They were going to be a bear to pull up and onto the boat when they were sodden with lake water. He heard Joe ask how many bottles were in a bundle. The answer was around twenty-five, many with short necks so they won't break so easy.

When the last bundle was stacked on the deck, Al appeared. Giuseppe was with him.

"I see you are co-piloting."

"Long enough to make sure everything and everyone is running smooth."

"Good, because you saved me a trip to Huron," Al said. "I have something for you and Petey." He motioned to Giuseppe who ambled like a bear into the warehouse. He returned moments later with a long object wrapped in a flannel blanket. Rusty had an inkling what it was the moment he saw Giuseppe emerge with it.

"This is a little gift to celebrate your maiden voyage with *New Moon*. Think of it as a boat warming gift." Al chuckled.

Rusty took the swaddled object from Giuseppe's extended hands, feeling the weight of it in his arms more than Giuseppe. He removed the cover. His guess was right. It was a rifle, but not just any. Al had given him a Browning Automatic Rifle—big, heavy and fearsome. It was a weapon that appeared on the scene near the end of the war and sent terror in the German ranks when they heard its distinct sound. The bullets were big and accurate at a mile and powered by energy forceful enough to blow holes through three men deep.

A thick canvas bullet belt with a dozen pouches was draped over Giuseppe's shoulder. In the pouches were empty clips for the B.A.R. He pulled it off and draped it over Rusty's shoulder. One of the warehouse men carried a wooden cartridge box from the shanty and loaded it with a thud onto the deck of the tug.

Al was grinning out of the side of his mouth. "Let's see Captain Kid sink you now."

***

The *Calamity Jane* churned its way southeast through Canadian then U.S. waters to fishing grounds located five miles north of the Ohio shoreline between Vermilion and Lorain. It was an area familiar to Rusty as it was a good fishing ground. Along the way, Rusty helped Joe and Lou secure the alcoholic bundles to the string line, keeping approximately fifty feet of space between bundles. When they reached the fishing spot they had previously decided upon, Davey gave them the go ahead and they began casting the bundles into the water, marking the spot with a net marker where each bundle dangled below the string line. Davey kept the pace steady as the string of bundles slipped one by one overboard and sunk into the water. What remained when the last bundle disappeared under water was an interval of net markers spanning 500' of underwater line masquerading as a string of gill nets.

Had the Coast Guard stopped them, they would have found nothing on the fish tug that would lead them to think nothing more than a group of fishermen had cast their nets, and with Rusty advising Joe and Lou prior how to dress the part of a fisherman and all the equipment aboard pointing to fishing—save Al's hardware and cartridges hidden in a double walled compartment within the gunwale, the charade was most convincing. Had the Coast Guard searched, they would have found a shotgun stored above Davey's head, not unusual to have aboard nowadays with the waters infested with lawless men.

The *Calamity Jane* put in to the port of Huron by noon. Joe's and Lou's spirits seemed uncharacteristically high and Rusty figured it was due to the fact that they had a half a day and all night open to them and having completed a job that paid over a week's wages for a few hours of their time.

Before they left, Joe told Rusty that he and Lou would join the tug on Middle Island from now on since they would be spending the summer months more on the islands than the mainland. Huron, he said, was a bit out of their way.

Rusty consented as he just as soon not have the Trapani clan hanging about his shanty especially with the bait shop man's reflection often appearing in the window anytime there was activity, but that left Davey to cross the lake alone and the thought of that made him cringe. Instead of telling the cousins of his concern—which most likely would fall on apathetic ears, he decided he would work the fish tug as well, co-piloting for Davey and stringing the nets along with Joe and Lou. If all went as it had this morning, he could sleep in the afternoon and early evening before making the runs with the speedboat. After all, it was to be two or three times a week unless Al decided to stack runs. But that would be a bridge he'd cross when and if it happened. Coming in from a night run and going straight out on the tug before dawn could be burning the candles at both ends. He did it before during the war only now he was a decade older and a lifetime wearier.

Chapter 54

He checked his watch. Ten past one. *Where in the hell was Pete?* In the other room he could hear Davey snoring loud enough to rattle the windows and he was glad the midnight alarm bell didn't wake him. He had only two and a half hours of sleep himself before the bell and most of that was tossing and turning.

He'd spent late afternoon and early evening going over the boat and outfitting it for the run. He had arranged his charts, maps and navigational equipment in the runner's armor plated wheelhouse and later, while Davey played a game of solitaire before bed, he had sat at the kitchen table and loaded each of the twelve clips with twenty rounds of 30-06, the whole time thinking if he had to use more than one clip, he may be in deeper shit than he could dig himself out of.

He heard the crunch of tires on gravel outside and a car door shut. Looking out the upstairs kitchen window to the shadowy cul-de-sac below, he recognized Pete's silhouette next to a dark car. He heard a woman's voice, and then the car pulled away, kicking up stones as it headed back towards town. He hurried down the steps into the yard.

"It's past one. Couldn't you and your bearcat cut your whoopee short for one night so you could be here on time? We're supposed to be heading out at one and it's fifteen after."

"Don't go castin' a kitten, I'm not that late. Besides, I gave that dumb Dora the icy mitt long ago. This is a new skirt, and I didn't want her to think I was giving her the bum's rush."

"Rush my ass, you keep that in mind when we're rushing back to port before the coasties have shift change and we're spotted." He stormed into the workshop and down the rustic steps leading to the boat garaged below the workshop with Pete in tow and pointed at the bow line. Pete untied it. He then tossed a long pole to Pete and Pete followed suit as Rusty, using the poles like a gondolier, pushed the freed boat back out of its shelter and down the short canal leading to the river.

"We should be well on our way to the pick-up, Romeo," Rusty continued to grumble as they entered the river.

"All right all ready, I get the message, captain."

Rusty shot him a look as he clamped his pole in place lengthways along the gunwale and indicated for Pete to do likewise with his pole on his side. He then ducked into the pilot house.

Al's gift was racked within arm's reach of the steering wheel and the canvas ammo belt was shelved under the dash.

Pete entered the pilot house and spotted the B.A.R. "How'd you like Al's present? Nifty, uh?"

“Let’s hope it is a waste of his money,” Rusty said as he pulled the choke and pressed the starter button. “Extra clips are loaded in the bullet belt there.”

Pete opened a pouch and took out a clip. “Ready for action.” He looked too eager when he said it.

The engine rumbled to life like tigers poked from slumber. Though at idle, Rusty could feel their vibration through his hands on the steering wheel and his feet on the deck. It was bridled raw power and energy that he had at his command and gave him a rush. He forgot he was mad at Pete and glanced at him and saw Pete grinning ear to ear.

He barely gave it throttle so that the engines would idle as quietly as possible as they slipped down the river towards the open lake.

“You packing?” Rusty asked.

Pete rummaged through his gear and pulled out a shoulder holster housing a Broomhandle Mauser—a side arm Rusty hadn’t seen since the war. He slipped it on. “When I ran before, we never carried weapons. Coasties shot warning shots and hijacking was rare. It wasn’t the big deal it is now. Now,” Pete’s voice sounded wistful, “everyone’s a gunslinger and keen to shoot. It’s gotten crazy.”

“Big business and stiff competition,” Rusty said. “And talk of repeal is ramping up activities before the bottom falls out and liquor prices crash.”

“That’s what Al says.” Pete lit a cigarette.

“Keep that confined to the pilot house,” Rusty said with a nod at the cigarette. “Doesn’t make sense to cut running lights if you’re waving a beacon like that about on deck.” He checked his gauges again as the boat cleared the breakwater. “I have a 16 gauge pump of mine I brought along, so we should be pretty set if things get hot and heavy.” He hesitated before throttling up to check his pants pocket to make sure the compass Uncle Fritz had given him was in there. He knew it was, but he needed the reassurance. Then he throttled up.

***

New Moon slipped through the lake water with the stealth of a phantom to the fishing ground where the string line from the fish tug had been strung earlier that morning. Her coal gray hull was lost against the lake and moonless sky and her engines purred quietly with ease. The only light came from a small red dash light in the pilot house like ships and submarines used so sailors could maintain their night vision while reading charts and instruments. But it would be shore lights that would be his real guides to locating the nets, using the same landmarks Davey used by day.

“There should be a marker about here,” Rusty said, eyeing the lights of the grain elevators in Huron, the lights of Crystal Beach in Vermilion, the lighthouse in Vermilion and the brightly lit *Castle Erie* on the shoreline. He aligned with harbor lights in between.

Time stretched and Pete was growing antsy.

“There it is.” He cut the engines and went to the gunwale and grabbed a hook on the end of a dragline. He dredged the water with it until he hooked the net line.

Pete also grabbed the line and together they pulled on it and heaved the first sodden burlap bundle aboard.

"You mean to tell me we have to do this ninety-nine more times?" Pete said. His pants and shoes were soaked from the dripping bundle.

It took them an hour to retrieve forty bundles and stow them in compartments below deck hatches. "Maybe we should reconsider this," Pete said, taking a seat on the rail. He wiped his brow which was a combination of sweat and lake water. "Why can't we take a chance and pick the damn things up at the fish shanty on Middle Island. The guys will load us in the evening, we shoot across the lake during the night and make our connection on shore and be back at port long before the crack of dawn."

Rusty took a seat beside him. He was dying for a cigarette. "This was decided so we don't draw attention to the warehouse and have to run through a dragnet of Coast Guard boats lining the border just chomping at the bit for speeding boats crossing over in the dead of night."

"So, this thing can outrun anything out there, can't it?"

"Did you listen to what I just said?"

Pete grunted.

They sat in the dark, listening to the occasional wave lap against the hull. The lake was so calm, the boat was almost still. The moonless sky was black and stars spread from horizon to horizon. For as far as he could see out into the lake, there was no light to be seen and it made for a feeling of emptiness that Rusty found strangely comforting.

"So what happened with your tomato?"

"She liked sucking the bamboo too much. She was wasted most of the time."

"Where'd you meet this one?"

"At a speakeasy in Bucyrus. I heard Capone's train car was sidetracked there two weeks ago and thought I'd check it out."

"Was it his car?"

"No. But the place was hopping and that's where I met this doll. She's not like that crazy flapper but she's a real hot mama."

"I wouldn't expect less," Rusty said standing. "Let's hit it again, we got a long night ahead of us."

An hour and twenty minutes later, they were loaded and low in the water. Rusty nosed *New Moon* south and it set out towards Erie's southern shoreline and the desolate dock at Beaver Creek.

***

Five hundred feet from the shoreline, Rusty flashed a spotlight—one flash, pause, followed by three rapid flashes. He and Pete strained their eyes into the darkness toward the area of the dock. A moment later, three rapid spotlight flashes followed by a pause and then another flash generated from the area of the dock, breaking the darkness.

New Moon approached as quietly as a stalking cat. Pete held the B.A.R. at ready.

"*Rising Sun*?" A voice called out to them from the dark shoreline.

"*New Moon*," Rusty answered.

Both parties were satisfied with the passwords. Pete racked the rifle as Rusty guided the boat to the dock.

A shadowy figured emerged on the dock. "Wow, you made it." The voice belonged to Vince.

Pete tossed a line to him and Vince snugged the boat to the dock. "How'd it go?"

"I'd say smooth as silk, but heaving these bags and taking a bath in lake water are a pain in the ass. Let's just say, Vinnie, I've earned my money."

Rusty passed the bundles to him and he loaded them on the dock while Vince returned to a parked vehicle. It was the old Paradise Farms milk delivery truck. He came back with a wheelbarrow.

"Christ, Vinnie, you alone?"

"Naw, Tony's riding shotgun. Here he is."

Tony appeared on the dock. He was carrying a World War 1 trench gun—a short barrel pump shotgun capable of 6 rounds counting the one in the chamber. "Hey, Petey, you been screwing around? We just about gave up on you." Pete and Tony embraced.

"Last time I saw you, you were at Al's party pissing in his fountain."

"Al would kill me if he knew. Between the alcohol and the ammonia I probably killed his goldfish," Tony laughed. He and Vince loaded the bundles into the wheelbarrow and began carting load after load to the truck, stacking them where milk once rode.

After he had passed off the last bundle, Rusty checked his watch. "Shit, Pete, its 4:30. We got to shake a leg."

"See you tomorrow, Vinne. Tony, catch you in three days." Pete jumped aboard the boat and Vince tossed him the lines as Tony hurried back to the truck.

Rusty fired up the engines. "Let's hope we can make time without too much racket." He throttled up and the boat cut an arc in the water as it accelerated from the dock. Pete lost his balance and fell to his seat. Without a load to burden it, it raced for the open water.

"Whoo-whee," Pete hollered over the engines roar.

Vince paused long enough on the bank to watch the shadowy boat fly into the darkness. The crescendo of the twin Liberty aircraft engines as they roared from the dock made the hair raise on his arms, and as the sound of their howls disappeared into the night, he laughed.

***

Every Monday and Thursday throughout April and most of May, the scenario repeated itself. Then Al upped the ante.

***

"I going to stop in and see Huddleson on Wednesday," Rusty said to Uncle Fritz as he loosened a bolt on a broken plow point. "I heard some chat in Port Clinton the other day and I want to know if Huddleson has an inside angle on it."

"I'd like to go along if you don't mind. I haven't seen him since the accident. How's he doing?"

"He's doing fine. Keeping his mouth shut and his eyes open, though."

"I bet." Uncle Fritz said as he passed him a new point followed by another bolt. "Coast Guard still running the light?"

"Yeah. What did you say you hit?"

"A rock the size of a small melon. I think they grow in the fields over winter."

"Frost heave."

"*Ja, ja.* Well, at least they let Huddleson stay at the keeper's house."

"Especially, since they really don't need him. The lights are going automated now," Rusty grunted as he tightened the nut.

"Well an automated light would not have seen you and Di and rescued you." Uncle Fritz sighed. "I don't know, everything is changing and not always for the better."

"I know a tractor would be better than a horse," Rusty said. He stood and brushed the dirt off his pants. "Especially for the horse since you like to rock hunt with your plow."

"Phtt! With a horse I can nod off and my plow lines will still be straight, a tractor I have to work with to keep straight."

Rusty smiled.

Uncle Fritz gathered the tools. "Does Huddleson know of your tomfoolery?"

Rusty's smile faded. He walked to the well pump, pumped it a few times and washed his hands under it.

"So what is it you heard in Port Clinton?" Uncle Fritz said, changing the subject back.

"Another incident on the lake similar to mine. Just west of Catawba off Scott Point."

"Isn't that out of Huddleson's way?"

"You fart on Cedar Point and they know it in Lakeside."

"Well then, all the more reason to see the keeper."

Huddleson was painting the picket fence surrounding the keeper's house when Rusty and Uncle Fritz drove up.

"Cap, I don't know if you remember my wife's Uncle Fritz—he was with me the day we found you injured…"

"Of course, I remember. You stopped by to see how I was doing in the hospital."

"You look much better than our last meeting," Uncle Fritz said, "And I see you have your petunias planted."

"Oh, yes. And how are you and the missus doing," Huddleson said turning to Rusty.

"We are fine."

"Time heals all wounds," Uncle Fritz said.

Huddleson studied Rusty, noting a glumness that surrounded him. "I have found the mind takes a little longer to heal than the body," he said in a soft voice. "Just give it time." He then brightened. "You fellas want some lemonade? I know I could use one."

"Thank you."

While Huddleson disappeared in the house, Rusty stared hard out into the water in the area where he and Di had sunk.

Uncle Fritz caught the look. "I would like a look at the automated light and see how it works—how about you?" he said, disrupting Rusty's focus.

"Sure. Before we leave," Rusty said returning from his thoughts.

Huddleson returned with a tray of glasses and a pitcher of lemonade. "So to what do I owe this pleasure?"

Rusty took a glass and filled it. "Well, first off, to see how you are doing."

"The gimp has left me a lot slower especially on the climb up and down the light. I guess you could say that is the one good thing about automation. As for my amnesia of the accident…it's still there." He winked at Uncle Fritz.

"Any more 'visitors?"

"No. Chief Stoddard stops in to see me as do Coast Guard personnel to check on the light. But no one shady. My heart would most likely stop, though, if Connors or his boys showed up here."

"That brings me to my other reason for dropping by…I heard another boat was sunk and an eyewitness fingered Connors."

Huddleson sat his glass down. His face turned grave. "You heard right. Do you also know that eyewitness is dead?"

Rusty face went ashen. He exchanged glances with Uncle Fritz who was equally as pale.

"It was near 3:30 in the morning. In this case, it was a rummy crossing over from Kingsville and headed for the Port Clinton area. Just as he gets west of Scott Point a Coast Guard picket boat opens fire. Direct hit, no questions asked. When the coasties pull up to the runner, he puts his hands up to surrender. That's when they open up with machine gun fire and he falls over board."

"Then who was the witness?" Uncle Fritz said.

"He was, because he wasn't dead- just playing dead. Of course, he was pretty shot up and bloody so they bought that he was dead. He watched as two coasties boarded the runner and sacked it. When they found the cases of gin, they loaded them onto the picket boat then shot up the runner until it sank. He thought for sure he'd be hit by flying bullets but luck was still with him. After the boat sank, they headed north. He found himself a piece of the boat's transom to hang onto and was able to propel himself towards Catawba where he washed up in the marshes south of Scott Point."

He paused for a breath, and Uncle Fritz leaned forward in eager anticipation for him to continue.

"He musters his strength and staggers toward the inland road where he collapses. God knows how he made it that far, half drowned and bleeding out his holes." He paused again and this time took a sip of lemonade to wet his throat.

Uncle Fritz glanced at Rusty to see if he was growing as impatient as he was for Huddleson to get through the story.

"It just so happens this motorcar comes along and of all people, it's the chief making his morning rounds. He rushes the fellow to the hospital, with the man ranting all the way there and at the hospital about the coasties shooting him up without warning. When the chief settles him down, the fellow tells him the gun that shot up the boat was a big one—a .30 caliber he is sure. Now get this, he overhears one of the coasties say, just before they shot him, 'get rid of the oil can, Bill'—Bill, that's the same name I heard before the tumble and then…then he sees the last two numbers on the bow…57!"

Rusty clenched his teeth. His face glowered. "Connors's boat is 157. And Bill is the name of his motor machinist."

"Uh-huh."

"When does the rummy die?" Uncle Fritz prodded.

"Not at that point. This is some tough bird. He makes it through surgery. Doc says he'll recover. The fellow bounces back, heck, he eats soup, wants to sit up, talks away, blah, blah then the second morning after surgery, a nurse finds him dead. Doc says he must have died in his sleep. *Most unexpectedly.*"

"You know all this for sure?" Rusty asked.

"Got it from the chief himself. Here's the interesting part. The chief goes to the Coast Guard station and asks if any boats made a bust that night. Dispatcher says no reports were filed. He goes back the next day and asks if any C.G. boats turned in confiscated contraband liquor in the last 24 hours. Dispatcher checks the records and says no arrests or seizes filed. Then the dispatcher asks the chief why the inquiries. The chief is button lipped. Says just looking into hearsay floating around. Tells the dispatcher it's probably just idle talk around the docks. Then, the next morning, this rummy is found dead in his hospital bed and the chief is kicking himself for not putting a guard in the room with this guy."

Rusty's face was drawn tight when he had finished.

"So the chief thinks maybe the same fellas that visited you, visited the rumrunner at the hospital, ja?"

"It's leaning that way."

"Why didn't the chief tell me?" Rusty said. "I have a right to know about this."

Uncle Fritz said, "What purpose would it serve? We already had our suspicions."

"The purpose is we'd have more proof. You keep harping on me that I need more evidence," he said, spinning to Uncle Fritz. "How much more evidence do I need?"

"The chief is on it, Rusty," Huddleson said. "Let's let him do his job and not get in his way. When he has something to tell you or ask you, he'll see you. And Fritz is right—what purpose would it serve other than to reopen wounds."

"Reopen? They never healed in the first place!"

"Come now, Rusty," Uncle Fritz said. "This is just what the chief was averting."

Rusty stormed to the water's edge where he and Di had made landfall that night. He could feel his pulse pounding in his temples.

Huddleson started after him, but Uncle Fritz waved him off. "Give him a minute."

Rusty glared at the water and clenched his teeth. He stomped back to Uncle Fritz and Huddleson. They watched him with anticipation. "We are dealing with very dangerous men."

"We know that," Uncle Fritz said.

"Deranged men."

"That's no secret," Huddleson added.

"You and I are in danger," Rusty said looking at Huddleson. "How long before they doubt the amnesia story or wonder if your memory will return? We are two more bodies that can finger them."

Huddleson's brows furrowed.

"What about the chief?" Uncle Fritz said. "He's got wind. Are they gonna kill him, too? People will start connecting the dots. Connors and his crew may be crazy, but they're not stupid."

"No. They're clever all right, but they're animals and if they feel cornered, there is no telling what they'll do and to whom. I for one don't want to live looking over my shoulder."

Uncle Fritz started to comment, but Rusty cut him off. "The chief can only do so much because the law has his hands tied. Where is the law out in the water?"

"The Coast Guard is the law."

Rusty snorted. "I rest my case."

Chapter 55

Al's latest pitch left a bad taste in Rusty's mouth. The original plan was running smooth. It made money and risk was low. But Al was making connections quickly and with first rate, brand name liquor and a reputation for square dealing, requests for their services were growing along the shoreline and that worried him. They had gone into this venture with similar objectives but different motives. Both wanted to make some smacks while putting the screw to Connors but with Al, money was the main reason while his was Connors.

The other reason that made him uneasy was competition with existing suppliers who would be more than curious to find out who was running them under the table. He didn't figure Al to be so naïve as to step on toes without having the heavier boot, but why take the risk? Hijacking and crossing territory lines were not as likely with the present runs, but the new dealings Al was orchestrating almost begged for it.

"Before you get your shorts in a knot, hear me out," Al said at the meeting at Sam's. His omnipresent shadow, Giuseppe stood somber faced and watchful from the back wall. The place was empty except for two men shooting pool in the back room. "I know I'm asking you and Petey to put your necks on the line but more money and more opportunities mean more risk, am I right? You said you felt an obligation to support all these folks and you need the money, right? You said you wanted to be on the lake. By hook or crook, you're on the lake, right? You said you wanted to take care of business with that coastie captain in your own way, right? Well, the door just opened wider for you, my friend."

Rusty grimaced. "I just wanted to keep this simple to pay off bills and make things right. Sure, I said all that, but I also said *I wanted to keep this simple.*"

"Well, it didn't work your way." Al said. He placed his arms on the table and leaned toward him. "I have an enormous amount of respect for you, Mr. Rusty. I wish I had a half dozen of you, but I don't so the one I got I want to keep and make happy so he stays with me." He leaned back in his chair. "I'm not just asking a lot of you, I'm asking a lot of my family. You forget those are blood kin of mine you're working alongside. I know what it looks like. I'm sitting up there in my big house on South Bass and making big plans, going to meetings at fancy restaurants and connecting with a lot of high hats while you... you, Petey, Joe, Lou, Vince...all of yous are doing the dirty work. But we're all in this together—nobody is top dog. I'm meeting fellas that make me sweat. I want you to understand that I want us *all* to live in a big house with fancy cars and no worries. This isn't greed on my part, it's seeing everyone is taken care of and happy." He removed his hat and rubbed his head. "Tell you what, my friend...give me six of these new runs and after that if they still give you the heebie-jeebies, you can quit. You can keep your usual circuit and I will find another pilot for these new connections though it will be tough finding a replacement as good as you. Just don't quit on me altogether. Come see me when you got a problem and we'll work it out. Just like today's meeting."

Rusty stared off into the pool room. A crack of cue balls and eruption of laughter from the pool room disrupted his thoughts. He heard Giuseppe blow his nose.

By the time the meeting was over, Al had him convinced this was sure fire.

***

"Anything?"

Pete scanned the horizon with the binoculars again. "Not yet."

"It's got to be near. We are practically on the border."

"There it is!" Pete pointed into the dark void of the lake.

Rusty crept *New Moon* over the invisible boundary onto the Canadian side of the lake. He had yet to see the ship, but Pete could see it thanks to the light gathering capacity of the binoculars. "Just keep scanning the entire horizon as well," Rusty said. "We don't want any surprises."

As *New Moon* advanced, a hulking dark shadow began to emerge from the darkness. Rusty flashed the spotlight twice, waited then flashed two again, this time, farther apart.

Four flashes of light in rapid succession replied from the shadowy form.

Rusty breathed a sigh which did little to quiet his pounding heart.

Meanwhile, Pete had traded the binoculars for the B.A.R. "Don't forget the passwords—*sailor, Gordon, mother...*"

"I remember!"

As they moved close, the dark form—a ship at anchor—loomed above them. It was a three mast schooner and it was uncomfortably quiet.

"Like a ghost ship," Pete whispered.

"Ahoy...*Isabeau*." Rusty called out.

"Ahoy."

"I'm looking for a sailor by the name of Gordon?"

"What do you want with him, *mon ami*," a voice replied from the ghostly schooner.

"His mother is dry and needs him home."

"I'll get him."

Pete relaxed his grip on the rifle.

Lantern light popped up along the ship's rail and figures began appearing in the glow.

Rusty flipped a small deck light on and it washed *New Moon*'s mid and aft deck in a soft glow. A hood over the light directed the beam downward to the deck, preventing any escape of its glow into the night.

"What's your pleasure?" A voice called from the schooner.

"Twenty cases scotch whiskey, ten Gordon gin, eight beer, five bourbon and two French champagne."

Quiet followed, then the voice said, "that will be $635.00."

A monkey rope ladder dropped over the ship's side. "Permission to come aboard with dough in hand," the voice called out again.

Rusty and Pete exchanged glances. Neither had planned to leave the boat so this was a new twist.

"I'll go," Pete said. "You need to stay with the boat." He handed the rifle to Rusty and unconsciously touched the Mauser in his shoulder holster for reassurance.

As he ascended the ladder he could hear shuffling and thumping from the deck above.

A figure stood near the ladder, reaching out with his hand and assisted him aboard. Once on deck, Pete could see the crates being assembled near the rail and a cargo net set in place.

A large, hairy man approached him. He had whiskey breath. "That will be $635.00, eh," he said shining a flashlight in Pete's face, then dropped the light onto Pete's hands as he reached for the money and counted it out slowly.

"Load 'em," the man bellowed as Pete passed the last bill. The man stashed the money in a pouch slung over his shoulder.

The cargo net was loaded with cases and crates of liquor and lowered over the side while Pete scrambled down the rope ladder. Once safely on deck, he helped Rusty offload.

With the final crate, Rusty shouted, "Clear," and the cargo net rose back to the mother ship.

"Pleasure doing business," the voice called from the rail. "Come again, eh?"

New Moon sat low in the water, but according to her painted watermark, she was right where she should be.

"Okay, Pete. Let's see if we can tiptoe into Lorain." Rusty killed all the lights and fired up the engines. He aimed *New Moon* south and they flew across the border and dark lake like a passing shadow.

"Well that went without a hitch," Pete said while marveling how quickly the shore lights popped into view.

"Not over yet. The tricky part is coming up."

"At least we know these waters. That ship gave me the creeps."

"You didn't piss yourself, did you?"

"Ha, ha. Wasn't your ass on that boat with Blackbeard."

Rusty nosed the boat just west of Lorain's harbor. It seemed surreal. These were the waters he plied as a tugboat seaman. He could see himself here on the dock and *Iroquois*. Now he was here as a rumrunner. He pushed the thought out of his head before it could root.

They passed the harbor and on the fringes of the city, a cluster of lights glowed on the shoreline, highlighting a stone fortress emerging high atop a rocky bank.

"There it is," Pete said. "*Castle Erie.*"

Rusty cut back the engines on the approach. "Stop gawking and keep watch on the surroundings." As they drew close, he grabbed the spotlight and flashed a signal. Moments later, the proper reply flashed from the castle's rampart. He idled down as he passed a rock jutting and searched the dark bank. A smaller light appeared on the bank below the castle. It swung back and forth like Al had said. He headed for the light, not realizing he was holding his breath. He reached for the shotgun and laid it across his lap.

"Pete, ready?"

Pete already had his Mauser in hand.

The light motioned them forward. There was a bend in the rocky bank where a soft glow emanated. On approach, they could see it marked the entrance to a small cave. A man with a railroad lantern stood at the cave's entrance, waving them in. A dim figure stood near him. As they passed into the mouth of the cave, they could see the second man was holding a Thompson submachine gun.

"Right up to the dock," the signalman was saying.

They looked in awe as they entered the illuminated cave. Up ahead, waiting on a stone dock, stood two men. Near them, two more stood with shotguns at ready.

"Remind me to thank your cousin Al for getting me into this," Rusty muttered, eyeballing the men with shotguns.

"You're not the one doing the dealing," Pete whispered back.

One man on the dock reached out for a line and Pete tossed it to him. He snugged up the boat.

Pete disembarked and handed the man a paper. "As ordered. Your people agreed to the cost as marked on the bottom and signed."

The man examined the paper. "Hey, Frog Eyes, pay the kid." He handed the man with the bulging eyes the paper. While Frog Eyes counted out the money, the man barking orders boarded the boat. "Let's have a look," he said to Rusty.

Rusty opened the hatches and lifted out a case. The man pried open the case and removed a bottle of gin. "A-1 sauce," he said with a nod. "Let's hope for your sakes it all is," the man said out of the side of his mouth to Rusty.

It took twenty minutes to unload the cases onto the subterranean dock.

Just as they were about to leave, the man said, "If the boss is happy with this, we'll be seeing you soon."

"We'll be seeing them soon if the boss ain't happy," Frog Eyes inserted. Both men laughed.

Rusty eased the boat from the dock. There was just barely enough room to jockey the boat around.

"You got some boat there, mister," the first man called out as he watched Rusty maneuver the boat. "I bet it can hum."

New Moon motored towards the cave's outlet at low throttle. They emerged with caution, keeping an eye on the men on the rocks and the surrounding shoreline. Rusty watched for any glint of reflected light out on the lake. When they cleared the rocky barricade, he hit the throttle and *New Moon* bolted from the shoreline like a horse bolting from a barn. He was never so glad to be out of a place.

"I don't know if I can do this," Rusty said.

"You didn't piss yourself, did ya?"

***

It was noon and he was still asleep when Eddie arrived.

When Davey answered the door, Eddie's first impulse was to bolt, but Davey's words snagged him. "Eddie, right? You want to see Rusty?"

"Is he here?"

"He's here, boy. Come on in." Davey left the door open and wheeled into the middle of the kitchen allowing Eddie space to enter.

Eddie stepped over the threshold cautious like a fox sniffing new ground.

Davey watched in silence as the boy's eyes scanned the room and finally came to rest on him and then the wheelchair. His black eye and split lip was a good indication this was not a social call. "Would you like a root beer, son?" Without waiting for an answer, he wheeled over to the icebox and got two bottles out. "Take a seat. I already got mine."

Eddie slid into a chair across from Davey and regarded him with watchful eyes.

"By the way, my name's Davey. I'm a friend of Rusty's. We worked together on the tugboats. I was the engineer." He cracked open the bottles and slid one across to Eddie. "So you're the one Rusty talks about, the famous Eddie. Says you have a dog for a shadow, and the two of you have more savvy than most grown-ups."

Eddie sat silent. He didn't touch the bottle of root beer.

"I'll ah…I'll get Rusty," Davey said. He backed his wheelchair up to the door of the bedroom and knocked on it with the back of his fist. "Rust! Wake up! You got a visitor." He knocked again. "Rust?"

There were some rustling sounds and then the door opened. Rusty looked heavy-eyed and hastily dressed. His sleepy eyes widened to alert when he saw his visitor. "Eddie?"

Eddie rose. "You said I could come anytime. You said if I needed help to come."

"Yes, of course, of course." He looked long and hard at Eddie's face. "What happened to you? Who did that?"

Eddie sniffed. Then he started to cry.

Rusty exchanged looks with Davey. "Take a seat, kid and tell me what happened."

Eddie brushed his tears and his bottom lip stiffened. "I was at the old lighthouse. Prince and I had been looking for bottles along the shore around dusk and it started to rain so we took cover inside the lighthouse. I must've fallen asleep because it was dark when Prince's barking woke me up."

Rusty sank into a chair across from him at the kitchen table. His eyes gobbled up every word Eddie spoke.

"Prince was barking towards the lake so I took a look. A small boat was docking at the lighthouse. It was still pouring rain. I quieted Prince and was set to high-tail it out of there when I heard someone coming into the lighthouse from the pier way so both exists were blocked. I headed for the trap door in the middle of the room, but when I opened it, I could see the boat tying off below it. The footsteps from the pier were coming closer so Prince and I were trapped. We backed into the old stairwell and crawled up as far as we could go before we hit rubble blocking the stairwell." He brushed a stray tear and set his jaw.

"I heard those footsteps head straight for the trapdoor and the sound of the trapdoor opening. A man from the boat said it was a shitty night but it made for good cover. He said he had twenty cases. I could hear shuffling and dragging sounds. I took a few steps down and peeked around the corner. In the lantern light, I could make out two men but there were too many shadows to see them well. One was handing crates up through the trap door; the other was taking them and stacking them on the floor next to it. The boat guy said he'd probably have a hell of a time finding the tug in all this pea soup. The guy inside the lighthouse answered him but I don't know what he said because..." Eddie's bottom lip started trembling," because when I heard his voice I recognized it—it was my old man's."

He choked back his tears and swallowed hard a few times before continuing. "I must've gasped or something because he stopped stacking and looked right at the stairway. I damn near pissed myself. I tried to back quiet-like up the stairs and that's when I bumped into the rubble, causing a couple of loose stones to roll down the stairwell. I saw the light from the lantern swing then the glow getting brighter as it neared the stairs but I couldn't go up any farther. The man—my father, stuck the lantern in the stairwell and saw me. He said, 'I'll be damned' and grabbed me by the leg and pulled me down the steps. Prince went wild and started barking and growling and trying to get past me to get to him. My old man grabs me around the neck, says 'you little shit' and tosses me onto the floor of the lighthouse. He yells to the boatman, 'it's okay—it's my stupid, big nosed kid.' "

At this point, Eddie eyes began to well with tears again. "He starts hollering that I'm a sneak and how he is going to lock me up. I get up to run but he grabs me and back hands me to the floor. Prince is jumping and barking and growling like crazy. I tried to scramble for the door to the pier, but he pulls me up and hits me across the face again. That's when I saw Prince leaping through the air—just like I always wished in my dreams. He grabs my old man's arm and begins shaking him like a rag doll. My old man punches Prince over and over again on the head but Prince hangs on, growling and tugging my old man all around by the arm.

I heard myself screaming *kill him, kill him, Prince.* The man from the boat comes running up with a shotgun. He points the gun at Prince. I screamed at him and lunged for the gun and wrestled him for it. The gun goes off. It spooks the guy and Prince. The guy runs for the trap door and says 'it's your problem' to my old man. I grabbed a case of liquor and smashed it into the backside of my old man and sent him head over heels. Then Prince and I ran. We ran till we got to the widow's place and told her what happened. She phoned the chief's house." By the stunned looks on Rusty's and Davey's faces, he felt his story must have had quite an impact.

"Where's Prince?" was the first thing Rusty could think of as he processed the story.

"Mrs. Donovan is hiding him for me. She told me to go to you—that you would know what to do and protect me."

"Will she be safe if the kid's father goes looking for him there?" Davey asked.

"She said if my old man pokes his head through the door or a window, he'll meet her iron skillet. Besides, Chief Bales put Ray Kruger to keep an eye on her place as this being serious business."

"Where was Hoot in all this?"

"Chief stopped by in the morning and I eavesdropped on his conversation with Widow Donovan. He told her that he found Hoot sitting under the eaves of the fishery in a puddle and four sheets to the wind that night. He said Hoot was so blotto he didn't even know he was soaked to the bone let alone anything else so he threw Hoot in the slammer for twenty-four hours so he could reflect on the *results of his dereliction of duty.*

Rusty's face was grim. He got up and walked to the window and stood looking out of it as the minutes silently passed.

Davey looked to him for a response.

"Eddie's old man doesn't surprise me," he said breaking the silence, still looking out the window. "Hoot either. But who is this mystery boat and what tug is its boatman talking about?"

***

The day after Eddie's account of his beating, Rusty asked Davey to oversee Eddie while he took a trip to Vermilion. He went directly to Chief Bales' office.

"I'd arrest that knucklehead if I could find him," the chief said. "I sent Ray Kruger to watch his place in case he shows up. I'm personally keeping an eye on Donovan's and the docks."

"What will you do with Hoot?"

"I don't know...got him in the back room sobering him up." Chief Bales sighed. "I gave that poor son-of—a-bitch a break when I kept him on as night watchman. Apparently, he can be had if a bottle is waved under his nose. What good is a watchman that can be had?"

"Can I talk to him?"

"Sure. He's awake. Refused breakfast. Probably got one hell of a hangover."

Bales unlocked the door to the room that held a small jail cell. "Company, Hoot."

Hoot was sitting on a bench along the side wall, his head hanging low. A high window with bars allowed a stream of sunlight into the cell, shining a beam on Hoot as if he was on the hot seat under cross examination.

He raised his head when he heard them enter the room. "Rusty? What are you doing here?"

"I came to see you and hear your side."

"My side? There's no side. I'm a damn fool. Got drunk and shirked my duty. Simple as that. Bales told *me* what happened. I let Eddie down. Poor Eddie. I'm a damn fool."

"What I want to know is what happened before you got drunk. Did you see or talk to anyone around the docks beforehand? Did someone give you the liquor?"

Hoot lowered his head into his hands. "I told Bales that I was walking my usual beat and was at the fishery making sure nothing was amiss. I rounded the corner and almost ran smack dab into Eddie's pa. Scared the hair off my head as it was dead of night and raining cats and dogs. He says, 'Hey, Hoot, I got me a bottle of *Templeton Rye* whiskey, wanna share?' I told him I was on duty, and he says 'sure, but a sip or two won't hurt—night like this a body can use a nip to buck up.' " Hoot paused. "We passed the bottle, but I must've taken more than a swig or two. Damn if I can remember anything after that until waking up here."

"Is that the first time you saw his pa while on watch."

"No."

"Has he offered you a drink those other times?"

Hoot fidgeted on the bench.

"Bales is in the other room, so it's between you and me and I won't tell him, so level with me, Hoot. Has his pa brought a bottle around to "share" those other times as well?"

Hoot stared at the floor.

"Please, Hoot. I'm not interested in whether or not your drinking on the job, I'm interested in Eddie's dad and what he's up to."

"Yes…yes…yes."

"Yes what?"

"Yes he shows up sometimes, yes he always has a bottle, yes I always drink it." Hoot's face was red and drawn. He stared at the floor, avoiding Rusty's eyes.

Rusty nodded. The frown line between his eyes deepened.

Hoot snatched a glance at him. "So you thinking his pa's a bootlegger?"

Rusty sighed. "It looks that way. A small timer I'm guessing by the size of the load. Seems he knows your Achilles Heel. He's probably getting you liquored up on the nights of delivery."

"He's not going to have it so easy next time—that is if Bales keeps me on."

"If you stay on, you're going to play dumb to his bootlegging if he comes around. If you spot him out and about around the shoreline or town during the night, go straightaway to Bales' house and wake him."

"And if he finds me first?"

“Refuse the drink. Tell him the last batch made you sick and you’ll pass. Act like nothing is wrong. Better yet, pretend to drink with him—like he pretends...*pretend* to be headed for a bender...for God’s sake, keep your head clear and your mouth shut or you might get a taste of what Eddie got...or worse.”

“Pretend? I get a whiff and I don’t know if I can pretend. I’m a sot... a souse. I fooled myself thinking I can pass it up, but I can’t, can I? And you want me to pretend?” Hoot scoffed. “That’s like telling a bee not to go to the flower.”

“Then you best spot him first and high-tail it to Bales. When you agreed to watchman, you agreed to watch over the people in this town. They, like Bales, are counting on you to keep them safe at night, and that includes Eddie.”

Hoot rose slowly and went up to the bars of the cell, his back to Rusty. “Bales says Eddie is not around. Ran off from old lady Donovan’s.” He grabbed hold of the bars and scrunched his face as if to squelch a cry. “Damn me to hell. Where could he have gone, the poor thing.”

“Eddie’s safe.”

“For sure?” Hoot’s voice brightened and he turned to Rusty.

“For sure.”

Hoots breathed a sigh of relief. “Is he okay? I heard his old man messed him up.”

“He’ll heal. He’s tough.”

Hoot hung his head again. “Eddie has always been good to me. He’s my friend, Rust. I can do this, for Eddie.”

Rusty nodded. “I’ll talk to Bales and see if he gives you that chance. Since this is getting sticky, it might not be a bad idea to add a second night watchman,” He headed for the doorway leading to Bales office and as he walked through it, Hoot added, “and it weren’t *Templeton Rye*... no sir. It was some panther piss he was passing off.”

***

Eddie spent two nights at the Huron boat house before he declared, “I got to get back to Prince.”

Rusty didn’t argue. Despite the risks in Vermilion, it was still a better environment than the rum running world he and Davey now occupied. Leaving the boy alone while they made runs and having iron-packing Sicilians around the dock and an unusual speedboat garaged under the boat shanty that headed out after midnight would have Eddie putting two and two together in a wink of an eye, so he drove him back to Mrs. Donovan the following day. But first, he sent a message to Al to have Joe and Lou come to Huron so Davey wouldn’t make the crossing into Canada alone that morning. Vince was sent in their place. He was okay with that. The departure of the fish tug with Vince aboard would not raise questions in Eddie. The last thing he wanted the boy to know was that he was a rumrunner.

The *Calamity Jane* was docking just as he returned from Vermilion. The three cousins, Vince with Joe and Lou, who Davey and Vince picked up at the Middle

Island warehouse, disembarked quickly and did their best to avoid Rusty, not wanting to be delayed with questioning or instructions. As usual after stringing nets and putting into port, they walked up town and caught the Lakeshore Electric to Sandusky, then took the ferry to the islands.

***

That night, on his run with Pete, he told him about the mysterious rumrunner and local bootlegger working Vermilion while they took a break from hoisting burlap bags from the lake.

Pete listened with rapt attention. "They sound small potatoes so it shouldn't be a problem," he said when Rusty had finished. "Vermilion has always been a drop-off hot spot for smugglers. Lots of barns and ice houses to stash the booze and back roads to get it out. They got only one cop and a watchman with one arm… or leg… or something who oils pretty easy with liquor. Besides, no syndicate really lays claim to this area and if they did it's not enforced like prime spots along the lake where the big thirst and the big money wait. Vermilion and the islands are for the small entrepreneurs which is why we're here. Al avoids territories."

"Still these rummies could draw attention to us."

"True, they already got the Vermilion bull on alert." Pete reached for his pack of cigarettes, hesitated as he remembered Rusty's warning about the glow from it, and took his hand away.

"He knows it's going on, but he's a one man show. He asks the feds for help and occasionally they show up but they are shorthanded and have bigger fish to fry. I plan to steer clear of Vermilion anyways since everyone knows me there. Hell, the chief just asked me if I wanted the job of night watchman."

Pete raised his brows. "Now that would be the fox guarding the hen house."

Chapter 56

"Petey tells me we got a couple of chiselers operating the Vermilion area. Trouble with these punks is they make mistakes and draw heat to guys like us." Al fell silent on the other end of the telephone and Rusty could tell he was thinking. "They're not a problem," Al concluded, "It's not like they're the Cleveland Syndicate which, in that case, we would avoid the area like the plague. No, these are small-timers running to make some dough like us. Now that the heat is on them, they'll avoid Vermilion unless they're as dumb as a rock. As for us, it's business as usual. Just keep your eyes peeled for coasties and feds. That bull might have contacted them and they could be sniffing around the area."

***

The runs were four times a week—staggered nights and alternating connections with some nights having double runs. The fish tug's schedule was more routine as fishing activity didn't attract the same attention as long as its habits and schedules were believable. With the warming of the waters in June, the lake saw an explosion in pleasure boat activity which made the Coast Guard's patrols more complicated in weeding out the rumrunners. For Captain Connors and crew, the problem was not as complex. As far as he was concerned, any boat was guilty until proven innocent and his .30 caliber discouraged any resistance to a random search and destroy. The latest furor to sweep the boating community was an innocent man who was shot and killed on a pleasure boat with people aboard when he reached for his boating registration under the dash. Three bottles of scotch were aboard for the revelers personal use. Some, a bit giddy in the head, thought it a joke when the CG 157 ordered them *to bring her to.* Panic set in when the boat started to be ripped apart in the futile search for stowed alcohol. If only the owner hadn't reached for his registration when the dogs were in a frenzy...

***

After reading the headline, Pete smacked the newspaper with the back of his hand.

State Prosecutor Tries to Sink Connors
Justice Department Throws Him a Life Line

"Nothing. Nothing more than a finger wagging. Imagine if one of us killed an innocent man, Rust, we'd be hanged, but that son of a bitch gets a two week suspension. An *accident* they're calling it—says the boater's actions appeared suspicious. Justice Department my ass. Talk about ballsy... they're backing Connors and blaming the boater for his own death. He and his dogs are murderers—a disgrace to the C.G. It's murder no matter how they box and wrap it." He tossed the papers into the corner of the booth.

A waitress brought more coffee and they sat silent as she poured it. When she left, Rusty said, "Look at it this way, we got two weeks sans Captain Kid."

***

The Calamity Jane had no sooner crossed the border out of Canadian water when a 75' Coast Guard cutter began trailing them.

"I think we are being cutterized," Davey said to Rusty as he watched his overhead mirror.

Rusty grabbed the binoculars. The rays from the rising sun glinted off the cutter's mast and one-pounder cannon. "Maintain speed and course," he said. "After all, we're just fishing."

Lou stepped into the cockpit, "We got a hound on our trail."

"We see that."

"What's the plan?"

"Davey here is going to proceed to the fishing ground and we are going to drop our nets."

"If he catches wind there's booze in those nets, we're busted."

"He can't arrest us if we don't unload."

Lou looked puzzled. "Am I missing something here?"

Davey glanced at Rusty. His brows were also raised in question.

"As long as we don't unload the booze, they can dog us all they want but not arrest us."

"I know that, I just want to know what the deal is."

He turned to Lou. "This is a fish tug—it still has gill nets aboard. We are going to cast the gill nets instead of the line with the booze nets."

"And if we get searched and they find whiskey instead of herring in the hold?"

"They may not search... the six bitters usually don't search—just wait for the off-loading before making their move." Rusty rubbed his chin. "We can do one of two things...take a chance they think we are real fishermen and not pull a search of the hold or...come about broadside and while two of us are busy on the near side casting the gill nets, one of us will jettison the booze on the far side, making sure a net marker is placed on the end of the line and hope like hell they don't figure it out it's a booze drop going on the other side."

"Either way sounds risky," Davey said, his brows still tightly drawn.

"A six-bitter might be slow but this tug cannot outrun it and we sure don't want to tip them off by crossing back into Canada and heading for the warehouse. These boys have enough provisions to shadow us for days so we might as well take our chances and see just how good our acting is. Joe, help Lou drag the gill nets to port side."

The fish tug reached the fishing ground and Davey cut back on the engines and swung the bow about so the tug was perpendicular to the approaching cutter.

"Okay, you boys start casting the gill net line. Remember nice and easy and keep cool. You're just fishermen doing your job. I'll be on starboard ditching the bundles."

"I don't think you're going to get that chance," Davey said. "They're coming on hard and appear to be coming along on our starboard."

The cutter gave one short blast on its horn. As it came within megaphone range, a voice from the cutter called out "Ahoy, *Calamity Jane*, bring her to."

Lou's eyes shot to Rusty. "I thought you said they didn't search."

"I said *usually*."

Davey cut the engines. Beads of sweat formed on his brow. He looked to Rusty.

"Davey and I'll do the talking," Rusty said to Joe and Lou. Their faces were tight and he could tell by the look in Joe's eyes he had no intention of being arrested. "You're fishermen," Rusty said. "Look cool or look surprised but for God sake don't look suspicious or like trouble." He turned to face the cutter as it pulled alongside. He waved his arm in greeting. "Ahoy," he yelled cheerfully.

"Come along side," the voice through the megaphone said.

Lines were thrown from the cutter to the tug and Rusty tied them off to the bow and stern of the tug. He was doing his best to act nonchalant despite his racing heart.

"How's the luck been?" the captain said from the rail.

"Good so far. Hope today is just as good or better."

A young looking surfman approached the rail alongside the captain. He grabbed the rail and leaned forward. "Rusty?"

Rusty stared at the young man in uniform while the wheels turned in his head. "Jimmy?"

The young surfman laughed. "Yes. Jimmy from Erie T."

"Rusty grinned. "Well, I'll be damn. Look at you. I knew you would make something good out of yourself."

"You know one another?" the captain asked Jimmy.

"Sir, this man taught me how to be a sailor. He's the best. We worked together on tugboats in Lorain harbor before the company went out of business. He taught me everything I know. If not for him, I may not have gotten into the guard."

The captain nodded. "You did a great job with him. I am pleased to have him aboard," he said to Rusty.

"Remember Davey the engineer?" Rusty said. "He's here—he's the pilot."

Davey stuck his head out. "Jimmy, good to see you, boy."

"Davey! Good to see you too. That guy's a wizard when it comes to mechanics," he remarked to the captain. "Gosh it's good to see you both. So you are fishermen now?"

"Yes, I lost my boat I used for fishing charters. Had to take another tack."

"Oh."

Davey chipped in. "I was whittling away. Not many jobs for a crippled man and then Rusty asked me to be his pilot for his fish tug. I jumped at the chance—pun intended, and I was as good as reborn."

Jimmy's grin extended ear to ear and his eyes filled with longing.

Rusty searched his eyes and knew how he felt—a flash to a time when life was good and labeled as *the best years of one's life* in memory's file. He drew a wistful breath and smiled back at Jimmy. "I'm proud of you, Jimmy. You got a good man here, captain."

The captain turned to Jimmy. "Since you know these men…"

"Sir, I'd vouch for them in blink of an eye. This tug will be shipshape and Rusty and Davey are two straight arrows."

The captain nodded. "Well, in that case, we best let you men get on with your business."

"Thank you, captain," Rusty said.

"Cast off."

Rusty untied the lines and threw them to the crew of the cutter and gave Jimmy one last wave. He watched him and the cutter grow smaller.

"Thank God for Jimmy," Davey said, exhaling loudly.

"It was good seeing him in more ways than one that's for sure. I'm glad he's done well for himself. That was a break," he added, looking relieved.

"So now what?" Joe said, interrupting his thoughts.

"Now we string our bottle line and get the hell out of here." As he helped Joe and Lou string the line a part of him felt relieved and a part of him felt guilty for betraying Jimmy's trust. Had the tug been searched and Jimmy learned he was a rumrunner it would have crushed Jimmy. He felt like a traitor—a turncoat to everything Jimmy valued and admired in him. Jimmy may have understood if he knew the circumstances but that didn't make it right and it sure in hell didn't earn respect. Still, the relieved part of him outweighed the guilt and he could still look at himself in the mirror.

Chapter 57

"So Tuesday when I asked Frogeyes if Capone ever dined at the castle he told me to shut up and mind my potatoes. I take that as a yes."

"Shut up," Rusty said, "your voice carries in the fog."

Pete gave him the brush off.

The fog entombed them in a shroud of gray like bed curtains drawn around a bed, confining the visibility to within the boundary of *New Moon.* The lake was flat as a sheet of glass, and the air thick and damp.

Rusty kept his eye on the boat's compass, keeping *New Moon* at a crawl on a heading due southeast.

"This is creepy," Pete whispered, gawking all around him at the walls of swirling gray mist. "I hope you know where we are." Ten minutes passed. "Do you think we're close to shore?"

"Ssshh. Listen."

There was a sound, then sounds. Water was being stirred. He recognized the lapping and swishing sound of a propeller. A faint rumble accompanied the sound of moving water. Rusty cocked his ear to starboard. The rumble, whose source was concealed by the thick, vaporous wall, was growing louder. A metallic clink followed. They strained their ears listening to the sounds. Then the sound of vibrating engines resonated in the murk. They were getting louder and louder.

Pete shot a glance to Rusty and saw him set his jaw.

Rusty cut the wheel hard to port. *New Moon* rumbled out of the fog and headed almost directly into the portside bow of a passing patrol boat. He cut the wheel harder to port and hit the throttle for power. *New Moon*'s throaty rumble rose as she barely cleared the Coast Guard vessel before she slithered back into the fog bank.

The patrol boat laid on the klaxon horn, piercing the air with its blast. It slipped into the fog after her. Search lights swept the air as they tried to cut their way through the thick gray murk, hunting down the *New Moon.*

Rusty eased back on the throttle and slipped quietly through the fog. Pete started to speak and he shushed him with his hand. They watched the searchlight, a weak glow, as it attempted to probe the thick mantle. He reversed course and followed the fog bank. Eventually, the lights grew fainter until they no longer saw the glow of searchlights.

Pete exhaled loudly. "Shit, that was close. Why in the hell weren't they ringing the fog bell."

"Probably the same reason we weren't."

They stayed in the fog bank as long as they could without veering too far off course. Then, as mysteriously as it arrived, the fog headed west for Michigan like a smoky sheet being pulled across the lake.

"Thank God we are out of the soup. I was beginning to think we died and went to purgatory or hell," Pete said.

Rusty didn't answer. He just motored up and headed for the shoreline toward their scheduled drop-off. They were an hour behind. Someone was sure to be pissed at the other end and there would be no excuses accepted. After all, it wasn't their ass out in the middle of the lake socked with fog and choked with patrol boats. He started to respond to Pete, but changed his mind. What he was going to say was they've been sliding toward hell since this deal began.

***

Middle Island Club wasn't very big but it was exclusive. Built by gangster, Joe Roscoe, it had electricity, marble fireplaces, bedrooms, a swanky dining room, a casino below carved out of solid bedrock and a spacious screened-in porch with sweeping views of the lake. Membership was restricted, and if one was lucky enough to gain access through a personal invite, he or she would still be patted down at the door. It was high class and chic where gaming tables sizzled like the filet mignons—thick as a fist—served up by black waiters in white coats. It was where men indulged in first rate, uncut booze and high class whores. It was also a place where wipers, goons and finger men rubbed elbows with kingpins, bootleggers, crooked politicians and corrupt cops. All one had to do to break into the club's circle was to know somebody and have that somebody vouch for him.

Fencers and rumrunners flocked to the place like flies to shit and among those flies were the Trapanis.

When Al left word for Pete and Rusty to meet him at Middle Island Club Friday afternoon, Rusty felt hesitant. The club, no matter how much crystal or high hat, was still what Di would call a den of immorality and to him nothing more than a fancy gangster hangout, and he stated emphatically to Pete that it was not a place where he wanted to mix. His gripe fell on deaf ears and Friday afternoon, after a morning of ferry jumping, he met Pete and Al at the infamous Middle Island clubhouse.

"Here's a new contact. We're not doing business with the Frenchies' schooner anymore. They're hard to work with," Al said. He spun a photograph that was torn out of a newspaper so Rusty and Pete could see it.

Pete leaned forward for a closer look. "What in the hell is that?" Pete said.

"A navy mine sweeper," Rusty said before Al could answer.

"It's a monster!"

Al grinned as he watched their faces. "These boys know how to do business. They're a floating warehouse of every brand of liquor and beer you can imagine. Got bootleg cigarettes and cigars, too. A regular one stop shop." He chuckled. "The point is, these fellas understand business. They provide a miscellany of products that are the real McCoy. You want *Cockspur Rum* from Barbados or

Templeton Rye—they got it or will get it! Now that makes good business for our clients who will in turn tell fellow entrepreneurs about the Trapanis' service and standing and good standing means good business."

Rusty scratched his head. "You're putting us in some hot grease. The waters around it have to be swarming with patrols."

Al leaned forward. "We've been through this before—making money takes some risk. I hired you, Mr. Rusty because you are a clever man and I can bank on you. And since you boys are sticking your neck out more, I'm adding an extra fifty smacks to the speedboat runs."

"Hot dog!" Pete said, clapping Rusty on the back.

"So what do you say?" Al said, studying Rusty's face as he settled back in his chair.

"I say you're making a hell of a profit for a man whose ass is not on the line."

Pete's eyes shot to Al's.

"So what would it take to make your ass feel like gambling?" Al said, his eyes narrowing.

Pete's eyes shot to Rusty's.

"One hundred smacks plus 10% of the cream."

Pete winced and checked Al's reaction.

Al sat quiet, sizing Rusty, and both men could tell the wheels were turning in Al's head, but neither could read him.

"Seventy-five and 5%," Al said with finality.

Rusty examined the photograph. It would be risky, but damn it, he could do it. *New Moon* was fast even with a load, and if Al would be flexible about the runs, they could use the weather to their advantage. Al could make his money and he could save his world. He nodded.

"Johnny, three beers!" Al called out as he lit his cigar. "Still fifty for you, Petey, after all it's his boat and he's the pilot."

As Rusty island hopped back to Sandusky he questioned himself over and over about the new run and came up with the same answers and excuses. *Di would pack it in if she knew about the clubhouse. And Fritz—his look alone would be an ass-kicking in itself.* He tapped his fist on the rail of the ferry. Not even the sun sparkling off the water or the cry of the gulls could lure him from his tumultuous thoughts. By the time, he stepped off the electric railway car at Huron he had pushed thoughts of their judgment and the risk of the run to the back of his mind. He had a job to do and his head had to be clear. He set his jaw and tramped back to his boat shanty.

Chapter 58

At least it was cloudy. That made all the difference. Al had scheduled a run on the night of June's waxing gibbous moon—a few days shy of a full moon and nearly as bright. The moonlight would make them visible for miles and highlighting their every move. He chewed Al for it, and Al's reply was he wasn't thinking and proceeded to reschedule the drop. That's when the clouds rolled in like a down comforter covering the moon and stars and blackening the waters. He called Al and told him they were on.

New Moon stumbled to life with a bumpy, pulsating throb that smoothed out to a throaty rumble as the engines warmed. She slipped out of the boat house and down the river under a mantle of clouds.

At 2: 45 a.m., she slinked across the boundary into Canadian waters on a NNE bearing. Ahead, out on the black water and yet to be seen, the World War I minesweeper was anchored.

Rusty grabbed the binoculars and scanned the northern horizon. A myriad of red and green running lights began popping into view, some closer to *New Moon* than others. They looked like bees in a swarm. As *New Moon* pushed northward, a speedboat zipped past them 300' off starboard, heading south.

"I think we found the minesweeper," Rusty said. He flipped his running lights on to avoid collisions with passing boats.

They approached the long, low rugged gray ship which was swarming with vessels of all shapes and sizes.

"Jeeze, oh man, it's like sales day at the May Company," Pete said.

A fish tug similar to *Calamity Jane* was just departing, leaving an opening and Rusty slipped *New Moon* into the spot, coming along the ship's side.

"Ahoy, *Virgo*. Permission to tie off."

"Identify yourself and state your business."

"*New Moon*. Hoover's as dry as hell in August."

"The king's wet. Tie off."

"Where's the paper for our order?" He said to Pete.

"They already have *New Moon*'s order. Al set it up." Pete took out a roll of money from his pocket as a bucket on a rope was lowered over the side. He dropped the money in the bucket and watched as it ascended the side.

As they waited for their payload, a fifteen-foot outboard runabout tied off near them. "Can you imagine being out here in that tin can?" Pete said as he lit a cigarette and took a drag. "If it floats, it's out here. Someone's even got an old tugboat," he said nodding toward it.

Rusty tapped a cigarette loose from the pack and glanced at the tugboat pulling away. He hesitated and narrowed his eyes.

Pete caught the look. "What?"

"That tugboat, there's something familiar about it. It's too dark and too far away to be sure."

"You've probably seen it before. You probably know all the tugboats from Sandusky to Lorain."

"Hand me the glasses."

Pete handed him the binoculars.

Rusty was silent for a moment, and then he mumbled, "I'll be damn."

"What? What?"

He lowered the binoculars. "I know that boat all right. It was one of Erie T's. It's the *Cherokee*."

A sharp voice from the rail broke his thoughts and a cargo net filled with cases of liquor and beer began lowering over the side of the ship. Once the bulging net was settled on the deck of *New Moon*, they started unloading. At one point, Pete grabbed a case of brandy. "Brandy?" Christ, you can buy this milk at the drugstore!"

"The order states two cases of brandy," a man yelled from the rail.

Pete shrugged and continued unloading.

All the while, Rusty's mind churned with thought of the *Cherokee*. The bullet holes made sense now. *Eliot must be involved- maybe even piloting the tug.*

His thoughts were again disrupted by the bow line being tossed aboard and a man in a loud voice saying "you're all set."

Rusty fired up the engines and *New Moon* backed away from the mine sweeper. He reached for the throttle to power up for their dash back across the lake just as the cloud cover parted unexpectedly and moonlight broke through. The pearlescent moonlight flooded the surroundings, sparkling off the water and glinting off the assembly of metallic hulls and masts.

It was his first good look at the big minesweeper and the school of vessels that collected about it like parasitic fish. The parting of clouds also revealed the silhouette of a large vessel on the southeast horizon off his port bow.

"Shit! We got company."

Pete followed Rusty's look. "Coast Guard?"

"Yeah. Six-bitter."

"Are you sure?"

"You better burn that silhouette in your brain if you call yourself a runner."

They sat idle as they calculated the course and speed of the cutter.

"You can give me my gold star now, teach, because I think I just spotted another one off starboard," Pete exclaimed.

Rusty looked to his right and saw the same distinctive silhouette. "Seems we're in shark infested waters."

"We gonna make a run for it?"

Rusty sized the two vessels, again calculating their speeds and proximity. "We got a lot of horse under us and the advantage of night despite the damn moon…unless you got a better idea, we have no choice but to make a dash."

"Between them?"

"Like I said, if you got a better idea sound off now. In the meantime, take your seat Pete and hang on." He switched off the running lights and *New Moon* became a shadowy silhouette. He glared at the moon and felt grateful for the flat charcoal paint that covered every inch of the runner. She would be a shadow at the most, and not a mirror reflecting the moon's light. He gave her throttle.

New Moon's throaty, throbbing growl rose in response. She rumbled forward as he sized up the two cutters one last time. They were about a mile apart, he guessed. He gritted his teeth, and throttled up. He could hear the sucking sounds of the carburetors as fresh air and more gas was dumped into them. The hungry engines gobbled up the surge of air and fuel, escalating in power and speed until they smoothed into the steady whirr of a fighter plane in flight for which they had been intended. *New Moon*, despite her load, rose in the water in response. Her razor-sharp bow parted the waves like a hot knife in butter. She flew across the dark water shimmering with moon light on a course dead center between the two cutters. If he could pass them, *New Moon* could easily outrun them but not their .30 caliber machine guns or one pounders. He needed to put over a mile between him and the cutters before *New Moon* would be clear of danger. But first, they had to spot him.

No sooner had he had that thought than a spotlight from the cutter off his portside burst on and split the darkness. It began sweeping the waters around them, searching for but not finding them.

"They must've caught wind of us," Pete said. He had a wild eye look about him.

"Probably we're the only ones dumb enough to attempt this," Rusty muttered.

Pete looked back to stern. "Nah…it looks like two more runners are dumb enough to follow us. The closest is about 300 yards back and falling behind."

The *New Moon* was almost between the two cutters when the searchlight swept across them, catching them in its beam as it passed. It stopped and immediately came back to rest on them, shining on them like stage players in a vaudeville show.

"Shit!" They said in unison.

The second cutter, off starboard, came to life and started towards them with its spotlight aiming directly on them also.

A straight line of red dashes raced over the water in front of their bow.

"Tracers- they're firing on us," Rusty shouted.

"Warning shots to get us to stop," Pete cried.

Another ribbon of red zipped before them, only this time over their bow.

"Don't stop," Pete cried, "they're trying to scare us."

The first cutter, off portside, fired its one pounder and the splash from the ball's impact was only a hundred feet in front of their bow. The booming report followed shortly.

Rusty felt the hairs on the back of his neck raise. "The hell with this…hold tight, Pete." He cut the starboard engine back on the throttle while cutting his wheel hard to starboard. The portside engine was still full power causing a lopsided reaction that pushed the boat instantly around almost 180 degrees in a power slide. As soon as the boat was spun about, he throttled up on the first engine so both engines were powered equally and then pressed the button on the dash to release a shot of castor oil into the carburetor. The oil was like a kick of adrenaline to the engines and *New Moon* lunged forward, the force of take-off pushing him and Pete deep into their seats. *New Moon* flew past the runner that had been following it.

Pete whooped wildly as Rusty made a wide arc, sweeping well beyond the stern of the second cutter.

He was still whooping and laughing as he glanced over his shoulder and saw the other rumrunner also turning to avoid the gauntlet of Coast Guard cutters. The other runner apparently didn't have a Davey for a mechanic, and he watched as it grew smaller and smaller as it fell further behind.

The second cutter, now on *New Moon*'s portside, began probing the waters again with its spotlight. It caught a brief glimpse of *New Moon* racing south. It fired its one pounder but it fell short.

New Moon flew across the water, her Liberty aero engines droning into the darkness.

It wasn't until Pete let out a sigh that Rusty realized how hard he had been gripping the steering wheel. He relaxed his grip.

"Hot damn!" Pete howled. "That oil shit really works."

"You can thank Davey for that. I know I will."

Ahead, the lights from the shoreline popped into view, marking the cities of Lorain and Vermilion. In between, was their destination—the dock at Beaver Creek where Vince and Tony would be awaiting their arrival.

About a mile from shore, Pete half stood and stared hard toward the southeast. "What's that?" He grabbed the binoculars. "Uh-oh, we got a patrol boat heading our way."

"Does he see us?"

"How in the hell should I know."

"Give me the glasses." Rusty studied the patrol boat. It was heading directly towards them and between the light from the moon and the light gathering capacity of the binoculars, he could see a seaman on deck looking through binoculars back at him.

Rusty jerked the glasses down from his eyes and thrust them at Pete. "They see us."

"Now what?"

"We head west and try to shake him and double back."

He cranked the wheel to the right and turned *New Moon* towards Vermilion. The patrol boat grew smaller, but not small enough. As they drew close to the village, about a half mile off the shore and to the west of the village, he spotted a picket boat. "Another coastie. That rumpus at the lighthouse with the rumrunners and the night watchman has got them sniffing around."

"Al was right," Pete said, "those numb nuts brought the heat around us."

"I think these boys were expecting us. Most likely the cutters radioed them that we were headed their way."

The picket boat picked up speed, heading right at them.

"Looks like we're caught between the shit and the sweat again."

"We gonna make a bolt for the lake?"

"We're running too low on fuel for another excursion," Rusty grumbled. "And the cutters may be lying in wait expecting us to head back out in the lake."

The Coast Guard boats were closing in, sandwiching *New Moon* right off the Vermilion shoreline.

"You're saying we're boxed in and low on fuel. Well that's just jake. I'm not going up the river for this."

Rusty had started to nose *New Moon* towards the open water and hesitated.

His face brightened. "You'rc right, Pete, we're both going up the river." He cut the wheel hard just as the picket boat fired its .30 caliber machine gun. The tracers flew past their stern. The hammering chug from the gun was almost simultaneous with the bullets. *New Moon* headed directly for the shoreline.

"What in the hell are you doing," Pete said as he watched as a blaze of white muzzle flash erupted from the gun and more red tracers streamed from its barrel. "You're gonna trap us for sure!"

Rusty ignored him as he increased the speed of *New Moon* and she raced towards the growing coastline. The space between them and decrepit lighthouse at the end of the pier was closing fast.

"Are you nuts?" Pete cried. His eyes grew like the rocks emerging along the shore. "You can't beach this and make a getaway- not here!"

"Dry up, Pete."

New Moon shot past the lighthouse and plunged into the mouth of the Vermilion River, leaving an undulating wake behind them. Rusty cut back on the throttle and *New Moon* idled down and glided up the river.

Pete exhaled. "Next time, cut me in on your plans."

"It was your idea."

Pete shook a cigarette free from the pack. "Shit." He paused, considered the cigarette, and stuck it unlit in his mouth anyway. "So now what, Cochise? We're trapped in the river."

"We hide up river. They can't follow us as they have no jurisdiction here. We'll hide the boat in a cove under hanging tree branches and cover it with brush. Then you'll go ashore and tell Sam to contact Vince and Tony and have them meet us at Belkopf's farm up river. Tell them to have enough money to grease Belkopf. Then we outwait the coasties and get this boat back to Huron."

***

Rusty stayed with the boat, cutting branches and brush to camouflage it while Pete headed up the bank and across pasture lands and backyards until he reached downtown and Sam's. A closed sign hung on the door, but he rattled the doorknob anyways and banged on the door. He hoped Sam was still there cleaning up, but no answer. "Shit." He checked his watch. It read 4:15. Ruth, the stout cook would be getting there closer to 5 to prepare for breakfast. He looked around at the silent streets and dark village lit here and there by street lights. His eyes fell on a Model A parked in front of a house two doors down from Sam's. He looked around again and crept towards the car. He hesitated, straining to hear. No dogs barked a warning and he recalled what Rusty had said about the dogs in Vermilion having been poisoned. He slipped into the car and started it up. Seconds later he was driving over the bridge out of town and headed for the dock at Beaver Creek.

When he pulled up to the dock there was no one. The milk truck was pulled off to the side as it always was. He got out of the car and instantly felt cold, hard, steel press against his temple.

"Grab air!" a thick voice said. It was Tony's voice.

"Tony! It's me, Pete. We ran into trouble." He felt the pressure of the gun barrel leave his temple. He dropped his hands and turned. "Shit, Tony, I thought you were the brass."

Tony shouldered the trench gun. "We thought you were a hijacker."

Vince appeared from the brush. "What's going on, Pete?" He was stuffing a .45 into his waistband.

"We had a close scrape with the coasties and had to hide the boat. Rusty's with it up the Vermilion River near Belkopf's farm. Said to meet him there to unload while we outwait the coasties."

Vince looked sideways at him.

"Don't sweat. Belkopf's place is one of the drop-off points for the river traffic. As long as you grease him, he looks the other way."

The strained look on Vince's face relaxed. "Okay, then, let's get going before it gets light."

"I'm going to take this auto back before it gets missed and hell is raised," Pete said. "Last thing we need is more attention. I'll join you shortly at Belkopf's farm."

Vince and Tony climbed into the milk truck and Pete tore off in the Model A. They parted ways at the bridge into town.

Pete drove the automobile into Vermilion's downtown. It was still dark and empty. He kept the motor at an idle as he crept down the street and parked it where he had found it. He got out and pressed the door shut with a quiet click, turned around and ran smack into Chief Bales.

Bales raised his heavy flashlight. When Pete came to, he was handcuffed and riding in the back of Bales's police car and his head hurt like hell.

***

"Where in the hell is Pete?" Rusty said. It was pushing 5:30 and a tint of pink was appearing on the eastern horizon.

"He should have been here by now," Vince said. The milk truck was loaded and ready to leave.

Tony was antsy. "We can't wait, Vince, we gotta go."

Vince sighed. "What are you going to do, Rust?"

"I'll wait and if he doesn't show up, I'll go see Sam."

"And the boat?"

"I'll keep it here and wait till dark again and take it back to Huron with or without Pete. Either I or Sam will be in touch as soon as we find out what happened."

The milk truck pulled away in a cloud of dust, leaving Rusty alone on the river bank. He rearranged the camouflaging brush and limbs over *New Moon* and took off up the bank towards Sam's, arriving there just as Ruth was turning over the sign to open.

"Is Sam around?"

"He won't be in till eleven today."

Rusty grimaced.

"Is it an emergency?"

Rusty hem-hawed before saying, "Have you seen Pete—Sam's cousin or nephew, I don't remember which he is?"

"Petey? Why no I haven't seen him for quite a while. Would you like to leave word for either him or Sam?"

Rusty rubbed the side of his face. "I'd like to talk to Sam directly and right away."

Ruth's brows furrowed. "He's asleep at this time, but if it's an emergency and can't wait, I'll ring him up."

"It's very important."

She went to the telephone and as she picked up the receiver, she said, "You're sure about an emergency?" One eye brow was raised as she looked at him.

"Yes!"

She gave Sam's number to the operator and waited. "Sam? I'm sorry to wake you, Sam, but I got a fella down here at the grill that said it's very important that he talks to you now. What's your name?" she asked Rusty. "His name is Rusty, he's a friend of Petey."

She handed Rusty the phone.

Rusty hesitated, looking at her until she sighed and walked over to the grill. He kept his voice low. "Sam, this is Rusty…listen, Pete and I had a problem and he went looking for you for help. He never returned from Vermilion, and I was hoping he was with you or contacted you. Vince and Tony saw him last heading into town in a Model A."

Sam coughed and cleared his throat. His voice was groggy, but clearing the more he spoke. "I haven't seen him at all. Do you think he ran into trouble?"

Rusty turned his back to Ruth. "I think he stole the Model A in town and was returning it."

"Whoever heard of returning a stolen car? Damn fool should have ditched it." Sam was wide awake now.

"Yeah, I know...that's what I said too."

"Okay, I'll check around. Meanwhile, you sniff around as well and keep in touch today at the grill. I'm on my way there now."

Rusty hung up the phone.

"Would you like breakfast?" Ruth said over her shoulder as she greased the grill.

"I suppose since I'm already here."

"Coffee will be ready in a few minutes. You look like you can use a whole pot."

He finished his breakfast and thanked Ruth again for her help and went outside. The sleepy town was beginning to stir. Rays of first light like pink fingers stretched across the sky. He walked down to the little beach where he and Di often sat on the bench overlooking the water. Ripples of waves, one after another rolled onto shore. His heart felt heavy. He smoked a cigarette and watched the gentle waves roll in. As though watching a moving picture, he saw himself and Di on the bench, then walking along the water. She was laughing and her hair tossed about her head as she did. He saw her slipping her arm around his and pressing her head into his shoulder. He could feel her soft hair cuddled against his cheek...

"You're back."

The sudden voice roused him from his thoughts with a jolt. He turned and saw Eddie and Prince a few feet away.

"I never said I wouldn't be. You're just usually not around when I stop by."

"So why you here now?"

"Making sure you and Prince are okay. I'm also looking for a friend."

"That's the real reason, isn't it?" Eddie scoffed. "What's he look like."

"Young guy—looks Italian. Not a local, but he's been around here before."

"Does your pal wear dough boy pants with an army buckle?"

He eyed Eddie and said with caution, "Yes."

Eddie walked to the water, picked up some stones and began skipping them across the surface.

Rusty pursed his lips and thrust his hands on his hips. Eddie had information and he was wielding it like a weapon. Punishment, no doubt, for abandoning him, he figured.

He waited and when it was apparent Eddie's pigheadedness was not about to yield, he said," Well, I guess I'll head up town and see if anyone there has seen him since you don't know." He started walking away.

"Better start with the chief and save yourself some time," Eddie said with a flip over his shoulder.

Rusty hesitated. "Was he arrested?"

Eddie concentrated on skipping the stones.

"Would a dollar jog your memory?"

Eddie didn't reply.

Rusty started walking again.

"Bales arrested him last night near Sam's. He's at the station."

"Well?" Rusty said.

"Well what?"

"Well, let's get going if I'm going to buy you and wonder dog breakfast."

They walked into Sam's and Sam was already there. Despite the dark bags under his eyes, he was wide awake.

"I found Pete," Rusty said.

"I found him," Eddie said.

Sam's eyes jumped between them.

"Eddie was on his rounds last night instead of staying safe inside Donovan's like he was told…"

"I was inside. I was watching from her window when Chief Bales got the jump on your friend. Then, I went to the station for a peek and I saw him inside with the chief—he was wearing handcuffs," Eddie said with a smug nod.

Sam and Rusty exchanged glances.

"I'll head over there," Sam said. "I'll tell Bales I heard about a rumpus around my place overnight and wanted to check it out."

"I'm going too," Eddie said, jumping off the counter stool.

Rusty grabbed him by the collar. "You're staying with me. You're going to eat and then we're going to buy dog food and groceries to take to Mrs. Donovan."

Eddie pulled loose and climbed begrudgingly back on the stool.

It was an hour before noon when Rusty, with Eddie still in tow, made it back to Sam's ahead of the lunch crowd. When he walked inside, Pete was there along with Al, Joe, Lou and Giuseppe. They were seated around a table with Sam and an impeccably dressed man.

"Vinnie called me about Pete missing," Al said to Rusty, motioning him to pull up a chair. "So I called Sam and me and the boys jumped on the first ferry to the mainland."

"Eddie," Rusty interrupted, "I forgot to buy milk for myself. Could you pick me up a quart bottle?" He dug some money from his pocket and handed it to Eddie. "There's extra here to get yourself some Coca Cola® while you're at it."

He waited till Eddie left and then turned back to Al.

"Kid's a whip, uh?" Al said

"He's the one who took a licking at the lighthouse with the rumrunners."

"You mean his old man," Sam blurted. "He's the one who did the beating. Beats that kid just for drill."

Al clicked his tongue. "A boy shouldn't be a punching bag. Sounds like the old man needs to go a few rounds with someone his own size." He looked at Rusty. "You look like you could tenderize some beef. You oughta give him a taste of his own medicine."

"That's what the law is for," Rusty said.

"Yeah, like they're doing such a great job protecting the innocents. Back to business. I then call Sam when we get to Sandusky and he says Petey's in the poke. I call my lawyer here," he said with a nod to the impeccably dressed man, "and tell him to meet me in the hamlet of Vermilion. We go to the police station, he throws out some fancy mumbo jumbo and Petey walks."

"No charges?" Rusty asked.

"Nope," Pete answered. "I didn't break any law so to speak. All he had was suspicious behavior and out after curfew—can you believe it—a curfew!"

"What about the stolen auto?"

"That's just it. He saw me after I returned the auto," Pete said. "I was leaving it, not taking it. There was never even a report about a stolen auto."

Al was chuckling. "Petey can weasel out of anything. Even as a *ragazzo* he could fall into shit and come up smelling like a rose."

Everyone snickered but Rusty.

Al stood and adjusted his hat. "My man here has got to get back to work," he said with another nod to the lawyer, "and so do I. Fellas, let's make some room for Sam's lunch crowd."

They walked out onto the sidewalk. "You sure you won't need Joe or Lou's help getting back with the boat?" he said, turning to Rusty.

"We'll be okay. Pete's going to hang out at Sam's and I' m going to catch the Lakeshore to Huron and come back on its last pass through Vermilion. We'll move out on the boat after dark."

"You're empty. Why wait till dark? If you get stopped, the authorities have nothing on you."

"We could be tailed or spotted heading into Huron and be put under surveillance."

A slow grin spread across Al's face. "That's why you're my man," he said. "You're always thinking and one step ahead. Clever man."

They parted ways, and Rusty hurried for the depot to catch the noon departure. He knew Davey would be anxious, wondering if the engines blew or worse.

Eddie caught up with him as he reached the station. He was carrying a bottle of milk. It had slipped his mind that he had sent Eddie after it.

"You leaving town?" Eddie asked.

"I got to get back to Davey. He might need a hand."

"On account of his legs being crippled?"

"I guess you could say that."

Eddie looked disappointed.

"Thanks for getting the milk." He fumbled to say something more.

The electric railcar approached the depot, sending sparks snapping and popping as it glided along attached to the electrical line overhead. It clanged its bell to announce its arrival.

He turned to Eddie. He didn't know what to say at the moment. Eddie looked at him with anticipation. "Next week is the 4th of July. I'm going with Di and her family to Crystal Beach for the fireworks. We are going to have a picnic and ride the amusement rides before the show. I was wondering if you'd like to go along."

Eddie's face brightened. "Can Prince come along?"

"I don't know if dogs are allowed in the amusement park, but to be safe, we'll ask Mrs. Donovan if she can look after him."

Eddie shook his head in agreement.

Watching Eddie's face beam made him realize just how much the boy needed him. He didn't need money, or a guardian or a friend. He already had a father. What he needed was a Dad.

He ruffled Eddie's head as the railcar came to a stop. He boarded it and as it rumbled and clattered its way to Huron, he hoped Di would be okay with Davey and Eddie tagging along.

Chapter 59

New Moon made three more runs between the minesweeper and the Beaver Creek dock—all uneventful—before word passed around the lake docks that Connors and his crew were back on the water and doing business as usual. In other words, rumrunner or not, the lake became risky again.

Over their fried chicken dinners at *Artie's Diner* in Huron, Rusty and Davey listened in as local fishermen concluded that Connors's two weeks hiatus only renewed his vindictive behavior and determination to make up for lost time. They knew it was only a matter of time before they crossed paths with the CG157 and there would be no warning shots to deter them and no Jimmy to bail them out.

They were making considerable money now, in fact, too much to bank without raising some eyebrows as to how two fishermen in a boat shanty could earn all that, and with the shanty unoccupied half the time, they decided burying the money to be the best solution. So on his last trip to the farm before the 4th of July, he asked Uncle Fritz for two quart size mason jars and received them without question. They each packed their respective jars with Jeffersons, Hamiltons and Franklins, and then Rusty buried them deep under the staircase below the second floor landing, leaving the top layer of sod intact so the ground did not look disturbed. Mad money was kept in coffee tins and oatmeal boxes, and money in line with the average worker's weekly salary was deposited at the Sandusky Bank and Lorain Bank each week in separate saving accounts for each man. When the runs, sleep and boat maintenance offered breaks enough for a game of pinochle or checkers, the topic of conversation nowadays was new and creative ways to disperse or hide the latest payouts. One night over pinochle, the topic shifted and Davey asked him if he felt like a criminal. His reply was the only thing he felt was guilty about was not telling Di the truth and not spending more time with her. Davey said he felt more dishonest than criminal and hoped his ma in heaven wasn't looking when he made his runs. But he didn't feel guilty like he thought he should, adding his life was over until Rusty asked him to join him.

***

On the same trip to the farm for the mason jars, he found Di picking strawberries in the strawberry patch. She wore a broad brim hat to shelter her from the morning heat, and with no dew on the berries and grass, he knew rain would be forthcoming. She was surprised to see him.

"You're here early," she said, looking up with a smile.

"I wanted to spend more time with you."

"I'm glad but I'm afraid you're going to have to spend the time in the berry patch as I have to get these picked before it rains."

"I know." He crouched down and began picking strawberries and placing them in her basket.

She indicated for him to open his mouth and she tossed a small berry into it. It was sweet and juicy.

"Going to make jam?"

"Jam and pies. Big ones will be for the pies and also to put on the ice cream that Uncle Fritz is going to make later today."

"What's the occasion?"

"No occasion except you being here. The possibility of ice cream, along with the pies and supper is how we entice you to keep coming," she said with a sly smile.

"I confess. I'm really here for the chow and am using you as an excuse to eat here, so I'll just head for the kitchen to check out what I'm really after." He pretended to start to get up and she threw a large strawberry and hit him in the forehead.

"Deadly accurate as always." He pawed through the plants looking for the berry.

"Be glad it wasn't a rock."

With that, he lunged playfully at her, grabbing her around the waist and they tumbled between the rows. She bumped the basket and all the berries spilled out.

"Oh crap," she said, eyeing the spill. "And here comes mom with an empty basket. She's gonna want to switch baskets."

She and Rusty scrambled to corral the berries back into the basket.

"They look okay, don't they?"

He inspected the berries in the basket. "Seem to be."

Mom walked up. "Good morning, Rusty. I should have brought another basket since you're helping. A lot of berries need picking and I can start the pies instead of helping Di pick. I'll fetch another basket for you."

After she was out of ear shot, Di peeked at him. "Not what you planned today, uh?"

"Not really. A walk down the lane, a ride to the river, swinging on the porch swing…"

"Think of the end result of your arduous labor."

"I am. Believe me, I am."

After Sunday's dinner was finished, Uncle Fritz made the ice cream and Di topped off each bowl with strawberries picked earlier in the day. She and Rusty sat on the porch steps to eat their ice cream, and he figured it would be a good time to tell her about Eddie and Davey. "Eddie is having a rough time."

"I know. His father should be in jail."

"Bales is walking a tightrope. If Eddie's dad and the runner thinks Eddie squealed about the rumrunning, the boy could be in real danger. Bales brought the old man in for questioning about the boys beating but, like always, had to release him with a warning."

"He actually thought Bales bought his cockamamie story about catching Eddie stealing and beating him for punishment?"

"Bales hopes he thinks that way. He put Krueger on as an extra night watchman along with Hoot to watch for the rumrunner and the dad's activities."

"I'm glad he gave Hoot a second chance."

"Me too." He paused. "Eddie's been down ever since I left Vermilion—now this."

"I know the feeling. I'm not happy about you moving either."

"I'm not happy as well but that's just the way things are now."

Her eyes fell and she grew quiet.

"Anyways, I feel sorry for Eddie and I thought since we all are going to Crystal Beach Park for the 4th, he could join us. He likes you Di, and you haven't seen him since the accident."

She stared hard at a clump of dandelions. "I didn't even think of him until the beating at the lighthouse."

"I know, but he thinks of you. Asks how you're doing each time I see him."

She bit her lip.

"I was wondering about asking him along if you don't mind."

She shook her head. "No, of course not. He needs to have some fun in his life. It really will be good seeing him." She paused. "I...I can't believe I haven't had him to the farm. He could have come with you once in a while."

"Well, it's understandable. We both have a lot on our minds. We need to sort out our lives before we take on his."

She sighed.

"And Di? I can't leave Davey alone on the holiday."

"You want to invite him, too?"

"Well... yes. Actually, I already did. He said no at first, but I told him you and the family wouldn't feel right about him sitting there all alone while we were celebrating the 4th."

She smacked at a biting fly. "That's true. Of course he should come along. He needs some fun, too. This is a family outing and he and Eddie are almost family now." She stopped abruptly. "How are we going to do this?"

"Davey and I will drive to Vermilion in the pickup truck and stop and get Eddie on the way. We'll meet you and the family at the park."

"Sounds like you already had this figured out."

"I knew it would be okay. It's not like it's a date."

She tightened her lips and nodded.

The air became heavy and suddenly cool.

"Rain's coming. We better help get this stuff inside," he said, starting to rise.

She placed a hand on his arm to stop him. "Why don't you move in here? The farmhouse is big and we can be together again."

"In your old bedroom?"

"Yes."

"What about Davey? I made him move to Huron. I can't abandon him after doing that."

"But it's all right to abandoned me?"

"I never abandoned you? Di, you pushed me away."

Uncle Fritz raised his head from hoeing in the garden nearby. He couldn't hear what was being said, but he could tell there was strain in Di and Rusty's rising voices.

Rusty noticed him looking and lowered his voice.

"I'm a patient man, Di, but I want my wife back and I don't want to live in a bedroom in a house I don't own. I thought spring would change things, but spring has turned to summer, and I am beginning to think you like this arrangement."

She sniffed. "I just want us to go back to the way we were."

"We can."

"It won't be the same! It can't be the same, and I don't want to live by that damn lake."

He was silent, and she bit her lip.

And then it rained.

***

The walk down the lane came after the rain shower ended when the lightning bugs began to rise from the grassy pastures and fields, blinking like released earthbound stars escaping into the twilight sky. Overhead, heavenly stars emerged one by one to a chorus of frogs from the pond and nearby wood lot as they walked side by side down the dusky lane. The rain had made the air heavy with scent, and the sweet smell of ripe timothy, clover and wild blackberry flowers filled the air.

Under the canopy of starlight and escalating firefly light, he pulled Di close and kissed her and she kissed him back.

***

Later, when they returned and he got into his pickup truck, he saw a package on the passenger seat. He looked inside. It was a whole strawberry pie.

***

It wasn't until the *Calamity Jane* docked late morning that the full impact of the heat and humidity hit Rusty. It was the day before the 4th and with a run scheduled that night to retrieve the bottles they had just cast plus having to deliver the cargo, he wondered out loud to Davey if the conditions might kick up a storm later and postpone the run to which Davey responded it was ripe enough.

Uncle Fritz would have said it was better to get the storm out of its system now rather than mess up the 4th, but Uncle Fritz didn't have a run to make tonight. He wondered how much good company he was going to be after being up all night pulling nets and delivering its contents. The plan was for all to meet at the pavilion at the park's entrance at eleven o'clock in the morning.

It would be Di's first time back to Vermilion and as much as she looked forward to going to the amusement park and watching the fireworks with Rusty and her family, she was apprehensive. When Uncle Fritz caught her face curdling at the mentioning of Vermilion, he told her to face her demons and beat them back—*the sooner, the better.*

Rusty pushed open the barn doors at either end of the shanty's workshop to allow a breeze to blow through the first floor. He pulled up a chair next to Davey's wheelchair, and the two of them watched as clouds, popping up like dandelions under a hot sun, sprouted in the western sky. The combination of the muggy heat and waking at 4 a.m. for the first run with the fish tug made them drowsy and they nodded off and on.

By two o'clock, cumulous clouds were packing into thunderheads and by four, a massive thunderhead towered before them, growing so high into the atmosphere that the top of it, like thick smoke hitting a ceiling, spread out into the shape of an anvil. It eclipsed the sun, and what sunlight seeped around its edges, outlined its dark mass with a shimmering thin glow of light as though the thunderhead was outlined with a pencil filled with light instead of lead.

"Depending on your frame of mind, you could say it's a cloud with a silver lining or a heap of trouble," Davey said to Rusty, watching the approaching storm cloud.

"You may be keeping in tonight," he added.

"I told Pete if it passed by midnight, we're on."

"Hmm…lake will be a mess...choppy, swells…"

"The boat can handle it. Then again, it might calm right back down. You and I both have seen the lake smooth out after a storm. It's not usual, but it can happen. It will be a wait and see."

"Nets will be shifted. You'll have a hard time locating them. We'll take the tug out and look for them at first light."

"Not much of a choice. This was a last minute order. Urgent, Al said. Some big 4th of July shindig in Bucyrus and the usual contacts didn't come through."

"Bucyrus? That's a long ways away from the lake! How can a little farm town have an emergency for booze let alone a big shindig?"

"There is supposedly a small underground city below the town with a popular speakeasy. There are even rumors that Capone stops by there when he's traveling through."

"I find that hard to swallow."

"Pete doesn't. Anyways, Bucyrus is not my concern. I'm just to meet some bootleggers at a boat launch up Old Woman's Creek."

"That's marshy as heck. The boat's got a shallow draft, but you're liable to get tangled up in the reeds and foul the engines."

"I told Al I wasn't keen on it."

"Talk costs of repairs and replacement parts with Al. He'll understand that."

A gust of wind kicked up the dirt in the pull-off in front of the shanty and dusted them. Rusty pulled the doors shut. By now, the massive thunderhead had completely blocked the sun, turning the land and water dark and quiet.

"I'm going to catch some sleep before the midnight run," Rusty said. "You coming up?"

"I'll watch the storm's approach for a bit and then head up. Play some solitaire."

***

Rusty woke before midnight and looked out the window of his bedroom. The storm had passed, dragging with it any trailing rain showers. He pulled on his pants and walked barefoot out into the night. Overhead, the clouds were breaking and starlight appeared in the gaps. The lake was agitated with choppy 3 footers, but he had seen it worse. He went back in and finished getting dressed, then headed down to the boat to wait for Pete who was suppose to arrive at 12:30 if the storm had cleared out.

A quarter to one, a Buick pulled up and deposited Pete.

"On time as always," Rusty said.

"Don't get your tit in a wringer, I was making sure the storm was over."

Rusty turned over the engines and waited for them to warm, and then they headed down river for the open lake.

When they cleared the breakwaters, the boat bucked when it hit the choppy waves. Rusty cut across the crests and the ride smoothed.

"This boat launch on Old Woman's Creek, is it on private property?"

"Not that I know of," Pete said over the drone of engines. "Runners and bootleggers use the spot as drop offs and pick-ups because it's so secluded."

"Doesn't sound so secluded if so many know about it. Who are our contacts?"

"Some boozehisters out of Norwalk. I guess their usual suppliers couldn't deliver and they needed the hooch in Bucyrus for the 4th."

Rusty frowned. "One, I hope we are not crossing territories and two, I don't want to take this boat into marshes."

"The channel is pretty clean because of the activity, and we're not taking territories. It's a one-time deal—their runners are unable to deliver for the 4th and we can. Hey, maybe it's the same runners that were at the Vermilion lighthouse, you know, that kid's pa and the rumrunner."

They reached the fishing grounds where the nets were strung earlier in that day.

"Shit. Just what I was afraid of," he said. "They're not here."

Pete flew to the side rail. "Some son-of-a-bitch stole them!"

"Relax, Pete. The currents created by the storm moved them," he said. "We got to search east of here and see if we can find where they drifted."

They searched in the darkness for an hour and twenty minutes, running a crisscross pattern.

"Let's take a chance and use the spotlight. We're wasting time," Pete said.

Rusty had the binoculars up to his eyes, hoping they would help spot the markers with what little light they could gather. "No, we're going to…hold on, there's our marker!"

The lake's chop made retrieving of the net line difficult and by the time the last bundle was hauled on deck, they were tired, soaked and running late.

"I hope these fellas are as patient as Vince and Tony," Rusty said, trying to check his watch in the soft red glow of the instrument dials.

"Screw 'em if they're not. They should be kissing our butts for saving their asses."

As Pete untied the last bundle, Rusty headed *New Moon* for the shoreline near Huron.

***

The sprawling mouth of Old Woman's Creek was choked with cattails, reeds and sedges. An aisle of clear, sluggish water ran through the center of the marsh that was just wide enough to allow a boat with a twelve foot beam up river. Once the tangled mouth was cleared, the river broke free of the jungle of grasses.

Rusty motored slowly up river, taking care to keep in the narrow channel of clear water. Frogs and insects of many sizes and shapes croaked, cheeped, clicked and shrilled so loud they could be heard over the drone of the engines.

Pete pointed out a silhouette of a Great Horned Owl high on a dead branch.

"The Indians believe if an owl calls your name you will die," Rusty said in a hushed voice.

"If that thing starts hooting, I'm shooting it."

A bend in the river hid the view beyond, and each man fell silent in anticipation of what or who lie just around the bend.

"That dock better be around the corner or I'm turning this boat around. It's getting narrower and shallower and I'm not getting in a jam," Rusty said. It was then he caught the smell of cigarette smoke wafting in the air. *New Moon* slipped around the bend and he caught the red glow from the butt of a cigarette.

A flashlight exploded light into the darkness with two sets of quick flashes.

"That's our contact," Pete said, and flashed a signal back using the boat's flashlight.

They motored up to a small, overgrown wooden dock where two men stood, one swatting wildly at mosquitoes. Pete tied off the boat.

"We were taking bets if it was the storm or the law that got you," the man with the cigarette said. "These damn mosquitoes are eating us alive."

"The storm shifted our nets and we had a …"

"Better late than never," Rusty blurted over Pete. "Let's stop beating the gums and get this load off. We're running late."

The men fell silent and the bundles of booze were quickly passed. After the last bundle, Pete lit a cigarette and waited as the man counted out the money. "Who usually delivers to you?" he asked taking the money.

"I don't know who they are. We just pick up and deliver. They have a smaller outboard—nothing like this boat. You guys must be big time. They use a tugboat to ferry the booze over, and then the smaller outboard to run the cases to shore. But, this is some boat you guys got. You'll make a lot of smiles tomorrow."

“One of those smiles wouldn’t belong to Al Capone by chance?” Pete asked.

“Scarface?” The men exchanged glances and burst into laughter.

“Pete, cast off and get in.” Rusty gave the engines a little throttle as Pete jumped in. He jockeyed the boat to turn it around and headed back down the creek, around the bend and out through the marshy shoreline. A hint of light seeped along the horizon. He frowned.

“I told you their suppliers were those Vermilion lighthouse dummies,” Pete said as they motored out into the lake. “Probably that same tugboat we saw at the minesweeper.”

“That’s not the only tug running. There’s dozens of them running booze with speedboats. Christ, Pete, do you realize we’re hitting the Coast Guard’s shift change?”

“No sweat. It’s just a short trip to Huron. Besides, the coasties will be on the other side of Marblehead.”

“They got to get there first. They’ll be coming in from all over the lake.”

Pete grabbed the binoculars and scanned the waters. “Nothing. Open her up and let’s go,” he said, swinging the binoculars towards the east. “Uh, oh, I think our buddy from Vermilion—that picket boat that chased us up river-is heading this way.”

“What’s her course?”

Pete was quiet as he studied the boat’s movement. “Yep, I think she spotted us because she was heading northwest and has just turned due west—right at us.”

“Dammit.”

“We can make it.”

“Rabbits run for their holes, and I am not giving away our hole.” He throttled up and headed north instead of west back to Huron.”

“What’s the plan?”

“We are going to lead her away from Huron, shake her and double back. This could get bad fast if she radios for support, which she most likely will do.”

“Damn it, I had big plans for today.”

“Dry up, you’re not the only one with plans.”

“So where are we headed?”

“We’ll make like we are heading for Pelee Point and head into Canadian waters if we have to. Once we shake her, we’ll swing wide to the east and circle back. In the meantime, start thinking of good hiding places along the shore and islands. You should know, you’ve ran before.”

As *New Moon* blazed north, the picket boat gave chase but the gap between the two boats was widening.

“She can’t keep up,” Pete said with a snicker over his shoulder.

They were almost past Kelleys Island, when another picket boat, hiding on Kelleys north side, flew towards them on an intercepting course, taking them by surprise.

"Our buddy must have radioed for backup." Rusty shouted over the engines roar as he cut the wheel hard. He doubled back then turned west to avoid the first picket boat closing in. *New Moon* bolted for the south side of Kelleys. She was light and agile as she roared through the Southern Passage between Marblehead Peninsula and Kelleys Island. Once clear of Kelleys, she turned and headed north again, flying past the Bass Islands off her portside. The sky and water brightened to soft blue light and visibility was far reaching even though the sun had yet to crest. Rusty felt like a vampire racing the sun. The lighter it got, the worse it would be for them for they would not only be visible, they could be easily identified.

That's when he heard it. He actually saw a pattern of water jets hitting all around them first and heard the sounds of ka-ping striking the boat's armor plating, but it was the sound that followed immediately, *chug-chug-chug-chug*, like a heavy anchor chain being dragged over a rail that made the hair stand on his neck. A third picket boat, newer and faster shot out from between South and Middle Bass Islands straight at them.

Chug-chug-chug-chug-chug-chug.

"The Belgian Rattlesnake," he said under his breath.

"What rattlesnake?" Pete cried.

"Lewis MK-1! .30 caliber machine gun."

"Connors!" Pete fumed. He reached for the B.A.R.

"No!" Rusty said. "Now is not the time."

"Not the time? He's shooting at us."

A burst of bullets raked *New Moon* with a series of thuds, cracking the small rear window. The pinging sound of ricochets was earsplitting

Rusty pressed the button that dispensed the castor oil. The oil dripped on the carburetors and *New Moon* shot forward throwing Pete backwards. She raced north towards the border.

Pete scrambled onto his seat. "We might be fast, but we can't outrun bullets," he cried. Sweat was pouring down his face.

"That's why I need you to pour oil on the manifolds. We need a smoke screen."

Pete looked stunned at him. "I'm not leaving this plated cockpit to go on deck."

The second picket boat had rejoined the chase, heading on a course to attempt to cut them off.

"Damn it, Pete, that's our way out of this. Now get your ass out there while I run a zigzag to dodge bullets."

"I'm not doing it."

"I'm the captain, and you'll do as told if you want to save our skins."

"Screw you. You're not my master. Who in hell do you think you're talking to?"

"Damn you, Pete…"

"I can't swim, asshole!" Pete shouted as if spelling it out. "If I fall over board, I drown. *Capisce!*"

Rusty tightened his jaw. "Take the wheel. Just keep her headed north-nothing tricky-just steer in a straight line."

Pete took the wheel as Rusty crawled out of the cockpit and onto the deck. The wind snapped his clothes and whipped his hair. He picked his way back to the engine compartment, steadied himself and raised the hatch covers. An oil can stood at ready in the compartment. He reached for it.

Bullets raked *New Moon* again with ricochets pinging and flying wildly. He ducked behind the open hatch covers, and as he did, he felt a stab of pain in his left index finger. He jerked his hand back and saw blood. He looked at his hand. The end of his index finger from the last joint up was missing. Stunned by the sight, he quickly shook off the shock of seeing the end missing and the pain that was accelerating as more bullets whizzed by him. He grabbed the oil can with his good hand and poured oil on the manifolds.

In an instant, a thick cloud of smoked rose from the engine compartment. It grew rapidly, engulfing the boat in an impenetrable gray fog that continued to increase and spread in size and scope until a wide area behind the boat was blanketed in dense smoke.

Rusty ripped a hunk of his shirt off and tied it around his throbbing finger dripping with blood. With one hand, he closed the hatches and steadied himself back to the cockpit.

"It's a whiteout behind us," Pete laughed as Rusty came into the cockpit. "They'll never find us in this smoke." He stepped from the wheel so Rusty could take over and saw the blood soaked cloth. "What the hell happened to your hand?"

"The tip of my finger got shot off," Rusty said with a grimace.

"Shit, you got to get to the hospital."

"We got to get out of this first." Rusty turned the boat on a wide arc to the west, and then south. "Let's hope they think we are heading for the border." He held his hand against his chest and blood seeped onto his shirt.

"We can't get back to Huron from here without passing too close to the C.G. station at Marblehead," Pete said, his voice anxious.

"I know. We're going to have to hide over on this side for a while and wait for it to cool." Pain shot up his arm like a giant needle being rammed from his finger to his shoulder. "Could you get me another cloth? This one's soaked."

Pete found a clean rag and ripped a strip off.

"Take the wheel."

Pete scrunched his face as he watched Rusty unwrap the blood soaked cloth, and then looked away before the finger was exposed. "That gives me the willies."

"You? How do you think I feel—I'm the one who lost my finger tip."

"So where are we headed?" Pete said, staring hard straight ahead. There was uneasiness in his voice.

"Port Clinton."

"Port Clinton? You need the hospital in Sandusky."

"There will be a report."

"Tell them it was fishing accident."

"And where do we hide the boat during all this? No, I know a guy in Port Clinton that I hope will let us hide our boat at his marina."

New Moon sped for the marina owned by Davey's friend, Mike—the same man who had helped them get the Liberty engines. The sun had crested as they pulled into the small harbor. Mike was walking across the boat yard and came to a stop when he saw *New Moon* pull up to the dock in front of his shop.

Pete jumped out and tied off the boat. "Mike, right? I'm a friend of Rusty and Davey. Rusty is hoping you can help us out. We had a bit of a problem."

Mike walked over to the boat as Rusty was crawling out. He spotted the blood soaked cloth wrapped around Rusty's shaking hand and the blood covering the front of his shirt. "What in hell happened?"

"We were coming in from a run late, almost dawn. Guard chased us."

"By the looks of you they did more than chase," Mike said.

"We ran into Connors," Pete said.

"That explains it. You're going to need that finger tended to."

"Could we dock here until nightfall? We need to keep this boat out of sight."

"I don't have a problem with that but with this being a holiday, this place will be crawling with boaters and your boat is quite a novelty." His face brightened. "I'll stick it down at the end behind some boats needing repairs. That way, it will be out of sight unless someone goes nosing around. You go on inside my shop so you don't spook the early birds with your bloody hand, and me and your partner here will take care of the boat. There's a bottle of scotch under my workbench in a tackle box. Take a few nips of that to help ease the pain."

Mike and Pete tucked *New Moon* between two boats docked at the end of a pier that ran perpendicular to a channel that led to the river and then headed back to the shop.

"Son, take my automobile and drive Rusty to the hospital," Mike said to Pete.

"No. Like I told Pete, it will raise too many questions. Conners will be sniffing around to hear if anyone showed up with gunshots or unusual injuries. I hear he's got a set of eyes and ears that works as a nurse in Sandusky."

Mike nodded and scratched his head. His face brightened again.

"My sister worked as a nurse. She used to assist with surgeries. She's been retired, but she's seen it all and she'd know what to do. Let me give her a call."

Rusty stepped between him and the phone. "Wait. How is she going to feel about this?"

"If you're asking about your finger, that's nothing to her. If you're asking about bothering her, she's a nurse and always will be. If you're asking abetting a law breaker," he flashed a smile, "Sis patched me up on occasion during my outlaw days until I got smart enough to know better and too old to care." He picked up the receiver.

Minutes later, they were on their way to his sister's house in Danbury Township.

***

It was almost mid-morning by the time sis had finished with the stitching and bandaging. "You keep that dry and see me in three days. I want to keep an eye on it so don't get septic or then I'll have to chop your hand off," she warned in her best nurse voice.

Her emphasis on chop your hand off made him cringe and he wondered if she was serious or laying it on thick with a trowel.

She went to the same cabinet that she had kept her medical supplies and selected a small vial. "A half teaspoon when the pain becomes unbearable. Don't make a habit of it. Use it sparingly." She made a sling that elevated his hand across his chest.

"How long for this?" he asked.

"A week, better two. I'll let you know when I check on your progress."

"At least it wasn't your trigger finger," Pete said as they headed back to Mike's automobile. "So now what?"

"We catch a ride back to Huron."

"I'll drive you to Sandusky and you can catch the trolley there," Mike offered. "I'd take you boys to Huron, but I need to get back to the marina. Busy day today. Probably already got a line of pissed off boaters wondering why I stepped out when they needed me to pump their gas and untangle their fishing line."

He drove them across Bay Bridge into Sandusky and up to the trolley depot. "Gee, you boys almost make me wish for the old days again. Notice I said, *almost*." He laughed. "Seriously, boys, you take care out there. It was a different ballgame when I ran."

"Here," Rusty said, handing Mike some bills. "For your trouble."

Mike shook his head. "No. It's not necessary."

"Then for docking fee. And since your sister wouldn't take anything for her services, get her some flowers from us as a thank you for her help."

Mike hesitated, then took the money and nodded thanks.

While they waited for the trolley to arrive, Pete turned to Rusty. "When Connors opened fire on us, you said, "rattlesnake." Were you meaning Rattlesnake Island or Connors?"

"The gun Connors uses. The Belgian Rattlesnake. It's a nickname the Germans gave the Lewis machine gun. MK-1 .30 caliber. We invented it, but the Belgians ran with it. We, meaning Savage Arms, perfected it later in the war and issued it to our soldiers."

"I damn near shit my pants when it went off. So, was that the old Belgian model or the improved Savage version?"

"Performed first rate to me," he said looking at his bandaged hand.

Pete paused, "Why did you stop me from shooting back? Isn't that why we have guns—to defend ourselves?"

"It wasn't the time or place."

"Time or place? Pete cried out. "This bird musta flown over my head because I can't think of a better time or place than when a maniac is chasing you down and shooting to kill you."

"We made it out."

"Sure, Rust, we made it out—just got the end of your finger blown off. Maybe next time it will just be my left nut, but hey—we'd a made it out! Or maybe next time it will be right here." He poked his finger between Rusty's eyes and Rusty reacted by smacking away his hand.

"Lay off."

The trolley pulled to a stop and a horde of high-spirited people piled out and headed for the ferry docks. He and Pete boarded. He checked his watch. It was almost eleven. He and Davey would be late. Better late than never took on a deeper meaning.

Chapter 60

"Good Lord, what happened to you," Davey exclaimed as Rusty came through the door. Rusty could see the alarm in Davey's face when he saw the hand and blood stained shirt. He was six hours later than usual from a run, and that alone would have been concern enough for Davey.

"We ran into Connors. He hammered us with that gun of his and shot the end of my finger off."

"Good Lord," Davey repeated.

"We were running late and by the time we made the connection, it was dawn."

"Nets… the nets made you late. The storm moved them."

"We had a hell of a time finding them."

Davey had an I-told-you-so look on his face, but didn't say anything.

"We got chased right after we left Old Woman's Creek."

"He was waiting for you there?"

"Not there. Up by the islands. That picket boat that ran us up river the other night spotted us coming out of the creek. She must have radioed because we had another boat on our tail when he joined in the fray. We made for the border, and then used the smoke screen to lose them. My finger tip got shot off when I was oiling the manifolds."

"That explains it. I thought maybe the armor plating and glass failed."

"They work perfectly. The boat is in good shape considering the rakes it took."

"You need a coat of armor for on deck."

"Amen."

Davey shook his head. "I should've rigged up a configuration that could be employed by you in the cockpit like the castor oil on the carbs." He looked dejected.

"Not your fault, Davey—mine for not listening to you last night about the nets."

"All the same, I'm going to work something out so we can get the oil onto the manifolds without stepping out of the protection of the cockpit." He looked at Rusty's hand, "You're not going to be able to work with that."

"I know, but I can still pilot." He looked at the kitchen clock. "Holy mackerel, we're suppose to be meeting them in Vermilion now!"

"You're planning on going? You should hit the hay instead."

"I can't miss. I don't want to miss it."

Changing his clothes and cleaning up was agonizing and slow and he wished Di was there because she would fuss over him and babying is what he needed from her more than ever.

“How are you going to drive the truck?” Davey asked as he slid himself onto the passenger’s seat.

“The same way I’m going to pilot the boat—with great difficulty,” he said, lifting the wheelchair with one arm into the truck bed.

“Why don’t we take the trolley?”

“No time for that. I told Eddie we’d pick him up and we are almost an hour late. That poor, damn kid can’t count on anything—not even me.”

Davey looked cockeyed at him. “I believe he’ll find your finger sufficient excuse.”

When they pulled up to Donovan’s, Eddie was seated on her front porch steps. His face brightened when he saw them.

“All aboard,” Davey called out the truck window.

Eddie hurried to the back of the truck and crawled into the bed. He never mentioned anything about them being late, but once out of the truck at the parking lot of the amusement park, he spotted Rusty’s hand.

“What happened to you?”

“I stuck my finger in the lake and a fish bit it off.”

Eddie’s eyes grew wide.

“He’s fooling with you,” Davey said with a wink.

“I got hurt working on the boat. I wasn’t being careful. Can you give me a hand getting this chair out?”

Eddie helped lift it out. “Did you chop it off?”

“Just the tip.”

“Did it bleed?”

“Like a stuck pig.”

“Woo,” Eddie said as he pushed the chair up to where Davey sat in the truck.

As they crossed through the park’s entrance gates, Di rushed to meet them on the other side.

“You’re an hour late. What happened?” She then spotted his hand. “Oh my God, what happened,” she said, her voice turning into alarm.

“My finger got in the way you could say.”

“How bad did it get in the way?”

“Enough to take the end of it off.”

She gasped and her eyes welled up.

“It will be all right. I had a nurse stitch it up. I’ll be okay.”

Tears rolled down her cheeks. “Does it hurt?”

“It hurts likc hell. But the nurse gave me something to help ease the pain.” He put his arm around her and kissed her forehead. “Let’s go join the others.”

They walked to the pavilion and Di’s mom and Uncle Fritz knew instantly something was wrong the minute they saw them. “He cut the end of his finger off, Mom,” Di said.

Di’s mother gasped and her hand flew to her mouth.

"Looks like you put your finger where it ought not have been," Uncle Fritz said. His face was grave.

"You got that right."

"You shouldn't be here," Di's mother said. "Look at him. He's been through the mill."

"No, I've been looking forward to this," he said looking at Di. "It'll get my mind off my hand, and if I need to rest, there are plenty of shade trees tempting enough for a nap."

"And you can count on me to keep you company under that shade tree," Uncle Fritz said.

Di's older brother brought his girlfriend along, and with Di's younger brother having an aversion to amusement rides, Uncle Fritz partnered with Eddie so Di and Rusty could be together. At first Eddie was quiet. Uncle Fritz was a portly man and unfamiliar to Eddie. Sensing his shyness, Uncle Fritz broke the ice by challenging him to a shooting match at the shooting gallery and bumper cars. By the time the first cotton candy was consumed, Eddie and him were pals. He drilled Uncle Fritz on everything from if he was the grandfather to Di to where he came from since he talked funny sometimes and said *ja* when he meant *yes.*

Rusty avoided the rides and focused on the side shows to get his mind off the throbbing pain. He felt content watching Di and Eddie share laughs as they partnered on rides and when it came time for the carousel and Ferris Wheel he joined in.

From high atop the Ferris Wheel which offered a panoramic view of the lake, Eddie asked Di why she liked being at the lake here and not at her cottage in Vermilion. Di bit her lip and did not answer, so Rusty inserted that she felt safe with all the people she loved around her. What he wanted to say was *good question, kid. If you can come up with the answer, we all would like to know.*

But he knew this was a big step for Di. He could almost feel her anxiousness and determination like it was his own. She had to walk before she could run, and she was taking her first big step.

***

"We are in a bit of pickle here, fellas," Al said, flicking his cigar ashes in the crystal ashtray in the center of the table. "The boat window can be fixed but our friend here is beyond fixing though his finger will heal. Now you said it would not be a problem for you to pilot the boat but hauling nets and getting that hand wet will be a problem, so that makes for another problem. It's like a domino effect. We'll either need a third man or another pilot with a good hand. But Petey said he won't run with any other pilot but you," he said turning to Rusty, "and I agree with him. So you think you will be up to the task?"

"Piloting will be no problem and the nurse said two weeks before the sling comes off and then limited use, so adding a third guy shouldn't be for more than three weeks."

"Bump that finger and you'll wish you waited four," Al said out of the corner of his mouth. He looked around the table at his kin who had gathered at Middle Island Club in response to his summons for a meeting. "We really can't spare an extra man," he said, taking a puff on his cigar and blowing out a ring of smoke. "Everybody is either at the fish house or running."

"What about Mario? He can pull nets," Pete said.

"No," Al said, jerking the cigar from his mouth. "My boy does not get involved."

The table fell quiet.

"Joe, Lou, you're big boys. You don't need Rusty to help you throw nets overboard and mark 'em. Tony, what if you caught a ride with Petey and joined the midnight runs for the next three weeks?"

"Who would ride shotgun for Vince? Not safe for one guy to deliver."

"Vince would only be alone until you got there with the boat and the load. Then after you've unloaded, you'll stay behind with him and ride shotgun on the delivery."

Tony grimaced about the extra workload, but nodded anyways.

"Now, what to do about this snake in the grass who won't play by the rules." Al's eyes began to darken. "This fruit salad who's passing himself off as a C.G. captain has crossed a line with me as he has with Rusty. I told you boys to avoid confrontation. I told you to cooperate if caught. Now I'm telling you if that son of a bitch comes near you, shoot back and give him a taste of his own medicine and we'll see how tough he is."

"Oh, he's tough," Rusty said. "To shoot back would be suicide."

Al stabbed his cigar in the ashtray. "To be a sitting duck is also suicide. At least make the pecker duck for Christ's sake. Pete! That B.A.R. is not a decoration for the boat. Use that god damn thing the next time you see the numbers CG157!"

"You'll get him killed for sure, Al. Let me handle this my way," Rusty said. "It's my ass on the line, too. Let me make the call. You said you wanted my services because you trusted me. Then trust me and let me be what I'm supposed to be out on the water—the captain."

Al inhaled deeply and seemed to hold his breath, before letting it out. He drummed his fingers on the table. The redness that had coated his face began to fade. "All right, Mr. Rusty… *Captain* Rusty. We'll do it your way for now. But if one of you so much as feels a breeze from a bullet from 1-5-7, we do it my way."

***

New Moon was no longer a phantom. The shadow that had eluded the Guard, dodged hijackers and consistently delivered A-1 quality when no one else could was not only real, but identifiable and those on both sides of the law that witnessed its mad run on the morning of the attack that cost Rusty his finger tip told their accounts of seeing the sleek and powerful shadowy rumrunner. Descriptions of its look, its sound and feats was told without little embellishment until the legend of the Shadow Runner, as it was dubbed, spread like a wildfire along the southern shore, the islands and central basin of the lake. Men boasted over beers that they were present when The Shadow Runner delivered, adding its crew was just as enigmatic. Al was uneasy that the boat had become a legend because, as he said, *there was always some nobody out there putting their crosshairs on legends in hopes of bringing them down just to make themselves famous* to which Davey added, like Bob Ford with Jesse James.

Tony joined the midnight runs and bitched so much that Rusty had to tell him repeatedly to pipe down as sound carried at night especially on the water. Coast Guard patrols had stepped up, so runs were fewer and more irregular and on more than one occasion, hiding in inlets or outfoxing guardsmen took bites out of the night causing them to just make it back to port before the first leak of daylight.

By week two, Rusty discarded the sling. His finger was healing nicely according to Sis, the nurse but he still had limited use and could not risk getting it wet. Despite the thick wad of bandaging encapsulating his finger, the mere thought of bumping it made him cringe. Shooting pain and throbbing had yet to cease although the edge was off. He wasn't sure if the healing process, Sis's pain killer or shots of whiskey and beer were to be credited.

It was week three of his recuperation, and it was business as usual at the farm, the boathouse in Huron, Middle Island and Vermilion. Then, in the wee hours of an unusually cool July night, the mysterious lighthouse rumrunner docked again at the crumbling Vermilion lighthouse.

***

The week had been sultry with humidity creating sauna-like conditions, so when an evening storm passed through bringing cooler temperatures on its backside, people in Vermilion slept deep for the first time in days as the cool breezes washed over them from open windows and sleeping porches.

The wind, like the heat of the previous nights, made Eddie restless. He tossed and turned until just before three when he finally yielded and got up and looked out his bedroom window of Mrs. Donovan's Cape Cod. He looked up and saw a million stars stretching across the black sky. Looking down from his second story perch, he could see a distant flashlight bobbing along the sidewalks, shining on each storefront as it moved down the street. *Ray Kreuger,* he thought. That meant Hoot was alone to patrol the docks.

He slipped out of his pajamas and into his clothes, grabbed his hat and lightly clapped his leg for Prince to follow. He unlatched the backdoor and he and Prince slipped into the night.

The town was dead to the world as he and Prince stole through the backyards and alley ways. The breeze rustled the leaves overhead and made their shadows dance below the street lights. Sometimes they played tricks on his eyes conjuring up rumrunners, dog poisoners and his pa tucked in the darkest corners, but with Prince at ease by his side, he knew it was only his imagination. They bee lined for the docks along the fishery where Hoot would no doubt be glad to see them.

The docks and fishery were dark, lit by only three lights- one over the main doorway and two along the riverfront dock, creating more shadows than they did light.

Eddie hurried down the bank to the fish house and as he was about to round the corner, Prince let out a low growl and his hackles stood on end. He screeched to a stop and silenced Prince with a hand signal. He knew right off that whoever was around the corner would not be Hoot.

With a *stay* hand signal, Eddie peeked around the corner. In the shadows on the far side of the building where boats of different sizes and shape were dry-docked, he could see shadowy movement and hear low voices but he was too far away to really see or hear. He doubled back to the rear of the building to avoid the lights on the dock along the river and crept around crates, coils of line and boat parts until he reached the corner closest to the activities within the shadows of the boats. Prince, sensing Eddie's covert mission, followed with head low and muscles tense.

The talking was louder, but just above a whisper. He still was unable to hear what was being said, but he recognized two of the four voices—Hoot's and his pa's. He signaled for Prince to stay. He darted from boat to boat till he was close enough to see and hear.

His pa was standing off to the side while two men sandwiched Hoot—one behind him and the other in front of him. The one in front had his face so close to Hoot's that Hoot was blinking from the spit.

Hoot was also begging. "I swear, I swear I'll be as silent as the grave."

The man in front of him poked Hoot in the chest. "You won't need to act, father time."

Eddie's pa was also pleading. "Please…just let him go. He won't talk. Can't you see he's scared shitless! You swear you won't talk, ain't that right, Hoot?"

"I swear. I swear on the bible itself."

"I'm afraid that boat already sailed, old man, because someone sang like a bird after that last fiasco and now we got heat all around us and are losing contacts. Grab him, Bill."

"No, please, I don't know anything about what happened. I was too drunk!"

The tall man stationed behind Hoot grabbed Hoot from behind and held him snug while the man in front, grabbed a full bottle of whiskey and pulled the cork off with his teeth.

Hoot began sobbing.

Eddie's pa stepped partly in front of Hoot. "Please …this will only make it worse."

"Worse?" the man with the bottle snapped. "How so? The town drunk got liquored up again and this time stumbled off the dock and drowned. That's all." He nodded to the tall man named Bill who pulled Hoot's head back. "You like to drink, old man? Then have a drink," and he began pouring the liquor down Hoot's throat.

Hoot coughed and choked, sobbed and slobbered as the alcohol was poured down his throat, splashing over his face.

Eddie's pa pressed the sides of his own head, "Stop, you're killing him!"

"Isn't that the point?"

Eddie began to rise to make a run, but his father's words ensnared him.

"I don't want to be a part of this. You said you only wanted to scare him."

The angry man yelled to his pa. "You shut your mouth. You're responsible for this getting botched just as much as him. I told you to keep the old man out of our hair, and what do you do? You let your kid get an eye and ear full and all this gets blown high."

Eddie squatted back down. His heart was pounding.

"Hey, listen, I did everything asked of me. I kept Hoot liquored up and I poisoned the dogs. I even help fence the stuff and for what—few bottles of booze and a couple of dollars? You got a bargain with me, buddy."

"Screw you and I'm not your buddy."

The words rang like a banging gong in Eddie's head: *I poisoned the dogs.* His pa was the culprit behind the dog poisonings. Eddie gulped and his eyes bugged. He wanted to run, scream, curse and beat his pa, but he remained still while his insides exploded.

Every fiber in Eddie told him to run for Chief Bales but he was too frightened to move. He was like a scared rabbit, afraid that his slightest move, even a breath, would give him away. If caught, would his pa save him from the angry man or would he just stand there like he was for Hoot? He didn't want to take that chance, but even if he wanted to run, he didn't think his legs could respond.

Hoot had grown quiet as the final contents of the bottle ran over his face. He slumped forward in the tall man's arm.

"Now you two drag him to dockside and dump him in the river."

Eddie's pa took hold of Hoot on one side and the tall man grabbed the other side, and together they dragged Hoot's limp body to the edge of the dock and tossed him into the river. Hoot swirled about in the current then sank.

It was Eddie's cue; he jumped up to run and tripped in a coil of line. The angry man spun around and spotted him. He lunged towards Eddie. Eddie jumped up and the angry man took after him. He was about to grab him when Prince bounded across the boat yard and knocked the man to the ground and they began to wrestle. The tall man and Eddie's pa, still at dockside, heard the commotion and came running. The tall one drew his pistol as he ran. Meanwhile, the angry man struggling with Prince was digging for his pistol, too.

Eddie yelled. "Prince, come."

But Prince wouldn't yield. He growled and shook the man and Eddie could hear the crunch of bones. The man let out a howl of pain and managed to wrestle the pistol from his holster.

Eddie reached for his back pocket and pulled out his slingshot. His hands were shaking. He fumbled in his front pocket for stones. He pulled out two and loaded one into the cup of the sling. His hands were trembling too much. *Take a deep breath, aim and fire as you breathe out, and remember, steady strain.* Rusty's words echoed in his head. The man fought his way to a sitting position and put the gun up to Prince's head. Eddie aimed between the man's eyes, pulled steadily, breathed out and released.

The man screamed and fell backwards, clutching his left eye.

The tall man aimed his gun at Prince but before he could pull the trigger, Eddie's pa knocked his hand away. "Run, Eddie, run," he yelled.

Eddie gave a sharp whistle and Prince broke away and bounded after him.

The last thing Eddie heard as he scrambled up the bank was his pa's voice yelling, "No Eliot, don't do it!"

Then there was a gunshot.

***

Ray Kreuger heard a shot down by the waterfront. He turned his flashlight off and ran for Chief Bales home. He arrived there the same time Eddie did.

"Eddie? What are you doing here?"

Eddie tried to talk but all he could do was gasp for air. Tears rolled down his cheeks.

Ray banged on the door, and then bent down to Eddie. "I heard a gunshot—do you know anything about it?"

Eddie nodded. "Hoot. They killed Hoot," he sobbed.

Ray rose and banged hard on the door.

The chief stuck his head out of an upstairs window. "Ray?"

"Chief, you better get down here quick. There's been a shooting."

Within minutes, the chief flung open the door and stepped out. He was in uniform and his holster with sidearm was strapped around his waist. He was carrying a 12 gauge double barrel shotgun. He took one look at Eddie, then Ray. "What's going on?"

"I heard a shot, Eddie here saw Hoot get shot."

"No. They drowned Hoot. The shot came when I was running away."

"Go get your rifle, Ray and call the state police." He looked at Eddie. "Tell me quick what happened."

"Two men and…and my pa are at the fishery. The men poured booze down Hoot's throat and threw him in the river. My pa didn't want to do it. One man came after me and I hit him in the face with my slingshot and ran. That's when I heard the gunshot."

"I ought to kick your ass for being there, but then they might have gotten away with it. Get back to Mrs. Donovan's, wake her and tell her what happened. Then you and Mrs. Donovan come here and wait with my wife just in case they go looking for you at Donovan's. And if I see you out and about before breakfast, I'll throw *you* in jail."

Eddie ran for Mrs. Donovan with Prince hot on his heels.

Chief Bales hurried through the night on the same route Eddie had taken earlier. As he approached the fishery, he slowed down and picked his way cautiously through the shadows, his shotgun at ready. He stopped and strained to hear for any sound. The fishery was dead silent, but in the distance he could hear the sound of a boat motor fading away. He crept among the dry dock boats towards the dock for a better look and could see the dark form of a boat heading out into the lake. Its course of direction and its wake told him it had departed the old lighthouse. He grimaced, and continued searching the area with his shotgun at ready.

Among the dry docked boats, a strong smell of liquor concentrated near one particular area. He approached the spot with caution and his foot kicked something. He clicked on his flashlight. A broken bottle lay upon the ground. What was left of its contents and the splatter nearby were still fresh. He shined the flashlight around the ground and the beam revealed a scuffle of footprints like a struggle had taken place here. He figured this was the spot Eddie saw the men with Hoot. He spotted drag marks. He followed their trail with his flashlight and tracked them to the dock. *They dragged Hoot to the dock and dumped him in the river,* Eddie had said. He shined his beam across the water, along the bank and around the moored boats docked on the riverfront. The beam hit an object bobbing in the water. It was bumping with a quiet tapping against the hull of a boat. He zeroed the beam of light on the object, not realizing he was holding his breath. It was driftwood, not a body. He sighed deeply. Then relief turned instantly to dread. The driftwood was Hoot's wooden leg. He felt his stomach turn. *Where was that damn state police?* He scanned the bridge over the river hoping to see their flashing light, knowing in his heart that not much time had passed between Eddie's report and now.

He crept through the boatyard and headed for the dark backside of the building, poking his flashlight's beam among the crates, coils of line and boat parts. Between an outboard motor and a discarded hull, his beam fell on a person sitting with his back up against the wall of the fishery, half hidden in junk. His heart leaped as he aimed the shotgun at the chest of the person—a man— a body. The body's head was cocked and a hole was at the temple. He shined his flashlight around the area and behind him in fear someone alive could be close and laying for him. He heard the slight sound of gravel kicked loose to his right and whipped his beam towards the sound. It landed on a fast approaching figure. He whipped the barrel of his shotgun onto the figure.

"Halt or I'll shoot!"

The figure froze and he instantly recognized the face."Ray!" He said in a loud whisper.

"Chief?"

"Yes, get over here quick." His voice was low.

Ray hurried over to Bales. "What's going on?" he whispered.

"I found a body here." He shined his flashlight beam on it.

"Is it Hoot?"

"No, it Eddie's pa."

"Sweet Jesus."

"Keep cover." Chief Bales knocked away lumber and a few crates to get to the man. "He's shot in the temple." He shined his light all over the body. "He's got a pistol in his hand. A .22 caliber."

"Holy mackerel, he committed suicide."

"No. Someone wants us to think that he did. There's no gunpowder smell on his hand. Someone placed it there afterwards. And there are also drag marks behind this building that lead right up to here. He was shot over there," he said using his beam as a pointer, "and dragged and stuffed back here. Look at all the scuffle marks and footprints. See the drag marks?"

"Jeepers! What about Hoot? Have you found him?"

"No, but his leg is floating in the river."

"Oh no."

Flashing lights and a siren alerted them to the arrival of the state police.

"Eddie said there were three men," Ray said.

"I saw a boat leaving the lighthouse when I first got here. I figure they must have been on it."

"Poor Eddie," Ray said.

"Poor Eddie has to get out of town."

***

There was a knock at the door. Rusty and Davey exchanged glances. Rusty crossed over to the door and brushed the curtain aside. It was the bait shop man. He opened the door.

"Rusty, I got a call for you. Here's the number you're suppose to call. Sounded urgent. Hey, Davey, how ya doing?"

"Thanks. I'm right behind you," Rusty said. He followed the bait shop man down the steps and to the shop. The morning was already hot and offered no relief to the stuffy apartment upstairs. Once inside the cooler bait shop, he headed straight for the telephone and asked the operator to connect him to the number. He waited for the connection, watching the bait shop man feigning to tidy his shelves in order to eavesdrop.

"Hello? Chief? Yes, this is Rusty." He listened quietly as the bait shop man stole glances, noting Rusty's face growing graver the longer he listened.

"Rusty, we're having a time here," the chief said over the telephone. "There was another incident at the fishery last night that appears to involve those rumrunners from before, only this time it went further. Eddie's pa was murdered and we just fished Hoot's body out of the river. Eddie said Hoot was also killed. He saw it happen. One of the men went after Eddie. He's safe, but he's got to get out of town. You're the only other person I know he's close to."

"I'll be right there." He hung up the receiver. "Thanks for the use of the telephone. What do I owe you?"

"Thank me by getting your bait and tackle here. Is everything all right?" the bait shop man fished.

"Yeah. You got two cold root beers in the icebox?"

"Sure do."

Rusty dropped two bits and a dime on the counter and the bait shop man produced two cold bottles. The clash of temperatures caused instant condensation on the bottles. "Keep the change for your troubles." As he hurried back to the boat shanty, he held one of the bottles up to his hot face. The fresh-out-the-box cold felt good.

Davey spotted Rusty's grim look when he walked in. "Uh-oh, what happened?"

"There was a ruckus at the docks last night in Vermilion involving rumrunners. Eddie's pa is dead. So is Hoot, the night watchman."

"The fella that was jailed for drunkenness?"

"That's him." He popped off the bottle caps and handed a root beer to Davey. "Here, it's cold."

Davey's face fell solemn. "That poor kid. I remember you saying Hoot was his buddy. To think he lost both his pa and buddy at once."

"The father's no loss. Probably a blessing," Rusty said taking a swig of pop. "That's not half of it, Eddie saw it happen and the fellas doing the killings saw Eddie. Now he's in hot grease. I got to get him out of there."

"Are you bringing him back here?"

"No. He needs to stay clear of runners and running. He needs to think I'm clean."

Davey looked at the floor. He hadn't taken a drink yet.

Rusty drained his bottle and belched. "I got to get to Vermilion. I might be gone for a while, will you be okay?"

"Sure don't worry."

"I'll ask the bait shop fellow to look in on you after he closes up. See if you need anything."

"I'll be fine."

"At least I don't have to worry about making a run tonight."

"Where will you take Eddie?"

"To the farm."

Davey nodded. "Remember Rusty—his father might have been a bad egg and whipped him, but he's still the boy's pa and Eddie might be pretty torn up about it."

Rusty hesitated at the door. "Di will know how to handle that, and I know how to handle those runners."

Chapter 61

Uncle Fritz, Di and her mother were waiting when Rusty with Eddie and Prince pulled into the farm drive. Since they had no telephone, he had called their neighbor from Chief Bales's office and asked the neighbor if she could contact the family and have them call him, giving her the telephone number of the station. Fifteen minutes later, the telephone rang, and the chief passed the receiver to Rusty. Di's mother was on the other end and after he explained the situation, she said yes without consulting the other family members.

Di rushed to Eddie the moment he got out of the truck and enveloped him in her arms. "Oh, Eddie, I am so glad you're safe." She hugged him while looking intently at Rusty, then rose and offered Eddie her hand, "Come inside, Mom and I have made you a sandwich and there's milk and cookies for you." He took her hand and she led him towards the house.

He looked over his shoulder, "Come on Prince."

Prince jumped out of the bed of the truck and trotted after Eddie.

Uncle Fritz stepped aside. "That dog isn't going to chase my chickens, is he?"

Di narrowed her eyes at him.

Her mother joined in. "Shush, Fritz, now's not the time to talk about that."

"Do I talk about it after I have dead chickens?"

"He doesn't chase gulls or ducks. He does what I tell him," Eddie said.

"If that's the case, if he chases my chickens you'll be the one I come see," Uncle Fritz said. "What?" he said, noticing the dirty looks from his sister and Di.

"Stay," Eddie said to Prince once they reached the porch, and Prince sat down on the porch next to the screen door.

"I'll bring him a bowl of water. Make him a sandwich, too," Di said. "Rusty, we'll need dog food," she said over her shoulder as she disappeared into the house with Eddie. Her mother was not far behind leaving Rusty and Uncle Fritz alone in the driveway.

"I'll go to the feed store with you," Uncle Fritz said. "We need to talk without all the ears."

They got in the truck.

"With the state police involved, I wouldn't think those men would be back especially after they killed Hoot and Eddie's pa," Uncle Fritz said. "The police chief might have hit a dead end."

"Chief Bales might very well have, but there's talk among runners and I'll be there with open ears."

"At that pirate den on the Canadian side you call a clubhouse?"

Rusty ignored the remark. "I got a gut feeling about who these runners could be."

"What does your gut say?"

"There has been mention of a tugboat that acts as a base for a speedboat. I saw a tugboat that I recognized from Erie T's fleet at one of the rendezvous. I don't know who is piloting it or who is in the crew. I don't even know if it's the same tugboat that has been working this area."

"What pieces of the puzzle lead you to believe who might have done this?"

"Something Eddie said. He said he heard his father say *no, Eliot*—Eliot is the name of the prick that worked at Erie T with me who was nothing but trouble. Eliot's old man owned the company. When the business went under, the tugboats were dispersed except for one—the *Cherokee.* The old man kept it. Guess the name of the tugboat I saw that night at the rendezvous?"

"The *Cherokee*?"

"The *Cherokee.*"

"So you think Eliot may be a runner using the *Cherokee* and he may be the killer of the watchman and the boy's father?"

"You have to admit there is a strong possibility."

"Possibly, but you will need some further evidence. Just because Erie T's old tugboat is being used in running doesn't mean it's the one involved in the murder, and as far as the name Eliot, there's probably half dozen Eliots rum running. It's a popular name—like Bill."

"Bill, that's another name Eddie mentioned. A tall, lanky guy named Bill was the third man."

Uncle Fritz snapped his fingers. "Wasn't that a Bill who tried to kill the lighthouse keeper on Marblehead after your accident?"

"Yes. Huddleson said he recognized the voice as belonging to a Bill that he often heard on the ship to shore radio."

"Bill is also a popular name."

"Yeah, well, Huddleson's Bill was also described as tall, lanky fellow too."

They exchanged looks.

"Another coincidence?"

Rusty shrugged. "It's something to chew on. Remember, who Huddleson said the voice sounded like? Captain Connors chief motor machinist's mate—Bill!"

Uncle Fritz's eyes widened.

"Uh-huh," Rusty said.

"So Eliot and Connors might be in cahoots?"

"Connors most likely shot up the *Cherokee* making a run while Erie T was still afloat and a deal might have been struck. Safe passage for a cut."

They remained silent the rest of the way to the feed store.

***

The clubhouse was packed. It was Friday night and two councilmen, a police chief, a mayor and a Broadway Star were among those rubbing elbows with rumrunners, bootleggers, kingpins and whores. A jazz band was cranking out hits in the bar and only missed a beat when a bleary-eyed dropper wanted to prove he could still sharp shoot drunk by blasting a hole through the dot over the letter "i" on the skin of the bass drum with his .45 automatic. Fortunately, the drummer saw him aiming and dove out of the way before the shot went off. Red-lipped flappers choked the bar, sucking on long cigarette holders and martinis, occasionally erupting into the Charleston or Shimmy while a white fog hung suspended above the bar.

Rusty bumped his way through the crowd to the back dining room where Al and his shadow, Giuseppe sat with Lou, Joe and two other men in three piece suits who Rusty did not recognize. When Al spotted him, he waved him over.

"Have a seat, Mr. Rusty. Gentlemen, this is the pilot who delivers your wares. He's my star player and first rate delivery man. Hey, Jerry, bring my man here a beer and get rid of these dead soldiers—your busboy must be napping." Al turned back to Rusty. "How's the hand coming along?"

"Good enough that we won't need Tony after next week."

Al turned to the two men. "He sacrificed his finger in a Coast Guard attack for the sake of the runs without missing a beat. He's like the U.S. Postal Service."

The men chuckled and one whose hair was parted down the middle and slicked tight against his head said, "thank you for keeping our patrons wet and happy, Mr. Rusty." He rose slightly to reach across the table and shook Rusty's hand. The other man did likewise. "Without men like you taking risks, we would be out of business and there would be a backlash of civil unrest." The other man nodded in agreement while Al beamed like a proud father.

The first man checked his watch. "Ooh, we got to be on our way. Now that we are on the same page, Al, I feel better." He rose and reached his hand towards Al's and shook it. "Thanks for the dinner. It's good to work with someone as straight and dependable as yourself and for that you have our loyalty." He turned to Rusty. "Thank you again." The second man nodded and repeated" thank you" to him.

After they left, Al turned to Rusty. "Petey says you smelled a rat with those snuffs in Vermilion."

"It's only a hunch. There are some dots that are starting to connect together."

"Those fellows that just left, they met with me because a couple of two-bit chiselers are trying to muscle onto our turf. Said these two men who looked like alley cats came to their joints offering to under bid the current suppliers, namely us. Said our product was cut and nothing more than bathtub gin. Then they wanted to know who we werc. The gentlemen said they didn't rat and thought I should know someone was fishing around. As perturbed as I am over this, I can't help but think what dummies they are—they tell the businessmen that our booze is rot gut and cut, and then they ask who we are. They're ass backwards!"

"Sounds like a couple of Joe Zilches."

"Yeah." Al lit a cigar and puffed on it before continuing, "But Joe Zilches have a way of blundering through, and a Joe Zilch can be a real thorn. You think there may be any connections?"

Rusty frowned. "That's hard to say. Then again, we could have pissed someone off that night we made the Old Woman Creek run. Even though their regulars were unable to deliver, it was still stepping on another's turf."

Al nodded. "And now that speakeasy wants to do business with us."

"That would mean taking over another's territory like those chiselers are trying to do to us. You said you were not going to do that."

"I know what I said. I haven't sent you back there, have I?"

"No."

"Then don't worry about it. You got enough to worry about with your regular runs. You hungry? You look like you could eat a horse."

Before Rusty could answer, Al shouted, "Jerry, get this man a rib-eye and make it medium."

It wasn't until he smelled the steak that he realized how hungry he was. He wolfed it down while Al groused about Pete's absence, Connors's sadism and the ballsiness of the Vermilion rumrunners.

"Here," Al said pushing an envelope towards him when Rusty got up to leave.

Rusty picked it up and looked inside. There was almost a quarter inch thick of twenty dollar bills. "What's this for?"

"For your finger tip. It can't buy it back or get you a new one but it may help ease the pain if you know what I mean."

He didn't protest, and stuck the envelope of money in his pocket. He nodded thanks.

Al nodded back and added, "If you see Petey out there, tell him to get his nose out from under a skirt and get his ass in here."

Rusty headed back through the bar area and spotted Pete at the bar necking with a flapper. He pushed his way through the crowd and got within two people deep of him.

"Pete, come up for air. Hey, Pete!"

Pete pulled back and looked for who was behind the voice.

"Pete!"

He spotted Rusty. "Ah no…I don't have to be to the boat till midnight," he yelled.

"Listen Valentino, Al wants to see you in the dining room."

Pete screwed up his face and looked at the flapper. "I won't be long so wait for me, July."

She pulled his ear. "It's June, my name is June, you goof."

"As hot as you are baby, you are pos-i-lute-ly a July." He half bit, half kissed her neck and pulled himself away.

A man near the bar with his back to Rusty appeared to be all ears when he heard the sound of Rusty's voice. The man turned around slowly for a look and

Rusty spotted him through the crowd. Their eyes locked. Rusty felt a surge of adrenalin shoot through his body like a bolt. The man was Eliot, the idiot troublemaker from Erie T. But what made him skip a breath was Eliot was wearing an eye patch.

His heart thumped in his chest. The slingshot. His hunch was right.

Eliot's good eye pierced Rusty. He stormed through the crowd towards Rusty. "What the hell are you doing here?"

"I would have asked you the same thing, but it explains the bullet holes the Erie T crew found in the *Cherokee.*"

"Screw you."

"Looks like you're the one screwed. What happened—pissed off a linchpin or bailed out on a hooker without paying?"

"None of your business, asshole."

"It might be my business. See, a rumrunner killed a friend of mine and a stone from a slingshot found its way into the killer's eye. I would suppose the killer would be wearing an eye patch."

Eliot tossed his drink in Rusty's face.

Rusty pulled out a handkerchief and methodically wiped off his face and stuffed it back into his pocket while Eliot watched in anticipation, his face red and his good eye bulging like it was about to explode. "Not only do you match the description of the killer, you're sporting an eye patch. I'd say adding it all up; the finger is pointing in your direction."

"And I say your adding is screwy."

"Is it? You and Bill have been regular late night visitors to Vermilion. It was working fine until Hoot couldn't be plied with alcohol. So you decided to drown him and make it look like an accident."

"You're full of shit. If you think you can frame me to get even about our problems at Erie T, you got another thing coming."

"I'm not setting you up. You're doing a good job of hanging yourself. In fact, you're going to hang for two murders that night, and Bill's gonna swing with you."

"A real eight minute egg, aren't you. You got nothing but wind."

"You're wrong. I got your eye for proof."

Eliot threw his empty glass to the floor with a crash and rushed him.

Rusty ducked under him and punched him hard enough to make Eliot gasp, clench his stomach and double over with the wind knocked out of him.

A flapper screamed and one man yelled "fight". Chairs tipped over as the crowd scattered, leaving an open ring around the two men.

Rusty waited with clenched fists, forgetting the pain of his left index finger.

Eliot reached for a bar stool to steady him, and gasped for air like a fish out of water. He remained doubled over, holding his gut as he struggled to catch his breath.

Someone in the crowd said, "he must be a boxer", referring to Rusty. Another voice said "killer upper cut".

He stood over Eliot, every muscle strung so tight it made his body slightly sway. But Eliot did not rise. He waited a few more seconds, anticipating him to rise any moment and attack, but it didn't happen. He breathed deep through his nose and relaxed his fists. Then he flung his hands at the crumpled body of Eliot.

"It's over, folks," the bartender said with assurance, returning a baseball bat under the counter.

Rusty turned to walk away and just as he did, Eliot rose and grabbed the bar stool and raised it over his head. The crowd gasped.

Rusty spun around and saw Eliot brandishing the bar stool high overhead on the brink of smashing it down on him. Before he could react, a set of bear paw-like hands grabbed the stool from behind and ripped it from Eliot's grip and sent it crashing to the floor. It was Giuseppe. He grabbed Eliot from behind, pinning his arms and raising him to his toes. Eliot winced. Then Giuseppe began bending Eliot's right arm at a wrong angle.

Eliot's face contorted in pain. Strange grunts and spittle leaked through his clenched teeth.

"Do you want me to break his arm, Mr. Rusty?" Giuseppe asked.

Rusty was stunned. "I think he got the message."

Giuseppe, having not made his point as much as he had hoped, spun Eliot around. His huge trap of a hand flew to Eliot's throat.

Eliot choked and turned red as Giuseppe throttled him. His hands clawed at Giuseppe's bear paw with the effectiveness of a dog scratching steel.

"You mess with him, I mess with you, *capisce?"* Giuseppe said, shaking Eliot like a rag doll. He threw Eliot to the floor like a bear discarding an empty container. Eliot's hands flew to his neck. Bands of scarlet ringed his neck. He gasped for air.

The crowd was silent. So were the jazz musicians who had stopped playing and stood on their chairs for a better look when Giuseppe entered the fight.

Rusty remained speechless.

Giuseppe looked to him for any new orders.

"Thank you…thanks for your help," Rusty said.

Giuseppe nodded. "I'll make sure he stays put while you leave," he said, looming over Eliot.

Rusty nodded *thanks* and left in a hurry, not knowing Pete was on his heels.

"Rust, wait, what happened back there? I left the bar and the next thing we hear is a rumpus in there and you're in the middle."

Rusty paused so Pete could catch up to him. Inside he could hear the band cranking up jazz again.

"We were right, Pete. Those chiselers that killed the night watchman and the kid's father—they're the ones' with the tugboat, *Cherokee.* It's Eliot all right-the shithead I worked with at the tug yards."

"The one Giuseppe wanted to bust up?"

"That's him. He has an eye patch, Pete. *An eye patch.* Remember the kid hit one of the killers in the eye with a rock from his slingshot?"

Pete's eyes grew wide.

"So I baited him. Said he was going to swing for the murders in Vermilion. I brought up the name Bill, too and instead of denying any of it, he blew his top. You know who Bill is?"

"The other rumrunner with Eliot," Pete said.

"Yeah, and the chief motor machinist's mate on CG157. It was Bill that tried to kill the lighthouse keeper on Marblehead after the attack on me and my wife. The lighthouse keeper recognized his voice from the radio."

Pete looked at him stunned. "Connors's is running?"

"At least Bill is, but I think Connors is involved. I think he's taking a cut from the *Cherokee.* I also think CG157 is hi-jacking runners. In one incident, Chief Stoddard on Marblehead said Connors confiscated liquor but never turned it in or recorded it dumped. There was no record on file of the search or seizure at the Coast Guard station."

Pete punched his own hand. "I told you that son of a bitch was a damn pirate."

"It explains his actions."

"What are we going to do about it?"

"I don't know."

"You know that Eliot fellow will have it in for you for sure."

"He's had it in for me since the day I met him."

"There's a lot of baked wind among runners. Most know your piloting for Al. Connors and Eliot are bound to find out that you are piloting for him. You can bet your mother that *New Moon* and *Calamity Jane* point to the Trapanis. Like you always say, 'just connect the dots'."

Rusty was quiet, but his face was grim.

"So what do we do?" Pete asked, throwing his hands on his hips.

"Not much except to island hop back to Huron and rest up for later." He looked sideways at Pete. "You better not be late."

Pete sighed. "You know that's not what I mean." He snorted. "And as far as that goes, in about ten minutes I expect to be in bed, all right."

"I mean it, Pete. We can't afford to screw up again. We got their appetites whetted and they'll be looking for us. Just be on time and watch your back." He started down the pier to a waiting ferry and paused. "As for what do we do? We pick our battles and when we do, we make Connors and Eliot wish they never picked this fight."

***

He took the ferry to Put-in-Bay where he caught another back to Sandusky an hour later. His pickup truck awaited him at the Sandusky dock. When he started it up, he paused before shifting it into gear to look at *Rising Sun*'s former slip. A sailboat occupied the space now. He shifted into gear and headed out the gravel drive- the same one Di had wobbled across in her high heels to get to *Rising Sun*'s slip the night of the attack. He could see her clearly in his mind's eye picking her way to the boat, her face anxious. He could hear himself say "come on, we'll be fine." He pulled onto the road and imagined himself heading back to Vermilion like he had done for so many years, but when the sign announcing the exit to Huron came up, he turned off but not without doubt. Was Huron and *New Moon* just a dream? He followed the road to the lake and to the boat house with his stamp of renovation. He knew then the nightmare was a reality.

He told Davey about Eliot, the fight, about Giuseppe saving him and CG157 almost certainly hi-jacking runners. He told him they would have to be vigilant. Then he went to bed.

Instead of sleeping, he tossed and turned. His mind raced with thoughts of Eliot, Connors, Huddleson, Hoot and Eddie. He replayed the sinking of *Rising Sun*, the hospital and the beating at the Coast Guard station. Di's screams played like a stuck needle on a Victrola.

Just when he thought his mind would explode from so many surfacing thoughts, the alarm went off. He had pissed away three hours of sleep with replay. He dressed and drank a glass of milk, and then went to the boat and sat on the aft deck, smoking a cigarette. The lake was calm and united in blackness with the sky above. Stars spread thick overhead, twinkling and blinking—some so bright, he felt if he reached up he could possibly touch one. He blew a stream of smoke into the dark sky and watched it rise and dissipate. Indians use smoke to carry prayers to the Great Spirit, he recalled. What would he pray for? But no prayer came to mind. His eyes traced the outlines of the dippers, Cygnus, Hercules and Scorpio. He gazed at the Seven Sisters, Pleiades and the planet, Jupiter, bright and constant.

"So what do the stars say? Good luck, I hope."

Pete's voice made him jump. *So much for being vigilant.*

Tony brushed past Rusty. "Three more runs and I'm outta here. Right? This shit gets old fast."

They headed out into the lake, invisible against the inky waters. The fishing ground where they were headed was mostly deserted except for two small boats outfitted with lanterns for night fishing. In the distance, they could see running lights from various vessels. Some would be pleasure boats still out and about, not wanting Friday night to end, some would be at anchor while the occupants slept off a drunk, while others would be returning from the dance hall on Put-in-Bay or Cedar Point. He knew Coast Guard harbor patrol and picket boats would be among the mix, tearing their hair out trying to weed out the good boats from the bad.

"I can see why we avoid the weekends," Pete said. "The lake is crawling with boats."

"Warm night, clear skies and a calm lake keep them out late."

"It's not the lake, it's the weekend. Dance halls, amusement parks, speakeasies all going hot and heavy like I would be if you hadn't told Al to schedule a Friday."

"The reason was laid out why. Was your head elsewhere when we discussed this?"

Pete hooked an underwater line with the grappling hook and pulled up a dripping bundle from the watery depths. "I'm not saying you're all wet. The hurly-burly out here is a distraction for us."

Tony grabbed the bundle as Pete lifted it to the rail.

Rusty was deep in thought as he looked out into the dark horizon on the opposite rail. "Pete, have you handled the Browning?"

Pete looked sideways at him. "Of course."

"I mean fired it. Target shooting. Know how to operate it. Know what to do if it jams? I assumed it has been sighted, but that's dumb of me—I should have target practiced with it and made sure."

Pete stopped fishing for the next line and leaned on the rail. He rolled his eyes at Tony. "Yes to all of the above. When Al first brought it to the warehouse on the island, we all shot it. What about you? You haven't shot it that I know of, I mean, you were in the war, but you were a merchant marine. What kind of experience with weapons is that?"

"Transporting troops gave me the opportunity to shoot all kinds of weapons including a B.A.R. and a submachine gun. I bet that's not on your resume."

"What do you think they're guarding the warehouse with? Pea shooters?" Tony said.

"Okay, wiseguy, just wanted to make sure you knew what you were doing. After all, I'll have my hands full piloting this boat if things get ugly and you'll be the ones doing the shooting if it comes to that." He paused and thought for a moment. "You know, I could have been shot worse than my finger and not been able to pilot the boat." He looked at Pete. "It's high time you learn how to run this. You've watched me—something had to sink in. After we've loaded, you take the wheel and make the delivery and then pilot her back to port. Handling this boat is just as important as handling a weapon."

What little facial expression Rusty could make out in the darkness, he swore he saw Pete all teeth.

***

Being a passenger was awkward for Rusty. He compensated by fussing over everything Pete did or did not do to Tony's amusement. Pete learned fast and was more astute than he gave him credit for and his opinion of him grew until Pete got cocky and almost swamped the boat at a high speed turn on the way back to Huron.

***

He knew exactly what to do with the money Al gave him for his finger. He drove to the farm and arrived just as Di and Eddie were heading for the pond for a swim.

"Where's your bathing trunks?" Di laughed as she hugged him. "Eddie has challenged me to a race across the pond. You can be referee." She pulled away and ran to catch up with Eddie. "Yell *go*," she hollered over her shoulder.

He walked to the pond's edge. Prince sensed the excitement and was prancing around Eddie. "On your mark…" he said.

Di and Eddie lined up at the pond's edge.

"Get ready…"

She assumed diving position and Eddie followed suit.

"Set…"

She bent low like a spring compressed, so Eddie did too.

"Go!"

Di sprang for the water and entered as smooth as a dolphin and Eddie belly flopped in like a frog. Prince smacked into the water as well, sending up a geyser of spray and dog paddled after Eddie.

He noticed Di had slowed to allow Eddie to reach the bank first. Eddie crawled out and began jumping up and down with his arms held up in victory. Di got out and Prince followed, shaking hard enough that his spray temporarily broke up the victory dance as they ducked for cover. He watched Di hug Eddie, then they waved at him and he waved back.

He turned, laughing to himself, and headed for the garden and found Uncle Fritz picking cucumbers.

"She's making pickles today," he said to Rusty.

"Di?"

"No, my sister. Di's been occupied with Eddie and I think she likes the excuse not to have to work. It's been good for them both. Do you see her face? I haven't heard her laugh so much since she came back here. She taught him how to swim."

"No kidding?"

"He helps me pick green beans and gather eggs and that makes him okay in my book. If only I can convince him how fun it is to clean out the chicken coop." He chuckled.

Rusty smiled.

Uncle Fritz straightened, mopped the sweat on his brow with a handkerchief and picked up the basket brimming with cucumbers of all sizes. "Let's get some lemonade. How's your finger?"

"As long as I don't bump the end of it, its fine. Skin has healed over."

Uncle Fritz nodded.

"How's Eddie doing? I mean, adjusting?"

Uncle Fritz shrugged. "At first it was hard on him. He had nightmares. Di could hear him crying at night. Clammed up about his father still. He's a fish out of water but he's coming around fast. Amazing what a warm, safe place can do a soul."

As they walked towards the house, Rusty said, "I have some money that I want to give you toward the care of Eddie. Towards Di's expenses as well."

Uncle Fritz slammed to a stop. "You make her sound as if she has been a burden."

"I didn't mean it like that. It's just that with an extra mouth to feed, expenses that I haven't kept up with…"

"I know she should be back with you, but to be honest, we enjoy having her back despite the circumstances. I know that sounds selfish on our part. I'm guilty of it the most. She's no burden." He started for the house again. "Someday she'll leave again, and you will also not be around as much. Am I wrong to want you both closer?"

Rusty sighed. "Well…there's Eddie I dumped on you."

Uncle Fritz stopped abruptly again. "Dumped? Dumped? That's one hell of a way to refer to a boy, especially in his predicament. What you call burdens and dumps, I call care and protection." He shook his head in disgust and started for the house again.

"I didn't mean it that way."

"There are a lot of things you've been saying and doing I hope you don't mean."

Rusty frowned. "To get back with what I was saying, here is some money for the boy… for dog food…for shoes. Boys are expensive. Hell, get him a fishing pole and bicycle." Rusty took out the envelope and handed it to him.

Uncle Fritz sat the basket down and leafed through the money. He looked up at Rusty. "Money you've been saving or is this what a run brings in?"

"It's money I earned."

Uncle Fritz looked accusingly at him.

"It's not my share of a liquor run, okay?" He put his hands on his hips. "Just keep it and use it for Di and Eddie. They're my responsibility and I made them yours. This is the least I can do for now, okay?"

Uncle Fritz scrunched his lips together. He hesitated, then nodded and stuck the envelope in his pocket. He picked up the basket again. "I like the part about the fishing pole and bicycle. *Ja*, I like that idea."

***

Rusty pulled the bolt back and let it slam shut. He nestled the stock into his shoulder, cocked his head and sighted down the barrel. One hundred yards away, an "x" painted white on the trunk of a 75' spruce tree appeared in the sights. He squeezed the trigger and a single round exploded from the muzzle. The recoil buried deep into his shoulder. The crack of the repercussion bounced off the side of the warehouse and echoed through the forest beyond the inlet.

"About 8 inches below center," Pete said lowering the binoculars. "You're gonna have to do better than that, Pop, if your tugboat pal tries to deep-six you next."

"Probably needs to be sighted," Rusty mumbled.

Pete laughed. "Don't go looking for excuses. It's been sighted. Only thing need sighting is you."

Rusty snapped the gun up to his shoulder, aimed at the "x" and squeezed off six rounds. He lowered the barrel as Pete checked out the target with binoculars.

"Oo-wee. Our aim improves as our temper rises," Pete said. He traded the binoculars for the Browning so Rusty could look.

He looked through the glasses and saw all six shots centered on and near the center of the "x."

"Guess you were just a little rusty, Rusty." Pete snickered. "Maybe you should handle weapons and I'll pilot."

"Thank you, but I think I'll keep my hands in both."

Pete grinned. "Try your hand at this." He picked up his Mauser, aimed at a lake gull on a pylon fifty feet away.

"Stop!" Rusty said.

Pete lowered the pistol before shooting off a round and looked at Rusty. "What?"

"Bad luck."

"Bad luck? What? You talking about the gull?"

"Yeah. Shoot that bottle floating in the water over there instead."

Pete snorted. "Killing an albatross is bad luck. I remember that from school when we were forced to listen to that dreary poem. Gulls are nothing more than garbage mongers." He leveled the pistol and fired off a round before Rusty could stop him again. The bullet slammed into the bird with an explosion of white feathers. It fell with a splash into the water."

"Sailors believe they are the souls of lost sailors," Rusty muttered under his breath.

"Lost souls? Who in the hell would come back as a garbage eating bird?"

Rusty picked up the B.A.R. and headed down the dock towards the warehouse.

Pete hesitated, shrugged, and then followed him."I don't know any lost sailors, so the bird couldn't be anyone I know."

Chapter 62

The Bass Islands were vague in haze as *Calamity Jane* passed them on her way to the fishing grounds. She churned her way across the flat lake, parting the blue-green waters with her bow.

Joe threw up twice over the side of the tug, not from seasickness but from a hangover from the previous night. Each time he vomited, Lou snorted in disgust. The second time he raised from the side, Lou flicked his spent cigarette at his head. When the Calamity Jane reached the fishing grounds, the two brothers set to work and began stringing the line and lowering the bundles of booze over the side.

Earlier that morning, Rusty was snoring loudly in his bedroom when Davey departed the boathouse on the *Calamity Jane.* For the last few nights, he could hear Rusty tossing and turning in the room next to his. No, he decided, he would not wake him. Not only did he know he could cross the lake to the fish shanty warehouse on the Canadian side himself, he wanted to prove to Rusty he could do it, so he let him sleep for what he felt by the snoring, was one of his more deeper sleeps in some time.

The run to Canada and the fishing grounds was uneventful and as Calamity Jane returned up the Huron River and neared the boat shanty, he spotted Rusty on the dock with his hands on his hips.

"He looks pissed," he overheard Joe say to Lou. "What's new?" he heard Lou mutter back.

Calamity Jane pulled up to the dock and Joe tossed mooring lines to Rusty who snugged the boat. Davey killed the engines and the boat floated to a stop, reined in by the mooring lines.

"What in the hell do you think you're doing?" Rusty said.

"The same thing we always do," Lou snapped.

"I'm not talking to you—I'm asking Davey." Rusty boarded and went to the wheelhouse. "Why did you skip out on me?"

"You needed the sleep."

"So you thought you could go it alone to Canada?"

"I didn't think I could, I knew I could and I did." Davey's voice was calm but resolute. He slid around the bench until he reached the side rail and hoisted himself up onto it. He swung his legs over and pulled the wheelchair towards him, and then lowered himself into it by use of his now muscular arms.

As agitated as he was, Rusty couldn't help but silently marvel at his friend's gained strength and agility, but he didn't allow the thought to disrupt his irritation for long. “What if a storm kicked up or the tug broke down? What if you ran into trouble?”

“Weather was calm, day clear and who better for mechanical repairs?”

“So you had a lucky shot, but I recall a certain engineer on the *Iroquois* that said never gamble if you can’t afford to lose. You took a gamble, Davey.”

“The tug is in topnotch condition. I should know that more than any one. The lake was calm. I didn’t throw caution to the wind.”

“You’re forgetting one thing—you’re a runner. If others haven’t already caught on, they soon will. You got Connors out there, hijackers and now Eliot. What would you have done if you have a run-in with them?”

“That’s why we got these,” Joe said, waving his .45 automatic.

“Davey is alone until he picks you up in Canada. He made the crossing alone.” Rusty turned back to Davey. “Eliot is going to fish around until he finds out who I’m running for and what boats I’m using, so where will that leave you if he learns about *Calamity Jane* and you’re out there all alone?”

“His fall out is with you, not me.”

“His fall out is with everyone. Look what he did to Hoot.”

“Davey has the double barrel shotgun at hand,” Lou said.

Still locked on Davey, Rusty’s reply was sharp, “So did Hoot. On the night he was killed, he was carrying a double barrel shotgun and he wasn’t crippled.”

The words bit hard on Davey. He scowled and grabbed the wheels of his chair and jerked them hard, brushing past Rusty without looking at him. He headed directly for the boat shanty. Joe and Lou exchanged glances, and Lou shrugged, grabbed his gear and disembarked, trailing Davey.

Joe was close behind. “Nice going, hard boiled,” he muttered as he passed Rusty.

***

“You’ve been there?” Di said.

“Sure. You mean you haven’t?” Eddie looked surprised.

“Uh, no.”

“I even slept overnight there.”

Di raised her brows.

“You should see it. Rusty built a swing for Davey so he can go up and down floors without help. It’s like the gizmos used by the Swiss Family Robinson in their tree house. They also got a garage underneath that you can drive a boat straight in from the river!”

“On my, it sounds mysterious,” Di said, laying it on thick, though her curiosity was peaked.

“It is. I was told not to go down to the boat garage, but there’s a trap door in the floor above the boat, so I opened it and looked down inside when Rusty was gone.”

“Hmm... so you admit guilt!”

“I didn’t go in there—just like I was told.”

"So what did you see when you were snooping about?"
"A racing boat the color of coal."
Di furrowed her brows. "They have a racing boat?"
"Yes, ma'm. They have two boats—a racing boat and a fishing boat."
"I knew about the fishing boat," she said. "Is Rusty racing?"
"I didn't ask…remember, I wasn't supposed to be in that area."
"Hmm…yes, that's right. Telling a boy not to go there was an open invitation."
"You ought to catch a ride with Uncle Fritz the next time he goes there."
"So he knows about this boat, too?"
"He's knows all about the swing gizmo, but I didn't bring up the racing boat 'cause..."
" Because you weren't suppose to know about it."
Eddie nodded. "Is it all right if I take Prince to the orchard to chase rabbits?"
"Sure," she said offhand, her mind abstracted.

For two days she mulled over in her mind about what Eddie had told her. She even quizzed Uncle Fritz about the boat shanty and then asked point blank if Rusty was doing anything other than fishing and boat building. Uncle Fritz offered to take her there so she could see the place for herself, and it was then she realized she'd been avoiding the place. In her mind, she visualized Rusty still at the cottage in Vermilion- waiting. She knew it wasn't so, but as long as she avoided the boathouse in Huron, the cottage in Vermilion with Rusty biding her return was the image she held tightly to. Seeing the boathouse would shatter all that.

She had a hair appointment in Elyria. Since she had the use of Uncle Fritz's Model A, she forewarned him that this time she was going to be gone for a while because she was getting the *works.* She did get her hair done, only it was a wash and style and she was in and out in a short time. But instead of heading back to the Model A parked in front of the beauty shop, she went to the trolley depot and caught the westbound Lakeshore Electric.

***

It was midafternoon when she disembarked at the little town of Huron. In Eddie's divulgence, he had described his route to the fishing pier and the layout of the area, so when she stepped off the trolley, she knew exactly how to get to the boathouse.

She headed down the dirt road towards the pier, removing her hat halfway there and used it to fan herself. She passed the bait shop and saw a 24- inch thermometer advertising Coca Cola® next to the shop door. It read 95 degrees. She passed two sail lofts and suddenly found herself before a gray painted boathouse. The doors of the lower floor were wide open. It looked dark and cool and inviting. Shading her eyes, she scanned the modest building and saw curtains blowing gently from the open upstairs' windows.

"Hello," a voice called from the dark interior of the bottom floor, "can I help you?"

Her eyes followed the voice to the lower floor. The open door at the other end silhouetted a figure seated in the interior, but it was too dark to see details due to the sun's glare. "Davey?"

"Yes! Di? Come on in and get out of that sun. You look like a wilted flower."

She walked inside and instantly felt relief from the shaded interior. A breeze blew through the open doors.

"Sit down and give your dogs a break," Davey said, "Let me get you a root beer."

He wheeled to the back corner and returned with a bottle. "It's cold. We got us an ice chest down here so we don't have to go up every time we want a drink." He popped off the cap. "I can go up and get you a glass to drink from if you like?"

"No, Davey, this is fine."

An awkward silence followed as Di sipped the root beer and looked about the workshop.

"Rusty's not here, I'm sorry to say. He should be back around 5 o'clock."

"I can't stay long. I just wanted to see the place, hoping I'd catch him here. Is he at work?"

"He went after some parts in Port Clinton and was stopping back in Sandusky to see his boss." Davey was glad he didn't have to lie. After all, Al was his boss in a way. "As far as seeing the place, look away all you like. The living quarters are upstairs. Your husband turned this rundown shack into a real nice place."

"He has a way of doing that." She walked around the shop with the bottle of root beer in hand. She paused at the workbench. "What are you working on?"

"A carburetor, ma'am. The bait shop man is having trouble with his boat's engine."

"Oh." She continued her tour and looked up and saw the harness and swing contraption Eddie had described. "This must be your gizmo for going between floors that Eddie was going on about."

"Yes, ma'am. Your husband built that for me so I can move between floors. If it wasn't for this, I'd be stuck up top… or on the bottom."

She examined the harness and swing. "You pull yourself up with this rope here, right?"

"Just like drawing a bucket from a well. When you go upstairs you'll see the pulley attached to the attic beams. Ingenious, uh?"

"Is it difficult for you? I mean, pulling up your body weight has to be hard."

"At first, I couldn't, but I've had six months to build up my arms."

"How are you doing overall?"

"I'm on top of the game as best it gets."

"I don't know how you do it."

"You'd be amazed at what you can do if you have to."

"I don't want to find out. I don't want to be tested!"

“But Di, you were and you pulled through. It was just in a different way. It takes strength up here,” he said tapping the side of his head, “to make the best of the situations we’ve been dealt.”

She smiled faintly. “You are an inspiration, you know. Do you mind if I go upstairs? I’d like to see what the place looks like.”

“Ma’am, it’s your husband’s place, too. You don’t need my permission.”

Di headed back out into the harsh sun and climbed the steps. She hesitated before opening the screen door, and then she stepped through into the kitchen. Despite the open windows, it was hot as an oven. The kitchen was basic. Her eyes trailed over an ice box, stove and kitchen table with two chairs and a bare light bulb with a dangling string hanging from the ceiling above the table. A deck of cards sat on the table. She was surprised to see curtains and an empty sink. She walked into a room off the kitchen and discovered a bedroom. A small bed sat between a night stand with a lamp and an open window. A dresser sat on the opposite wall with a wheelchair nearby and next to the chair was a hole cut through the floor.

She walked over to it and followed the ropes up through the ceiling where a pulley was attached securely to the attic’s joists. She looked down at the hole in the floor. It was wide enough for a seated man to fit through. Her eyes followed the ropes down through the hole to the workshop below where she saw the top of Davey’s head. He was back to work on the carburetor.

She went into the other bedroom. This had to be Rusty’s, she figured. The bed looked bowed, but it was made and covered with sheets. There was no bedspread, coverlet or quilt. She sighed heavily. A folded blue wool blanket sat on a dresser by the door. There was also a nightstand with a lamp and windup alarm clock upon it. A window opposite the bed had curtains blowing in. The room was absent of anything that identified it as being his. Tears welled in her eyes. *So this is what it has come down to*, she thought. She took one last look around the room, and dried her eyes, and then she took a few deep breaths before heading back down to the workshop.

“So what’s the feminine verdict of the place?” Davey said when she returned.

“A bachelor’s pad none-the-less, though I must say it’s clean and I’m surprised about the curtains.”

Davey grinned. “We’re not wholly without hope.”

She spotted the trap door in the workshop floor. “Does that lead to the boat garage below?” She asked with innocence in her voice.

“Sure does, handy as all heck. You don’t have to go outside to get to your boat plus it shelters it from the elements.”

The rope handle seemed to beckon to her like it must have done to Eddie.

“Go on, you can open it and have a look,” Davey said.

Di hid her surprise at the invitation. She reached for the rope handle and jerked it open. Below, she saw water. There was no boat. “Is this where you keep your fishing boat,” she said, trying not to act disappointed.

“Shoot, no, the fish tug is too big for that.”

“So nothing is stored here?”

Davey chose his words. “We have a smaller boat—a runabout that we use to get around as the fish tug is not practical to use for anything other than fishing.”

“Did he take that runabout to Port Clinton today?”

“As a matter of fact, he did. We needed some parts for the engine and there’s a fellow there that specializes in that type of engine.”

She nodded and lowered the trapdoor shut, disappointed that no coal colored racing boat was garaged below. *Perhaps runabout hidden below a trapdoor was too humdrum for a boy’s imagination.*

She turned to Davey. “I should get back. I didn’t tell anyone I was coming, and they’ll be getting worried.”

“I’ll tell Rusty you were here. He’ll be really disappointed he missed you.” He followed her to the big open doorway. “Ma’am, I just want to let you know what a good man your husband is. When I said it takes strength up here to pull through, I should have added it helps when you got someone to help you pull and he did just that for me.”

Her eyes began to well again. She nodded. “Goodbye, Davey. I’ll see you Sunday-you’re coming to supper.” She hurried down the gravel road back to town and caught the trolley back to Elyria. When she drove into the yard, Uncle Fritz was sitting on the porch steps with Eddie by his side. They each had new fishing poles.

“I was wondering if your beauty shop was in Timbuktu. Eddie and I are going up to Rusty’s place and try these new poles out on the fishing pier. Want to come along?”

***

“Al thinks we should have a third man on the boat,” Pete said landing a soggy bundle of bottles he fished out of the lake. “Says things are heating up.”

“That’s added weight on the boat. She’s at capacity now,” Rusty said. “Adding another person would mean cutting back on the bottles.”

“What should I tell him?”

“Just what I said, we are operating at weight capacity. It has to be one or the other. Can’t do both.”

They fished and stacked the bundles in silence under a canopy of stars. Pete noticed Rusty was quieter than usual, unaware that missing Di‘s visit in the afternoon was the reason he was so sullen.

“So what did you do in the war on the merchant ship?” Pete said, breaking the silence.

Rusty was silent as he dragged the water with his hook, fishing for the line attached to the next bundle. He hooked it, pulled it towards the boat and hoisted it up the side as Pete reached for it. “I was a deckhand. We transported fresh troops, artillery, supplies- even horses and mules to Europe on a 125-foot steamer. It was originally a cargo freighter used for hauling lumber to Great Britain before she was commissioned for war duty. On the return trip back to the states, we brought back injured soldiers and dead bodies." He fell silent again.

"Damn, what a turnaround," Pete murmured. He waited for Rusty to continue.

"On the trip over, the troops were lively... an eagerness to cope with the nerves. Most were scared though they wouldn't admit it...sea sick was the worst thing happening at that point, but the return trip back to the states...," he shook his head, "those faces ...even those alive were dead in spirit." He hesitated and Pete paused with the bundle before taking it to the hold. Rusty continued. "When I first met you, you said you dressed like a doughboy because you thought it made you look keen and attractive to the ladies. I guess I saw too many missing limbs, mangled bodies and shell-shock faces to have keen come to mind."

Without saying a word, Pete carried the bundle to the hold. Two bundles later, he asked Rusty if he ever saw a Heinie submarine.

Rusty looked at him with surprise. "Hell, yes. The Atlantic was full of them. Thick as sharks. Transports were ripe pickings. Stop the troops and supplies from reaching the front—that was their mission as well as terrorize and destroy moral. Shake up the home front by sinking returning ships. We didn't have the fire power or training of a battleship or destroyer. Even though we had destroyer escorts, we felt like sitting ducks. The u-boats prowled the shipping lanes and coastlines hunting for us. They thought of us as sitting ducks, too."

"Were you ever scared?"

Rusty glared at him. "What do you think? Christ, wouldn't you be scared? We were all scared shitless."

"Were you ever hit?"

"Hit? Yeah, we were hit a number of times."

"Which was the worse?"

Rusty snorted. "The one that sunk the ship."

Pete fell quiet. As he hauled the next bundle to the hold, Rusty overheard him mutter, "Two sinkings...not sure I want to be on the same boat with this guy."

***

Something woke him. Davey sat up on his elbows. Was it the breeze rustling the curtains...a dog barking in the distance...a boat on the river? His ears strained for any sound in the darkness, but he heard nothing. He fumbled for his watch on the nightstand and clicked on the lamp. It was 3:28 a.m., too early for Rusty to be back. He clicked off the light and lay back in bed. It was damp with sweat and felt clammy. No breeze floated through the open window but a mosquito did, and it whirred at his ear. He brushed it, knocking it away for the moment and closed his eyes.

The careful sound of the sliding door rolling on its rail sounded from below. His eyes flew open. A faint "clunk" came from the workshop below him. He held his breath and listened. Another clunk. His first thought was Rusty came back early—perhaps a mechanical problem, a connection cancellation or change of plans. He listened in darkness to see what would happen next and more rummaging sounds came from below. He pulled himself up and to the edge of the bed as quietly as he could and peeked out the window by the bed that faced the river. The night held deep shadows and was still save the croaks of frogs along the banks and clicks and whirrs of insects concealed in foliage. He drew a breath and was about to call out *Rusty?* when he spotted a shadowy silhouette of a speedboat with an outboard motor tied at their dock. He narrowed his eyes, searching along the river's bank and the back of the boathouse for signs of life.

As he peered into the darkness, a figure emerged through the doors of the workshop below his window. Despite the obscurity of night and the vantage point from overhead, he knew the figure below was not Rusty, Pete, Joe nor Lou. The figure hesitated outside the doors, scanning up and down the river bank and then the figure turned and began looking up towards his window. Davey pulled his head back into the darkness of the room, hoping the curtains concealed him. He caught his breath, straining to hear. He heard the crunch and scuffle of gravel and guessed the figure to be on the move. He dared a peek out the window and saw the figure disappearing around the corner of the shanty and realized the figure was heading for the staircase.

Davey's heart began thumping. Swiftly he pulled on his trousers and reached for the wheelchair and slid himself into it as quietly as he could. The creak of each step as the figure cautiously ascended the staircase increased the speed of his heartbeat. He wheeled towards the hole in the floor and grabbed the seat to the harness and wrestled it under his rear end. His ears picked up the sound of the kitchen doorknob turning. With trembling hands, he grabbed the rope as the sound of squeaky hinges conveyed the opening of the kitchen door.

He listened as footsteps crisscrossed the kitchen. He took a couple of deep breaths to steady himself and heard the sound of liquid splashing about the kitchen. He smelled gasoline. His heart thumped madly. He pulled himself up from the wheelchair until he was free of it, and then he swung himself into position over the hole and began lowering himself down hand over fist. As he descended through the hole, he heard the footsteps head for Rusty's room and the same splashing sound. With hand over fist in rapid succession, he lowered himself, his sweaty hands slipping on the rope two thirds of the way down. He started to free fall but seized the rope tight with both hands and caught himself before plummeting to the workshop floor swaying below him. He grunted as he caught the brunt of his weight and at the same moment, heard above him the door to his bedroom open. His heart raced and his chest felt tight for want of more oxygen as he placed each trembling hand carefully one after the other to continue downward. The footsteps were now overhead.

Davey reached the workshop floor. If the figure looked down the hole in the bedroom floor, he would surely see him fumbling for his second wheelchair on the shop's floor. Sweat dripped from his face as he reached for the chair and pulled it under him. He released the harness strap and freed himself from the swing, all the while listening to the sound of liquid splattering in his room. Davey settled into the wheelchair and unlocked the wheels and backed away from the hole opening overhead. As he did, he heard the splashing sound stop, a pause, and then footsteps cross towards the hole in the bedroom floor. Davey noticed the harness and ropes were still swinging—the intruder would notice it too.

His heart skipped a beat. He pulled back hard and fast on the wheels and rolled for the open back door of the workshop. The intruder would either come down the hole in the floor or take the stairway to investigate the swinging rope—either way, he figured, the back doors, already opened enough for him to squeeze through, was his best chance at escape. As he listened to the footsteps racing down the stairway, Davey plunged out the opening into the backyard of the shanty. He pulled and pulled on the wheels, rolling and bumping his way at a break neck pace over the terrain as he headed for the dock until a patch of sand froze the tires to a stop. He gritted his teeth and heaved back on the wheels until he thought the veins in his neck would burst. The wheels slowly cut through the sand. He pulled and pulled until the muscles in his arms burned and finally, the wheels grabbed solid ground and he rolled onto hard packed dirt. With a smooth, hard surface under his wheels, he made time to and up the wooden ramp of the dock. He pulled alongside *Calamity Jane* and hoisted himself onto her rail, swung his legs over and lowered himself onto the bench. With the last bit of strength left in his arms bolstered by adrenalin, he lifted his wheelchair over the gunwale, and then slid himself along the rail and untied the mooring lines. His hands fumbled so much he cursed them as he slipped the lines, but once slipped, the fish tug was free. He pushed himself along the bench to the wheelhouse and grabbed the double barrel shotgun from its rack above the windshield. Just as he did, the figure popped out the back of the workshop. He prayed the darkness concealed him at the helm.

Sweat dripped off his nose and ran in streams down his back. He swung the barrel in firing position with his fingers on the triggers and waited.

The figure stood as still as a statue as he surveyed the backyard, dock and along the river bank and Davey guessed he was listening for any sound that would tip off a presence. After a few moments passed, the figure ducked back inside the shanty without noticing *Calamity Jane* drifting from the docks.

Davey acted fast. He turned over the engine and it barked to life, but not before he heard a crash of glass from within the shanty. He looked and saw an orange glow emitting from the workshop. Then he spotted the figure, silhouetted against the glow, running across the backyard and onto the dock heading for the *Calamity Jane*. Davey gave the engine throttle and she pulled away, picking up speed as she headed up river towards the marina and town.

He glanced over his shoulder and saw the shadowy figure jump into the speed boat. It sped towards the *Calamity Jane*. He gave the engine more throttle and realized it was pegged. Looking over his shoulder again, he saw the speedboat coming along side on his starboard. He hoisted the shotgun off his lap and pointed the barrel at the approaching speedboat and fired off one shot. The speedboat cut sharp and took off down river at a break neck speed and disappeared into the lake.

Davey kept his course up river heading towards the marina. As he did, he looked back in horror as flames licked through the shanty.

***

The drop off at *Castle Erie* went routine. On their return home to Huron, Rusty and Pete took turns with the binoculars, watching the running lights of harbor patrol passing north of Vermilion.

Farther up the shoreline, Rusty noticed a faint orange glow. "Pete, see if you can tell what that glow is up ahead."

Pete looked through the binoculars. "It looks like a fire."

"Fire?"

Pete handed him the binoculars. "I think so."

Rusty looked through the glasses. "Looks close to Huron." His voice hinted concern. He studied a bit longer, and then handed the binoculars back to Pete. "It's in Huron." He gave *New Moon* more throttle and she picked up speed.

"It looks like it's a big one," Pete said he took a turn with the binoculars. "Closer to the lake than to town."

Rusty felt the blood drain from his lips. He pressed *New Moon* for speed and she rose in the water, roaring across the inky lake in total darkness towards the orange glow on the horizon.

Pete lowered the binoculars and saw the anxious look on Rusty's face. "It's close to the boat shanty, isn't it?"

Rusty's face was stone. "Too close."

As *New Moon* raced towards Huron, the orange glow intensified and spread further into the sky.

Rusty's heart pounded in his chest. The closer they got, the more his stomach knotted. It was clear to him now that the fire was near the mouth of the river. Without another word, they flew towards the Huron River.

It didn't take long before the skeletal frames of three shanties, engulfed in a raging infernal of orange, became evident. Yellow flames leaped into the night sky.

"Oh, God," Rusty said. His pounding heart sank into his stomach, "Oh, God."

Pete clasped his head; no words came out of his gaping mouth, but he heard Rusty whisper, Davey.

New Moon idled down as it approached the river's mouth. They could see a fire truck and crowd of people, some with buckets and shovels in hand, running down the peninsula dirt road headed for the fire. The river, docks, buildings and running crowd were illuminated by an eerie orange glow. Gray smoke boiled upwards into the night sky.

Rusty passed the mouth and beached the boat on a shadowy slip of sand he knew was there. He and Pete jumped off the boat and joined the surge of people running toward the blazing shanties.

The heat—like the great furnaces of the steel mill, grew intense the closer they got. When they arrived on the scene, they saw pandemonium. People were yelling and running while firemen got down to the business of fighting the fire. The police chief arrived and quickly organized bucket brigades and squads of shovelers to save the nearby structures.

Rusty rushed towards the fire. “Davey!” he yelled as hard as he could over the din. “Davey!”

Pete grabbed him and pulled him back, and Rusty wrestled to free himself, but Pete held on, dragging him away from the flames.

“Davey!” Rusty howled.

His voice sent shivers up Pete’s spine. “Rusty, you can’t do a damn thing now. If he was in there, he…he wouldn’t know a damn thing now. It would be over.”

“No!” Rusty cried. He ripped himself free from Pete, but he stayed in place. He watched in horror as the skeletal remains began to collapse.

“There’s a chance he might have got out,” Pete said.

“He’s crippled, Pete. Just how fast do you think he can get out of a second story burning building?”

Pete’s face was grim. “Give him more credit than that, Rust.”

“Rusty!” A voice shouted in the commotion. The bait shop man came running up. “Rust…I got Davey at the shop. He’s okay. He’s worried sick that you’ll think he’s burned up.”

“*He’s* worried?” Rusty ran to the shop with Pete and the bait shop man on his heels and found Davey sitting in his wheelchair in front of the store. He embraced him. “God, I’m glad to see you.” He was half crying, half laughing.

Pete grabbed Davey’s hand and patted his back. “You’re one lucky skunk, fella.”

Davey looked drained but he was grinning. “I was afraid you thought I was crisp as burnt bacon.”

“ *You* were afraid?”

They turned and watched the fire consume the remains of the shanties.

“Thank the Lord the places on either side were empty,” the bait shop man said.

They stood in silence and watched, and then Rusty turned to Davey. “Do you know what started it?”

Davey looked at him, raised one brow and his face darkened. “More like who than what.”

Rusty looked shocked. “You saying someone started this?”

“I’m saying someone’s out to get us.”

Rusty went ashen.

“That *someone* broke in and spread gasoline around in the rooms and set the place afire. He arrived alone by speedboat with an outboard motor around 3:30 in the morning.”

Rusty was speechless at first. “Did you see his face?”

Davey shook his head. “It was too dang dark. But I can tell you this much, he had no intentions of letting me get away.”

“How did you get away?” Pete asked.

"I heard him break in. At first, I thought it was you and was going to holler out, but my gut told me to stay quiet. I heard what sounded like water sloshing about. Then I smelled gasoline. I knew I had to get the hell out of Dodge fast. I escaped down the hatch and out the back doors and made for *Calamity Jane*."

"Is she okay?"

"Got her out in the nick of time and took her up river to the marina. That scoundrel came after me in his speedboat and I discouraged him by blasting at him with the shotgun."

"Hot dawg! Good for you, Davey," Pete said."

"Did you hit him?"

"I don't know, but he was able to turn tail and run. It was pretty dark and I had no intention of letting him get close enough to shoot me."

"Christ, Davey, I don't know how you managed."

"What do you mean?" Pete said. "Davey manages as well or better as the rest of us. Got more brains than most of us put together, too. I would have thought it was you coming home early, too and walked right into it."

"You'd have slept through it and burned up," Rusty said.

"Davey's escape is quite a tale," the bait shop man said. "Let's go inside and I'll put on some coffee and he can tell more of his hair-raising account."

Rusty pushed Davey into the shop. "I think I'll take a rain check on the coffee," he said. He felt antsy and wanted to get back to the fire.

"Sit for a minute and have a cup with me," Davey said. "It's been a long night."

Rusty paused, then relinquished. Davey looked like he needed his company. "Okay, one cup."

"You boys are going to need a place to stay," the bait shop man said as he lit the stove and put the coffee pot on the burner. "I got some cots I'll set up in the little store room in back and you can stay here until you find a place."

"Thanks, but we can stay on the *Calamity Jane*," Rusty said.

"I'm sure you can, but why not stay out of the elements? Your friend here looks pretty beat."

Rusty looked at Davey. His face was pale and drawn and big bags puffed under his eyes.

Pete rubbed his chin. "It might not be a good idea to sleep on the boat. That asshole is liable to come back and burn it, too."

"Pete has a good point, Rust," Davey said wearily.

"Then it's settled. I'll set up the cots and you fellas stay here. Sleep in as long as you like—you won't be in the way. I'll have the coffee pot on all day so when you wake up you can have some."

"Thanks," Rusty said. "We won't be in your hair long."

"It's no problem at all," the bait man said as he poured the readied coffee, "Just as long as this arsonist doesn't decide to come after you here."

Rusty took a sip. "Have you seen anyone unusual poking about?"

The bait shop man hesitated with the coffee pot and skewered his face in thought. "No, just the regulars. Most out-of-towners fish other places." He sat the pot down. "Oh, there was a young fellow in here yesterday morning asking if you lived nearby. Said he heard you were in Huron now. He used to work with you at the tug yards in Lorain and wanted to stop by and say hello. I showed him which place was yours and told him I saw you and Davey leave by boat and you weren't back yet, so he said he'd stop by again next time he was passing through."

Rusty sat his cup down. "Did he leave a name?"

The bait shop man skewered his face again. "No, don't recall a name. He was an average size fellow with dark hair, but he was distinct all right. Had a black eye patch on his left eye."

Rusty stiffened.

Pete and Davey exchanged quick glances and looked at Rusty.

"You know the guy?" the bait shop man asked.

Without saying a word, Rusty bumped past Pete and flew out the door. He broke into a run, heading towards the cove where he had beached *New Moon.*

"Go after him, Pete," Davey said, "and throw water on his fire!"

"Is the co-worker the arsonist?" the bait shop man asked.

Pete took off after Rusty. He caught up to him before he reached the boat.

"Have you lost your marbles? You can't go out there," he said, panting. "That would be like looking for a needle in a haystack."

He ignored him, so Pete grabbed his arm and pulled him around abruptly. "Don't make me tackle you. Eliot will be long gone—hiding no doubt and if he's not, then he's lying in wait for you expecting you to do just this."

He pulled away from Pete but did not continue on. He put his hands on top of his head. He was breathing hard and began pacing in circles. He reminded Pete of a riled dragon.

Pete approached with caution. "It's probably a trap. Don't you see, the fire might be bait to draw you in…or out. He expects a backlash, hoping you'll be blind with rage and walk right into his trap so don't take the bait, Rust. We need to clear our heads and get together a plan."

"God dammit! God dammit! God dammit!" Rusty shouted. He threw wild punches into the air. "Aaaarrrghh…."

Pete clenched his teeth and watched at a safe distance as Rusty stormed about.

With both fists clenched, Rusty started shaking and biting back sobs.

That unnerved Pete more than the yelling and cursing. He watched in silence as Rusty struggled to gain control. Finally, to his relief, Rusty took a few deep breaths and straightened.

"Come on, Rust, let's head back. Davey's probably casting kittens."

"I feel like I am being ripped apart. I just want to get a hold of that son of a bitch." He turned to Pete. "I should've wrapped the anchor line around his leg and dropped it into the sink when he was screwing with me at Erie T."

"You may get your chance yet. Come on, Rust. Let's call it a day, and then tomorrow we'll put our heads together when we're thinking clearer and go catch us a rat."

Rusty heaved a sigh. "You're right. I know you're right."

Without a word, the two of them headed back to the fire. Rusty's guts were a mixture of rage and frustration. Finding Eliot would have fixed that and more. But Pete was right—the lake was vast and it was ludicrous to think he could find Eliot tonight, and baiting him with the fire made perfect sense. For once, Pete was making more sense than him. As they walked back, he said, "Thanks for stopping me and making sense out of all this."

"Usually it's the other way around—you're suppose to be older and wiser."

"Wiser, but watch the older part, bub."

Neither laughed or mustered a smile.

By the time they arrived back at the scene, orange flames no longer jumped into the night sky. The shanties were now smoldering heaps of charred wood fragments and ash, peppered with fires no larger than camp fires. The area, earlier aglow in an eerie orange light, had reverted back to darkness, and the cries and hustle on the bank were now still as silent sentries watched the blaze slowly die.

"What are you going to do with *New Moon*?" Pete asked.

I'll camouflage her with some brush. Maybe see if I can dock it in Port Clinton until I find something more permanent. Try to get it out of here at nightfall."

The sun was about to break the horizon and the void left by the fire was made glaringly clear by the dawn's light.

Pete clapped Rusty on the back. "Well, old salt, the interurban should be up and running. I'm gonna catch it to Sandusky and take the ferry over to Al's place and tell him what happened, then I am going to look at the inside of my eyelids. You need to do the same thing, pal. Ring Al after you wake—he'll want a meeting for sure." He patted Rusty's back again. "That rat won't get away with this. Oh, and better let Davey know you didn't run willy-nilly all over the lake." With that, he headed towards town.

Rusty remained, staring at the embers. The last thing he wanted to do was sleep.

***

A half mile off Huron's shore, in the twilight before dawn, a picket boat started its engines and slowly headed back to Marblehead.

Chapter 63

With Davey safe and the *Calamity Jane* unscathed, Rusty ruminated not just on the fact that Eliot wanted him dead or scared off at the least, but on the loss of his pickup truck and tools that burned in the fire. He couldn't decide which made him angrier. The tools were expensive and unique to boat building. He had selected, modified or assembled each one to his personal specifications. The furnishings and appliances could be replaced, but the tools were years of accumulation. They were old friends—familiar and true in his hands. As for the pickup truck—it was more than transportation. It evoked a better time. He had taken a wreck, rebuilt it and shared its seat with the love of his life. Eliot destroying the shanty made him smolder as much as the lingering embers, but the thought of him destroying the tools, truck and last vestiges of his and Davey's home life made him burn like the raging inferno that engulfed the shanty.

The other thought that picked at him was whether or not Connors and crew were in on Eliot's scheme. When he wondered out loud to Davey whether or not it was personal or a joint conspiracy, Davey's answer was that anything and everything Eliot did was personal.

Along with Davey's being alive and well, Rusty considered what small blessings he could salvage, like the decision made months ago to bury the money in the yard and not in the shanty's walls or floorboards. When the people and embers had faded away, he return to the site and dug up their jars with the money safely stowed inside, and then he and Davey set out on *Calamity Jane*, on a course northwest to Put-in-Bay and Al's vineyard haven.

***

A maid led Rusty and Davey to the back of Al's two story house where a veranda was tucked between fragrant flowers and sheltering trees. It offered a peek-a-boo glimpse of the vineyards beyond. The dappled shade was an instant respite from the beating sun that bounced off the water on their trip over.

The talking ceased when they arrived at the veranda. Al was seated with his backside to the house, allowing him a commanding view of the vineyards. Also at the table sat Pete, Joe, Lou, Vince and Tony, positioned so as not to obstruct Al's view, thus averting a *why do I want to look at your pumpkin heads when I can be looking at my grapes* tirade. Missing from the group was Giuseppe.

Al's face was grim. "Saints be praised you boys were not hurt. Pete filled me in. The question is whether this diabolical deed was directed at Rusty personally or was it aimed to scare us from doing business?"

No one offered an answer and Al wasn't expecting one. He continued. "My gut feeling is they are one and the same." He turned to Rusty and Davey. "First order of business is you are now homeless and need a place to stay. You can't stay in Huron."

"We plan to stay on the trap net fishing tug and dock here and there," Rusty said.

"What are you? A couple of gypsies? You might as well go buy yourself a tent—same thing. No, Lou says there's an old trapper's shack on Middle Island close to our warehouse. It has a small dock for the runner. The fish tug can dock at the warehouse. When you think about it, it actually makes sense."

Davey and Rusty exchanged glances. Rusty could tell that Davey was thinking the same thing he was, that crossing over was as much figurative as it was literal.

"We prefer to stay stateside."

"What's the difference?"

"A different country for starters. The mainland is our home, whether or not we actually have one, and our families and friends are there."

"Jeez, it's not like I suggested China. Middle Island is in the middle of the pond just a couple of miles from here. What is it—5 or 6 miles northeast?" he said, looking at Lou and Joe who shrugged. "We're doing business out of there and we don't consider ourselves Canucks."

"Davey and I will look for a cottage with a dock to rent somewhere between Port Clinton and Lorain."

Al folded his hands. He frowned. "Let's be logical. It's not safe for you boys around that neck of the woods. You operate out of that area again and the next thing you know we're fishing your dead bodies out of the lake. Middle Island is secluded and safe and until things cool off or get corrected, it just makes commonsense. Rusty, I can see it in your eyes you're bucking me, but this is a quick fix. Just think of it as temporary. As for your former coworker, Eliot…"

"Leave him to me."

Al shook his head. "I'm afraid I can't. We're in this together. He not only interrupted my business, he screwed with my employees and friends and therefore he's screwing with me. Now this thing has been building and it's getting uglier. It's hard to figure who's in cahoots with whom, who's doing business together and why, and who's trying to muscle us, but I do know that every time shit hits the wall, the same names and faces stick. We're going to cool off for a bit with our runs and let our enemies think we turned tail and ran. I want eyes and ears out there. I want palms greased. I want you boys to dig deep and I want to know names." He turned to his family seated around the table, "Let's go hunting, boys."

***

At Al's directive, the runs temporarily ceased, and the Trapani clan spent the short hiatus rubbing shoulders, buying drinks and tailing anyone that might possibly offer them information. The reports trickling back to Al always pointed to a tugboat moored in Lorain on the Black River, a man with an eye patch named Eliot and a tall, bullying man called Bill who was rumored to be Coast Guard. Bill had been spotted more than once with Eliot. But the most interesting report came from a runner who spotted a picket boat off loading crates from a tugboat.

"Was it an arrest? Confiscation?" Tony had asked.

"It was a confiscation all right. But it didn't go back to the station and it didn't end up in the sink," the runner said, slipping Tony's twenty dollar bill in his pocket.

Meanwhile, Rusty and Davey made the trapper's shack as comfortable as possible.

***

Uncle Fritz was grim-faced as he looked over the charred remains of the shanty. If Rusty hadn't telephoned the neighbor who in turn walked over to the farm to inform the family of the fire and their safety, he would have more than likely had a stroke reading about it first hand in the "other area news" tucked in the local daily. As it was, he had found himself taking bicarbonate of soda on a frequent basis to quiet the burn in his stomach.

He sighed as he stared at the sooty shell of the pickup truck. He was suppose to be enjoying the freedoms that come with bachelorhood, but with his brother-in-law and nephews working twelve hour shifts, often seven days a week at the mill, he felt he alone was left to ride herd on the family. The minute he let his guard down, someone always strayed or messed up. The burden of being the voice of reason in all this chaos as well as the half-truths and secrets that infected his principles came with a price—colic being one of them. He wanted to both hug Rusty and kick him square in the seat of his pants.

Di was hell-bent on accompanying him to the scene of the fire, but he and his sister talked her out of it, assuring her Rusty would not be there and she would see him the next day. The fire, the article had read, was the act of an arsonist and he knew no doubt that Rusty's endeavors were at the root and the last thing he wanted was Di in the mix. She was still buying into the idea that he was working for Lyman's Boatworks and that bothered him. It's no wonder men drink, he concluded. As he headed back to his Model A, he made up his mind it was time for the farm to have a telephone installed.

***

Rusty came the next day. He drove up the driveway in a '29 Ford Roadster. Not the dream automobile he had coveted a lifetime ago at the dealership in Vermilion, but another that brought equal satisfaction. He blew the horn incessantly as he drove up the drive.

"Who is that?" Di's mother said as she parted the curtains.

Eddie rushed to the window. "It's Rusty!"

Di burst out the door and raced Eddie to the roadster. "What on earth?"

"Say hello to your new roadster."

"Rusty?"

"We have to replace the truck, so I figure if we have to, let's go for it."

Di placed her hand over her heart. "I don't know what to say."

"Say you like it."

"I do. But the money—you lost everything."

"I didn't lose you and that's what counts. You always wanted a sporty breezer."

"I'm not sure this is the right time. I mean, Rusty, we don't even have a house."

"Hey, there's a rumble seat for me and Prince," Eddie said.

"Jump inside and we'll take her for a spin," Rusty said to her.

Uncle Fritz and Di's mother came out onto the porch and watched as Di, Eddie and Prince jumped into the car.

"A motor car like that doesn't make any sense," Di's mother said half under her breath.

"Sense flew out the window long ago," Uncle Fritz muttered.

Di waved to her mother and Uncle Fritz and the roadster sped out the driveway.

They drove around the countryside until it was almost time for supper.

"You drive it back," Rusty said. "It's your car."

"It's our car," she said sliding into the driver's seat. She popped the clutch and hit the accelerator and the car lunged forward jerking Rusty's and Eddie's head.

"Light foot, old girl—it's not the pickup truck," he said laughing.

"Indeed it's not. She drove it home, gaining more confident as the miles flew by.

They pulled into the driveway and when she braked, Eddie jumped out and ran to the house to report the adventure to Uncle Fritz.

"Since you aced the handling, you can drive me to the depot tomorrow so I can catch the trolley to work," Rusty said as she turned the car off.

"What do you mean? You need this for work and to drive to the farm."

"No, I don't need it. Besides, I bought this for you. It's all yours to take to the beauty shop or Eddie to the park or wherever your heart desires."

She looked at him blankly. "My heart's desire is sitting next to me. How are you getting to the farm?" Her eyes suddenly brightened. "Are you moving in? After all, you don't have a place now."

"There's Davey to think about. He's my responsibility. How do you think they would feel about two more moochers when I already saddled them with Eddie and his dog? That's asking a lot of their hospitality."

"But that's what families are for."

"No, it's my mess, my responsibilities and I need to see to it."

"You're not a moocher. Neither is Davey nor Eddie. Mmm, maybe Prince, though he does let us know when someone drives in the yard." She suddenly pouted. "What about me? You're so busy with all your 'responsibilities.' Where do I fit in the mix?"

"You know where you stand, Di. You've always been front and center."

"Sometimes I don't feel like I am."

"You are behind everything I do. Any feelings you have otherwise are baseless."

She fell quiet.

"Listen, my work is coming to an end. There won't be any more of this back and forth between places and work. I have a couple more things to do and then it's over. I want you to keep the vehicle because I won't have need for it and because it's my gift to you to remind you that I have always put your needs and wants first."

She looked puzzle. "Have you been fired?"

"No. The job's coming to an end."

"Then you're moving back to the farm?"

"I'll build you your own palace."

"I don't want a palace—I want you."

***

Before he left the next morning, he motioned Uncle Fritz to follow him away from the house. He told Di to wait in the roadster.

He handed Uncle Fritz a cardboard shoebox. "Here. I want to give this to you for safe keeping. It's for Di and Eddie." He patted Uncle Fritz on the shoulder. "Thanks, Uncle Fritz, thanks for being the port in the storm." He headed for the car and got into the passenger seat. Di tooted the horn *goodbye* and Uncle Fritz gave a wave.

As they pulled out onto the road, he opened the box. It was stuffed with twenty, fifty and one hundred dollar bills. His eyes grew wide as he leafed through the bills. There were no small ones. On the bottom of the box, under the stack, he found two little bank statement books. He took them out and threw privacy to the wind. He opened them. Di's name was listed as savings holder. He flipped through until he found the entries listing the latest balances. His jaw dropped. Stunned, he stuffed the statements back under the bills and placed the lid back on the box.

The fact that the box held a fortune was overshadowed by Rusty's sudden entrustment of it to him. *Why did Rusty do this? Did Di say something about Rusty's job ending? What did that mean?*

Uncle Fritz tucked his arm around the box and hurried towards the house. What alarmed him the most was that he didn't know how to reach Rusty and if he couldn't reach him, how could he stop him?

Chapter 64

"I thought Al said we were to hunker down," Davey said. His voice was urgent as Rusty poured gasoline into *New Moon*'s fuel tanks. He noticed a .45 automatic tucked in Rusty's waistband.

"I'm done hunkering." Rusty sat the gas cans down on the small wooden dock of the trapper's shack and wiped his hands off on a rag, then tossed the rag into the wheelhouse.

"He's not going to like you taking off like this." He watched as Rusty retrieved two more gas cans and two whiskey bottles and carried them into the cockpit. When he emerged, Davey continued. "Pete's going with you, right?"

"No."

Davey frowned. "You're not making a run on your own, are you?"

"No."

"Then where are you going?"

Rusty didn't answer, but said instead, "You got that double barrel from the *Calamity Jane*, but I want you to also carry this with you at all times." He handed Davey a .38 revolver and a cartridge box.

"Where did you get this?"

"I told Giuseppe I was looking for a piece that would make a good side arm for you. It appeared on the pilot seat of *New Moon* the next day. A box of cartridges was next to it."

Davey raised his brows. He took the gun and looked it over. "I don't know about this, Rusty. I don't like how this is turning."

"I should be back before daybreak."

"Should? And if not?"

Rusty looked across the water towards Pelee Island. It was lost in the evening dusk. "Then you better tell Al I broke his curfew."

"Can you at least tell me where you're going so we have a starting point where to look for your body?"

"Giuseppe knows. A little bird told him where the *Cherokee* would be tonight. For a man of few words he sure has a way of encouraging people to talk."

"What makes you think this snitch will not about face and rat on Giuseppe's inquiry?"

"Inquiry?" Rusty snorted a laugh. "I'd call it grilling myself." He boarded the boat. "That canary won't be singing any time soon—not for tonight at least." He ducked inside the wheelhouse.

"Bear in mind, if you end up in hot grease or worse, I'm stuck here with no boat, no telephone—no one. I'll be stranded!" Davey called out. He frowned as Rusty started the engines.

***

It was 10 p.m. when *New Moon* passed east of Kelleys Island on a SSE course for Old Woman's Creek. She ran without running lights as usual making her virtually invisible. With no load to drag her speed, she made the trip to the south shore in little time.

He cut the engines just off shore and listened intently as he scanned the water and coastline with the binoculars. The night was too late for boaters and fishermen, too early for runners and their connections. Like him, the Coast Guard would be scouting and settling into position. CG157 would be volunteering to watchdog this area tonight—Connors wouldn't want any bona fide law enforcing guardsmen to mess up the drop off.

Rusty lowered the binoculars, started the engines and idled towards the marshes up the shoreline from the creek's mouth. He backed the boat into a marshy cove and winced as a couple of mallard ducks squawked in protest. They swam deep into the marsh and fell quiet again. He found the spot he had scouted out weeks ago, hidden in black shadows by tall reeds and sedges growing higher than the top of the boat. His shallow draft allowed him to put in deep. He cut the engines, dropped anchor and covered himself with a mosquito net. Then he sat and waited, staring out into the dark lake with the binoculars that gave his eyes an edge.

As the night wore on, a picket boat passed a mile off shore. He watched it until it disappeared to the west. It returned a half hour later heading east, only this time about a half mile out. There was nothing secretive about it as its running and mast lights were on. If it was the CG157, it was likely demonstrating a show of force to anyone who may have been in the vicinity.

The soft night under the canopy of stars went unnoticed by him. The lap of gentle waves and serenade of frogs—usually music to his ears, he regarded as interference.

An hour passed, and the picket boat returned. This time it snaked its way along the coastline. A high beam spotlight on its foredeck swept the banks, lingering longest on shadowy nooks. When the light beam approached him, Rusty's instinct was to duck, but he chose to trust the thick reeds, the concealing-effect of the gray mosquito net and the flat paint and lack of detailing on the *New Moon* to make him undetectable among the marshes. The spotlight moved on heading up the coast. He was safe.

He waited until he was out of reach of the spotlight and retrieved the binoculars. He watched the picket boat go up the coast until it was almost out of view, and then watched it turn and head out into the lake. About a mile off shore, it stopped and its lights went out. He smiled crookedly. The guard dog is in place.

A half hour passed, and he wished he would have splurged on padding for the seat. His ass felt flat and numb. He shifted his position and yawned, and then took the binoculars and scanned the lake's horizon again. A black blob on the north horizon caught his eye. He watched it grow. It was running without lights and was on course for the mouth of Old Woman's Creek. He was wide awake now and his sore ass no longer concerned him.

The shadowy boat approached slowly and he could hear its throaty diesel engine. When it got a quarter mile off shore, it came to a stop. Through the binoculars, he could clearly make out the dim shape of it—a harbor tugboat like those of Erie T. The tugboat had placed itself between Rusty and the picket boat. Perfect!

The snitch was straight with Giuseppe, but then who wouldn't be? Two men operated the *Cherokee*, he told Giuseppe. They anchor off shore and use the speedboat to transfer the cases of alcohol to the shallow shoreline or as in this case, up creeks and rivers. Tonight the drop-off was the spot where *New Moon* had delivered once before as a substitute.

Is Connors's chief motor machinist, Bill, the second man on the tugboat?

No. He stays with the picket boat—the crew stays together. Don't know who the second guy is, but the tug's pilot wears an eye patch like he's some frigging pirate.

Rusty pulled off his mosquito netting, weighed anchor, and continued watching through the binoculars.

Fifteen minutes passed and he saw a small shadow depart from the tugboat. It made its way across the water at a fair speed on a direct course for the inlet of Old Woman's Creek. The shape of a speedboat took form, and as it reached the halfway point, he could finally hear the outboard motor. He followed its approach with his binoculars and as the speedboat reached a point just off shore, he could make out the shape of two figures on it and hoped the night was not playing tricks on his eyes.

The speedboat plunged into the inlet and was swallowed up by the jungle-like reeds as it went up the creek towards the dock around the bend.

Rusty wasted no time. He coaxed the engines to life, avoiding throttle and slipped out of the marshes. When he had cleared the shoreline, he gave a little throttle and glided as quietly as a cat's purr towards the tugboat that anchored between him and the Coast Guard picket boat on the opposite side.

He came alongside the tug and saw the bow numbers identifying it as the *Cherokee*. Even in the dark, he could see the big black letter "E" on the side of the wheelhouse. He felt a tug on his heart. Though it wasn't the *Iroquois*, it was still an old friend.

He strained his ears for the slightest of sound, but the only sound was the lap of waves against the hulls, so he threw a line from *New Moon* over the rail of the dark *Cherokee* and crawled aboard it and tied off *New Moon*. He paused and gazed about the silent deck and looked up at the dark wheelhouse. In his mind's eye, he could see Frankie Kopinski seated behind the wheel and leaning out the window yelling, "steady strain, boys."

He sighed. Frankie was long gone, replaced by a heart as dark as the wheelhouse. The muscles tightened in his face. He re-boarded *New Moon* and retrieved the cans and lifted them carefully onto the deck of the *Cherokee*. He lugged one of the cans up the stairs of the wheelhouse, unscrewed the cap, paused again for one last look around and began tossing the contents about, giving extra attention to the pilot's chair. The severe smell of gasoline pervaded the air. He backed down the staircase, soaking each step until he reached the deck, then uncapped the other gasoline can and proceeded to empty its contents about the deck. He soaked the ropes draped over the bow, and coils of line on the aft deck then flung a final wash of gasoline across the deck. He freed the line tethering *New Moon* and jumped aboard her. On her deck were two gas filled whiskey bottles and the rag he had tossed aboard at the trappers' shack. He uncorked the bottles, releasing the smell of gasoline and ripped the rag in two pieces, stuffing their ends into each whiskey bottle. He flicked his lighter and lit the ends of one rag, waited for the flame to get a good bite and threw the bottle into the open window of the wheelhouse. Then, without hesitation, he lit the other and threw it onto a coil of gasoline saturated lines on deck. The flames leaped to life and sped across the boat like a hungry piranha consuming the gasoline. He turned over the engines, throttled up and sped west, keeping the tugboat in line between him and the picket boat. After he got a half a mile away, he brought the boat down to idle and turned to face the cremation of the *Cherokee*.

The tugboat—like the shanty—was of aged, dry wood, and the flames swept over and through it quickly, consuming the lines, the stairwell, and the wheelhouse. As the fire fed off the hull and decking, the flames leaped into the dark sky and set the water around the tug aglow in orange light. The glow could be seen for miles in all directions.

The men in the speedboat would not know it yet since they were imbedded in the marshy cove, but the picket boat couldn't miss the fire. CG157 would by now be on its way to check out the burning tugboat, he figured, passing its investigation off as a legal duty.

Just then an explosion blew apart the *Cherokee*, and he knew the flames found the diesel tank in the engine room. Pieces of flaming wood and hunks of metal blasted into the sky as glowing ash and embers mixed with the stars above and then rained down around the tug.

If Eliot hadn't known before, he ought to know there's trouble at the tug now. He watched for another minute before turning the boat north for a wide berth towards the Canadian border.

***

The incident of the burning tugboat slipped newspaper reporters, but word of it swept through the runners and made its way into the Coast Guard report. Luckily, the CG157 happened to be in the area to rescue two men from the burning boat.

The boat, a charter fishing vessel, was completely destroyed and remnants sunk to the bottom of Lake Erie, the report read.

Back at Middle Island Clubhouse, the clientele were abuzz over the incident. They knew the boat was a tugboat—not a charter, that it belonged to Eliot and that it was running, but no one—not even Connors, Eliot or Al knew if the fire was anything other than an accident started by a fuel leak or a burning cigarette or any numerous causes. Davey, on the other hand, had a pretty good hunch that he kept to himself.

When Al heard the news of the *Cherokee*, he was ecstatic. "Couldn't happen to a nicer guy," he proclaimed as he passed cigars around the table. "It's back to work boys."

***

Rusty stood up with paint brush in hand as Joe approached him.

"This'll be ready for morning, right?"

"It's done now," Rusty said. Al had re-registered the *Calamity Jane* and Rusty painted the new numbers and name on her. Davey re-named her, *Annie O* after Annie Oakley, only he regretted the boat was not the straight shooter of her namesake.

At 4 a.m., she left Middle Island for the fishing grounds with Lou, Joe and Davey. Rusty, Al advised, should sit it out as inspections of fishing boats were on the increase and they could not risk Connors or Eliot or anyone that recognized Rusty as connected to the trap net fishing boat. "There is no such thing as being too cautious. We have to tiptoe with eyes wide open."

That night, after midnight, *New Moon* left the trapper's dock and headed for the fishing grounds. Al didn't hesitate reducing a couple of cases so Joe could continue to ride along with Rusty and Pete. *Preventative measure* was the words he used. Joe brought along a Tommy gun, and Rusty raised his brows when he saw the machine gun. "If the action ever gets that close," he said to Tony, "I prefer my pump action 16 gauge."

New Moon, now with a crew of three, passed within binocular sight of a row of mother ships anchored just over the border and Rusty pointed out a U.S. Coast Guard Six Bitter shadowing the flotilla. More concerned with a show of force than surprise and pursuit, its spotlights punctuated the darkness.

New Moon flew over the border and into open U.S. waters, heading SE towards the fishing grounds. In the far distance off starboard, they spotted a Coast Guard cutter heading north. The night was theirs.

Joe marveled at the speed and smooth ride of *New Moon* and the mystery that came with the empty, dark lake. "If we go back to two on the crew, I'm going to switch jobs with you, Petey," he said at one point.

"Tell me that after you've hauled up hundred soggy bundles."

They reached the fishing ground where *Annie O* strung her line and began hauling nets filled with bottles of liquor. By 3:30 a.m., they were on their way to the desolate dock at Beaver Creek near Lorain. They off loaded, and Vince and

Tony drove the bundles away in the milk delivery truck while *New Moon* headed back for Middle Island across the border.

The night went without a hitch and Joe said if he had known it would be this much of a lark, he would have insisted Al assign him the runner instead of the fishing boat.

***

A quarter mile away, hidden behind a wooded cove, the captain of a picket boat watched the exchange between *New Moon* and the milk delivery truck. He trained his binoculars on *New Moon* as she pulled away and watched until the night swallowed her.

Chapter 65

"Dammit, Pete, what were you thinking?" Al cuffed him alongside his head to the amusement of Vince and Joe who snickered.

"What are you talking about? I am thinking! Tell me this is not going to give us an edge?"

"Oh this will give us an edge all right, it will also get big noses poking up my ass, wise guy."

Vince and Joe turned sober.

Rusty walked into the warehouse with Davey following behind. A small cluster of Trapanis were gathered around a packing table.

"Come see what your partner did," Al said with sarcasm when he spotted them. "Too bad he didn't have a zipper in his head so I could stick some brains in it."

Rusty and Davey approached the table and saw a radio as the focus of the Trapanis' attention.

"Ship to shore?" Rusty asked.

"Lifted from a Coast Guard boat by yours truly," Al said with a nod towards Pete.

Davey raised his brows and Rusty snorted. Vince and Joe exchanged glances.

"That could come in handy," Rusty said, looking the radio over.

Pete shot Vince and Joe a smug grin.

"How did you get your hands on that?" Davey said.

"Tell 'em Houdini."

"I waited till the coastie crew came ashore then I slipped on board, popped some screws and took it."

"No, no, that's not the whole picture," Al cracked. "Tell 'em where this took place—that's what's got me hot under the collar."

All eyes riveted on Pete. "The boat was docked at the South Bass lighthouse station …"

"Which," Al interrupted, "happens to be located down the road from my home." He frowned at Pete.

"What's this have to do with you and the vineyard?"

"Come on, Petey, it's a small island. It would have to be someone close by to know when the boat was there and empty. I'm a vintner with a booming grape juice business. You pilfered equipment belonging to the feds. They are going to be sniffing around to see if anyone knows or sees anything, and who do you think they will start with?"

"You're not the only one that lives in that area."

"But maybe they figure that I am the only one that may have need to eavesdrop on coasties. How do you know that we are not already suspected of running? There are a lot of runny mouths and open ears at the clubhouse."

"Thick as thieves, Al."

"Bullshit, Petey. You're a dupe if you believe that. Reality among rumrunners and bootleggers is copping territories and eliminating competition. It doesn't matter if that's not our agenda because there is a dozen more bad asses doing business here that would like nothing better than to present your head on a platter in order to take over your contacts."

The grins and smirks suddenly stopped, and Al allowed his words time to sink in. "We may be working the fringes, but this is no lark. We are in the manure and no matter how clean we try to stay, we are going to get dirty and attract shit flies."

The gathering remained quiet and Rusty finally broke the silence. "We got this radio now, so we might as well use it. If we are suspect, we'll have a heads up. If not, we'll know where the patrol boats are."

He looked at Al and Al nodded begrudgingly.

"All right, then. The runner is the logical choice for having the radio which also gets it away from my place," Al said.

Pete flashed a grin at Vince and Joe.

"Don't go patting yourself on the back, pal," Al said to him. "And don't ever jeopardize my vineyard and our family again."

***

Rusty and Davey spent late afternoon wiring the radio in *New Moon*. The August sun was setting earlier now and despite daytime temperatures still climbing into the 80s and 90s, the nights were cooler and Rusty found it easier to sleep before a run.

They finished the wiring before dusk and then turned the radio on. Static transmitted from the speaker and Davey did some adjusting with the wires and knobs. There was a crackle, then a broken voice. Davey played again with the knobs and a voice came over clear.

"...capsized. Two in water. Over."

"That's affirmative. No assistance required. Over."

Davey and Rusty exchanged looks and smiled.

"Sure you don't want to leave this with me at the trapper shack? Could be quite entertaining," Davey said.

"Maybe we can talk Pete into lifting two more so you and Al can each have one."

Davey chuckled. "I'm sure Al would go for that."

Rusty pan-fried a supper of fish and diced potatoes after the mosquitoes drove them inside, and when they finished the meal, he went out to the small dock for a last smoke.

The sun had long set and all that remained of day was a ribbon of bright blue along the western horizon. He wondered if Di saw it too. He smoked his cigarette and watched the light fade to dark. In another month, it would be one year that the world turned upside down. *Or did it really start unraveling before that? Davey's accident...Erie T going under...the grape juice runs with Rising Sun...*

He examined his remaining half finger in the last light, and then headed back to the shack.

Davey had lit the kerosene lanterns and started a game of solitaire. He looked up from the cards when Rusty came in. "Hitting the hay?"

"Last year at this time, could you have pictured yourself doing this?"

"Last year at this time? Mmm, I was in a nursing home—yeah, I could picture myself playing solitaire." Then he saw Rusty's sober face and fell serious. "You mean running?"

"I mean all of it."

"Well, my prospects were quite dim at this time last year, Rust. Could I picture myself piloting a trap net boat? No. Could I picture myself living in a trapper's shack? No. Never could picture rubbing elbows with rumrunners and the Trapanis—it just wasn't in my circle. But then, I couldn't picture myself anywhere but in a bed at a nursing home. You have some regrets?"

"I regret letting this go on so long and losing my focus."

After a moment of silence, Davey asked, "And what exactly is your focus?"

"I built the boat for Connors. I agreed to rum running to get me near him but instead, I got caught up in running."

Davey remained quiet.

"Good money."

Davey nodded. "And a thrill for two ex—tugboat salts."

Rusty smiled but it was fleeting. His frown returned. "It's getting dirty and nasty."

"The wrong side of the track tends to be that way. Maybe you didn't lose your focus...maybe you just wised up. Di and Eddie should be your focus anyways."

Rusty nodded. "I'm going to tell Al we're packing it in after August. Give him a heads up so he can make other arrangements. He said we are free to quit when we want unless you want to continue piloting for him?"

"No. We are set for life. Time to get while the getting is good. What about *New Moon*, though? They'll want the boat...can't see them letting us and the boat go."

"It's my boat, Al and I agreed on that, but I'll sell it to them. I won't have need for a boat like that anymore and they got the money to buy it. Running has been lucrative for all of us. Pete's capable of running the boat. I've let him handle it and he's a quick study."

"And Joe and Lou can handle *Annie O.* Made sure they knew how in case something happened to me."

Rusty nodded.

"And Connors?"

Rusty was quiet. "I wanted nothing more than to kill that son-of-a bitch. Now…I want nothing more than to be back with Di. I guess I lost my heart."

"No, you found it again. Your moral compass kicked in."

Rusty half smiled, as he imagined Uncle Fritz's compass snug in his watch pocket. "Then it's settled. I'll talk to Al and tell him we will run until the first of September and leave the Trapanis to bigger profits." He gave Davey's shoulder a pat, and Davey could see his spirits were lighter.

"Besides, I got to focus on you, too, buddy, see here," he pointed out the Queen of Diamonds on top, "You holding on to that Jack of Spades for a reason?"

***

Al listened with intent as Rusty informed him he and Davey would be calling it quits after the August runs. Without blinking an eye, he upped their share and when Rusty had convinced him it wasn't about money, he said he understood and eventually the frown faded from his face. He hated to see them go and was grateful for their services, but they had an agreement and he would honor it, he said.

Before Rusty could mention selling *New Moon*, he offered to buy her. She was born to be a runner, he said and not only would it take time to find a replacement, there was nothing out there her equal. She was one of a kind, he added, like Rusty—both legends on the lake.

Chapter 66

Davey was going to miss old *Jane* or *Annie* as she was now called. He savored each run to string line. He loved the lake as much as Rusty—the rock of the boat, the lap of waves, the sun sparkling off the crests, the stretch of endless water, the cries of gulls, the unbroken wind and the thrill of whitecaps. He hoped Rusty's plans for the future included boats and him. If not, he would look for a cottage on the water near Port Clinton and see if Mike could use an extra hand at the marina. Maybe build a dock with a ramp and buy himself a boat for fishing. That is if Rusty would be willing to help set him up initially. He could afford anything he wanted now—just couldn't afford total independence and that was one burr under his saddle he would have to ignore.

Lou seemed less sullen on the runs and Davey wondered if it was because Lou was glad to soon be rid of him or happy that he was to be the new pilot of *Annie O.* It wasn't until one morning after their line was strung, that Lou told him he was going to miss him and asked if he would still fix their boats. Lou's sentiment nearly floored Davey who had come to think of Lou as emotional as a boot.

Giuseppe seemed to mellow a bit as well. He even left Al's side long enough to join Rusty at the clubhouse bar and buy him a beer one evening much to Rusty's amazement. Halfway through the beer, Rusty asked him how long he had known Al, and Giuseppe looked surprised that Rusty didn't know.

"Since we were teeny *ragazzos.* My padre and his were cousins. My family went back to Sicily when I was eight; I come back at twenty-one and Al's padre gives me a job. Then I work for Al."

"For cousins, you and Al don't look anything alike," Rusty said as he sipped his beer.

"I take after my *madre.*"

Rusty nearly choked on his beer and hoped Giuseppe didn't take notice.

***

Like Davey, Rusty also savored the August runs. No matter what course his life took after month's end, he was pretty sure it wouldn't include racing across the lake under a canopy of stars. The allure of the run was as powerful as the money was lucrative and he beat guilt down every time it tried to rear its sanctimonious head.

***

New Moon coursed its way through the dark rocks and slipped into the dimly lit tunnel under *Castle Erie.* On board was $50,000.00 in booze cargo. Rusty and Pete kept an eye on the boat's relation to the tunnel's stone walls while Joe gaped in awe at the subterranean passageway.

"It's one thing to hear about this, but to see it is mind-boggling," he said. "Do you think this tunnel was built because of Prohibition?"

"The bartender told me it was built for runaway slaves. Said this place was a station on the Underground Railroad," Pete said.

"Fat chance," Rusty said. "The castle was built in 1894. That's thirty years after the war." He slowed the boat to almost a stop as they approached the underground dock and he and Pete with the Mauser in hand, scanned the area. The men that usually greeted them to unload the boat were not there. The empty dock made Rusty uneasy. "Pete, do you recall the sentry at the entrance to the tunnel?"

Pete thought for a moment. "Come to think of it, no."

"I don't like this," Rusty said narrowing his eyes to probe the shadows. "Where's Joe?"

"He went on deck to tie off."

"Tell him to get his ass back in here quick and be quiet about it." He glanced down and saw the Tommy gun on the passenger seat where Joe had left it and then returned to scanning the area, his eyes darting to all the shadowy places.

"Joe...Joe," Pete whispered, sticking his head out the cockpit. "Get in here."

"What about tying off?"

"Forget about it. Just get in here now!"

As Joe crossed the deck, Rusty spotted a sharpshooter in the shadowy rafters over the dock. His rifle was aimed on Joe. Rusty's heart jumped to his throat.

At that same moment, there was a commotion on the dock. One of the men who usually greeted them stumbled out onto the platform. His face was bloody. "Get out of here. Cops. It's a trap."

A shadowy figure struck him from behind and he collapsed to the dock.

"Hit the deck," Rusty yelled, and cranked the wheel and threw the throttle into reverse.

The maneuver caused Joe to fall to the boat's deck just as a shot went off with a loud crack, missing him. He scurried on his belly like a lizard towards the cockpit.

Another shot glanced off the side of the cockpit and the echo rang through the tunnel.

The dock suddenly erupted with men brandishing weapons. They opened fire upon *New Moon* with handguns, shotguns and rifles. The tunnel was thick with flying lead that whizzed and pinged past *New Moon* and those that found her, struck with dull, heavy thuds.

Rusty gritted his teeth as he jockeyed the boat about face. Every shot that rang out was like an electrical shock to his heart. Seconds felt like minutes.

It took him a moment to realize that Pete had grabbed the Tommy gun and was strafing the dock and rafters. The noise was deafening and fearsome as the machine gun hammered away with rapid fire and staccato, brilliant bursts of muzzle flash.

The whole tunnel came alive with blinding muzzle flashes and ear splitting weapon reports, and he felt like he was inside a fireworks storeroom that had been torched.

With Pete alone returning fire, he wrestled *New Moon* around until her bow faced the entrance. *Where the hell was Joe?* Ricochets continued to ping around the tunnel and strike the boat's armor plating. He winced each time one hit the cockpit or ricocheted off the windows. He knew Pete couldn't hold off the shooters alone and was putting them in jeopardy by firing out the open side window that would allow bullets to find their way into the cockpit. He was about to yell for Pete to shut the window when he spotted the boat's flare gun attached to the cockpit's wall- *a diversion to buy time.*

He grabbed it and cocked it. "Step back, Pete." He aimed past Pete and out the open window beyond the boat's stern towards the dock. He fired.

The tunnel exploded into a huge ball of blinding orange light that sent sparks showering the dock and channel. He slammed the throttle up and *New Moon* lunged forward. He could hear Pete's voice lost in the commotion yelling for Joe as they sped through the rolling bright orange smoke.

New Moon roared through the tunnel and burst out the opening under a barrage of bullets fired from the rocks that guarded the opening. The bullets struck off her plating and pierced her sides. Up ahead, he saw a wall of lights instead of the black void of the lake and realized something was blocking their way out of the rocky maze. It only took a second for him to realize it was a boat setting crossways. The words, Lorain Harbor Patrol were emblazed on its side.

"Fuck!" Pete yelled.

Rusty could see muzzle flash sprout along the patrol boat's side.

He jammed the throttle and *New Moon* picked up speed and bore down on the starboard side of the patrol boat.

"Are you crazy?" Pete screamed.

"Hang on, Pete, I think we can squeeze past!"

"You are crazy!"

The patrol boat opened fire with a mad minute of rifle and handgun rounds, the bullets barely clearing the top of the cockpit. Rusty ignored the warning and pressed on. The patrol boat, seeing *New Moon* wasn't deterring, lowered its aim and bullets began striking about the cockpit with clinks and thuds.

"You're going to kill us," Pete hollered at Rusty as he ducked for cover.

Rusty whipped the wheel starboard at the last minute and when the crew of the patrol boat realized *New Moon*'s intent was to squeeze between their bow and the rocks, the skipper moved the patrol forward to cut him off.

Rusty, seeing this, pressed *New Moon* faster as he raced to beat the patrol boat to the rapidly narrowing opening. He clenched his teeth and held tight to the wheel.

Pete raised his head to look and saw both boats bearing down on the small space. He fell back to the floor and covered his head.

New Moon, with her steel plated razor sharp bow, smashed through the advancing bow of the patrol boat, shirring the end off. The sound of wood splitting and metal grating joined the bullet din. She cut through the bow's tip without slowing down under a shower of wood splinters and roared off into the cover of night.

The roar of the wide open Liberty engines and the diminishing gunshots, made Pete raise his head for a peek. "I can't believe you did that. I can't believe we are in one piece," Pete gasped as he pulled himself up. His relief didn't last long. "Joe's back there. He fell off in the cave. I don't know if he got shot or just fell off the boat."

"Did you see him fall?"

"No, but I saw him in the water. He was alive. He was splashing about. We got to go back for him before they kill him, Rust."

"We can't go back. You said he was alive in the water, right? Then Joe will be taken alive."

"He's my cousin, Rust!"

"Pete, listen. It was a raid. Those were cops. They are not going to kill Joe—they'll want to pump him for information. They'll arrest him and if he's hurt, they'll do something about it, but they're not going to kill him. Putting him in the slammer is good publicity."

"You better be right because if we abandoned him and they torture or kill him, there will be hell to pay and it will include more persons than those buttons."

Rusty's jaw stiffen. "You're going to have to trust me on this one, and if I am wrong, let the chips fall where they may. But I won't be wrong."

Like a shadow skimming over the water, *New Moon* raced for the Canadian border.

***

Wounded Rum-runner Escapes Hospital

Rusty looked up from the newspaper as the waitress poured coffee into his cup. She saw the headlines.

"They say he tied bed sheets to a steam pipe by the window and that a black car was waiting for him."

"Says here, a man walking his dog saw the whole thing and called police," he added.

"I heard cops had a dragnet set up from Sandusky to Avon."

"Coast Guard, too."

"Did you read his armed guard left long enough to just get a sandwich at the hospital cafeteria? Wasn't gone for more than five minutes." She shook her head.

"They don't say *letting your guard down for a second* for nothing."

She laughed. "And to think the most exciting thing in my life is a perm and a hair color. Hubba-hubba," she said as she turned away.

He smiled. What he could have told her was the black get-away car was a Packard, and that the armed guard took a piss break, not a lunch break. He could have also told her that the escapee never got farther than *Sam's* in Vermilion.

***

Joe had taken a bullet in his right side and his thigh. As luck would have it, no organs or arteries were involved. The cops had fished him out of the tunnel's channel and took him to the same hospital in Lorain Davey had been sent when he was injured. He had surgery and recovered quickly, but had bouts of pain and blackouts every time a police detective came into his room for questioning. His handsome looks and puppy dog eyes made the nurses all the more protective of his peace, quiet and rest.

Pete had sent June, his squeeze he had met at Middle Island Club, in as the grieving sister who couldn't understand how her brother could have been led astray by demon rum. So convincing was her distraught and so distracting were her charms, she was more comforted than questioned by law officials.

While Joe monitored the habits of his guards and nurses, the Trapanis hatched a plan, using June as their liaison. When opportunity knocked, the black Packard was waiting, and all June asked in return was a ring of engagement from Pete, or she would sing like a canary.

***

Rusty stuck the tip of his little finger in one of the dents in the armor made by the bullet strafe that had peppered *New Moon.* "Pretty good dent for what they were using."

Davey raised his brows. "Imagine if they had some real meat on them."

Rusty spotted Al approaching and stood up. Giuseppe, Tony and Pete accompanied him.

"Hey, you're not selling me a bum boat, are you?" Al cracked. "This animal was mint when I agreed to buy it."

"She took some fire that's for sure."

"So much for bullet proof glass," Al said looking over the cockpit's shattered rear window.

"It did its job all right. If it hadn't been for that, Pete and I would have taken hits—maybe killed."

"Well, we'll get this glass taken care of before the next run," Al said. "The holes and dents can stay. They give her character."

"How's Joe?"

"Mending and crabby. We have an aunt who's a nurse who checks in on him. Says the crabbier they are, the faster they mend." He propped himself against a dock pylon. "I talked with the proprietor of the castle and told him the tunnel was too risky with just one way out- just like you said originally. So our arrangement is for Vinnie and Tony to deliver the goods in the milk truck. Milkmen making their rounds, delivering milk, butter and cream to the restaurant at cock's crow. Tony will take Joe's place on *New Moon* and you'll drop off the castle's booze at the Beaver Creek dock. He will then disembark and he and Vinnie will take it from there. Sound good to you?"

Rusty nodded.

"I know Petey will sleep a whole lot better with this arrangement," Al said.

"Yeah? You would have shit yourself if you had been there," Pete said.

Al snickered. "That's why it's good to be the top dog."

***

When Uncle Fritz read the headlines, his heart skipped a beat. The police did not release the name of the wounded runner to the newspaper, but he was pretty sure Rusty would be involved because of the area concerned. He rubbed his hands over his face and mumbled *scheisse.*

Di came into the room. "Are you okay, Uncle Fritz?"

"It's nothing, *liebste.* I shouldn't read the news when I already have a headache." He folded the newspaper. "I think I'll go to my shed and see if there's a beer with my name on it." He tossed the newspapers onto the chair and left the parlor.

Di, half concerned and half puzzled, watched him leave. She picked up the papers and opened it to the article he was reading. It was about an escaped rumrunner that had been wounded in a raid in Lorain. She skewered her face in puzzlement and placed the papers back to the chair. Then she headed for the shed.

She found Uncle Fritz not with a beer but lost in his thoughts. His brows were drawn taunt and his face ashen. She startled him when she entered the shed. "What's going on? You look like someone walked on your grave."

"Not mine."

"What's that mean?" She looked confused.

"Nothing."

"Uncle Fritz, I know something's wrong. Is Rusty okay?"

He sighed. "I don't know where he is or how to contact him so how should I know? If he shows up Sunday, we know he's okay, ja?"

Di folded her arms. "I'm not stupid. I know something about Rusty has had you in knots for the past six months. I can see the strain in both your faces when you are together. Something is vexing you. Don't think Mom and I haven't noticed your bicarbonate sodas." She dropped her arms and marched over to him. "Level with me, Uncle Fritz. He's my husband. Don't you think I wonder why he hasn't found a place for us by now or come live at the farm? He's got a separate world he's shut me out of and I demand to know why, so if you know something, tell me...please."

Uncle Fritz turned to her. "Ask him what you asked me next time you see him."

She looked taken back. "Is there another woman?" There was panic in her eyes.

"Good God, no!" Suddenly, the running didn't seem so bad to him. "No, no, that's not it at all." He crossed over to her and put his arms around her. "He loves you dearly, and that's why he's doing what he does."

She raised her head from his portly chest. "What does he do?"

He released her and scratched his chin. "He should be the one to tell you, but I'm sick of secrets."

Her eyes grew large. "Secrets? What secrets?" Her eyes suddenly narrowed. "I have a right to know!"

"God, how do I say this?" he mumbled.

She flew in front of him as if to block his escape. Her eyes were demanding. "Give me some credit. We've been through a lot this past year. I can handle anything but another woman."

He sighed heavily. "I thought he would tell you in time or you would have questioned his actions by now. Maybe we all are trying to sweep things under the rug, ja?" He sunk to his stool by the work bench. "Let me start this way, Rusty is making a lot of money—for *you*, and it's not by building boats for Lyman or anyone else." He felt like both fink and louse. He was ratting out Rusty and was about to destroy her safe world and he resented his position. "The kind of money he makes cannot be made building boats...or by working at the mill..." Her eyes were boring into him. He couldn't stop now if he had wanted to. "Di, remember he is doing this for you."

"What is he doing?" She emphasized each word like a hammer strike.

"Running."

"Running?"

"He's rum running. Davey, too."

Di's hand flew to her mouth. Silence followed as she absorbed what he had said.

He studied her reaction with unease.

"Well," she sighed finally, "Guess Eddie was straight after all when he told me of the racing boat in the boat shanty."

He raised his brows in surprise. "Eddie saw the boat?"

"Yes. I went to Huron to see for myself...the shanty, the boat, Rusty's corner of the world..."

"And what did you find?"

She was quiet for a moment. "Sadness...and compassion."

Her reaction wasn't what he expected but it relieved him. She looked pale however. She raised her eyes to him and he saw deep sadness.

"How dangerous is this?" she asked.

He shook his head. "I think it may be turning ugly."

She gasped and tears welled in her eyes but she did not crumble like he had expected and feared. "We need to stop him. I don't give a hoot about money or a roadster...I don't care if I don't have a child...I just want him. *Him.* With me!" A stray tear ran down her cheek. "We got to stop him, Uncle Fritz!" She brushed the stray away.

"I would if I could, but I don't know where to find him or Davey. He left me with no way to contact him after the fire. I'm beside myself."

"Do you think that runner who escaped from the hospital was him?"

He shook his head. "I don't know. All I know is he works for a vintner on one of the Bass Islands. He hasn't told me much."

"The fire…was it meant to kill him?"

"I don't know but I have my suspicions especially with him going into hiding." He heard her sniff and saw her nose red and tears coursing down her cheek. He pulled a handkerchief from his pocket and handed it to her. "Be strong, *liebste*. You've always been strong, so don't stop now. We'll wait for Sunday. If he comes, we will get this out on the table once and for all."

"And if he doesn't?"

"I got an idea where we can start looking."

Chapter 67

Al waited until the Trapani clan, Rusty and Davey had gathered at the warehouse before speaking. Rusty could see Al's usual jovialness had fizzled out like left-over champagne. He even looked older.

When the last man took his seat on a packing table, Al began. "There was a problem, but by God's good Grace, it worked out. You see, this is what I was talking about…about not being careful. You smelled a rat," he said to Rusty, "therefore Joe should have stayed in the cockpit. If it doesn't feel right, get the hell out. We can always make a sale, but we cannot bring back the dead." He paced the floor. "From here on out, wait for the pilot to give an 'all clear' before blundering onto the deck," he said, looking at Joe. "If you had sat tight in the armored cockpit this incident would not have gotten out of hand and Pete wouldn't have the buttons all worked up by returning fire. Thank God, it wasn't the federal boys or we would really be up shit creek."

"What was I suppose to do, Al, let 'em waste us like sitting ducks? They opened fire on us without warning," Pete said.

"And now they have it out exclusively for the *Shadow Runner* or whatever the hell the boat has been tagged."

"Big fucking news—CG157 has had it out for us right from the get go. Before *New Moon*!"

"Clean out your ears, Pete! Be careful and pay attention out there. The buttons are just doing their job. Are you forgetting? By the laws of the land, we are the bad guys now. You break the law, you risk getting busted."

"Then why in the hell did you arm us if we can't shoot back? When Connors shot Rusty, you asked me why I didn't return fire. You said, and I quote, 'that B.A.R. was not for decoration.' "

Al face turned red. "Because," he shouted, "Rusty made sense when he said shooting back at Connors or any fed for that matter would be suicide. Shooting is to be the last resort when all other avenues have been exhausted and our lives are in danger. Are you forgetting we had discussed this? We don't want shoot outs with badges or to muscle territories. We are runners supplying a need—staying low, but making money."

"We were trapped and taking fire and Joe was taking hits. It was the last resort." Pete shouted back.

"If he had stayed inside the cockpit, you could have gotten out of the situation."

Joe jumped in. "Are *you* forgetting, Al, that cops broke my arm at the warehouse in Sandusky and now put two bullets in me at the castle? I didn't get a warning and I sure wasn't resisting. They had no reason to rough me up at the warehouse as I was cooperating and they found nothing. As for the other night, there was no warning, no chance to surrender. Hell, we could have been delivering root beer or herring for all they knew."

Al was quiet and the red began to fade. "They knew. We're no saints." He paced the floor again while all eyes followed him. "Our man, Rusty here, told me he wants out because he has gone off course. Says this is not what he wanted. I didn't want it either. I wanted to listen to the birds and make wine on my island. Have my family work in the business. Make a wine that turns the French green and makes my nonno proud." His tone softened. "The Trapanis have made wine for generations. Our vineyards in Sicily had a reputation. You want a great wine with your Pollo al Marsala or lamb chops, you buy a bottle from *Cantine Trapani*. I don't have to tell you how we lost our vineyards and were forced out—you all know." He sighed. "This lake region, these islands were perfect for starting a vineyard in the new world. My dream, like *nonno's*, was to rebuild the Trapani reputation for wine here in America. It's what we know—it's who we are." He began pacing again and his voice got tense. "That is until some Einstein invented the 18th Amendment and the Volstead Act saw to it. Why? Because some jerks couldn't hold their liquor or refrain. So now we all pay. And good guys become bad guys at a stroke of a pen."

"So what's your point, Al?" Tony asked.

Al snorted. "My point? My point is we stay safe, make ourselves small and make money before the repeal which is around the corner. Hold together, make our fortunes and then go back to making wine legitimately after the repeal. Or in your, Petey's and Joe's case, live off your hay made running until you blow it all." He turned to Rusty. "You also told me after your finger was shot off that you were the captain and called the shots. I would say that makes you responsible, but I also know my brother and cousin are impetuous and pig-headed. Next time you feel uneasy, screw the delivery and get out. And I don't want anyone so much as blowing their nose on board without asking Rusty if it's okay." He scrutinized the group and waited for a response. There was none, so he clapped his hands. "Now, let's go. We got a run tonight."

Rusty pushed Davey out of the warehouse and onto the dock.

"After that speech, I feel like I should be wearing a black hat and bandana," Davey said.

"Let's get you back, Black Bart. I gotta run to make tonight."

***

Tony boarded *New Moon.* He was carrying the machine gun Joe had with him on the runs, leaving his WWI trench "broom" with Vince in the milk delivery truck. He wasn't happy about replacing Joe and returning to the runs and did little to mask his unhappiness.

The night was dark as ink and just seeing one another aboard was a challenge. When Pete stepped on Tony's toes, he snarled and Pete grumbled he couldn't see his hands in front of his face let alone Tony's big elephant feet. Rusty knew it was going to be a long night.

New Moon slipped through the veil of darkness to the fishing ground and retrieved the sunken bundles of liquor with some measure of difficulty due to the blackness that enveloped them. It took longer than usual and when the last bundle was being stowed, *New Moon* coursed her way to the desolate dock at Beaver Creek.

On approach, Pete flashed the usual signal. There was no return signal from the dock so Pete flashed again. Still no response.

It was too dark to see if the milk truck was even there.

"Maybe he's late…had a break down or something," Tony said.

"Knowing Vince, he probably fell asleep without your big mouth keeping him awake," Pete said.

Rusty remained silent. His eyes bored into the darkness around the dock. He pushed Pete's arm down as Pete was about to flash the signal again.

"You got a bad feeling?" Pete's voice fell to a whisper.

"No one leaves the cockpit. I'm going to hit the dock with the spotlight. Pete, you on the B.A.R.?"

"You bet."

Rusty flipped the spotlight on, piercing the blackness with a sharp, harsh light that highlighted the side of the milk delivery truck. At the wheel, with his head cradled in his arms resting upon the steering wheel sat Vince.

"Christ, he fell asleep," Pete said, lowering the automatic rifle. Tony laughed.

"Tony," Rusty whispered. "I'm going to idle over to those rocks. I want you to jump off. I'm going to move my position and then I'll hit the truck with the spotlight again. Wait before approaching the truck. Make sure it's Vince. If things don't look or feel jake, beat it back and I'll pick you up at the rocks and we'll get the hell out of here."

"What about Vince?" Pete said.

"You heard me, Tony—be alert."

Rusty, using as low as throttle possible, moved to the outcrop of rocks about 150 feet from the dock.

Tony, with machine gun in hand, jumped overboard onto the rock jutting, and then Rusty idled the boat away as quietly as possible to a position almost perpendicular to the dock so when he hit the truck with light, its side would be highlighted with a clear view of Vince at the wheel. He flipped on the switch.

With the spotlight flooding the truck, the dock was lit up like a stage in a dark theater. Tony cautiously approached the door. It was Vince all right, asleep at the wheel. "Vince, get your ass up!" He poked Vince's shoulder. "Vince, you jerk, wake up." He grabbed him by the arm and Vince tumbled out of the doorway onto the dock unconscious. Had Tony took notice before, he would have seen the small hole in Vince's temple and the blood and brains that splattered the truck's passenger side. With Vince lying on his left side, Tony clearly saw the right side of his face blown out.

Tony jumped back in horror and faced the spotlight. “He’s dead!”

“Get out,” Rusty cried, killing the light to avoid highlighting Tony.

Pete screamed *no*, shouldered the B.A.R. and swept the darkness surrounding the dock. He couldn’t see, but he was jacked up and Rusty feared he would fire haphazardly into the dark, jeopardizing Tony.

“Hold fire, Pete, until we know were Tony is.” Rusty moved *New Moon* to the rock cropping where Tony had disembarked.

“How’s Tony going to see his way back in the dark?” Pete asked. His voice was shaking and Rusty could hear him sniffing back snot.

“He’ll manage. We can’t highlight him.”

A quick burst of muzzle flash pierced the darkness accompanied by a staccato burst of machine gun fire. It was short. Then it was quiet.

“Tony?” Pete screamed.

No reply.

Then the headlights of the milk truck came on.

Pete buried the butt of the B.A.R. deep into his shoulder, taking aim at the lights. “Tony!” His frantic voice sent shivers up Rusty’s spine.

They waited.

“Rusty?” A voice called from the shadows beyond the headlights. “Tony’s here. See?” Two figures, one tall and lanky and the other medium built, pulled Tony in front of the headlights. He was on his feet but he sagged between the two figures holding him up. His head hung down. “Tony’s okay—just a bump on the noggin, right Tony?”

Tony raised his head. His voice cracked and sounded weak. “Pete, it’s a trap, they killed Vinnie.”

“Who? Who are they?” Pete cried.

The tall and lanky figure punched Tony in the stomach, causing him to double over.

“Take the wheel and give me the rifle,” Rusty whispered to Pete. By the sound of Pete’s sobs and shaking voice, he knew he may not be steady on the aim. “Be ready to roll.”

He leveled the barrel and put the cross on the tall figure that punched Tony. In his mind’s eye, he saw himself taking each man out. *Would he be forced to kill?*

Just then a third voice surprised him as it called from the shadows beyond the headlights.

“Rusty. I know it’s you.”

Rusty hesitated. His ears strained for all sounds in the darkness.

“Your partner won’t get hurt if you cooperate,” the voice continued. “All we want is the cargo. Dock, off load and you can have Tony in return.”

“You expect us to believe you after you killed Vince. If you wanted to bargain you would have used him.” Rusty raised the barrel and took aim again at the tall figure supporting Tony. Tony was already a dead man as far as he was concerned. "I got me a clear shot. How about if I take out your two men and we call it even?"

"Wait," Pete said, "we can't take that chance with Tony. Even if you shoot those two there's the guy in the shadows and he'll kill Tony sure as hell."

Rusty gritted his teeth.

"So, *Shadow Runner*, is it a deal? Tony for the goods. You and your crew sail away and me and my boys drive away."

The voice from the dark was sounding more and more familiar.

"I'm growing impatient," the voice said.

Rusty's mind sorted through names. The voice was too familiar. It hit him like a flash. "You're not here to deal," Rusty called out. His voice had a new edge to it. "You're intention is to kill us just like you did Hoot and tried to do to Huddleson and Eddie. Am I right, *Eliot*?"

Movement and then a figure appeared behind Tony. He and Pete could see a hand at the back of Tony's head.

"I have the barrel of a .45 pressed against the back of your friend's head. You'll have to shoot through Tony to get me and if you fire at one of my men, you'll be scrapping Tony's face off the dock."

"I know your hand, Eliot. Tony is already a dead man. So am I if I dock."

"If that's the case, you can tell your boss man you killed Tony."

"Don't do it, Eliot," a voice supporting Tony pleaded. "This is going too far."

Rusty felt charged hearing the pleading voice and the verification of the name of Eliot and his senses sharpened moreover. "When I say now, switch on the spotlight," he whispered to Pete. "I'm taking that son of a bitch out."

"Are you nuts? He's behind Tony," Pete whispered back.

"I'm going to drop the big guy to the left of Tony first. Tony will slump forward leaving Eliot open."

"You may get two, but you can't get all three. And maybe there's more hiding in wait."

"Can't you see he's suckering us in? He's going to kill us all. That's his intention. Tony is a dead man already. At least this is a chance." He took aim at the tall, lanky man holding Tony.

"Can't take that chance, Rust."

"We have to!"

Eliot, the voice behind the pistol, called out again. "So this means no deal, uh? Well, it looks like another poor sucker takes the rap for you, Rusty. Just like poor Davey. That line was meant for you, you know. Or didn't you? I rigged that line to get you, and that dumb bastard got in the way. It was suppose to be you with the broke back and you in a wheelchair…or worse. Well, here's another one you can chalk up and feel all bad and sad about."

"Now!"

Pete switched on the light. It flooded the area and blinded the men on the dock and revealed a fourth man standing close by on the rocks with a machine gun aimed at *New Moon*. The machine gunner opened fire on them. Rusty swung the barrel of the B.A.R. around towards the machine gunner and fired back in rapid fire. Meanwhile, everyone scattered from the front of the headlights into the shadows at the eruption of gunfire but not before a pistol crack sounded among the din. Pete watched in horror as Tony fell. He yelled. Rusty felled the machine gunner and immediately swung the barrel back to the dock. No one was there except for Tony lying motionless in a heap.

Eliot's voice called from the darkness. "Your luck has officially run out. We know who and where you are. Hope Davey doesn't get in the way again."

Rusty strafed the dock and surrounding darkness with B.A.R. fire.

When he ceased sweeping the area with bullets, he could hear the sound of engines. He strained over Pete's screaming curses and cries to hear the direction the vehicles were heading. They were heading west towards Huron and Sandusky. The road leading there was deserted this time of night. It tightly followed the shoreline—water on one side, marshes and open farm ground on the other through dark and sparsely populated countryside. There was a bridge four miles up the road the vehicles would have to cross.

Rusty knocked Pete away from the wheel as he watched the headlights of the vehicles course their way along the shoreline road. He gunned the engines of *New Moon*. She carved a deep arc in the water as he nosed her west and gave her full throttle. Her wake boiled and rolled behind her as she flew westward along the dark shoreline, sweeping undetected past the vehicles on the road above.

Pete grew quiet as he surmised Rusty's plan and he prayed Rusty knew the shoreline and what lie beneath the surface better than him. Finally, Rusty idled down, and motored to a spot on the shore. Pete could see it was a creek with a bridge above it. Rusty tucked the boat underneath it. He killed the engines. He grabbed a flashlight and stuck it in his back pocket. The headlights of the two vehicles were growing brighter on the shoreline road above.

Before Pete could say or do anything, Rusty grabbed the B.A.R. and jumped off the boat into knee high creek water. Pete started after him with the shotgun.

"Stay with the boat, Pete, we may need a fast get away."

Pete started to protest, but in the darkness could feel rage radiating from Rusty so he backed off. He listened to the sound of Rusty sloshing hurriedly through the water and then heard him climb the bank. The croaking of frogs farther up creek were soon drowned out by the rattling of the milk truck and following vehicle as they approached the bridge. Pete felt like he was going to explode. He held the shotgun tight and fought the urge to run up the bank behind Rusty.

Streams of sweat ran down Rusty's face as he scrambled up the bank to beat the vehicles before they crossed the bridge. He fought through the tangle of brush and weeds covering the steep incline and before he could reach the road, the first vehicle, the milk delivery truck, started onto the bridge. He clenched his teeth and raised the B.A.R.'s barrel to the bridge and opened fire, strafing the milk truck from below as it reached the halfway point of the bridge. The deep thunderous staccato thud-thud-thud of the B.A.R. was deafening in the night air and the echoes reverberated like lightning claps. A bullet found the gas tank and the milk truck blew up in a ball of flames. Without a break in action, he swept the bullet barrage back towards the second vehicle. The second vehicle, having just started onto the bridge, weaved erratically and broke through the bridge's wooden rails, plunging to the creek below, landing on the up side of the creek thereby not blocking the mouth for *New Moon*'s escape.

Pete's heart landed in his throat when the automobile came crashing to the creek bed. He wrestled with leaving the boat to inspect the vehicle or stay tight like Rusty had ordered him. He could see the flames of the burning milk truck overhead through the slats of the bridge and readied the boat in case he had to move quickly from underneath the bridge while keeping his eye and the shotgun trained on the overturned vehicle in the creek.

Rusty scrambled to the top of the bank and approached the bridge with the rifle leveled at the burning milk truck. Movement in the milk truck caught his eye. He zeroed in on the movement with gun at ready and watched as a figure, his pants aflame, rolled out of the milk truck. The man was moaning and near death. He approached cautiously with rifle still leveled at the figure. He clicked on his flashlight. He saw the man's shirt soaked in blood; he then shined the light on the man's anguished face and gasped. "Lloyd Robson? What the…" It was Lloyd Robson, crew mate from the late Erie T. Rusty lowered the rifle and beat the flames out on Lloyd's clothing. He raised Lloyd's head. "Lloyd…are you with…Eliot?"

Lloyd gasped for air and his eyes rolled over to Rusty's. "Rust, I'm sorry. It… wasn't suppose to go like… this." He coughed up blood. "Just make… some money. Not hurt… anyone." His body quivered and he went limp. His eyes stared blankly into the beam of the flashlight.

Rusty lowered Lloyd's head and rose stunned. He swept the area with his rifle barrel and then searched around the milk truck with his flashlight beam and headed back down the bank. "It's Rusty," he whispered to Pete as he passed the boat. "I'm going to check out the vehicle in the creek."

He sloshed through the water and shined the flashlight's beam on the driver side and then around the interior. No one was inside. Where was the driver? He shined the beam up and down the stream and around the banks. He felt the hair prickle on his neck. Where was Eliot? Did he even come with them? And where was the third man- the tall one? Was he the driver? He continued sweeping the banks and shoreline with his flashlight beam. He jumped at any sound, swinging the light beam here and there in the surrounding darkness.

"You looking for me?" A voice in the dark said from behind him.

Rusty heard the click of a hammer being cocked. He could almost feel the barrel at the back of his head. He felt the blood drain from his face. "Eliot."

"Who's the idiot now?"

"Why Lloyd, Eliot? He was a good man." Every hair on his body was raised.

"Why not? He crewed with me on the *Cherokee*. Made peanuts busting his ass on the scrap barges. I needed someone familiar with the tug—he wanted to make money. As simple as that."

"I was wrong…you're not an idiot, you're scum."

"Call me want you want, dead man."

A booming blast of gunshot with a blinding flash punctured the darkness. It blinded Rusty and deafened him. He waited for sharp pain or was he dead already?

"Fucking scum alright." It was Pete's voice.

Rusty turned and slowly raised the flashlight. Pete was near him holding the 16 gauge pump shotgun. He shined the light down and behind him and saw Eliot in a heap, his face and upper body looked like raw hamburger.

Pete leaned over and spit a wad of spittle on Eliot's bloody face.

Rusty felt suddenly weak in the knees. His face felt bloodless.

"You all right?" Pete asked. "You don't look so good."

"I am just thinking how glad I am you didn't follow my orders and stay with the boat." He took a deep breath, not realizing he had been holding it. "Be on guard. The tall man is missing. I don't know if he was in the vehicles or still at the dock."

"Maybe there was a third car. Maybe he was waiting for a pickup?"

"Maybe a boat pickup?"

They fell into an uneasy silence as they turned and headed for the boat. Neither spoke as Rusty turned over the engines and headed for open water at half throttle.

"I can't believe it," Pete muttered, breaking the silence. "Vinne…Tony…"

With the adrenalin fading away, the deaths were settling in on him and Rusty could hear him sniffing again.

"How do I tell Al and the family? Christ, this is bad…real bad." His voice was breaking.

"Tell him their deaths were avenged."

"That don't bring 'em back, Rust. This is a nightmare I can't wake up from." He started softly sobbing and Rusty could hear he was fighting to stifle it, but was not having success. "I'm going on deck for fresh air."

"Just for a moment and don't smoke. Anyone out tonight on land or water would have heard that rifle's report for over a mile. I'll turn the radio on and see if there's any coasties chattering."

He clicked on the radio and it was silent except for a few crackles. Pete was right—it was a nightmare that he too could not wake from. He played the dock and bridge scene over and over in his head to see if he could have done anything different. That's when he heard it—a big boom. Then *New Moon* shuddered. He spun his head about searching the darkness.

"Boat…close off portside…one pounder!" Pete yelled scrambling towards the cockpit door.

Rusty looked to port side and saw a muzzle flash followed by another boom. *New Moon* rocked. The phantom boat was close. *How did it get so close without them noticing?* As he throttled up, machine gun fire opened on them. *Chug-chug-chug-chug-chug.* It was Connors's Savage Lewis .30 caliber machine gun.

Rusty cut hard to starboard and gunned the engines. *New Moon* peeled away from CG157. *Where in the hell was Pete?* "Pete, get your ass in here." It was too dark to see Pete or CG157.

A large, bright spotlight mounted on the CG157 switched on. Apparently, it too had trouble seeing and had lost *New Moon.* The brilliant beam swept the waters hunting for her. *New Moon* was still within the beam's boundary and that made him cringe, but it also revealed Connors' position. He struck a course at a 90 degree angle and planned to double back when the beam hit directly on *New Moon.* It was like being shot with a bullet of light.

"Pete?" *Where in the hell is he?* "Forget about hanging on, the light will highlight you. Crawl in on your belly and keep a good grip. Pete?"

The light beam remained fixed on *New Moon* and no matter how he tried to shake it, he couldn't lose it. It was like a rope made of light that was attached to him. Connors, or whoever was manning the light, seemed to anticipate his every move.

He looked over his shoulder at the highlighted deck of *New Moon.* His heart skipped a beat. Pete was not on deck. "Oh God."

The .30 caliber opened up again and the bullets strafed *New Moon*'s armored hull and ricocheted off her steel plated cockpit. Despite his perilous situation, his mind was clouded with Pete's whereabouts. Was he shot? Did he fall overboard? Did he take cover in the hold? He had to do something to shake Connors off him so he could look for Pete. He pressed the dash button that shot castor oil onto the carburetors and *New Moon* bolted out of the beam of light into the darkness. But instead of disappearing into the night, he doubled back and approached CG157's stern well beyond the beam of light and sound of idle engines. The Coast Guard vessel's spotlight was still probing the surrounding waters, concentrating on the area the crew had last seen *New Moon.* He had to find Pete but first he had to get rid of Connors.

He backed off the engines, bringing *New Moon* to a stop and keyed the ship to shore radio. He spoke into the microphone. "We spotted a runner heading north-northwest off Lorain. It appears to be heading towards the border at a high rate of speed."

The spotlight switched off the CG157. He waited in the darkness to hear if she would take the bait.

"Where is your location?" a voice came over the radio. He recognized it as Connors's.

Rusty keyed the microphone. "Three miles north off Vermilion. She's running without lights and is very difficult to see. Can you assist?"

"Roger."

He watched as a scant number of lights flipped on the Coast Guard vessel and listened to her engine motor up. CG157 turned and started into the lake at a NNW bearing. Connors had taken the bait.

He waited until Connors was well enough away and then he climbed on deck with his flashlight. He searched the deck and sides with the beam and then opened the hold and engine compartments. "Pete? Pete?" The flashlight beam probed every nook in case Pete was lying unconscious. There was no Pete. He remembered what Pete had said and his words echoed in his head-" I can't swim". Rusty's stomach turned.

He crawled back to the cockpit and headed *New Moon* back to where he had last seen Pete. He cut the engines and called into the darkness. "Pete? Pete?" He grabbed the boat's spotlight knowing CG157 would be far enough away not to see it but still kept the beam low on the water's surface. He swept the black waters over and over where the action with Connors took place. He searched the banks and rocky outposts with the spotlight beam, calling into the darkness and repeating the process again and again, ignoring the voice in his head that said Pete was lost and possibly drowned. He checked his watch. In one hour it would be daybreak. He cursed. With little time remaining before first light would expose *New Moon*, he headed for Beaver Creek dock and tied off to retrieve the bodies of Vince and Tony. To his shock and relief, Tony gave a moan when he grabbed him. He had taken a shot in the chest and was barely alive but alive.

Rusty retrieved clean rags and hastily dressed Tony's wound, and then carried him to the boat and placed him next to Vince's body. Unlike Vince, he made Tony comfortable as possible. In his rush to cast off, he paused and shone the flashlight on the rocks where the machine gunner fell. There was no body, but a lot of blood. He shone the light around. His ears ached for the sound of brush, a splash in the water or Pete's voice. But none came. He made a final sweep of the area and with heavy heart and blurry eyes, he headed WNW for Middle Island. The lake was crawling with Coast Guard searching for him and daylight would soon erase his shadowy advantage. It became not only a race to get Tony help, but to beat the light. He pushed *New Moon* hard and with the weight of the cargo still in her hold, her engines labored and gobbled fuel. Like vampires, they raced the light for the sanctuary of the Canadian waters.

By the time he crossed the Canadian border, the sun had crested the horizon. He had to switch on the auxiliary fuel tank as he crossed the border and sweated whether or not he could make it back to the dock. On fumes, he was sure, she reached the warehouse's dock. Now came the truly hard part—breaking the news to the Trapanis.

Lou met him on the dock. He was grouchy as usual. "Where in the hell have you guys been? The castle called and said the delivery didn't show up. We haven't heard from Tony and Vince either." He stopped his tirade abruptly when he saw Rusty's face. "What happened?" His eyes drifted back to the boat.

"It went bad," was all the words Rusty could muster.

Lou rushed to the boat and looked into the cockpit and saw Vince and Tony lying on the floor. There was no question that Vince was dead. Lou cried out and slammed his fist against the cockpit's steel plating and climbed into the cockpit.

Rusty listened to Lou's sobs and waited with unease. Finally Lou emerged on deck. "Where's Pete?"

"I can't find him. I searched, God knows I searched and...I can't find him, Lou. He fell over board when Connors was chasing us."

Lou struck the side again and moaned.

Rusty bit his lip then looked towards the warehouse. "Is there anyone here that can help us with Tony and to look for Pete?" he asked Lou cautiously.

"You mean who's left of us?" Lou moaned. He wiped his forearm under his nose. "Giuseppe. He's inside."

In an odd way, Rusty was relieved. What Giuseppe did best was look after the family and that included him now. He retrieved Giuseppe and it was the first time he saw a crack in the big Sicilian's stoic expression. Without a word, Giuseppe charged down the dock and entered the cockpit. He gathered up Tony like a child and carried him to the warehouse. Rusty and Lou followed with Vince suspended between them. They placed Vince's body and Tony on the packing table and Giuseppe folded Vince's hands on his chest. Tony was groaning and his makeshift bandages were soaked in crimson.

"We got to get Tony help and tell Al what happened," Lou said.

"I have to go back and search for Pete right away. I'm going to use the fish tug and have Davey help me." Lou's eyes shot to him. They were red and burning. Rusty swallowed hard. "Tell Al I will explain everything when I get back. Tell him, it was Eliot and his partners—the ones that killed Hoot killed Vince and wounded Tony at the dock. There was also a fourth gunman with them and we killed him right off, I'm sure. Someone carried his body off after we went after Eliot and his partner. Pete and I caught up with them. Pete killed Eliot and I got the other one."

"And the third?"

"He disappeared but I think I know how to find him. He had to have a way out of there and whoever picked him up most likely retrieved the machine gunner."

"Tell me who and where." Giuseppe eyes were fierce and black and he was ready to act.

"Lou, after you break the news," Rusty was cautious as if he was handling dynamite, "send some men to search for Pete on shore around Beaver Creek ...Vermilion, Lorain."

Giuseppe stepped in front of Rusty. It was like standing face to face with a riled grizzly bear. "I said tell me who and where."

Rusty swallowed hard again. "I'm almost positive the third man was Bill from CG157 and 157 just happened to be in the immediate area when they ambushed us. Not only did they cause Pete's fall, I'm pretty sure they were behind the dock shooting. I'm gonna make 'em pay, all right, Giuseppe. When I need you I'll let you know but right now you got to help Lou."

Giuseppe grunted and backed away.

"You," Lou said stabbing his finger at Rusty, "are gonna drop Tony and Vinnie off at Al's and take Giuseppe with you while I'll take our motorboat on ahead break it to Al and get help."

With Vince and Tony loaded onto the fish tug, Rusty and Giuseppe headed for the trapper's shack to retrieve Davey.

Davey met them on the dock. "Where's *New Moon*, what's going on? I've been worried."

"You got a lot more to worry about than you think," Rusty said quickly tying off the fish tug. "Come on, I'll help you board. I need you to help me look for Pete."

"What's going on?"

"Let's get going and I'll explain on the way."

Davey cut him off with his wheelchair. "Rust," he said. His voice was stern. "What happened?"

"Pete's in the water. We were being chased by Connors and he fell overboard. It was too dark to see and Connors was on me like stink on shit. Tony's been shot and Vince is dead."

"Lord Almighty."

"The kid can't swim." Rusty's voice broke when he said that. "Please, Davey, I need your help to search for him. The fish tug won't draw suspicion."

"That's a long time to be in the lake even if you could tread water."

"Never mind, I'll go myself." Rusty hurried back to *Annie O.*

"Wait!" Davey called. "I'll go. Help me in." He saw Giuseppe as he was boarding, dark with blazing eyes. He didn't acknowledge him and Davey thought it best not to say anything.

"We're dropping them off at Al's."

"Does Al know about Pete?" Davey asked.

"He doesn't even know about Tony and Vince," Giuseppe muttered. He headed for the stern of the tug, distancing himself from Rusty and Davey.

No one spoke another word on the trip to South Bass Island.

Lou met them at the dock near Al's vineyard with the flatbed truck used for the crates. He had Mario, Al's son who had drove Rusty and Di to the dock from the harvest party last fall, with him. As soon as Vince's body and Tony were placed on the truck bed, Rusty cast off and headed for the waters off Lorain. On the way, he told Davey the whole story. He was relieved it was Davey and not Al that he had to tell at this point. A recount of last night to Al would come later.

They searched for hours, following currents that could have carried Pete. Just off shore near Sugar Creek Bridge, they watched as patrol cars came and went and men collected on the bridge and beneath it, investigating the murder scene. A tow truck arrived, and work began on retrieving the vehicle underneath the bridge where Eliot was killed. At one point, they passed near shore off Lorain and could see men milling about on the dock at Beaver Creek. They knew it would be the Trapanis as no one outside of them knew about the murders at the remote dock. The big bear would be Giuseppe. Rusty knew the blood stains would both infuriate and agitate them like fighting pit bulls. There would be a reckoning for sure.

As the afternoon wore on, Davey called a halt to the search. With reluctance, Rusty agreed. They docked in Vermilion, and got coffee at a family diner in view of Sam's eatery. The dining room was abuzz with the talk of the bridge murders and the theories behind it. They sat in silence sipping coffee and eavesdropping on every word.

All the while Rusty kept his eyes glued on Sam's entrance. As the hot steam curled about his face, he prayed Pete would come bounding out the door.

***

"Rusty, good to see you, how are you doing?"

Chief Bales almost ran into them as they were leaving the diner. So startled was Rusty, the chief might as well have been Tony or Vince. "Fine. I'm doing well." He hoped his voice or face didn't betray his uneasiness.

"What a mess we got on our hands. Did you hear about the two men shot a couple miles up the road? The state police say they were bootleggers and that someone most likely had a score to settle with them. It may even have been a hijack. You know what I think? I think they could be those bootleggers that killed Hoot. The one guy had an eye patch. Remember how Eddie shot that one fellow in the eye with the slingshot? It was a direct hit according to Eddie so most likely he lost his eye. They also matched Eddie's descriptions of two of the men." Chief Bales seemed pleasingly satisfied for a man who had two bullet riddled corpses near his jurisdiction."

"Sounds like the guys, all right." Rusty said and began pushing Davey down the sidewalk.

"Got a call from the Coast Guard," the chief continued. "Told me to keep my eyes peeled for a rumrunner that fell overboard in that same area. They said they saw the runner's boat leave the scene of the shooting and when they gave pursuit, the runner fell overboard. Picket boat couldn't find him so they don't know if he drowned or swam ashore, but I'm to keep my eyes open for him. He's wanted dead or alive."

Chapter 68

Upon Lou's report, Al instructed Tony to be taken to a spare bedroom and then immediately telephoned the family's physician. Constance Trapani, frozen with shock at the news and seeing the bodies carried in, jumped into action when Al yelled at her to get water and bandages for Tony.

Vince was laid out in the same grand foyer where he had danced the night away at the harvest party months earlier while Constance blubbered about a death certificate and his burial. "We just can't stick him in the ground and keep him a secret!" She said between sobs.

"The certificate needs a coroner's signature and a coroner will make a report and there will be an investigation. You know what that means?" Al said. "Get back to Tony and let me clear my head so I can think."

Lou called Joe and told him to round up the men and meet at the grape press. After breaking the gut wrenching news, the men broke into two teams: one group would search for Pete on land; the other would take the motorboat and search the waters while Al, Lou and Giuseppe would head for Beaver Creek dock to the scene of the executions. Constance, meanwhile, would receive and aid the physician.

***

Uncle Fritz's face turned ashen. He had promised to take Eddie with him to the hardware store in Vermilion and stop by for an ice cream soda at the drugstore. The plan included stopping by Widow Donovan's for a visit. He first heard the news at the hardware store when he overheard the excited chatter between the clerk and a small gathering at the register. When he went to pay, he asked if anything new was going on in town and the gathering, all talking at once, told him their versions of the shooting at the bridge up the road. *Gang warfare, bootleggers, rumrunners, hijacking, murder, bloody corpses*—he picked out the key words as his head swam with trepidation. He paid, grabbed his package and placed his arm around Eddie and hustled him out. He felt dazed and numb until Eddie reminded him of the soda. Perhaps the drugstore would have more information.

As Eddie slurped his soda, Uncle Fritz listened in on the pockets of conversation concerning last night's shootings. When the soda jerk asked if they wanted another refill, Uncle Fritz asked him if the bodies had been identified.

"Chief Bales is pretty sure they were the runners that killed Hoot on the account that they matched the boy's description and one had an eye patch," the soda jerk said.

Eddie looked at Uncle Fritz and grinned. Uncle Fritz felt sudden relief that it was an eye patch and not a wheelchair that was involved. But his relief was fleeting when the clerk added rumrunners were suspected of the murders as a shadowy runner was seen leaving the area at a high rate of speed with a Coast Guard picket boat giving chase.

Uncle Fritz drummed his fingers while Eddie relished his second soda. With the final slurping of froth and air, he told Eddie it was time to get back home.

"What about Widow Donovan? Ain't we gonna see her?" Eddie said, lagging behind.

To Uncle Fritz's relief, she was not home and he assured Eddie they would come back the following week. When he pulled into the farm, Eddie reminded him he had forgotten to stop at the feed store in Kipton before going home.

The more he thought about the suspect shadowy rumrunner, the more he grew troubled. Even if Rusty was not involved in the shootings, the Coast Guard as well as law enforcement and government men would be stepping up the hunt for rumrunners and bootleggers as murders and suspicious activity along the southern shoreline was mounting. Rusty was in the soup and it angered him he no longer had contact with him. He was sick and tired of sitting on his hands and waiting for Sundays to see if Rusty would show or not. He was tired of it, tired of it all. He would put a stop now to this nonsense running. Stop it now before the next body found was Rusty's. He waited until Eddie went outside and then he told his sister he forgot to stop at the feed store. He also told her since he was out and about he was going to see Rusty in Sandusky. Icebox my supper as I may get back late, he said. He grabbed his hat, climbed in his Model A and headed west.

***

The sun was setting behind a veil of clouds when Rusty tied off *Annie O* at the trapper shack's dock. "I'm docking her here instead of the fish warehouse so you have a way off the island."

"You plan on leaving me?"

Rusty didn't answer.

"Are you going to Put-in-Bay to talk to the Trapanis? You know they'll be expecting you to give a full account."

Rusty disappeared around the trapper's shack and when he came back, he was carrying a gasoline can. "I was riding on fumes when I came in last night. I don't even have enough to make it over to the fuel tank at the warehouse dock."

"It would be more inconspicuous if you took Annie to the island. She's got plenty of gas." Davey said. A deep furrow had formed between his brows.

Rusty emptied the can of gas into *New Moon*'s fuel tank and sat the empty can on the dock. He checked the oil levels including the castor oil. "Keep your side arm on you all times, Davey. There is still a third man out there that's behind the killings." He jumped on board *New Moon* and went into the cockpit.

Davey wheeled over to the edge of the dock and looked inside. Rusty was checking the B.A.R. and the shotgun for ammunition, making sure they were fully loaded. He then wrapped the belt of magazine cartridges around him.

"What in God's name are you up to?" Davey cried. "God damn, Rust, don't you do what I think you are about to do! You get that notion out of your head right now, do you hear me?" He wheeled to a closer position. "You got to live with your decision."

"I'm going to fuel up at the warehouse dock. If the Trapanis show up here, tell them..." he paused, "tell them Pete's been like a kid brother to me." He cast off the lines and fired up the engines.

"Rusty, Rusty...wait. Listen, when Wyatt Earp avenged his brothers, the guilt of revenge followed him to his grave. Can you live with that?"

"If I'm not back by tomorrow night, I want you to take *Annie O* to Mike's in Port Clinton. Call my Uncle Fritz and tell him where you are."

"And what do I tell him about you? Where will you be?"

"Tell him you don't have a clue."

"I don't!" As he watched Rusty pull away from the dock he yelled, "Think of Di and Eddie. They need you." *New Moon* rumbled out the cove. "I need you, too," he said as she disappeared around the bend.

Rusty fueled up at the warehouse dock. It was odd not seeing any activity there. He throttled up *New Moon* and rumbled southeastward. Behind him, heat lightning flashed low in the western horizon.

Davey found a letter on the table in the shack. It was addressed to Di. Next to it a note read, "Davey, see that Di gets this if I don't return." He angrily crumpled the note. A commotion outside caught his attention. He grabbed the letter and slipped it into his shirt pocket and wheeled out of the shack. Lou was tying off the Trapanis' motorboat and Al, Joe and Giuseppe were disembarking.

"Where's Rusty?" Al said.

"You just missed him."

"Is he headed for my place?"

"I don't think so."

"God damn it!" Al said. "I need to know what exactly happened last night." He pointed his finger at Davey. "That boy should have seen me after he finished searching."

"You didn't find Pete?"

"No." Al rubbed his face. "This is making me crazy." He turned back to Davey. "So where did Rusty go?"

"He didn't tell me what he was doing or where he was going but I got a pretty good idea."

"And?"

"I think he's going after Connors. He armed himself pretty good and fueled up *New Moon*. Said if he didn't return by tomorrow night, I was to figure on him not coming back."

"Sure he didn't just turn tail and run?" Lou said.

Al shot him a look that silenced Lou. "Did he tell you what happened?"

Davey nodded. He recounted in detail the incidents of last night as told by Rusty. He started with Rusty's suspicion and unease when *New Moon* arrived at Beaver Creek dock, the shootings at the dock and the executions at the bridge. He gave a full account of the chase by CG157 and Pete's disappearance. Al wanted every detail and he gave it to him. The Trapanis listened with rapt, almost spellbound attention and when he finished, they absorbed the account in silence.

"Rusty's pretty sure the tall man holding Tony was Connor's chief motor machinist?" Al said breaking the quiet.

Davey nodded.

"So CG 157 did not just cause Petey's disappearance, it was in on Vinnie's murder and Tony's shooting?"

"Rusty says so. Said the CG157 has been covering for the tugboat right along and it just happened to be right in the area last night."

Giuseppe straightened and looked at Al.

Davey could tell the wheels were turning in Al's head.

"How about Giuseppe and I pay a visit to the Coast Guard Station," Lou said.

"Is CG157 on patrol tonight?" Al asked.

"Rusty must think so," Davey said.

"We can hang at the dock out of sight and wait for 157 to come in," Lou continued.

"No," Al said. He narrowed his eyes. "We need a plan."

Davey turned to Lou. "Rusty wouldn't run away. That's not him. There's not a yellow bone in that man's body. He told me to tell you that Pete is like a kid brother to him." He turned back to Al. "He said we cannot live looking over our shoulder. Said we'll never be safe as long as Connors and his mates are out there. They know he can finger them and they got him marked."

Al said, "So Rusty's going to beat them to the punch." He walked to the edge of the deck and looked out over the water. He lit his cigar and puffed on it like a steam locomotive building pressure. "If that fool would have waited and talked to me first, we could have worked out a plan. Bait and catch." He sighed and looked at each man. "We'll need a mayday rescue this evening."

Joe and Lou exchanged glances.

"There's no guarantee Rusty alone will get him," he continued. "He may even get killed right off the bat. I say we bait Connors with a mayday and do him in ourselves just in case. Look, there is a storm on the horizon. It's a ways off. We could say we broke down and need help before the storm hits." He looked at Davey. "We can take the *Annie O.* She's bigger with more protection, and can ride out the storm better than our motorboat if we get caught in it. Meanwhile, we fake a mayday call. You in, Davey?"

Davey's face squirmed. "I'd rather wait for Rust to return."

"And if he doesn't?"

"You will remember I'm here, right?"

"Sure. We'll even leave you the motorboat if it makes you feel better. You *can* get in it and operate it with your...?" Al motioned his cigar at Davey's legs.

"I'm able."

Satisfied with their plan, the Trapanis returned to their motorboat and grabbed weapons they had brought along. Davey watched as they stashed a Thompson submachine gun, a sawed off double barrel 12 gauge shotgun and a Remington .30-06 aboard *Annie O.* Hand guns were already in their belts and holsters.

"My shotgun is under the steering wheel," Davey said, "and I wouldn't mind having it with me."

Joe brought him the shotgun. "Same gauge as ours only ours is sawed off," he said handing it to Davey.

"How's the gas," Lou asked.

"She's full up," Davey said.

With all aboard but Davey, Joe cast off.

Like he did with *New Moon*, Davey watched until *Annie O* was out of sight. There was a lot of lightning flashing in the distance clouds but he had yet to hear the thunder. He wished he was on the mainland.

***

Uncle Fritz crossed the long span of bridge over Sandusky Bay onto Marblehead Peninsula. The sun had slipped behind a cloud bank on the western horizon. As he made his way to the eastern tip of the peninsula, he began having reservations about his mission. The clouds, though still a distance off, looked dark and the last place he wanted to be was on a peninsula or an unfamiliar stretch of road during a night storm. He pulled up to the lighthouse just as Cap Huddleson was crossing over to it from the keeper's house.

"There's a blow on the way," Huddleson said as he headed for the lighthouse. "Can I help you?" The husky man exiting the Model A became suddenly familiar to him. "Hey, hello there, aren't you Rusty's uncle?"

"Fritz."

"Fritz, yeah." His smile was wide. "What are you doing here?"

Uncle Fritz did not know where to begin or even what to say. He began to doubt if he should have come at all. "Is the storm going to be a bad one?" It sounded lame.

Huddleson, with a look of puzzlement, scratched his chin. "I've seen the barometric reading worse. She'll most likely be fast and furious, but she won't be the storm to end all storms if that's what you mean. But you're not here about the storm are you?"

Uncle Fritz swallowed his bottom lip. "I have to see Rusty and I don't know how to find him. I don't remember where he lives now. I was hoping you knew how to reach him?" The words felt foreign and clumsy. "He's moved and he comes to visit on Sundays...but I have to find him tonight."

A look of concern crossed Huddleson's face. Uncle Fritz looked troubled. "No, I'm sorry; I don't know where he is. I haven't seen him in a while. In fact, the last time I saw him was when he was here with you. Spring, wasn't it?" His voice was concerned.

Uncle Fritz wrung his hands and looked towards the cloud bank. He could see heat lightning in the clouds.

His fretting made Huddleson uneasy, and the keeper waited with as much patience as he could muster for him to continue.

"I think he is out on the lake tonight and I was hoping you could reach him on your radio."

"I can try. Do you have his call numbers?"

"Numbers? No."

"Name of vessel?"

"No. I thought maybe you would know. Maybe seen his boat from your tower."

"I knew he had a fish tug, but I lost track of him after the fire in Huron." Huddleson held open the door to the lighthouse for Uncle Fritz to follow him inside. "Let's see what we can do." He started up the winding staircase and Uncle Fritz huffed and puffed his way behind him.

When they reached the cramped "office," Uncle Fritz was breathless. He looked around the little quarters while he caught his breath and saw a small desk with the ship to shore radio upon it, a telephone, a pair of binoculars, a flare gun and a small electric fan. There was a stack of papers also on the desk and a box underneath with miscellaneous items whose contents he could not discern. There was a window to the north and he could see in the growing dusk that they were only halfway up the lighthouse.

"Light is automated now, so I don't need to light the lanterns like I did when I first came here," Huddleson said turning on the ship to shore radio. Instant chatter between Coast Guard vessels followed. "Let's monitor this a bit and see what we pick up."

They listened as a lake freighter discussed the approaching weather with its sister ship. That was followed by a returning fishing fleet comparing catches.

"Perhaps we'll pick up Rusty," Uncle Fritz said.

"Not unless he calls in for a weather update. Generally, the only time you overhear the private vessels is when they are checking on conditions, school locations for fish and maydays. He may get a weather update—a lot do."

"He better have his eye on the sky," Uncle Fritz said, watching the growing lightning flashes in the wall of clouds. Over the sporadic crackle of the radio he heard a low rumble of distant thunder.

Minutes passed slowly and Uncle Fritz was getting antsy. "Can't you just call on that and ask if there is a man named Rusty on the lake tonight?"

All of a sudden a voice blurted from the radio.

"Mayday, mayday." The radio crackled.

Uncle Fritz froze.

"We receive you. This is CG157. State your mayday and location," a voice said.

"That's the Coast Guard," Huddleson whispered.

"Mayday. We're a fishing tug and uh, we broke down and there's a damn storm coming." Pause. "Our engine is dead."

"We need your location and name of vessel."

"I'm in the fucking water north of Kelleys Island! Wait a minute." Long pause. "I got it. Wait, what is it? Oh yeah. We're N 41° 50" by W 82° 45"'. North of Kelleys like I said."

"We are on our way. What's the name of your vessel?"

Silence.

"Vessel's name, sir?"

"*Buffalo Bill.*"

***

Rusty thought it was his imagination but the more he listened to the radio stolen by Pete, the more he was sure. It wasn't the fact that a fish tug was in distress…it was the voice on the mike and the vessel's name: *Buffalo Bill*? Couldn't they be more original than a name associated with Annie Oakley? He now was certain the voice on the mike was none other than Al's. But what was he doing on the *Annie O* and was Davey piloting her? And was she really in distress? He chartered the co ordinances for her exact location. She would be about 4 miles NNW off Kelleys Island. And who of all else was going to her rescue? CG157. *What in hell was going on?* He scowled. This changed everything. He cuffed the steering wheel and weighed whether he should sit and wait it out or find the fish tug and see if it really was *Annie O* in trouble? He was close enough that he could beat Connors to her. Thunder rumbled. He decided to check out the fish tug in distress.

By the time he got north of Kelleys, lightning was lacing the sky and the wind had picked up. In the dusky blue of the lake, he could see the profile of a fish tug sitting idle and riding the building waves. He fought the urge to radio the vessel. To do so would give himself away to CG157. He circled her stern from afar and looked through the binoculars. The spray from the waves and the closing dusk made it difficult to focus. There. He saw it. *Annie O* on the stern. The name reverberated through his head. "What in the hell?" he muttered. He swung the binoculars and swept the horizon. A vessel was approaching hard and its silhouette disclosed it as a Coast Guard picket boat. He started *New Moon* forward and distanced himself so that *Annie O* would block him from the picket boat's approach. With visibility reduced, *New Moon* blended into the environment of gray overcast and murky lake. He waited, not sure what to do next.

***

Joe lowered the binoculars. He had spotted an ash colored speedboat circling his stern some distance away. He reported it to Lou and Al.

“That could be Rusty,” Lou said.

Giuseppe relaxed his grip on the shotgun under his overcoat.

Joe watched as the boat faded into the mist and then continued scanning the horizon until he spotted another vessel on a fast approach. “Big boat off starboard heading for us.”

“Where’s starboard?” Al asked Lou and Lou pointed. “Is it Captain Kid?”

Joe studied the boat and then lowered the binoculars. “It’s a Coast Guard picket boat all right, but I can’t make out the number yet.”

Lou turned to face the approaching boat so that the machine gun hanging behind his shoulder wouldn’t be visible.

“We make sure.” Al looked at Giuseppe. “I’ll light my cigar when I’m sure.”

Giuseppe nodded.

“You heard me, Lou, Joe?”

Both men nodded.

The picket boat drew close and out of the mist and spray the numbers on its bow emerged—CG157. The Trapanis exchanged looks.

“Ahoy, *Buffalo Bill.*” The voice came from a megaphone in the wheelhouse. “This is Coast Guard vessel 157. Toss us a line and we’ll see what the problem is.”

“The problem is the engine is dead.” Al called out.

“If it can’t be fixed we’ll tow you to harbor,” the megaphone voice reassured.

Joe tossed the bow line to one of the men at the rail. There were two guardsmen standing there—one short and built like a bulldog, the other tall and lanky. As far the Trapanis could see, the voice in the wheelhouse made three. He had to be the captain—Captain Connors.

“Did you check your fuel level?” The megaphone voice asked.

“We got plenty of gas,” Al called out. “We checked everything and it don’t make sense.”

“All right, I’m going to send my motor machinist mate aboard to have a look.”

“Sure. Just make it snappy. That storm is about to crawl up our ass.”

The two guardsmen tossed bumpers over the rail, pulled on the bow line and snugged *Annie O* close. The tall, lanky man started over the side and the short guardsman said, “Hold on, Bill—the tool box.”

Hearing the name *Bill* made Al’s heart skip a beat. His eyes narrowed and turned cold. He watched Bill climb down the picket boat and onto the deck of *Annie O* with the interest of a lion watching an irritating hyena. He took a cigar out of his coat pocket as Bill approached him.

“Maybe we can get you under way before this hits,” Bill said with a nod to sky.

“You’re Bill?” Al asked.

“Yeah. Chief motor machinist’s mate.”

“So your captain,” Al thumbed towards the wheelhouse, “would be Connors then, right?”

“Yeah, that’s him.”

"I've read about you boys in the paper. You have a pretty impressive record catching rumrunners." Al took out his matchbook.

"That's because we are serious about getting rid of shit on the water," Bill grinned.

Al struck a match. "So am I." He lit his cigar and stepped away.

Giuseppe lifted the sawed-off shotgun barrel from under his coat and leveled it at Bill. A fiery blast roared out one barrel. Bill never knew what hit him.

Lou, meanwhile, had swung the machine gun around and riddled the smaller guardsman at the rail with bullets. The guardsman did a violent dance and fell backwards, and Lou continued strafing the deck. He then joined Joe in shooting up the wheelhouse. Joe, when the action started, had placed the rifle's crosshairs on Connors's silhouette. The same moment of the shotgun blast, he had he fired his semi-automatic at Connors.

The sound of weapons discharge was deafening and drowned out the sound of thunder and lightning claps. When the guns fell silent, the fury of the approaching storm could be heard.

But Connors, from his perch above, had had a feeling. It was his *every vessel is a trap* feeling. And like always, he was right again. He had spotted Joe raising the rifle and taking a bead on him but he didn't have time to warn Bill or his mate. Just time enough to duck for cover. He dove and flattened himself on the floor of the wheelhouse until the shooting stopped, and then he cautiously raised just enough to reach the controls and shove CG157 to full throttle. So determined was he to escape the range of bullets, he forgot the *Annie O* was still tied to his vessel.

Annie O jerked violently, causing Joe and Giuseppe to fall to the deck while Al had managed to catch himself. Lou, at the wheel, was the first to realize that *Annie O* was being dragged by the picket boat and that Connors was still alive.

The picket boat, its engine roaring at full speed, dragged *Annie O* in a wild, out of control tow and Lou knew it would be a matter of time before she capsized or ripped apart. He pawed frantically through her toolbox then spotted an ax on the side wall of the wheelhouse. He yanked it off the wall and ran out on the bow. By now, Joe had found his footing and was firing the rifle with no success at the wheelhouse.

Lou steadied himself next to the cleat where the line attached to the fish tug, raised the ax and began whacking at the line. The rain now struck with a fury and waves tossed the two speeding vessels about. With the third whack, the ax chopped through the line and *Annie O* broke free. She glided until she came to a stop. She was now at the mercy of the slamming waves which tossed her about. Lou ran back to the wheelhouse, crossed himself and pressed the ignition. *Annie O's* trusty engine turned over. She had power. He looked to the heavens and whispered "thank you."

Al, Joe and Giuseppe, meanwhile, took cover under the canopy of the wheelhouse as the rain swept across the boat in sheets.

"He's alive and he has that one pounder," Lou said. "He can reach us, but we can't reach him save for the rifle and that has to be an accurate shot. He doesn't need to be accurate with the cannon to sink us.

"Do you think he'll come back for us?" Joe asked.

"He has to," Al said flatly.

***

Through his binoculars, Rusty had seen small flashes from the *Annie O.* He thought he heard gunshots over the thunder. There was a sinking feeling in his gut. Connors was attacking *Annie O.* He fired up the Liberty engines and throttled them to power. *New Moon* roared to life and raced across the water towards the two distant vessels. To his surprise, both vessels seemed to be moving. He grabbed the binoculars and saw the picket boat was speeding with *Annie O* close behind—too close. There could only be one reason, the fish tug was being towed at break neck speed by CG157. He keyed the mike on the ship to shore radio.

"CG157, this is *New Moon.* I'm the shadow runner you have been chasing all summer. You remember *Rising Sun*—the Lyman you sank last fall? Do you remember its pilot that you and your crew thrashed at the station and called a liar? Tell me, do your fellow guardsmen know about your skimming and hijacking from runners? Do they know about the murders you're behind, you son of a bitch?"

***

Uncle Fritz's jaw dropped. It was Rusty's voice loud and clear over the ship to shore radio. He looked at Huddleson. "It's him. That's Rusty."

Huddleson shook his head. "Connors is sure to kill him with that disclosure."

"Radio him so I can to talk to him."

Huddleson held up his hand for quiet. Another voice came across the radio.

"CG157, do you hear me. This is CG149. Give us your location."

No response.

"CG157. This is CG149. What is your location?"

Still no response.

"The CG149 is heading out," Huddleson whispered. "She's got a good crew. I know the captain. He' s aboveboard. Told me his misgivings about Connors."

"And Rusty—where does that leave him?"

Huddleson shook his head. "Let's hope CG149 gets there before anything happens."

"Let me have the mike. *New Moon*, this is Uncle Fritz. I am worried sick over you. Stop this nonsense and come home." There was no response. A bolt of lightning hit close to the lighthouse and made him jump. "What do we do now?"

Huddleson shook his head again. "All we can do is make sure the light is there to guide him home through the storm."

Rusty caught up with CG157 as Connors was bringing the vessel about and heading back towards *Annie O.* It was no mystery as to what Connors intentions were. As CG157 came within cannon range of the slower moving fish tug, Rusty flew past the bow of the picket boat and circled to her stern.

"Do you remember me now?" he chided over the radio. He doubled back and did a close sweep along her starboard side and cut past her bow a second time then circled back again. "Is the fish tug next on your hit list? That would be like shooting a sitting duck. But then, I wouldn't expect anything less from a freebooting, lowlife scoundrel."

The bow of the CG157 turned off her present course towards *Annie O* and headed towards *New Moon.*

Rusty snickered.

***

"Give me that damn thing," Al said snatching the binoculars from Lou. "What's going on?"

"Rusty's running rabbit," Lou said.

"Rabbit? What's that mean—running scared?"

"No. He's running interference. He's leading Connors away from us."

"I'll be damned." Al handed the binoculars back. "I told you from the get go I liked that man. Straight-shooter and clever he is…and loyal."

They took turns with the binoculars, watching the two boats speed eastward until the rain and wind-whipped mist swallowed them up.

***

He could easily out distance the picket boat, but instead stayed just enough in front of her to tempt her. The one pounder was easily within range as was the .30 caliber Savage Lewis machine gun which concerned him more, so he ran a zigzag course, losing himself in the misty rain, and then reappearing again. It had to be driving Connors crazy. His destination was Gull Island directly to the east—an island so tiny only gulls could inhabit it. It was surrounded by shallow rings of shoals with each ring getting progressively shallower as it neared the island. In some places, there was only 1-3 feet of water above the sand and rock and with the undulating waves caused by the storm, the depth would even less. If there was one thing he could count on with men like Connors was their fanatic obsession with the hunt that blinded them to their surroundings, causing them to make stupid choices and costly mistakes. He was counting on Connors's lust for blood to blind him.

The combination of following 6-7 foot waves and *New Moon*'s erratic course made for a bronco-like ride and as he sweated at throttle control and steering, he noted the picket boat was plowing easily through the choppy waves. Unlike his, her course was more steadfast.

As they approached the tiny island, he allowed the gap between *New Moon* and CG157 to close. It would be like dangling meat in front of a hungry dog. CG157 bore down on him and he heard the pinging of bullets on the exterior of the cockpit. Connors had taken the bait, but how many hits could *New Moon* take before one or more bullets found her Achilles heel, he wondered. In the driving rain he made out the tiny bump of Gull Island. He cut close to her eastern coast line and headed on a short north course then doubled back towards Connors. He was now on a collision course with CG157 and the distance between the two boats closed rapidly. Muzzle flashes from the picket boat's wheelhouse sprouted as he raced towards her and then, at the last minute, he made a hard cut to port. *New Moon* shot across the shoals. He dodged the rocks visible below the surface and barely cleared the sand bars and prayed *New Moon*'s draft was shallow enough to cross without going aground. To make sure Connors's attention was locked on him and not on the precarious surrounds, he fired a couple of pot shots out the cockpit window with his handgun.

The CG157, in hot pursuit with her machine gun blazing, followed *New Moon* across the shoals.

Rusty cut sharp and *New Moon* bogged down, her propeller churning through sand. She was still moving, but only at half the speed and CG157 was bearing down. He cut back on one engine so the thrust of the other would shift the boat around, then he switched engines. The propeller churned up sand and broke free and *New Moon* gained speed but not soon enough. CG157's bow rammed him aft on starboard. She shuddered violently and there was a rip of metal that he could hear above the wind and thunder. At that same moment, CG157 struck an out cropping of rocks. The sound of scraping metal screeched above the weather. She came to an abrupt stop and immediately yawed to port.

Rusty looked over his shoulder and saw both the gaping hole gouged in the side of *New Moon* and the listing picket boat that was dead atop the shoals. Water, pushed by the wave action, poured into the hole near *New Moon*'s stern and he knew it was beyond the capabilities of his bilge pump. He closed the scruppers to keep more water from finding its way in, but he knew sinking was inevitable. He removed the cartridge belt and put on a life vest and then stuck a flashlight and flare gun in his belt. Movement on the deck of CG157 caught his eye. It was Connors with the Savage Lewis machine gun making his way towards the bow.

As Rusty gave the engines throttle, what relief he felt that there was still power was diminished by the fact that *New Moon* was still in shallow water and in danger of going aground.

Connors opened fire and bullets struck the cockpit with thuds and clanks. The chugging sound of the big gun and pinging of ricochets was nerve wracking and intense.

Rusty reached for the B.A.R., realized it would be too cumbersome in the close situation and grabbed for the shotgun. At that moment, the back and starboard port hole shattered. He dove to the floor as bullets pinged, whizzed and clanked inside the cockpit. He reached up and gave the engines throttle. He would have to take his chance with the shoals as he could not raise enough to return fire.

New Moon started, bogged and shifted. He alternated engines, fearful his hands would be shot under the mad barrage of gunfire. *New Moon* shifted again.

He then felt her break free of the sand. He dared not raise, but trusted his memory as to his location in the shoals. He gave both engines throttle and she surged forward, clear of sand. But he could feel her low in the stern and swampy in the way she handled. Connors may have been immobile, but his bullets were not. There would be no time to put enough distance between him and the .30 caliber bullets before *New Moon* sank.

He moved *New Moon* forward and rose up just enough to sneak a peek at CG157. A shower of bullets sprayed the back of the cockpit, forcing him to hit the deck again. He snarled. His options were few if any, but *New Moon*'s windshield was strong and intact and could deflect the close range bullets for a short term.

"Hang with me old girl," he muttered as he turned her around to face the rain of bullets. He jammed the throttles to full power. The Liberty engines roared and *New Moon* bolted forward. Her engines howled over the storm as she raced towards the side of CG157.

Connors, realizing Rusty's intentions, intensified his firing, concentrating on the pilot side windshield of the runner.

The shoals were getting increasingly shallower. Rusty waited and at the last minute, jumped out the passenger side door of *New Moon* into the water. *New Moon* ramped up the shoals and plunged into the side of CG157. Her fuel tanks ruptured and a giant fire ball blasted into the sky as both boats exploded.

He watched with astonishment as the boats burned furiously, unhampered by the rain. Then without warning, CG157, with *New Moon* buried inside of her, rolled onto her side and the pounding waves pushed what was left of her off the shoals into the deeper water. He was dumfounded as the boats quickly sank beneath the stormy waves.

He was alone now bobbing in choppy waters. Gull Island was close. He swam half way and then waded the rest to the tiny island. When he climbed up on it, he immediately pulled out Uncle Fritz's compass and was relieved water had not infiltrated the works. He checked the compass's bearing and while doing so, spotted a vessel approaching. The rain had let up enough that he could make out in the twilight it was the *Annie O.* He fired off a flare and by the time *Annie O* reached Gull Island, the storm was over.

He swam out to meet her and when Joe and Giuseppe raised him up and over the rail bringing him face to face with Al he said, "All I ever wanted to do was fish."

***

They passed CG149 as they headed back to Middle Island. Rusty sat at the stern and watched her go by and wondered what if anything they would find. When he told the Trapanis CG157 had blown up and sunk with no survivors not one of them spoke a word but he saw a gleam in their eyes. He even caught a gleam in Giuseppe's eye or maybe it was his imagination, but he swore he saw one corner of the big Sicilian's mouth curl up in a fleeting half smile.

It was dark by the time *Annie O* reached the trapper's shack. As she docked, Rusty jumped off and ran to the shack. Davey was sitting in the doorway backlit by lantern light from within with his shotgun across his lap. He watched the fish tug dock and spotted a flashlight coming towards him. "Davey," the voice behind it said. Davey breathed a sigh of relief. It was Rusty.

"Davey, we're going home. I'll gather our gear."

"I'm not sure just where home is." Davey said.

"The mainland. The Trapanis are going to drop us off at Marblehead Light."

"Marblehead Light?"

"I have a hunch Uncle Fritz is there."

Annie O crossed the international boundary and chugged past Kelleys Island. All on board looked in silence at the sparse scattering of lights dotting the dark island and upon rounding her tip, a shaft of bright light cut through the night. The Marblehead Lighthouse was showing the way into the Southward Passage.

***

Chief Stoddard of Marblehead Peninsula had joined Uncle Fritz and Huddleson at the lighthouse. He had a call from the Coast Guard alerting him to a runner who might come ashore in his jurisdiction. He was to keep his eye open for his boat named *New Moon* and any suspicious characters. They told him the runner was suspected in the disappearance of CG157. A third vessel, *Buffalo Bill* was missing as well.

Chief Stoddard said that was a turnaround—CG157 missing. He asked Uncle Fritz about his radio call to a Rusty. "That was the fellow that sank in *Rising Sun* with his wife last fall, right?"

"He is out fishing and I presume caught in the storm. I am concerned for his safety," Uncle Fritz said.

With that being said, the fish tug, *Annie O* pulled up to the dock near the lighthouse. The three men watched as a wheelchair was unloaded and two men helped a man off the boat into it. Behind them, another man disembarked.

"Rusty and Davey," Uncle Fritz said. The three men hurried to the dock.

Uncle Fritz got there first. "Rusty, you know better than to keep fishing when a storm is on the way. You had us worried sick." He winked hard in view of Rusty, Davey and the Trapanis.

Huddleson and Stoddard caught up.

"There was a mayday call from a fish tug named *Buffalo Bill.* Apparently she got caught in the storm, too. CG157 went out to assist. By chance did you boys come across them or see any signs of them?" Stoddard asked.

The Trapanis shook their heads.

"No," Rusty said. "We didn't see anything. Visibility was low and we had our hands full with the storm. It's a big lake out there."

Chief Stoddard frowned. "They're both missing."

"The storm was bad on the lake."

Huddleson interceded. "I could see the storm was a lot worse over the lake. We only caught its fringe."

Stoddard nodded. "Well then, glad you boys made it in safely. They'll show up. A cutter is headed that way and they'll find them." He sighed. "Well, I got to get on patrol. Looking for a runner that may come my way."

Rusty instantly thought of Pete and exchanged glances with Al who was thinking the same thing.

Stoddard continued. "This runner was out on the lake same time as you boys. He was goading CG157 and Captain Connors. Called his boat *New Moon.* The authorities believe he may be involved in CG157's disappearance." He paused and looked at Rusty. "Oddly, he mentioned *Rising Sun* and her sinking. Why would he do that?"

Rusty raised his brows in surprise. "I don't know."

"That's no surprise," Davey said. "*Rising Sun* represents all of Connors' innocent victims. If you mixed it with the boaters and fishermen like I do, you would know she's still in the hearts of pilots and sailors and most likely runners as well. She's like a rallying cry—like *remember the Alamo.*"

Chief Stoddard frowned and looked at him askance. "Alamo or not, there's a government vessel and crew that's missing. Federal agents will be crawling all over the area. They'll be crawling up my ass and dissecting me for information and hunches as well." He looked at Rusty. "They will be hot and heavy after that *New Moon* runner. If he's smart, he'd pack it in and stay clear of the lake."

"If he's smart," Rusty said, taking hold of the wheelchair's handles. He began pushing Davey towards the lighthouse. "Good luck with your runner and the agents, Chief. And chief," he paused and looked back at Stoddard, "thanks for keeping the pot stirred at the Coast Guard Station. You turned some heads. Thank you—for everything."

Stoddard half smiled. "Get out of here and go home."

Chapter 69

Saying good-bye to the Trapanis was harder than he thought. He had shared a lifetime with them in the year he had known them. They may not have been like family to him, but they most certainly were good friends—good people, he would come to call them.

Al had a thick envelope for him at their parting. "Your share of the business and a little reward money for ridding the lake of a heinous man." When Rusty protested the reward money as blood money, Al changed it to compensation for the loss of *New Moon* and Rusty accepted it.

Eliot's wild shot to Tony left a bullet behind in his chest. Lodged next to his spine and inoperable, the doctor warned if it moved, Tony could have permanent numbness or worse, paralysis. He recovered but avoided any kind of labor to be sure.

Rusty would not hear from the Trapanis again until after the repeal of the 18th Amendment when Giuseppe startled him by driving up the driveway to hand deliver an invitation from Al to an "End to Prohibition Party" at the vineyard.

Meanwhile, Pete had yet to be found. Whether he was lying comatose in some hospital, washed up dead on a remote beach or a hostage of the lake that refused to give him up, it drove the Trapanis crazy with grief and uncertainty and awoke Rusty many a night in sweat. The nightmare was always the same—images of Pete reaching to him as the waves slowly engulfed him.

Huddleson wasn't sure what had happened on the lake that night of the storm when CG157 went missing, but he slept a little deeper feeling confident he wouldn't have to look over his shoulder anymore.

***

After the storm, Uncle Fritz drove Rusty and Davey back to the farm. When they got out of the Model A, Rusty handed Uncle Fritz his compass. "I don't need it now."

Uncle Fritz gave him a wary look when he took back the compass.

"It's late; I'll explain everything in the morning."

Uncle Fritz held up his hand. "I don't want to know anything. The only thing I want to hear from you is that it's over and you're staying put—here!" He emphasized by pointing his finger at the ground.

"It's over."

Uncle Fritz gave a terse nod. "Good."

Di and Eddie exploded from the door with the rest of the family close behind.

Kisses, scoldings, hugs and cross-examinations washed over Rusty all at the same time. It never felt so good to be back.

***

A month later, with some of his money, Rusty bought the adjoining farm next to Di's family when the owner, an elderly widower, took ill and moved in with his son near Toledo. It more than doubled the size of the family's farm. He knocked down the old farmhouse and built a two story, five bedroom Arts and Craft kit house from Sears in its place. It had two bedrooms downstairs which worked well for Davey. A wide porch across the entire front offered respite from sun and rain and became a favorite spot for Uncle Fritz and Davey to share afternoon lemonades. Di decorated it in Art Deco and furnished it Arts and Crafts.

Di and Rusty turned the third upstairs' bedroom into a sewing room. Though they hoped for a child, they did not plan for one. Besides, Eddie, they would joke, was like getting three for one. Di became a dressmaker for a boutique in Elyria. Using fashion and movie magazines as her reference, she gained a local reputation for cutting edge fashion and was in demand by women of affluence in the area. She never gave another thought about the lake—it seemed like another life.

They officially adopted Eddie and Eddie, with Uncle Fritz's tutelage, turned his street smarts into book smarts.

Prince had house privileges which included Eddie's bed, and when he killed a fox outside the chicken coop at the turning of the leaves, Uncle Fritz rewarded him with a T-bone steak. Prince would continue to collect such rewards.

Behind the house, a loft barn was built to house a Paint horse for Davey and a Welsh pony for Eddie. The Paint did not have four white socks but its name was Chief. Like the dock ramp at Huron, Rusty built a ramp for Davey to reach his horse's back although Eddie had thought a swing pulley system like in the boathouse would have been nifty.

Uncle Fritz told Rusty of his vision of a vineyard in the back twenty and Rusty convinced him a patch for barley and a couple of beef steers would be better.

When the leaves began to fall and Rusty cut field corn with the new tractor and corn harvester, Uncle Fritz rushed over to tell him the stock market had crashed. Black Friday it was called. They didn't feel the effects of the depression at the farm.

In November, The Witch hit the lake and the counties inland. The blow lasted three days and when it was over, the Vermilion lighthouse toppled after battering by the gale winds and powerful fifteen feet high waves. A few days later, the headline in the newspaper read that a Coast Guard life ring and part of a picket boat's transom was found washed up on shore near Bay Village in the storm's aftermath. The Guard confirmed it was from CG157. There would never be another thing found or bodies recovered.

On Valentine's Day three months later, Rusty took Di to dinner at The White Oaks just across the county line. There was a slight commotion—most diners didn't notice, as four men in suits and overcoats walked into the room and spread out. They had that Chicago-look Pete had always talked about and it made Rusty uneasy. A moment later another man walked in, a big, robust man in a fedora with thick lips and a scar down his left cheek. He was jovial and the owner, brushing aside the maître'd, personally sat the man and the four suits with him. He overheard the owner instructing the maître'd to bring their best wine. He heard one at the table say Big Al. Rusty grabbed Di's hand. Pete would have been in Seventh Heaven.

Throughout the winter, Pete invaded his dreams until one day a small article on the front page of the newspaper read *Decomposed Body Found Incased in Ice Off Vermilion.* He read further. The body, that of a man, was believed to have been a rumrunner. The only thing of identity about him was a WWI belt and buckle.

***

Spring came early. As Rusty broke ground with the plow, the lake gulls, searching inland for worms and bugs in the fresh turned dirt, swooped about his tractor and plow, cawing and meowing like they had when he rode the lake. It caused a yearning in him and a bit of melancholy. One particular gull flew close a number of times, and then boldly landed at the nose of the tractor. It looked him straight in the eye. He whispered Pete and the gull spread his wings.

Afterward

Prohibition was a failure. It brought out the rebel, the criminal and the crooked side of the American public. It was said that it was "harder to find a drink before Prohibition than during it."[1] Even Presidents Wilson and Harding had prohibited alcohol in the Whitehouse. Harding, ironically, voted in favor of Prohibition as a senator.

When the law first went into effect, alcohol consumption fell but it steadily rose to pre-Prohibition levels. People wanted not just to drink, they wanted the right to drink and the forbidden fruit of alcohol became all the more desirable. Only now people were drinking hard liquor as bootleggers favored hard liquor over beer because profits were higher and it was easier to import. Consequently, the higher alcohol content of hard liquor made people drunker than they would have been on beer.[2]

Law enforcement, undermanned and underfunded, became impossible as gangsters became crime syndicates and law abiding citizens became criminals for chasing the Demon Rum. Corruption at local, state and federal levels grew either through bribes or smuggling by law enforcers themselves. A thousand dollar bill hidden under a speakeasy's bar glass could buy a corrupt cop's silence; a brewery's bribe of a couple hundred thousand dollars could make an agent look the other way. In one city, the Prohibition Bureau captain called together his officers and promptly fired those wearing diamond rings knowing that an agent could not afford diamonds on an agent's wages.[3] One newspaper editor asked in his editorial, "who's watching the Coast Guard while the Coast Guard is watching the coast?"[4] Bootlegging became the largest business in the country and everyone involved was making money except for the government who lost out on alcohol taxation.

Despite Prohibition advocates predictions that crime would decrease, prisons overflowed, courts were overloaded and trials became backlogged for years. Not until the appeal of the 18th Amendment would the numbers fall back to pre-Prohibition levels.

With a new administration in 1927, Secretary of Treasury Lincoln C. Andrews, at a Senate committee hearing on crime, testified that bootleggers and rum runners were hauling an estimated $3 billion a year while the government confiscated only 5%. Upon hearing this, President Calvin Coolidge committed $30 million in equipment and manpower to combat bootlegging and related crime.[5] It helped to a degree but it was like closing the barn door after the horses had already escaped.

Alcohol became lethal. The harder it was to find top shelf alcohol and the bigger the demand grew, had people turning to substandard alcohol. It was dubbed bathtub gin, monkey rum, needled beer and jake (tainted Jamaican Ginger) among other names. Wood (methyl) alcohol, acid compounds and the neurotoxin TOCP were just some of the poisons intentionally added by bootleggers and moonshiners to cut or add kick to the drink. Without any regulations, cutting liquor with dangerous chemical and distilling and storing liquor in filthy conditions (often with dead rats and snakes found in stills and barrels) was not uncommon. The result was blindness, paralysis and even death for those who drank the contaminated alcohol. During Prohibition, It is estimated that 30,000-50,000 people died as a result of adulterated alcohol. But the biggest shock was the deaths caused by the government poisoning alcohol allocated for industrial, medical and scientific use in an effort to prevent people from obtaining and drinking it. The tainted alcohol was responsible for killing 400 people and sickening 1200 in New York City on New Year's Eve 1926. Despite outcries from the medical community to halt the addition of methyl alcohol to the alcohol, the government continued to contaminate and 700 more died the following year. Figures estimate that 10,000 died from this poisoning alone during the course of Prohibition.[6] People grew wary not just of law enforcement, but of the government.

Meanwhile, innocent people were being killed by crossfire, mistaken identity and drive-by shootings. Organized crime, rooted in Prohibition, ran and controlled gambling, prostitution, drugs and extortion. Headlines of criminal activity splashed newspapers' front pages. People, weary and skeptical, had had enough.

Industrialist, Pierre du Pont- an adamant supporter of Prohibition in the beginning, reversed his stance and called for repeal. In 1926, he and the newly formed AAPA (Association Against the Prohibition Amendment) argued for the repeal of the 18th Amendment. This organization consisted of industrialists (many like du Pont who had originally campaigned for its passing) called Prohibition "sheer lunacy." Their campaign was joined by another organization for repeal, the Women's Organization for National Prohibition Reform. After the stock market crash, these and other organizations for repeal argued that the government needed money and men needed work. Alcohol taxation would create revenue, and breweries, distilleries and the ensuing jobs would create work. The same effort used for the law's passing was now being used for its repeal.

Franklin D. Roosevelt, in his 1932 campaign for presidency, pledged the repeal of the 18th Amendment if elected. He won the election. On March 12, 1933, he signed the Beer and Wine Revenue Act which legalized the sale and taxation of 3.2 beer and light wine. Upon signing he declared, "I think this would be a good time for a beer." Then, on December 5, 1933, he signed the 21st Amendment proclamation ending national Prohibition. It was said that a carnival atmosphere followed. The "Great Experiment" had failed.

Prohibition was as awful flop,

We like it.

It can't stop what it was meant to stop,

We like it.

It's filled our land with vice and crime,

It's left a trail of graft and slime,

It don't prohibit worth a dime,

Nevertheless we're for it.

—Franklin P. Adams

[1] Wayne Lewis Kadar, "The Prohibltion Era: 1920-1933," *Great Lakes Crime and Villains,* (Gwinn, Michigan: Avery Color Studios, Inc. 2009) 171.

[2] Kadar, 171.

[3] Frederick Stonehouse, "Prohibition," *Great Lakes Crime II*, (Gwinn, Michigan: Avery Color Studios, Inc. 2007), 150.

[4] Stonehouse, 155.

[5] Schreiner, Jr., Samuel A. *May Day! May Day!* (USA: Donald I. Fine, Inc. and Canada: General Publishing Co., Limited, 1990).

[6] Deborah Blum, "The Chemist's War: The Little Told Story of How the U.S. Government Poisoned Alcohol During Prohibition with Deadly Consequences," *Slate*, 19 February 2010, retrieved 27 May 2014 <http://www.slate.com/articles/health_and_science/medical_examiner/2010/02/the_chemists_war.html>

About the Author

R. C. Durkee is both a writer and an artist who blends the love of history, nature and the country life into her creative projects.

The sixth generation to have lived on the family's 180-year-old Ohio farm, she has raised draft ponies, horses, sheep, cows and crops. She is also an avid gardener.

An award winning artist, her artwork has appeared on magazine covers and art books, and at galleries in Ohio and beyond.

Her interests are historical buildings and places, century farms, old post and beam barns, classic cars, and visiting Civil War sites. She enjoys hiking and biking with her husband, cross country skiing, star-gazing, movies and reading fiction and non-fiction.

She is presently working on *Looking for Hiram,* a novel based on a Civil War soldier's diary that led to a mystery and life-long quest.

CPSIA information can be obtained at www.ICGtesting.com
Printed in the USA
BVOW05s2015091114

374237BV00004B/9/P